What
abo

"R.J. Patterson does a fantastic job at keeping you engaged and interested. I look forward to more from this talented author."

- ***Aaron Patterson***
bestselling author of SWEET DREAMS

DEAD SHOT

"Small town life in southern Idaho might seem quaint and idyllic to some. But when local newspaper reporter Cal Murphy begins to uncover a series of strange deaths that are linked to a sticky spider web of deception, the lid on the peaceful town is blown wide open. Told with all the energy and bravado of an old pro, first-timer R.J. Patterson hits one out of the park his first time at bat with *Dead Shot*. It's that good."

- ***Vincent Zandri***
bestselling author of THE REMAINS

"You can tell R.J. knows what it's like to live in the newspaper world, but with *Dead Shot*, he's proven that he also can write one heck of a murder mystery."

- ***Josh Katzowitz***
NFL writer for CBSSports.com
& author of Sid Gillman: Father of the Passing Game

"Patterson has a mean streak about a mile wide and puts his two main characters through quite a horrible ride, which makes for good reading."

- ***Richard D.***, *reader*

DEAD LINE

"This book kept me on the edge of my seat the whole time. I didn't really want to put it down. R.J. Patterson has hooked me. I'll be back for more."

- ***Bob Behler***
3-time Idaho broadcaster of the year
and play-by-play voice for Boise State football

"Like a John Grisham novel, from the very start I was pulled right into the story and couldn't put the book down. It was as if I personally knew and cared about what happened to each of the main characters. Every chapter ended with so much excitement and suspense I had to continue to read until I learned how it ended, even though it kept me up until 3:00 A.M.

- ***Ray F.**, reader*

DEAD IN THE WATER

"In Dead in the Water, R.J. Patterson accurately captures the action-packed saga of a what could be a real-life college football scandal. The sordid details will leave readers flipping through the pages as fast as a hurry-up offense."

- Mark Schlabach,
ESPN college sports columnist and
co-author of *Called to Coach*
and *Heisman: The Man Behind the Trophy*

THE WARREN OMISSIONS

"What can be more fascinating than a super high concept novel that reopens the conspiracy behind the JFK assassination while the threat of a global world war rests in the balance? With his new novel, *The Warren Omissions*, former journalist turned bestselling author R.J. Patterson proves he just might be the next worthy successor to Vince Flynn."

- ***Vincent Zandri***
bestselling author of THE REMAINS

OTHER TITLES BY
R.J. PATTERSON

Cal Murphy Thrillers

Dead Shot
Dead Line
Better off Dead
Dead in the Water
Dead Man's Curve
Dead and Gone
Dead Wrong
Dead Man's Land
Dead Drop
Dead to Rights
Dead End

James Flynn Thrillers

The Warren Omissions
Imminent Threat
The Cooper Affair
Seeds of War

Brady Hawk Thrillers

First Strike
Deep Cover
Point of Impact
Full Blast
Target Zero
Fury
State of Play
Siege
Seek and Destroy
Into the Shadows
Hard Target
No Way Out
Two Minutes to Midnight

SEEK AND DESTROY

A Brady Hawk novel

R.J.
PATTERSON

Seek and Destroy

First Print Edition 2018

Cover Design by Books Covered

Published in the United States of America
Green E-Books
Boise Idaho 83713

For Don, an incredible mentor and an even greater friend

CHAPTER 1

Istanbul, Turkey

BRADY HAWK CREPT DOWN THE SIDEWALK with Shane Samuels a few feet behind him. Using the natural cover of the tree limbs growing overhead, Hawk and Samuels remained in the shadows and out of view from the sparse streetlights. The precautionary exercise seemed unnecessary given that the time was just past 2:00 a.m. But considering the target of the operation, Hawk insisted they couldn't be careful enough.

The aim of their mission was to break into the home of Bartu Kemal, whose house was situated along a hill near Emigran Park and provided a breathtaking vista of the Bosphorus Strait. Officially, Kemal was a security guard at a small research facility located in downtown Istanbul. But after admiring the posh neighborhood and all it provided, Hawk wondered just how many people were falling for Kemal's lie. The truth about Kemal's occupation explained how he could afford such a place. But keeping his identity a secret was paramount to his success in his daily task of keeping Katarina Petrov and The Chamber offices safe.

Hawk and Samuels reached the edge of the property and leapt over the fence. They stole across the yard and headed to the back where Hawk determined they would lie in wait.

"Are you sure about this plan?" Samuels whispered.

"Every night at 2:15 a.m., without fail," Alex Duncan chimed in over the coms.

"It's those details that make your sister the best operational commander in the world," Hawk said as he eyed Samuels.

"Let's watch that hyperbole there, Hawk," Alex said, pausing before she continued. "Best operational commander in the universe."

Hawk looked at his partner, whose eyes were still trained on the house.

"After all these years, you suddenly find out you have a sister and then you quickly learn she's insufferable," Hawk said.

Samuels nodded toward the back door. "I think I see some movement."

The back door creaked open and out bounded a Maltese. Hawk watched as the fluffy white dog bounced around the yard before venturing into the shadows to take care of business.

"Now," Hawk whispered.

Samuels then tossed a dog treat near Kemal's pet and waited.

"Come on, girl," Hawk said underneath his breath.

The dog scratched around in the dirt and circled around several times.

"What's the backup plan?" Samuels asked.

"That is Berk's favorite treat," Alex said over the coms. "Just be patient. She'll go for it."

"The dog's name is Berk?" Samuels asked incredulously.

"It's a Turkish dog, bro. Not all of them are given American names like Oscar or Timmy."

"Who names a dog Timmy?" Samuels asked.

"Me. That was my last dog's name," she said.

"Timmy? Really?"

"Dang right. Best Yorkie on the planet."

Hawk watched as the dog noticed the treat and bounded toward it. He tapped Samuels on the shoulder. Yanking the string tied to the treat, Samuels lured the dog right next to them. Berk let out a yelp.

Kemal pulled his robe tight and peered out into the yard.

"Berk! Berk!"

Nothing.

Kemal ventured down the steps off the deck and headed toward the last location where Berk was—in the scope of the outdoor floodlight on the corner of the house. The moment he stepped into the darkness, Hawk and Samuels grabbed him. Samuels clamped his hand across Kemal's mouth.

Hawk jammed his gun into Kemal's back. "Not another word. Understand?"

Kemal nodded.

"Don't kill my dog," Kemal whispered.

Samuels patted Kemal on the shoulder and exhaled.

"What do we look like to you? Terrorists? We wouldn't hurt your dog, man."

Kemal wasn't interested in hearing a response. He twisted free and attempted to escape back to the house. Hawk lunged for the security head and swatted at his feet. With his feet tangled, he tumbled to the ground. Hawk and Samuels pounced on Kemal, securing him with a piece of para cord, which Samuels wrapped around his wrists within seconds. Samuels took hold with a firm grip.

"Where'd you learn to do that?" Hawk asked, his mouth agape.

"Cattle ranching one summer in Colorado," Samuels said. "You should tap into your western American roots sometime. Want me to do his ankles?"

Hawk chuckled. "I think this will do."

Kemal wriggled on the ground. "What do you two cowboys want?"

"We need some information and a little help," Hawk said, pulling Kemal to his feet. "Let's step inside your garage and talk for a moment."

"What about Berk?" Kemal asked.

"Berk isn't going anywhere," Hawk said, nudging Kemal toward the house with his gun. "Let's make this quick."

Once they were inside the garage, Hawk initiated the interrogation.

"We've been watching you for quite some time."

Kemal placed his hands in the air. "Let me turn on the light."

He reached behind him and pressed a button on a panel that Hawk presumed was the garage door opener. However, after a few seconds a red light started blinking.

"What did you do?" Samuels asked.

"You have five minutes to leave before the police arrive and arrest you for trespassing," Kemal said. "Plus, I doubt that you have passports that match your fingerprints in Interpol. God knows how much trouble you'll be in and how long you'll be apprehended here. So, I suggest you leave right now."

Hawk put his hand on Kemal's chest. "I think you might want to reconsider that play."

Hawk nodded to Samuels, who pulled out a laptop from his backpack.

"Alex? Are you getting all this?" Hawk asked.

"Almost done with the transaction," she said.

Samuels showed the screen to Kemal.

"That's your bank account," Hawk said. "From the looks of it before, you liked money. Now you have none—and it will stay that way until you notify the police that there's been a mistake."

Kemal depressed a few buttons on the panel next to the door. The red light stopped blinking.

"Is that all you need to do to make sure the police don't come?" Hawk asked.

Kemal nodded. "They will think it was a false alarm."

"No phone call."

"This isn't America," Kemal growled.

"No, it sure isn't," Hawk said. "Because you'd never be able to get away with there what you're getting away with here."

"What do you want, Mr. Hawk?" Kemal asked.

"Every day your employer disappears between 3:00 and 4:00 p.m.," Hawk said. "We need to know where she goes and how to find her."

"Where she goes is a simple answer," Kemal said. "How to find her there? That's not something I'll be able to help you with."

Hawk glared at Kemal. "Let's start with the simple answer first."

"Ms. Petrov is very concerned about her security, as well she should be. You being here is proof that her fears aren't unfounded."

"Skip the commentary, Mr. Kemal," Hawk said. "My time is very valuable."

"She has a bunker where she conducts more sensitive matters. Meetings with heads of state all take place on secure channels in that building where attempts to intercept signals or tap into the video and audio feeds are impossible."

"How do we get in?"

Kemal shook his head. "You can forget about it. Most people that work for The Chamber do not know where she goes, much less have access to the bunker."

Samuels smiled and slapped Kemal on the back.

"But we're bettin' you do, *partner*," Samuels said.

"I suggest you return to the range where you can roam free before this mission gets you killed," Kemal said.

"This guy here sure does have a sense of humor," Samuels said.

Hawk held up his index finger. "The way I see it, Mr. Kemal, is you have limited options. One is to help us; the other is to become a well-known philanthropist throughout Europe where we give away all your money to various causes if you don't comply. And based on your past record for abusing women, I think we'll start with a nice donation toward an organization that helps battered women. Don't get me wrong, I'd love to give your money away to such great causes, but I'd rather pay Ms. Petrov a little visit. What sounds more appealing to you?"

Kemal sighed. "What is it you want me to help you do?"

"I think it should be pretty clear by this point," Hawk said. "You're going to escort us into Ms. Petrov's bunker when we ask you to. In the meantime, you better not breathe a word of this to anyone—or try to move your money. We've got the best computer wiz on our team when it comes to tracking funds in overseas bank accounts. Any tinkering with your accounts will lead to an immediate release of all your funds to various NGOs of our choosing. Do I make myself clear?"

Before Kemal could answer, Hawk heard the sound of tires skidding to a halt on the pavement just outside the garage.

"You *sonofabitch*," Hawk said.

"Good luck, Mr. Hawk, Mr. Samuels," Kemal said. "I believe you might want to leave now."

Hawk and Samuels eased out the side door leading to the back yard. Their movement in the field of a motion detector activated the floodlight, signaling their presence to the police. Hawk heard heavy footfalls racing in his direction.

He wasted no time in leaping over the fence and

heading toward the street. Samuels followed closely behind him with both men using the cars parked along the curb as cover as they tried to distance themselves from the pursuing officers.

They reached a small wooded lot nestled between two houses and ducked behind a felled tree. Hawk could feel his heart beating so strongly that he would've sworn it was audible to Samuels.

"Now what?" Samuels asked.

"We sit here and wait," Hawk said. "The van is almost a mile away. We'll never be able to reach it now without igniting a chase through the streets of Istanbul. Now, I don't know about you, but I'm not very comfortable with that."

"That makes two of us," Samuels said. "I'm never comfortable when you're driving anywhere."

Hawk put his finger to his lips, signifying for Samuels to be quiet.

Along the sidewalk in front of their brief sanctuary, a policeman shined his flashlight everywhere in search of the escapees. Then he stopped and pointed his light at Hawk and Samuels. Neither of the men moved, both easing their heads down and hoping the officer didn't see them.

"Is he gone?" Samuels asked after a few minutes.

Hawk peeked his head up. "It appears so. But let me go clear the area first. If they're still milling around, at least one of us will have a chance to escape."

Hawk ventured out to the sidewalk and noticed that the police car was no longer parked outside Kemal's house. Signaling for Samuels, Hawk stealthily darted from one cluster of shadows to the next.

"You still there, Alex?" Hawk asked.

"I haven't gone anywhere," she said. "I've just been pondering where to dump all of Kemal's money."

"Give it back to him," Hawk said. "We need him to at least be amenable to our demands the next time we approach him."

"He almost screwed you over," she said.

"And that surprised you?"

"Never mind that," she said. "Just get back to the van as quickly as possible."

Hawk glanced over his shoulder to see Samuels creeping along the sidewalk.

"You ready?" Hawk asked.

Samuels nodded.

"This isn't going to be nearly as easy as I thought it would be," Hawk said.

Samuels leaked a guarded smile, barely visible in the darkness.

"It never is, is it?"

CHAPTER 2

Lyons, France

KATARINA PETROV LICKED HER FINGER and turned the page of her book while she waited for her appointment. While she spoke a handful of different languages, she found that reading in English at least a half-hour each day kept her communication skills sharp. She needed them now more than ever after the setback she'd experienced in recent weeks.

Narrowly escaping right from underneath the noses of the President's personal detail was an accomplishment to revel in. However, if anyone knew about what she'd done, she'd be dismissed from serious consideration regarding the one world currency she'd been so desperate to create. While she projected all the bravado of a heavyweight boxer when she discussed her economic plan, she knew the truth deep down. She needed the United States' involvement if the idea was to ever gain momentum and take flight.

But before she reached that point, she needed someone else on board. She needed new European Central Bank head Gaspard Fournier.

Fournier hobbled through the door ten minutes past their scheduled time. He said something to the host at the front, who then directed Fournier to Petrov's table.

"I apologize for being late, I—"

"Save it," Petrov said. "I don't have time for excuses. And if you're going to be that way, perhaps it's best that we part ways right now."

Fournier leaked a smile. "It'd be a shame that we never got to have this conversation because a terrorist attack in downtown earlier has traffic at a standstill. It's awful outside."

"I do enjoy a brisk walk twice a day," Petrov said. "However, I didn't ask to meet with you to discuss traffic patterns or terrorism—both of which are problems to the average person. But let's face it, Mr. Fournier, I'm not average and neither are you."

He wagged a finger at her.

"Flattery isn't the way to curry my favor nor is a lack of decorum," he said.

She glanced at the glass of alcohol she'd ordered for him.

"Will bourbon work?" she said with a smile.

"It's a start, but I must warn you that I don't have much time."

"In that case, let me get straight to the point, Mr. Fournier. In my final conversation with Henri Dubois, he agreed that the European Central Bank was in dire need of a fresh start, something that only a brand new currency could give it. So, he and I discussed the details of what that would look like and how the ECB could move forward in this new economic environment."

"Your point, Ms. Petrov?"

"My point is that if it made good sense for your predecessor to join this burgeoning movement, it makes good sense for you now as well."

"I'm not my predecessor," Fournier said. "And since you didn't do your due diligence before having this conversation—in which case you would've saved yourself plenty of time and a trip to Lyons—I disagreed with Mr. Dubois on many fronts, most notably the notion that the ECB needs to transition to a new currency."

"I'll give you a moment to reconsider," she said flatly. She fidgeted with the edge of a file folder while awaiting his response.

He sighed as his gaze met hers.

"Frankly, that's never going to happen," Fournier said. It's why I was selected to assume Mr. Dubois' position. The rumor had spread rampantly that he was going to lead Europe into a new economic era with that decision. It's likely the board, at the time, would've ratified the proposal, but that's not the case anymore. Apparently, several members of the board were indebted to you, but that debt has been eliminated. What you held as leverage before is dead weight now. You won't pull the strings any longer with the ECB."

Fournier leaned back in his seat and grabbed his glass of bourbon off the table. Petrov thought he looked like a lawyer who'd just decided to rest after making a strong case. She waited until he was finished with his drink before sliding the folder across the table.

Fournier snatched the folder off the table and opened it. His eyes widened and his forehead scowled as he flipped through the pictures.

"What is the meaning of this?" he said, slamming the stack of pictures onto the table.

"You're a smart man, Mr. Fournier. I think you know all too well what the implications of those photos are."

"Enlighten me, Ms. Petrov."

"That is your daughter, Amelie, is it not?"

Fournier nodded.

"And that's her attending her classes at Le Rosey in Rolle, correct?"

"And?"

"Mr. Fournier, you spend a fine fortune to send your daughter to one of the most elite prep schools in the world. I'm sure you also know how important privacy is to the families of the students who attend there. It might even be one of the main reasons why you enrolled your 15-year-old daughter there."

"I don't like what you're suggesting."

"The Chamber has people everywhere, even at Le Rosey. You may attempt to protect your family every way you can, but I can assure you that you're not as safe as you think you are. And if you aren't willing to agree to my terms, perhaps we can find a new head of the European Central Bank."

Fournier stared at the table, rotating his glass a quarter and pausing before repeating. He continued in this manner for half a minute.

"In the end, Dubois didn't actually agree with your plan, did he?"

She shrugged. "If only you could ask him."

"You overplayed your hand, Ms. Petrov. You could've coerced Dubois to bring this issue to the board and more easily persuaded it to join in. But instead, you tried to strong arm him and look where that left you."

"Look where it left him," she said. "I believe I'm in much better shape today than he is. Wouldn't you agree?"

"Let's not belabor the point. You made a dreadful mistake, one that you will not be able to come back from."

Petrov smiled. "I'm afraid you're not quite as intelligent as I once thought."

"Resorting to insolent comments won't persuade me to acquiesce. I'm afraid you've been terribly wrong when it comes to reading me."

"And I'm afraid you've been quite mistaken when it comes to my resolve in getting what I want."

Petrov pointed at the photos.

"You might want to consider very carefully what you're about to say next because those pictures aren't just glamour shots of your daughter enjoying her time at a ritzy private school on daddy's money. I hope you understand what it is exactly that those pictures suggest."

"Are you threatening me, Ms. Petrov?"

She smiled and subtly shook her head.

"Oh, no. I never threaten anyone, Mr. Fournier. But I do make promises. And here's the promise that I'll make you: If you do not choose to join the new world currency, I'm afraid you'll not only find Europe isolated economically, but you'll also find your family far more fragmented than you ever imagined. *That* is my promise to you."

She raked the folder of pictures toward her across the table and stuffed them in her bag before standing up.

"You have forty-eight hours to think about it, Mr. Fournier. I expect you'll be able to encourage others on the ECB board to join you in helping bring the European banks into the 21st century and stabilize all those floundering economies. Forty-eight hours. Good day."

She glanced over her shoulder at Fournier, who was still eyeing the bottom of his bourbon. He then raised his hand and ordered another shot.

Petrov smiled. She knew she wouldn't have to wait that long for his answer.

CHAPTER 3

Lisbon, Portugal

STRETCHED PRONE ON THE MASSEUSE table, J.D. Blunt looked up at the scene in front of him. The Tagus River finishing its long journey across the Iberian Peninsula by pouring into the Port of Lisbon was long one of Blunt's favorites. He'd worked in the country before with some high-ranking officials in the Portuguese government. Blunt found that extending several off book favors went a long way in keeping friends. He groaned as the woman worked over his shoulder muscles.

"So this is how you spend all your free time?" Hawk asked as he sauntered onto the veranda, accompanied by Alex and Samuels.

"If you'll excuse us for a few minutes," Blunt said to the woman. She nodded and shuffled back toward the house.

Blunt sat up and pulled a robe around him.

"Are you jealous, Hawk?" he asked.

Hawk smiled. "Of this? Who could be jealous of this incredible view of an old European port city from the terrace of a multimillion-dollar home? I mean, I'd much rather be tangling with demented psychopaths in a Middle Eastern desert somewhere with my life on the line any day of the week."

Blunt sauntered over to the wet bar and poured himself a drink. He shot a glance at the television in the corner rolling through the most recent noteworthy news events.

"Help yourself," he said, turning back toward the team and raising his glass.

"I swear, you live the life," Alex said. "Were you getting bored with your place in Morocco?"

Blunt laughed heartily. "I don't own *all* these places, especially not this one. But I do have friends. You should try it sometime."

"How about you just let us try your friends' houses. How does that sound?" Hawk asked.

"I'm not sure you'd be willing to do what I did in order to become pals with some of these people," Blunt said. "And you're better off for it."

Samuels threw up his hands. "I don't wanna know. Please just keep that to yourself."

Blunt ignored Samuels. "The last time I was here, one of my friends in the Portuguese government had a problem with a relentless mistress. She threatened to expose their affair to the world just a few months before the general elections. So, I was asked to take care of it."

Slack-jawed, Alex stared at Blunt. "You killed her?"

"Oh, no, no, no," Blunt said before tossing back the rest of his glass. "I can be cold and calculated when I need to be, but that wasn't necessary in that case."

"Okay," Samuels said. "I'm officially interested now."

Blunt continued. "Well, this government official—who will remain nameless—set up a rendezvous with his mistress in an attempt to smooth things over. He gave the address of a quaint villa on the beach and told her to meet him there the next evening. However, he never showed. But I *just so happened* to be at the cottage next door out on the porch taking in the waves all by my lonesome. When the mistress came to the realization that she'd been stood up, she wandered onto her back porch and started crying. Of course, I hate to see a woman cry, so I trekked over to her to see if I could comfort her. It wasn't long before we were doing more than that—and my friend's secret service detail captured some of the intimate moments on film."

"You knowingly let them photograph you?" Alex

asked.

"Well, I was a gentleman, but I allowed them access long enough to get the suggestive shots my friend needed to make her disappear—well, that and a hefty payout."

"The things you did for your country," Hawk said.

Blunt laughed. "The things I did to earn the trust of friends who own places like this, places far off the beaten path where President Michaels would never think to look for us."

"Is President Michaels really the one we need to be concerned about right now?" Hawk asked. "What about Petrov? Saving Michaels' life should at least buy us some time. But Petrov seems determined to advance her cause based off all the news I've read lately."

Blunt nodded and sighed. "Petrov is a legitimate concern at this point, and quite possibly a higher priority from a global perspective. But our first mission is to defend our country—and sadly, the biggest threat to America right now is our own president. Michaels has resisted Petrov's plans so far, but that won't last long. He is going to ruin our nation if he gets the idea that the U.S. should join all the other nations Petrov has coerced into signing on to her scheme of a one-world currency. It's going to decimate our economy and weaken our security. The more control we give up, the more vulnerable we become."

"That much should seem obvious to anyone," Hawk said. "But it's as if Petrov has brainwashed all the heads of state."

"Or blackmailed them," Alex quipped.

Blunt whipped his head back toward the television as a few phrases caught his ear.

"Turn that up," he said to Samuels, who was standing closest to the remote on a nearby table.

The Spanish news anchor, Maria Vasquez, recounted the breaking news that just rolled across the wire. With her normal smooth delivery disrupted by the hastily written update, she struggled to disguise her shock, though a pleasant one from her perspective. Her faint smile and subtle nod indicated that the news she was reporting was something she agreed with.

Blunt found the report so troubling that he threw his glass.

"What did she say?" Samuels asked. "I think I missed it."

"Just watch," Blunt said, maintaining a steely gaze on the screen.

Vasquez alerted viewers that they would be taken live to a press conference in Beijing. The next image on the screen was the Chinese prime minister explaining his country's decision to ditch the yen and join the single-currency movement that was gaining steam. He pronounced that China would be early adopters instead of waiting for everything to come online. It would begin within the next couple of months as currency production ramped up. Vasquez interjected how long experts believed it would take for that amount of money to be printed and distributed through the world's elaborate banking system. Some projections claimed it would take upwards of five years before all the banks would receive enough money to continue doling out cash.

Vasquez then cut away to a quick interview with an economics professor who wrote a recent book on the demise of cash in our society and how no one would carry paper money and coins within the next decade.

"Fascinating," Blunt said.

"Or terrifying," Alex added. "If the world takes the bait with Petrov's proposition, what's going to back up all this cash? The world is going to be her oyster when it comes to money."

"Even more disconcerting is how there won't be a need for cash ten years from now," Samuels said. "It'll be like Bitcoin for everyone."

"The biggest thing to be on guard about is Petrov's play here," Hawk said. "Whatever she's doing, we know it's not altruistic. Her end game isn't simply to make banking easier for everyone and to help lift other nations out of abject poverty. I'd bet that what she wants to do is actually quite dire."

"Hawk's right," Blunt said. "Petrov has become

a serious threat on the world stage. However, her growing popularity makes her more difficult to dismiss in the public sphere. We're going to have to fight her from the shadows."

"So, we're going after her next?" Hawk asked.

Blunt shook his head. "Never deviate from the course. Michaels is still our top target. If we can stem the tide here, we might be able to demonstrate just how bad of a deal this is for the rest of the world, not to mention how Petrov is quietly wresting power out of the hands of free nations and placing them under her thumb. One day you could be wealthy, but the next you could be practically broke—and all due to the whims of an easily manipulated market."

Before anyone else could say another word, Blunt's head snapped back toward the television where Vasquez announced another breaking news.

"We're going to join another press conference already in progress live from Tokyo," Vasquez said, "where the Japanese prime minister is speaking to the media along with South Korean government officials about the two nations' pending transition to the one-world currency as well."

"This is outrageous," Blunt said.

"Before too long, the U.S. will be the only one left," Samuels said.

"That's exactly what Petrov wants to happen," Blunt said. "She's hell bent on forcing the hand of the

U.S. government—and we're not going to let that happen."

Hawk picked up a copy of the Lisbon newspaper *Expresso* and tapped the headline of a front-page article. Hawk translated from Spanish to English as he read: "The End of Poverty? One-world currency will reduce poverty, experts say."

"It's already begun," Blunt said. "The endless propaganda designed to render the opinions and even the studies from those who reach contrary conclusions. And in the end, it'll make the wealthy feel better about themselves, while the poor get no relief—and Petrov and The Chamber will ascend to an untold position of power."

"So you still think we need to get to Michaels first?" Hawk asked.

Blunt sighed and stared out across the water. A barge loaded with shipping containers pulled away from a dock, where another boat was waiting to take its place.

"We've become so consumed with stuff that the whole world has lost its soul," Blunt said.

"I didn't mean for this to turn into a philosophical discussion," Hawk said. "I was just wanting to know if we should—"

"Ultimately, what we do in this world today has a profound impact on future generations. It doesn't matter what the nature of your work is, it all adds up.

And I'll be damned if I'm going to ignore the fact that the greatest nation on planet earth is getting destroyed from the inside out, its power likely to be stripped by the very man the American people voted to uphold the most ingenious document ever written solely by man, the U.S. Constitution. Michaels will spit on it and mute America's standing and influence globally just to enjoy a more prominent status, personally. If the rest of the world goes to hell in a hand basket, so be it. But if we're not careful, our once-proud nation will be reduced to a footnote in the annals of history by an arrogant self-righteous bastard."

"So, Michaels it is," Hawk said with a grin.

"If we take him down, we might be able to stem the tide of all these nations foolishly ditching their currencies."

Before another word was said, a bullet tore through Blunt's chest. He collapsed to the ground, his face pressed against it. While Blunt struggled to breathe, he watched as Hawk sprang into action. It was the last thing he remembered before everything went dark.

CHAPTER 4

Camp David
Catoctin Mountain Park, Maryland

PRESIDENT CONRAD MICHAELS stretched out on a chair near the pool and read through a recent education bill the Senate had hammered out and was about to put to a vote. The Senate speaker wanted to know if they could count on the president's support before they introduced it. But Michaels was smart enough to avoid walking into a trap, especially so close to the election cycle. Even if the bill looked great on the surface, if it proved to be a dismal failure, Michaels knew his primary opponents would seize on it and use it to challenge his competency in office. However, Michaels never liked reading legislation. He tossed it aside after several minutes of perusing it and then got up to get a refill of bourbon.

As Michaels finished topping off his glass, one of the Secret Service agents approached him with a letter in his hand.

"Sir," the agent said, "this came for you."

Michaels scowled. "So, now you're a mailman? You just hand me random notes without any context or clue of who it came from?"

"One of the kitchen hands asked me to pass it along to you, sir."

"Well, why don't you open it then?" Michaels asked, gesturing toward the letter. "I believe your job is to keep me safe, is it not?"

"I just thought—"

"Open the damn letter," Michaels growled.

The agent complied and handed the handwritten note to Michaels. Almost immediately, Michaels' face fell.

"Is everything all right, Mr. President?" the agent asked.

"Who'd you say gave this to you?"

"One of the kitchen hands, sir."

Michaels wadded up the piece of paper and threw it in the trash. Without hesitating, he stormed into the kitchen.

"Who sent that note to me?" Michaels demanded as he pushed through the swinging door.

However, instead of finding a staff busily preparing food for the next meal, Michaels noticed just one lone chef whacking off the fat from a large steak with a butcher's knife.

"I take it you received my note," the man said in

a thick Russian accent.

"Who are you? And how'd you get in here?" Michaels demanded.

"My name isn't all that important, though if it makes you feel better, you can call me Ivan or Boris or whatever you wish."

"This is one of the most secure locations in the world. How'd you get in here?"

The man laughed before chopping off another strip of fat and tossing it to the side.

"You act surprised, Mr. President. Were you under the impression that being here makes you safe?"

"What do you want?"

"I'm not here to hurt you, but I am here to deliver a message from a mutual friend of ours—Ms. Katarina Petrov."

"I'm not really inclined to hearing anything she has to say."

"Mr. President, did you know that there are almost 19 billion chickens on earth? That's nearly three times as many chickens as people. You would think the chickens would revolt when they realize what is happening to them. They're simply being raised to fill the bellies of man and women, boys and girls. If the chickens are well fed and modestly cared for, the chickens remain happy even as they're led to slaughter."

"Your point, *Boris*?"

"There's only a handful of government bureaucrats able to control the American people. And as long as you keep the people rich and well fed, you can control them. But what happens when they wake up and realize that they aren't rich any longer, that the American dream was—and always has been—a big lie? They won't be so easily controlled. It will be your worst nightmare, this much I can promise you."

"I'm going to call for the Secret Service if you don't hurry up."

The butcher didn't look up, keeping his eyes focused on the meat lying across his cutting board. He swung the knife down hard, trimming a thin slice of fat along the left edge.

"Ms. Petrov would like to strongly urge you to reconsider your position on the one-world currency," the Russian said. "The execution of her plan is going along as expected with one exception—you. If you continue to prevent the U.S. from joining, there will be dire consequences for both you and your country. However, if you change your mind, you'll be compensated handsomely for your efforts. The Chamber holds fast to the belief that happy leaders make the best leaders."

Michaels shook his head. "More like the most compliant ones . . . as you lead them to slaughter."

"President Michaels, feel free to draw any conclusions that you so desire from our conversation, but know that this offer will not remain on the table for very long."

The butcher came down even harder on the meat again.

"Sorry, not interested."

"It's a shame that you are making such a curt dismissal," the Russian said. "It will be tragic for you once you leave office. All that money that you saved up will be gone, rendered as worthless as the paper it is printed on. On the other hand, Ms. Petrov can secure a wealthy future for you by way of this deal."

"And how does she intend to do that?"

"A favorable exchange rate should suffice."

"How much are we talking about here?" Michaels asked.

"Now you're asking the right questions, Mr. President. I knew you'd come around. I'm sure the equivalent of a hundred billion dollars should suffice."

"So, what do you want me to do?"

The butcher trimmed the last side of the piece of beef in front of him.

"Why, Mr. President, I never thought you would ask."

CHAPTER 5

Istanbul, Turkey

KATARINA PETROV FLICKED HER LIGHTER and ignited another cigarette. She took a long drag and threw her head back as she blew a long plume of smoke into the air. She ran her tongue across her top teeth and leaned forward at the table, peering at the laptop in front of her.

"What exactly am I looking at here?" she asked.

Bartu Kemal scooted closer to her and pointed at the screen.

"This is a list of all the files that we know Ahmet Polat accessed," Kemal said. "However, we were able to recover the flash drive he used to download all the files and didn't find any trace of them on his computer."

"So, what you're saying is that he never knew that you switched his flash drive?" Petrov asked.

"That was our goal. We monitored him for several weeks and once we learned of his connection to Blunt, we lured them in."

Petrov took another drag and released the smoke out the side of her mouth.

"And yet we still have no idea how successful your operation was. It's still possible that he was able to get a copy of the device to the Americans, no?"

"It's highly unlikely," Kemal said. "He was a trained analyst with a background in computers, not a highly-skilled operative. He would've had to have given my men the slip one night and figured out a way to mail the drive back to Blunt, all without us seeing, knowing, or suspecting anything. The chances that happened are extremely rare."

"So what you're saying is that you had eyes on him all the time?"

"Ears too. We had a surveillance team listening around the clock. There were no phone conversations. I don't even think Polat had any friends. The only people who came by his house were people delivering food. And we vetted them all. Nothing."

"This whole situation still makes me nervous," Petrov said. "It's a loose end and you know how much I hate loose ends. We need to tie it off quickly."

"What do you suggest?" Kemal asked.

Petrov stared pensively out of the window as she filled her lungs with smoke. She then exhaled slowly. The smoke rolled out of her mouth and settled in a low-hanging haze above the table.

"There is no easy answer here," she said. "If

Polat stole the information and transmitted it back to the U.S., all of our assets could be burned."

"And if not, we'd be the ones burning them."

She nodded. "Do you see my dilemma here? It's very perplexing."

"I could set up something in our server that would alert us if an outside party with access to any of our files attempted to breach our system."

"And how long would it take you to do that?"

"I could finish it in a day or so."

"Good," Petrov said. "Make it happen. I don't want to let this linger for long."

"But that's not the only issue we're facing as it relates to your security," Kemal began.

"Do you think Brady Hawk is going to come for me?"

"I'm almost certain of it," Kemal said.

"What changed your mind? Because you dismissed my inquiry into it just yesterday."

"Just a gut feeling I have," he said. "I don't really know how else to describe it."

"So, he's coming for me—as the Americans would say, sarcastically of course, *big deal*."

"I wouldn't be so flippant about it," Kemal said, choosing his words carefully. "If they capture you, you will have a difficult time launching anything else in the near future, perhaps even the distant future, too."

"I have a feeling you're not telling me everything.

What else are you holding back?"

"Nothing, I swear. I've just worked in this business long enough to know that the Brady Hawks of this world will stop at nothing to capture you and persuade you to think differently about your position."

Petrov smiled. "I welcome the challenge. It's not as if I'm going to be laying down for him, allowing him to run roughshod over me."

"So you have a plan?"

"It's not fully formulated yet, but I do have an idea."

Kemal stroked his chin and stared at Petrov. "Okay," he said. "Let's hear it, shall we? Your partially formed plan is better than anything I've come up with."

"I won't dispute that fact," she said with a wry smile. She stood up and began pacing around the room.

"If Mr. Hawk is going to come for me, let him come for me," she said. "We may not know when he's going to arrive, but if we plan accordingly, he'll walk right into our trap."

"You want to set a trap?" he asked.

She nodded. "And then I want to personally dismember him *slowly*, piece by piece."

CHAPTER 6

Lisbon, Portugal

HAWK SHIFTED IN HIS SEAT in the waiting area of St. Mark's Hospital. He cracked his knuckles and looked at the ground. Then he stood up and paced around for several minutes before restarting the endless cycle of fidgeting. When he returned to his chair, he looked at the row directly across from him and noticed a young boy whose eyes drooped along with the corners of his mouth.

"It's going to be okay," Hawk said in Portuguese.

The boy gave Hawk a faint nod and then resumed staring blankly around the room.

Hawk cracked his knuckles again before Alex grabbed his hands.

"Maybe you should take your own advice," she said.

"This is Blunt we're talking about here," he said. "It's not just an exercise in patience. If he doesn't make it out of this alive . . ."

She patted his hands. "You're right. This *is* Blunt

we're talking about. How many times has he been in a situation like this? Three? Four? Five? He's going to pull through."

"That was a lot of blood at the villa. I don't think I've ever seen him bleed like that."

"Just don't think about the terrible outcomes so much, okay? Worrying about things that haven't happened yet is a waste of time."

Hawk stood up. "I'm going to the chapel to pray."

"You? Pray?" she asked.

"God knows, I'm not the religious type. But there comes a time when you realize that you need help in this messed up world."

"And you're just going to rub the little bottle and God will come out like a genie and make everything better?"

Hawk shrugged. "I don't know about that, but I do know I need some peace right now. Praying is one way I find that."

She forced a smile. "Then you go pray. Pacing around here certainly isn't going to change anything or bring you what you need."

* * *

ALEX WATCHED HAWK exit the waiting room before she turned to Samuels, who was hunched forward in his chair, elbows resting on knees.

"Want some coffee?" she asked.

Samuels shook his head. "I'm fine. I don't need any jitters right now."

"Are you as worried as Hawk?"

"I never feel completely at ease when someone is in surgery for getting shot, but it didn't look that bad to me. Then again, I'm not a doctor. But from my experience, Hawk is probably taking this way too hard. I understand that Blunt is like a father to Hawk in some respects. And I can see how that might make it more stressful."

"But Blunt's going to be okay," she said.

"Is that a question, or are you trying to convince yourself?"

"Maybe a little bit of both? I don't know. I know he's pulled through worse than this before."

"The waiting is the hardest part. You always feel so helpless."

"Sounds like you've spent plenty of hours in a hospital anticipating a report from a surgeon."

Samuels nodded. "I had one of the best big brothers a guy could ask for. Matt was a godsend to me. He used to pick me up from college on the weekends and take me out to eat. He knew I was barely making it, trying to work to pay for school and keep up my grades. He graduated just before I started my freshman year at the University of Texas and started working straight out of school as a pharmaceutical rep. He used to mail me letters once a week. Some of the guys teased me about it and would say it was from my secret admirer. I guess Matt's handwriting wasn't exactly what you'd consider masculine, which stood in stark contrast to his 6-foot-4, 220-pound frame. But I didn't care that they teased me about. I loved it."

"What happened?"

"We were at a club late one night a few months after I'd graduated and started working for this security firm in Austin. I wanted to leave early, but he wanted to stay. We were celebrating his friend's twenty-fifth birthday and I'd had enough. I certainly didn't want to go to work with a throbbing headache the next morning, so I caught a cab home. But Matt stayed and partied with his friends."

Samuels paused and took a deep breath, exhaling slowly before continuing.

"The bar we were at wasn't even in a sketchy part of town, but pipe bombs can be placed anywhere. And the shrapnel packed inside doesn't discriminate either. Four people died aside from the coward who hurled it and then later took his own life after the cops pinned him down."

"Who was the bomber?"

"You think this is the part where I tell you it was a Muslim kid and that's why I wanna fight terrorism, right? But it wasn't. Just some mentally ill bartender who'd been fired from the club they were at. He wanted to strike back at them, make them pay for what they did. In the end, all he did was make a mess of several families' lives before losing his own. And what for? Because he lost his crappy job serving alcohol to people trying to forget about the reality of their lives for a few hours every night. There were no winners in that situation."

"Your brother died at the hospital?"

Samuels nodded. "It was intense. Initially, they were optimistic that he'd be able to pull through, but as they opened him up in surgery, they found shrapnel had ripped through several organs creating some intense internal bleeding. There was nothing they could do in that situation. He died right there on the table."

"You seem pretty calm right now considering what you went through," Alex said, putting her arm around Samuels.

Samuels fought back tears and sighed. "He was your half brother, too. You would've loved him. He reminds me of Hawk."

"Tough as nails?"

"A compassionate warrior. And the world is in short supply of those in this day and age."

A doctor entered the room and studied a chart before speaking.

"Is a Mr. Hawk here?" he asked.

"I'll go get him," Alex said as she stood up. "He's in the chapel."

* * *

HAWK FINISHED HIS PRAYER and stared up at the crucifix attached to the wall behind the lectern. While Hawk proclaimed he wasn't the religious type, he'd spent plenty of hours in church as a kid. The iconic image of Jesus reminded Hawk that even a man who lived a perfect life was tortured and mocked. Suffering was part of the journey, like anything else. But even as Hawk realized it was necessary, he loathed it.

The door to the chapel swung open and Alex strode in.

"The doctor's here and out of surgery," she announced.

Hawk nodded and stood up. "And Blunt?"

"The doc hasn't said anything yet. I wanted to wait until you were done."

"I'm ready. Let's go."

Hawk followed Alex while glancing at his right hand. It was trembling. Holding it steady by using his left hand, Hawk tried to keep pace with Alex. He put his shoulder into the door and pushed it open.

Alex stopped and turned around. "Are you all right back there?"

"I'll be all right," he said. "I'm just moving a little slow."

Alex resumed her pace and turned sharply to the right before coming to a stop with Hawk just a few steps behind her. The doctor was seated in a chair against the hallway wall, studying a chart. When he realized he had company, he shut the chart and rose to meet them.

"Dr. Almeda," he said, offering his hand to Hawk and Alex.

"We appreciate your help, doc," Hawk said as he shook hands with the surgeon.

"Well, you'll be pleased with the news," Dr. Almeda said. "Mr. Blunt was incredibly lucky as the bullet went clean through him without nicking any major arteries. There was only some minor internal bleeding, but nothing that we couldn't quickly get under control."

Hawk sighed and cracked a faint smile. "So, he's gonna be okay?"

"He just needs some rest, but he should be back to full strength in a couple of weeks."

"You don't know him like we do," Alex said. "He'll be fine within the next three days."

Dr. Almeda lowered his chin and cast a quick glance at Alex over the top of his glasses.

"Even the fastest healers need plenty of rest. Discourage him from any strenuous activity for at least two weeks. His body needs time to repair itself."

"Do you have a straightjacket we can borrow?" Alex deadpanned.

The doctor scowled and shook his head. "You can go in and see him now if you like."

"Thanks again," Hawk mumbled before sliding

past Alex and beating her to Blunt's room.

Hawk eased into the room and slowly peered around the corner. Propped up in bed, Blunt was hardly visible, his face covered by the large newspaper he held out in front of him.

"I told you I'm not hungry," Blunt groused without moving the paper to see who'd entered his room.

"Then it's a good thing I'm not bringing you any food," Hawk said.

At the sound of Hawk's voice, Blunt dropped the paper and folded it up before tossing it onto the bedside table.

"You *care* about me," Blunt said, a smile spreading across his face. "If you agents were worth a damn you'd have already caught the bastards who did this to me."

Hawk came around to the side of Blunt's bed and sat in a chair next to him. Alex occupied the other seat facing the foot of the bed before Samuels wandered in.

"The gang's all here, I see," Blunt said.

"But not for long," Hawk said. "We've got to get you out of here."

Blunt laughed. "You think someone is still watching me? Because if they were, I'd likely already be dead by now. I've made you far too suspicious."

"Suspicion is what keeps me alive on most missions—that and Alex being my eyes and ears everywhere," Hawk said.

"It's probably more to do with Alex," Blunt said. "I know she's saved your bacon more times than you care to admit."

"We're a team," Alex said with a grin. She flashed a wink to Hawk.

"And seeing that we're a team, we need to get you out of here because I'm not staying any longer in this petri dish of germs and diseases," Samuels chimed in.

"Hear, hear," Blunt said as he picked up a small paper cup with a couple of pills and raised it in the air. "So, what's the plan?"

Before Hawk could spell it out, Blunt's phone buzzed.

"Hold that thought," Blunt said before answering.

Hawk leaned forward in his chair, elbows resting on his knees. He clasped his hands and looked down at the tiled floor. It was scuffed and dirty, certainly not like any hospital he'd ever visited in the U.S. He halfway listened as Blunt responded with one-word answers and plenty of "yes sirs." And within thirty seconds, the call was over. Blunt hung up and placed his phone back on the tray in front of him.

"That was President Michaels," Blunt said, his face turning dour. "He wants us to stand down in our pursuit of Petrov."

"Did he give you a reason?" Alex asked.

"Does he need to?" Samuels said. "He's the President of the United States."

Hawk stood up and sighed. "I don't like this."

"What?" Blunt said.

"Something just feels off to me. He knows where we are now."

"So?" Alex said. "We're back in his good graces."

"We *were*," Hawk said as he started to pace around the room. "Seems like he's reached some sort of understanding with Petrov."

"You're probably right, Hawk," Blunt said, shoving the tray to the side. "I need to get out of here."

"We all do," Hawk said. "But let's don't make this easy on Michaels. Alex, you're with me. Samuels, you stay with Blunt. We'll bring the SUV around. I'll text you when to start heading downstairs so we can get the hell outta here."

"Sounds like a plan," Blunt said. "Better hurry."

Hawk and Alex walked quickly down the hall, careful not to attract attention by breaking into a slight jog.

"You really think something is up?" Alex asked.

"Blunt always told me to trust my gut. And I'm not about to ignore his advice when it might be his life on the line."

In less than five minutes, they made it their vehicle. Alex texted Samuels to let him know they were driving to the front.

* * *

"IT'S TIME TO MOVE," Samuels said as he hurried across the room to help Blunt out of bed.

Blunt swung his feet around and planted them firmly on the floor. He winced as Samuels grabbed his arm.

"Be careful," Blunt instructed. "It's still tender."

"I thought you were supposed to be battle-axe tough," Samuels said. "Guess you never really know a man . . ."

Blunt groaned. "Let me shoot you through the chest and see how you feel."

An orderly was stationed just outside of Blunt's room and approached the duo.

"Would you like some help getting down?" the orderly asked.

"Absolutely," Blunt said, wasting no time settling into the orderly's wheelchair.

"Where to?" the orderly asked.

"The lobby, please," Samuels answered. "And we're kind of in a hurry, so if you can please speed it up, okay?"

The orderly nodded and guided Blunt down the busy corridor until they reached the elevators. Once inside, Samuels repeatedly hit the button for the lobby.

"You only need to press it once, sir," the orderly said.

Samuels shot the orderly a sideways glance and stepped back from the control panel. Seconds later, the doors eased shut and the elevator began its descent.

Blunt twiddled his thumbs and watched the orderly's hands. They were gnarled, likely from years of hospital work. But still, there was something about him. As the floors ticked past, Blunt studied the man's hands. They appeared steady and calm, not the hands belonging to anyone who was anxious. And Blunt took that as a sign that it was all the more reason to be anxious.

Third floor, second floor, first floor.

Ding.

The elevator slowed to a halt and waited a couple of seconds before opening. Without hesitating, the orderly gestured for Samuels to exit first. But Samuels insisted on trailing.

"Suit yourself," the orderly said as he pushed Blunt forward.

They exited the hospital and reached a small pickup area just outside.

"Is your car here?" the orderly asked.

"There it is right there," Samuels said, pointing toward a black SUV.

Samuels hung back and intensely watched the orderly. Everything appeared normal until the orderly made a sudden move. He reached for a pouch attached to the back of the wheelchair and pulled out a syringe. Ripping the cap off, he tapped it to make sure it was flowing and prepared to jam it into Blunt's neck.

In an instant, Samuels figured out what was happening and dove for the man. In the ensuing scuffle, the orderly lost his grip on the syringe and it bounded away down the sidewalk. Samuels kicked the man in the ribs before scrambling to get the needle. Using his fast reflexes, Samuels rolled the man over and rammed it into his neck. Samuels stood up and eyed the man closely.

"What have you done?" the man gasped.

Samuels watched as the man writhed in pain, grabbing different parts of his body and letting out shrill screams. A small crowd standing nearby had gathered and witnessed the debacle. The man twisted and turned before breaking into what looked like a seizure. Samuels knelt down next to the man and pretended to give him CPR.

"Who sent you?" Samuels asked, gritting his teeth.

The man attempted to flail around.

"I said *who sent you*?" Samuels asked again.

A second later, the orderly's body fell limp.

"Damn it," Hawk said as he rushed up to the scene. "He's gone."

Samuels looked up at Hawk and shook his head.

"All's not lost, Hawk. Trust me on this one."

The small crowd that had been watching the scene unfold buzzed with questions while one person ran off to get a doctor.

"Let's get out of here before the circus arrives," Hawk said.

Samuels and Hawk hustled toward the waiting SUV and drove off.

"We could've used him," Hawk said to Samuels.

Samuels held up the orderly's phone. "We weren't going to get anything out of him anyway through conventional interrogation tactics. But at least we've got this."

"Nice work," Blunt said. "And by the way, thanks, Samuels. I'm pretty sure I would've been the one thrashing about on the ground until my death if you hadn't stopped that man in time."

"No need to thank me, sir," Samuels said. "Just doing my job."

"Speaking of our job," Hawk said. "We apparently don't have one at the moment. And based on what just happened out there, it shouldn't come as a surprise to any of us. However, we do need a new plan—and fast."

CHAPTER 7

Washington, D.C.

PRESIDENT MICHAELS DONNED a hat and sunglasses as a serviceable disguise. Knowing that the Secret Service wasn't hovering over his shoulder or standing guard just outside the room was an enormous relief. While Michaels enjoyed the power and other perks that accompanied his position, he never understood just how intrusive a security detail could be. Without them around, Michaels felt human again for the first time in several years.

Finding a place in Washington where Michaels could meet incognito wasn't easy. However, masquerading as a non-descript man going about his business through the vast network of the Library of Congress' underground tunnels wouldn't earn him a second glance. Employees mindlessly pushed carts along corridors that extended a quarter of a mile or more. Researchers and library employees chatted with one another, unaware of who was in their midst.

Michaels used his burner phone to call and reserve one of the conference rooms in the Jefferson building. He didn't even get much pushback either from the woman who answered the phone. She happily booked it for him and asked him to make sure he had his driver's license with him when he checked into the front desk. When Michaels reached the front desk, he pawned off his fake credentials to gain access without as much as a second glance.

"There you go, Mr. Orwell," she said. "Or would you prefer I just call you George?"

"I'll leave that up to you," Michaels said, amused that the secretary asked him that without even a hint of irony. He understood she had no inkling of an idea who George Orwell was.

I really need to get to work on our education program.

"Just sign right here," she said, pointing to the clipboard on her desk.

Michaels scrawled his fake name and then took the key off the counter. He wound his way through the maze of rooms until he arrived at the conference room. Eight chairs surrounded a table comprised of fabricated dark wood. It was simple, devoid of any of the touches that always accompanied his meetings in the White House. Although, Michaels didn't mind. He reveled in the raw moment, one devoid of people fussing over him in an effort to gain more favor within the White House hierarchy.

He slung his briefcase onto the table and sat down. Exhaling a long breath, he opened up his attaché and studied the stack of papers he'd placed inside before giving the Secret Service the slip.

After a half-hour, the first person opened the door, tentatively poking his head inside.

"Am I in the right spot?" the man asked with a furrowed brow.

"Absolutely," Michaels said. He'd yet to remove the disguise.

"Care to tell me what this is all about?" the man asked.

"What is this all about? It's about accountability—and an incredible opportunity for you to change the course of world history. Please, have a seat, Justice Kellerman."

Kellerman hesitated for a moment before pulling out a chair and sitting down.

"Who are you?" Kellerman asked.

"In due time, Justice Kellerman, in due time."

Michaels leaned back in his chair and templed his fingers as he awaited the arrival of the others justices.

Justice Frank Kellerman had been the justice Michaels was the most familiar with. At age 84, Kellerman was not long for the Supreme Court, if not the world. His thick glasses betrayed his attempts to act as if his vision was sufficient. The gangly hearing aid devices affixed around each ear were necessary for distinguishing any sounds. Using a cane to support, he hobbled around Washington, oblivious to the glances and fingers pointing at him. Not that Kellerman would've cared if he could've seen the looks of pity and heard the whispers. In his prime, he was a battering ram to congressional laws run amok, outspoken in his criticism of lower court judges attempting to legislate from the bench. To consider him a strict constitutionalist was a gross understatement. Kellerman established the bar on what it meant to be the kind of judge who interpreted the U.S. Constitution—nothing more, nothing less. He revered the past and worshipped the framers from long ago who crafted the enduring laws of the land.

Kellerman was the one justice Michaels needed to convince the most to correct a gross injustice from years ago and help pave the way for a more stable—and just—future.

"If there was one thing you wish you could change about the Constitution, what would it be?" Michaels asked.

Kellerman looked up and scowled as he shot a glance at Michaels.

"Did you say something?"

"Yes, Justice Kellerman," Michaels answered, careful to enunciate precisely and speak loudly, "I did. I asked you if there was one thing you could change about the Constitution, what would it be?"

Kellerman glared at him. "It's perfect as it is."

"Perfect? Are you sure?"

"Perfect as something made by men could be."

Michaels' eyebrows shot upward. "So, you're implying that it's not *exactly* perfect?"

"What are you getting at Mr.—"

"Orwell."

"What are you getting at, Mr. Orwell?"

"I'm just wondering if there is something worth changing in the Constitution—and if you'd help me do that."

"How the hell am I supposed to do that? I'm a justice on the Supreme Court, not a legislator. Damn kids today don't even know how the branches of government work. Stupid education system. We've got a nation full of dummies, I tell ya."

Before Michaels could respond, the next justice walked in and then another. By the time the fourth justice filed in, Kellerman raised his objections.

"What is this all about anyway, Mr. Orwell? This is starting to feel very strange to me, and I don't like it."

Then the fifth justice walked in.

Michaels stood up and walked over to the door, shutting it and then locking it. Once he pulled the blinds, he proceeded to take off his disguise.

"Gentlemen and *lady*," Michaels said, giving a distinct nod toward Justice Camille Williams. "I know this is very unorthodox, perhaps even political suicide should anyone ever learn about this meeting. However, I'm trusting that you will all keep the details of this meeting and the fact that it even happened confidential. Can I trust you to do that?"

All the justices nodded, except for Kellerman. He stared at Michaels, making the President wonder if Kellerman knew who he was.

"Justice Kellerman," Michaels said. "It's me, the President."

"Where'd that Orwell guy go?"

Michaels suppressed a smile. "He was just standing in for me until I could get here and didn't want to cause a scene when he left."

"What are we doing here?" Kellerman asked. "I demand to know right now or I'm gonna get up and walk out."

"Settle down, Justice Kellerman," Michaels said. "I need to give you all a little context first before continuing this unorthodox meeting."

"By all means, continue," Kellerman grumbled. "You are the President, for god's sake."

Michaels put on his best politician face and smiled.

"Thank you. Now, the reason you're all here today is because we're facing a crisis of epic proportions. And this is not just hyperbole. In days of old, our freedoms were under assault from madmen wielding weapons of mass destruction. Today, this evil takes a different shape and form, but it's just as devastating in nature. I'm talking about the financial sector."

Michaels paused to pull five packets out of his briefcase and hand them to the justices.

"Make sure Justice Kellerman gets the thick one on the bottom," Michaels instructed. "It was printed specially for him in a large font."

Justice Williams gave Michaels an exaggerated eye roll before fishing the stack of papers off the bottom and handing them to Kellerman.

"Now, what you'll see in here is a brief history of how the Federal Reserve Act came to be—and how it never should have," Michaels continued. "A small segment of private banks have been controlling the entire U.S. economy for over a century with limited abilities to curb this *carte blanche* power the Supreme Court approved of on several occasions despite convincing challenges. I'd argue that those justices who caved did so under immense threat and danger to their own families."

"Do you have proof of this?" Williams asked.

Michaels shook his head. "However, if you look at the voting records of the justices who sided with Congress to uphold the Federal Reserve Act of 1913, you'll find that it was a departure from their usual voting patterns. It's an anomaly if you've ever seen one. Flip to page seven."

Michaels directed them to view the chart that showed the justice's record on cases dealing with fiscal activity—and based on the information presented, Michaels appeared to have a compelling case.

Justice Horford, the junior member of the Supreme Court—and a Michaels' appointee, scratched his neck as he held up his hand.

"Did you have a question?" Michaels asked.

Horford nodded. "So, how exactly does any of this relate to what you suggested at the beginning of the meeting, that there's an *attack* coming?"

"Good question," Michaels said. "In fact, it's already begun. With the one-world currency gaining momentum, the United States and all her assets abroad are at extreme risk to becoming devalued almost overnight. If we're not on board with this, the global board that will be setting the exchange rates for nations that choose to retain the current fiscal system will be at the mercy of this small group of decision makers."

"Sounds exactly like what we have now," Williams said. "Why would you want to go along with this? Seems to me that you simply want to move the country from one failed system to another."

"No, no, no," Michaels said. "This is different. The U.S. government will actually have people on this board if we decide to switch over our currency."

"Then why not petition Congress to do this?"

Horford asked.

"Because it will trigger lawsuits and immense pressure from the group of banks and their shareholders who benefit from the current arrangement," Michaels said. "If we don't get in on the ground floor, we could get shut out or minimized. And I believe that the United States, the one great harbinger of freedoms in this world, needs to be leading in this arena."

Kellerman tapped his cane several times and took a deep breath.

"Did you want to say something, Justice Kellerman?" Michaels asked.

"I don't know," Kellerman said. "It just seems off to me. I don't like getting involved in affairs such as these. It's why we rarely cross paths with the President in public—and never in private. If the public found out about this meeting, they would hang us all, not to mention the fact that even if we agree to overturn the Federal Reserve Act, you still don't have the authority as President to make decisions about currency."

"You just leave that to me, Justice Kellerman," Michaels said with a wink. "I don't need you to figure out everything for me. But I need you to listen to this case in an emergency hearing. Get it on the schedule. Let the two sides present their cases. And make a decision pronto."

"How quickly were you thinking?" Williams asked.

"Almost immediately," Michaels said. "And if you

do, there's going to be some nice perks for you."

"Go on," Horford said. "I'm listening."

"As the world moves in this direction, there's going to be a clarion call to reorganize our justice systems as well, make sure they're all in line with one another. And there's going to be a big need for judges to help fashion and shape global laws. Some of you will have the ability to be on that initial panel to create this new judicial system."

"Intriguing," Williams said. "But be careful about mentioning this to anyone. It could qualify as bribery."

Michaels smiled. "You know I'd never do that. I'm a patriot. I care about making this country the best it can be—and keeping it safe. With our currency as part of this new one-world system, I'll be going a long way in making good on my promise to improve this already great nation better and keep it even safer."

Kellerman cleared his throat, arresting the attention of everyone in the room.

"Did you have something you wanted to say, Justice Kellerman?" Michaels asked.

"I hope you'll be prepared for all the constitutional challenges in court that a change of this magnitude will bring," Kellerman said. "The kinds of lawsuits that will be filed almost certainly demand that we issue a stay. Anytime a new law will create that kind of upheaval, the kind that will affect every financial institution in this country, you have to wait."

"It won't matter," Michaels said. "Trust me."

"I'm no constitutional scholar, but—"Kellerman said, pausing as he put his finger in the air before a wry smile spread across his lips. "No, wait. I am a constitutional scholar and you're going to be in for one hell of a fight."

"That's why I'm giving you a heads up about this now, so it won't be such a battle," Michaels said. "We have enough division in this country as it is. And I'm well aware that this likely won't be a 9-0 decision, though that would be nice. However, we need to come together around something like this. This is one of those times where the American people and all the pundits in the media have no idea how devastating remaining under our currency will be to the financial sector."

"I hope you aren't just doing this to get re-elected because you have no idea how to jumpstart the economy," Horford said. "That was one of your key campaign promises."

Michaels paced around the room as he talked.

"Getting elected and making this country great—or in this case, keeping it from going off the rails—are vastly different things," Michaels countered. "Of course I know that I'll get re-elected if the economy isn't falling apart. That's Presidential Campaigning 101. But I'd do this if I were at the end of my second term. We all have wealth we want to protect. Every single

American who's working or has a bank account does. To not make a move of this nature would be like taking all the money they worked so hard to earn and rendering it useless. And that's not even to mention what it would mean for the U.S. dollar overseas. Our people wouldn't be able to travel. Businesses with an international presence would be devoured almost overnight. We'd be condemned to the poor

3..house—but I'm refusing to stand by and let that happen, re-election or no re-election."

"Fair enough," Horford said.

"Can I count on all of you to make sure you'll take up this challenge and seriously consider righting one of the greatest wrongs in this country?" Michaels asked.

Four of the five justices bobbed their heads in agreement. Kellerman was the lone dissenter.

"Justice Kellerman," Michaels began, "is there something you find objectionable about this?"

"Aside from this whole dog-and-pony show right now," Kellerman said. "I'll need to be convinced in court."

Michaels nodded. "I understand. You don't want to violate your conscience—and you shouldn't have to. None of you should. But just consider what's happening now and think about it. The framers of the constitution couldn't have imagined a scenario like this and they certainly wouldn't have given the power to

Congress if they ever thought Congress would be crooked and inept as it is today."

"I'll consider it," Kellerman said.

Michaels gave a hint of a smile. "That's all I can ask—legally, that is."

A knock at the door for all intents and purposes ended the meeting. Michaels gestured for everyone to exit out of the door on the opposite side of the room, one by one. He told them to scatter about the building and suggested that they check out some legal books from briefs written a couple of hundred years before.

When the last justice was gone, Michaels sauntered over to the door and opened it.

"Mr. President," the Secret Service agent said. "What are you doing here? And why did you give us the slip?"

"Don't worry," Michaels said. "It wasn't anything important. I just needed to feel normal again, not like I needed a damn babysitter to walk down the street."

"I understand, sir, but—"

"Save your lecture on protocol for someone else," Michaels said. "Perhaps for someone who cares because I simply don't."

"It's our job to keep you safe," the agent said.

"And I'm in no danger here, okay? You can wait outside while I finish some reading here."

The agent didn't argue. He was trained to do everything the President said and when the President said it. And Michaels knew it. Without another word, the agent slunk outside and took up his post outside the door before closing it.

* * *

BIG EARV WAITED IN THE HALLWAY while one of his fellow Secret Service agents retrieved the Red Ranger, the name Michaels selected for himself to be used among those protecting him. At first Big Earv thought it was merely a coincidence that he happened to see Justice Kellerman in a rare public sighting, even though the annals of the Library of Congress hardly qualified as such. Then Big Earv saw Justice Williams.

When Justice Horford strolled by, keeping his head down and refusing to look up, Big Earv knew something strange was happening. The fact that he was at the Library of Congress retrieving the President meant something had gone terribly wrong. The trio of justices he spotted only made the situation more suspect.

Big Earv picked up his cell phone and called Vice President Noah Young.

"Do you know where Red Ranger is?" Young asked once he answered the phone.

"Probably in the Caves of Alhambra by now," Big Earv said, using Michaels' personal nickname for the White House. "But that's not where he was a half-hour ago."

"What was he doing? Nothing was on his schedule."

"He was at the Library of Congress."

"The Library of Congress. What for?" Young asked, his voice rising an octave.

"I can't be sure, but I also think it can't be a coincidence that I just saw three Supreme Court justices wandering the halls within minutes of one another, coming out of the same area where Red Ranger was."

"Whatever it is, he's up to no good."

"Roger that."

CHAPTER 8

Melbourne, Australia

KATARINA PETROV SAUNTERED AROUND the room and sipped her tea. The glass wall overlooking Port Phillip Bay was one of the best settings she'd encountered outside of Europe for a meeting of this importance. Usually she would've preferred a boardroom at the top of a building without any windows. But this wasn't a banker or some business powerbroker she was meeting with. Malcolm Tabart wasn't the kind of person she wanted the public to know she was conspiring with. Her conversations with him needed to be held in person and in private, away from prying eyes and loose lips.

Petrov had stopped her pacing, mesmerized by a catamaran with full sails slicing through the water.

"It's beautiful, isn't it?" Tabart asked as he entered the room, interrupting Petrov's contemplative moment.

"How could you ever leave this place for a far

less picturesque home in Canberra?"

"To be the prime minister of Australia, one must make sacrifices."

"There are some sacrifices that seem too great."

Tabart laughed as he finger combed the sparse strands of silver across the top of his head.

"It's also as private of a place as I'll ever have. Keeps all those nosey photographers out with their zoom lenses, trying to land a picture of me on the front page of some rubbish tabloid."

"I'm sure Sandra appreciates the ability to get away from the political spotlight."

"Yes, my wife very much enjoys this place—when she's not traveling with her business. Quite frankly, I come here more often than I should, and definitely more often than my critics feel is necessary. There's always some columnist in *The Herald* yammering on about my gross abdication of responsibility. I used to take those comments seriously, but I've learned that my style of governance is more effective when I'm focused on doing what's best for the people as opposed to trying to appease the rabble-rousers."

"Speaking of which, have you had time to consider our proposal?"

Tabart gestured toward the couch. "Please, have a seat and let's talk about it."

Petrov complied and placed her teacup and saucer on the coffee table in front of her.

"I sense some hesitancy in your voice, no?" Petrov said.

Tabart shrugged. "Hesitancy, uncertainty, fear—call it whatever you like, but there is definitely an uneasiness about introducing this to Parliament."

"Why not? The Australian dollar has languished behind other currencies when compared to global market. This could be just the opportunity Australia needs to regain influence economically."

Tabart leaned back in his seat and stared out the window, remaining pensive for a moment before responding.

"I've worked hard to keep this country from spiraling into a recession. While the rest of the world was in panic mode, we stayed true to the path set out before us. Build slowly to go fast, as the Americans say. Over there, it's a meaningless axiom, betrayed by their culture of having everything right now. But under my leadership here, it's become a mantra embraced by all. There's not a bloke with a business who doesn't know that phrase. They teach it in the universities now, business schools have created t-shirts with the saying on it. It's just everywhere. And then if I were to suddenly announce a shift in our currency?"

Petrov cocked her head to one side. "If you don't, you'll be building with worthless material—unless you're comfortable entering into an isolationist phase here. I know Australia has plenty of natural resources, but you don't have everything you need here to build a robust infrastructure. And the last thing you want is to be held hostage by a worthless currency."

Tabart narrowed his eyes. "That sounds vaguely like a threat, Katarina. And how long have we been friends?"

"For many years, Malcolm. However, this is not a threat. It's a warning of what will happen. Market forces will be out of my hands once the new currency is enacted. For those nations who adopted early, wealth will be built immediately. For those who waited or chose to remain in an antiquated system, fortune will not smile upon them. They will be enslaved by their poor choices due to how the global economy works. You'll only have yourself to blame."

"When do you need to know?" he asked.

"As soon as possible. There is a council forming that will help determine the exact date for when and how everything will be enacted. We're working with private banks and governments from all the countries embracing this change. It's the way of the future, Malcolm. You don't want to get left behind."

He sighed. "I'll give it some more thought. I'm on holiday next week and I'll discuss this with some of my aides and solicit their input."

"That would be wise," she said. "However, don't wait too long. I refuse to work with a table that's overcrowded, especially filled with obstinate people who joined to further their personal agendas. I know you're not like that, Malcolm. You're different. You want what's best for Australia, and deep down you know this is what's best, even if it might be a painful transition."

"What you're saying makes sense, but still there's—"

"What? An election to consider? Don't think I won't be able to help have your political campaign coffers filled should you decide to go along with this idea."

"I promise you that I will seriously consider this decision and notify you of my intentions as soon as possible."

Petrov stood up and smoothed out her skirt. "Very well then. I do have one more piece of information to help you make your decision."

"Oh?"

Petrov walked across the room toward the chair in the corner where she'd placed her briefcase. Tabart followed her closely.

"It's in here somewhere," she said, rifling through the bag. "Oh, here it is."

She collected the folder and handed it to Tabart.

He opened it, and immediately his mouth fell. His right hand trembled while his left hand covered his mouth.

"How dare you?" Tabart said, refusing to look at the pictures anymore as he slapped the folder shut. "I will not be subject to your extortion."

Petrov shrugged. "It's not extortion. It's simply a picture. You are free to infer from it whatever you wish. But I will warn you that your window isn't as blacked out as you might think. Someone on the beach with the right type of equipment could easily snap photos of you through the window, as you can see right here."

She flipped open the folder in his hand and peered at one of the photos.

"Must've been one of those weekends when Sandra wasn't here," Petrov said.

"Get out," Tabart growled.

Petrov turned toward the door and grabbed the knob before leaving her parting shot.

"One week," she said. "That's all you've got. After that, I'm going to consider Australia to be a lost cause and share as much with the world. One week."

She closed the door behind her and walked down the steps toward her car and driver. A faint smile spread across her lips.

Australia? Check.

CHAPTER 9

Portree, Isle of Skye
Scotland

BLUNT STARED WIDE-EYED at the heaping plate of breakfast food in front of him. Bacon, scrambled eggs, hash browns, black coffee—Blunt found it all to be perfect. He placed his napkin in his lap and picked up his fork, anticipating what he suspected would be a delightful meal.

"How did you do this, Hawk?" Blunt asked as his agent entered the dining room.

"Is this place safe?" Hawk asked. "I remember what happened here last time."

"Can you answer my question first and then leave? I simply want to savor every bite. It's been far too long since I had a breakfast like this. If Texas could knight someone . . ."

Blunt picked up the bottle of hot sauce on the table and grinned.

"You thought of everything, didn't you?"

Hawk forced a smile. "I figured you needed some comfort food, Texas style."

"It's perfect."

"So, what about your security here?"

Blunt shook his head. "Do you ever listen to me? What don't you understand about the word *leave*?"

"I heard you loud and clear, but after what happened the last time we were here."

"Don't worry. The house has been sold twice since we were last here. Once to an old friend of mine here who The Chamber would never be able to link us together and then to a shell corporation I created. It's a non-profit that helps kids. They won't touch us here."

"You still didn't answer my question about the security."

"It's been upgraded, state of the art. Now, will you either shut up about all that so I can eat in peace this incredible breakfast you made or go pester someone else?"

Hawk exited the room, where Blunt spent the next ten minutes scarfing down every morsel on the plate. For a few fleeting seconds, he contemplated licking it but decided against it in the off chance that one of the Firestorm team members would walk in and catch him in the act. Ultimately, he didn't want to endure endless teasing for a momentary pleasure.

"Hawk, I'm done," Blunt announced loudly.

He stood up and lumbered over to the kitchen

sink where he placed his dishes.

"There is no kitchen fairy here," Alex said, watching him from the doorway. "Those dishes don't magically float into the dishwasher."

"That's not how that works?" Blunt asked with a wink.

"No, it's not," Hawk said as he joined them. "And when I've made a big meal like I did this morning, I don't feel like it's my job to clean everything else up. If you partook of the fruits of my labor, the least you can do is the dishes."

"My, you're jumpy today, Hawk," Blunt said. "I know it's only eight-thirty in the morning, but do you need a beer?"

Hawk headed straight toward the kitchen table and took a seat. Samuels pulled out the chair next to him and sat down.

"We're safe here," Samuels said, giving a reassuring pat on the back to Hawk.

"In this world, we're never safe," Hawk said. "There's always something or someone lurking around the corner. Forgive me for refusing to join in your giant relaxation party, but I'm just anxious to get back out there and put an end to this once and for all."

Blunt poured himself another cup of coffee and took a seat at the head of the table, opposite of where Alex had settled.

"If you ever think of this job as a task to be finished, you're never going to be satisfied with your work," Blunt said.

"Then what's even the point?" Alex asked. "I mean, even if we are successful in taking down Petrov, does that really matter? Will the one-world currency movement live on after she dies?"

"That's not something I can answer right now, but I hope to make this less of a hypothetical question and find out exactly what will happen in short order," Blunt said.

"I think we should still go after Petrov," Hawk said, tapping the table for emphasis. "She's the one person holding this whole thing together for The Chamber. If she goes away, so does the momentum for this crazy plan that's going to either set the U.S. back to the Dark Ages or put us under the thumb of an oppressive leader—and I'm not comfortable with either of those outcomes."

Blunt's phone rang and he snatched it up off the table.

"I need to take this," he said.

Staggering to his feet, Blunt shuffled into the study and shut the door behind him.

"There's something big happening in Washington right now," said the man on the other end. "Very big."

"Slow down, Noah," Blunt said, determining quickly it was the Vice President, Noah Young. "What's going on?"

"I just got a call from our mutual Secret Service

friend," Young said. "Apparently, Michaels just slipped his security detail and went down to the Library of Congress for a special meeting. But you won't believe who he met with."

"The Russians? The North Koreans?"

"Nothing quite that disturbing from the arena of global politics, but a group that makes meeting with him far more sinister."

"You got me."

"The Supreme Court."

Blunt let out a long slow whistle. "I need more details on this."

"I wish I had more, but I don't. All I know is that one of our agents knew Michaels donned a disguise and proclaimed to be a man named George Orwell, using his false identity to book a meeting room at the Library of Congress. The agents found him, but only after the meeting had dispersed. A few minutes later, our mutual contact identified three Supreme Court justices in the building."

"Perhaps the justices were there for research," Blunt countered.

"You know how big that place is, which means you know how preposterous those words sound coming out of your mouth."

"So, what if he did meet with them? What does that prove?" Blunt asked.

"The scuttlebutt around Washington right now

is that the Supreme Court is going to agree to listen to a challenge to the Federal Reserve Act of 1913."

"A law that's been intact for over a century?"

Young forced a laugh. "Uh-huh. My sentiments exactly. I'm betting Michaels had to convince them just to take the case."

"Not to mention get assurances that the votes will fall in his favor."

"If not, why even go through all the trouble in the first place? The only thing that makes sense is that Michaels is mounting this challenge with the express purpose of wresting control away from Congress."

"But he'd still need an amendment to give that power to the executive branch."

Young hesitated. "Not exactly. There are other ways to exert your authority if you're President."

Blunt's mind whirred as he tried to conceive of what pathway would provide Michaels with the clout to seize governance over the country's finances. Then it dawned on him.

"He wouldn't?" Blunt said, half asking, half stating.

"He'll kill me, given the chance," Young said. "Do you really think he'd stop at nothing to make this a reality?"

"But why? I don't understand it. Petrov tried to kill him."

"Petrov is playing him for the fool that he is.

Michaels is very concerned with getting re-elected right now. But that will be the least of his concerns once this story leaks out. Jail will be a likelier option if the FBI has the guts to launch an investigation against him. The lying and the coercion will barely cause someone to arch an eyebrow once the rest of what he's done comes to light."

"This is a mess," Blunt said.

"You're telling me. Just go figure out a way to fix this fiasco."

"Roger that," Blunt said before he hung up.

He rummaged through his desk drawer before finding a lighter. However, he'd been looking for his cigar cutter for days and figured this was as good of a time as any. After a few minutes of fruitless searching that included loud swearing and the intermittent pounding of fists, Blunt slumped back in his chair. He was already irate over Michaels' attempt to usurp the Constitution in a sneaky—albeit it, legal—way.

A knock at the door interrupted his frantic search.

"Looking for these?" Hawk asked.

Blunt turned around to see Hawk holding up a cigar cutter in one hand and a cigar in the other. Forcing a smile, Blunt nodded.

"Well, I was looking for the cigar cutter, but that stogie looks far fresher than this one which was hanging out in this drawer for who knows how long."

"Rough phone call?" Hawk said as he strode across the room and handed both objects to Blunt.

"Yeah, let's talk about it with the rest of the team."

Blunt stood up and returned to the dining room with Hawk.

"We have a serious problem," Blunt said as he clipped one end of the cigar and then jammed it into his mouth. "Michaels held a secret meeting with several members of the Supreme Court today. Nobody outside of a handful of Secret Service agents even know about this."

"And now us," Hawk said.

Blunt nodded. "Now that we do, we must act immediately. There isn't time to waste here."

"So, we're officially done with Petrov?" Samuels asked.

Blunt chewed hard on his cigar. "We're never going to be done with her, but for now? Yes. We're going to lay off her for the time being. We need to weaken her position first and at least give Michaels the illusion that we're on his side."

"He has to know that we figured out he ordered some agent to kill you," Hawk said.

Blunt shrugged. "Maybe, maybe not. My money would be on Michaels who initiated the hit, mostly because he's probably the only person who could've tracked us there. But he needs to take a number and get in line behind a slew of others who want me dead. The best thing for us to do right now is to act as if we're following his orders and falling in lockstep with his commands."

"That move will certainly play to his ego," Alex said.

"But that means we'll be back in Washington with big targets on our backs," Samuels said. "I don't know how comfortable I am with that plan."

"If you think things are bad for us now, I can promise you our situation will be a hundred times worse if Petrov has convinced Michaels to join her on this fool's errand," Blunt said. "We have to lay low and bring Michaels' scheme to light."

"It's all so dizzying," Alex said. "What could my mother—Petrov—have done to get Michaels back on board? She tried to *kill* him a few weeks ago."

Blunt shook his head. "Petrov has a knack for finding just the right pressure point."

"You mean she has blackmail material for everyone?" she asked.

"Same difference. In the end, she's going to get her way. She's always been like that."

"Unfortunately for her, she's running up against her own daughter who has inherited her mother's resolve," Hawk said with a smile and a wink.

"So, this is settled?" Samuels asked.

Blunt nodded. "We're going to go stop Michaels first."

CHAPTER 10

Washington, D.C.

THE NEXT COUPLE OF DAYS in Washington were filled with enough news to dominate the national headlines. President Michaels watched the cable news channels and wondered how many CEOs would choose a time like this to announce a recall or some other news that would normally result in severe damage to their company's reputation. But in a week where Washington politics were front and center? No one would likely notice.

The news about dustup on the House floor between two congressmen resulted in an enormous number of commentaries, not to mention enough memes and gifs to saturate social media for weeks to come. Almost lost in the throwback to the 19th century era of American politics was what caused the fight to begin with: Two bullheaded politicians trying to gain the political high ground in the debate over the Federal Reserve's reluctance to embrace the one-world currency. Politicians had held their finger to the wind of American sentiment, anxious to determine which way the public was swaying before taking a position. And in classic 21st century politics, the two prevailing parties couldn't reach a consensus and work together. Credit had to trump cooperation.

Michaels smiled as the news unfolded. Every last piece of news was playing into his hands. Lost in raucous was the fact that in the lower courts, two attempts to challenge the constitutionality of the Federal Reserve Act of 1913 had been dismissed. There wasn't even a mention in *The Washington Post*'s political round up, apparently deemed as some moronic crusade unworthy of the public's time and attention.

However, that all changed the following morning when the Supreme Court announced it would hear briefs in the case and would hold them in two days in an emergency hearing. The announcement caught everyone off guard. Journalists scrambled to report who was behind the challenge and what the potential fallout of a reversal of the law could mean, a law that had withstood far more aggressive challenges throughout history than this one.

Michaels sipped on a cup of coffee as he flipped the channel across several news channels to listen to what commentators were saying. Some agreed with the challenge and said it should've been overturned years ago. Others thought the lawsuit was ridiculous, as was the "antiquated" Supreme Court justices for agreeing to take it up. But regardless of what any pundit thought about the situation, Michaels' name was glaringly absent. Not even a mention of what the president might think about a potential landmark change to the law.

With Washington abuzz over the news and impending case, Michaels recorded his weekly radio address to the nation. He didn't have the flair Roosevelt did with his fireside chats, but Michaels found the opportunity to speak his mind directly to the American people without a filter quite refreshing. He liked using social media as well, but he found messages were often lost or misinterpreted in the small number of characters allowed to craft his idea. He also felt any form of digital communication was often subject to the loss of tone, giving the user the power to determine the intent of whatever was conveyed. Michaels found utilizing social media oftentimes counterproductive. But the radio address was golden.

He entered the studio to record something he'd written himself. No speech writers, no input from aides. Just Michaels and a pen with some paper. He'd never felt so proud of his oratory skills than he did when he read what he'd written. Everything he said, he did so with conviction and passion.

For the first time since he'd been elected, Michaels felt like he was poised to make a difference.

He was convinced that his leadership for the country was necessary in a time like this.

In a moment of gut-wrenching honesty, Michaels realized he was overselling his importance. And his leadership was little more than dancing to the tune Katarina Petrov commanded him to. But no one had to know. He'd gone to great lengths to make sure he was shielded from any controversy. The only people who could blow the lid off his plan were the five justices he'd asked to attend a secret meeting. And if one of them dared to expose Michaels, they'd all be considered equally guilty by the public and perhaps even by governing law boards. If any of the justices cared about their position and reputation, they would never breathe a word of what happened to anyone—and Michaels knew they all cared deeply about legacies. All judges with aspirations for the Supreme Court eyed their place in U.S. history with great contemplation. But Michaels escalated their dreams by offering the proverbial carrot on the stick: Vote for me and you will find yourself on the first world court.

Michaels had no idea if it would come to pass or not—at least not while he was in office. But his offer was compelling enough to sway any fence sitters. Ultimately, how the justices voted regarding the challenge to the Federal Reserve Act was all that concerned Michaels. There would be no going back for them once the law was struck down, clearing the path for the next phase of Michaels' plan.

Everything was falling in to place. And as long as nothing went wrong, Michaels would be celebrating an unprecedented political coup in less than a week.

Michaels listened to his recorded address several times before signing off on it. Satisfied with the tenor of his recording, he returned to his office. He hadn't been sitting down more than two minutes before his secretary buzzed him on his phone.

"Mr. President?" she asked.

"Yes, Heather. What is it?"

"You've got a call on line 2. It's urgent."

"Who is it?"

"Just take the call," she said before hanging up.

Michaels pressed the blinking light on his phone and answered.

"This is President Michaels."

"Who knew it'd be so easy to reach you?" said a woman.

"Justice Williams, what a fine pleasure it is to speak with you today. It's been quite some time. What is it I can do for you?"

"Quite some time?" she said. "Cut the bullshit. I don't care if this conversation is being recorded or not."

"No need to dispense with proper decorum or begin with such hostility. However, I can tell that something isn't right."

"You know damn well something isn't right," she said. "I know what you're up to."

"Of course you do," Michaels said. "I shared it with you."

"No, that's not what I'm talking about. I figured out what your end game is and I'm not going to be party to these shenanigans that are making a mockery of our Constitution."

"What are you going to do, Justice Williams? Report me? Need I remind you that I buried plenty of skeletons from your past when I was on the Senate Judiciary Committee that was working hard to get your nomination cleared?"

"You didn't bury anything," she said. "You keeping a few embarrassing things from my past personal life out of the mainstream media could hardly be considered *burying* something. That was a professional favor. I could've endured it, though it doesn't matter now that Henry's dead."

"So you think now that your husband is dead that it wouldn't be any less embarrassing to you if it became public?"

"Do whatever you wish, but I'm not on board with what you're trying to do here. And I can promise you that—"

"Save your angry rhetoric and empty promises for the brief, Justice Williams. And if it's not in favor of what I suggested, I hope it's for the dissenting opinion."

Michaels hung up and stewed for several minutes. He hadn't anticipated any defectors so soon. But there were other ways to deal with Justice Williams and the problem at hand.

Michaels picked up his phone and buzzed his secretary.

"Heather, get me Frank Stone at the Pentagon on the line. Let him know that I have an urgent matter to discuss with him."

CHAPTER 11

Milan, Italy

KATARINA PETROV SURVEYED the group of leaders she had assembled in pressing forward with her plan to initiate the one-world currency. In a conference room atop the UniCredit Tower, the diversity of the people gathered around the table was vast, as were their feelings toward her. Against her better judgment, she strong-armed Fournier and Tabart into compliance. The Chinese and South Korean delegates had been willing participants, eager to join a seismic shift in global economics. But Petrov held fast to the belief that the ends justified the means—and this was just the first step.

She stood up from her seat at the head of the table and leaned forward on her knuckles.

"Thank you all for coming together for this truly historic meeting," she said. "There's little doubt in my mind that years from now what happens in this room today will be written about in the annals of history. It will be the moment described as when the world banded together, all for the good of the whole."

She started to pace, her tone measured as she spoke.

"For some of your countries, the decision to make this shift will mean your economy will suffer in the short term," she continued. "It's not easy to convince your fellow citizens that even though it's not immediately in their best interest to do this, it will be better for the world as a whole. Most people care more about their current state of affairs than anything else. But you—you are all visionaries, people with a dream about what this world can become. And it is because of you and your ability to set aside poll numbers and public opinion in favor of simply doing what is right. Every one of you is a hero. And while you may not feel like it now, in due time, you will. People will celebrate your courageous leadership for years to come."

She cast a glance at Malcolm Tabart, who refused to make eye contact with her from the moment he entered the room. She scanned the table and locked eyes with Gaspard Fournier, who forced a smile, though his narrowed eyes betrayed him.

"As we gather here in Milan, just north of one of the most famed cities in the world, we are aware of a famous axiom about this city: Rome was not built in a day," Petrov said. "In fact, Rome was built over many years of hard work by ambitious politicians and generals who imagined an empire that would benefit the entire world. That is our aim as well. We know that what we are on the cusp of doing is not something we can accomplish by signing a document and making a statement in front of journalists. No, what we decide today in this room is just the beginning."

She walked back to the head of the table and eased into her chair.

"Now, before we construct the final agreement to all sign, are there any issues we need to discuss before we move forward?"

The room remained silent for several seconds other than a few men restlessly shifting in their seats. Claude Bertrand, the director of the French banking system, finally spoke.

"I know this might sound ironic coming from a Frenchman, but I can't help but notice the glaring absence of a delegate from the United States around this table. They have not been what I would consider cooperative under President Michaels, but they are still an economic power in the world today. What happens if they decide to downgrade the one-world currency?"

Petrov shrugged. "Why do we need the United States? They do far more importing than exporting. If they want the goods our countries produce, they will have to pay the market rates that we determine."

Ville Löfström, a diminutive Finnish man, cleared his throat before responding.

"If I may," he asked, nodding toward Petrov.

She gestured for him to continue.

"I find the exclusion of the United States from this one-world currency proposal somewhat problematic," Löfström said. "They import a large number of electrical equipment we produce, not to mention some of our machinery as well. They are our third largest importer. If we lose them as a partner, it will make a significant dent in our economy. I am not sure we can afford to lose them without suffering needlessly."

"This new arrangement will not prevent Finland from trading with the United States," Petrov said. "Let me be very clear on that point."

"But when the exchange of goods ceases to be economically feasible, we will in essence lose them," Löfström said as he pushed his glasses up on his nose.

"In that case, it will be business as usual, Mr. Löfström," Petrov said. "Every country knows that trading partners come and go. Perhaps this new currency will open new doors for Finland."

"The Finnish people are a fickle lot. Signing on with this plan has the potential to cripple our exports. I am not so sure this is in our best interest."

Petrov leaned back in her chair and folded her arms.

"And what about all your other trading partners?" she asked. "If you think this will make it more difficult with the United States, consider how much more difficult it will make trading with European countries. The ECB has already announced it will make this change, so the euro as we know it will cease to exist. Are you prepared to return to the markka if you fail to join?"

"I will not sign," Löfström said. "Not today anyway. We still need to debate this in parliament."

"That would be ill-advised," Petrov said. "Besides, there is still time for the United States to join. They may not receive the prominent standing its leaders are accustomed to because of their refusal to become a charter member, but they are always welcome to unite with the rest of the world in this groundbreaking movement."

Stephan Fischer, a member of the German contingent, raised his hand.

"Mr. Fischer, do you have a question?" Petrov asked.

He nodded. "I was wondering what the next steps are. Germany is anxious to move forward."

"I would like to make a formal announcement tomorrow," she said. "And I would like to have full participation from everyone represented here. It will be very important for the media to portray the one-world currency initiative as united on all fronts. Perhaps it will be enough to persuade our American friends to change their minds when they see what they will be missing."

Löfström pushed back from the table. "In that

case, I will not be able to stand with you tomorrow or sign any agreement."

"We are not asking you to sign a legally enforceable contract, Mr. Löfström," Petrov said. "We are simply asking that you sign a document stating the intention of Finland to join all the other signatory nations. But if you simply must dissent—"

"I must," Löfström interrupted. "It would be unwise for me to do anything else."

Petrov shrugged and continued with the meeting.

"It's settled then," she said. "I will have a document prepared for everyone to sign in the morning ahead of our announcement that we will make to the press. Meet me here tomorrow at nine and we will address the media at ten."

The group of leaders stood up and exited the room, some more jovial than others. Amidst the low, dull murmur of conversations, Petrov listened for any open dissenters or grumbling. She was serious about her desire to present a united front—and nothing was going to stop that.

* * *

THE NEXT MORNING in the lobby of the UniCredit Tower, Petrov watched the signatories to the one-world currency initiative file in with somber faces. She never once considered postponing the announcement, even though she anticipated requests to do so.

But no one complained.

"Can you believe what happened last night?" Claude Bertrand asked Petrov. "I mean, we were just sitting around the table with him yesterday."

Petrov shook her head and looked down, not out of shame but out of duty. She needed Bertrand and anyone else watching her to believe she had nothing to do with the death of Ville Löfström.

"I have been to Milan many times," she said, "and I have never feared for my life while walking the streets. To think that he was murdered for a couple hundred euros just goes to show how dangerous the world is becoming. It has never been more evident to me than it is now how important our work is. The inequality we face in wages will tear people apart if we do not take swift steps to correct this."

Bertrand nodded. "Perhaps we should name the agreement after him."

Petrov flashed a faint smile. "That is an excellent idea. The Löfström Agreement—it has a nice sound to it."

"We are ready to begin," said the media relations expert Petrov had hired for the event. "The press will wait until your opening statement and then they will begin to funnel questions through me. Understand?"

Petrov nodded. She had been waiting for this moment for a long time.

CHAPTER 12

Washington, D.C.

HAWK FELT UNEASY about leaving Blunt by himself in Scotland to recover, but he insisted it was best for the team. Blunt explained that he would be a liability since his skills weren't what they used to be. While Hawk didn't like the idea, he couldn't argue with Blunt's reasoning. From a strategic standpoint, leaving Blunt behind certainly made the most sense. Hawk finally agreed, but not without plenty of handwringing and suggested alternative ideas. In the end, Blunt's stubbornness—and good sense—trumped Hawk's desires to keep Blunt protected by the Firestorm team.

"I didn't bring this team together to protect me," Blunt said in his closing argument. "I brought it together to help protect the United States of America. And that's exactly what you're going to do."

Hawk and the rest of the team took Blunt's jet back to Washington and went to work immediately on how they would shut down Michaels' plan. Their first step was to meet with Vice President Young to discuss any new developments that occurred since Blunt's shooting. The team arranged an unorthodox meeting in the men's room with him, Hawk and Samuels during a fundraiser Young was hosting at a downtown hotel.

Hawk and Samuels hid in a janitor's closet while two Secret Service agents cleared the room.

"Clear," Hawk heard one of the agents shout.

Once the door slammed shut, Hawk heard the shuffle of feet. After a few seconds, he and Samuels stole across the room and waited for Young.

"I bet you didn't expect to conduct meetings in the bathroom when you became vice president, did you?" Hawk said when Young walked in.

Young chuckled. "I can honestly say this is not something I ever thought would happen." His face fell. "Unfortunately, it's necessary given what Michaels is attempting to do to this country."

"We understand the consequences," Hawk said. "Petrov has been relentless in her march toward pushing this currency idea beyond backroom conversations among political powerbrokers and into the public."

Samuels kept an eye on the door in case the agents posted outside decided to come in and check on Young.

"Things have gotten worse in the past few days," Young said. "Petrov made a big announcement in

Milan earlier this week. She called it the Löfström Agreement."

"The what?" Hawk asked.

"The Löfström Agreement, in honor of Ville Löfström, the Finnish delegate who lost his life in a senseless murder on the streets of Milan the night before the big announcement."

"Senseless, my ass. He probably dissented openly."

"That's what I thought, though no one is talking," Young said.

"And does that surprise you? Would you talk if you knew the lone objector was dead the next morning?"

Young shook his head. "Things are going to get worse if something isn't done. Michaels' about-face on this currency issue means that he's angling for something with Petrov. She is either threatening him with something or making a grandiose promise of power."

"Michaels is a fool if he believes anything she says. He's going to be her puppet."

"I agree, which is why you need to stop him."

"We're open to suggestions on how to do that," Hawk said. "Just point us in the right direction."

"Excellent," Young said. "There's someone you need to meet."

* * *

SITTING OUT THE MEETING with the vice president rankled Alex at first, but she understood. Grabbing a few minutes alone with him was difficult enough in a public men's restroom, but adding her to the mix would've made it next to impossible without increasing the likelihood of getting identified or even arrested. Instead, she told Hawk that she was going to do what she did best: dig around.

Holed up in an FBI safe house that was no longer active, Alex cleared off the dining room table and opened her laptop. She needed to focus and use her critical thinking skills to unearth what was going on with Michaels. If he was indeed making a power play, angling to assert his leadership as president into the currency issue, he wasn't doing it via any traditional route. Everything Michaels was doing appeared to be akin to guerilla tactics where everything of importance was handled in the shadows.

"So if I wanted to control the Supreme Court justices, how would I start?" she said aloud. After about a minute, she let out an exasperated breath and resorted to tapping mindlessly on the keyboard.

Alex took a deep breath, regrouped, and realized she was asking herself the wrong questions. She would never be president, so she needed to think more like a detective instead.

"What would Michaels do to control the justices?" she asked aloud again, this time narrowing her focus.

"He would do what he always does—intimidate, threaten, and lie . . . just like every other politician."

What Alex needed was evidence linking them all together. She needed to show that Michaels was exerting undue influence on the justices. But how? If Michaels could keep his meetings secret, Alex assumed it'd be simple for him to avoid any kind of potential pitfalls with regards to this information going public.

Then Alex realized she was ignoring her best resource in a time that absolutely required assistance.

"Mallory Kauffman," Alex said aloud.

She picked up her phone and dialed former CIA colleague, Mallory Kauffman, who'd recently joined the National Security Agency. In a text to Alex, Kauffman explained that she had finally seen the light as it pertained to their former supervisor and wasn't going to stand for it another week. Once she contacted the NSA and inquired about any openings, she switched agencies with no resistance. Alex assumed it was because their former supervisor was eager to see both women leave.

If anyone could help Alex, Mallory Kauffman could.

"Long time, no see," Kauffman said when she answered Alex's call.

"Definitely longer than it should be—and technically, this is still just a phone call," Alex said.

"Well, since you're calling me at home, I'm assuming this is a work related request."

"Of course."

"If I can assist you, I'm going to require you to buy me at least two drinks when you get an opportunity."

"If I survive, you're on," Alex said flatly.

"You're not joking, are you?" Kauffman asked.

"I wish I was, but we're in some deep trouble. To be honest, we're all in deep trouble."

"Do I really want to know what's going on?"

"I'm sure you can figure it out after I make my request."

"Lay it on me."

Alex took a deep breath. "I need you to search the phone records of Supreme Court justices over the past week. Look for any numbers that seem out of the ordinary. Can you do that for me?"

"For you, anything. Now that everyone knows what kind of information we collect, I'm sure I'll be getting more requests like this."

Alex laughed. "I don't want to be *that* kind of friend, the kind that only calls you when she needs something."

"Better than never getting a call at all," Kauffman quipped. "I'll call you back after I'm done searching. It shouldn't take too long."

Five minutes later, Alex's phone rang and "unknown number" appeared on her screen.

"Hello," Alex said as she answered.

"I found something that might interest you," Kauffman said.

"I was hoping you would."

"Well, it certainly makes me a little bit nervous."

"Yeah?"

"According to Camille Williams' phone records, she received a call recently from someone at the Pentagon."

"The Pentagon? Calling a Supreme Court justice?"

"Yeah. A guy by the name of Frank Stone. Ever heard of him?"

Alex nodded even though she knew Kauffman couldn't see her.

"Stone is a close ally of President Michaels."

"There's your link then," Kauffman said. "Good luck uncovering whatever it is. And the next time you're free and we can meet up, you owe me two drinks."

"Sounds like a fair trade to me," Alex said. "I appreciate it."

"Stay alive out there. And I mean that—I'd hate to have done all this work and not get my two drinks."

"You're incorrigible," Alex said.

"I've been called worse."

Alex hung up and contemplated the result of Kauffman's search. It confirmed—at least in her mind—that Young was on the right track about the purpose of the meeting: Michaels was trying to influence the Supreme Court.

CHAPTER 13

Portree, Isle of Skye
Scotland

BLUNT STUDIED THE SECURITY MONITOR in his bedroom, unsure if he could trust his eyes. The man standing outside his home ringing the doorbell appeared to be longtime friend, General Van Fortner. But Fortner commanded Camp Lemonnier in Djibouti, thousands of miles away from Scotland. Past experience of counterintelligence tactics and the familiar face out of place were enough to make Blunt think twice about answering the door.

"General Fortner?" Blunt asked. "Is that you?"

"In the flesh," Fortner responded, looking up at the camera and smiling.

Blunt was still unsure. "Who did we leave buck naked outside of Tangiers one night?"

"That little twerp Teddy Myers," Fortner said, breaking into a chuckle. "The poor sot couldn't keep his mouth shut and hurt your chances with that waitress broad."

Blunt's doubts were quieted with Fortner's answer.

"I'll come open the door in just a minute."

Blunt opened the door slowly and motioned for Fortner to come in.

"There's nobody out there," Fortner said as he stepped inside. "I wouldn't have even considered venturing near this place if there was. I'd never put you at risk like that."

Blunt broke into a smile and shook Fortner's hand. After securing the door, Blunt gestured toward the living room.

"We can have a seat in here," Blunt said. "Would you like something to drink?"

"I'm good," Fortner said. "And I'll keep this brief."

The pair sat down across from one another, the smiles that were on their faces just moments ago had vanished.

"Were you just in the neighborhood and decided to pop in?" Blunt asked.

"I'm being transferred to Ansbach and thought I'd pay you a visit."

"Ansbach? That sounds like a nice cushy gig."

"I wish," Fortner said. "It's going to be nose to the grindstone Army counterintelligence. A sentence to a Siberian work camp might be more relaxing than what I'm in for."

"I'm sure you'll manage," Blunt said, shifting in his seat. "But I take it this is more than a social call to catch up on work."

Fortner nodded. "Unfortunately, it is. There are some serious issues we need to contend with, all of which begin and end with Katarina Petrov. Seems she's hell bent on taking over the world."

"That's nothing new," Blunt said. "I suspected that when I first got mixed up with her and The Chamber. It was a damn fiasco."

"Well, I don't know what you've heard, but I suspect that you don't know about the latest bit of intel we picked up in the past few days."

"Fill me in."

"This one-world currency fiasco is a smoke screen to what's truly happening behind closed doors," Fortner said. "We've learned from several strategically placed assets in multiple foreign governments that Petrov is making a play to create a united government, banding countries together with common laws. The economy is just the beginning. Pretty soon, any nation that aligns with this ridiculous plan is going to be subject to a plethora of edicts without a legitimate way to appeal them. At least now, citizens can travel to centrally located sites to air their grievances. But that's going to go away. She's ginning up support for a judicial system that will trump anything we have in place today. It's going to be a disaster."

"That would help explain Michaels' sudden change of heart regarding Petrov and The Chamber,"

Blunt said. "He's trying to stay out of the picture now and put his finger to the wind to determine which way the court of public opinion is blowing. The moment it shifts toward one world, it's over. He's going to steamroll ahead—and likely retain some prominent position of power on the new governing cabinet."

"Honestly, Michaels is the least of our worries. To me, the most troubling aspect of what I've heard is Petrov is angling for a world military force next," Fortner said. "She wants, in essence, a world police organization that will keep everyone in line."

"Any ideas on how to stop this?" Blunt asked.

Fortner sighed. "You mean aside from putting a bullet in Petrov? I'd love to take her out right now."

"You and me both."

"Unfortunately, I don't want to engender any sympathy for that woman or give fuel to our detractors. We have to prevent The Chamber from getting its hooks in the U.S. government, first and foremost. After that, we can expose Petrov before we take her out."

Blunt shook his head and forced a laugh. "And to think that just a few months ago, all we concerned ourselves with were madmen running around in the Middle Eastern desert."

"It's always like that, isn't it?" Fortner asked rhetorically. "You think there's one thing that's going to get you—but it never is. The thing that gets you is the thing you never see coming."

"Fortunately, we've seen Petrov in time."

Fortner nodded. "And now it's time to show the world who she really is."

"The Firestorm team is back in Washington, trying to figure out a way to prevent the Supreme Court from giving Michaels the win he needs to push this one-world currency initiative forward, but after they're done . . ."

"You just let me know if and when you need any help," Fortner said. "My men will be there to assist."

CHAPTER 14

Istanbul, Turkey

KATARINA PETROV CLOSED HER EYES and tilted her head back as the makeup artist dusted powder on her face. A natural beauty, Petrov loathed wearing anything on her face. She insisted foundation and other products made her face itch. But she relented due to the pressure of a producer who insisted by telling her that her face would wash out beneath the lights.

Petrov didn't care, but she cared what the producer thought. More to the point, Petrov was concerned with the general public's perception of her. Winning them over was critical to building an unstoppable momentum.

Once the lemmings realize this is the way to go, no politician will want to stand against them—even if elected officials know their offices will be vanishing.

"Press your lips together like this," the makeup artist said, closing her mouth and then making a soft popping sound.

Petrov mimicked the woman several times before she nodded her head approvingly.

"That's it," she said. "Perfect."

She handed a mirror to Petrov, who took it and studied herself for several seconds.

"I hate it," Petrov said. "Think there's something else we can do? Another color perhaps? I look like a clown."

"But that bright red screams power," the makeup artist said.

Petrov pointed at her face. "I don't need anything but my mouth to put people under my thumb. It's not what I look like, but what I do."

The artist shrunk back before rushing to finish the job. She slipped out of the room without speaking another word.

"Are we ready?" asked Janet Hubbard, as she poked her head in the door. "Interview is set to go live in five minutes. Tut, tut."

Hubbard, the vivacious host for *Good Day, Britain*, winked at Petrov and exited the room. Petrov agreed to appear on the show with Hubbard, who was famous worldwide, though Petrov assumed Hubbard's popularity had more to do with her bust size than her journalistic prowess. Petrov had watched more than a dozen episodes of Hubbard's favorable handling of her guests. Hubbard's easy questions accompanied by plenty of slack-jawed expressions and effusive praises made Petrov comfortable about sitting across from her.

Petrov walked into The Chamber's makeshift offices and took a seat in the director's style chair opposite Hubbard. Surveying the surroundings, Petrov smiled. She'd managed to secure the offices a week before the interview in order to give The Chamber a more legitimate presence. Her underground operation hidden well out of sight from the people of Istanbul and guarded night and day would've sent a chilling message, along with creating plenty of other questions. They were questions even Hubbard would've felt compelled to ask.

The corporate feel to the temporary offices ensured that everyone involved on the production team would feel safe and welcome. Carpeted floors, big windows, plush furniture, modern light fixtures, soothing music piped into the lobby—everything anyone would've expected in a serious business environment.

"Nice digs," Hubbard said as she glanced around the room. "I love how you designed your logo with the T and the C. They go together so effortlessly. It's incredibly thoughtful, like you, I suppose."

Petrov smiled, reaching deep to turn on the charm. She had it when she wanted it. Her KGB training had taught her that much.

"You're very kind," Petrov said. "But I'm just trying to do my part and help the world get along. I've been fortunate enough to get into a position where I can influence change. And that's what I want to do."

"On that note, let's jump right into the questions I have for you regarding history of The Chamber and what your role is here and what you see this organization doing in the future."

"I guess I could talk for half an hour on those topics, so stop me if I'm getting long or veering off topic, will you?"

"Of course, of course," Hubbard said, tilting her head and smiling. "By all means, continue."

"Well, The Chamber has an interesting history, one that I wasn't a part of when it originally was founded," Petrov began. "Initially it was created as a charity, designed to help those in floundering countries, mostly poor people who were destined to die far before their time. The Chamber's founder, Lord Byron Cornwall, had that in mind when he started. And initially that's all The Chamber did—deliver food to the poor in developing nations through many different technological means. The organization also founded medical clinics, providing health care to those who'd never even seen a doctor, much less been to one."

Hubbard put her hand out, signifying her desire to speak. Petrov had seen enough of Hubbard's interviews to know what she meant. "But why the change in recent years? Can you tell us about what prompted all that?"

"About seven years ago, The Chamber had an identity crisis. We didn't know if we wanted to be a charity or something more. In many of the different governments, we identified rampant corruption, which we determined was one of the main factors that people in those countries couldn't escape cycles of poverty. The idea that we could help them seemed like a daunting one at first. I mean, really, what could we do about it? But that's when we took our relationships with the common people—the people we were helping—to a deeper level. Instead of just helping them, we sought to understand what was causing all these problems."

"And what did you find?"

"Exactly what I mentioned before—government corruption. Once we realized that, we understood that we'd be doing the same thing in a hundred years that we're doing now. It'd be a constant refrain of helping people live hand to mouth. And that was never the vision for The Chamber. So, we sought ways that we could more seriously effect change."

"What specific ways do you now plan to address this issue?"

Petrov looked pensively at her interviewer before answering.

"That, of course, was the million dollar question—or in today's environment, the billion dollar question," Petrov said with a hint of a smile. "Overcoming corruption isn't something you can merely do by snapping your fingers and bobbing your head like you're Mary Poppins. And honestly, corruption is part of human nature. Rooting out such systemic depraved behavior would take several generations, if it was even attainable at all. That's why we realized the only way to put a dent in this behavior is to remove the human gatekeepers that make this possible."

"And based on some comments you've made in the media, you believe economic bodies in various countries to be the people you're referring to. Am I right in making such an assumption?"

Petrov nodded vigorously. "Absolutely, Janet. These people are the ones doing favors for the banking industry titans. All the while—to borrow the vernacular of our American friends—the little man is getting screwed."

Janet narrowed her gaze as curious lines flashed across her brow.

"But haven't you befriended bankers? How is what you're doing different?"

"That is a good question, Janet. And the truth is, I've vetted and targeted only bankers I deemed to be honest ones. In my dealings with them, I've only tried to persuade them that this will be best for everyone, even if their bottom line will take a hit."

"And they're still willing to go along with your plan?"

"I think most people in the banking industry realize that if the world enters into an economic downturn, nobody benefits. Economies are only as strong as the speed through which money is exchanging hands. If someone doesn't understand that, they are being intellectually dishonest. And unfortunately, our current system allows those charlatans to prosper. But not anymore under this new proposal."

Janet nodded and eased back in her seat, glancing at her notes before she asked her next question.

"You have an impressive lineup of nations who have publicly stated they will adopt your plan for a one world currency. But what about the United States? It seemed like they remain hesitant for whatever reason. How do you plan to win them over?"

"I don't," Petrov said flatly. "It's their choice, not mine. If they want to be the lone outlier in the global market, that decision is to their detriment. They will be forced to accept what the new market says in relation to exchange rates. I can promise you that resisting will result in painful upheaval in the U.S. economy."

Janet nodded and smiled. "Well, we will all be sure to keep an eye on those developments as the plan to adopt a one world currency continues to move forward."

Petrov watched as Janet turned directly toward the camera and wrapped up the interview with a few pithy comments and a prediction about how a one world economy would make the world a safer place as well as reduce poverty, which she reminded her viewers was the ultimate mission of The Chamber. It was unscripted television, but Petrov smiled knowing she couldn't have chosen better questions to help further her agenda.

It's only a matter of time now.

CHAPTER 15

Washington, D.C.

MOMENTS AFTER JANET HUBBARD'S INTERVIEW with Katarina Petrov hit the airwaves, snippets of their conversation were condensed and posted on social media. Less than an hour later, every live talk show on radio and television, was discussing the fallout of Petrov's one world currency plan and her dire forecast about the U.S. economy should it maintain its isolationist economic policy. Hosts whipped their audiences up into a frenzy over the issue, leading to angry rants by callers who demanded wholesale changes in Washington. The internet was ablaze with opinions about the government leaders who were willfully walking Americans down a metaphoric plank.

The furor across the country was just the kind of fuel President Michaels needed to get his way. And he didn't have to wait long to get it either.

By 1:00 p.m. on the East Coast, the Supreme Court made an unprecedented announcement that it would hear a case about the constitutionality of the Federal Reserve Act. And talk shows turned a raging fire into a wildfire powered by crosswinds. Anything else that happened that day would be forgotten in the annals of history.

At 3:00 p.m., President Michaels climbed onto the podium and stepped behind the lectern. He remained stoic, trying to hide his pleasure regarding the Supreme Court's announcement.

"For years, this great country has relied upon trusted harbingers of the Federal Reserve to keep our financial institutions secure and trustworthy. But that time might be coming to an end."

Michaels straightened his tie and cleared his throat before continuing.

"No country's economic market can exist in a bubble, no matter how much we might wish it did. The truth is many of the jobs so many hardworking Americans rely upon to feed their families are the direct result of consumer purchases and businesses thriving beyond our borders. We cannot ignore those people, those same people who might be our neighbors across the street. And even if we did, we'd be fools to think we wouldn't be negatively impacted in one way or another."

He paused to drink a glass of water and quickly survey the press corps eyeing him carefully. Assessing a crowd's mood was a vital tool in delivering a successful speech, and Michaels excelled at it. From the looks on the faces of the reporters scattered in front of him, he could tell they were eating up his rhetoric and itching to share their thoughts with viewers.

Just keep it simple.

"As a country, we owe a great debt to those Americans who've served admirably on the Federal Reserve's board. For over a century, the Federal Reserve has provided the stability necessary to help this country get through several trying economic periods and usher us into prosperous times again. But times have changed and it's time for the Federal Reserve to change with it. A private body that is unwilling to change puts us all at risk and we can't afford this type of leadership anymore. At some point, leadership that was once helpful often grows stale, fixated more on its power than its ability to guide others through unprecedented challenges. What we are facing now both as citizens of this country as well as wayfarers on planet earth is something no one has ever experienced before—and what worked in the past isn't guaranteed to work in the future. In short, the future is happening now, and the Federal Reserve stands for a bygone era. It's time for new economic leadership in this country."

He paused and took a deep breath, satisfied that he'd won over the vast majority of the reporters present.

"Now I'll take your questions," he said.

A cacophony of voices erupted as hands shot

skyward. Michaels surveyed the eager inquirers for a friendly face. He settled on Tegan Volker from *The New York Times.*

"Ms. Volker," Michaels said, silencing the chorus of competing voices.

She smiled and nodded. "Thank you, Mr. President. If this situation is as dire as you've painted it, why not let the legislative branch rescind the Federal Reserve Act of 1913 and strip the board of its power? Wouldn't that make more sense?"

"If we had the time, it would," Michaels answered. "But I've come to the conclusion through the sage advice of many trusted economic advisors that to delay any action could result in catastrophic consequences for the U.S. Waiting simply isn't something we have the luxury of doing in this case. There will be plenty of time to rewrite the laws as we know them regarding who sits over the governing financial body. But in the interim, we need to act quickly and decisively."

A few seconds of silence were interrupted by hand-waving troops chomping at the bit to get the president's attention.

"Yes, Mr. Hartman. You're next," Michaels said.

Kyle Hartman, NBC's Washington correspondent, had been mostly friendly in the past toward Michaels, which was why the following question stunned Michaels so much.

"Is it true that you will assume a leadership position during the interim?" Hartman asked. "Seems a little bit beyond your purview, don't you think?"

The first question was a good one that every journalist needed answered. But Michaels took offense at quasi-question Hartman posited, which sounded more for his benefit than for helping clarify things for Michaels. But Michaels was ready for him.

"Quite honestly, Kyle, I find that there are things that are beyond my purview each and every day as I hold this powerful office. There is no college course on how to become president. It's just something you do—and you figure it out as you go along. I know that may not come as much comfort to you or many Americans, especially the ones who think I'm unqualified to hold this position. But I've already won the popularity contest, and my decisions from here on out are about doing the best job I can to prove to those who voted for me that they were right to trust me. If I don't do that, I fail. However, it's in my failing that I gain strength."

"But, sir, I—"

Michaels held up his hand, which silenced Hartman for the moment.

"My point is that I'm no more capable of handling this situation than I am selecting the best color to paint my bedroom to make sure it matches with the comforter on my bed. But like everything else I do, I'm going to do my best, which includes listening to seasoned veterans around me who are experts in this field and taking their advice to heart."

Hartman wasn't satisfied with Michaels' explanation.

"But, sir, from what I've heard, the experts you've surrounded yourself with don't seem to be interested in rocking the status quo. They hold fringe views that aren't generally shared among the vast majority of the economic community. How can you really consider all sides of an issue if you have loaded your cabinet and advisory boards with *yes* men?"

Michaels clenched his fists, trying hard to keep them hidden behind the lectern and out of sight from the opportunistic photographers' pool, which would relish the chance to document his anger. He sifted through the notes on the podium, giving him time to cool down. After a deep breath, he responded to Hartman's aggressive line of questioning.

"The only thing these men say *yes* to is sound economic policy," Michaels said calmly. "They aren't in anyone's pocket. They aren't here because they agree with my overall economic policy. They serve at my pleasure because they're the best at what they do. You and I may disagree over how effective their track record is in averting crisis and navigating through new challenges, but I wouldn't have them advising me if I didn't believe they had our country's best interest at heart."

Michaels scanned the audience of reporters once

more as their hands shot up haphazardly around the room and shouting recommenced. The faces turned, all eager to learn about the president's response to the Supreme Court's apparent attempt to overturn an act put into law by Congress more than 100 years prior. All Michaels saw were narrowed eyes and a press corps ready to pounce.

"Mr. President," one reporter shouted loudly over the crowd, "is there any truth to a secret meeting you held recently with a select group of Supreme Court justices at the Library of Congress?"

That was Michaels' cue to leave.

"No more questions. Good day," he said.

He exited to the left and didn't breathe until he was a few steps down the hall and out of sight. Pulling out a pocket square, he mopped his brow and held up his hand, signaling his Secret Service detail to stop. Michaels rested against the wall and took a deep breath before resuming his march back toward his office.

He needed an update on Justice Williams.

CHAPTER 16

Great Falls, Virginia

HAWK EYED JUSTICE CAMILLE WILLIAMS through his binoculars in preparation for making a dash across her sprawling property. The 15 acres she inherited along with an 8,000-square-foot mansion from her late husband Harold Wannamaker wasn't easily accessible to any would-be intruders. A 10-foot stone wall enclosed the property and created a formidable perimeter. The only portion of the land that wasn't walled in was the backside, which abutted a manageable cliff overlooking a roiling portion of the Potomac River.

"Do you see any guards?" Alex asked. "I can't see any on the thermal imaging cameras I'm using."

"From what I've observed, Williams only has a pair of guards and they're both in the front of the property."

"And that cliff didn't give you any problems?" Samuels asked.

"Piece of cake," Hawk said, pressing his eyes

against his binoculars once more. "I see her in her study reading a book."

"Be careful, Hawk," Alex said. "If this goes sideways, you'll be lucky to get out alive. Her security guards are former military who served several tours in Iraq."

Hawk shoved his binoculars into his backpack. "If I can keep the justice quiet enough to explain myself, everything will be just fine."

He scanned the grounds once more before striking off toward Williams' house.

"Bet you ten bucks Hawk gets attacked by some dogs," Samuels said.

Hawk stopped near a tree and adjusted his ear piece. "I can hear everything you're saying, Samuels. Nice to know you're rooting for me."

"Who says I'm not rooting for you?" Samuels asked. "Besides, what's wrong with me hoping for a little more action on this assignment?"

"Your bark is definitely more ferocious than your bite," Hawk fired back.

Alex chuckled.

"Whose side are you on anyway?" Samuels said. "Hawk's or your brother's?"

"I'm on the side of getting this job done without incident," she snapped.

"Roger that," Hawk said before he continued his stealthy approach to the house.

Once Hawk reached the house, he inched along

with his back to the wall. He froze when he heard heavy footfalls nearing the door.

"Guys, did either of you pick up a third person in the house?" Hawk asked.

"Nope," Alex said. "Just the two guards and Justice Williams. No, wait."

She paused. Hawk didn't need to wait for her reply to know they'd missed something. The screen door creaked as it swung open and out stumbled another security agent. At 6 foot 6 with the physique of a power lifter, he was an intimidating wrench thrown into Hawk's plan. Hawk wasn't used to facing larger men, but he knew his only advantage was surprise.

Hawk kicked the man in the back of his knees, forcing him to the ground. Without waiting for him to fall, Hawk pistol whipped the man, knocking him out with two successive blows.

"I won't have long now," Hawk said, pausing before the entrance. "Are you two positive only Justice Williams remains in the house?"

"I'd stake my life on it," Samuels said.

"Good," Hawk said. "At least I'll have something to look forward to if I'm able to survive this mess."

"Just stay focused," Alex said. "Second floor, back right corner of the house for the study."

"Roger that," Hawk said before quietly opening the door.

He slipped inside and crept up the stairs toward

Williams' study. As he reached the door, one of the boards creaked rather loudly beneath his step.

"Thomas? Is that you?" Williams called.

Hawk took a deep breath and peered around the corner. Still seated with her back to the door, Williams' head barely poked above the back of her chair.

"I'm afraid not," Hawk said as he strode into the room.

Williams turned around frantically. "Who are you? And how did you get in here?"

Hawk continued moving slowly toward her until she brandished a gun. He raised his hands in the air and took a step backward.

"I'm not the one you need to be worried about," Hawk said. "I'm here to warn you that your life might be in danger."

She glared at him. "Who are you? One of Michaels' thugs? You can tell him I won't be intimidated."

"No," Hawk said as he eyed her weapon. "I'm here to warn you about what Michaels might do to you."

"To me? If he's going to do anything, he's going to threaten my family. Now tell me who you are before I fill you full of lead."

"My name is Brady Hawk and I'm a former Navy Seal. I care about this country and I care about what happens if Michaels gets his way with the case you'll be hearing tomorrow. I want to make sure that you make it there alive."

"Protect my children or my grandkids," she said, lowering her gun. "That bastard is more likely to use them against me."

"No, he needs your vote. And if he thinks you're not going to vote his way, he will eliminate you and appoint someone who will do what he wants."

She sighed and waved dismissively at Hawk. "And then what? The bench will have a split verdict and nothing will happen."

"And if one of the other judges recuses himself?"

Williams chuckled again. "And who would do that, not to mention why?"

"Justice Scarborough stands to profit greatly if the one world currency becomes a reality in the U.S.," Hawk said. "Rumor has it that his family's bank, which hasn't been allowed to participate on the Federal Reserve's committee, would be tapped to help lead the currency exchange here."

"But I know him," Williams snapped. "He's an honorable man and would never do anything like that."

Hawk shrugged. "Perhaps not, but once Michaels' minions spread that information around to the press, he'd have to recuse himself, leaving Michaels with a 4-3 decision in his favor to overturn the Federal

Reserve Act of 1913. And guess who will then be leading our country through this transitional time period?

"Damn him," Williams said.

"You've just got to make sure you stay alive so you can oppose him—if that's what you intend to do."

"Our founding fathers are rolling over in their graves right now," she said. "If I step outside on my back porch, I might even be able to hear George Washington spinning all the way from here."

In the next instant, the sound of shattering glass filled the room. Hawk instinctively dove toward Williams, covering her up by placing his arm around her. A second shot tore through the remaining glass.

"That was just a warning shot," Hawk said, his face pressed against the floor. "If they wanted you dead, you'd be dead right now."

"Why not just kill me?" she asked, her lips quivering.

"It's far more convenient for you to just vote the way he wants you to without creating a conspiracy or a congressional investigation. But if push comes to shove, he'll forge ahead and deal with the fallout later."

Alex's voice squawked in Hawk's earpiece.

"Who's that?" Williams asked, cutting her eyes toward the cord.

"A friend," Hawk said to Williams. "Where is he, Alex?"

"The target is heading toward the water," Alex said.

"And the guards?"

"He tranqed them both," Samuels said.

"How did you guys miss him?" Hawk asked, leaping to his feet and racing toward the back.

"I-I don't know," Alex said. "I don't know how he slipped onto the screen without me seeing him."

"Don't let me get surprised like that again," Hawk said as he sprinted toward the back of the property. "Now, where is he?"

"He appears to be scaling the wall down to the water," Samuels said. "Maybe thirty meters northeast of your position."

"Roger that."

Hawk reached the edge of the craggy cliff just in time to see the rope loosened and pulled down.

"I'm going after him," Hawk said.

"Come on, Hawk," Alex pleaded. "That's not a good idea. It's dark and he's got the advantage."

"The moon is bright and calling this thing a cliff is a generous description. Just follow me."

Hawk proceeded to scramble down the rocks. In less than a minute, he was standing along the shore, searching for the gunman. Hawk noticed the man look back over his shoulder before he dashed farther upstream. Without hesitating, Hawk went after the man.

Hawk's pursuit lasted less than thirty seconds, halted by the crack of a rifle. The man staggered to the ground, collapsing face first into the water.

Immediately, Hawk took cover and waited for a few moments before saying anything.

"What just happened, Hawk?" Alex asked. "Why'd you stop moving?"

"Someone just shot our gunman and I'm hiding."

"Just leave him there," Samuels said. "Wait until it's safe and come back to the house. I'm sure Justice Williams will appreciate what you did."

"But I didn't do anything. We need to find out who that was so we can tie Michaels to all of this," Hawk said. "It might be another way we could take him down."

"Do you think anyone is going to believe that story?" Samuels asked. "It'll be dismissed before the story gains any traction."

"When did you get all negative on us?" Alex asked. "This isn't like you."

"I'm just concerned, that's all."

Hawk sighed. "It's been a few minutes. I'm gonna go take a look now."

Hawk's attempts to discover the man's identity ended sharply when a warning shot whistled off a nearby rock. Slipping back behind a boulder, Hawk reconsidered.

"Maybe you're right, Samuels," Hawk said. "It's obvious someone doesn't want me inspecting the body."

"Better get back here," Alex said. "You'll have

some more explaining to do if you don't."

"You're right," Hawk said. "This isn't ever going to end, is it?"

"I'm afraid not," Alex said. "At least, not until you finish this."

"Easier said than done."

Hawk crouched low as he eased his way toward the back of Williams' house. He glanced over his shoulder a final time, waiting until there was a moment of cloud cover from the moon. After climbing up the rocks, he reached the back of Williams' grounds. Alex greeted his arrival loudly with a warning.

"The police just arrived," Alex said. "Better skip that explanation for now and sneak out of there before the place is crawling with cops."

"Roger that," Hawk said.

He crept to the woods surrounding the justice's house and eased back to the main road where he reunited with Alex and Samuels in their van.

"You all right?" Alex asked.

Hawk shook his head. "I thought Michaels was unhinged before, but that was nothing. We've got our work cut out for us if we're going to stop him this time."

"Any regrets over saving his life?" Alex asked.

Hawk nodded. "I'm regretting it more and more with each passing second."

CHAPTER 17

Portree, Isle of Skye
Scotland

BLUNT TUNED IN to an international cable news channel and watched as political and legal pundits broke down proceedings in the U.S. Supreme Court earlier that day. He grunted as one of the British commentators explained how the forthcoming ruling could help the U.S. maintain its prominence globally. While Blunt had been around long enough to know television experts often got it wrong, he winced when several of the panel members broke into giddy laughter. He knew exactly what they were thinking—the Supreme Court was going to disband the Federal Reserve Act of 1913.

I'd like to wipe that smug smile off your face, son.

Blunt considered hurling his glass at the screen before deciding against it.

"I've covered this particular Supreme Court bench enough to know what they are thinking based on their mannerisms and their questions," Dr. Titus Wellman, one of the panel members said from a television studio in Washington, D.C. "And I can promise you right now that they are weighing the consequences of ruling that the Federal Reserve Act was unconstitutional. Who will handle all the duties that will be relegated when this announcement is made? What about setting interest rates? What governing body will do that now? It's going to be a mess logistically for a while, but I can assure you this is the way the court was leaning after watching the judges' body language and line of questioning."

The show's host, a sophisticated brunette named Darcy Barrow, furrowed her brow and cocked her head to one side.

"Dr. Wellman, was there any indication that perhaps one judge's vote may swing the ruling and uphold the Federal Reserve Act?" she asked as she looked directly into the camera.

Wellman chuckled and shook his head.

"Not a chance," he said.

"Not even Justice Williams? I know several other legal experts seem to believe she might side with those in favor of upholding the century-old piece of legislation."

"Based on what I witnessed today, she's in President Michaels' pocket."

"Thank you for your time, Dr. Wellman," she

said. "We look forward to your report tomorrow when the U.S. Supreme Court issues their ruling in this all-important emergency hearing."

"Thank you, Darcy."

Blunt clenched his fists before letting out a frustrated scream. Without any nearby neighbors, he felt comfortable in getting out his aggression in the privacy of his cottage overlooking the water. He turned off the television and struggled to stand up.

The Firestorm team hadn't checked in since the previous night to update him on what happened at Justice Williams' house. Based on that conversation, Blunt was convinced that Williams would do the right thing. After pondering the situation for a few more minutes, he concluded that maybe she still would. Tipping her hand too early wouldn't be in her best interest if Michaels had put her in his crosshairs. Blunt met Williams on several occasions in formal settings at Washington galas and benefits. He found her to be delightful and kind as a person, yet direct and fair as a judge. In short, Blunt didn't figure her to be the kind of judge who would cave with a little bit of pressure. Yet, he had to acknowledge that anyone would cave with the right kind of pressure.

Then he had a thought.

I need to tell Hawk.

He hobbled across the room toward his phone. Despite his latest setback, Blunt felt as good as he had since his surgery and wondered if he might be able to run again soon.

Blunt reached the table and placed his palms on top of it, bracing himself. Drawing in a deep breath, he reached for the phone only to feel a strong hand grab his wrist that prevented him from making the call.

"What the—" Blunt asked aloud.

He turned around to see what was happening, but he didn't get a good look at his captor before Blunt suffered a swift blow to the side of his head, rendering him unconscious.

CHAPTER 18

Washington, D.C.

HAWK SAT IN HIS CAR parked at the bottom of a deck, awaiting Big Earv. While Hawk appreciated the recently rekindled friendship, he still held everyone suspect. He'd grown accustomed to the constant state of suspicion, though he wished he didn't have to live his life that way. But serving his country required sacrifices, sacrifices that Hawk willfully chose. Even so, Big Earv would've been the last person Hawk would've suspected, which was precisely why he felt more guarded around the secret service agent.

Big Earv pushed his way through the door, casting a looming silhouette. He paused for a beat and looked to his left and right. Satisfied that he wasn't being observed, he strode toward Hawk's car and climbed in.

"Sorry to have to meet you like this," Hawk said as he shook hands with Big Earv. "I'd prefer to do this in a bar over a couple of bottles of beer."

"That was another lifetime ago for both of us," Big Earv said. "Maybe we'll be able to do it again one day, but not now."

"I know. Just wishful thinking."

"I'm assuming this wasn't a social call. So, what can I help you with?"

Hawk pulled out *The Washington Post* and folded it back to one section before pointing at one of the articles. He handed the paper to Big Earv.

"Are you working Michaels' fundraising gala tonight?"

Big Earv nodded subtly but remained quiet.

"I need some helping getting in."

Big Earv chuckled and looked wide-eyed at Hawk.

"You? You're going to crash this black tie event full of million-dollar donors?"

"Don't be ridiculous. Your friends at the Secret Service would riddle me with bullet holes before I had a chance to speak."

"So, what's your play?"

"Have someone swap out the president's watch so we can record his conversations and his movements."

Big Earv stroked his chin and glanced over his shoulder as if he were still scanning the deck.

"That's a bold move, Hawk. Who's hustling this swap?"

"Alex Duncan."

"Alex? Your handler?"

"I know. Shocking, isn't it? Turns out she's got some skills that extend beyond writing code and monitoring CIA intelligence satellites."

"She better have more than just skills—she better be like a goddess when it comes to swapping out the Michaels watch. Our guys will be looming over him. If they suspect anything, she will get arrested immediately. And I suspect that's not something you'd want."

"Alex is a pro. She'll be careful. If she has to abort, she will."

"I'll get her name on the list and have an invitation left at will call. Just be careful, okay? There's only so much I can do to protect her, especially when my sole responsibility is to protect Michaels."

"Use the legend of Christina Harper. She'll be posing as a philanthropic CEO of a new startup that's worth millions after just one year of operation."

"And she'll be able to substantiate that with documentation should anyone look?"

Hawk nodded and handed his phone to Big Earv.

"She's already created a company site along with inserting several dummy articles on major news channels."

"Impressive," Big Earv said as he scrolled through the list. "This should be sufficient. I'll make sure she gets in. After that, it's up to her."

"Understood," Hawk said as he took his phone

back.

Big Earv moved toward the door when Hawk put a hand on his friend.

"Thanks," Hawk said. "I really appreciate this. You know if it wasn't important, I wouldn't ask for your help."

"I know. You can count on me."

Hawk watched Big Earv get out of the car, scan the deck, and walk casually back to the stairwell entrance.

Once Big Earv disappeared, Hawk dialed Alex's number.

"You're in," he said.

* * *

THE NATIONAL BUILDING MUSEUM sparkled beneath the glare of the spotlights casting their beams on the magnificent structure. The red carpet event attracted some of the city's most powerful political brokers along with a fair share of A-list celebrities. Elegant music pumped through the speakers as attendees presented their invitations before making their way inside.

Alex, wearing a tasteful sequined black gown, sidestepped the welcoming party, posing as a journalist. If she intended to avoid drawing scrutiny, the last thing she wanted was to be photographed at the event. Slipping behind the gawkers and celebrity critics, she ditched her microphone in a nearby potted plant and pulled out her identification.

"Christina Harper," she said, holding out her fake credentials for the woman managing the will call table.

The woman leaned forward, peering over her glasses while she read the name. Methodically, she flipped through the stack of envelopes until she stopped and pulled one out.

"Sign here, ma'am," the woman said, pointing to the back of the envelope.

Alex complied with the instructions.

The woman handed Alex her invitation. "Enjoy the event."

A pair of Secret Service agents almost immediately approached Alex.

"Good evening, gentlemen," she said. "Is there a problem?"

"Just protocol, ma'am," one of the agents said as they began waving their wands around the contours of her body.

"You're free to proceed," he said after a few seconds.

She exhaled slowly and handed her invitation to a woman before entering the event.

"Just breathe," Hawk said over the com tucked inside Alex's ear.

"So, this is what it's like to be on a mission and have someone in your head the entire time," she said. "I should've never put you in that truck."

"I'm enjoying this," Hawk said. "I've got a full

selection of security cameras to choose from and a microphone to use if I want to bug you."

"This isn't a game, Hawk."

Hawk chuckled. "I know. But it sure is fun to be on the other side of this for once."

"I prefer we not make a habit of this, okay?"

"Roger that."

Alex proceeded to get a drink and strike up a conversation with a leading political author she'd seen on television before. He droned on about his latest project and how the "the other side" was unfairly lambasting it just because it didn't agree with their political position. After three minutes, she moved on.

"There's a reason I never pay attention to politics," Alex said. "Too many petty people bickering over things that don't matter."

"Meanwhile, nobody pays attention to the things that do matter," Hawk added.

"Exactly."

Alex glided from one dull conversation to the next until she grew tired and sat down.

"What's the matter?" said a man, who took a seat next to Alex. "Nobody here interesting enough for you? Some people are just too enamored with their own brilliance to bother to even take notice of the world around them."

Alex cast a glance at him before returning her gaze to the sea of people.

"You've noticed this too?"

He shrugged. "At times, but I know it must be true since there's an exquisitely beautiful woman sitting all alone here."

Alex blushed. "At least someone noticed."

"Yes," he said. "Would you look at her?"

He pointed across the room toward another woman sitting by herself.

"Not a soul around her."

Alex felt sheepish for even considering that the man was referring to her before he broke into a laugh. She hung her head and nodded with him in agreement, trying to play off what she'd just done.

"I'm teasing you," he said. "Of course I was referring to you. Besides, that woman is my wife and I know for a fact that she'd rather be alone in a room with a book than talking with some stranger about the latest scandals in the political cycle."

"Charles Freeman," he said, offering his hand. "MIT, Professor of Thermodynamics."

"Impressive," she said, trying to avoid a discussion that involved talking about herself.

"And you are?"

A short pause. "Parched and dying to meet President Michaels. Isn't that the only reason anyone ever comes to these things anyway? To drink and meet famous politicians?"

Alex got up and walked toward the bar to order

a drink. But she didn't make it that far. A man wasn't looking where he was going and spun around, crashing into her and spilling his drink.

"Oh, I'm so sorry," the man said. "Here let me help you."

He rushed over to get several napkins from a nearby waiter carting drinks.

Alex eyed the man closely before studying the drenched portion of her gown. It wasn't that noticeable given the dark color, and she was getting far more attention than she wanted. A small crowd had gathered around her, mostly women gasping and murmuring about the horror of getting a dress soiled.

"I'm really sorry," the man said, returning with a stack of napkins.

"It's okay," Alex said as she took the napkins and blotted her gown.

"No, it's not. I wasn't paying attention and should have been more cautious. The fact that I didn't see a beautiful woman like you means that I really am completely self-absorbed. Shame on me. Let me make it up to you."

"Don't fall for it, Alex," Hawk chimed in.

"Wait, I know who you are," Alex said. "You're the actor who—"

"Stop right there," the man said. "Just call me Brad. Don't look at me any differently just because you've seen one of my films. I'm just a normal person, just like everybody else."

"Oh, no, I haven't seen your movies, but I've heard about you," Alex said.

He laughed nervously. "You can't believe what you read in the tabloids."

"Well, Brad, thank you for the napkins," Alex said, satisfied that she'd thwarted his aggressive advances in an effort to remain virtually invisible.

"That's not all you're going to thank me for, Ms. —"

"Harper. Christina Harper," she said offering her hand. "Really, I must be going."

"Nonsense. I'm going to make it up to you by introducing you to the president."

Alex swallowed hard. "What did you say?"

"Let's go meet the president," Brad said. "I hosted a fundraiser for him in Hollywood last election. We filled his coffers with fifty million dollars. I'm sure he'll take a minute to speak with me."

Alex's original plan to meet the president consisted of befriending—and charming—Francine Dobbs, a senator from New Hampshire, who had Michaels' ear on all things related to women. Alex aimed to share with Dobbs her equal pay campaign that included a green wristband to signify standing in solidarity with women fighting to reduce the gender pay gap. Michaels had sung a constant refrain on the campaign trail about reducing the pay gap. He'd yet to take any action, but it was a popular stance among his constituency—even though his opponent held the same view on the issue.

But Alex opted to go a more direct route when she realized that she might actually be able to get an audience with Michaels in a different manner, especially one that included an A-list celebrity standing right next to her. With the agents likely to be focused on and enamored by her superstar escort, she figured she'd be able to accomplish what she needed to do with a simple handshake.

"I take that back, Alex," Hawk said. "Roll with it."

A faint smile spread across Alex's lips. She was already thinking the same thing.

"In that case, you better buy me a drink first," Alex said to Brad. "I wasn't prepared to meet the most powerful man in the world like this."

"Of course," he said as he hustled off to the bar.

He returned shortly with her drink before placing his hand on the small of Alex's back to guide her toward President Michaels.

"The president is a really nice guy," Brad said. "He can be a little moody sometimes, but I think that's how all politicians get. I'm sure he'll be giddy tonight."

"He is smiling," Alex said.

"They're like actors, too," he said. "They know how to give the public a show."

After speaking with one of the president's handlers, Brad and Alex were ushered into a roped off area where Michaels stood, flanked by a pair of Secret Service agents.

"Mr. President, I want you to meet someone," Brad said as he shook Michaels' hand. "This is my good friend Christina . . ."

"Harper," Alex said as she offered her hand to shake his.

Michaels pulled back and folded his arms. He narrowed his eyes and stared at her while pursing his lips.

"You look vaguely familiar," Michaels said.

"I don't think we've met," she said while forcing a laugh. "I probably would've remembered that."

"No, no," he said, pointing at her. "I know where I know you from."

Alex swallowed hard and held her breath.

There's no way he recognizes me.

"Stay cool, Alex," Hawk said over the coms.

"Little Rock, three years ago," Michaels said. "You were working for my campaign there, weren't you?"

Alex shook her head. "I'm afraid you've got me mixed up with someone else."

"No," he said, refusing to admit defeat. "I know you from somewhere. I just can't put my finger on it."

Alex put her hand out again. "Either way, why don't I give you a chance at a fresh start?"

Michaels shrugged. "Well, alright. I guess I can

go along with that. It's always a pleasure to meet a smart and sophisticated woman," he said before dropping his voice to a whisper. "Not to mention drop dead gorgeous. But don't tell anyone else I said that."

They shook hands, and Alex went to work. She gave his hand a squeeze and then patted the outside of his hand with her left hand. Then she winked at him.

"Your secret is safe with me," she whispered back.

The latch on the watch broke free and slipped off Michaels' wrist and onto the floor. Just as she'd practiced, Alex knelt down and made the switch, right underneath the eyes of the watchful Secret Service agents.

Michaels joined her close to the floor.

"Here, let me get that," he said. "That was awfully clumsy of me."

Michaels picked up the watch and tightened the band around his wrist, giving it a swift tug before threading the extra band into place.

"There," he said, giving the watch a little twist as he stood up. "That won't happen again, will it?"

Alex shook her head. "I think your watch is secure now."

"So, Miss Harper," Michaels said. "I hope you're enjoying yourself at this fine gala this evening and finding my administration to suit your interests."

Alex smiled. "Absolutely. Just keep doing what

you're doing. And don't let those Europeans steal all our wealth."

"You mark my words," Michaels said. "It'll be over my dead body that those running the Federal Reserve cabal will continue to exert such undue influence and control over our country's financial system."

Samuels joined in on the coms. "Michaels better be careful what he wishes for."

"I'll let you get to more important guests," Alex said. "Thank you for your time. It was a great honor to meet you."

Brad leaned in and gave Michaels another hug.

"Thank you for the introduction," Michaels said to the actor.

"Any time, Mr. President."

With that exchange, Brad ushered Alex out of the roped area and toward a buffet of hors d'oeuvres.

"You sure know how to make it up to a girl," Alex said to Brad. "I appreciate it."

"My pleasure," he said. "You know, later on me and some of my friends who are working on my latest film are going to be hanging out. I'd love it if you would join us."

Alex's eyes widened. "Me?"

"Yeah, you," he said. "I'd love to get to know you better."

"I'm sure he would," Hawk said.

Alex chuckled. "Well, that's quite flattering and

all but—"

"She's coming with us," said a man behind her.

Before Alex could turn around, she felt a firm hand grab her bicep and give it a swift tug.

"What's the meaning of this?" she said.

"It's best that you didn't ask any questions or make a scene," the agent said.

"What makes you think you can just cart me off like some common criminal?" Alex said, her volume rising with each passing second.

"Order of the president, ma'am," the agent said. "Now, let's not make this any more difficult than it has to be."

Alex resisted, attempting to shake free. "I demand to know where you're taking me right now."

"Ma'am, if you want to maintain your dignity, I suggest you pipe down before we take more drastic measures."

"Stay cool, Alex," Hawk said on the coms. "I'll get you out of this."

"You better," Alex said.

"Excuse me," the agent said. "Did you say something?"

Alex looked up and glared at the man.

"Nothing," she said.

"Good," he said. "Let's keep it that way."

He gave her a firm shove and urged her ahead through the crowd. Alex could feel the eyes of the fundraiser attendees following her with every step.

So much for staying invisible.

"You're going to be okay, Alex," Hawk said. "I won't let Michaels do anything to you. I swear on my father's grave."

"Don't take your pledges lightly," she said. "I'm going to hold you to it this time. I guess we're going to find out how good you really are."

CHAPTER 19

HAWK AND SAMUELS WATCHED the security feeds until the agents and Alex disappeared from the screen. Clicking through every camera, Hawk was frustrated after realizing she was nowhere to be seen.

"Where could they have taken her?" he asked aloud.

"There are only so many ways out of that building," Samuels answered. "Unless there's an underground route we don't know about."

Hawk sighed. "This is Washington. The entire city is practically sitting on top of a vast network of underground tunnels."

"So, getting her back just became much more complicated."

"That's one way to put it," Hawk said. "More like next to impossible."

Samuels patted Hawk on the back. "Since when did you let a little challenge get you down? My sister will be fine."

"You don't know Michaels like I do. I just saved

that bastard's life, but he's going to ruin the people who are the reason he's breathing on the planet at this very moment."

"*Ruin* isn't the same as *murder*."

"You're right," Hawk said. "One can be more painful than the other, which is why we need to stop him—not only for Alex's sake but for the good of the country. This situation is starting to spiral beyond our control."

Hawk fired up the van and headed back toward their safe house. He needed to regroup and think of a way to draw Michaels out in order to get Alex to safety.

"This might all be pointless," Hawk said as he bumped along the pothole-laden streets of the capital.

"Pointless? What do you mean?"

"Even if we get Alex back, the damage might already be done. Even if we somehow survive this ordeal, our lives as we know them could be destroyed."

"That doesn't sound like you, Hawk. Sure something else isn't bothering you?"

Hawk seethed as he drove, incessantly checking his mirrors to make sure they weren't being followed.

"It's Big Earv," Hawk said. "He should've stopped this. And I can't believe I haven't heard from him by now."

"Maybe he got hung up or didn't know what was

going on," Samuels said.

"No, even if he was on duty, he would've heard over their secure channel what was happening. Two agents wouldn't have acted on their own and just grabbed Alex."

Samuels shrugged. "Perhaps. Or maybe the president ordered them to capture her. Don't rush to judgment."

Before Hawk could say another word, his phone buzzed.

"Who is it?" Samuels asked.

Hawk shot a sideways glance at Samuels and answered the phone.

"It's about time I heard from you, Big Earv," Hawk said.

"Hawk, I'm sorry about all this," he said. "I was on break when he gave the order."

"And you didn't hear what was going on?"

"I did, but it was too late," Big Earv said. "I couldn't just run in there like a cowboy and snatch her away. If I'm going to avoid drawing suspicion, I have to follow protocol."

"And what kind of protocol is it to arrest an innocent young woman?" Hawk asked.

"You're using the wrong word. We don't *arrest* anyone; we *detain* them. President Michaels does it all the time. It's how he manages to keep all his affairs discreet."

Hawk chuckled. "So, the president talks with a

beautiful woman and then moments later has her *detained*—that doesn't look suspicious to anyone?"

"I don't make the rules," Big Earv said. "And if I want to continue to be your eyes and ears here and shut this maniac down, I need to make sure I'm not creating suspicion by following orders as long as I can."

"I understand, but you know as well as I do that we can't let this thing drag out. The longer Alex is in custody, the longer Michaels' minions have a chance to trump up some charges against her."

"We better get to work then."

Hawk's phone buzzed with a call from an unknown number.

"I've got another call I need to take. An unknown number. These calls rarely have good news."

"Call me back."

"Roger that," Hawk said before answering the incoming call. "This is Hawk."

"How pleasant to hear your voice, Mr. Hawk," said Katarina Petrov.

"To what do I owe the pleasure of your call?"

"It seems that I've found one of your friends—and we need to make a deal."

Hawk drummed his fingers on the steering wheel.

"Who is this friend?"

"Mr. Blunt," she said. "I just so happened to

catch him in Scotland recovering from a most unfortunate injury. And now his condition has been upgraded to critical."

"I don't know what kind of sick game you think you're playing, but I can assure you that it won't end well for you."

"Perhaps, but I'm going to have to adjust your friend's condition to fatal should you choose not to play. Meet me at my offices in Istanbul if you ever want to see him alive again. Be prepared for a trade—you for your friend."

"I need proof of life before I'm going anywhere."

"Fine. Suit yourself. Mr. Blunt, there's someone who wants to speak with you. And no funny business."

A few seconds later, Blunt came on the line.

"Hawk," he said. "Don't come. It's a trap. Just get your old van and get out of town. She's going to—"

"That's enough," Petrov said as the rest of Blunt's words grew muffled.

"Satisfied, Mr. Hawk?"

"He better not be hurt," Hawk said.

"You have forty-eight hours."

The line went dead.

Hawk pounded his fist on the dashboard.

"What is it?" Samuels asked.

"I've got forty-eight hours to get to Istanbul and

trade myself for Blunt," he said.

"We better not waste any more time then."

Hawk called Big Earv and told him the timeline needed to be moved up to as soon as possible. They made plans to meet in half an hour and discuss how they would break Alex out of Secret Service custody.

"Don't worry," Samuels said. "She's going to be okay."

"You don't know that," Hawk said. "If Michaels learns who she really is, he'll use her as bait for me before killing all of us."

"You're right. I don't know if she'll survive—or if any of us will. But I know we'll all give them one hell of a fight."

"Damn right," Hawk said.

CHAPTER 20

ALEX TWISTED HER WRISTS in an attempt to assuage the itching and the burning caused by the rope used to confine her to the chair. Her arms had almost fallen asleep and she was thirsty. While she wasn't in the mood to give out compliments, she admired the precision that Secret Service agents worked with. They behaved like consummate professionals in whisking her away from the event. Despite being alert for the entire trip, Alex had no idea where she was.

She glanced around the room, which was stark and dimly lit. There were no windows and only one entry point. The cinder block walls were unpainted and the floor was concrete. Her best guess was that they were in the basement of a building.

After Alex sat alone for a half-hour, an agent walked into the room and asked her who she really was.

"I already told the last guy that I am Christina Harper," she said.

The agent paced around the room before stopping directly in front of Alex.

"Yes, but this time I want the truth," he said.

"I don't understand what's going on or what I've done."

"I'm the one asking the questions here," he said. "Now, what's your real name?"

Prior to Alex's decision to participate in the operation, Hawk emphasized the importance of sticking with her legend should she get caught and talking as little as possible.

"Well, Christina Harper, I noticed you have quite an impressive resume online."

"Thank you. Now will you please untie me?"

The agent narrowed his eyes. "But it's too impressive. I didn't believe this for one minute. It's obviously some fabricated cover if I've ever seen one."

"My name is Christina Harper, I swear."

"If I didn't know any better, I'd think you were some sort of computer savant. You set up a company website and a fake resume. I'm guessing you had some help on the inside to secure a ticket to the fundraiser because all the attendees are thoroughly vetted. Am I barking up the right tree here, *Mrs. Harper*?"

"I'm sorry that you find my accomplishments so unbelievable," she said, fully embracing her legend. "Most men feel threatened by strong women, especially in the marketplace. You're probably feeling threatened right now."

The agent laughed and shook his head.

"I'm afraid you've got it all wrong, sweetheart," he said. "You're the one who should feel vulnerable right now—because you are. I could make you disappear in an instant. And you know how I could do that?"

Alex remained silent and kept her gaze fixated on the wall in front of her.

"I could do that because Christina Harper doesn't exist. Nobody will come looking for a woman who is a figment of your imagination. So, save all your feminist talk for someone who cares. It doesn't intimidate me. I'm going to find out who you really are. And when I do, it's not going to be good for you."

The agent glared at her and shook his head.

"Now, why don't you make it easy on all of us and start talking, you little impostor?"

Alex continued looking forward and resisted the temptation to talk.

"Suit yourself," the agent said before punching her in face.

Alex's head rocked back due to the blow. The powerful punch stung and her face burned. Before she had time to fully comprehend what was happening, the agent delivered another hit to the other side of Alex's face. She teetered to the side in her chair before all four legs landed on the ground with a thud.

"Enjoying this, sweetie?" he asked.

Alex felt blood oozing from the corner of her mouth. She used her shoulder to temporarily stop the flow, brushing it against her face.

"There's a lot more where that came from," he said with a sneer.

"Bring it," she said. "You're only going to end up with a giant lawsuit on your hands when this is all over with . . . if you survive."

The agent stared at her. "Are you threatening me, little lady?"

"Damn right, I am," she said. "You'll be lucky to survive this ordeal if you're not careful."

"And who's going to stop me? You?" he asked mockingly.

"I'd be careful if I were you."

The man threw his head back and laughed. He then recoiled and slammed his fist into the side of Alex's face again. Alex regrouped from the blow as the agent broke into a maniacal laugh. He drew back and prepared to dish out another punch.

Then the lights went out.

CHAPTER 21

Istanbul, Turkey

BLUNT COULD FEEL ALL the blood draining from his arms as he hung suspended six feet in the air. A searing pain persisted around his ribs from his earlier injury. With his hands bound and tethered to a metal pipe attached to the wall, he glanced around the room and was certain he wasn't the first person to experience similar treatment from Petrov. He wondered how many of Petrov's enemies had taken their last breath in the room before considering the odds that he would do the same.

While Blunt had utilized government channels and legislation during most of his time working with Petrov, he knew she was prone to exert more direct means of pressure when necessary. She asked him to engage some black ops units in the past when traditional methods of achieving her objectives had failed. Blunt had been leery of complying, but on more than one occasion he obliged her. Those decisions were some of the few he'd come to regret during his time with The Chamber. Blunt considered how hanging in a painful position for long stretches of time had a way of making him reevaluate his life—or at least particular decisions he'd made.

But there was nothing he could do about any of it now. He concluded that regret was a worthless emotion when stuck in a helpless situation. Instead, he decided to turn his thoughts toward more hopeful ones, imagining how Hawk might be able to rescue him. It wasn't likely given the circumstances. He could only hope the secret message he tried to pass along was received and understood by Hawk.

An hour ticked slowly past before the door swung open and a streak of bright light flooded the room. He didn't have to guess whose silhouetted figure darkened the door and proceeded to march toward him.

"Nice of you to join me, Katarina," Blunt said. "I saved a spot for you up here."

"Ever the gentleman, J.D.," she said. "But I think I'll decline your invitation. We have some pressing matters to discuss before I trade you for your little soldier boy."

"Trade?" he asked. "You're really going to follow through on your promise?"

"As long as the exchange doesn't get messy, and there are no guarantees that it won't."

Blunt shook his head. "You're going to turn this

into a blood bath, aren't you?"

"It doesn't have to be. You tell me what I need to know and it'll just be a single sniper shot to his head. Very clean and quick. He'll be dead before he hits the ground."

"You think it's going to be that simple to kill Hawk?" Blunt said, breaking into a laugh. "You really are delusional."

"One person's delusion is another person's reality. Besides, the reality is you're not going anywhere unless you tell me what I want to know."

"I doubt I'll be able to pass along any useful intel to you. It's hard to think when your hands are hanging above your head."

Petrov walked toward the wall and pressed a button. A small pulley motor began to hum, lowering Blunt to the ground. Petrov grabbed a chair that was against the wall and used her foot to slide it to him.

"Have a seat and collect your thoughts," she said. "Your life depends on it."

Blunt sat down and moaned. He took a few deep breaths and threw his head back, grateful for a respite.

"All better now?" she asked.

Blunt nodded. "Thank you, Katarina. Kindness is very becoming on you."

She narrowed her eyes and glared at him before pushing the button on the wall. The motor sputtered to life again and hoisted Blunt back to his previous position.

"It didn't have to end this way," Petrov said. "We could've been doing this together."

Blunt situated himself again and struggled to get a deep breath before speaking.

"When I agreed to join The Chamber, this was never the mission."

She laughed. "Oh, you poor naïve man, J.D. This has always been the mission. But like any good leader, the soldiers only need to do their job to accomplish the overall objective. The bigger picture isn't of consequence to them."

"I thought The Chamber was going to be a force of good in this world, a last line of defense against ruthless dictators," he said. "Never did I dream for a minute that it was actually a vehicle for creating a totalitarian regime."

"In the annals of history, it won't matter what you thought. All that anyone will ever remember about J.D. Blunt was that he was a traitor to his country. Because if I go down, you will go down as well."

"So, you have a dead man's switch? Clever."

She smiled and nodded. "You know me. I always think of everything. Three days after I die, someone from my office will anonymously release mountains of documents on all of the people involved in The Chamber. My legacy will remain heroic within the Russian border, which is all I care about. You, however, will be viewed quite differently after your death."

"I doubt anyone will care that much about me after I die. Hell, no one probably even cares if I'm alive or dead."

"Brady Hawk cares, which is the only reason you're alive right now—and quite possibly the only reason you'll survive, if I decide to let you."

"You better kill me now because I assure you that if I live, I'll do whatever I can to make sure that you won't live to see the end of the week."

She shrugged. "By that point, everything I was assigned to do might already be completed. You'll only be feeding your rage and anger."

"No, I'll be getting justice, justice for all the terrible things you've done."

"J.D., I'm disappointed in you, trying to claim some moral high ground like that. You know that everything is relative and highly subjective according to your perspective. One man's traitor is another man's hero."

"You're no hero, Katarina."

"I suppose the Russian history books will differ with you and thus prove my point. So, you cling to your hope up there, but you've done nothing to persuade me to change my mind. Hawk is going to die."

"Aren't you even going to attempt to interrogate me?" Blunt asked. "Maybe I'll give you what you want to know."

She shook her head. "No, you've made it very

clear where you stand on everything. And I'm a big fan of not wasting everyone's time, though you arguably have more to waste than I do at this point. So, consider this an act of grace that I don't treat you like you deserve right now."

"I'm so grateful," Blunt sneered.

"I'm in the position of power, not you, J.D. Your angry words and threats ring hollow as you hang up there. Enjoy what time you have left. Your mind will torture you far more brutally than I ever could."

"I doubt that. My conscience is clear."

"Don't be absurd. In how much denial do you have to be to even believe such a statement like that? Your conscience is clear? What a ridiculous claim. We both know the truth. Pakistan, Yemen, Libya, El Salvador—you mean to tell me you have a clear conscience about what you did on each of those operations?"

"I wasn't perfect, but I didn't kill innocent people and their families just because they got in my way."

"And that's why I'm standing down here and you're hanging up there," she said as she turned out the lights. "Sweet dreams, J.D."

Blunt summoned all his strength to draw another deep breath as he watched her silhouette vanish down the hall before the door closed behind her.

Hurry up, Hawk.

CHAPTER 22

HAWK EASED HIS WAY along the darkened corridor in the bowels of the Library of Congress. The four buildings that comprised the world's largest library were interconnected through a series of tunnels. And while the library was closed to the public, employees worked through the night to fulfill requests and shuttle books back and forth between the various reading rooms. As a result of the graveyard shift staff, Hawk exercised caution as he moved toward the target.

Samuels was fulfilling Alex's role, watching the security feeds and warning Hawk about any potential dangerous situations lurking around the next corner. Big Earv, who'd filled Hawk and Samuels in on the Secret Service's clandestine holding facility just a few blocks away from the White House, took up his position just outside the doors to prevent any suspicion being cast on him. If video cameras showed he was overcome by Hawk, no one would suspect Big Earv's involvement.

Hawk reached the entry point into the interrogation

room, which was well disguised by a stairwell door. Big Earv had explained that one floor below the bottom basement level was a secure holding area for people that the President wanted detained for whatever reason. While the facility remained Secret Service lore to the public, Big Earv confirmed what Hawk had long believed to be true.

The plan consisted of Big Earv relieving the current guard on duty before Hawk would stage an attack and subdue his accomplice. However, the guard was still at his post when Hawk slipped into the hall. He hid behind a cart loaded with books as he waited.

Big Earv strode up to the man about a minute later and Hawk watched intently.

"You're relieving me of my duties?" the guard asked.

Big Earv nodded. "That's what I was told. Here's the text I received right here." He showed his phone to the other guard.

"How come I wasn't notified about this? You know protocol."

"Check again," Big Earv said. "Maybe you missed the message."

Hawk grew uneasy with the situation.

"Samuels, did you forget to send a text to the guard on duty?" Hawk whispered over the coms.

"Just sent it again," Samuels said. "I'm not sure what happened."

"Try not to let that happen again," Hawk said. "We're counting on you."

Hawk turned his attention back toward the guard post.

"Oh, there it is," the guard said after scrolling through his phone for a few second. "Sorry about that, Big Earv."

"No worries. It happens. Have a good night."

"You, too," the guard said with a wave as he spun and walked toward the exit.

Big Earv assumed his position and looked imposing. Hawk waited for a couple of minutes before taking a deep breath and sprinting toward his friend. After the altercation ended with Big Earv on his back, Hawk deemed their performance was Oscar worthy. He took the keys off Big Earv and entered the stairwell.

He maneuvered down the steps and determined to follow Big Earv's advice about killing the lights. Hawk was about to turn them off when he heard cries coming from the interrogation room down the hall. He crept up on it and saw an agent draw back before striking Alex. Hawk felt the blood rush to his face.

That bastard is gonna pay for that.

Hawk hustled back down the hallway and killed the lights. He waited for a few seconds before easing into the room. He slipped on his infrared glasses and located the man who'd hit Alex. However, he wasn't the only man in the room. Two other agents were also nearby. They were both groping against the wall in search of the light switch.

Perfect.

Taking two of the guards by the back of their shirts, Hawk slammed them into one another. Unable to see who hit them, they both started swinging wildly. Hawk then turned his attention to the agent who'd been striking Alex. While Hawk considered how unfair the fight was for a moment, he justified it since it was as fair as the agent torturing an innocent woman bound to a chair.

Hawk's first punch was straight to the man's throat. The next was a swift kick to his midsection. Hawk followed that with a series of blows to the man's face, finishing him off by placing him in a sleeper hold.

Glancing at the other two guards, Hawk watched as they continued to blindly fight one another.

Hawk pulled out his knife and began to cut through Alex's bindings.

"Sorry about taking so long to get here," he whispered after the blade severed the rope. "Let's get out of here."

He led her toward the door.

"Wait here for just a minute."

Hawk rushed over to the two men and delivered a pair of haymakers, knocking them both to the floor.

He ran back to Alex and grabbed her by the hand.

"Let's go. We don't have much time."

They hustled up the stairwell, stepped over Big Earv's body, and raced toward the exit.

"How are we looking, Samuels?" Hawk said over the coms.

"So far so good," Samuels answered.

Hawk yanked Alex close as they rounded hard into a corridor on the left. Within a few seconds, they'd both reached top speed.

"Hold on," Samuels said. "You're about to have company."

Hawk threw his hand out to slow Alex as he tried to stop. But it was too late. A security guard roaming the halls stepped into the hallway and saw both of them. The guard fumbled for his nightstick, but he wasn't able to get a good handle on it before Hawk kicked it free. After two vicious punches, the man toppled to the ground unconscious. Hawk grabbed the man's radio and resumed running toward the exit.

"What are you trying to do, Samuels? Get us arrested again?" Hawk asked.

Samuels was slow to respond.

"Samuels? Samuels? Are you there?" Hawk asked.

"I'm here. Sorry about that. I'm still new to this whole monitoring thing."

"Don't worry," Hawk said. "Just be a little more

vigilant until we get out of here. And then I'm going to permanently relieve you of that duty."

A few minutes later, Hawk and Alex were climbing into the van with Samuels.

Samuels rushed over to Alex, giving his sister a tight hug.

"Thank God you're okay," he said. "What happened?"

Alex sat down and buried her head in her hands before she began to cry softly.

"I didn't think I'd ever see either of you two again," she said. "How did you find me? Big Earv?"

Hawk nodded as he cranked the van and started driving.

"The most important thing is you're okay because we need our entire team running on all cylinders if we're going to be successful on our next mission."

Alex dried her eyes and took a deep breath.

"So, what's next? Back to protecting Justice Williams?"

Hawk shook his head. "No, Justice Williams is on her own now."

"We can't just leave her alone," she said. "Michaels is obviously unhinged. He's going to kill her tonight if he thinks she's going to vote against him."

"From the news reports I heard, she did a pretty good job of tipping her hand. She appears to be voting in lockstep with the president. Besides, we have a far more important operation ahead of us."

"More important than making sure the U.S. doesn't adopt Petrov's one world currency plan?"

Hawk nodded. "Petrov kidnapped Blunt. She wants me to trade myself for Blunt in less than forty-eight hours. If not, she's going to kill him."

"Saving Blunt is more important than saving the justice? Hawk, you know what Blunt would want us to do—and saving him isn't it."

"We're going to put an end to this thing once and for all."

"And how do you plan on doing that?"

"I'm going to kill Petrov."

CHAPTER 23

ON THE PLANE RIDE to Istanbul, Hawk worked with Alex and Samuels to develop a plan to infiltrate Petrov's compound using information off the thumb drive Polat had sent them. Hawk insisted on going over every piece of intel Polat had sent them and found a few hidden gems.

"Polat gave his life to get these plans to us," Hawk said. "Let's make sure it doesn't go to waste."

As she dug through the files, Alex found a blueprint that contradicted what was officially on record with Istanbul's planning website.

"Would you look at that?" she said.

Hawk leaned over her shoulder and studied the plans carefully.

"What am I looking at?"

Alex pointed at the screen. "See this hallway right here?"

"Yeah."

"That's not on the originals. I've combed through all of these plans, and this is the only area that deviates from the official ones."

"Think this is where they're holding Blunt?"

"I'd bet my life on it," Alex said.

"Great," Hawk said. "So, how do you recommend we sneak into this room?"

Alex scrolled through several pages before answering.

"Right here," she said. "The ventilation shaft on the second floor runs all the way down to this room. It's your best bet at sneaking into The Chamber's offices without getting caught."

Hawk stood up and stroked his chin, his eyes still roaming over every inch of the screen.

"And how do you suggest we penetrate their state-of-the-art security system?"

She smiled and pounded out a few keystrokes on her computer.

"You're going to have to access this passageway from inside the building—right here."

Hawk's eyes widened as he drew a deep breath.

"That's a suicide mission, Alex," he said. "I want to get Blunt out of there alive. And I'd like to join him."

"What makes you think you can't get inside without them noticing?"

"For starters, I'm sure she has her security team on high alert for me. Her guards probably have contour on my face memorized by now."

Alex turned toward Samuels and gestured to him.

"Enter the Magic Man."

Hawk glanced at Samuels. "Do you have some skill you've been hiding from me?"

Samuels smiled and winked at Hawk.

"Not a hidden skill, but a hidden piece of tech," Samuels said, opening a briefcase. "This will make you look like someone else entirely."

Hawk hovered over the briefcase and studied the machine.

"What does it do?"

"It creates a mask that so alters the outside of your face that even the best facial recognition software will be fooled by it."

"You'd bet your life on it?" Hawk said.

"Absolutely," Samuels said. "And to prove it, I'm going to join you on this operation."

Hawk shook his head. "No, I need you helping Alex in case things go sideways."

"She can handle herself. I think she's proven that to us time and time again. But you're going to be outgunned and outmanned. Without me, you don't stand a chance."

"Maybe, but this is the kind of mission where not everyone comes back alive. Think you can handle that?"

"I'll take my chances."

"Fine," Hawk said. "Let's do it. Any idea who we should look like?"

"I've got just the face for you," Samuels said.

Hawk retreated to the back of the plane to place a phone call. He was sure he understood a secret message Blunt was trying to pass to him. When the man on the other end answered, Hawk knew he'd interpreted the message correctly.

* * *

ONCE THEY LANDED, they went straight to a hotel, where they finalized their plans. Hawk asked everyone if they felt confident about their roles in the operation, which was met with assured nods.

"Excellent," Hawk said. "Let's get some rest before we head over this afternoon. I have a feeling it's going to be a long night."

"Agreed," Alex said. "But before we do, I want to check the news. The Supreme Court was supposed to render its judgment by now."

She re-opened her computer and started to scour news websites. In a matter of seconds, she found the story she was looking for blaring in large type across the front of one of her favorite news sites.

"Scarborough recuses himself, court split on revoking Federal Reserve Act," she read.

"What does that mean?" Samuels asked.

Hawk watched Alex's eyes speed back and forth across the screen.

"It means that the efforts to rule the act unconstitutional are dead—for now," she said. "And that means that Justice Williams' life is in grave danger."

"Not yet. Michaels will need to regroup before going back in front of the Supreme Court and asking it to review its ruling."

"So, you're saying that she's safe?"

"Not indefinitely, but it means that what we're doing tomorrow has grave consequences for our own country as well as Justice Williams," Hawk said. "If we can finally put an end to Petrov and her attempts to dupe the world's financial leaders into signing up for her scheme, Michaels won't care anymore. It'll all be moot at that point."

Alex continued to hammer away on her keyboard.

"What are you doing now?" Samuels asked.

"Michaels must be livid," she said. "I'm sure he's scrambling and trying to figure out a way to get what he wants by some other means."

"Time to see if that watch works," Hawk said.

"Exactly what I was thinking," Alex said. She continued typing until she accessed the feed and heard Michaels' voice.

"Worked like a charm," Samuels said.

Hawk smiled. "Turn it up."

Alex adjusted the volume and the Firestorm team listened in, getting a rare live account of the inner workings of the president's office. Hawk appreciated the voyeuristic nature of taping Michaels. All they needed was one mistake out of the president and they would be able to safely return to the U.S.—if they survived their impending clash with Petrov.

Michaels' voice was silent for a few moments before it came back on and he started talking. Based on the nature of the call, Hawk could tell it was a phone call. Then Michaels said he was going to place her on speaker phone. When the other voice became audible, the entire team gasped.

"Petrov," Alex said.

They listened for another minute before the pair created a new plot.

"Can you believe that?" Alex asked, her mouth agape. "The public is going to go berserk if they hear this."

"Just what I'm counting on," Hawk said.

CHAPTER 24

Istanbul, Turkey

TWELVE HOURS BEFORE PETROV'S imposed deadline, Hawk and Samuels entered The Chamber's headquarters, posing as computer repairmen and donning their masks. They stopped at the front desk and spoke with a receptionist, who wasn't eager to let them enter.

"Who are you here to see again?" she asked.

"You're there to see Ms. Ibrahamovic in accounting," Alex said over the coms.

"A Ms. Ibrahamovic in accounting," Hawk said, parroting back the instructions.

"Ah, just one moment," the receptionist said. "Let me try her office."

She dialed the number and Alex intercepted the call, posing as the accountant on the other end.

"Are you expecting some computer repairmen?" the receptionist asked.

"But of course," Alex said. "Send them on through."

The receptionist looked up at the men and unenthusiastically waved them inside.

"Follow those signs to the elevator. She's on the second floor."

"Thank you so much," Hawk said.

Hawk and Samuels followed suit, confidently striding down the hallway toward the elevators. Less than a minute later, they were both standing on the second floor and ready to get to work.

Samuels served as the lookout on the floor, while Alex was watching through The Chamber's security feeds.

"Make it quick, Hawk," she said. "Two employees about ten seconds from coming around the corner."

Hawk nodded slightly to acknowledge her comment and continued working on the lock. After a few tense seconds, he managed to gain access. He and Samuels eased inside and proceeded to the next part of their plan.

Hawk and Samuels worked quickly to open an access panel to the ventilation shaft. Once they unscrewed the door, they climbed inside.

As planned, Hawk went first and was to drop down and rescue Blunt. Samuels was to stay put and hoist them back up. Only in the event of an emergency was he to leave his post.

Hawk crawled slowly through the shaft until he reached the one that dropped down into the hidden basement. Easing his way down, Hawk applied pressure against both sides of the aluminum structure to slow his fall. Samuels stayed at the top and secured a cord with a winch. Once Hawk reached the floor, he listened for a moment in an attempt to determine if anyone else was in the room. The only sounds Hawk heard were Blunt's moans.

Hawk kicked the vent door open and dropped to the floor. A rope followed quickly behind him. Looking up the shaft, he flashed the thumbs up sign to Samuels.

Hawk ripped off his mask. He rushed over to Blunt and started to untie him.

"You made it," Blunt said followed by a groan as Hawk worked feverishly to release his boss.

"You didn't think I was going to leave you here, did you?" Hawk asked.

"No, but I was afraid you might try to trade yourself for me."

Hawk chuckled. "I wasn't born that long ago, but it wasn't yesterday. Petrov would never let you live if I did that."

"Good boy," Blunt said as his hands finally came free and he dropped to the floor. He hit the ground hard and moaned as he tried to clamber to his knees.

"Are you okay?" Hawk asked while rushing over to attend to the elderly man.

"You'll have to be more specific," Blunt said. "I've got some broken ribs from a previous incident, while my arms feel like they've been yanked out of their sockets. I'm dehydrated and I'm not entirely sure I can run. Other than that, I'm feeling just dandy."

"Well, let's get you out of here," Hawk said, helping Blunt to his feet.

"I hope you have a good plan for escaping this fortress."

Hawk nodded and looked upward.

Blunt waved dismissively at the rope hanging from the ceiling.

"If you think I'm climbing up that thing, you're crazy," he said.

"Samuels has a winch," Hawk said. "He'll pull you up."

"A guard will be back in ten minutes to check on me," Blunt said. "No way we've got enough time to get out that way."

"Got any better ideas?" Hawk asked.

"There's a door in that corner over there that might be easier for us to get out of and onto the street."

"And what about Samuels?"

"Tell him to get his ass down here and join us. It'll give us the best chance," Blunt said.

"Did you hear that, Samuels?" Hawk shouted up toward the shaft.

"Roger that," Samuels said over the com.

Blunt followed Hawk over toward the door and

reached to open it. But the door crashed open and a dozen armed guards rushed inside. Hawk turned toward the back door and took a few steps before it flung wide and another dozen guards flooded the room.

In a matter of seconds, the guards formed a circle around Hawk and Blunt.

"I'd advise you to stay put," one of the guards said.

"Great advice, too," said Petrov, who strode through the front door clapping slowly.

Hawk cast a quick glace toward Blunt before turning an icy stare toward Petrov.

"Two for the price of one," she said. "Mr. Hawk, I can't thank you enough for making this far easier for me than it was going to be. I have to admit that you do know how to make an entrance."

Hawk stopped and spun around, surveying the situation. Two dozen guards holding guns all trained on him and Blunt. Hawk's options had dwindled to a prayer.

"Talk to me, Hawk," Alex said over the coms. "I'm flying blind here. There are no security cameras in that room."

"We're trapped," he said.

CHAPTER 25

Washington, D.C.

PRESIDENT MICHAELS FUMED over the Supreme Court's split decision, grousing about the outcome to one of his aides. After throwing several books across the Oval Office, Michaels calmed down and fell into his chair.

"I swear I'm going to ruin Williams," he said as he looked up at his aide. "She's going to pay dearly."

"What exactly would you like for me to do, sir?" the aide asked.

"Get out," Michaels growled.

Michaels waited until the aide left the room before moving. Surprised that Petrov hadn't called, Michaels scrolled through his address book in search of one name: Frank Stone. He finally found it and dialed the number again.

"We have some things to discuss," Michaels said as Stone answered.

"Apparently our warning wasn't strong enough

for Justice Williams," Stone said.

"That's one way to put it, but we'll have to wait and address it at a later time."

"You have a more pressing matter?"

"Yes, and it's not one that we can afford to have screwed up this time. No excuses. Do you understand?"

"Don't accuse me of not doing my job," Stone said. "You were the one who told me only to scare Williams. I could've just as easily had them kill her that night."

Michaels bristled. "My orders were to persuade her to vote in my favor. Your *persuasion* didn't accomplish the intended goal."

"I think I've established with you well by now that persuasion isn't my specialty. I deal better when it comes to finite directives with results that are easier to measure."

"Take this order as a more permanent one with only a single outcome that will satisfy me," Michaels said. "In other words, if you don't fulfill the mission, don't come home."

"Who's the target?" Michaels asked.

"Brady Hawk," Michaels said. "I want him dead."

"Where is he?"

"At the moment, he's in Istanbul. Not sure if he'll be there long—or survive, for that matter. But you better go and bring back pictures of his dead body.

This is your final chance. Got it?"

"Loud and clear."

Michaels hung up and then leaned back in his chair. He stared at the ceiling and pondered his next move.

CHAPTER 26

Istanbul, Turkey

HAWK RAISED HIS ARMS IN THE AIR and stared at Petrov. He'd hoped for a clean getaway but would've settled for a messy one under the circumstances. Scanning the room, he realized he'd likely get neither. He stood in the middle of a tinderbox. One itchy finger was all that was between his hope of a miracle and utter annihilation.

"Seems like you've won and congratulations are in order," Hawk said.

Petrov wagged her finger. "Mother Russia has won. I have simply fulfilled my role in a greater plan."

"So, now what? A bronze bust of you in Moscow or St. Petersburg? A university named in your honor?"

"That'd be nice," she said with a smile. "But I'd settle for a nice little home somewhere along the Black Sea. But enough about my retirement plans. Let's discuss yours, which are limited at this point to either a quick death or a slow one."

"I was hoping you'd just let me walk out of here," he said. "A little catch and release. Without me in your life, things wouldn't be very interesting."

She circled Hawk, her heels clicking against the concrete floor.

"Believe it or not, Mr. Hawk, I prefer life to be less interesting. Whenever people do exactly what I say, I find that my stress level goes down. But when you are around, somehow I'm constantly on edge. So, I'll decline your proposal, which puts us back to what I originally asked you—quick death or slow death?"

Hawk shrugged. "Dealer's choice."

"Very well then," she said. "But before I make my decision, there's something I want you to see."

Petrov turned and nodded at one of the soldiers, who pressed a button on the side of the wall. A large screen dropped down from the ceiling along with a camera. Next, a row of lights flashed on. Petrov moved toward the middle of the room.

"Keep those two over on the side. I don't want them in the shot," she instructed, gesturing toward Blunt and Hawk.

She pulled out her smart phone and began dialing. Seconds later, a video conference feed appeared on the screen with a simple name beneath it: Michaels.

After a few seconds, the screen blinked alive and President Michaels was sitting in the Oval Office, hunched forward, his elbows resting on the desk, hands clasped together.

"Ah, Katarina, how are you? I've been expecting your call."

"I'm sure you've been looking forward to it too given your failure to uphold your end of the bargain."

Michaels winced. "Unfortunately, this isn't Russia. In a democratic republic, sometimes things don't end up going your way."

"Your type of government isn't an excuse," she said. "When you promise results, you should deliver. Now, you've put me in a less than desirable position."

"I'm sorry about that, Katarina. Is there any way I could make it up to you?"

"Since you asked, I'm willing to give you one more chance."

"Just tell me what I need to do."

Katarina laughed mockingly and turned toward her guards. "American men are so weak."

"What was that?" Michaels asked.

"Never mind. Here's what I'm going to need you to do: Convince the Federal Reserve to disband on their own and place temporary decision-making power back into your hands."

"Disband? You can't be serious? There's a better chance that Kim Kardashian would—"

"Shut up," she said. "You asked for one more chance. I'm giving it to you."

"But how am I supposed to convince the entire

Federal Reserve to give up all their power and disband? They already hate me as it is."

"Good," she said. "Then you won't lose any friends over the deal since they loathe you so. I hate losing friends."

"How quickly do you want this done?"

"I'll give you three days," she said.

"Three days? Are you out of your mind? These are busy people. There's no way I can schedule meetings that quickly with all of them."

"I can't hold off initiating the one world currency any longer than that. But to assist you in this manner, I'll have my office send over some compromising material on all the board members momentarily."

"I'm not sure that will still be enough time, but I'll try."

"A skillful politician could have this wrapped up in a day."

Michaels loosened his tie. "Fine. I'll do my best. What about our other little problem?"

"Firestorm?"

"More specifically, Brady Hawk."

"Consider him taken care of."

"So, he's still alive?" Michaels said. "I thought you were going to handle him."

"I'm always mopping up after you, Mr. President. For someone who claims to be the leader of the free world, you are quite terrible at your job."

She grabbed Hawk by the collar and dragged him into the picture.

"Satisfied?" she said.

Michaels' face lit up when he saw Hawk.

"Excellent," Michaels said. "Just make sure that bastard is filled with lead as quickly as possible."

"It will be my pleasure," she said. "I'll see to it personally. Three days, Mr. President. Three days or else the United States will be left behind as the world forges ahead into a new era of economic prosperity."

She tapped her phone and the overhead screen went dark before ascending up into the ceiling along with the camera.

"So, it's going to be a quick death," Hawk said.

"Oh, no," she said. "It's going to be slow and painful. And you're going to wish our paths never crossed."

She looked at a couple of the guards.

"Attach them to the pipe and get me a knife," she said. "I'm going to enjoy this."

Blunt looked at Hawk as the guards ushered them back toward the pipe and started securing them.

"This was your big rescue plan?" Blunt asked softly. "Didn't you get the message I sent you?"

"Now would be as good of a time as any, Samuels," Hawk said.

"Had to get all my weapons ready," Samuels said over the com.

Seconds later, Samuels repelled from the

ventilation shaft and started shooting. The gunfire momentarily distracted the guards, who had to turn their attention to the back door. An elite team of Army Rangers under the direction of General Van Fortner stormed into the room and started shooting.

Hawk ripped free from the bindings and helped Blunt get away before sprinting for cover behind several crates stacked near one side of the room. Offered a gun by one of the soldiers, Hawk grabbed it and began looking for Petrov.

"Where is she?" Hawk asked.

Blunt peered into the room filled with smoke and gunfire, which had started to die down.

"I don't see her," he said. "Wait, I think that's her over in the corner."

"Where?" Hawk asked, his nose burning from the smell of gunpowder.

Blunt pointed. "Right there."

Hawk turned his steely gaze toward the place Blunt directed him. Before Hawk could put Petrov in his sights, a flash bang exploded in the room. More chaos and confusion. Hawk put his hand on Blunt's back and the two stayed low for a few seconds while waiting for the smoke to clear.

"Samuels!" Hawk said, peeking up to see his fellow agent gasping for air in the middle of the room. "I've got to pull him out of there."

Blunt took a fistful of Hawk's shirt and pulled

him back.

"You can't. He's already gone, Hawk."

"You don't know that. We could save him."

"Petrov is going to get away if you don't move."

Hawk crouched low as he re-entered the line of fire. He grabbed Samuels by the ankles and pulled him back toward the line the Rangers had formed.

"Get him some help, will ya?" Hawk said to one of the soldiers.

The soldier nodded.

Hawk then counted in his head. Ten seconds had elapsed since the last bullet shot.

"What's going on in there, Hawk?" Alex said over the coms. "Can you give me some kind of update? I'm flying blind here."

"I think we've eliminated all the hostiles, except for Petrov," he said. "But I'm going after her now."

CHAPTER 27

HAWK SPRINTED AFTER PETROV, slipping into the stairwell that led up to the obscure street level entrance Alex identified on the plans. As Hawk ran, he wondered about Samuels' status. Even though he'd only been a part of the Firestorm team for just a few weeks, Hawk had taken to him, if only for the fact that he was blood kin to Alex. Samuels had made a heroic move—Hawk only hoped it wasn't a costly one.

Meanwhile, Hawk tried to stay focused on the task at hand, keeping pace of Petrov as he refused to lose sight of her. She'd dashed around several corners but had been unable to shake him. She paused for a few seconds to ditch her shoes, allowing Hawk to gain more ground briefly. But she quickly rebuilt her lead running barefoot.

"Alex, are you still with me?" Hawk said.

"Of course," she said. "But before you ask, her phone is off. I can't track her."

"Well, stay close by," he said. "I might need you soon."

"Roger that."

Despite Petrov's winding route through the city to evade capture, Hawk figured out where she was ultimately headed. He figured he'd go to the same place, too—the Grand Bazaar.

The vast network of covered streets packed tightly with shops would give anyone a fighting chance to disappear. After a few minutes, Hawk's suspicions were confirmed when Petrov entered the Grand Bazaar at the Nuruosmaniye Gate. The market hadn't been open more than an hour but was already bustling with local shoppers and curious tourists. Vendors lined the major thoroughfares, hawking goods outside their shops. Several shopkeepers grabbed Hawk forcefully by his sleeve in an attempt to pull him inside their shop. Keeping his eyes focused on Petrov, he resisted and kept moving forward.

As Hawk closed in on her, she made a sharp turn and approached a pair of police officers. She waved her arms frantically and then pointed at Hawk. The officers looked right at Hawk, and one of them started speaking into his radio.

Hawk glanced at Petrov, who shot him a satisfied grin before she started running again.

Turning his back on the officers, Hawk started running back along the main street. He immediately cut down an adjacent street that led back toward Petrov's direction. Ducking into one store, Hawk hastily overpaid for a shawl and wrapped himself in it before returning to his pursuit.

He'd managed to avoid several officers, who still appeared to be intent on finding him, but he lost Petrov.

Where could she be?

Hawk had been to Istanbul several times, though he'd never been thrust into a situation that required extensive knowledge of the city. Taxi cab drivers and public transportation handled getting him where he needed to go. Knowing Petrov like he did, Hawk figured she would try to cut off any potential public relations nightmare and would need to get out in front of a workplace shooting at The Chamber's main offices.

"Alex," Hawk said over the coms, "can you still hear me?"

"Yes," she said. "I'm still tracking you."

"Great. I need your help."

"Tell me what you need this time."

"If you were needing to get out of the bazaar and find the nearest television station, where would you go and what's the fastest way to get there?"

"Give me a second."

Hawk continued moving along the outside of the bazaar, scanning the streets for any sign of Petrov. But she was gone.

"Come on, Alex. I can't lose her."

"I wouldn't do it on foot. I'd use a ferry. There's a

terminal a few blocks from you that would be ideal. You could get to a couple of TV stations easily—and the international airport is on the west side of the Bosphorus."

"You're a genius, Alex. Now, tell me how to get there."

Alex gave him directions and Hawk didn't hesitate. He raced toward the Sirceki ferry terminal five blocks away. However, when he was within two blocks of the location, he spotted Petrov walking hurriedly in a throng of people moving along the sidewalk. Periodically, she glanced over her shoulder as if she were still looking for Hawk.

"Found her," he said to Alex.

"Be careful, Hawk. You know how dangerous she is."

"This is going to end today."

Hawk increased his pace and followed her onto the ferry headed across the Bosphorus for the Harem terminal.

Less than five minutes after Hawk bought a ticket and got on board, the ship's crew began to initiate the departure process. They removed the ropes tying them to the dock and drew in the pedestrian and auto ramps. The engines chugged to life and the ferry wasted no time in putting distance between itself and the terminal.

Hawk hunkered down on the automobile deck and considered his next move. He needed to coerce her somehow into a private place. Hawk kept his head down but his eyes focused on the ferry passengers. After several minutes, he located Petrov and started following her. She sat down several times but wouldn't remain in any seat for very long, getting up and pacing around the deck. She constantly scanned the room and glanced over her shoulder.

Hawk followed her for 10 minutes before she got up and decided to go below the passenger deck. Continuing her nervous behavior, she wove her way through the cars lined up and ready to depart. Most of the cars' owners had joined the other foot passengers above. Hawk raced around the outside of the deck and positioned himself near the set of stairs she was likely to use. There was a janitorial closet around the corner from the stairs, which Hawk discovered was unlocked.

He took a deep breath and exhaled slowly, waiting for Petrov. She eased her way through the cars, keeping her head on a swivel. But Hawk remained invisible right up until the moment he grabbed her by the arm.

Petrov gasped and her eyes widened. Hawk shoved his free hand over her mouth and shoved her into the janitorial closet.

"It's over," he said.

"It's not over until I say it's over," she said, reaching for her gun.

Hawk reacted quickly, hitting her arm with such force that she dropped her weapon.

"No, it's over, Katarina."

"I will scream. People will come running. I will tell them that you tried to rape me."

"You will be dead before anyone arrives," he said. "Everyone will see a woman who tragically took her own life."

She glared at him for a few seconds before relaxing her shoulders, a sign that she had admitted defeat.

"Killing me won't stop what's already been set into motion," she said. "The one world currency will become reality. Your children and your grandchildren—if you live that long to see them—will all speak Russian. You will see."

"Your persistence and dedication to your cause is to be admired, but you have failed. You intended to trap me but didn't account for everything."

"Even a broken clock is right twice a day."

"I think it's safe to say I've been right more than that," Hawk said. "But it doesn't matter because I was right today and your plans stop right here with you."

"You won't get away with this," she said. "I'm too famous to just go missing. People will search for me. Governments will want to know what happened to me."

"Oh, they will search for you, but not in an effort to rescue you. They will be looking for the woman who stole all their money and vanished into thin air. Trust me. We've thought of everything."

"You bastard. I swear on my mother's grave—"

"I'd advise you against making any promises you can't keep," Hawk said. "However, I will keep one promise I made to your daughter a long time ago. I told her that I wouldn't kill you without letting you speak to her one final time."

Hawk took an extra earpiece out of his pocket and handed it to Petrov.

"Go on," he said. "Put it in your ear. Alex wants to speak with you."

"So this is goodbye?" Alex said.

"Unless you can convince your madman friend to let me go, it would appear that way," Petrov said.

"I wish I had the chance to really get to know you," Alex said. "I don't believe you're as horrible of a person as you portray yourself to be."

Petrov forced a nervous laugh. "Well, I don't portray myself to be any such way. I am simply a servant to my country, doing whatever is asked of me. When I was married to your father and became pregnant with you, I did what was asked, which was to raise you up and love you as I would any child I gave birth to. And I did it well. While I hate to disappoint you, I don't feel the same way as you. Getting to know you was never a priority of mine. You were nothing more than a mistake, an extra burden to my assignment."

Alex's voice quivered. "I don't believe you."

"I can't make you believe it, but it doesn't matter. It's the truth. I'm not sorry for abandoning you or anything that I did. To be honest, you're lucky to be alive."

"What is that supposed to mean?" Alex said.

"If you haven't learned by now, if you don't want to hear the answer, don't ask the question."

Alex relented. "We will work hard to show the world what your true legacy is—and that your biggest 'mistake' turned out to be the only good thing that came from you."

"Goodbye, Alex," Petrov said. "You probably deserved better, but it doesn't change the fact that you were a mistake."

"Just do it, Hawk," Alex said.

Petrov ripped out the earpiece and threw it at Hawk.

"Make it quick," she said.

Hawk obliged, putting a bullet in the center of her forehead. Petrov crumpled to the ground. He grabbed a rope and tied it to both of Petrov's legs. Then he found a sandbag and tethered it to her body. Moving swiftly, he peeked out the door. With no other pedestrians lurking around, he rushed to the deck and dropped Petrov's body into the water. She sank fast and went unnoticed by anyone on the observation deck.

"She's gone," Hawk said over the coms. "And she's never coming back."

Alex's sigh was audible followed by a whispered "thank you."

Hawk returned to the top of the ferry with the rest of the pedestrians. He sat down but couldn't relax. He still had plenty of work to do.

CHAPTER 28

LATER THAT EVENING, Hawk reunited at a hotel with Blunt, Alex, and General Van Fortner. Fortner explained how Samuels had been flown back to the military hospital on his base and was in critical condition.

"What are the doctors saying?" Hawk asked.

"It's still touch and go at this point," Fortner said. "The surgeon I spoke to said he'd give Samuels a 50-50 chance of surviving."

"He sacrificed everything for this mission. Keep us posted, will you?"

Hawk glanced at Alex, whose eyes welled up with tears.

"Stay strong," Hawk said. "He could still pull through."

Hawk then recounted for everyone how he killed Petrov. Sensitive to Alex, he didn't go into all the details, sticking to the basics. He could see relief on the faces of everyone in the room. Then Hawk proceeded to share his final conversation with Petrov.

"She said that we wouldn't be able to stop the one world currency movement at this point, even with her out of the way," Hawk said.

"I hate to say this, but she's probably right," Blunt said as he sat propped up in one of the beds. "There are a lot of moving parts in this push to change, and she did a great job at generating momentum in all of the sectors that mattered most. The financial decision makers, the court of pubic opinion, the international political bodies—she approached this like a pro and certainly understood what she was doing."

"In that case, we simply need to reverse everything she did," Hawk said. "I'm sure there were plenty of people who felt cajoled by her actions, if not outright threatened."

Fortner nodded. "Probably true, but she's done a great job at creating a groundswell of support among the general public. Any politician worth his weight in salt isn't going to ignore that at this point."

"You're not suggesting we give up, are you?" Hawk asked.

Fortner shook his head. "At times, we need to be shrewder in how we solve a problem."

"So, what do you suggest?" Hawk asked.

Fortner paced around the room. "We need to undermine the movement and expose it for what it really is—a Russian attempt at a power grab of the global economy. Nobody has made much of the Russian banks being the ones with all the power in setting the conversion rates when countries exchange their money in for the new one world currency."

"And each nation has to have their share backed up by gold, trading for it," Blunt said.

"Once Russia gets control of all the gold, they could bankrupt their own system and leave the other nations broke," Hawk said.

"That's precisely why this is such an important issue."

"But wouldn't such a move likely leave Russia with more enemies than it could possibly fight off?" Hawk asked. "It'd be the world against Russia."

Blunt shrugged. "But how would these countries pay their soldiers if their coffers are bare? No one would accept that worthless money, making the buildup of an effective campaign that much more difficult."

"Petrov's bosses really thought of everything, didn't they?" Hawk asked.

"Yes, but they didn't count on a small force like Firestorm being so disruptive," Blunt said. "We can still stop this before everyone transfers their gold to the Russians."

"That looks like it's our only shot," Hawk said.

"We need ironclad proof that leaders are being tricked and manipulated into doing this," Blunt said.

After listening in silence, Alex finally spoke up.

"We already have some," she said. "If we can show everyone that Petrov had Michaels under her thumb, we'll be able to convince journalists and other world leaders."

"And we know some well-placed journalists," Hawk said.

"Where is all this information? And how did you get it?" Blunt asked.

"You don't want to know the answer to your second question," Hawk said.

Alex glanced at her computer. "The info is all stored on my computer. I've been collecting it ever since we activated that watch on the President, which oddly stopped working a few hours ago."

"Were you able to capture Michaels' conversation with Petrov from earlier today?" Blunt asked.

"Oh, yeah," Alex said, patting the top of her computer. "It's all right here."

A knock at the door interrupted their brainstorming session.

"Does anyone know we're here?" Blunt asked.

Hawk pulled out his gun and screwed a silencer on the end of it. Then he eased the safety off.

"Why don't you take it, General?" Hawk said.

Fortner shrugged and walked over to the door. He looked through the peephole.

"Did either of you order room service?" he asked.

The remaining trio all shook their heads.

"Who is it?" Fortner shouted through the door.

"Room service," came the reply.

"Sorry, we didn't order any."

"That's not what I have on my ticket," the waiter replied. "This is room 345, isn't it?"

"Yes, but we'll decline it," Fortner said.

"Sir, I can't return with this bottle of wine that's worth 300 euros, nor can I leave it out in the hall since it's alcohol, hotel policy."

"One moment please," Fortner said. Turning toward Blunt, he asked, "What now?"

"Just take it," Blunt said. "We'll pour it down the drain."

Hawk nodded but backed into the bathroom and trained his gun on the door.

"Okay, I'll take it," Fortner said, checking the peephole one final time. He proceeded to remove the panic chain and turned the deadbolt. However, the door crashed into him and a pair of soldiers wearing body armor stormed into the room.

Hawk fired two shots at the men before one of the men hit Hawk in the shoulder with a tranquilizer. He fell to the ground and his gun fell from his hand.

"Now, no one else move," said Frank Stone as he entered the room wearing a hotel staff uniform. He kicked Hawk's gun aside.

Hawk tried to sit up as his vision blurred.

"Take every piece of electronic equipment in this room," Stone ordered the other soldiers. "Every watch, every phone. Nothing that runs off power is to be left behind."

Alex glowered at Stone. "What are you going to do to us?"

"Nothing," Stone said. "Unlike some people in this room, I know how to follow orders." He nodded at Fortner. "Your presence here will be passed along to your superiors, as well as your unauthorized use of a Ranger team."

"Screw you," Fortner said.

Stone wagged his gun at Fortner.

"Settle down, General. You made these decisions, not me."

The soldiers ripped cords out of the wall and piled all of Alex's computer equipment on the waiter's cart. In less than a minute, they had gathered everything.

"Evening, gentlemen," Stone said before glancing at Alex, "and lady."

The door slammed shut behind them.

Hawk's eyes grew heavy and he decided to lie on the cold bathroom floor.

"Please tell me you made a copy of everything," Blunt said as he looked at Alex.

She took a long breath and hung her head.

"I didn't have a chance yet."

"All our evidence is gone," Blunt screamed. He then launched into an expletive-laden tirade.

The reality of what had just happened dawned on everyone in the room—any chance of showing the American public as well as the global community what President Michaels had been up to just vanished.

Hawk closed his eyes and passed out.

CHAPTER 29

Washington, D.C.

THREE DAYS LATER, Hawk stumbled out of bed in one of Blunt's safe houses in Washington, D.C. He started a pot of coffee and picked up a copy of *The Washington Post* sitting on the kitchen table. Next to it was a note from Blunt, who said he'd gone to the store but would return in half an hour.

Hawk knocked on Alex's bedroom door.

"Come in," she said.

Hawk entered the room and found her sitting at her desk. She typed furiously and didn't even look up.

"How'd you sleep last night?" she said.

"Better. And you?"

"Couldn't sleep. I get restless when I don't have my equipment up and running."

Hawk sat down on her bed. "Configuring all your new equipment?"

She nodded and continued typing.

"I'll let you get back to it then," he said. "Want

me to fix you some breakfast?"

She nodded before stopping and spinning around in her chair to face him.

"Did you read the paper yet?"

Hawk shook his head. "I was just about to sit down and see if I could find anything interesting to read."

"Front page, below the fold," she said. "Apparently, they found parts of my mother's body floating in the Bosphorus, but no head."

"So, no way to tell what happened to her?"

"No left arm or right foot either. She was quote-unquote *chewed to pieces by marine animal life*, according to the article."

"That should shake some people up," Hawk said.

"Hopefully that will *wake* some people up and they'll realize what she was trying to do."

"If anything, it gives me a good opening to speak with our reporter friend today. Little things matter more to a reporter than timeliness of a story."

"Good luck with that," she said. "I'm going out later on to grab a few things to finish building my computer."

"Breakfast should be ready in fifteen minutes," he said before closing the door and returning to the kitchen.

Hawk read the front page story detailing the discovery of Katarina Petrov's death. There was an accompanying article that discussed what bearing her death would have on the formation of the one world currency. Another story on the opinion page outlined President Michaels' options to get the U.S. in line with the rest of the countries signing up for the new global economic policy. One sentence stood out to Hawk.

"While Michaels' attempt to persuade the Supreme Court to rule that the Federal Reserve Act was unsuccessful, it'll be a footnote in the annals of U.S. history if he can persuade the Federal Reserve's board to relinquish its power or direct Congress to adopt Petrov's vision for a one world currency."

Hawk's eyes widened.

If he can pull that off, there's nothing we can do about it. We're all screwed.

Discouraged, he closed the paper and started making breakfast.

* * *

LATER THAT AFTERNOON, Hawk donned a disguise and walked several blocks to a run-down laundromat. Thumbing a card in his pocket, Hawk made sure to keep his head down to avoid any facial recognition scans Michaels might be running through any of the city's publicly placed cameras. He tugged his hat low on his face and wore large sunglasses.

He found the lone pay phone around the side of the building. Covered in graffiti, Hawk picked up the receiver and was pleasantly surprised to find it in working condition. The numbers and letters on the keypad had been worn off and were difficult to see without a close examination. He pulled the card out of his pocket and dialed the number of *New York Times* reporter Lee Hendridge.

"Hi, Lee. This is your favorite government source," Hawk said.

"Who?"

"I'd rather not say, but I'm pretty sure you recognize my voice."

"Yeah, okay. I know who this is. What do you want?"

"I was wondering if you'd be interested in a big story, a blockbuster story, the kind that could make your career explode."

Hendridge remained silent.

"Lee, are you still there?"

"Yeah, I'm here. Just not sure I want anything to do with something that will make anything in my life explode. I've had enough of that."

"Are you all right?" Hawk asked.

"Yeah. Just kind of busy with some other stories right now. Maybe in a couple of weeks. I'm just tied up at the moment."

"This story will be old news by then," Hawk said.

"Well, give it to someone else then. I'm trying to tell you as politely as possible that I'm not available to look into whatever story you're pushing right now."

"Got any suggestions for who might be willing to run with something like this?"

"Do your own research," Lee said. "Gotta run."

Hendridge hung up and Hawk followed suit.

On his way back to the safe house, Hawk replayed the conversation in his head a couple of times. Something definitely felt off. Hendridge acted cold and almost indifferent to the story. The reporter Hawk had met earlier was far more engaging and winsome. And he would've pursued any tips Hawk passed along like a wild animals on a fresh carcass.

Hawk considered that perhaps Hendridge thought his phone was tapped. Given the recent history of presidential administrations tapping journalists' phones, such paranoia was completely justifiable. A simple "no thank you" would've sufficed if Hendridge truly wanted to distance himself from Hawk's lead. But the evasive answers and foggy memory made Hawk wonder if something else was going on.

Back at the safe house, he reported what happened to Blunt and Alex. Neither of them had any better theories than Hawk, just wild speculation as to what could've been the reason for Hendridge's behavior.

"I'm going to find out what's really going on and pay him a visit tomorrow," Hawk said.

"Be careful," Blunt said. "I'm not sure that type of risk is worth it."

"At this point, we're running out of time," Hawk

said. "I can't sit around and do nothing."

"If you must," Blunt said. "But exercise extreme caution. Michaels is unhinged and who knows what he's got planned for us. But I can promise you that whatever it is, it won't be good."

CHAPTER 30

THE FOLLOWING MORNING, Blunt received a text message requiring an urgent response. He hadn't even finished his morning cup of coffee or read his copy of *The Washington Post*, self-imposed prerequisites before he spoke to anyone at the start of a new day. He groaned as he eased out of his chair and paced around the room. The combination of rest and painkillers helped him recover more quickly than he'd anticipated, but he was still far from feeling back to his old self.

"Good morning," Hawk said as he entered the kitchen.

"Wish I could say the same," Blunt grumbled.

"You feeling okay?"

"General Fortner has an urgent message for me. Those are never good."

Blunt ambled back to his room and placed the call to Fortner.

"Thanks for getting back to me so quickly," Fortner

said after he answered.

"What's so urgent?"

"I just saw a kill order for Brady Hawk, and I thought you'd want to let him know."

"Who signed it?"

"The president."

Blunt unleashed a string of expletives. "I guess saving the life of that sorry pathetic excuse for a leader was only worth a slight reprieve in his vendetta against Hawk."

"Did you expect Michaels to suddenly be filled with gratitude? That man is about as self-absorbed as they come, and he's going to ruin our country if he gets his way."

"If he thinks killing Hawk is going to solve all his problems, Michaels has another thing coming. He's also got a short memory, too, if he thinks murdering Hawk is going to be easy."

"From what I've seen in the field, Hawk can handle himself. I don't know any Special Forces agent who would hold the upper hand against Hawk, and I know some damn good ones."

"It still worries me," Blunt said. "All Michaels has to do is fabricate some evidence against Hawk like he did before, and the whole world will be looking for Hawk. He's good but nobody could last long when you're on every criminal watch list with every known law enforcement agency in the world."

"There has to be another way to bring Michaels down first," Fortner said. "I'm sure you'll think of something. You always do."

"You have far more confidence in me than I have in myself."

"You faked your own death once, and now you walk around a free man."

Blunt chuckled. "You say this as I'm holed up in a safe house hiding from my own government."

"Well, until recently, you were."

"Yes, but here I am now, and it's not a good place."

"Things can change quickly. You ought to know that as well as anyone by now."

"Usually for the worse."

"Look, if you need my help with anything over there, I'm not sure what I'll be able to do from here in Europe, but I will do whatever I can."

"I appreciate that. Any word on Samuels?"

"Still the same. He's in a medically induced coma right now, but the doctors are monitoring his healing process."

"So, no updated prognosis on his survival?"

"Nope," Fortner said. "Docs are optimistic but still concerned."

"Thanks, Van . . . for everything."

"Any time, J.D."

Blunt hung up and returned to the kitchen.

"So, was it the good news you were expecting?" Hawk asked after he looked up from reading *The Post*.

Blunt shook his head and topped off his coffee. "Not good at all, especially for you."

Hawk wrapped his hands around his mug and stared at Blunt.

"What do you mean?"

"Samuels is still in a medically induced coma and his prognosis for survival hasn't changed."

"He's got to pull through."

"I think he will. But that wasn't the only bad news."

"What could be worse than that?"

"Fortner told me that he saw a kill order for you."

"A kill order? So, what's new?"

"Michaels signed it."

"Ungrateful bastard," Hawk said. "I save his life and this is how he repays me."

"Don't disparage ungrateful bastards by comparing them to Michaels," Blunt said.

Hawk grinned. "I'm not sure who dislikes the president more—me or you."

"If he gets his way, I'm sure you'll edge me out in that department."

"Well, I'm not going to let that happen."

Alex sauntered into the kitchen, her hair still matted to her face.

"Why are you two carrying on like this so early

in the morning?" she asked.

"Too much bad news before breakfast," Hawk said.

"Don't hold out on me. What's going on?" Alex said.

"Samuels is in a medically induced coma, and he's still about 50-50 for survival," Blunt said.

"Oh, come on," she said. "You have to start my day off like this?"

"That's not all," Hawk said.

"It's Michaels," Blunt said. "We just learned that he issued a kill order for Hawk."

She scowled. "I would curse but I have a rule against doing that until I've eaten breakfast."

"That's okay," Hawk said. "Blunt has done enough swearing for all three of us this morning."

"So, what are you going to do?" she asked.

"I'm going to disappear, for the good of the team," Hawk said.

Alex shook her head. "I don't think that's a good idea. We're stronger together."

"Yeah, but as it stands now, if they find me, they find you," Hawk said. "You don't honestly think they're going to just let you go on your merry way, do you? If they're focused on capturing me and you remain well hidden, at least you'll both be safe."

"It's sound thinking," Blunt said. "But if they catch us, they're going to use us as bait to draw you out."

"I'll just have to get to them first," Hawk said.

"Them?" Blunt asked. "It's not like this will be a single agency hunt. Everyone will be looking for you."

"I'll disappear."

"And then what?" Alex asked. "Just wait for Michaels to leave office?"

"If I have to, though I have other plans."

Blunt cocked his head to one side. "Such as?"

"Such as plot my revenge on Michaels."

"You already did that one," Alex said. "And he survived it. Politically, the man is made out of Teflon."

"There are other means to exact revenge and take someone down."

"Even while you're in hiding?" she asked.

Hawk nodded. "The less I tell you, the better."

He glanced at his watch and threw back his coffee.

"Now, I've gotta run," Hawk said. "I still need to do one last thing before I vanish."

"Where are you going?" Alex asked.

"Where I said I would go yesterday. I'm gonna go see Lee Hendridge."

* * *

HAWK LEFT THE SAFE HOUSE on foot just after 8:30 a.m. He walked three blocks, doubling back several times before entering a Metro station and catching a train to Georgetown where Hendridge lived.

Hawk tugged his hat down low and used his sunglasses to conceal his constant scanning of the surrounding passengers. One man stood out to Hawk, which made him antsy. Two stops from his destination, Hawk got up and stepped off the train just as the doors started to close. The man Hawk had noticed followed him.

Hawk maintained a steady pace, searching the dark corridors of the station for a place to evade the man. After several turns, Hawk found an unlit hallway that had several closed doors. Hawk jiggled the handle on one and found it unlocked. Inside were electrical components for powering the station.

Hawk left the door cracked in hopes that he'd draw the man into the room. As Hawk anticipated, the man entered the room, gun drawn. Hawk kicked the gun loose before the man could make eye contact. The man responded by landing a combination of body punches, but Hawk fought back with a devastating throat punch followed by a sharp kick to the man's abdomen. Hawk finished him with two more kicks to the head, knocking the man out.

Hawk decided to exit the station and walked several blocks to the next one before re-entering the Metro system. Once aboard the train, he took off his hat and glasses, removed his jacket, and walked from the front to the back in an effort to throw off anyone trying to follow his movements on security cameras.

Once Hawk found Hendridge's apartment, he

slipped inside as a woman was leaving to walk her dogs. He walked through the lobby and waited for the elevator. When it opened, he stepped in alone and pressed the button for Hendridge's floor. The elevator whirred as it jerked Hawk up 14 stories.

After Hawk got off the elevator, he strode down the hallway and knocked on Hendridge's door. Half a minute passed before Hawk knocked again. Finally, Hawk heard footsteps shuffling toward him from the other side. Hendridge opened the door and shook his head.

"I'm not interested in speaking with you," he said. "I thought I made that clear yesterday. I don't have time for your bullshit story."

"This is important," Hawk said. "If you've ever wanted to write something that mattered, this is it."

"I've already done that, thanks to you. Seriously, I do appreciate you helping me make my career, but I'm not interested in jeopardizing my life again."

"What are you working on?" Hawk said as he pushed his way past Hendridge into the apartment.

Hendridge closed the door. "I'm serious, Mr. Hawk. I am entrenched in this story and don't have time to be unearthing any more conspiracies at the moment."

Hawk walked over to the kitchen table, which was covered with pages of notes. He glanced at the computer and scanned the words on the screen.

"This is big," Hawk said.

"Mr. Hawk, please," Hendridge said. "Please stop looking at that. And I'm serious when I say that I need you to leave. They'll kill me if they see me talking to you."

"Nobody is going to kill you," Hawk said. "Stop being so paranoid."

"My paranoia is totally justified. Now will you please leave?"

Hawk glanced up at Hendridge. "What I've got is even bigger. Just hear me out, okay?"

Without waiting for an answer, Hawk launched into a truncated version of President Michaels' plan to get the Federal Reserve Board to relinquish its control and turn it over to him.

Hendridge's eyes lit up for a moment.

"That's definitely some Pulitzer-worthy material there, but I'll need more evidence to substantiate your claims before I start slinging them around in the paper."

"I can get that for you, but you need to work fast on this before Michaels upends our entire economy and hands the power over to the Russians."

"The Russians? They're behind all this?"

"They're the one pulling the strings right now—and as soon as Michaels green lights the U.S. joining the one world currency movement, the Russians are going to pull the rug out from underneath our entire country. We'll go from being one of the wealthiest nations to one of the poorest overnight, and we'll be beholden to the wishes of the Russians."

"You're leveling some serious accusations," Hendridge said. "Are you sure you can get me evidence to prove all of this?"

"Positive," Hawk said.

"Get it to me as fast as you can and I'll talk with my editor about cobbling together this story as fast as possible. But I can assure you they're going to want to move slowly on this. Plenty of legal ramifications if all your allegations aren't true."

"I understand. Just push hard to get your editor to run this the moment it's ready to go."

Hawk headed toward the door and stopped, spinning around to address Hendridge once more.

"Is everything okay?"

"I'm tired—and I think someone is out to get me."

Hawk shrugged. "It's the nature of the business, I suppose."

"No, I think someone is trying to kill me. I hear strange noises when I'm on the phone. Some of my friends have told me that they've been questioned about me by some suits."

"I feel your pain. Just be vigilant and keep doing what you do. Our freedoms depend upon serious journalists like yourself."

"Be careful out there."

"You do the same."

Hawk exited the apartment and only went a few steps before he heard Hendridge's deadbolt click behind him.

As he approached the elevators, one of them dinged and doors slid open. A man in a dark suit brushed past Hawk and kept his head down.

"Excuse me," Hawk said.

The man didn't look up. Hawk sensed something was wrong.

"Hey, sir," Hawk said, "I'm talking to you."

The man glanced over his shoulder at Hawk but kept walking.

Hawk didn't waste another second. He broke into a dead sprint and hit the man from behind with a flying leap, sending the pair crashing to the ground. Hawk rolled up onto his knees and delivered two ferocious punches to the man's head. The man scrambled to his feet and kicked Hawk in the chest. On the man's second kick, Hawk grabbed the man's foot and spun him around, knocking him off balance and sending him crashing against the wall.

The man then unholstered his gun and warned Hawk to stay put.

Meanwhile, Hendridge opened his door and shouted from down the hall. He clutched a gun and trained it on the man in the suit.

"That's enough," Hendridge said. "I suggest you leave right now."

The agent dropped his guard for a second, just long enough for Hawk to kick the gun out of the man's hand. After two more punches, Hawk subdued the man, knocking him out cold.

Hawk looked back down the hall at Hendridge.

"Good work," Hendridge said.

The faint smile on Hawk's face faded as he noticed another man in a dark suit, who'd just entered the hallway from the stairwell.

"Look out," Hawk said.

By the time Hendridge turned around, the man was only a few feet away. He shoved Hendridge into his apartment and locked the door behind him. Hawk grabbed the agent's gun and rushed down the hall. But before Hawk reached the apartment, he heard a single gunshot.

Hawk stood frozen, realizing that if he attempted to break into the apartment, he'd be walking into a kill zone. Instead, he decided to make a quick exit. He wiped his prints off the agent's gun and placed it in his hands. Hawk then used the stairwell to exit onto the street.

He put on his sunglasses again and pulled his hat down over his eyes.

"Damn you, Michaels," he muttered to himself.

CHAPTER 31

DISAPPEARING WASN'T HAWK'S first choice when it came to addressing the news that President Michaels had put out a kill order. During his Navy Seal training, he'd learned the finer points of going dark if his situation ever required it. And while he knew what details needed to be attended to in order to achieve a vanishing act, he wasn't keen on the idea. He'd suggested it but only because it was the only way to make sure Alex and Blunt remained safe.

After the incident at Hendridge's apartment, Hawk found a consignment shop and purchased some clothes. He needed every advantage he could in avoiding detection by Washington's vast network of cameras that government law enforcement agencies all had access to. Hawk then spent the rest of the day dirtying up his clothes and changing his appearance. He dyed his hair blond and then sought out some of the areas in the city where the homeless congregated.

Hawk needed the better part of the afternoon to

identify a strategic public park that appeared to have a significant homeless population. He spent the night staying warm by a fire that a couple of guys had built in an old oil drum. Using a coat he'd purchased as a blanket, he finally fell asleep.

When he awoke in the morning to a chorus of birds singing in the tree overhead, he decided to take a walk. He walked by a newsstand and froze, stopping to read the headlines.

Federal Reserve Board Mulls Dissolving Amid Growing Concerns

But it was a smaller headline below the fold that Hawk found more intriguing. He read it twice just to make sure he wasn't imagining things.

NY Times Reporter, Pulitzer Winner Commits Suicide

Suicide? Unbelievable.

He found a pay phone and placed a call to Blunt's secure line.

"You know I haven't had my coffee yet," Blunt said as he answered.

"They killed him," Hawk said, ignoring Blunt's grouchy greeting.

"I already read this morning in the paper. How'd

they do it?"

"Bastards ambushed him. They sent two agents. I stopped one in Hendridge's hallway outside his apartment, but Hendridge came out with a gun when he heard the commotion going on. When he did, another agent who used the stairwell snuck up behind him and forced Hendridge back inside before shooting him."

"CIA?" Blunt asked.

"That's what they looked like to me."

"Damn. That kid didn't deserve that."

"They're going to do the same to us if we aren't careful. And that's why I'm calling to say goodbye. I'm going off the grid and I'll contact you once I figure out a way to regain our freedom."

"There's only one way that's going to happen."

"I know. Tell Alex I love her and I'll reach out once I have a better idea of how I need to do what needs to be done."

"Good luck, Hawk. And be careful."

"Always."

Hawk hung up and headed to the bus station. He needed to get out of the city. He needed to get out of the country.

Then he needed to plot his revenge.

THE END

ACKNOWLEDGMENTS

I am grateful to so many people who have helped with the creation of this project and the entire Brady Hawk series.

Krystal Wade has been a fantastic help in handling the editing of this book, and Dwight Kuhlman has produced another great audio version for your listening pleasure.

I would also like to thank my advance reader team for all their input in improving this book along with all the other readers who have enthusiastically embraced the story of Brady Hawk. Stay tuned ... there's more Brady Hawk coming soon.

ABOUT THE AUTHOR

R.J. PATTERSON is an award-winning writer living in southeastern Idaho. He first began his illustrious writing career as a sports journalist, recording his exploits on the soccer fields in England as a young boy. Then when his father told him that people would pay him to watch sports if he would write about what he saw, he went all in. He landed his first writing job at age 15 as a sports writer for a daily newspaper in Orangeburg, S.C. He later attended earned a degree in newspaper journalism from the University of Georgia, where he took a job covering high school sports for the award-winning *Athens Banner-Herald* and *Daily News.*

He later became the sports editor of *The Valdosta Daily Times* before working in the magazine world as an editor and freelance journalist. He has won numerous writing awards, including a national award for his investigative reporting on a sordid tale surrounding an NCAA investigation over the University of Georgia football program.

R.J. enjoys the great outdoors of the Northwest while living there with his wife and four children. He still follows sports closely. He also loves connecting with readers and would love to hear from you. To stay updated about future projects, connect with him over Facebook or on the interwebs at www.RJPbooks.com and sign up for his newsletter to get deals and updates.

Made in the USA
Coppell, TX
30 March 2022

75753997R00152

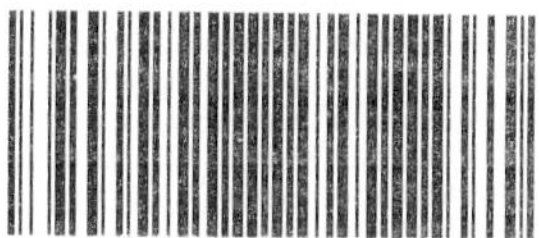

はじめての日本語能力試験

N2単語 2500

2500 Essential Vocabulary for the JLPT N2

アークアカデミー

英語・中国語・ベトナム語訳 + 赤シート

with English Translation

另附中文翻译

Có bản dịch Tiếng Việt

ask

はじめに

Introduction / 前言 / Lời nói đầu

この本は、日本語能力試験のレベル別シリーズの一冊となっており、本書はN２合格を目指すためのものです。

日本語能力試験によく取り上げられ、毎日の暮らしにも役立つ単語をリストアップしました。チャプター・セクションごとにテーマがあり、それぞれの場面をイメージして学べます。英語・中国語・ベトナム語の対訳がついているので、単語や例文の意味もスムーズに確認することができます。N２レベルの基本単語に加え、「同義語」「反義語」「関連語・類義語」、コラムで挙げた単語・表現を含め、約2,500語を収録しました。

すべての漢字にルビがついているので、辞書なしで勉強できるのも魅力です。また、赤シート、単語と例文の音声、チャプターごとの模擬試験も用意しました。

日本で学習している方はもちろん、日本以外の国で学習している方にもイメージしやすい内容になっています。この単語帳は試験対策だけではなく、日本語を学習する皆さんにとって心強い一冊になります。合格を心から祈っています。

2016年10月

著者一同

This series is divided into levels corresponding to the levels of the Japanese Language Proficiency Test. This volume is for learners aiming to pass the N2 level of the JLPT.

This book presents vocabulary words found commonly on the Japanese Language Proficiency Test and used in daily life in Japan. Each section of every chapter has its own theme to help you study efficiently while visualizing each setting. English, Chinese and Vietnamese translations are included so you can study smoothly and with ease. Along with the basic vocabulary for the N2 level, the book presents 2,500 words including synonyms, antonyms, related words and quasi-synonyms, as well as words and phrases mentioned in the column.

This book also includes the readings for all of the kanji, so we hope that you are able to make use of this handbook of sorts without the additional aid of any dictionary. Furthermore, a red sheet and audio files for every vocabulary word and example sentence have been provided for further assistance, along with practice tests for each chapter.

These books are easy to follow and understand for those studying both inside and outside of Japan. We strongly hope that they serve to not only help you prepare for the JLPT, but also help you study Japanese.

October 2016

From the Authors

本书为日语能力考试分级别系列之一，专为以 N2 为目标的学习者而制作。

本书汇集了日语能力考试中频繁出现的、日常生活中也能用到的单词。每个章节、每个部分都有不同的主题，可通过想像不同的场景来学习。配有英语、中文、越南语的对照翻译，可即时确认单词、例句的意思。本书除 N2 级别的基本单词以外，加上“同义词”、“反义词”、“关联词・类义词”专栏中的单词及表达，共收录了 2500 词。

所有的汉字上都标有假名，不用查字典就能自学也是本书的魅力所在。另附红色卡片、单词及例句的音频，每个章节还配有模拟试题。

本书内容不但适用于身在日本的学习者，对在海外的学习者来说也同样明了易懂。这本单词书不仅是一本考试对策书，对于日语学习者来说是能让日语水平更上一个台阶的不可多得的参考书。我们衷心期待大家的好成绩。

2016 年 10 月

全体著者

Đây là một quyển thuộc bộ sách được chia theo cấp độ của Kỳ thi Năng lực Nhật ngữ và quyển sách này dành cho các bạn đang hướng đến mục tiêu thi đậu N2.

Chúng tôi đã lọc ra danh sách các từ vựng thường xuất hiện trong Kỳ thi Năng lực Nhật ngữ và cũng có ích trong sinh hoạt thường ngày. Có đề tài theo từng chương, từng phần, để các bạn có thể vừa hình dung các tình huống vừa học. Vì có kèm theo bản dịch tiếng Anh, tiếng Trung Quốc và tiếng Việt nên các bạn có thể kiểm tra ý nghĩa của từ vựng và câu ví dụ một cách dễ dàng. Có khoảng 2.500 từ bao gồm phần “Từ đồng nghĩa”, “Từ trái nghĩa”, “Từ liên quan – Từ tương đương” của các từ vựng căn bản cấp độ N2 và từ vựng, mẫu câu được đưa ra ở Góc kiến thức.

Tất cả các chữ Kanji đều có phiên âm cách đọc nên bạn có thể học mà không cần đến tự điển cũng là điểm hấp dẫn của cuốn sách này.

Ngoài ra, chúng tôi cũng đã chuẩn bị cả tấm bìa đỏ, phần phát âm từ vựng và câu ví dụ, bài thi thử trong từng chương.

Đây là bộ sách có nội dung mà đương nhiên các bạn đang học tập tại Nhật và cả các bạn đang học tại các nước ngoài Nhật Bản đều có thể hình dung dễ dàng. Sổ tay từ vựng này không chỉ là đối sách luyện thi mà còn là một quyển sách hỗ trợ tinh thần mạnh mẽ cho các bạn học tập tiếng Nhật. Chúng tôi thành tâm chúc các bạn thi đậu.

Tháng 10 năm 2016

Nhóm tác giả

この本の使い方

How to Use This Book / 本书的使用方法 / Cách sử dụng quyển sách này

▶ テーマ別単語学習

Study vocabulary by theme / 分主题学单词 / Học từ vựng theo đề tài

日本語能力試験で取り上げることが多い単語がテーマ別にチャプター・セクションでまとめられています。チャプターの順どおりに進めてもいいですし、興味のあるチャプターから始めてもいいでしょう。

Vocabulary words often used on the Japanese Language Proficiency Test are divided into various themes organized into chapters and sections for ease of study. You may progress sequencially through each chapter, or begin from whatever chapter interests you.

我们把日语能力考试中频繁出现的单词分为不同的主题，汇总成了各章节及各部分。大家使用时可按照章节的顺序，也可从感兴趣的章节开始学习。

Những từ vựng xuất hiện nhiều trong kỳ thi năng lực tiếng Nhật sẽ được tóm tắt theo đề tài trong từng chương - mục. Bạn có thể học theo thứ tự chương hay bắt đầu từ chương nào bạn thích cũng được.

▶ 模擬試験で腕試し

Use the practice test to gauge your progress / 通过模拟试题自我测试 / Thử sức với bài thi thử

日本語能力試験の語彙問題の模擬試験がウェブサイトにあります（PDF / オンライン）。くわしくはウェブサイトをご覧ください。

https://www.ask-books.com/jp/hajimete-jlpt/

The Japanese Language Proficiency Test practice test is available at our website for PDF download or use online. Please see the website for more details.

网站上附有日语能力考试的词汇部分的模拟试题（PDF/ 在线）。详情请查看官网。

Bài thi thử môn Từ vựng của kỳ thi năng lực tiếng Nhật có trên trang web (PDF/ trực tuyến). Vui lòng xem trang web để biết thêm chi tiết.

▶ 赤シートの活用

Use the red sheet / 活用红色卡片 / Sử dụng hiệu quả tấm bìa đỏ

付属の赤シートで、単語と例文中の単語を隠して学習できます。訳を参照して、隠れている語がすぐに思い出せるか確認しましょう。

Use the attached red sheet to hide vocabulary words and example sentences for studying. Try showing the translation while trying to guess the hidden vocabulary word.

可将随书附赠的红色卡片用于遮盖单词及例句来学习。参考译文的同时，测试自己是否能马上联想到被遮盖的部分。

Bạn có thể học từ vựng và từ vựng trong câu ví dụ bằng cách che chúng bằng tấm bìa đỏ kèm theo sách này. Tham chiếu với phần dịch và kiểm tra xem mình có nhớ ra ngay từ đã che hay không.

音声の活用

Use the audio files / 活用音频 / Sử dụng hiệu quả phần âm thanh

単語と例文の音声がウェブサイトにあります。くわしくはウェブサイトをご覧ください。https://www.ask-books.com/jp/hajimete-jlpt/

Audio files for the vocabulary words and example sentences are available on the website. Please see the website for more details.

网站上附有单词与例句的音频。详情请查看官网。

Phần phát âm từ vựng và câu ví dụ có ở trang web. Vui lòng xem trang web để biết thêm chi tiết.

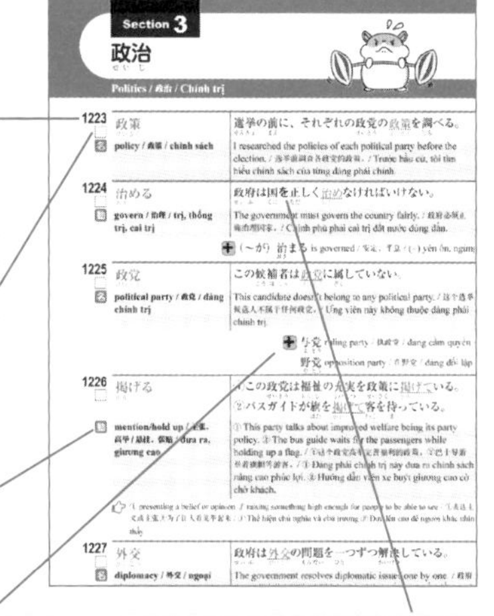

単語の番号です。
This is the vocabulary word number. / 单词编号 / Số thứ tự của từ vựng.

覚えたら、チェックボックスにチェックを入れましょう。
If you have memorized it, check the box. / 记住后请在确认栏上做上标记。 / Nếu nhớ rồi, hãy đánh dấu vào ô vuông.

単語の品詞です。
This is the part of speech of the vocabulary word. / 单词词性 / Từ loại của từ vựng.

一緒に覚える単語と、注意点や説明などです。
These are related vocabulary words, points to keep in mind and explanations. / 需要同时记住的单词、注意点、说明等。 / Từ vựng nhớ cùng nhau, và các điểm cần lưu ý, giải thích v.v.

- ➕：関連語・類義語など
  Related words or similar words / 关联词・类义词等 / Từ liên quan - Từ tương đương v.v.
- 〓：同義語　Synonyms / 同义词 / Từ đồng nghĩa
- ↔：反義語　Antonyms / 反义词 / Từ trái nghĩa
- 👉：注意点や説明
  Points to keep in mind or explanations / 注意点、说明 / Điểm cần lưu ý và giải thích

自動詞・他動詞の助詞、または主に否定文で使われることを示す「ない」は太字で表記しています。
The word ない in bold is the particle used for transitive or intransitive verbs, or in negative sentences. / 自动词・他动词的助词，以及主要用于否定句中的“ない”，都用粗体字表示。 / Trợ từ của tự động từ - tha động từ, hoặc phần 「ない」 được sử dụng chủ yếu trong câu phủ định được thể hiện bằng chữ đậm.

▶ この本で使用する品詞の一覧 All of the parts of speech used in this book / 本书中使用的词性一览表 / Danh sách từ loại sử dụng trong sách này

名：名詞 Noun / 名词 / Danh từ

動：動詞 Verb / 动词 / Động từ

副：副詞 Adverb / 副词 / Phó từ

代：代名詞 Pronoun / 代名词 / Đại danh từ

接続：接続詞 Conjunction / 接续词 / Từ nối

連語：連語 Copula / 连词 / Cụm từ

接辞：接辞 Affix / 词缀 / Phụ tố, Tiếp từ

慣：慣用句 Idiom / 惯用语 / Thành ngữ

ナ形：ナ形容詞 Na-adjective / na 形容词 / Tính từ loại "Na" (Hình dung từ "Na")

イ形：イ形容詞 I-adjective / i 形容词 / Tính từ loại "I" (Hình dung từ "I")

連体：連体詞 Adnominal adjective / 修饰词 / Liên thể từ

感：感動詞 Interjection / 感叹词 / Từ cảm thán

目次 Table of Contents / 目录 / Mục lục

コラム 目次(もくじ)

N2

Chapter 1

人と人との関係
ひと　ひと　かんけい

Relationships Between People / 人际关系篇 / Quan hệ giữa người với người

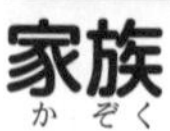

家族（かぞく）

Family / 家人 / Gia đình

1 □ 名	一家（いっか）	兄（あに）が私達（わたしたち）一家（いっか）を支（ささ）えてくれている。
	family / 一家子，全家 / một nhà, cả nhà, cả gia đình	My older brother supports the family. / 是哥哥一直在支撑着我们整个家庭。/ Anh tôi cáng đáng cả gia đình chúng tôi.

＝ ファミリー　＋ 一家団（いっかだん）らん happy family gathering / 全家团圆 / quây quần một nhà

2 □ イ形	ありがたい	家族（かぞく）は本当（ほんとう）にありがたい存在（そんざい）だ。
	grateful / 值得感恩的，难得的 / biết ơn, hạnh phúc, đáng quý	I am really grateful to my family. / 有家人真好。/ Gia đình thật sự là sự tồn tại đáng quý.

＋ ありがとう thank you / 谢谢 / cám ơn

3 □ 動	向（む）き合（あ）う	家族（かぞく）みんなで問題（もんだい）に向（む）き合（あ）っている。
	face / 直面，面对面 / đối mặt, đối diện	We are trying to face the problem as a family. / 全家人一起面对问题。/ Cả gia đình đối diện với vấn đề.
4 □ 副	つくづく［と］	最近（さいきん）、家族（かぞく）のありがたさをつくづくと感（かん）じる。
	deeply, greatly / 痛感，深切地感到 / sâu sắc, tỉ mỉ, thấm thía	I feel deeply grateful to my family these days. / 最近深切地感受到了有家人真好。/ Gần đây, tôi cảm nhận sâu sắc sự quý giá của gia đình.

＋ しみじみ［と］ deeply / 深切，恳切 / sâu sắc, thấm thía

5 □ 動	養（やしな）う	父（ちち）は一生懸命（いっしょうけんめい）に働（はたら）いて、家族（かぞく）を養（やしな）っている。
	provide for / 养育，供养 / nuôi, nuôi dưỡng	My father works hard to provide for the family. / 父亲拼命工作养活我们全家。/ Cha tôi làm việc cật lực để nuôi gia đình.
6 □ 名	役目（やくめ）	子（こ）どもを育（そだ）てることが親（おや）の役目（やくめ）だ。
	duty / 职责，任务 / trách nhiệm, vai trò, nhiệm vụ	It is the parents' duty to raise their children. / 养育孩子是父母的职责。/ Nuôi dạy con là trách nhiệm của cha mẹ.
7 □ 動	甘（あま）える	妹（いもうと）は子（こ）どもの頃（ころ）から、母（はは）に甘（あま）えている。
	to be spoiled, to be dependent / 撒娇，受宠 / làm nũng, nhõng nhẽo	My little sister has been dependent on our mother ever since she was a child. / 妹妹从小就爱跟母亲撒娇。/ Em gái tôi từ nhỏ đã nhõng nhẽo với mẹ.

＋ 甘（あま）え lack of self-reliance / 娇气 / người nhõng nhẽo, tính nhõng nhẽo・
甘（あま）やかす to spoil / 娇纵，娇惯 / nuông chìu, chìu chuộng

8 ☐ 名 **世間知らず**（せけんし）
ignorant of the outside world, inexperienced / 不谙世故，没见过世面 / khờ khạo, ngây thơ

父に「おまえは世間知らずだ」と言われた。
My father told me, "You are ignorant of the world." / 父亲说我不谙世事。/ Tôi bị cha nói "con thật khờ khạo".

9 ☐ 名 **しつけ**
discipline / 教养，管教 / sự dạy dỗ, việc giáo dục (khuôn phép, nề nếp)

子どものしつけは、親の義務だ。
Disciplining their children is the parents' duty. / 管教孩子是父母的义务。/ Việc giáo dục khuôn phép cho con cái là nghĩa vụ của cha mẹ.

➕ しつける to discipline / 管教，教育 / dạy dỗ, giáo dục (khuôn phép, nề nếp)

10 ☐ 動 **言いつける**（い）
tell / 告发，打小报告 / méc, mách

兄は妹のいたずらを母に言いつけた。
My big brother told his mother about his little sister's prank. / 哥哥向妈妈告状说妹妹恶作剧。/ Anh tôi méc mẹ về việc em gái nghịch ngợm.

11 ☐ 名 **自立〈する〉**（じりつ）
independence / 自立 / tự lập

兄は自立して、一人暮らしをしている。
My big brother has left home and lives on his own. / 哥哥已经自立，现在一个人生活。/ Anh tôi tự lập, sống một mình.

12 ☐ 動 **言い出す**（いだ）
start saying / 说出口，提出 / nói ra, ngỏ ý

妹はアメリカに語学留学したいと言い出した。
My younger sister started to say she wants to study English in the United States. / 妹妹提出想去美国留学，学习外语。/ Em gái tôi ngỏ ý muốn đi Mỹ du học để học tiếng (Anh).

13 ☐ 名 **意思**（いし）
intention / 想法，打算，意思 / ý chí, ý muốn

親に自分の意思を伝えるのは難しい。
It is difficult to tell your parents of your intentions. / 想要让父母了解（我自己）的想法很困难。/ Thật khó để truyền đạt ý chí của mình cho cha mẹ biết.

14 ☐ 名 **尊重〈する〉**（そんちょう）
respect / 尊重 / sự tôn trọng

両親はいつも、私の意見を尊重してくれる。
My parents always respects my opinion. / 父母一直都很尊重我的意见。/ Bố mẹ luôn tôn trọng ý kiến của tôi

15 ☐ 名 **説得〈する〉**（せっとく）
convince / 说服，劝导 / sự thuyết phục

父は私の留学に反対だったが、母が説得してくれた。
My father was against me studying abroad, but my mother convinced him. / 虽然父亲反对我去留学，但母亲帮我说服了他。/ Bố phản đối việc du học của tôi nhưng mẹ đã thuyết phục giúp tôi.

16 ☐ 名 **納得〈する〉**（なっとく）
acknowledgement / 同意，认同 / sự đồng ý

父は私の留学を、やっと納得してくれた。
My father finally agreed to my studying abroad. / 父亲终于同意我去留学了。/ Cuối cùng bố cũng đồng ý với việc du học của tôi.

17 □ **逆らう**（さか）

①若いときは、よく親に逆らった。②強い風に逆らって歩く。

動 **to go against / 违背，违抗 / 逆（方向），反 / chống đối, ngược lại**

① I often rebeled against my parents when I was young. ② I walk against the strong wind. / ①我年轻时总是违抗父母的意思。②顶着强风前行。/ ① Khi còn trẻ, tôi thường chống đối bố mẹ. ② Đi bộ ngược cơn gió mạnh.

＋ 抵抗（ていこう）〈する〉 resistance / 抵抗 / kháng cự, chống cự

① to take a rebellious attitude toward one's parents and seniors ② to move in the opposite direction to the flow / ①违抗亲人或是上级②与事物行进的方向相逆 / ① Có thái độ phản kháng với bố mẹ, người trên. ② Tiến về hướng ngược lại với dòng chảy của sự vật.

18 □ **反省**（はんせい）〈する〉

昔親に逆らったことを、今は反省している。

名 **reflection / 反省 / sự phản tỉnh, suy nghĩ lại**

I am now sorry that I rebeled against my parents when I was young. / 如今反省了自己当年违抗了父母的意愿。/ Nay tôi phản tỉnh việc chống đối bố mẹ ngày xưa.

＋ 反省会（はんせいかい） reflection meeting / 反省会，检讨会 / buổi đúc kết, đánh giá (sau một sự kiện, công việc nào đó)

19 □ **放っておく**（ほう）

父はいちいちうるさい。放っておいてほしい。

動 **to leave alone / 搁置，放着不管 / bỏ mặc, phớt lờ**

My father is always nitpicking. I want him to leave me alone. / 爸爸很啰嗦，真希望他能不要管我。/ Bố tôi nhặng xị đủ chuyện. Mong (ông) phớt lờ tôi.

20 □ **介護**（かいご）〈する〉

家族みんなで祖母を介護している。

名 **nursing / 护理，照顾 / sự chăm sóc, điều dưỡng**

The entire family helps in nursing our grandmother. / 全家一起照顾奶奶的生活。/ Mọi người trong gia đình cùng chăm sóc bà.

＋ 介護士（かいごし） nurse / 介护士（照顾病人的护工）/ điều dưỡng viên

21 □ **ホームヘルパー**

週に3回、ホームヘルパーに来てもらう。

名 **home helper, home care worker / 家庭护理人员 / người trợ giúp (chăm sóc) tại nhà**

The home helper comes three times a week. / 每周请家庭护工来三次。/ Một tuần 3 lần, nhờ người trợ giúp đến.

＝ ヘルパー

22 □ **世代**（せだい）

世代が違うと、話が合わないこともある。

名 **generation / 世代，辈分 / thế hệ**

It's difficult to communicate among different generations. / 不是一代人，说话有时候会有代沟。/ Thế hệ khác nhau thì cũng có khi nói chuyện không hợp nhau.

＝ ジェネレーション　＋ 世代交代（せだいこうたい） generation change / 世代更替 / chuyển giao thế hệ

23 継ぐ（つ）

動 **to inherit / 继承 / tiếp nối, kế thừa**

来年、父の会社を継ぐことになった。（らいねん　ちち　かいしゃ　つ）

I will inherit my father's company next year. / 明年我将继承父亲的公司。/ Sang năm, tôi sẽ kế thừa công ty bố tôi.

➕ 受け継ぐ（う　つ） to inherit / 接管，继承 / kế thừa, thừa hưởng

24 妊娠〈する〉（にんしん）

名 **pregnancy / 怀孕，妊娠 / sự mang thai**

妹は妊娠3か月だ。（いもうと　にんしん　げつ）

My younger sister is three months pregnant. / 妹妹怀孕 3 个月了。/ Em gái tôi mang thai 3 tháng.

➕ 産婦人科（さんふじんか） obstetrics and gynecology / 妇产科 / Sản phụ khoa・
妊婦（にんぷ） pregnant woman / 孕妇 / phụ nữ có thai

25 出産〈する〉（しゅっさん）

名 **child birth / 生育，分娩 / sự sinh, đẻ (con)**

実家の近くの病院で出産することにした。（じっか　ちか　びょういん　しゅっさん）

I decided to give birth at a hospital near my parents' home. / 我决定在娘家附近的医院生孩子。/ Tôi quyết định sinh ở bệnh viện gần nhà bố mẹ ruột.

➕ 出産祝い（しゅっさんいわ） baby gift / 庆祝新生儿 / chúc mừng sinh em bé

26 産む（う）

動 **to give birth / 生，分娩 / sanh, đẻ**

姉は二十歳のときに長男を産んだ。（あね　はたち　ちょうなん　う）

My older sister gave birth to her eldest son when she was 20 years old. / 姐姐二十岁时生了她的大儿子。/ Chị tôi đã sanh con trai trưởng khi 20 tuổi.

➕ 生まれる（う） to be born / 出生 / chào đời

これも覚えよう！（おぼ） ❶

➕ 接辞（せつじ）：程度（ていど）① Affix: Degree / 词缀：程度 / Phụ tố: Mức độ

・高〜（こう）

高学歴（こうがくれき）	well-educated / 高学历 / Học vấn cao
高学年（こうがくねん）	upper grade / 高年级 / Cấp lớp cao
高収入（こうしゅうにゅう）	high income / 高收入 / Thu nhập cao
高性能（こうせいのう）	high performance / 高性能 / Tính năng cao
高気圧（こうきあつ）	high atmospheric pressure / 高气压 / Khí áp cao
高血圧（こうけつあつ）	high blood pressure / 高血压 / Cao huyết áp

Section 2

友達(ともだち)

Friends / 朋友 / Bạn bè

27 □ 名

友人(ゆうじん)

friend / 朋友，友人 / bạn thân

国(くに)から友人(ゆうじん)が遊(あそ)びに来(き)た。

My friend from my home country came to visit. / 有国内的朋友来玩。/ Bạn thân từ nước sang chơi.

➕ 友人達(ゆうじんたち) friends / 朋友们，友人们 / những người bạn thân

28 □ 名

仲(なか)

relationship / 关系 / tình cảm, mối quan hệ

このクラスの生徒(せいと)は、とても仲(なか)がいい。

The students of this class are close to each other. / 这个班级的学生大家关系都很好。/ Học sinh lớp này rất thân thiết.

➕ 仲良(なかよ)し friends / 好朋友 / quan hệ tốt, thân thiết

29 □ 名

縁(えん)

fate / 缘，缘分 / duyên

縁(えん)があって、彼女(かのじょ)と親友(しんゆう)になれた。

It was fate that I became best friends with her. / 我与她有缘，成为了挚友。/ Có duyên mà tôi trở thành bạn thân với cô ấy.

30 □ 名

ニックネーム

nickname / 小名 / biệt danh, tên thân mật

彼(かれ)と私(わたし)はニックネームで呼(よ)び合(あ)っている。

He and I call each other by nicknames. / 他和我用昵称称呼彼此。/ Anh ấy và tôi gọi nhau bằng biệt danh.

＝ 愛称(あいしょう)・あだ名(な)

31 □ 名

大半(たいはん)

most of / 大半，大部分 / hơn nửa, phần lớn

一日(いちにち)の大半(たいはん)の時間(じかん)を友達(ともだち)と過(す)ごしている。

I spend most part of the day with my friends. / 一天中大部分的时间我都和朋友一起度过。/ Tôi dành phần lớn thời gian trong ngày với bạn bè.

32 □ 動

恵(めぐ)**まれる**

to blessed with / 受恩惠，富足 / được ban cho, may mắn

私(わたし)は、いつも友人(ゆうじん)に恵(めぐ)まれている。

I am always blessed with friends. / 我人缘很好。/ Tôi luôn may mắn có được bạn bè.

33 □ 動

頼(たよ)**る**

to depend / 依靠，依赖 / trông cậy, dựa vào

私達(わたしたち)は親友(しんゆう)なのだから、困(こま)ったときは頼(たよ)ってほしい。

We are best friends, so I want you to depend on me when you are in trouble. / 我们是好朋友，有什么难处就来找我。/ Chúng ta là bạn thân nên khi gặp khó khăn, mong bạn dựa vào tôi.

➕ 頼(たよ)りにする to rely on / 作为依靠 / trông cậy vào・
頼(たよ)りになる to be reliable / 可靠 / có thể trông cậy

34 □ イ形	頼もしい (たの) **dependable / 可靠的，有出息 / đáng tin, đáng trông cậy**	彼女は何でも相談できる頼もしい存在だ。(かのじょ なん そうだん たの そんざい) She is a dependable friend and I can confide in her with anything. / 她很可靠，任何事都能跟她商量。/ Cô ấy là người đáng trông cậy, có thể trao đổi bất kỳ chuyện gì.
35 □ 動	見習う (みなら) **to emulate / 学习，以…为榜样 / noi gương**	私には見習うべき友人が何人かいる。(わたし みなら ゆうじん なんにん) I have some friends that I should emulate. / 我有好几个值得学习的朋友。/ Tôi có mấy người bạn phải noi gương học tập.

➕ 見習い (みなら) apprentice / 见习，模仿 / sự học theo, noi gương

36 □ 動	打ち明ける (う あ) **to confess / 吐露，坦言 / nói thẳng, bày tỏ, mở lòng**	親友だけに秘密を打ち明けた。(しんゆう ひみつ う あ) I shared my secret only with my best friend. / 我只对好朋友吐露了秘密。/ Tôi chỉ bày tỏ bí mật với bạn thân.
37 □ 動	励ます (はげ) **to encourage / 鼓励 / động viên, khích lệ**	私が試験に落ちたとき、友達が励ましてくれた。(わたし しけん お ともだち はげ) My friend cheered me up when I flunked the test. / 我考试不及格的时候，朋友鼓励了我。/ Khi tôi thi rớt, bạn bè đã động viên tôi.
38 □ 副	あえて **venture to, daringly / 硬是，敢于 / dám, mạnh dạn**	大切な友達だから、あえて厳しい忠告もする。(たいせつ ともだち きび ちゅうこく) I dare to offer bitter advice since he is an important friend to me. / 正因为是很重要的朋友，我才会说一些逆耳忠言。/ Vì là bạn bè quan trọng, mới dám cảnh báo nghiêm khắc.
39 □ 動	なぐさめる **to console / 安慰 / an ủi, động viên**	彼女にふられたとき、友達がなぐさめてくれた。(かのじょ ともだち) My friend comforted me when I got dumped by my girlfriend. / 被女朋友甩了 的时候，朋友安慰了我。/ Khi bị bạn gái chia tay, bạn bè đã an ủi tôi.
40 □ 動	察する (さっ) **to infer / 揣测，察知 / thông cảm, đồng cảm**	彼女の気持ちを察して、何も言わなかった。(かのじょ きも さっ なに い) I didn't say anything because I understood how she felt. / 我体谅她的心情，什么也没说。/ Đồng cảm với tâm trạng của cô ấy, tôi đã không nói gì.
41 □ 名	思いやり (おも) **thoughtfulness / 体谅，体贴 / sự quan tâm**	周りの人への思いやりを大切にしたい。(まわ ひと おも たいせつ) I want to be thoughtful of the feelings of people around me. / 我想要好好珍惜这份为周围人着想之心。/ Tôi muốn gìn giữ cẩn thận sự quan tâm đến người chung quanh.

➕ 思いやる (おも) to be thoughtful / 体谅，设身处地为他人着想 / quan tâm

42 ☐ イ形

何気ない(なにげ)

友達(ともだち)との<u>何気ない</u>(なにげ)会話(かいわ)が楽(たの)しい。

casual / 不经意，若无其事的，没有特别的企图 / thoải mái, vô tư

Casual conversation with friends is fun. / 和朋友漫无目的地聊天很开心。/ Những cuộc trò chuyện vô tư với bạn bè thật vui.

43 ☐ 動

からかう

彼女(かのじょ)ができて、友達(ともだち)に<u>からかわれた</u>。

to tease / 嘲弄，开玩笑 / trêu chọc

I got a new girlfriend, and my friends made fun of me. / 交到了女朋友，被朋友调侃了。/ Có bạn gái rồi thì tôi bị bạn bè trêu chọc.

44 ☐ 名

幹事(かんじ)

仲間(なかま)の飲(の)み会(かい)では、いつも私(わたし)が<u>幹事</u>(かんじ)だ。

organizer, person in charge / 干事，负责人 / cán sự, quản lý

I'm always in charge of arranging drinking parties with friends. / 和同伴们出去喝酒时，经常由我负责组织。/ Những buổi ăn uống với bạn bè, tôi luôn làm cán sự.

45 ☐ 動

呼(よ)び出(だ)す

夜遅(よるおそ)く、親友(しんゆう)に「飲(の)みに行(い)こう」と<u>呼び出された</u>(よ・だ)。

to send for, to summon / 叫出来，传唤 / gọi, kêu ra

My best friend called me out for drinks late at night. / 深夜，被好朋友叫出来喝酒了。/ Tối khuya, tôi bị đứa bạn thân gọi "đi nhậu thôi".

46 ☐ 動

盛(も)り上(あ)がる

①パーティーは<u>盛り上がって</u>(も・あ)、夜中(よなか)まで続(つづ)いた。

②地震(じしん)で道(みち)が<u>盛り上がった</u>(も・あ)。

to liven up/to surge / 气氛高涨 / 凸起，隆起 / hào hứng, dâng lên, sôi động

① The party livened up and continued till midnight. ② The road surged up because of the earthquake. / ①派对气氛很热烈，一直进行到深夜。②路面因地震鼓起来了。/ ① Bữa tiệc trở nên sôi động, kéo dài đến nửa đêm. ② Mặt đường dâng lên do động đất.

☞ ① become excited ② expand and rise / ①气氛、心情很高涨②鼓出来，高起来 / ① Trạng thái tình cảm, cảm giác hào hứng, sôi động. ② Phồng lên, trở nên cao lên.

47 ☐ 動

あきれる

彼(かれ)はいつも遅刻(ちこく)するので、<u>あきれて</u>しまう。

to be appalled/to surge / 吃惊，厌烦 / ngạc nhiên, sốc

I am appalled at how he is always late. / 他老是迟到，真是不像话。/ Anh ấy lúc nào cũng trễ giờ, thật đáng ngạc nhiên.

48 ☐ 動

ふざける

友達(ともだち)と<u>ふざけて</u>いたら、転(ころ)んで足(あし)の骨(ほね)を折(お)った。

to fool around / 开玩笑，打闹，嘲弄 / hiếu động, đùa giỡn

I fell and broke my leg because I was fooling around with my friend. / 和朋友打闹的时候，不小心摔倒腿部骨折了。/ Tôi đùa giỡn với bạn, té ngã và gãy xương chân.

49 ☐ イ形

久(ひさ)しい

高校時代(こうこうじだい)のクラスメートと<u>久しく</u>(ひさ)会(あ)っていない。

long time / 许久，久违 / lâu ngày, đã bao lâu

I haven't met my classmates from high school for a long time. / 我好久没和高中同学见面了。/ Đã lâu tôi không gặp lại bạn bè thời cấp III.

➕ 久(ひさ)しぶり long time no see / 好久不见 / lâu ngày, lâu nay

Section 3

知人・付き合い

ちじん　つ　あ

Acquaintances / 熟人・交际 / Người quen - Mối quan hệ giao tiếp

50 □ 名	初対面 しょたいめん **first meeting / 初次见面，第一次见面 / lần đầu gặp mặt**	山田さんとは初対面だったので、あいさつした。(やまだ／しょたいめん) I greeted Mr. Yamada, as I have never met him before. / 因为我和山田是第一次见面，所以去打了个招呼。/ Vì lần đầu gặp mặt anh / chị Yamada nên tôi đã chào hỏi.
51 □ 名	自己紹介 じこしょうかい **self-introduction / 自我介绍 / sự tự giới thiệu**	合コンでお互いに自己紹介をした。(ごう／たが／じこしょうかい) We introduced ourselves to each other at the party. / 在联谊会上，大家互相介绍了一下自己。/ Chúng tôi đã tự giới thiệu với nhau ở tiệc gặp mặt làm quen.

➕ 自己流 (じこりゅう) own method / 自己的风格，自成一派 / theo kiểu của mình

52 □ 名	おじぎ〈する〉 **bow / 鞠躬，行礼，点头寒暄 / sự cúi chào**	朝、大家さんに会ったので、おじぎした。(あさ／おおや／あ) I greeted the landlord with a bow when I met him in the morning. / 早上见到了房东，我点头行了个礼。/ Hồi sáng, vì gặp chủ nhà nên tôi đã cúi chào.
53 □ 名	近所付き合い きんじょづあ **interaction with neighbors / 和邻居相处 / mối quan hệ láng giềng**	できるだけ近所付き合いを大切にしている。(きんじょづあ／たいせつ) I take interacting with my neighbors very seriously. / 我尽量和邻居们和睦相处。/ Tôi cố gắng hết sức gìn giữ mối quan hệ láng giềng.

➕ 友達付き合い (ともだちづあ) interaction with friends / 和朋友相处 / mối quan hệ bạn bè

54 □ 名	大家 おおや **landlord / 房东 / chủ nhà**	私のアパートの大家さんは、とても親切な人だ。(わたし／おおや／しんせつ／ひと) My apartment's landlord is very kind. / 我公寓的房东是个特别热心的人。/ Chủ căn hộ của tôi là người rất tử tế.
55 □ 名	飼い主 かぬし **owner / 饲养主 / người chủ (nuôi thú cưng)**	犬の飼い主同士が公園でおしゃべりをしている。(いぬ／かぬし／どうし／こうえん) The dogs' owners are chatting at the park. / 一些养狗的人在公园里聊天 / Những người cùng là chủ nuôi chó trò chuyện ở công viên.
56 □ 動	交わす か **to exchange / 交换，相交 / trao đổi, trao qua lại**	近所の人達に会うと、笑顔であいさつを交わす。(きんじょ／ひとたち／あ／えがお／か) When I meet my neighbors, we exchange greetings with a smile. / 我见到邻居的时候，会笑着和他们互相打招呼。/ Mỗi lần gặp những người hàng xóm là tôi thường tươi cười chào hỏi.
57 □ 動	呼び止める よと **to stop / 叫停，叫住 / gọi chặn lại**	アパートの前で管理人さんに呼び止められた。(まえ／かんりにん／よと) The super stopped me in front of the apartment. / 在公寓前被楼管叫住了。/ Trước căn hộ, tôi bị người quản lý gọi chặn lại.

58 ☐ 動

振り返る (ふりかえる)

①後ろから名前を呼ばれて、振り返った。
②学生時代を振り返ると、なつかしい。

to look back/to reflect / 回头 / 回顾，回忆 / ngoảnh lại, nhìn lại, quay lại

① Someone called my name and I turned around. ② Reflecting on my days in school brings back good memories. / ①后面有人叫我名字，我回头看了一下。②回首学生时代，感到非常怀念。/ ① Bị gọi tên từ phía sau, tôi ngoảnh lại nhìn. ② Nhìn lại thời sinh viên, thấy thật nhớ nhung.

① to look behind by moving one's face or body ② to remember the past / ①脸或身体朝后看②回忆过去 / ① Quay mặt và cơ thể lại, nhìn về phía sau. ② Nhớ lại quá khứ

59 ☐ 名

再会〈する〉 (さいかい)

以前お世話になった人に再会した。

reunion / 再相见 / sự gặp lại

I reunited with someone who was very good to me before. / 和以前关照过自己的人重逢了。/ Tôi gặp lại người mình đã chịu ơn lúc trước.

60 ☐ 名

覚え (おぼえ)

田中さんとは会った覚えがない。

recollection / 记忆 / nhớ, trí nhớ

I don't recall meeting Mr. Tanaka. / 我不记得和田中见过面。/ Tôi không nhớ mình đã gặp anh / chị Tanaka.

➕ 記憶 (きおく) memory / 记忆 / ký ức, trí nhớ

61 ☐ 名

心当たり (こころあたり)

心当たりのない番号から電話が、かかってきた。

known of, something that comes to mind / 头绪，猜想 / biết, ý kiến (về vấn đề gì đó)

Someone called me from a number I have no knowledge of. / 一个不认识的号码打来了电话。/ Một cuộc điện thoại từ số mà tôi không biết gọi đến.

62 ☐ 動

結びつく (むすびつく)

川田さんの名前と顔が結びつかない。

to link, to be put together / 关联，结合 / liên tưởng, nhớ

I can't put together the name and face of Mr. Kawada. / 川田的名字和脸我对不上号。/ Tôi không nhớ ra khuôn mặt anh / chị Kawada dù biết tên.

➕ (～を) 結びつける (むすびつける) to link, to put together / 把…联系起来 / gắn, kết nối (~)

63 ☐ 名 副

とっさ［に］

隣の人に会ったとき、とっさに名前が出てこなかった。(副)

instant/in a split second / 猛然间，刹那间 / ngay lập tức

When I met the person next to me, I couldn't recall their name at that moment. / 见到旁边的人时，我一下子想不起他的名字来了。/ Khi gặp người hàng xóm, tôi không thể nhớ ra tên người đó ngay lập tức.

64 ☐ 副

てっきり

てっきり彼らを兄弟だと思っていた。

assumed / 以为一定 / chắc chắn

I assumed they were brothers. / 我一直以为他们俩是兄弟。/Tôi nghĩ chắc chắc họ là anh em.

65 ☐ 動

思い込む (おもいこむ)

私は木村さんが独身だと思い込んでいた。

to be under the impression / 以为 / tin rằng, cho rằng

I was under the impression that Mr. Kimura was single. / 我一直以为木村是单身。/ Tôi cứ cho rằng anh / chị Kimura độc thân.

➕ 思い込み（おもいこみ） assumption / 坚信，固执的想法 / sự tin rằng, sự cho rằng

66 □ コミュニケーション

名 **communication / 交流，沟通 / giao tiếp**

いろいろな国（くに）の人（ひと）とコミュニケーションを持（も）ちたい。

I want to communicate with people from different countries. / 我想和各个国家的人交流。/ Tôi muốn giao tiếp với người của nhiều nước khác nhau.

67 □ ネットワーク

名 **network / 网络 / kết nối, mạng lưới**

将来（しょうらい）のために、知（し）り合（あ）いのネットワークを広（ひろ）げたい。

I want to expand my network of acquaintances for my future. / 为了自己的将来，想拓宽自己的人脉。/ Vì tương lai, tôi muốn mở rộng sự kết nối với người quen.

👉 original meaning comes from radio and television networks / 原来指广播网、电视网等播送网 / Vốn có nghĩa là "mạng lưới phát sóng truyền thanh và truyền hình"

68 □ 直接（ちょくせつ）

名 副 **direct/directly / 直接 / trực tiếp**

彼（かれ）とは直接（ちょくせつ）の友達（ともだち）ではない。（名）

I am not a direct friend of him. / 我和他不是直接认识。/ Tôi không phải là bạn trực tiếp với anh ấy.

↔ 間接（かんせつ）

69 □ 接（せっ）する

動 **coming in contact with ~ / adjacent / 交往，打交道 / 相连，相接 / tiếp xúc, tiếp giáp**

①敬語（けいご）が下手（へた）なので、目上（めうえ）の人（ひと）と接（せっ）するのが苦手（にがて）だ。
②私（わたし）のアパートは、隣（となり）のビルと接（せっ）している。

① I can't speak honorifics well so I am not good at talking with my seniors. ② My apartment is adjacent to the building next door. / ①我敬语用不好，所以不善于和上级打交道。②我住的公寓和隔壁的大楼是连在一起的。/ ① Tôi dở kính ngữ nên ngại tiếp xúc với người trên. ② Căn hộ của tôi tiếp giáp với tòa nhà bên cạnh.

👉 ① exchange with people ② almost touching; adjacent / ①和人交流②中间没有间隙，非常靠近，相邻 / ① Giao lưu với người khác. ② Gần sát không có khoảng cách. Cạnh nhau

70 □ 招（まね）く

動 **invite / 邀请，招呼 / 招致，招来 / mời, kéo theo, dẫn đến**

①先日（せんじつ）、部長（ぶちょう）のお宅（たく）に招（まね）かれた。
②彼（かれ）の言葉（ことば）が大（おお）きな混乱（こんらん）を招（まね）いた。

① I was invited to the manager's home a few days ago. ② His words caused major confusion. / ①前几天我受邀去了部长家。②他的话招致了巨大的混乱。/ ① Hôm trước, tôi được mời đến nhà trưởng phòng. ② Những lời nói của anh ấy đã dẫn đến sự hỗn loạn lớn.

👉 ① invite ② be the cause of an unfavorable result / ①招待②导致不好结果的原因 / ① Chiêu đãi, mời. ② Trở thành nguyên nhân của kết quả không tốt.

71 □ 気配（きくば）り〈する〉

名 **consideration for others' feelings / 照顾，用心周到 / sự chu đáo, sự quan tâm**

アルバイト先（さき）の先輩（せんぱい）の気配（きくば）りを見習（みなら）いたい。

I want to emulate the consideration for others that my senior co-worker at my part-time job shows. / 打工时遇到的前辈待人周到细心，我想向他学习。/ Tôi muốn học hỏi sự chu đáo của người đàn anh ở chỗ làm thêm.

72 □	込める(こ)	感謝(かんしゃ)の気持(きも)ちを込(こ)めて、先生(せんせい)へのプレゼントを選(えら)んだ。
動	**infuse, insert, put in / 倾注，满怀 / với, bao gồm**	I chose a present for the teacher that is infused with a sense of gratitude. / 我满怀着感激的心情为老师挑选了礼物。/ Tôi đã chọn quà tặng cho thầy / cô với tất cả tấm lòng biết ơn.
73 □	同期(どうき)	彼(かれ)は会社(かいしゃ)の同期(どうき)と、とても仲(なか)がいい。
名	**colleague / 同期，同时期进入公司的同事 / cùng kỳ, cùng thời gian**	He has a good relationship with his collegues that entered the coampany at the same time as he. / 他和同批进公司的同事们关系非常好。/ Anh ấy là bạn cùng kỳ ở công ty, rất thân thiết.
74 □	ぐち	毎晩(まいばん)居酒屋(いざかや)で同期(どうき)とぐちをこぼしている。
名	**complaint / 牢骚 / sự than vãn**	My colleague and I vent our complaints every night at a Japanese-style pub. / 每天晚上和同批进公司的同事们一起在居酒屋发牢骚。/Mỗi tối, tôi than vãn với bạn cùng kỳ ở quán nhậu.
75 □	大(おお)いに	今日(きょう)は大(おお)いに飲(の)んで楽(たの)しもう。
副	**very / 非常，很 / nhiều, rất**	Let's drink and enjoy today to the fullest. / 我们今天尽情喝个够吧。/ Hôm nay uống thật nhiều cho vui nào.

これも覚(おぼ)えよう！ ❷

接辞(せつじ)：程度(ていど)② Affix: Degree / 词缀：程度 / Phụ tố: Mức độ

• 低(てい)〜

低予算(ていよさん)	low budget / 低预算 / Dự toán (ngân sách) thấp
低学年(ていがくねん)	lower grade / 低年级 / Cấp lớp thấp
低血圧(ていけつあつ)	low blood pressure / 低血压 / Huyết áp thấp
低姿勢(ていしせい)	low profile / 低姿态 / Tư thế thấp, khiêm nhường, thái độ nhún nhường
低次元(ていじげん)	trivial matter / 低层次，低级 / Tiêu chuẩn thấp
低レベル(てい)	low level / 低水准 / Trình độ (mức độ) thấp

恋人（こいびと）

Lover / 恋人 / Người yêu

76 □ 名	カップル **couple / 情侣，一对 / cặp, cặp đôi**	彼（かれ）らは似合（にあ）いのカップルだ。 They are a cute couple. / 他们是很般配的一对。/ Họ là một cặp đẹp đôi.

➕ ペア pair / 一双，成双 / cặp, cặp đôi

77 □ 名	愛（あい） **love / 爱意，爱 / tình yêu**	愛（あい）を込（こ）めて、彼女（かのじょ）にメッセージを送（おく）る。 Send her a message with love. / 满怀爱意地给女朋友发信息。/ Tôi gửi tin nhắn cho bạn gái với tất cả tình yêu.

➕ 愛（あい）する to love / 爱 / yêu・愛情（あいじょう） affection / 爱情 / tình yêu, tình thương

78 □ 名	同士（どうし） **each other / 同伴，同好 / cùng là ~**	恋人同士（こいびとどうし）が見（み）つめ合（あ）う。 The lovers gaze at each other. / 恋人互相凝视对方。/ Những người đang yêu nhìn nhau say đắm.

➕ 友達同士（ともだちどうし） friends / 朋友之间 / cùng là bạn bè・
他人同士（たにんどうし） strangers / 别人之间 / cùng là người dưng

79 □ 名 副	［お］互（たが）い［に］ **each other/mutually / 互相 / cùng nhau**	二人（ふたり）はお互（たが）いの性格（せいかく）が気（き）に入（い）った。（名） 私達（わたしたち）は会（あ）ったときから、お互（たが）いに好（す）きだった。（副） They liked each other's personalities. We liked each other from the moment we met. / 那俩人中意对方的性格。我们自见面以来就互相喜欢上了。/ Hai người đều thích tính cách của nhau. Chúng tôi thích nhau từ khi gặp mặt.
80 □ 動	つり合（あ）う **suitable / 均衡，相当，和谐 / hợp**	僕（ぼく）が彼女（かのじょ）とつり合（あ）っているかどうか心配（しんぱい）だ。 I am worried whether I'm suitable for her or not. / 我很担心自己能否配得上她。/ Tôi lo không biết có hợp với cô ấy không.
81 □ 副	むしろ **rather / 比起…更，与其…不如 / ngược lại, thà~ hơn là**	完（かん）ぺきな人（ひと）より、むしろ欠点（けってん）のある人（ひと）の方（ほう）が好（す）きだ。 I prefer someone who has faults rather than someone who is perfect. / 比起完美的人，我更喜欢有缺点的人。/ So với người hoàn hảo, tôi thà thích người có khuyết điểm hơn.
82 □ 副	いわば **so to speak, as like ~ / 可以说是，换言之 / có thể nói, như là ~**	彼女（かのじょ）は僕（ぼく）にとって、いわば太陽（たいよう）のような人（ひと）だ。 She is like the sun to me. / 她对我来说，可谓太阳一般的存在。/ Với tôi, có thể nói cô ấy như vầng thái dương.

83 □ 名	視線(しせん)	二人(ふたり)は、しばらく視線(しせん)を合(あ)わせなかった。
	line of sight / 视线 / ánh mắt	The two refused to look at each other for a while. / 他们俩许久没有正视对方。/ Hai người không nhìn vào mắt nhau một thời gian.
84 □ 動	見(み)つめる	彼(かれ)は彼女(かのじょ)をじっと見(み)つめていた。
	stare / 凝视，注视 / nhìn chằm chằm	He was staring at her. / 他目不转睛地注视着她。/ Anh ấy nhìn chằm chằm vào cô ấy.

➕ 見(み)つめ合(あ)う stare at each other / 互相凝视 / nhìn nhau chằm chằm

85 □ 動	そらす	彼女(かのじょ)に気(き)づかれて、目(め)をそらした。
	look away / 转移 / lảng tránh	She noticed me, and I looked away. / 被她发现了，我赶紧移开了视线。/ Bị cô ấy nhận ra, nên tôi lảng tránh.
86 □ 副	ちらっと	好(す)きな人(ひと)が隣(となり)の席(せき)に座(すわ)ったので、ちらっと見(み)た。
	peek / 一扫，一瞥，一闪 / liếc nhìn, nhìn thoáng qua	Someone I like sat next to me, so I took a peek. / 喜欢的人坐在旁边，所以我瞥了（他 / 她）一眼。/ Vì người tôi thích ngồi ở ghế bên cạnh nên tôi đã thoáng liếc nhìn.

= ちらりと

87 □ 副	もしかすると	もしかすると、彼(かれ)は私(わたし)のことが好(す)きかもしれない。
	maybe / 也许，或许 / biết đâu chừng, có lẽ	Maybe he likes me. / 或许他喜欢我。/ Biết đâu chừng, có lẽ anh ấy thích tôi.

= もしかしたら・もしかして・ひょっとすると

88 □ 動	探(さぐ)る	①友達(ともだち)に頼(たの)んで、彼女(かのじょ)の気持(きも)ちを探(さぐ)ってもらった。 ②ポケットを探(さぐ)ったら、500円玉(えんだま)が出(で)てきた。
	search / 试探 / 摸，掏 / thăm dò, lục lọi	① I asked my friend to ask whether she liked me or not. ② I searched my pocket and found a 500 yen coin. / ①我拜托朋友去试探了一下她的想法。②掏了掏口袋，摸出来一枚 500 日元的硬币。/ ① Tôi nhờ bạn thăm dò tình cảm của cô ấy. ② Tôi lục túi thì phát hiện ra ra đồng 500 yên.

👉 ① check out without having others notice ② search for something one cannot see / ①不被人发现的情况下调查②看不见的东西用手或脚摸 / ① Điều tra sao cho không bị người khác nhận biết. ② Tìm đồ vật không thấy được bằng tay, chân.

89 □ 示す（しめ）
動 show/point / 表露 / 举出，示出 / thể hiện, đưa ra

①彼は彼女に自分の気持ちを示せない。②例を示して、文法を説明する。

① He cannot show his true feelings to her. ② Explain the grammer by showing an example. / ①他无法对她表露自己的心意。②举例说明语法。/ ① Tôi không thể hiện tình cảm của mình cho cô ấy. ② Tôi đưa ra ví dụ để giải thích văn phạm.

① convey one's feelings to the someone else ② show something clearly to others so they can understand / ①向对方表达自己的心情②清晰地呈现给对方 / ① Truyền đạt tình cảm của mình cho người đối diện. ② Cho người đối diện thấy rõ.

90 □ 口実（こうじつ）
名 excuse / 借口 / viện lý do

試験勉強を口実にして、彼女と図書館で会った。

I used studying for an exam as an excuse to meet her at the library. / 我以备考为借口，和她在图书馆见了面。/ Viện lý do học thi, tôi đã gặp cô ấy tại thư viện.

91 □ うつむく
動 look down / 低下头 / nhìn xuống, cúi xuống

彼女は恥ずかしそうにうつむいた。

She shyly looked down. / 她很不好意思地低下了头。/ Cô ấy cúi xuống trông có vẻ xấu hổ.

92 □ こそこそ〈する〉
副 sneakily / 偷偷摸摸 / lén lút, vụng trộm, thì thào

親に内緒にして、こそこそ付き合うのは嫌だ。

I don't want to keep our relationship a secret from our parents. / 我不想瞒着父母偷偷摸摸地谈恋爱。/ Tôi ghét việc giấu bố mẹ, lén lút quen nhau.

➕ こっそり［と］ secretly / 偷偷地 / lén lút, lén

93 □ ささやく
動 whisper / 喃喃细语 / thì thầm, nói khẽ

彼は、やさしい声で「愛してる」とささやいた。

He whispered, "I love you," in a gentle voice. / 他温柔地轻声说"我爱你"。/ Anh ấy thì thầm bằng giọng nói dịu dàng "anh yêu em".

➕ つぶやく mutter / 嘟囔 / thì thầm, nói khẽ

94 □ 禁物（きんもつ）
名 taboo / 忌讳，禁忌 / điều cấm kỵ

私達の間で、うそは禁物だ。

There should be no lies between us. / 我们之间切忌说谎。/ Giữa chúng tôi, nói dối là điều cấm kỵ.

➕ 禁句（きんく） taboo words / 禁忌，避讳的言词 / từ cấm, từ kỵ húy

95 □ 許す（ゆる）
動 forgive / 原谅 / tha thứ, cho phép

彼にうそをついたことを謝って、許してもらった。

He apologized for lying and was forgiven. / 我向他道歉，之前对他撒了谎，得到了他的原谅。/ Tôi xin lỗi anh ấy về việc nói dối và nhận được sự tha thứ.

96 □ 名	合コン（ごう） mixer / 联谊 / tiệc gặp mặt làm quen	二人（ふたり）は合（ごう）コンで知（し）り合（あ）ったそうだ。 They met at a mixer. / 他们俩好像是在联谊会上认识的。/ Nghe nói hai người quen nhau tại tiệc gặp mặt làm quen.

＋ コンパ party / 联欢会，茶话会 / buổi tiệc

97 □ 名	アプローチ〈する〉 approach / 接近 / sự tiếp cận	先（さき）にアプローチしたのは彼（かれ）だった。 He was the one who approached first. / 是他先接近我的。/ Người tiếp cận trước là anh ấy.
98 □ 名	運命（うんめい） destiny, fate / 命运 / định mệnh, số phận	彼女（かのじょ）こそ、僕（ぼく）の運命（うんめい）の人（ひと）だ。 She is my soulmate / 她才是我命中注定的人。/ Cô ấy chính là người định mệnh của tôi.
99 □ 名	決意（けつい）〈する〉 determination / 决意 / sự quyết ý, quyết định	ついに彼女（かのじょ）との結婚（けっこん）を決意（けつい）した。 I finally decided to marry her. / 我终于下决心要和她结婚了。/ Cuối cùng tôi đã quyết định kết hôn cùng cô ấy.

＋ 決心（けっしん）〈する〉 resolution / 决心 / sự quyết tâm

100 □ 名	プロポーズ〈する〉 proposal / 求婚 / lời cầu hôn, sự cầu hôn	指輪（ゆびわ）を贈（おく）って、彼女（かのじょ）にプロポーズした。 I gave her a ring and proposed to her. / 我送了她戒指，向她求婚了。/ Tôi gửi tặng chiếc nhẫn và cầu hôn cô ấy.
101 □ 動	誓う（ちか） swear, promise / 发誓 / thề	みんなの前（まえ）で愛（あい）を誓（ちか）った。 We pledged our love in front of everyone. / 在大家的面前宣誓我们的爱。/ Trước mọi người, chúng tôi thề nguyện tình yêu.
102 □ 名	花嫁（はなよめ） bride / 新娘 / cô dâu	彼女（かのじょ）の花嫁姿（はなよめすがた）は、きっと美（うつく）しいだろう。 She will no doubt look beautiful in her wedding dress. / 她穿婚纱的样子一定很美吧。/ Hình ảnh cô dâu của cô ấy chắc chắn là đẹp lắm.

＋ 花（はな）むこ groom / 新郎 / chú rể

これも覚えよう！❸

接辞：程度③ Affix: Degree / 词缀：程度 / Phụ tố: Mức độ

● 好～

好印象	good impression / 好印象 / Ấn tượng tốt
好条件	favorable terms / 好条件 / Điều kiện tốt
好成績	good grades, good results / 好成绩 / Thành tích tốt
好景気	booming economy / 经济繁荣 / (Tình hình) kinh tế tốt
好人物	good-natured person / 好人 / Nhân vật tốt
好都合	convenient / 好时机 / Thuận lợi, thời điểm tốt

● 悪～

【あく～】

悪条件	unfavorable conditions / 恶劣条件 / Điều kiện xấu
悪趣味	bad taste / 恶趣味，低俗趣味 / Sở thích xấu
悪影響	bad influence / 恶劣影响 / Ảnh hưởng xấu
悪天候	bad weather / 恶劣天气 / Thời tiết xấu
悪習慣	bad habit / 坏习惯 / Thói quen xấu
悪循環	vicious cycle / 恶性循环 / Ách tắc, tuần hoàn không tốt

【わる～】

悪知恵	crafty / 阴谋诡计 / Khôn lỏi, khôn vặt, xảo quyệt
悪酔い	sick from overdrinking / 酒后身体不适，耍酒疯，酒品差 / Say xỉn
悪ふざけ	prank / 令人厌恶的恶作剧 / Tinh quái, nghịch ngợm thái quá

Section 5

関係悪化(かんけいあっか)

Bad Relationship / 关系恶化 / Mối quan hệ (trở nên) xấu đi

103 □ ナ形	ささいな **petty / 小小的，微不足道 / nhỏ nhặt, vụn vặt**	ささいなことが原因(げんいん)で、彼女(かのじょ)とけんかになった。 I argued with her about something petty. / 我因为一点鸡毛蒜皮的小事和她吵架了。/ Vì một nguyên nhân vụn vặt mà tôi đã cãi nhau với bạn gái.
104 □ 動	避(さ)ける **avoid / 避开，避免 / lảng tránh**	私(わたし)は彼(かれ)のようなタイプが苦手(にがて)で、つい避(さ)けてしまう。 I am not good with people like him and tend to avoid such people. / 我不太擅长和他这种类型的人打交道，总是能避则避。/ Tôi ngại những kiểu người như anh ta nên lảng tránh.
105 □ 名	誤解(ごかい)〈する〉 **miscommunication / 误解，误会 / sự hiểu nhầm, ngộ nhận**	小(ち)さなことが彼女(かのじょ)の誤解(ごかい)を招(まね)いてしまった。 Something minor caused her to misunderstand me. / 因为一件小事招致了她的误解。/ Một việc nhỏ đã dẫn đến sự hiểu nhầm của cô ấy.
106 □ 名	勘違(かんちが)い〈する〉 **misunderstanding / 错误判断，误解 / sự hiểu nhầm, phán đoán nhầm**	私(わたし)の勘違(かんちが)いで、親友(しんゆう)とけんかになった。 I fought with my best friend because of my misunderstanding. / 因为我的误解和朋友吵架了。/ Do hiểu nhầm mà tôi đã cãi nhau với người bạn thân.
107 □ 名	言(い)い訳(わけ)〈する〉 **excuse / 借口，辩解 / sự phân trần, biện bạch**	彼女(かのじょ)は言(い)い訳(わけ)が多(おお)い人(ひと)だ。 She always gives excuses. / 她是个满嘴借口的人。/ Cô ấy là người nhiều biện bạch.
108 □ 副	きっぱり［と］ **firmly / 断然，干脆 / dứt khoát**	彼(かれ)に食事(しょくじ)に誘(さそ)われたが、きっぱり断(ことわ)った。 He invited me to dinner/lunch but I firmly refused. / 他邀请我一起吃饭，但我干脆地拒绝了。/ Tôi được anh ấy mời dùng bữa nhưng đã dứt khoát từ chối.
109 □ 慣	ばかにする **make fun of / 欺负，贬低，轻视 / xem thường**	あの人(ひと)は、いつも私(わたし)をばかにしている。 That person always makes fun of me. / 那个人总是瞧不起我。/ Người đó lúc nào cũng xem thường tôi.
110 □ 名 ナ形	いやみ〈な〉 **sarcasm/sarcastic / 另人不愉快的 / mỉa mai, châm biếm**	彼(かれ)の言(い)い方(かた)はいやみに聞(き)こえる。(名) The way he says it always sounds sarcastic. / 他说话的方式令人不快。/ Cách nói của anh ta nghe như lời mỉa mai.

111 □ 動	責める せ accuse / 责备 / đổ lỗi, quy kết	一方的に人を責めるのはよくない。 いっぽうてき　ひと　せ It is not good to accuse someone one-sidedly. / 一味地责备别人不好。/ Việc chăm chăm đổ lỗi cho người khác là không tốt.
112 □ 動	けなす belittle / 贬低，诽谤 / gièm pha, bôi nhọ	彼は人をほめず、いつもけなしている。 かれ　ひと He always criticizes people and never commends them. / 对他人，他从不表扬，总是贬低。/ Anh ta không khen ngợi mà luôn bôi nhọ người khác.
113 □ 動	だまる be quiet / 沉默 / im lặng	彼女が怒っているときは、だまるしかない。 かのじょ　おこ When she is angry, all you can do is stay quiet. / 女朋友生气的时候，只能沉默。/ Khi cô ấy tức giận thì chỉ có im lặng mà thôi.
114 □ 動	にらむ glare / 怒目而视，瞪眼 / liếc, lườm	彼女は怖い顔で、じっと彼をにらんだ。 かのじょ　こわ　かお　かれ She stared at him with a furious expression. / 她用很凶的表情直直地瞪着他。/ Cô ấy chăm chăm lườm anh ấy với nét mặt đáng sợ.
115 □ 動	裏切る うらぎ betray / 背叛 / phản bội	信じていた人に裏切られてしまった。 しん　ひと　うらぎ I was betrayed by someone I trusted. / 被一直都很信任的人背叛了。/Tôi bị người mình tin tưởng phản bội.
116 □ 動	だます trick / 欺骗 / lừa gạt	知り合いにだまされて、お金を貸してしまった。 し　あ　かね　か I was tricked by an acquaintance and lent him money. / 被认识的人骗了，借了钱给他。/ Tôi bị người quen lừa, cho mượn tiền mất tiêu.
117 □ 名	せい fault / （不好的）缘故，原因 / vì ~ (lý do xấu)	うそをついたせいで、彼とけんかになった。 かれ I fought with him because of a lie I told. / 都怪我撒了谎，结果和他吵架了。/ Vì nói dối mà tôi đã cãi nhau với anh ấy.

➕ おかげ thanks to / （好的）缘故，原因 / nhờ ~ (lý do tốt)

118 □ 名	行為 こうい action / 行为 / hành vi, hành động	彼女の行為が、どうしても許せない。 かのじょ　こうい　ゆる I simply cannot forgive her actions. / 她的所作所为我无论如何都无法原谅。/ Hành vi của cô ấy thật không thể tha thứ được.

➕ 迷惑行為（めいわくこうい） nuisance / 给人添麻烦的行为 / hành vi phiền toái

119 □ 名	口論〈する〉 こうろん argument / 口角，争吵 / cãi nhau	こんなことで友達と口論したくない。 ともだち　こうろん I don't want to argue with friends about something like this. / 我不想因为这种事和朋友发生口角。/ Tôi không muốn cãi nhau với bạn bè vì một việc như thế này.

＝ 口（くち）げんか〈する〉

120 □	怒鳴る（どなる）	父が大声で怒鳴るのを初めて聞いた。（ちち おおごえ どな はじ き）
動	yell / 吼叫，生气 / gào lên, hét lên	I heard my father yell in a loud voice for the first time. / 我还是第一次听到父亲这么大吼大叫。/ Lần đầu tiên tôi nghe bố hét lên bằng giọng thật lớn.
121 □	殴る（なぐ）	友達に殴られて、大けがをした。（ともだち なぐ おお）
動	hit / 揍，殴打 / đấm	A friend hit me, and I was severely injured. / 被朋友打了，受了重伤。/ Tôi bị bạn đấm bị thương nặng.
122 □	貸し借り〈する〉（か か）	友達とは、お金の貸し借りをしない方がいい。（ともだち かね か か ほう）
名	lend or borrow / 借来借去 / cho vay và vay, vay mượn	It is better not to lend or borrow money from friends. / 朋友之间最好不要有金钱上的往来。/ Bạn bè thì không nên vay và cho vay tiền.
123 □	ばらす	①人の秘密をばらすなんて、彼は最低だ。（ひと ひみつ かれ さいてい） ②引っ越しで、ベッドをばらして運んだ。（ひ こ はこ）
動	reveal (the truth), disassemble / 透露，泄露 / 拆开 / tiết lộ, tháo rời ra	① He's horrible. He revealed people's secrets. ② We disassembled the bed and carried it out when we moved. / ①竟然泄露别人的秘密，他真是太差劲了。②搬家时我是把床拆开了搬运的。/ ① Gì chứ tiết lộ bí mật của người khác, anh ta thật tệ hại. ② Vì chuyển nhà nên tôi tháo rời giường ra để khiêng.

☞ ① reveal to others things that are not meant to shared ② to disassemble what was originally in one piece / ①把秘密跟别人说②把一件完整的东西拆开 / ① Nói với người khác chuyện nếu bị biết thì phiền phức. ② Làm một vật thành ra nhiều mảnh.

124 □	気まずい（き）	口論の後、二人は気まずくなった。（こうろん あと ふたり き）
イ形	awkward / 尴尬 / khó xử, ngại ngần	The two felt awkward after the argument. / 争执过后，两人都感到很尴尬。/ Sau khi cãi nhau, hai người trở nên khó xử.
125 □	今さら（いま）	今さら彼に謝られても、すぐには許せない。（いま かれ あやま ゆる）
副	now that / 现在才，事到如今 / giờ này (mà ~)	I cannot forgive him immediately just because he apologized. / 事到如今，即使他道歉，我也无法马上原谅。/ Giờ này anh ấy có xin lỗi thì tôi cũng không thể tha thứ ngay được.
126 □	台無し（だいな）	けんかをして、親友との友情を台無しにしてしまった。（しんゆう ゆうじょう だいな）
名	totally ruined / 糟蹋，白费 / công cốc, trắng tay, không còn gì	I ruined my friendship with my best friend because of a fight. / 我和好友的友情就这么因争吵而断送了。/ Cãi nhau rồi thì tình bạn với người bạn thân cũng không còn nữa.
127 □	うらむ	彼女に裏切られたが、うらむ気にはなれない。（かのじょ うらぎ き）
動	blame / 怨恨 / căm ghét, hận	She betrayed me, but I don't feel like blaming her. / 虽然她背叛了我，可我却对她恨不起来。/ Tuy bị cô ấy phản bội nhưng tôi không thể có cảm giác căm ghét.

➕ うらみ blame / 怨恨 / sự căm ghét

128 □ 動	追い出す (おいだす) **drive someone out / 逐出，赶出 / đuổi đi**	父とけんかして、家を追い出された。(ちち、いえ、おいだ) I fought with my father and he drove me out of the house. / 我和父亲吵架，被赶出了家门。/ Tôi cãi nhau với bố và bị đuổi ra khỏi nhà.
129 □ 名	仲間外れ (なかまはずれ) **leaving someone out / 被删除，被排挤 / lẻ loi, không có bạn, ra rìa**	私は、SNSで仲間外れにされてしまった。(わたし、なかまはず) I was being left out on social networks. / 我在社交网站上被孤立了。/ Tôi bị cho ra rìa trên mạng xã hội.
130 □ 名	あいつ **him/her, that person (derogatory) / 那个家伙 / thằng đó, hắn, nó**	あいつとは、もう二度と会いたくない。(にど、あ) I don't want to ever see him again. / 我再也不想见到那个家伙了。/ Tôi không muốn gặp hắn ta lần thứ hai.

➕ やつ person (derogatory) / 家伙 / thằng đó, hắn, nó

👉 An informal way of saying "that person," used when you are in a superior position to the person or you are very familiar with the person / 是「あの人」的粗俗的说法。看低对方或者是和对方非常亲近时使用 / Cách nói "người ấy" một cách suồng sã. Dùng trong trường hợp coi thường người đó hoặc trong trường hợp thân mật đặc biệt.

131 □ 名	他人 (たにん) **stranger / 别人，外人，陌生人 / người dưng**	兄はけんかすると、他人のような態度になる。(あに、たにん、たいど) My big brother acts like a stranger when we fight. / 哥哥一吵架，就会表现得像个陌生人一样。/ Anh tôi hễ cãi nhau là có thái độ như người dưng.

これも覚えよう！❹

接辞：程度④ Affix: Degree / 词缀：程度 / Phụ tố: Mức độ

・**名〜**

名案	good idea / 好点子 / Đề nghị (ý kiến) hay
名作	masterpiece / 名作 / Danh tác, tác phẩm xuất sắc
名画	masterpiece painting / 名画 / Danh họa
名曲	famous song, famous composition / 名曲 / Bản nhạc nổi tiếng
名所	place of interest / 名胜 / Danh lam (thắng cảnh)
名人	master / 名人 / Danh nhân, người nổi tiếng
名産	local specialty / 名产 / Sản vật nổi tiếng
名医	good doctor / 名医 / Danh y
名文	fine prose, famous literature / 名句，美文 / Câu (đoạn) văn nổi tiếng, xuất sắc
名著	great book, masterpiece / 名著 / Cuốn sách nổi tiếng, xuất sắc
名声	fame / 好名声，美誉 / Danh vọng, danh tiếng
名場面	famous scene / 为人熟知的经典片段 / Cảnh (phim, truyện v.v.) nổi tiếng
名女優	great actress / 著名女演员 / Nữ diễn viên nổi tiếng, minh tinh

N2

Chapter 2

暮らし

くら

Livelihood / 生活篇 / Đời sống

住まい

Housing / 居住 / Nơi ở

132	一人住まい（ひとりずまい）	このアパートは学生（がくせい）の一人住まい（ひとりずまい）が多（おお）い。
名	living alone / 一个人住 / việc sống một mình	There are many students living alone in this apartment. / 这个公寓里有很多一个人住的学生。/ Chung cư này có nhiều sinh viên sống một mình.

➕ 一人暮らし（ひとりぐらし） live on your own / 一个人生活 / việc sống một mình

133	賃貸（ちんたい）	去年（きょねん）から賃貸（ちんたい）のアパートに住（す）んでいる。
名	rent / 租赁，出租 / sự cho thuê	I have been living in this rented apartment since last year. / 我从去年开始在租的公寓里居住。/ Tôi sống ở căn hộ cho thuê từ năm ngoái.

➕ 賃貸住宅（ちんたいじゅうたく） rented house / 出租屋，出租房 / khu nhà cho thuê

134	敷金（しききん）	このアパートは借（か）りるときに敷金（しききん）が必要（ひつよう）だ。
名	deposit / 押金 / tiền cọc	You need a deposit to rent this apartment. / 这个公寓在租住时需要支付押金。/ Căn hộ này cần đặt tiền cọc khi thuê.

➕ 礼金（れいきん） key money / 礼金 / tiền lễ

135	更新（こうしん）〈する〉	ここに住（す）んで2年（ねん）経（た）ったので、もうすぐ更新（こうしん）だ。
名	renewal / 更新合约，续约 / sự gia hạn, đổi mới	It's been two years since I moved in here so it's almost time to renew the contract. / 我在这里租住了两年了，马上就该续约了。/ Tôi đã sống ở đây 2 năm rồi nên sắp gia hạn (hợp đồng).
136	ローン	会社（かいしゃ）の先輩（せんぱい）が30年（ねん）ローンで家（いえ）を買（か）った。
名	loan / 贷款 / sự vay nợ	My senior co-worker took out a 30-year loan to buy the house. / 公司的前辈贷款30年买了房。/ Người đàn anh trong công ty đã mua nhà bằng cách vay nợ 30 năm.

➕ 住宅ローン（じゅうたく） housing loan / 住房贷款 / sự vay nợ (mua) nhà ở

137	決まり（き）	ここではペットを飼（か）ってはいけない決（き）まりがある。
名	rule / 规定 / quy định	Pets are not allowed here. / 这里规定不能养宠物。/ Ở đây có quy định không được nuôi thú cưng.

➕ ルール rule / 规定，规则 / luật lệ

138	一戸建て（いっこだ）	先生（せんせい）が東京（とうきょう）に一戸建（いっこだ）てを買（か）ったそうだ。
名	house / 独栋别墅，独门独户的房子 / nhà riêng, nhà biệt lập	Our teacher bought a house in Tokyo. / 听说老师在东京买了栋独栋别墅。/ Nghe nói thầy / cô đã mua nhà riêng ở Tokyo.

➕ 一軒家（いっけんや） a single-family detached home / 独栋别墅，独门独户的房子 / căn nhà riêng

139 □ 名	マイホーム **my home / 属于自己的房子 / nhà (của tôi - phân biệt với nhà thuê)**	日本（にほん）でマイホームを買（か）うのが夢（ゆめ）だ。 It's a dream to buy my own house in Japan. / 在日本买房是我的梦想。/ Mua nhà riêng ở Nhật là mơ ước của tôi.
140 □ 名	我が家（わがや） **my home / 自己家 / nhà mình, gia đình tôi, nhà chúng ta**	やっぱりふるさとの我が家（わがや）が一番（いちばん）だ。 My home in my hometown is the best. / 还是故乡自己的家最好。/ Đúng là nhà mình ở quê vẫn là nhất.

➕ 我が町（わがまち） my town / 自己的城市 / thành phố chúng tôi, thành phố chúng ta・
我が国（わがくに） my country / 自己的国家，我国 / đất nước chúng tôi, đất nước chúng ta

141 □ 名	家屋（かおく） **house / 房屋，屋宅 / nhà cửa (nói chung)**	実家（じっか）は家屋（かおく）は大（おお）きくないが、庭（にわ）がとても広（ひろ）い。 My parents' house is not big but it has a large garden. / 我老家的房子不大，但院子很宽敞。/ Nhà bố mẹ ruột tôi nhà cửa không lớn nhưng vườn rất rộng.
142 □ 名	屋根（やね） **roof / 屋顶 / mái nhà**	あの青（あお）い屋根（やね）が山田（やまだ）さんの家（いえ）です。 That house with a blue roof is the Yamada family's residence. / 那个蓝色屋顶的就是山田家。/ Mái nhà xanh đó là nhà anh / chị Yamada.
143 □ 名	洗面所（せんめんじょ） **washroom / 洗手间 / nơi rửa mặt, phòng rửa mặt**	この家（いえ）には洗面所（せんめんじょ）に洗濯機（せんたくき）を置（お）くスペースがある。 This house has space to put the washing machine in the washroom. / 这个房子的洗手间里有放洗衣机的地方。/ Nhà này có khoảng trống ở phòng rửa mặt để đặt máy giặt.
144 □ 名	物置（ものおき） **storage / 库房，杂物间 / nơi (phòng) để đồ**	使（つか）わない物（もの）は物置（ものおき）に入（い）れておく。 Unused items will be left in storage. / 把不用的东西都收到杂物间里。/ Những gì không dùng đến thì cất vào phòng để đồ.
145 □ 名	間取り（まどり） **floor plan / 房间布局，房型，格局 / cách bố trí phòng ốc trong nhà, sơ đồ nhà**	我が家（わがや）の間取り（まどり）は４ＬＤＫだ。 Our house has four rooms, including a living room, dining room and kitchen. / 我们家的房型是 4 室 1 厅。/ Sơ đồ nhà chúng tôi là 4LDK.
146 □ 名	空間（くうかん） **space / 空间 / không gian**	この部屋（へや）は、空間（くうかん）を広（ひろ）く見（み）せる工夫（くふう）をしている。 This room is designed to look spacious. / 这个房间在如何呈现更大的空间上下了功夫。/ Căn phòng này có dụng công để cho thấy không gian rộng rãi.

147 □ **奥**（おく）

名 **innermost/in back / 最里面，深处 / 后面，里屋 / góc (nhà, phòng), trong sâu**

①寒くなったので、押し入れの奥からふとんを出した。
②田中さんの家を訪ねたら、奥の部屋に通された。

① It became cold so I pulled out the futon from the back of the closet. ② I visited the Tanaka family and they showed me to the room inside. / ①天气变冷了，我就从壁橱的最里面把被子翻出来了。②我去田中家拜访，被他们请进了里屋。/ ① Vì trời lạnh rồi nên tôi lấy mền từ trong góc tủ âm tường ra. ② Đến thăm nhà anh / chị Tanaka thì được đưa đến căn phòng bên trong.

① the innermost place of something ② the farthest from the entrance of a given room / ①某样东西的深处 ②离某个空间的入口较远的地方 / ① Chỗ sâu trong nơi nào đó. ② Nơi cách xa từ cửa vào của không gian.

148 □ **手前**（てまえ）

名 **toward oneself / 跟前，靠近自己这边 / phía trước**

そのドアは手前に引いてください。

Pull that door towards you. / 开那扇门的时候请朝自己这边拉。/ Vui lòng kéo cánh cửa đó về phía trước.

149 □ **南向き**（みなみむ）

名 **facing south / 朝南 / hướng nam**

この部屋は南向きで暖かい。

This room faces the south and is warm. / 这个房间朝南很暖和。/ Căn phòng này hướng nam nên ấm áp.

＋ 北向き（きたむ） facing north / 朝北 / hướng bắc・西向き（にしむ） facing west / 朝西 / hướng tây・東向き（ひがしむ） facing east / 朝东 / hướng đông

150 □ **温もり**（ぬく）

名 **warmth / 温暖，暖意 / sự ấm áp, hơi ấm**

この家は木の温もりが感じられる。

You can feel the warmth of wood in this house. / 这个房子里能感受到木头的暖意。/ Ngôi nhà này có cảm giác ấm áp của gỗ cây.

151 □ **頑丈な**（がんじょう）

ナ形 **sturdy / 结实 / vững chắc**

うちは頑丈なので、地震が起きても大丈夫だ。

Our house is sturdy so it can survive earthquakes. / 我家的房子很坚固，就算发生地震也没事。/ Nhà tôi vững chắc nên động đất có xảy ra cũng không sao.

152 □ **点検〈する〉**（てんけん）

名 **check-up, maintenance / 检查 / sự kiểm tra, bảo dưỡng**

今日はマンションのエレベーターが点検中で、動かない。

The elevator in the apartment building is not operating because it is going through maintenance today. / 今天公寓的电梯在检修，用不了。/ Hôm nay thang máy của căn hộ đang trong thời gian bảo dưỡng nên không hoạt động.

＋ 点検中（てんけんちゅう） conducting a check-up / 检查中 / đang kiểm tra

153 □ **停止〈する〉**（ていし）

名 **stop / 停止 / sự dừng, ngưng hoạt động**

今、エレベーターが停止している。

The elevator is not moving now. / 现在电梯停运了。/ Bây giờ, thang máy đang ngưng hoạt động.

154 □ 物音（ものおと）
名 **sound / 声响，声音 / tiếng động**
上の部屋で大きな物音がする。
I heard a loud noise from the room above. / 楼上的房间传来很大的声响。/ Phòng trên có tiếng động lớn.

155 □ 防犯（ぼうはん）
名 **crime prevention / 防盗 / sự phòng chống tội phạm**
防犯のために、ドアに特別な鍵をつけた。
I installed a special key as to prevent break-ins. / 为了防盗，在门上装了特制的门锁。/ Để phòng chống tội phạm, tôi đã khóa cửa bằng chìa khóa đặc biệt.

➕ 防犯ベル burglar alarm / 防盗铃 / chuông phòng chống tội phạm・防犯カメラ surveillance camera / 监控摄像机，防盗摄像头 / máy ghi hình phòng chống tội phạm

156 □ ぞっと〈する〉
副 **get the chills / 毛骨悚然，害怕 / run sợ, sợ**
同じアパートに犯人が住んでいたなんて、ぞっとする。
It's frightening to think that the criminal lived in the same apartment as I do. / 我居然和罪犯住在同一栋公寓里，想想就毛骨悚然。/ Gì chứ tên tội phạm đã sống cùng căn hộ thì sợ ghê.

157 □ 警備（けいび）〈する〉
名 **security / 警备，安保 / sự bảo vệ**
このマンションは警備が厳しい。
This mansion has tight security. / 这栋公寓里警备森严。/ Căn hộ này bảo vệ rất nghiêm ngặt.

➕ 警備会社（けいびがいしゃ） security company / 安保公司 / công ty bảo vệ・警備員（けいびいん） security guard / 保安，安保人员 / nhân viên bảo vệ

158 □ 新築（しんちく）〈する〉
名 **newly built / 新建公寓 / mới xây dựng**
このアパートは新築ではないが、建ってからまだ2年だ。
This apartment is not newly built, but the building is only two years old. / 这栋公寓虽然不是全新的，但建成也只有两年。/ Căn hộ này không phải mới xây dựng nhưng cũng mới xây 2 năm thôi.

➕ 築年数（ちくねんすう） age of building / 建成年数 / số năm xây dựng, số tuổi của tòa nhà

お金
かね

Money / 金钱 / Tiền bạc

159 **収入**
しゅうにゅう

名 **income / 收入 / thu nhập, khoản thu (chưa trừ các phí tổn)**

アルバイト生活なので、毎月の収入が違う。

My monthly income varies because I only work part-time. / 因为是靠打零工为生，所以我每个月的收入都不稳定。/ Vì là cuộc sống làm thêm nên thu nhập hàng tháng khác nhau.

↔ 支出（ししゅつ） ＋ 所得（しょとく） earnings / 所得，收入 / thu nhập・年収（ねんしゅう） annual income / 年收入 / thu nhập cả năm

160 **ごく**

副 **very / 极，非常 / cực kỳ, vô cùng**

ごくわずかだが、給料が上がった。

My salary increased a tiny bit. / 我涨工资了，虽然就涨了一点点。/Tiền lương đã tăng lên dù cực kỳ ít ỏi.

161 **せいぜい**

副 **at the very best/do one's best / 最多，充其量 / 尽可能 / nhiều nhất là, tối đa, trong mức có thể**

①私の給料はせいぜい月20万円くらいだ。
②あきらめずに、せいぜい頑張りなさい。

① My monthly salary is 200,000 yen at the most. ② Don't give up and do your best. / ①我的工资每个月充其量也就20万日元左右。②不要放弃，尽全力去做吧。/ ① Tiền lương của tôi nhiều nhất khoảng 200.000 yên một tháng. ② Không được bỏ cuộc mà hãy cố gắng trong khả năng có thể.

☞ ① at the maximum ② as much as one can allow/do / ①最多也就②在可行的范围里 / ① Có nhiều cũng ② Trong phạm vi có thể

162 **出費〈する〉**
しゅっぴ

名 **expenditure / 开销 / chi tiêu**

一人暮らしは出費が多くて、大変だ。

Living alone is hard as there are many expenses. / 一个人生活开销很大很辛苦。/ Sống một mình thì chi tiêu nhiều, thật vất vả.

＋ 経費（けいひ） expense / 经费 / kinh phí

163 **赤字**
あかじ

名 **deficit/red letters / 赤字 / 红色的字，校正部分 / lỗ (âm), chữ đỏ**

①困った。今月もまた赤字だ。
②レポートが返ってきたが、赤字が入っていた。

① I'm in trouble. I'm in red again this month. ② The report came back with comments in red from the teacher. / ①真让人头疼，这个月也是入不敷出。②报告发回来了，但上面有红字的批注。/ ① Thôi rồi! Tháng này lại âm rồi. ② Bài báo cáo đã được trả lại, có chữ đỏ.

☞ ① expenditure exceeding income ② marks made to correct errors / ①出账比入账要多，入不敷出②批改时用红色字标注出错误的地方 / ① Chi tiêu nhiều hơn thu nhập. ② Đánh dấu để sửa sai.

164 **大金**
たいきん

名 **lot of money / 一大笔钱 / số tiền lớn**

私にとって1万円は大金だ。

To me, 10,000 yen is a lot of money. / 对我来说，1万日元是一大笔钱了。/ Với tôi, 10.000 yên là số tiền lớn.

165 □ 名	税金（ぜいきん） tax / 税金 / tiền thuế	市役所（しやくしょ）から税金（ぜいきん）の支払（しはら）い通知（つうち）が来（き）た。 The city office sent me a notice demanding I pay my taxes. / 市政府发来了税金支付通知函。/ Có thông báo yêu cầu thanh toán tiền thuế từ văn phòng ủy ban thành phố.
		➕ 税込（ぜいこみ） tax included / 含税 / bao gồm thuế
166 □ 動	納（おさ）める pay / 缴纳 / nộp, đóng	私（わたし）は税金（ぜいきん）を、きちんと納（おさ）めている。 I pay all my taxes. / 我一直都认真履行纳税义务。/ Tôi nộp thuế đầy đủ.
167 □ 動	含（ふく）む included / 含，包含 / bao gồm	税込価格（ぜいこみかかく）は消費税（しょうひぜい）を含（ふく）む。 The price includes tax. / 含税价格里包含了消费税。/ Giá gồm thuế là bao gồm thuế tiêu thụ.
		➕ 含（ふく）める include / 包含，加入 / bao gồm
168 □ 名	公共料金（こうきょうりょうきん） utility charges / 公共费 / tiền công cộng, tiền điện nước ga (nói chung)	日本（にほん）の公共料金（こうきょうりょうきん）は私（わたし）の国（くに）よりずっと高（たか）い。 Japan's utility charges are much more expensive than those in my country. / 日本的公共费比我们国家的贵得多。/ Tiền công cộng ở Nhật cao hơn hẳn so với nước tôi.
169 □ 動	払（はら）い込（こ）む make payment / 交付，缴纳 / thanh toán	商品（しょうひん）の代金（だいきん）をコンビニの ATM で払（はら）い込（こ）んだ。 I paid for the product using the ATM at a convenience store. / 在便利店的 ATM 机上支付了商品的货款。/ Tôi đã thanh toán tiền hàng bằng ATM ở cửa hàng tiện lợi.
		➕ 振（ふ）り込（こ）む deposit / 汇款，缴款 / chuyển khoản
170 □ 名	引（ひ）き落（お）とし withdrawal / 从账户上扣款，划账 / sự rút (tiền từ tài khoản)	光熱費（こうねつひ）は銀行（ぎんこう）の引（ひ）き落（お）としにしている。 I have my utility bills withdrawn from my bank account. / 我的电费和煤气费是直接从银行账户上扣款的。/ Tiền điện nước ga được rút từ ngân hàng.
		➕ 引（ひ）き落（お）とす withdraw / 扣款，划账 / rút (tiền từ tài khoản)
171 □ 名	手数料（てすうりょう） fee / 手续费 / lệ phí, phí dịch vụ	この時間（じかん）に ATM を利用（りよう）すると、手数料（てすうりょう）がかかる。 You will be charged a fee if you withdraw from the ATM at this hour. / 这个时段使用 ATM 机需要支付手续费。/ Nếu dùng ATM vào giờ này thì sẽ tốn phí dịch vụ.
172 □ 名	出（だ）し入（い）れ〈する〉 deposit and withdrawal / 存取 / việc rút và gửi (tiền)	銀行預金（ぎんこうよきん）の出（だ）し入（い）れは、コンビニでもできる。 You can withdraw and deposit money at convenience stores. / 银行账户的存取款在便利店也能办理。/ Có thể rút và gửi tiền từ tài khoản ngân hàng ở cửa hàng tiện lợi.

173 □ 慣
高くつく（たか）
cost a great deal / 开始是想要精打细算的，但后续费用很高 / đắt tiền, đắt đỏ

一人暮らしの自炊は高くつくこともある。
It could be costly to cook for yourself when living alone. / 一个人生活自己做饭，有时反而比较贵。/ Việc tự nấu ăn khi sống một mình cũng có khi đắt đỏ.

⇔ 安く済む（やすくすむ）

174 □ 名
残高（ざんだか）
balance / 余额 / số dư

ときどき銀行の残高をチェックする。
I check my bank balance periodically. / 我会时不时查询一下银行账户的余额。/ Thỉnh thoảng, tôi kiểm tra số dư trong ngân hàng.

175 □ 副
せっせと
busily / 孜孜不倦地 / chăm chỉ, siêng năng

せっせとバイトして、少しでも貯金したい。
I want to save money by keeping busy with part-time work. / 我想通过拼命打工，尽量存一点钱。/ Tôi chăm chỉ làm thêm để tiết kiệm dù chỉ một chút.

176 □ ナ形
大まかな（おお）
roughly / 粗枝大叶，粗略 / đại khái, ước chừng

大まかに1か月の生活費を計算すると、10万円だ。
I calculated my one month spending to be roughly 100,000 yen. / 粗略计算下来一个月的生活费大概10万日元。/ Chi phí sinh hoạt 1 tháng ước chừng 100.000 yên.

177 □ 動
差し引く（さしひく）
deduct / 扣除，抵扣 / trừ đi

給料から生活費を差し引くと、貯金はできない。
I can't save money if I deduct living costs from my salary. / 从工资里扣除生活费后就存不下钱了。/ Nếu trừ đi chi phí sinh hoạt từ tiền lương thì không thể tiết kiệm.

178 □ 動
努める（つとめる）
work on / 尽力，努力 / nỗ lực, cố gắng

いつも節約に努めている。
I make an effort to be thrifty. / 我总是尽力节省。/ Tôi luôn cố gắng tiết kiệm.

＋ 努力〈する〉（どりょく） effort / 努力 / nỗ lực, cố gắng

179 □ 動
立て替える（たてかえる）
pay on behalf of / 垫付，代付 / tạm ứng, ứng trước

友達に飲み会の勘定を立て替えてもらった。
My friend paid the bill on my behalf at the drinking party. / 请朋友帮忙垫付了聚餐的钱。/ Tôi nhờ bạn tạm ứng trước tiền buổi ăn uống.

180 □ 名
援助〈する〉（えんじょ）
aid / 支援，支持 / sự viện trợ

生活が苦しくて、親に援助してもらった。
Life was difficult, and my parents helped me financially. / 生活过得太苦，只好去向父母求援了。/ Đời sống khó khăn nên tôi được bố mẹ viện trợ.

181 □
返済〈する〉（へんさい）

次のボーナスで親に借金を返済しよう。

名 **repayment / 还，偿还 / sự trả, hoàn trả**	I will repay my debt to my parents when I receive my next bonus. / 用下次发的奖金来还向父母借的钱吧。/ Tôi sẽ trả tiền nợ cho bố mẹ bằng tiền thưởng lần tới.
182 □ 安定（あんてい）〈する〉	①やっと、日本（にほん）での生活（せいかつ）が安定（あんてい）してきた。 ②この機械（きかい）は安定（あんてい）したところに置（お）いてください。
名 **stability / 稳定，安定 / 平稳，稳当 / ổn định**	① I finally started to settle down in Japan. ② Please set this machine is a stable place. / ①在日本的生活终于安定下来了。②请把这台机器放在稳当的地方。/ ① Cuối cùng thì cuộc sống ở Nhật cũng đã ổn định. ② Hãy để cái máy này ở chỗ ổn định.

➕ 安定感（あんていかん） sense of stability / 安定感 / cảm giác ổn định・不安定（ふあんてい）な unstable / 不安定 / không ổn định

👉 ① no major change ② physically stable, does not wobble or fall when placed somewhere / ①没有很大的变化②放东西的时候不会掉下来或是摇摆不定 / ① Không có thay đổi lớn. ② Khi đặt đồ vật, không làm cho đồ ngã hay lắc lư.

これも覚（おぼ）えよう！ ❺

➕ **接辞（せつじ）：金銭（きんせん）①** Affix: Money / 词缀：金钱 / Phụ tố: Tiền bạc

• ～費（ひ）

教育費（きょういくひ）	education fee / 教育费 / Chi phí giáo dục
学費（がくひ）	tuition / 学费 / Học phí
会費（かいひ）	membership fee / 会员费 / Hội phí
食費（しょくひ）	food expenses / 伙食费 / Tiền ăn
交際費（こうさいひ）	entertainment expenses / 交际开销 / Tiền lễ tiết, giao tiếp
住居費（じゅうきょひ）	housing expenses / 住宿费 / Tiền nhà, phí cư ngụ
光熱費（こうねつひ）	cost of heat and electricity / 电费及煤气费 / Tiền điện, nước, ga
生活費（せいかつひ）	cost of living / 生活费 / Chi phí sinh hoạt
人件費（じんけんひ）	labor costs / 人工费 / Tiền thuê nhân công, phí nhân công
医療費（いりょうひ）	medical expenses / 医疗费 / Chi phí y tế

Section 3

食事（しょくじ）

Food / 用餐 / Bữa ăn

183 ☐ 名	好き嫌い（すききらい） likes and dislikes / 偏好，好恶；挑肥拣瘦，挑剔 / ý thích yêu ghét, kén cá chọn canh	子どもの頃から好き嫌いが多かった。（こ ころ すききらい おお） Even as a child, I was picky. / 我从儿时起就很挑剔。/ Từ lúc nhỏ tôi đã kén cá chọn canh.
184 ☐ 名	好物（こうぶつ） favorite thing / 喜爱的食物和饮料 / món yêu thích	私の好物は肉料理と甘い物だ。（わたし こうぶつ にくりょうり あま もの） My favorite foods are meat and sweets. / 我喜欢吃肉食和甜食。/ Món yêu thích của tôi là món thịt và đồ ngọt.

➕ 大好物（だいこうぶつ） most favorite thing / 最喜爱的食物和饮料 / món cực kỳ yêu thích

185 ☐ 動	飽きる（あ） get bored with / 腻，厌烦 / chán, ngán	味の濃い料理は、すぐ飽きる。（あじ こ りょうり あ） I get tired of dishes that taste too strong. / 重口味的菜一下子就吃腻了。/ Món ăn đậm đà thì ngán liền.
186 ☐ イ形	物足りない（ものた） feel like something is missing / 美中不足，欠缺 / thiếu thiếu, không thỏa mãn	この料理は、まずくはないが、物足りない気がする。（りょうり ものた き） This dish doesn't taste bad, but something seems to be missing. / 这道菜不难吃，但总觉得少了点什么。/ Món ăn này không dở nhưng cảm thấy không thỏa mãn.
187 ☐ 名	ボリューム volume / 分量 / 音量 / phân lượng, âm lượng	①この店の料理は、とてもボリュームがある。（みせ りょうり） ②すみませんが、少しボリュームを下げてください。（すこ さ） ① The food at this store comes in large portions. ② Excuse me, but please lower your volume. / ①这家店的菜品分量十足。②不好意思，请把音量调小一些。/ ① Món ăn ở tiệm này lượng rất nhiều. ② Xin lỗi, vui lòng hạ âm lượng xuống một chút.

👉 ① amount ② audio volume / ①一口吃掉②音量 / ① Phân lượng ② Âm lượng

188 ☐ 名	一口（ひとくち） a bite / 一口 / 一点点 / một miếng	①彼は寿司を一口で食べた。（かれ すし ひとくち た） ②彼女は納豆を一口食べて、二度と食べなかった。（かのじょ なっとう ひとくち た にど た） ① He ate the sushi in one bite. ② She took one bite of the natto and never ate it again. / ①他一口就吃掉了寿司。②她尝了一点纳豆，之后就再没吃第二口。/ ① Anh ấy ăn một lần là hết miếng sushi. ② Cô ấy ăn một miếng natto rồi không ăn thêm miếng nào nữa.

👉 ① eat in one bite ② eat or drink little by little / ①一下子一口吞②只尝一点点 / ① Ăn 1 lần một cách hùng hổ, mạnh bạo. ② Chỉ ăn, uống một chút

189 □ かじる	りんごを一口(ひとくち)かじってみたが、固(かた)くて食(た)べられなかった。
動 bite / 咬 / cắn	I took a bite of the apple but it was too tough to eat. / 我咬了一口苹果，但太硬了吃不下。/ Tôi thử cắn một miếng táo nhưng cứng quá không thể ăn được.

190 □ ひとたび	この肉(にく)は、ひとたび食(た)べたら、また食(た)べたくなる味(あじ)だ。
副 once / 一旦，一次 / một lần	The taste of this meat makes you want to eat it again. / 这个肉的味道，吃过一次之后就还会想吃。/ Món thịt này ăn một lần rồi là lại muốn ăn nữa.

a formal expression for いったん and 一度 / "いったん" "一度" 的生硬表达 / Cách nói cứng nhắc "tạm, một chút", "một lần".

191 □ うまい	①こんなにうまいラーメンは食(た)べたことがない。 ②スピーチがうまい人(ひと)が、うらやましい。
イ形 tasty/good / 好吃 / 厉害，高明 / ngon, giỏi	① I have never had ramen that tasted this good before. ② I envy people who are good at giving speeches. / ①我从没吃过这么好吃的拉面。②我很羡慕那些擅长演讲的人。/ ① Tôi chưa từng ăn món mì ramen ngon như thế này. ② Thật ghen tị với người giỏi hùng biện.

① tasty ② good way of doing something / ①好吃②技艺精湛 / ① Ngon ② Cách làm giỏi

192 □ いける	①彼女(かのじょ)はお酒(さけ)が、かなりいける。 ②彼(かれ)はスポーツなら、何(なん)でもいける。
動 good at / 会，能行 / 很好，擅长 / có thể (làm gì đó)	① She can drink quite a lot of hard liquor. ② He can play any sport. / ①她很能喝酒。②他什么运动都很擅长。/ ① Cô ấy có thể uống rượu khá nhiều. ② Thể thao thì anh ấy có thể chơi môn gì cũng được.

① can drink alchohol ② can do well (don't use negative form " いけない ") / ①能喝酒②擅长（但是否定形式いけない没有这个意思）/ ① Có thể uống được rượu. ② Có thể làm / chơi giỏi. *Không sử dụng ở hình thức " いけない "

193 □ 渋(しぶ)い	①お茶(ちゃ)は渋(しぶ)い方(ほう)が好(す)きだ。 ②まだ30代(だい)なのに、彼(かれ)の趣味(しゅみ)はとても渋(しぶ)い。
イ形 bitter/refined / 涩 / 古朴，素雅 / đắng, chát, già dặn	① I prefer bitter tea. ② He's only in his 30s but his hobbies are refined. / ①我更喜欢带一点苦涩的茶。②虽然只有三十多岁，但他的爱好很古雅。/ ① Tôi thích trà đắng hơn. ② Còn ở độ tuổi 30 mà sở thích của anh ấy rất già dặn.

① a tingling sensation on the tongue ② an impression of being calm and collected / ①涩舌头的味道②沉稳的感觉 / ① Vị như làm tê lưỡi. ② Có ấn tượng trầm tĩnh.

194 くどい

イ形 strong/repetitive / 过浓，太重 / 罗嗦，冗长 / nặng mùi, dai dẳng

①この料理（りょうり）はおいしいが、ちょっとくどい味（あじ）だ。
②また同（おな）じ話（はなし）をしている。本当（ほんとう）にくどい人（ひと）だ。

① This dish is tasty but a bit strong. ② He is repeating himself. He's really verbose. / ①这道菜挺好吃的，就是味道有点太重了。②又在重复说一样的话了，他这个人真啰嗦。/ ① Món ăn này ngon nhưng hơi nặng mùi. ② Lại nói cùng một chuyện. Thật là người dai quá.

① a color or taste that is too strong ② doing the same thing over and over / ①颜色或味道太浓重②同样的事情重复很多遍，很难缠 / ① Mùi, màu quá đậm. ② Dai, làm một chuyện không biết bao nhiêu lần.

195 ファミレス

名 casual restaurant (for families) / 家庭餐厅 / nhà hàng, nhà hàng gia đình

昼（ひる）ご飯（はん）はファミレスで食（た）べた。

I ate lunch at the casual restaurant. / 今天的午饭是在家庭餐厅吃的。/ Tôi đã ăn trưa ở nhà hàng gia đình.

= ファミリーレストラン

196 フルコース

名 full-course meal / 西式全餐 / bữa ăn nhiều món (từ khai vị đến tráng miệng)

彼（かれ）にフランス料理（りょうり）のフルコースを、ごちそうしてもらった。

He treated me to a full-course meal of French cuisine. / 他请我吃了法式全餐。/ Tôi được anh ấy đãi bữa ăn Pháp.

197 オーダー〈する〉

名 order / 点单 / sự gọi, đặt món

オーダーをうかがって、よろしいでしょうか。

Are you ready to order? / 请问您需要点单了吗？ / Xin phép hỏi anh / chị dùng gì?

198 催促（さいそく）〈する〉

名 reminder / 催促 / sự hối thúc, thúc giục

料理（りょうり）がなかなか来（こ）ないので、催促（さいそく）した。

I wasn't served the ordered dish so I reminded (the waiter) of the order. / 点了的菜一直没上，我催了一下。/ Mãi không thấy thức ăn đem lên nên tôi đã hối thúc.

199 会計（かいけい）〈する〉

名 payment / 付账，买单 / sự tính tiền

カードで会計（かいけい）を済（す）ませた。

I paid by credit card. / 我刷卡结的账。/ Tôi tính tiền bằng thẻ.

＋ 勘定（かんじょう）〈する〉 bill / 结账，买单 / sự tính tiền

200 バイキング

名 all-you-can-eat / 西式自助餐 / ăn tự chọn

お昼（ひる）はバイキングで、食（た）べ過（す）ぎてしまった。

I had a buffet lunch and ate too much. / 中午吃了自助餐，吃撑了。/ Buổi trưa ăn tự chọn nên tôi đã ăn quá nhiều.

＋ ビュッフェ buffet / 冷餐会，自助餐 / ăn buffet

201 トレイ
名 tray / 托盘 / khay, mâm
ビュッフェでトレイの上(うえ)に食(た)べたいものを載(の)せた。
At the buffet, I put food that I wanted to eat on my tray. / 吃自助时把想吃的东西放在托盘里了。/ Ăn buffet nên tôi đã cho những gì muốn ăn lên khay.

can also be written トレー / 也写作"トレー" / Cũng viết là "トレー"

202 器(うつわ)
名 serving dish / 器皿，容器 / đồ đựng, chén, bát nói chung
美(うつく)しい器(うつわ)で食(た)べる料理(りょうり)は本当(ほんとう)においしい。
Food eaten on a beautiful plate is really tasty. / 用好看的器皿装菜会让人觉得更好吃。/ Ăn đồ ăn trong chén bát đẹp thì thật ngon.

203 重(かさ)ねる
動 pile on top of something/ repeat / 重叠，叠加 / 反复，重复 / chồng, chất lên
①回転寿司(かいてんずし)では、重(かさ)ねた皿(さら)を数(かぞ)えて代金(だいきん)を払(はら)う。
②わがままだった弟(おとうと)が、年(とし)を重(かさ)ねて立派(りっぱ)な人(ひと)になった。
①Payment at a conveyer-belt sushi restaurant is made by counting the number of plates that are piled up. ② My selfish younger brother turned into a good man as he grew in years. / ①旋转寿司店是通过数叠起来的空盘子数量来算钱的。②曾经很任性的弟弟随着年龄渐长成为了一个很优秀的人。/ ① Ở sushi băng chuyền, người ta đếm số dĩa chồng lên nhau và trả tiền. ② Em trai tôi vốn bướng bỉnh, nay tuổi đời chồng chất (lớn lên) đã trở thành người tuyệt vời.

① place something on top of something else ② repeating something / ①在东西上放别的东西②事物反复发生 / ① Đặt vật này lên trên vật khác. ② Lặp đi lặp lại sự vật, sự việc.

204 ずらり［と］
副 line up / 一大排，成排的 / hàng dài, trải dài
パーティーの会場(かいじょう)にずらりとごちそうが並(なら)んだ。
Fancy food was lined up at the party room. / 宴会会场内，摆着一长排佳肴。/ Ở hội trường bữa tiệc, thức ăn được bày biện trải dài.

＋ ずらっと in a row / 一长排 / hàng dài

205 主食(しゅしょく)
名 main dish / 主食 / thức ăn chính
日本人(にほんじん)の主食(しゅしょく)は米(こめ)だ。
The staple food for Japanese people is rice. / 日本人的主食是米饭。/ Thức ăn chính của người Nhật là cơm.

206 生(なま)
名 raw / 生的 / sống, tươi sống
この魚(さかな)は新鮮(しんせん)なので、生(なま)で食(た)べられる。
This fish is fresh, so it can be eaten raw. / 这条鱼很新鲜，可以生吃。/ Con cá này còn tươi nên có thể ăn sống.

＋ 生野菜(なまやさい) raw vegetables / 生的蔬菜 / rau sống・生(なま)ビール draft beer / 生啤 / bia tươi

207 なま物(もの)
名 raw food / 生的食物 / đồ sống
夏(なつ)はなま物(もの)が腐(くさ)りやすいので、注意(ちゅうい)する。
Raw food spoils easily in the summer, so we should be careful. / 夏天生的食物容易坏，要注意。/ Mùa hè đồ tươi sống dễ bị hư thối, nên lưu ý.

208 □	特製(とくせい)	私(わたし)の特製(とくせい)ケーキで彼(かれ)の誕生日(たんじょうび)を祝(いわ)う。
名	**special / 特制 / sự đặc chế, món đồ làm đặc biệt**	I will celebrate his birthday with a special cake I made. / 用我特制的蛋糕为他庆祝生日。/ Tôi chúc mừng sinh nhật anh ấy bằng chiếc bánh kem làm đặc biệt.
209 □	粗末な(そまつ)	①最近(さいきん)、粗末(そまつ)な食生活(しょくせいかつ)が続(つづ)いている。 ②親(おや)を粗末(そまつ)にしてはいけない。
ナ形	**miserable, shabby / 简陋，粗糙 / 粗暴，疏忽 / sơ sài, đạm bạc, thờ ơ**	① My diet these days is shabby. ② You should not treat your parents so poorly. / ①我最近一直吃得很简单。②对待父母不能怠慢。/ ① Gần đây, việc ăn uống sơ sài cứ tiếp diễn. ② Không được thờ ơ với bố mẹ.

①the end result and quality is not good②not treating something properly and being careless / ①做工不好，品质不好②不珍惜，得过且过地处理 / ① Độ hoàn thiện, chất lượng không tốt. ② Đối xử hỗn xược, không tôn trọng.

これも覚(おぼ)えよう！ ⑥

接辞(せつじ)：金銭(きんせん)② Affix: Money / 词缀：金钱 / Phụ tố: Tiền bạc

• ～代(だい)

電話代(でんわだい)	phone bill / 电话费 / Tiền điện thoại
部屋代(へやだい)	rent / 房费，房租 / Tiền phòng
電気代(でんきだい)	electricity bill / 电费 / Tiền điện
ガス代(だい)	gas bill / 煤气费 / Tiền ga
バイト代(だい)	paycheck from a part-time job / 打工工资 / Tiền làm thêm
バス代(だい)	bus fare / 车费（公共汽车）/ Tiền xe buýt
電車代(でんしゃだい)	train fare / 车费（电车）/ Tiền xe điện
食事代(しょくじだい)	cost of a meal / 餐饮费 / Tiền ăn
品代(しなだい)	bill for article / 货款 / Tiền hàng

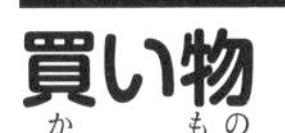

Section 4 買い物（かもの）

Shopping / 购物 / Mua sắm

210 □	購入（こうにゅう）〈する〉	重（おも）たい物（もの）はインターネットで購入（こうにゅう）する。
名	**purchase / 购买，购入 / sự mua**	I purchase heavy things on the Internet. / 重的东西就在网上买。/ Những đồ nặng, tôi mua qua mạng internet.
		⟷ 販売（はんばい）〈する〉
211 □	［お］買（か）い得（どく）	スーパーのお買（か）い得（どく）商品（しょうひん）を毎日（まいにち）チェックしている。
名	**bargain / 划算，特价 / sự mua với giá hời, mua rẻ**	I check for bargain products at the supermarket every day. / 我每天都查看一下超市的特价商品。/ Tôi theo dõi hàng giá rẻ của siêu thị mỗi ngày.
212 □	手頃（てごろ）な	あの店（みせ）には、学生（がくせい）に手頃（てごろ）な値段（ねだん）の物（もの）がたくさんある。
ナ形	**affordable / 适合，称手 / vừa phải, phải chăng**	There are many items at that shop that are affordable for students. / 那家店学生买得起的东西很多。/ Cửa tiệm đó có nhiều đồ giá phải chăng với sinh viên.
213 □	値引（ねび）き〈する〉	デパートの食品（しょくひん）売（う）り場（ば）は夜（よる）8時（じ）になると、値引（ねび）きする。
名	**discount / 打折 / sự giảm giá**	The food floors of department stores offers discounts after 8:00 p.m. / 商场的食品柜台到了晚上 8 点就打折。/ Ở quầy đồ ăn của trung tâm thương mại, cứ đến 8 giờ tối là giảm giá.
		＝ まける
214 □	おまけ〈する〉	①近（ちか）くの八百屋（やおや）で100円（えん）おまけしてくれた。 ②りんごを買（か）ったら、みかんをおまけしてくれた。
名	**extra / 折扣 / 赠品 / sự giảm giá, khuyến mãi**	① The vegetable shop nearby gave me a 100 yen discount. ② The shop gave me an extra orange for purchasing apples. / ①在附近的蔬果店买菜时，老板给我便宜了 100 日元。②买了苹果，店家还送了我橘子。/ ① Tiệm rau gần đây đã giảm 100 yên cho tôi. ② Mua táo thì được khuyến mãi quýt.

☞ ① giving a special discount ② giving away extra products as a service / ①商品优惠②销售某个商品时另外付赠的东西 / ① Bán sản phẩm với giá rẻ hơn một cách đặc biệt. ② Khuyến mãi món khác kèm món hàng.

215 □	返品（へんぴん）〈する〉	ネットの写真（しゃしん）と違（ちが）う商品（しょうひん）が届（とど）いたので、返品（へんぴん）した。
名	**returns / 退货 / sự trả lại hàng**	I returned the product that arrived because it was different from the photo on the Internet. / 收到的商品跟网上照片上的不同，所以我退货了。/ Vì sản phẩm khác với hình trên mạng nên tôi đã trả lại.

216 □ 返金〈する〉 へんきん
商品の代金は返金してもらえたが、手数料を取られた。
（しょうひん　だいきん　へんきん　てすうりょう　と）

名 **repayment / 退钱，退款 / sự hoàn tiền**
The shop returned the money for the product, but they charged me a fee. / 商品的货款是给我退了，但是被扣了手续费。/ Được hoàn tiền mua hàng nhưng bị lấy tiền phí dịch vụ.

217 □ 価格 かかく
二つのスーパーが価格の競争をしている。
（ふた　かかく　きょうそう）

名 **price / 价格 / giá**
The two supermarkets are competing with their prices. / 两家超市在打价格战。/ Hai siêu thị đang cạnh tranh giá cả.

218 □ 高価な こうか
ネットでは高価な物は買わないことにしている。
（こうか　もの　か）

ナ形 **expensive / 高价 / cao giá, đắt tiền**
I do not purchase expensive products on the Internet. / 我一般不在网上买高价商品。/ Tôi quyết định không mua hàng đắt tiền qua mạng.

⟺ 安価な あんか

219 □ 金額 きんがく
この店では買った金額によって、くじ引きができる。
（みせ　か　きんがく　び）

名 **amount of money / 金额 / số tiền**
This shop offers a lottery depending on the amount of purchases you make. / 这家店根据消费金额可以抽奖。/ Tiệm này có rút thăm tùy theo số tiền đã mua.

220 □ 価値 かち
この絵は 20 年後には価値が上がるだろう。
（え　ねんご　かち　あ）

名 **value / 价值 / giá trị**
The price of this drawing will probably rise 20 years from now. / 这幅画 20 年后一定会升值。/ Hẳn là 20 năm sau, giá trị bức tranh này sẽ tăng lên.

➕ 価値観（かちかん） values / 价值观 / giá trị quan

221 □ 品質 ひんしつ
品質のいい物を買うようにしている。
（ひんしつ　もの　か）

名 **quality / 品质 / chất lượng**
I try to buy good quality buy products. / 我尽量买品质好的东西。/ Tôi cố gắng mua đồ chất lượng tốt.

222 □ 消費税 しょうひぜい
この価格には消費税が入っていますか。
（かかく　しょうひぜい　はい）

名 **consumption tax / 消费税 / thuế tiêu thụ**
Does this price include tax? / 这个价格包含消费税了吗？ / Giá này đã có thuế tiêu thụ chưa?

223 □ オークション
ネットオークションでバッグを買ってみた。
（か）

名 **auction / 拍卖 / đấu giá**
I tried purchasing a bag on an Internet auction site. / 试着通过网上的拍卖买了一个包。/ Tôi đã thử mua túi xách qua đấu giá trên mạng.

224 名物（めいぶつ）
名 **specialty / 特产，名产 / đặc sản, sản vật nổi tiếng**

最近（さいきん）は、地方（ちほう）の名物（めいぶつ）がネットで買（か）える。
We can now buy local specialities over the Internet these days. / 最近，网上也能买得到各地的特产。/ Gần đây, đã có thể mua được đặc sản địa phương qua mạng.

➕ 特産（とくさん） local specialty / 特产 / đặc sản・名産（めいさん） specialty / 名产 / đặc sản

225 取（と）り寄（よ）せる
動 **purchase by backorder / 调货，订购，让寄来 / đặt hàng đem đến, gửi đến**

一年（いちねん）に数回（すうかい）、北海道（ほっかいどう）のお菓子（かし）を取（と）り寄（よ）せている。
I purchase desserts from Hokkaido by backorder serveral times a year. / 我每年都订购几次北海道的点心。/ Một năm mấy lần, tôi đặt mua bánh kẹo Hokkaido gửi đến.

➕ [お] 取（と）り寄（よ）せ〈する〉 purchase by backorder / 订购 / đặt hàng

226 扱（あつか）う
動 **handle/treat / 销售 / 对待 / thụ lý, đặt, bán, đối xử, xử lý**

①あの店（みせ）では食品（しょくひん）は扱（あつか）っていない。
②子（こ）どもでも、一人（ひとり）の人間（にんげん）として扱（あつか）うべきだ。
① That shop does not have any food. ② Children should be treated as independent people. / ①那家店不卖食品。②即使是孩子，也应该把他当成是一个独立的人来对待。/ ① Cửa tiệm đó không bán đồ ăn. ② Dù là trẻ em cũng phải đối xử như một người (độc lập).

➕ ①取（と）り扱（あつか）う handle / 经营；对待 / thụ lý, đặt, bán, đối xử, xử lý

👉 ① sell as a product in stores ② take appropriate measures while also taking one's situation or status into consideration / ①作为商品销售②对待某人（站在其立场上，为其考虑）/ ① Bán ở tiệm như là sản phẩm. ② Nghĩ đến vị trí của người đó và đối xử thích hợp.

227 買（か）い換（か）（替（か））える
動 **purchase a replacement / 更新，买新的 / mua mới, mua đổi**

そろそろ車（くるま）を買（か）い換（か）えようと考（かんが）えている。
I am thinking of replacing my car soon. / 我在考虑差不多该换辆车了。/ Tôi đang định chuẩn bị mua đổi xe hơi.

➕ 買（か）い換（か）（替（か））え replacement purchase / 更新，买新的 / sự mua mới, mua đổi

228 売（う）り出（だ）す
動 **sell / 开始出售 / bán, bán ra**

A社（しゃ）から新（あたら）しい車（くるま）が売（う）り出（だ）された。
A new car has been put on sale by Company A. / A公司开始销售新车了。/ Xe hơi mới đã được công ty A bán ra.

➕ 発売（はつばい）〈する〉 on sale / 开始销售，开始贩卖 / sự bắt đầu bán

229 チラシ
名 **flier / 传单 / tờ bướm quảng cáo**

デパートのチラシでバーゲンを知（し）った。
I learned of the bargain through a department store flier. / 我看了百货商场的传单得知现在正在打折。/ Tôi biết chương trình giảm giá nhờ tờ bướm quảng cáo của trung tâm thương mại.

230 切り取る（きとる）
動 cut out / 剪下，撕下 / cắt lấy

支払いのときに、この券を切り取って出すと安くなる。

Present this ticket when paying and you will get a discount. / 撕下这张券，付款时出示能便宜一些。/ Cắt phiếu này đưa ra khi trả tiền sẽ rẻ.

231 パック〈する〉
名 pack/facial treatment / 盒，包 / 面膜 / gói, hộp, đắp (mặt)

①いちごを2パック買った。
②お風呂の後、パックしてから寝る。

① I purchased two packs of strawberries. ② I do facial treatments after taking a bath before I go to sleep. / ①买了两盒草莓。②洗了澡以后，敷个面膜再睡。/ ① Tôi đã mua 2 gói dâu. ② Sau khi tắm, tôi đắp mặt rồi ngủ.

① sell in a single bundle ② a facial skin-care treatment item / ①包装成一体销售的东西②用于护养皮肤的美容用品 / ① Món đồ được gói gọn lại thành một rồi bán. ② Món đồ làm đẹp để chăm sóc da.

232 包装（ほうそう）〈する〉
名 wrapping / 包装 / sự gói

家で使う物は包装を簡単にしてもらう。

I will ask that the products for home-use be wrapped simply. / 自己家用的东西就简单包装。/ Những gì dùng ở nhà thì tôi nhờ gói đơn giản.

233 試食（ししょく）〈する〉
名 tasting / 试吃 / sự ăn thử

デパートで試食してから、お菓子を買った。

I bought the dessert at the department store after tasting it. / 在商场试吃之后买了点心。/ Ở trung tâm thương mại, tôi đã mua bánh sau khi ăn thử.

➕ 試飲（しいん）〈する〉 tasting / 试饮 / sự uống thử

234 試着（しちゃく）〈する〉
名 trial fitting / 试穿 / sự mặc thử

スカートは試着して買わないと心配だ。

I get worried if I don't try on skirts before purchasing them. / 裙子没试穿过的话不敢买。/ Tôi thấy lo lắng nếu mua váy đầm mà không mặc thử.

➕ 試着室（しちゃくしつ） fitting room / 试衣间 / phòng thử đồ

235 わりあい［に］
副 kind of, sort of / 比较 / tương đối, tỉ lệ (so với)

いい物がわりあい安く買えた。

I was able to purchase a good product for a reasonable price. / 以相对便宜的价格买到了好东西。/ Tôi mua được món hàng tốt mà tương đối rẻ.

236 ダブる
動 have two of the same thing / 重复 / trùng, trùng lắp

同じ本をダブって買ってしまった。

I bought the same book twice. / 同一本书买重了。/ Tôi lỡ mua trùng cuốn sách giống nhau.

237 □ 動	よす **quit / 停止 / ngưng, bỏ**	無駄づかいはよしなさい。 Don't waste your money. / 不要乱花钱。/ Hãy bỏ thói tiêu xài hoang phí đi.
238 □ 副	わりと **quite / 比较 / khá là, tương đối**	あの店は広くないが、わりと商品が充実している。 That shop is not that large, but it has a fairly substantial variety of products. / 那家店虽然不大，但商品却还挺丰富。/ Cửa tiệm đó không rộng nhưng hàng hóa khá là đầy đủ.
239 □ 名	実物 **actual product / 实物 / hàng thật, đồ thật**	届いた商品の実物が写真と全く違う。 The actual product that arrived is totally different from the picture. / 实际收到的商品和照片上的完全不同。/ Sản phẩm thật được gửi đến hoàn toàn khác với trong hình.
240 □ 名	粒 **grain of, bead of, sand of / 粒，粒头 / viên, hạt**	粒が大きい真珠は値段が高い。 Pearls of large beads are more expensive. / 颗粒大的珍珠价格很高。/ Trân châu hạt to thì giá cao.
241 □ 名	スペース **space / 空间，区域 / khoảng trống, không gian**	ここは障がい者が駐車するスペースです。 This is parking space for the disabled. / 这里是残障人士停车的区域。/ Đây là khoảng trống để người khuyết tật đậu xe.

Section 5

時を表す言葉
ときあらわことば

Words Expressing Time / 时间 / Từ thể hiện thời gian

242 現在 げんざい
名 **the present / 现在 / hiện tại**

実家を出て、現在は一人暮らしです。
じっか で げんざい ひとりぐ

I left home and am now living on my own. / 我离开了老家，现在一个人生活。/ Tôi rời khỏi nhà bố mẹ ruột và hiện tại sống một mình.

243 過去 かこ
名 **past / 过去 / quá khứ**

過去は忘れて、未来に向かって進もう。
かこ わす みらい む すす

Forget the past and move towards the future. / 忘记过去，迈向未来。/ Hãy quên đi quá khứ, hướng về tương lai mà tiến thôi.

244 年月 ねんげつ
名 **years / 年岁，岁月 / tháng năm, thời gian**

長い年月をかけて、この木はこんなに成長した。
なが ねんげつ き せいちょう

This tree grew so large over the years. / 经过这么多年，这棵树已经长得这么大了。/ Trải qua những tháng năm dài, cái cây này đã trưởng thành như thế này.

245 月日 つきひ
名 **days / 日子，时间 / ngày tháng, thời gian**

月日が経つのは本当に早いものだ。
つきひ た ほんとう はや

The days pass really quickly. / 时间过得真快啊。/ Thời gian trôi qua thật là nhanh.

246 日時 にちじ
名 **time and date / 日期 / ngày giờ**

忘年会の日時はメールでお知らせします。
ぼうねんかい にちじ し

I will notify you about the date and time of the year-end party by e-mail. / 年终联欢会的具体时间会发邮件通知。/ Tôi sẽ thông báo ngày giờ tiệc tất niên bằng e-mail.

➕ 日程 にってい schedule / 日程，日期 / lịch trình

247 今日 こんにち
名 **today / 今天，现在 / hôm nay, ngày nay**

今日の世界には多くの問題がある。
こんにち せかい おお もんだい

There are many problems in today's world. / 当今世界存在着很多问题。/ Thế giới ngày nay có nhiều vấn đề.

248 年代 ねんだい
名 **era/age / 年代，年纪 / những năm, thế hệ**

①これは1980年代に流行したファッションだ。
ねんだい りゅうこう

②彼女と私では年代が全く違う。
かのじょ わたし ねんだい まった ちが

① This is the fashion that was popular in the '80s. ② Her age and mine are completely different. / ①这是二十世纪八十年代流行过的时尚。②她和我完全不是一个年龄层的。/ ① Đây là thời trang thịnh hành vào những năm 1980. ② Cô ấy và tôi, thế hệ hoàn toàn khác nhau.

👉 ① the period of a particular era ② about the same age (20s, 50s etc.) / ①时代中的某个阶段 ②年龄层（"20多岁""50多岁"等）/ ①Khoảng thời gian trong một thời đại. ②Độ tuổi như nhau. ("độ tuổi 20", "độ tuổi 50" v.v.)

249 □	年間(ねんかん) 名 annual / 一年，年间 / trong năm	年間(ねんかん)の訪日観光客(ほうにちかんこうきゃく)が急(きゅう)に増(ふ)えた。 The number of foreigners visiting Japan annually increased suddenly. / 全年访日观光客人数剧增。/ Số khách du lịch thăm Nhật Bản trong năm đã tăng đột ngột.
250 □	年中(ねんじゅう) 名 副 all year round/all year / 一整年 / suốt năm, quanh năm, cả năm	この店(みせ)は年中無休(ねんじゅうむきゅう)だ。(名) 父(ちち)は年中(ねんじゅう)ゴルフばかりしている。(副) This store is open all year. My father plays golf all year round. / 这家店全年开休。父亲一整年光打高尔夫了。/ Cửa tiệm này suốt năm không nghỉ.Bố tôi chơi gôn quanh năm.
251 □	本年(ほんねん) 名 this year / 今年 / năm nay	本年(ほんねん)もよろしくお願(ねが)いします。 I look forward to spending as much time with you this year as last year. / 今年也请多多关照。/ Năm nay cũng xin được giúp đỡ.
252 □	日中(にっちゅう) 名 daytime / 白天 / trong ngày	日中(にっちゅう)は天気(てんき)がよく、暖(あたた)かかった。 The weather was nice and warm. / 白天天气很好，也很暖和。/ Trong ngày thời tiết đẹp và ấm áp.
253 □	夜間(やかん) 名 nighttime / 夜晚 / buổi tối	この辺(あた)りで夜間(やかん)の一人歩(ひとりある)きは危険(きけん)だ。 It's dangerous to walk alone at night around here. / 这附近夜晚一个人走很危险。/ Đi bộ một mình buổi tối ở khu vực này thì nguy hiểm đấy.
254 □	ただ今(いま) 名 副 now/currently / 现在，当前 / bây giờ, câu chào khi về đến	田中(たなか)はただ今(いま)席(せき)を外(はず)しております。(副) Tanaka is not as his desk right now. / 田中现在不在。/ Bây giờ Tanaka đang vắng mặt ạ.
255 □	先(さき)ほど 副 earlier / 刚才 / lúc nãy	先(さき)ほどアメリカ出張(しゅっちょう)から戻(もど)りました。 I just returned from a business trip to the United States. / 我刚从美国出差回来。/ Lúc nãy, tôi đã quay lại từ chuyến đi Mỹ công tác. ⇔ 後(のち)ほど
256 □	近々(ちかぢか) 副 soon / 近期，最近 / sắp tới	近々(ちかぢか)そちらにお邪魔(じゃま)したいと思(おも)います。 I would like to visit you soon. / 近期我想去拜访您一下。/ Sắp tới, tôi định sẽ làm phiền anh / chị.

Section 5

257 □	後日（ごじつ）	詳しいことは後日決めましょう。
名	later date / 日后，将来 / sau này, về sau	Let's decide the details at a later date. / 详情日后再决定吧。/ Những việc chi tiết để sau hãy quyết định.
258 □	やがて	今は小雨だが、やがて雨も風も強くなるだろう。
副	before long / 不久，马上 / chẳng mấy chốc	It's only drizzling now, but it will rain harder later. / 现在虽然是小雨，但过一会风和雨都会大起来吧。/ Bây giờ mưa nhỏ nhưng chẳng mấy chốc cả mưa lẫn gió sẽ mạnh lên không chừng.
259 □	いずれ	いずれ子ども達も自立して、家を出ていく。
副	eventually, some day / 反正，终究 / rồi thì, một ngày nào đó	The children will eventually leave home and be on their own. / 孩子们终究也会独立，然后离开家。/ Rồi thì con cái cũng sẽ tự lập và rời khỏi nhà thôi.
260 □	今後（こんご）	今後の連絡は、新しいアドレスにお願いします。（名）
名 副	hereafter/from now on / 今后 / từ nay về sau, tương lai	Hereafter, please forward correspondence to the new e-mail address. / 今后请用我的新地址联系我。/ Việc liên lạc từ nay về sau, xin vui lòng gửi đến địa chỉ mới.
261 □	すでに	日本に来たとき、すでに桜の季節は終わっていた。
副	already / 已经 / đã từ lâu	The cherry blossom season was already over when we arrived in Japan. / 我来日本的时候，樱花开放的季节已经过了。/ Khi tôi đến Nhật, mùa hoa sakura đã kết thúc từ lâu.
262 □	あらかじめ	会議の予定をあらかじめ教えてください。
副	in advance / 预先，事先 / trước	Please let me know the meeting schedule in advance. / 请事先告知我会议的安排。/ Vui lòng cho biết trước dự định của buổi họp.

＝ 事前に（じぜん）

263 □	従来（じゅうらい）	従来のやり方を、そろそろ変えた方がいい。（名）
名 副	past/up to now / 以往，直到现在 / lâu nay, từ trước đến nay	We should start changing the ways of the past. / 是时候改变一下一直以来的做法了。/ Nên chuẩn bị thay đổi cách làm lâu nay.
264 □	あくる〜	大雪が降った。あくる朝、外は真っ白だった。
連体	next / 第二，下个，次 / tiếp theo, sau đó	It snowed heavily. The next morning, everything was white outside. / 下了一场大雪，第二天早上外面一片雪白。/ Tuyết rơi nhiều. Sáng hôm sau, bên ngoài trắng xóa.

＋ あくる日（ひ） next day / 第二天 / ngày hôm sau

265	一時（いちじ） 名 副 **moment/momentarily / 短时间，一时 / nhất thời, tạm trong thời gian ngắn**	事故（じこ）で一時（いちじ）、電車（でんしゃ）が止（と）まった。（副） The train stopped momentarily due to the accident. / 电车因事故停了一段时间。/ Tàu điện tạm dừng do tai nạn.
		➕ いっとき moment/a while / 一时 / nhất thời, khoảnh khắc
266	一生（いっしょう） 名 副 **all one's life/rest of my life / 一生，一辈子 / cả đời, suốt đời**	一生（いっしょう）のお願（ねが）いです。私（わたし）の話（はなし）を聞（き）いてください。（名） この感謝（かんしゃ）の気持（きも）ちは一生（いっしょう）忘（わす）れません。（副） Please do me the biggest favor ever. Please listen to me.I will never forget this feeling of gratitude. / 这是我此生最大的请求。请听我说。这份感激之情我终生难忘。/ Đây là nguyện vọng cả đời tôi. Hãy vui lòng nghe tôi nói.Tấm lòng biết ơn này cả đời tôi không quên.
267	永遠に（えいえんに） 副 **forever, eternally / 永远 / vĩnh viễn**	この愛（あい）は永遠（えいえん）に続（つづ）く。 Love lasts forever. / 此爱永存。/ Tình yêu này sẽ kéo dài vĩnh viễn.
		➕ 永久（えいきゅう）に forever / 永远，永久 / vĩnh cửu

これも覚えよう！ ❼

接辞：金銭③ Affix: Money / 词缀：金钱 / Phụ tố: Tiền bạc

• ～料

使用料	usage fee, rental fee / 使用费 / Phí sử dụng
保険料	insurance fee / 保险费 / Phí bảo hiểm
授業料	lesson fee / 学费，课时费 / Tiền học
サービス料	service fee / 服务费 / Phí dịch vụ
送料	shipping fee / 运费 / Tiền cước, tiền gửi
手数料	commission, handling fee / 手续费 / Tiền lệ phí, phí thủ tục
入場料	entrance fee / 门票 / Phí vào cổng
レンタル料	rental fee / 租赁费 / Tiền thuê

• ～賃

家賃	rent / 房租 / Tiền thuê nhà
運賃	transportation fare / 交通费，运费 / Tiền vận chuyển
電車賃	train fare / 电车费 / Tiền tàu xe

N2

Chapter 3

At Home / 家庭篇 / Ở nhà

朝（あさ）

Morning / 早晨 / Buổi sáng

268 **夜明け**（よあ）
名 **daybreak / 拂晓，黎明 / ban mai, rạng sáng**

最近、夜明け頃に一度目が覚める。（さいきん　よあ　ごろ　いちどめ　さ）
I wake up once before daybreak these days. / 最近，清晨天亮的时候我会醒一次。/ Gần đây, khoảng rạng sáng là tôi thức dậy 1 lần.

➕ 明け方（あがた） dawn / 拂晓，黎明 / bình minh, rạng sáng

269 **起床〈する〉**（きしょう）
名 **uprise / 起床 / sự thức dậy**

毎朝、6時に起床している。（まいあさ　じ　きしょう）
I wake up at 6:00 a.m. every morning. / 我每天早上 6 点起床。/ Mỗi sáng, tôi thức dậy lúc 6 giờ.

↔ 就寝〈する〉（しゅうしん）　➕ 起床時間（きしょうじかん） time to wake up / 起床时间 / thời gian thức dậy

270 **もたれる**
動 **lean on something/being heavy / 靠，依靠 / 不消化，积食 / dựa vào, nặng (bụng)**

①壁にもたれて、歯をみがく。（かべ　は）
②この料理は胃にもたれる。（りょうり　い）
① I brush my teeth while leaning against the wall. ② This food is heavy on the stomach. / ①靠着墙刷牙。②这道菜不容易消化。/ ① Tôi dựa lưng vào tường và đánh răng. ② Món ăn này nặng bụng.

👉 ① lean against something firm ② a feeling of undigested food in the stomach / ①依靠着某物②吃下去的食物消化不良，积在腹中的感觉 / ① Dựa vào vật gì có thể đỡ được. ② Cảm giác món đã ăn không được tiêu hóa mà còn trong bụng.

271 **フレッシュな**
ナ形 **fresh / 新鲜，清新 / tươi ngon, tươi mát**

毎朝、フレッシュな野菜ジュースを作って飲んでいる。（まいあさ　やさい　つく　の）
I make fresh juice and drink it every morning. / 我每天早上榨新鲜蔬菜汁喝。/ Mỗi sáng, tôi làm nước trái cây tươi để uống.

272 **乳製品**（にゅうせいひん）
名 **dairy product / 乳制品 / sản phẩm làm từ sữa**

朝ご飯は乳製品とサラダだ。（あさ　はん　にゅうせいひん）
Breakfast is dairy products and salad. / 早餐是乳制品和沙拉。/ Cơm sáng là sản phẩm làm từ sữa và rau trộn.

273 **洗い物**（あらもの）
名 **dirty dishes, laundry (for clothes) / 洗东西 / đồ để rửa, việc rửa**

食事が終わったら、洗い物をする。（しょくじ　お　あら　もの）
I wash the dishes after meals. / 吃了饭之后洗碗。/ Sau khi ăn xong, tôi rửa chén bát.

274 **欠かす**（か）
動 **miss / 缺，停止 / thiếu, khuyết, bỏ sót**

毎朝欠かさず、ジョギングをする。（まいあさ　か）
I jog every morning without fail. / 我每天早上都一定要跑步。/ Mỗi sáng tôi không bỏ việc chạy bộ.

275 □ 名 配達〈する〉 はいたつ
delivery / 配送 / sự phát, phân phối

朝、新聞配達のバイトをしている。
I have a part-time job of deliverying newspapers. / 早上兼职配送报纸。/ Buổi sáng, tôi làm thêm công việc phát báo.

➕ 新聞配達 (しんぶんはいたつ) newspaper delivery / 配送报纸 / phát báo

276 □ 名 見出し みだ
headline / 目录，索引 / đầu đề

ネットニュースの見出しをざっと見る。
I browse through the news headlines on the Internet. / 大致扫一眼网络新闻的标题。/ Tôi đọc sơ các đầu đề tin tức trên mạng.

277 □ 副 一切（～ない） いっさい
totally / 完全，一切（都不）/ hoàn toàn (không ~)

私は新聞を一切読まない。
I don't read newspapers at all. / 我完全不看报纸。/ Tôi hoàn toàn không đọc báo.

👉 Also a noun meaning "all" / 也有"所有，全部"意思的名词用法 / Cũng có danh từ với nghĩa "tất cả, toàn bộ"

278 □ 名 合間 あいま
in between / 空闲间隙 / thời gian trống, thời gian rảnh

洗濯の合間にネットでニュースを読む。
I read the news on the Internet in between doing the laundry. / 在洗衣服的间隙上网看新闻。/ Trong lúc giặt đồ, tôi đọc tin tức trên mạng.

279 □ 副 てきぱき［と］〈する〉
swiftly / 利落，爽快 / nhanh chóng, mau lẹ

家事をてきぱきと片付け、出かける準備をする。
I will finish my household chores quickly and prepare to leave. / 麻利地做完家务，准备出门。/ Tôi nhanh chóng làm việc nhà để chuẩn bị đi ra ngoài.

280 □ 名 間 ま
interval, opening, gap, pause / 间隙，时间 / thời gian, khoảng trống

出かけるまでに少し間がある。
There is still some time before I leave. / 离出门还有一点时间。/ Có chút thời gian trống cho đến khi ra ngoài.

281 □ 名 周辺 しゅうへん
surroundings/surrounding area / 周边 / xung quanh, quanh

毎日、公園の周辺を30分歩く。
I walk around the park every day for about 30 minutes. / 我每天在公园周围走30分钟。/ Mỗi sáng tôi đi bộ vòng quanh công viên 30 phút.

282 □ 名 周囲 しゅうい
circumference / 周围 / xung quanh, chu vi

朝ご飯の前に、家の周囲を犬と散歩する。
I walk with the dog around the house before breakfast. / 我早饭前在家附近遛狗。/ Trước bữa sáng, tôi dắt cho đi dạo quanh nhà.

283 □ 副 あと
after, later / 剩下的 / nữa, sau

あと5分でバスが来る。急がなきゃ。
The bus will arrive in five minutes. I have to hurry. / 再过5分钟公共汽车就要来了，得抓紧时间了。/ Còn 5 phút nữa là xe buýt đến. Phải mau lên.

284 □	すれ違う(ちが)	ごみを出し(だ)に行く(い)と、いつも隣(となり)の人(ひと)とすれ違う(ちが)。
動	**pass by one another / 错过，交错 / (đi, gặp) ngược chiều**	I run into my neighbor every time I go to throw away the garbage. / 出去丢垃圾时，总是会和邻居擦肩而过。/ Khi đi đổ rác, tôi luôn gặp người hàng xóm đi ngược chiều lại.
285 □	はう	コンタクトを落(お)として、床(ゆか)の上(うえ)をはって探(さが)した。
動	**crawl / 趴 / bò ra**	I dropped my contact lenses and crawled on the floor to look for them. / 隐形眼镜掉在地上了，趴在地上找。/ Tôi đánh rơi kính sát tròng nên bò ra sàn để tìm.

➕ はいはい〈する〉 crawling / 爬 / bò

286 □	替える(か)	出(で)かける前(まえ)にバッグを替(か)えた。
動	**change / 换，更换 / thay, đổi**	I changed my bag before leaving. / 出门前换了一个包。/ Trước khi đi ra ngoài, tôi đổi túi xách.

➕ 換(か)える switch / 换，交换 / thay, đổi

287 □	整える(ととの)	①服装(ふくそう)を整(ととの)えて、出(で)かける。 ②この病院(びょういん)は最新(さいしん)の設備(せつび)を整(ととの)えている。
動	**straighten, tidy, set / 整理 / 备齐 / chỉnh đốn, trang bị**	① I got dressed up and left. ② This hospital is equipped with cutting-edge facilities. / ①整理好衣服出门。②这家医院配备了最新的设备。/ ① Tôi chỉnh đốn trang phục để đi ra ngoài. ② Bệnh viện này trang bị thiết bị tối tân.

➕ (～が) 整(ととの)う is set / 齐全，齐备 / (~) chỉnh tề, trật tự, đầy đủ

👉 ① to make soemthing look proper ② to be equipped with ~ / ①整齐的状态②备齐，凑齐 / ① Làm để ở tình trạng, trạng thái đàng hoàng. ② Trang bị

288 □	ろくに（～ない）	この頃(ごろ)ろくに寝(ね)ていないので、午前中(ごぜんちゅう)は眠(ねむ)い。
副	**properly / (不能) 很好地 / đầy đủ, tốt**	I haven't been sleeping well recently, so I'm sleepy in the mornings. / 这段时间一直没睡好，上午都很困。/ Thời gian gần đây, do không ngủ đầy đủ nên buổi sáng tôi buồn ngủ.

➕ ろくな（～ない） proper / (没有) 很好的 / đầy đủ, tốt

日課（にっか）

Daily Routine / 每日惯例 / Công việc hàng ngày

289 □ 名	めりはり **modulation / 张驰 / nhịp độ, sự rõ ràng, tách bạch**	日課を決めて、生活にめりはりをつけている。 I have my routine set to lead a modulated life. / 决定好每天必须完成的事情，让生活张弛有度。/ Quyết định công việc hàng ngày để tạo nhịp độ trong cuộc sống.
290 □ 副	何度も（なんど） **many times / 好几次 / bao nhiêu lần**	一日に何度も歯をみがく。 I brush my teeth many times a day. / 一天刷好几次牙。/ Một ngày tôi đánh răng không biết bao nhiêu lần
291 □ 副	ほぼ **almost / 基本上，大致 / hầu như**	ほぼ毎日、彼にSNSでメッセージを送る。 I text him using social network almost every day. / 我基本每天都在社交媒体上给他发信息。/ Hầu như mỗi ngày, tôi đều gửi tin nhắn SNS cho anh ấy.
292 □ 名	寄り道（よりみち）〈する〉 **dropping by / 顺道去 / sự tiện đường, ghé ngang, ghé qua**	帰る途中でスーパーに寄り道する。 I drop by the supermarket on my way home. / 回家的途中，顺道去超市。/ Trên đường về nhà, tôi ghé siêu thị.
293 □ 名	食物（しょくもつ） **food / 食物 / đồ ăn**	食物アレルギーの表示を見ながら買い物をする。 I look at the allergen labels while shopping. / 买东西时看看食物所含的过敏成分提示。/ Tôi vừa xem nhãn hiển thị dị ứng đồ ăn vừa đi chợ.
294 □ 名	換気（かんき）〈する〉 **ventilation / 换气，通风 / sự thông gió**	家に帰ったら、まず窓を開けて換気する。 I open the window first and change the air when I get home. / 回到家先打开窗户通风。/ Sau khi về nhà, trước tiên tôi mở cửa sổ để thông gió.

➕ 換気せん（かんき） ventilator / 排风扇 / quạt thông gió

295 □ 副	いったん **temporarily / 姑且，暂且 / tạm, một chút**	いったん家に帰ってから、食事に出かける。 I will return home once and leave again to eat outside. / 先回一趟家，再出去吃饭。/ Tôi về nhà một chút rồi ra ngoài đi ăn.
296 □ 名	物干し（ものほし） **drying rack / 晒台 / dây, chỗ phơi đồ**	洗濯物を物干しから外して、中にしまう。 I take in the laundry from the drying rack and bring it inside. / 把洗好的衣服从晒台上拿进来。/ Tôi rút đồ giặt từ dây phơi và cất vào trong.

➕ 物干しざお（ものほ） drying pole / 晒衣竿 / sào, mắc phơi đồ

297 □	食卓 しょくたく	ご飯を食べる前に、食卓をきれいにふく。 はん た まえ しょくたく
名	**dinner table / 饭桌，餐桌 / bàn ăn**	I wipe the dinner table clean before eating meals. / 吃饭前把餐桌擦干净。/ Trước khi ăn cơm, tôi lau bàn ăn cho sạch.
298 □	後回し あとまわ	食事を後回しにして、宿題を片付ける。 しょくじ あとまわ しゅくだい かたづ
名	**postpone / 推迟 / sự để sau, hoãn**	I postponed eating to finish my homework. / 先把作业做完再吃饭。/ Việc ăn uống để sau, tôi làm cho xong bài tập.
299 □	削る けず	①寝る時間を削って、受験勉強をしている。 ね じかん けず じゅけんべんきょう ②弟は鉛筆が上手に削れない。 おとうと えんぴつ じょうず けず
動	**cut back/shave / 减少 / 削 / cắt bớt, gọt**	① I cut down on my sleep to study for the entrance exams. ② My little brother can't sharpen his pencil properly. / ①我一直在减少睡眠时间来备考。②弟弟削铅笔削得不好。/ ① Tôi cắt bớt thời gian ngủ để học thi đầu vào. ② Em trai tôi không gọt bút chì giỏi được.

☞ ① delete a portion of something from the whole ② cut out something using a knife / ①去掉全体中的某个部分②用刃器去除表面 / ① Bỏ một phần có trong toàn thể. ② Cắt bỏ bề mặt bằng dao

300 □	かなえる	夢をかなえるために、毎日一生懸命勉強している。 ゆめ まいにちいっしょうけんめいべんきょう
動	**make come true, grant / 实现 / đạt nguyện vọng, mục đích**	I study hard every day to fulfill my dream. / 为了实现梦想，每天拼命努力学习。/ Để đạt được ước mơ, hàng ngày tôi cố gắng học hết sức mình.

➕ (〜が) かなう come true, be granted / 实现 / (~) đạt được

301 □	調節〈する〉 ちょうせつ	エアコンの温度を調節する。 おんど ちょうせつ
名	**save, economise / 调节 / sự điều chỉnh**	Save on the use of air conditioning by adjusting the temperature. / 调节空调的温度。/ Tôi điều chỉnh nhiệt độ của máy điều hòa.

➕ コントロール〈する〉 control / 控制 / sự điều khiển

302 □	ゆったり[と]〈する〉	①家に帰ったら、ゆったりした気分で過ごす。 いえ かえ きぶん す ②このパジャマはゆったりしている。
副	**relaxed/loose / 闲适 / 宽松 / thong thả, chậm rãi, rộng rãi**	① I relax when I get home. ② These pajamas are loose. / ①悠闲地度过回家以后的时间。②这件睡衣很宽松。/ ① Về đến nhà rồi thì cảm giác thong thả. ② Bộ đồ bộ này rộng rãi.

☞ ① having a lot of time and relaxing ② clothes that are not tight-fitting / ①时间上有余地，很悠闲②衣服等不贴身 / ① Có thời gian dư dả, chậm rãi. ② Áo quần v.v. không chật chội

303 □	売り買い〈する〉 う か	毎日ネットのオークションで売り買いしている。 まいにち う か
名	**sell and buy / 买卖，做生意 / sự mua bán**	I sell and buy things on the Internet auction site every day. / 每天通过网络拍卖来买卖东西。/ Hàng ngày tôi mua bán đấu giá trên mạng.

304 □ 動	思い浮かべる (おも う) recollect / 想起，忆起 / nhớ ra, hồi tưởng	その日の出来事を思い浮かべて、日記を書く。 I think back on the day's events and write in my diary. / 我回想起那天发生的事，并写成日记。/ Tôi hồi tưởng những sự kiện trong ngày và viết nhật ký.
		➕ (～が) 思い浮かぶ recall (it) / 想起 / (~) hiện ra, hồi tưởng, nảy ra
305 □ 名	独り言 (ひと ごと) talking to oneself / 自言自语 / sự nói một mình	テレビを見ながら、つい独り言を言ってしまう。 I have a habit of talking to myself while watching TV. / 我总是会边看电视边不禁自言自语起来。/ Tôi vừa xem tivi vừa nói chuyện một mình.
306 □ 名	風呂場 (ふろば) bathroom / 浴室 / phòng tắm	毎晩、風呂場で歌を歌っている。 I sing in the bathroom every night. / 我每天晚上都在浴室里唱歌。/Mỗi tối tôi đều hát trong phòng tắm.
307 □ 動	かぐ smell / 嗅，闻 / ngửi, hít	ハーブの匂いをかいで、リラックスする。 The smell of herbs makes me relax. / 闻着药草的清香，放松一下。/ Tôi hít mùi thảo mộc và thư giãn.
308 □ 名	寝つき (ね) quality of sleep / 睡眠，入睡 / sự ngủ, dỗ giấc ngủ	寝つきが悪いので、寝るときに薬を飲む。 I usually don't sleep well, so I take medicine before I go to sleep. / 我睡眠不好，所以睡前要吃药。/ Vì khó ngủ nên tôi uống thuốc khi ngủ.
		↔ 寝起き (ねお)
309 □ 名	用心〈する〉 (ようじん) caution / 小心，警惕 / sự chú ý, cẩn thận	一人暮らしなので、いつも用心している。 I live alone so I'm always cautious. / 我因为是一个人生活，所以总是小心警惕。/ Vì tôi sống một mình nên luôn cẩn thận.
		➕ 用心深い (ようじんぶか) wary / 小心谨慎 / chú ý kỹ
310 □ 名	メッセージ message / 消息，留言 / thông điệp, tin nhắn	寝る前に、国の家族からメッセージが届いた。 A message from my family back home arrived before I went to sleep. / 睡前收到了国内的家人发来的信息。/ Trước khi ngủ, có tin nhắn từ gia đình bên nước gửi đến.

Section 3

料理(りょうり)

Cooking / 料理 / Nấu ăn

311	炊事(すいじ)〈する〉	家事(かじ)の中(なか)で炊事(すいじ)が一番(いちばん)好(す)きだ。
名	**cooking / 做饭，烹饪 / nấu ăn, việc bếp núc**	I like cooking the best among all of my household chores. / 家务活里我最喜欢做饭。/ Tôi thích nấu ăn nhất trong các công việc nhà.
312	献立(こんだて)	毎日(まいにち)献立(こんだて)を考(かんが)えるのは大変(たいへん)だ。
名	**menu / 食谱 / thực đơn**	Thinking about the menu everyday is hard work. / 每天考虑吃什么是一件很麻烦的事。/ Hàng ngày, suy nghĩ thực đơn thật vất vả.
313	リクエスト〈する〉	家族(かぞく)のリクエストで、メニューを決(き)める。
名	**request / 要求 / yêu cầu**	I decided on the menu based on the family's request. / 根据家人的要求决定吃什么。/ Tôi quyết định thực đơn theo yêu cầu của gia đình.
314	流(なが)し	流(なが)しで野菜(やさい)を洗(あら)う。
名	**sink / 洗碗池 / bồn rửa**	I wash the vegetables in the sink. / 在洗碗池里洗菜 / Tôi rửa rau ở bồn rửa.

➕ 流(なが)し台(だい) sink / 洗碗池 / bồn rửa

315	ちぎる	キャベツをちぎって、鍋(なべ)に入(い)れる。
動	**tear / 撕成小块，撕碎 / xé**	I tear the cabbage by hand and put it in the pot. / 把卷心菜撕碎了放进锅里。/ Tôi xé bắp cải cho vào nồi.
316	冷(さ)ます	材料(ざいりょう)を冷(さ)ましてから、野菜(やさい)で包(つつ)む。
動	**cool down / 冷却，弄凉 / làm lạnh, làm nguội**	I cool the ingredients and wrap them in vegetables. / 把食材晾凉后用蔬菜包起来。/ Sau khi làm nguội nguyên liệu thì cuốn bằng rau.
317	煮(に)える	魚(さかな)が煮(に)えて、いい匂(にお)いがする。
動	**boil / 煮熟，煮烂 / nấu chín**	The fish has been boiled and smells good. / 鱼煮熟了，香气四溢。/ Cá chín rồi tỏa mùi thơm.
318	味付(あじつ)け〈する〉	我(わ)が家(や)の味付(あじつ)けは、ちょっと薄(うす)い。
名	**seasoning / 调味 / sự nêm nếm**	Our family uses light seasoning. / 我家做菜口味比较清淡。/ Nhà tôi nêm nếm thức ăn hơi lạt một chút.

319 □ 動	薄める うす dilute / 稀释，弄淡 / làm cho lợt, nhạt, loãng	味が少し濃いので、水で薄めた。 あじ すこ こ みず うす It tasted a little strong, so I diluted it with water. / 味道有点太重了，加了点水稀释了一下。/ Vị hơi đậm nên tôi đã làm nhạt bằng nước.
320 □ 名	甘み あま sweetness / 甜味，甜度 / vị ngọt	ケーキをよく作るが、甘みは控えている。 つく あま ひか I often bake cakes, but I don't make them too sweet. / 我经常做蛋糕，不过会注意控制甜度。/ Tôi thường làm bánh kem nhưng giảm vị ngọt.
321 □ 名	工夫〈する〉 く ふう device, solving ingeniously / 工夫 / công phu, bỏ công	安い材料でも、工夫すれば、おいしくなる。 やす ざいりょう く ふう Inexpensive ingredents will be tasty if you think out ways to cook them. / 即使是便宜的食材，只要动脑筋去烹调，也能做得好吃。/ Dù nguyên liệu rẻ tiền nhưng nếu bỏ công một chút sẽ trở nên ngon.
322 □ 動	添える そ garnish / 添加 / thêm vào, đính kèm	ハンバーグに、にんじんを添える。 そ Garnish the hamburger with carrots. / 在汉堡肉饼里加上胡萝卜。/Tôi thêm cà rốt vào thịt hăm-bơ-gơ
323 □ 動	挟む はさ insert, interpose / 夹入，插入 / kẹp	パンに、いろいろな材料を挟む。 ざいりょう はさ I sandwich different ingredients in the bread. / 往面包里夹各种食材。/ Tôi kẹp nhiều loại nguyên liệu vào bánh mì.
324 □ 名	加減〈する〉 か げん degree, just the right amount of / 程度 / mức độ, sự điều chỉnh, tăng giảm	この料理は調味料の加減が、ちょうどいい。 りょうり ちょうみりょう か げん The flavoring of this dish is just right. / 这个菜调味调得刚刚好。/ Món ăn này mức độ gia vị vừa ngon.
		➕ 味加減 あじかげん seasoning / 味道的好坏 / sự điều chỉnh vị, vị・ 塩加減 しおかげん saltiness / 咸淡 / sự điều chỉnh muối, mức độ muối
325 □ 動	固まる かた harden, become firm / 凝固 / đông cứng	冷蔵庫に入れておいたゼリーが固まった。 れいぞうこ い かた The jelly in the refrigerator is firm now. / 放在冰箱里的果冻凝固了。/ Món rau câu cất trong tủ lạnh đã đông lại.
		➕ (～を) 固める かた make firm / 使…凝固 / làm (~) đông cứng
326 □ 動	なめる lick / 舔，尝 / liếm, nếm	ソースを作りながら、少しなめて、味を確かめる。 つく すこ あじ たし I taste the sauce to check it while cooking it. / 做酱汁的时候，舔一点尝尝味道。/ Tôi vừa làm nước sốt vừa nếm một chút để kiểm tra vị.

327 □	臭い (くさ)	魚が焦げて、台所が臭い。(さかな こ だいどころ くさ)
イ形	smell / 臭，有异味 / hôi, thối	Fish was burned, so the kitchen smells. / 鱼烧焦了，厨房里弥漫着一股味道。/ Cá bị cháy nên nhà bếp bị hôi.
328 □	冷める (さ)	スープが冷めたので、食事の前に温めた。(さ しょくじ まえ あたた)
動	become cold / 变冷，凉 / nguội	The soup got cold, so I warmed it up before the meal. / 汤凉了，所以吃饭前热了一下。/ Vì phần canh đã nguội nên trước bữa ăn tôi đã hâm nóng lại.
329 □	余分な (よぶん)	少し余分にカレーを作って、冷凍しておく。(すこ よぶん つく れいとう)
ナ形	extra / 多余，剩余 / phần dư, thừa	I will cook extra curry and freeze the leftovers. / 多做了一些咖喱，冷冻保存起来。/ Tôi làm cà ri hơi dư một chút và để đông.
330 □	容器 (ようき)	この容器は料理を冷凍するのに便利だ。(ようき りょうり れいとう べんり)
名	container / 容器 / đồ đựng	This container is convenient for freezing dishes. / 用这个容器冷冻保存饭菜很方便。/ Đồ đựng này tiện cho việc làm đông thức ăn.

➕ 入れ物 (いれもの) container / 容器，装东西的 / đồ đựng, hộp đựng

331 □	賞味期限 (しょうみきげん)	この缶詰は賞味期限が切れている。(かんづめ しょうみきげん き)
名	expiration date / 保质期（最佳食用期）/ thời hạn sử dụng tốt nhất	This canned food is past its expiration date. / 这个罐头过保质期了。/ Món đồ hộp này đã hết hạn sử dụng tốt nhất.

➕ 消費期限 (しょうひきげん) expiry date / 保质期（安全食用的期限）/ thời hạn sử dụng

332 □	手作り (てづく)	姉の手作りケーキはプロのような味だ。(あね てづく あじ)
名	handmade / 手工制作 / tự tay làm, làm thủ công	My sister's handmade cake tastes like it was made by a professional. / 姐姐手工制作的蛋糕味道堪比专业人士。/ Bánh kem em gái tự làm có mùi vị như của đầu bếp chuyên nghiệp làm.

➕ 手料理 (てりょうり) handmade dishes / 亲手做的菜 / món ăn tự tay làm・
お手製 (てせい) handmade / 自制 / đồ làm bằng tay

333 □	もてなす	先日、手料理でお客様をもてなした。(せんじつ てりょうり きゃくさま)
動	entertain / 招待，请客 / đối đãi, tiếp đãi	The other day, I entertained my guests with homemade dishes. / 前几天自己做菜招待了客人。/ Hôm trước, tôi đãi khách bằng đồ ăn tự nấu.

➕ [お] もてなし hospitality, entertainment / 款待，招待 / sự tiếp đãi (ân cần, chu đáo, thành tâm)

家事（かじ）

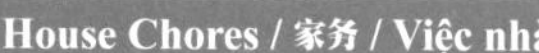

House Chores / 家务 / Việc nhà

334 □ もれる

動 **leak / 漏 / 泄露 / rò rỉ, bị lộ**

①洗濯機のホースが壊れて、水がもれてしまった。
②いつの間にか、私の秘密がもれてしまった。

① The washing machine hose broke and water leaked. ② Before I knew it, my secret had leaked out. / ①洗衣机的软管坏了，漏水了。②不知道什么时候，我的秘密被泄露出去了。/ ① Ống nước máy giặt bị hư, nước bị rò rỉ. ② Tự lúc nào, bí mật của tôi đã bị tiết lộ.

➕ (～を) もらす to leak / 漏出，泄露 / làm rò rỉ, tiết lộ

👉 ① water or sound leaks out ② someone's secret is revealed to others / ①水或声音漏出去②秘密等被人知道 / ① Nước, âm thanh xuất hiện ra bên ngoài. ② Bí mật v.v. truyền đến người khác.

335 □ ごちゃごちゃ〈な / する〉

ナ形 副 **messy/messily / 乱七八糟 / lộn xộn, xáo trộn, lung tung**

彼の机の引き出しの中は、いつもごちゃごちゃだ。（ナ形）

The inside of his desk drawer is always messy. / 他的书桌抽屉里总是乱七八糟的。/ Bên trong hộc bàn của anh ấy, lúc nào cũng lộn xộn.

👉 also an adverb meaning "griping about it" / 也有"不停唠叨"意思的副词用法 / Cũng có phó từ với ý nghĩa "nói ồn ào nhặng xị"

336 □ 元（もと）

名 **original, origin / 原来，原状 / 开始，起初 / vốn, cũ, ban đầu**

①使ったものは元の場所に戻してください。
②元は、ここも海だった。

① Please return what you used to where it belongs. ② This place used to be the sea. / ①请把用过的东西放回原处。②起初这里也是海。/ ① Vui lòng trả lại những gì đã dùng về chỗ cũ. ② Ban đầu nơi đây cũng là biển.

➕ もともと originally / 原来 / vốn, cũ, ban đầu

👉 ① basics ② origin / ①基本，原本②开始，起源 / ① Căn bản ② Bắt đầu

337 □ 自動的な（じどうてき）

ナ形 **automatically / 自动的 / tự động**

この掃除機は自動的に部屋をきれいにしてくれる。

This vacuum cleaner automatically cleans the room. / 这个吸尘器会自动地把房间打扫干净。/ Cái máy hút bụi này tự động làm sạch phòng.

338 □ さっと

副 **quickly / 突然，瞬间 / nhanh chóng**

人が来たので、洗濯物をさっと隠した。

I quickly hid the laundry because someone came over. / 有人来了，我赶紧把要洗的东西藏了起来。/ Do có người đến nên tôi nhanh chóng giấu đồ giặt đi.

339 □ 名	清掃〈する〉 せいそう	年末の掃除は清掃会社に依頼する。 ねんまつ　そうじ　せいそうがいしゃ　いらい
	clean-up / 清扫 / sự dọn dẹp, làm vệ sinh	I will ask the cleaning company to do the year-end cleaning. / 年底的大扫除委托清洁公司来做。/ Việc dọn dẹp cuối năm sẽ nhờ công ty vệ sinh.

➕ 掃き掃除（はきそうじ） sweeping / 扫除 / quét dọn・拭き掃除（ふきそうじ） wiping / 擦干净 / lau chùi

340 □ 動	取り除く と　のぞ	掃除機のごみを取り除く。 そうじき　と　のぞ
	remove / 去掉，除掉 / bỏ, lọc bỏ, loại trừ	I remove the dirt in the vacuum cleaner. / 把吸尘器里的垃圾倒掉。/ Tôi loại bỏ rác trong máy hút bụi.
341 □ 名	素材 そざい	洗濯の前に服の素材をチェックする。 せんたく　まえ　ふく　そざい
	material / 材料，面料 / chất liệu	I check the material of the clothes before washing them. / 洗衣服之前，确认一下面料。/ Trước khi giặt, tôi kiểm tra chất liệu quần áo.
342 □ 名	表示〈する〉 ひょうじ	この服には素材の表示がない。 ふく　そざい　ひょうじ
	label / 标示 / nhãn biểu thị, thể hiện	There is no label showing what material these clothes are. / 这件衣服上没有标示出面料。/ Cái áo này không có nhãn biểu thị chất liệu.

➕ 表示価格（ひょうじかかく） list price / 标价 / bảng giá

343 □ 名	分類〈する〉 ぶんるい	表示を見ながら、洗濯物を分類する。 ひょうじ　み　せんたくもの　ぶんるい
	category / 分类 / phân loại	I categorize the laundry by checking the label. / 一边看标示一边把衣服分类。/ Tôi vừa xem nhãn vừa phân loại đồ giặt.
344 □ 動	すすぐ	①洗濯機で洗濯物をすすぐ。 せんたくき　せんたくもの ②歯医者に行く前に、口をすすぐ。 はいしゃ　い　まえ　くち
	rinse / 漂洗，洗涮 / 漱，洗漱 / súc, xả	① I rinse the laundry in the washing machine. ② Rinse your mouth before going to the dentist. / ①用洗衣机漂洗衣物。②去看牙医之前先漱口。/ ① Tôi xả đồ giặt bằng máy giặt. ② Trước khi đi nha sỹ, tôi súc miệng

☞ ① rinsing with soap and water ② clean inside the mouth by gargling, etc. / ①用水把肥皂清干净②通过漱口清洁口腔 / ① Rửa trôi xà bông bằng nước. ② Làm sạch miệng bằng cách súc

345 □ 名	ネット	これはネットに入れて洗った方がいい。 い　あら　ほう
	net / 网 / lưới, túi lưới	This needs to be put in a net before washing. / 这个最好放在洗衣网里清洗。/ Cái này nên cho vào túi lưới để giặt thì tốt hơn.

➕ あみ net / 网 / lưới

346 吸収〈する〉 きゅうしゅう
名 **absorption / 吸收 / sự hấp thụ, sự hút**

このタオルは水分(すいぶん)をよく吸収する(きゅうしゅう)が、乾き(かわ)やすい。
This towel absorbs water well and dries fast. / 这种毛巾吸水性很强，却很容易晾干。/ Cái khăn này hút nước tốt nhưng dễ khô.

➕ 吸い込む(すいこ) absorb / 吸收 / hút vào, hấp thụ vào・吸収力(きゅうしゅうりょく) absorbive power / 吸收力 / sức hấp thụ, sức hút vào

347 泥 どろ
名 **mud / 泥 / bùn**

靴(くつ)についた泥(どろ)が、なかなか落ち(お)ない。
The dirt on the shoes doesn't come off easily. / 鞋子上沾到的泥怎么也弄不掉。/ Bùn dính ở giày mãi không rớt ra.

➕ 泥(どろ)だらけ covered in mud / 满是泥 / toàn bùn・泥(どろ)んこ muddy / 满是泥 / bùn đất

348 知恵 ちえ
名 **wisdom / 智慧 / trí tuệ**

家事(かじ)には昔(むかし)の人(ひと)の知恵(ちえ)が生き(い)ている。
In daily household chores live the wisdom of our forebearers. / 家务活中凝结着前人的智慧。/ Trí tuệ của người xưa tồn tại trong việc nhà.

349 可燃ごみ かねん
名 **combustible waste / 可燃垃圾 / rác đốt được**

ここでは火曜日(かようび)と金曜日(きんようび)が可燃(かねん)ごみの日(ひ)だ。
Tuesdays and Fridays are when combustibles is collected around here. / 这片区域周二和周五收可燃垃圾。/ Ở đây, thứ ba và thứ sáu là ngày rác đốt được.

⟷ 不燃(ふねん)ごみ

350 資源ごみ しげん
名 **recyclable waste / 资源垃圾, 可回收垃圾 / rác tái sinh**

資源(しげん)ごみはリサイクルできるごみのことだ。
Recyclable waste means garbage that can be recycled. / 资源垃圾是指可回收再生的垃圾。/ Rác tái sinh là rác có thể tái sử dụng.

➕ アルミ缶(かん) aluminum can / 易拉罐，铝罐 / lon

351 粗大ごみ そだい
名 **oversized trash / 大件垃圾 / rác cỡ lớn**

粗大(そだい)ごみを捨て(す)るときは有料(ゆうりょう)だ。
You need to pay a charge to throw away oversized waste. / 扔大件垃圾是需要付费的。/ Khi vứt rác cỡ lớn thì tốn tiền.

352 古新聞 ふるしんぶん
名 **old newspapers / 旧报纸 / báo cũ**

古新聞(ふるしんぶん)が、たくさんたまっている。
Old newspapers are piling up. / 积攒了很多旧报纸。/ Báo cũ dồn đọng nhiều quá.

➕ 古雑誌(ふるざっし) old magazines / 旧杂志 / tạp chí cũ

353	分別〈する〉（ぶんべつ） 名 sort / 分开，分类 / sự phân loại, phân chia	日本（にほん）は、ごみの分別（ぶんべつ）がとても大変（たいへん）だ。 Sorting the garbage is a lot of work in Japan. / 在日本，垃圾分类很繁琐。/ Nhật Bản rất khó khăn việc phân loại rác.
354	ごみ袋（ぶくろ） 名 garbage bag / 垃圾袋 / bao rác, túi rác	スーパーでごみ袋（ぶくろ）を買（か）う。 I buy garbage bags at the supermarket. / 在超市买垃圾袋。/ Tôi mua bao rác ở siêu thị.
355	生臭い（なまぐさ） イ形 smell fishy / 腥，腥臭 / mùi hôi tanh	台所（だいどころ）のごみが生臭（なまぐさ）い。 The garbage in the kitchen smells fishy. / 厨房的垃圾很臭。/ Rác ở nhà bếp hôi tanh.
356	大小（だいしょう） 名 large and small / 大小 / lớn nhỏ	テレビは大小（だいしょう）に関係（かんけい）なく、ごみに出（だ）せない。 Televisions cannot be disposed of as normal waste, regardless of their size. / 电视机无论大小都不能作为垃圾直接扔掉。/ Tivi dù lớn hay nhỏ cũng đều không thể bỏ rác.
357	しゃぶる 動 suck on / 含，吮 / mút, ngậm, bú	この子（こ）はまだ指（ゆび）をしゃぶっている。 This child still sucks on his finger. / 这个孩子还在吮手指头。/ Đứa bé này vẫn còn bú tay.
358	おむつ 名 diaper / 尿布 / tã	そろそろおむつを取（と）り替（か）える時間（じかん）だ。 It's about time to change the diaper. / 差不多到该换尿布的时间了。/ Sắp sửa đến giờ thay tã rồi.
		＋ 紙（かみ）おむつ paper diaper / 纸尿裤 / tã giấy
359	双子（ふたご） 名 twins / 双胞胎 / trẻ sinh đôi	双子（ふたご）が生（う）まれると、育児（いくじ）も2倍（ばい）大変（たいへん）だ。 When you have twins, raising them is twice as difficult. / 生了双胞胎，育儿也加倍辛苦。/ Khi sinh đôi thì việc nuôi con vất vả gấp 2 lần.
360	衣類（いるい） 名 clothes / 衣服，衣裳 / quần áo, y phục	暑（あつ）くなってきたので、夏（なつ）の衣類（いるい）を出（だ）そう。 I will bring out the summer closes because it is getting hotter. / 天气热起来了，把夏天的衣服拿出来好了。/ Trời đã trở nên nóng, hãy lấy quần áo mùa hè ra thôi.
361	入れ替える（いれかえる） 動 interchange, replace / 更换 / thay đổi	年（ねん）に2回（かい）、夏物（なつもの）と冬物（ふゆもの）を入（い）れ替（か）える。 I switch winter clothes and summer clothes twice a year. / 每年更换两次夏季衣物和冬季衣物。/ Một năm 2 lần, tôi thay đổi đồ mùa hè và đồ mùa đông.

362 □ 狂う（くる）

①最近忙しすぎて、気が狂いそうだ。
②時間が足りなくなって、予定が狂った。

動 **go crazy/fall apart / 发疯，疯狂 / 混乱，打乱 / điên khùng, loạn xạ, trục trặc, xáo trộn**

① I'm so busy these days, I feel like I'm going crazy. ② My schedule fell apart because I ran out of time. / ①最近太忙，感觉快疯了。②时间不够了，计划都打乱了。/ ① Gần đây bận quá đến sắp phát khùng. ② Thời gian không đủ nên dự định bị xáo trộn hết.

① losing mental stability ② unforseeable changes in schedule / ①失去精神的稳定性②计划打乱 / ① Đánh mất sự ổn định tinh thần. ② Dự định bị lệch

これも覚えよう！ 8

接辞：用途① Affix: Usage / 词缀：用途 / Phụ tố: Ứng dụng

• ～用（～のための）

家庭用（かていよう）	for family use / 家用 / Dùng cho (dành cho) gia đình
自宅用（じたくよう）	for home use / 自己用 / Dùng cho (dành cho) nhà riêng
外出用（がいしゅつよう）	for outside use / 外出用 / Dùng (dành) khi ra ngoài
婦人用（ふじんよう）	for ladies / 妇女用，女性用 / Dùng cho (dành cho) phụ nữ, quý bà
女性用（じょせいよう）	for women / 女用 / Dùng cho (dành cho) nữ giới
男性用（だんせいよう）	for men / 男用 / Dùng cho (dành cho) nam giới
大人用（おとなよう）	for adults / 成人用 / Dùng cho (dành cho) người lớn
子供用（こどもよう）	for children / 儿童用 / Dùng cho (dành cho) trẻ em
公用（こうよう）	for official use / 公用 / Dùng vào việc công
私用（しよう）	for private use / 私用 / Dùng vào việc tư

Section 5

引っ越し

Moving / 搬家 / Chuyển nhà

363 □	処分〈する〉	①壊れたコピー機を処分した。②学校の規則を破ったので、処分を受けた。
名	**dispose/penalized / 处理 / 处分 / sự bỏ đi, xử lý, giải quyết, xử phạt**	① I got rid of the broken copy machine. ② I was punished because I broke the school rules. / ①把坏掉的复印机处理掉了。②因为违反了学校的规定，受到了处分。/ ① Tôi đã bỏ cái máy photo bị hư đi. ② Vì vi phạm kỷ luật nhà trường nên tôi chịu xử phạt.

① throw away something unnecessary ② punish someone who broke the rules / ①丢掉不要的东西②处罚违反规定的人 / ① Vứt những thứ không cần thiết. ② Phạt những người vi phạm luật lệ v.v.

364 □	不用品	不用品はリサイクルショップに売ろう。
名	**useless things / 闲置，不用的东西 / đồ dùng không cần thiết**	Let's sell all of the stuff we don't need at a recycle shop / 把闲置物品都卖到旧货商店去吧。/ Hãy bán các đồ dùng không cần thiết cho cửa hàng tái chế (tiệm ve chai).
365 □	はがす	ポスターを壁からきれいにはがす。
動	**peel / 剥下来，撕下 / gỡ ra**	Peel the poster cleanly off from the wall. / 从墙上把海报干净地撕下来。/ Tôi đã gỡ tấm áp phích ra khỏi tường sạch sẽ.
366 □	束	本は束にして、ひもでしばる。
名	**bundle / 捆 / bó**	Bundle the books and tie them with a string. / 把书叠成摞，用绳子捆扎起来。/ Sách thì bó lại và cột bằng dây.

➕ 花束 flower bouquet / 花束 / bó hoa・札束 wad of bills / 成捆的纸币 / xấp tiền

367 □	しばる	荷物のひもを、きちんとしばって運ぶ。
動	**tie / 捆，绑 / trói, bó, buộc**	Tie the luggage with a string firmly and carry it. / 把行李用绳子认真地捆好搬运。/ Tôi buộc dây hành lý lại thật chặt và khiêng đi.

↔ ほどく ➕ 結ぶ tie / 扎，系 / buộc, cột

368 □	段ボール	本を段ボールに入れて、トラックに積む。
名	**carton / 硬纸板，纸板箱 / thùng các-tông, thùng giấy**	Put the books in the box and load it onto the truck. / 把书装在纸板箱里再堆到货车上。/ Tôi cho sách vào thùng các-tông và chất lên xe tải.
369 □	ガムテープ	段ボールのふたをガムテープで留める。
名	**packing tape / 胶带 / băng keo vải**	Close the lid of the carton using packing tape. / 把纸箱的上盖用胶带封起来。/ Tôi đóng nắp thùng các-tông bằng băng keo vải.

370 □ 動	押し込む（おこ） push in / 塞入 / nhấn vào, ấn vào, nhét vào	段ボールに洋服を押し込んだ。（だん ようふく お こ） I pushed the clothes into the cardboard box. / 把衣服塞进了纸板箱里。/ Tôi đã nhét áo quần vào thùng các-tông
371 □ 名	リスト list / 名单 / danh sách	引っ越しのときに、することをリストに書く。（ひ こ か） Write a to-do list when moving. / 搬家的时候，把要做的事情列成清单。/ Khi chuyển nhà, viết danh sách những việc cần làm

➕ リストアップ〈する〉 draw up a list / 列出，列表 / sự lên danh sách

372 □ 動	引っ掛かる（ひ か） get stuck/tricked / 卡住 / 中计，受骗 / mắc phải, vướng	①机の脚が引っ掛かって、部屋に入らない。（つくえ あし ひ か へ や はい） ②あんな話に引っ掛かってしまうなんて。（はなし ひ か） ① The desk cannot get into the room because its legs get stuck. ② I can't believe I was tricked by such a story. / ①桌子脚卡住了，搬不进屋。②真没想到竟然会被那种话给骗到。/ ① Chân bàn bị vướng nên không vào phòng được. ② Không ngờ lại vướng phải chuyện như thế.

➕（～を）引っ掛ける（ひ か） hook / 挂，骗 / treo, móc

👉 ① unable to move something because it is caught on something else ② be tricked / ①被什么东西卡住不能动②被骗 / ① Bị mắc vào vật khác, không nhúc nhích. ② Bị lừa

373 □ 動	持ち上げる（も あ） lift / 抬起来，拿起来 / cầm lên, nâng lên	ベッドを持ち上げて、掃除機をかける。（も あ そうじ き） Lift the bed to vacuum the floor. / 把床抬起来吸尘。/ Tôi nâng giường lên để hút bụi.
374 □ 動	担ぐ（かつ） carry / 担，扛 / vác, nâng	隣のアパートに引っ越したので、荷物は担いで運んだ。（となり ひ こ にもつ かつ はこ） I moved to the apartment next door so I hand-carried the luggage over. / 因为搬到了隔壁的公寓，所以行李是自己扛着搬过去的。/ Vì đã chuyển nhà sang căn hộ bên cạnh nên tôi vác hành lý chuyển đi.
375 □ 動	くたびれる get tired/worn out / 累，疲劳 / 用旧 / mệt nhoài, kiệt sức, tả tơi	①くたびれたので、少し休もう。（すこ やす） ②このコートは10年着たので、くたびれている。（ねん き） ① I'm tired, so let's rest. ② I wore this coat for 10 years, so it is worn out. / ①累坏了，休息一下吧。②这件大衣穿了10年了，已经穿旧了。/ ① Đã mệt nhoài rồi, hãy nghỉ ngơi chút nào. ② Tôi mặc cái áo khoác này 10 năm rồi nên nó đã tả tơi.

👉 ① physically or mentally fatigued ② the shape of something is lost because it has been used for a long time / ①身心疲惫②东西用久了之后变形了 / ① Cơ thể và tâm hồn đều rất mệt. ② Tình trạng món đồ sử dụng lâu năm thay đổi cả hình dáng.

376 □ 名 **すき間(ま)**

家具(かぐ)のすき間(ま)にたまったほこりを掃(は)く。

gap, crack / 间隙，缝隙 / khoảng trống

Sweep the dust that has built up between the furniture. / 打扫家具缝隙里积下的灰尘。/ Tôi lau bụi phủ ở các khoảng trống giữa đồ gia dụng.

377 □ 名 **中身(なかみ)**

段(だん)ボールから中身(なかみ)を出(だ)して、引(ひ)き出(だ)しに入(い)れる。

inside / 内容，里面装的东西 / bên trong

Take the items out of the cardboard box and put them in the drawer. / 把纸箱里的东西拿出来放进抽屉里。/ Tôi lấy đồ bên trong thùng các-tông ra cho vào ngăn kéo.

also written 中味 / 也写作"中味" / Cũng viết là " 中味 "

378 □ 副 **さっさと〈する〉**

さっさと荷物(にもつ)を片付(かたづ)けて、のんびりしたい。

quickly / 迅速地 / mau chóng

I want to clean up the luggage quickly and rest. / 想赶紧把行李整理好，然后好好休息。/ Tôi muốn mau chóng dọn dẹp hành lý rồi thong thả nghỉ ngơi.

379 □ 動 **つるす**

クローゼットに服(ふく)をつるす。

hang / 挂，吊 / treo

Hang the dress in the closet. / 把衣服挂进衣橱里。/ Tôi treo quần áo vào tủ.

＋ つる suspend / 悬挂，吊 / treo

380 □ 副 **まさに**

①この部屋(へや)は駅(えき)が近(ちか)いし家賃(やちん)も安(やす)い。まさに理想的(りそうてき)だ。

②まさに家(いえ)を出(で)ようとしていたとき、地震(じしん)が起(お)きた。

truly / 实在，真正 / 正当 / đúng là, chính xác, đúng lúc

① This room is trully ideal because it's near the station and the rent is inexpensive. ② Just when I was about the leave the house, the earthquake hit. / ①这个房间离车站近，房租也便宜，条件真是非常理想。②正当我要离开家的时候，突然地震了。/ ① Căn phòng này tiền thuê vừa rẻ vừa gần nhà ga. Đúng là lý tưởng. ② Đúng lúc định rời khỏi nhà thì động đất xảy ra.

① without doubt, truly ② just, just at that moment / ①无疑，真的②刚好，正当此时 / ① Không sai, thật sự là ② Đúng ngay lúc đó

381 □ 名 **居心地(いごこち)**

今度(こんど)の部屋(へや)は、とても居心地(いごこち)がいい。

comfortableness / 心情，感觉 / ở cảm thấy thoải mái, dễ chịu

The room I'm in now is very comfortable. / 这次的房间，住起来非常舒适。/ Căn phòng lần này cảm giác ở rất dễ chịu.

＋ 座(すわ)り心地(ごこち) comfortableness when sitting / 坐着的感觉 / ngồi thấy thoải mái, dễ chịu・
乗(の)り心地(ごこち) comfortableness when riding / 乘坐的感觉 / đi (xe, tàu) thoải mái, dễ chịu・
着心地(きごこち) comfortableness when wearing / 穿着的感觉 / mặc thấy thoải mái, dễ chịu

382 一変（いっぺん）〈する〉

名 completely changed / 完全改变 / hoàn toàn thay đổi

日本（にほん）で暮（く）らし始（はじ）めた日（ひ）から、生活（せいかつ）が一変（いっぺん）した。

My life changed drastically from the day I started living in Japan. / 从开始在日本生活的那一天起，一切都改变了。/ Từ ngày bắt đầu sống ở Nhật, cuộc sống đã hoàn toàn thay đổi.

383 アンテナ

名 antenna / 天线 / 搜寻信息的能力 / ăng-ten

①テレビのアンテナが古（ふる）かったので、取（と）り替（か）えた。
②彼女（かのじょ）は好奇心旺盛（こうきしんおうせい）で、いつもアンテナを張（は）っている。

① I changed the TV antenna because it was old. ② She is very curious and always stays alert. / ①电视机的天线很旧了，所以换了个新的。②她的好奇心很旺盛，随时留意收集着各种信息。/ ① Ăng-ten tivi đã cũ nên tôi thay. ② Cô ấy cực kỳ hiếu kỳ nên lúc nào cũng sẵn sàng nghe ngóng.

① a device to catch radio waves ② the ability to seek information and catch it / ①接受信号的装置②搜寻信息及获取情报的能力 / ① Thiết bị bắt sóng điện. ② Năng lực tìm kiếm, tiếp nhận thông tin

384 いっそ

副 rather, preferably / 干脆，索性 / thà vậy, thà rằng

また海（うみ）に行（い）ったの？ いっそ沖縄（おきなわ）で暮（く）らしたら？

You went to the sea again? Wouldn't you rather just move to Okinawa? / 你又去海边了吗？要不干脆去冲绳生活得了。/ Lại đi biển nữa à? Vậy thà sống ở Okinawa luôn đi?

これも覚（おぼ）えよう！ ❾

接辞（せつじ）：用途（ようと）② Affix: Usage / 词缀：用途 / Phụ tố: Ứng dụng

• ～向（む）き（～に適（てき）している）

子供向き（こどもむき）	for children / 适合儿童 / Phù hợp với trẻ em
高齢者向き（こうれいしゃむき）	for the elderly / 适合高龄人群 / Phù hợp với người lớn tuổi
老人向き（ろうじんむき）	for the aged / 适合老人 / Phù hợp với người già
独身向き（どくしんむき）	for single people / 适合单身人士 / Phù hợp với người độc thân
単身者向き（たんしんしゃむき）	for single people / 适合独自生活的人 / Phù hợp với người một mình

これも覚えよう！ ⑩

接辞：用途③ Affix: Usage / 词缀：用途 / Phụ tố: Ứng dụng

• **～向け（～を対象にした）**

子供向け	for children / 面向儿童 / Dành cho (hướng đến) trẻ em
若者向け	for the young / 面向年轻人 / Dành cho (hướng đến) giới trẻ
学生向け	for students / 面向学生 / Dành cho (hướng đến) sinh viên, học sinh
女性向け	for women / 面向女性 / Dành cho (hướng đến) nữ giới
男性向け	for men / 面向男性 / Dành cho (hướng đến) nam giới
主婦向け	for housewives / 面向家庭主妇 / Dành cho (hướng đến) các bà nội trợ
ＯＬ向け	for working women / 面向 OL，面向职业女性 / Dành cho (hướng đến) các nữ nhân viên văn phòng
国内向け	for domestic / 面向国内 / Dành cho (hướng đến) trong nước
外国人向け	for foreigners / 面向外国人 / Dành cho (hướng đến) người nước ngoài
海外向け	for overseas / 面向国外 / Dành cho (hướng đến) hải ngoại

N2

Chapter 4

Town / 城市篇 / Phố xá

Section 1

町（まち）

Town / 城市 / Phố xá

385 □ 名	街（まち） town / 街道 / phố, thị trấn, khu phố	午後（ごご）から街（まち）にショッピングに出（で）かけた。 I left in the afternoon to go shopping in town. / 下午外出上街购物了。/ Từ buổi chiều, tôi ra phố mua sắm.
386 □ 名	都市（とし） city / 城市 / thành phố, đô thị	この町（まち）は人口（じんこう）も増（ふ）えて、立派（りっぱ）な都市（とし）になった。 The town turned into a major city as the population increased. / 这个地方的人口也逐渐增长，成了一座气派的城市。/ Thành phố này dân số cũng tăng lên, trở thành một thành phố tuyệt vời.

➕ 大都市（だいとし） large city / 大都市 / thành phố lớn, đô thị lớn・地方都市（ちほうとし） local city / 地方城市 / thành phố địa phương・都会（とかい） urban city / 都市 / đô hội, thị thành

387 □ 名	下町（したまち） downtown / 庶民区，平民区 / khu phố chợ, phố cổ	私（わたし）は東京（とうきょう）の下町（したまち）生（う）まれだ。 I was raised in downtown Tokyo. / 我出生在东京的平民区。/ Tôi sinh ra ở khu phố cổ Tokyo.
388 □ 名	土地（とち） land / 土地 / đất, đất đai	東京（とうきょう）は土地（とち）の値段（ねだん）がとても高（たか）い。 Land prices in Tokyo are very expensive. / 东京的地价很高。/ Giá đất ở Tokyo rất đắt.
389 □ 名	活気（かっき） liveliness / 生动，活力 / sức sống, hoạt bát	若者（わかもの）が多（おお）い町（まち）は活気（かっき）がある。 Towns that have lot of young people are lively. / 年轻人多的地方很有活力。/ Thành phố có nhiều người trẻ thì có sức sống.
390 □ 名	人通り（ひとどお） pedestrian traffic / 人流量 / người đi đường	商店街（しょうてんがい）は人通（ひとどお）りが多（おお）くて、にぎやかだ。 This shopping street sees a lot of people go by and is very lively. / 商业街的人流量很大，十分热闹。/ Phố mua bán thì đông người qua lại, nhộn nhịp.
391 □ 動	絶（た）える die off / 消失，断绝 / hết, ngưng	電車（でんしゃ）が出発（しゅっぱつ）すると、駅前（えきまえ）の人通（ひとどお）りが絶（た）えた。 No one passed by the station front once the train left. / 电车一发车，车站前就没什么行人了。/ Khi tàu điện xuất phát, người đi qua lại trước ga cũng hết hẳn.
392 □ 名	坂（さか） hill / 坡道 / dốc	ここは坂（さか）の多（おお）い町（まち）として知（し）られている。 This town is known for having many hills. / 这个地方因坡道很多而闻名。/ Nơi đây được biết như là thành phố có nhiều dốc.

393 □ 名 辺り (あた)
around / 附近，一带 / chung quanh, quanh
この辺り(あた)は公園(こうえん)が多(おお)く、散歩(さんぽ)にぴったりだ。
There are a lot of parks around, so it is perfect for going on walks. / 这一带有很多公园，很适合散步。/ Chung quanh đây có nhiều công viên, rất hợp với việc đi dạo.

394 □ 名 付近 (ふきん)
nearby / 附近 / khu vực lân cận, gần
公園(こうえん)の付近(ふきん)に桜(さくら)が咲(さ)いている。
The cherry blossoms are blooming around the park. / 公园附近盛开着樱花。/ Khu vực gần công viên, hoa sakura đang nở.

395 □ 名 住宅 (じゅうたく)
house / 住宅 / nhà ở
この辺り(あた)は高級(こうきゅう)な住宅(じゅうたく)が多(おお)い。
There are many luxurious houses around here. / 这一带有很多高级住宅。/ Khu vực này có nhiều nhà ở cao cấp.

➕ 住(す)まい residence / 居所，住房 / nơi sinh sống, nhà ở・住宅街(じゅうたくがい) residential area / 住宅区 / khu nhà ở, khu dân cư sinh sống

396 □ 名 地区 (ちく)
district / 地区 / khu vực
ここは学校(がっこう)や幼稚園(ようちえん)が多(おお)い地区(ちく)だ。
There are many schools and kindergartens in this district. / 这个地区有很多学校和幼儿园。/ Đây là khu vực nhiều trường học và mẫu giáo.

397 □ 名 エリア
area / 区域 / vùng, khu vực
公園(こうえん)の中(なか)に入(はい)ってはいけないエリアがある。
There is a restricted area in the park. / 公园内有个禁止入内的区域。/ Trong công viên có khu vực không được vào.

➕ 区域(くいき) area / 区域 / khu vực・地帯(ちたい) zone / 地带 / vùng, vành đai

398 □ 名 中間 (ちゅうかん)
half-way, middle / 之间，中途 / khoảng giữa, giữa
家(いえ)と駅(えき)の中間(ちゅうかん)に、おしゃれなカフェがある。
There is a fancy café located half-way between the house and station. / 家和车站之间有一家很高级的咖啡店。/ Giữa nhà và nhà ga có quán cà phê sành điệu.

399 □ 名 境 (さかい)
border / 边界，交界 / ranh giới
隣(となり)の町(まち)との境(さかい)に川(かわ)が流(なが)れている。
There is a river running along the border to the neighboring town. / 在和相邻城镇的交界处流淌着一条河。/ Ở đường ranh giới với thành phố bên cạnh có dòng sông chảy qua.

400 □ 名 ナ形 斜め〈な〉 (なな)
diagonal/diagonally / 倾斜 / xéo, chéo
郵便局(ゆうびんきょく)の斜(なな)め前(まえ)に新(あたら)しいコンビニができた。(名)
There is a new convenience store diagonally in front of the post office. / 邮局的斜前方新开了一家便利店。/ Xéo phía trước bưu điện có cửa hàng tiện lợi mới.

➕ 斜(なな)め後(うし)ろ diagonally behind / 斜后方 / xéo phía sau, chéo phía sau

401 □ **抽選〈する〉**
ちゅうせん
名 **drawing / 抽签，抽奖 / sự bốc thăm**

商店街の抽選で温泉旅行が当たった。
しょうてんがい　ちゅうせん　おんせんりょこう　あ

I won a a hot springs vacation at a lottery organized by the shopping street. / 在商店街的抽奖活动中中奖了，奖品是温泉旅行。/ Tôi trúng chuyến du lịch suối nước nóng nhờ bốc thăm ở phố mua bán.

➕ くじ引き lottery / 抽签 / sự bốc thăm
び

402 □ **避難〈する〉**
ひ なん
名 **evacuate / 避难 / sự lánh nạn**

地震のときは、近くの公園に避難する。
じ しん　ちか　こうえん　ひ なん

In the event of an earthquake, evacuate to the nearby park. / 发生地震时去附近的公园避难。/ Khi có động đất, lánh nạn ở công viên gần đó.

➕ 避難場所 evacuation area / 避难场所 / nơi lánh nạn
ひ なん ば しょ

403 □ **訓練〈する〉**
くんれん
名 **drill / 训练 / sự huấn luyện, tập huấn**

この町では一年に一回、避難訓練を行う。
まち　いちねん　いっかい　ひ なん くんれん　おこな

This town conducts evacuation drills once a year. / 这座城镇一年会举行一次避难演习。/ Ở thành phố này, 1 năm 1 lần, tổ chức tập huấn lánh nạn.

404 □ **見回る**
み まわ
動 **patrol / 巡逻，巡视 / nhìn quanh, theo dõi**

毎晩パトカーが住宅地を見回っている。
まいばん　じゅうたく ち　み まわ

The police car patrols the residential area every night. / 每天晚上警车都会在住宅区巡逻。/ Mỗi tối, xe cảnh sát theo dõi quanh khu nhà ở.

➕ 見回り patrol / 巡逻，巡视 / sự nhìn quanh
み まわ

405 □ **築く**
きず
動 **build / 修建，建立 / xây dựng**

ここでは住民同士がいい関係を築いている。
じゅうみんどう し　かんけい　きず

The residents have a good relationship with each other here. / 这里的居民之间构建了良好的关系。/ Ở đây cư dân với nhau xây dựng được mối quan hệ tốt đẹp.

406 □ **見当**
けんとう
名 **guess / 估计，推断 / sự dự đoán, tiên đoán**

この町が20年後にどうなっているか、見当がつかない。
まち　ねん ご　けんとう

I have no idea what this town will be like 20 years from now. / 这座城镇20年之后会怎么样，无法预料。/ Không thể đoán được thành phố này 20 năm sau sẽ ra sao.

407 □ **落書き〈する〉**
らく が
名 **sketching, graffiti / 涂鸦，乱涂乱画 / sự viết, vẽ bậy**

近所で何軒かの家が壁に落書きされた。
きんじょ　なんげん　いえ　かべ　らく が

The walls of some of the houses in this neighborhood were scribbled with graffiti. / 附近有几栋房子的墙壁被画上了涂鸦。/ Có mấy nhà hàng xóm bị viết bậy trên tường.

408 □ 強化〈する〉

名 **strengthen / 强化 / sự đẩy mạnh**

最近犯罪が多いので、住民が見回りを強化している。

The residents are reinforcing their patrol because of the recent increase in crime. / 最近犯罪行为频发，所以居民们加强了安全巡视。/ Gần đây do có nhiều tội phạm nên cư dân đẩy mạnh việc theo dõi.

これも覚えよう！ ⑪

接辞：とき① Affix: Time / 词缀：时间 / Phụ tố: Thời gian

• **今～**

今世紀	this century / 本世纪 / Thế kỷ này
今年度	this fiscal year / 本年度 / Năm tài khóa này
今学期	this school term / 本学期 / Học kỳ này
今大会	this tournament / 本次大会，本届大赛 / Đại hội này

• **現～**

現時点	at this point / 当前 / Thời điểm hiện tại
現段階	at this stage / 现阶段 / Giai đoạn hiện tại
現住所	current address / 现住址 / Địa chỉ hiện tại
現政権	current government / 现政权 / Chính quyền hiện tại
現物	actual article / 实物 / Hiện vật
現品	actual goods / 现货 / Hàng hiện có, hàng hiện đang trưng bày

Section 2

役所（やくしょ）

City Office / 政府机关 / Ủy ban (văn phòng Nhà nước)

409 **自治体**（じちたい） 名
municipality / 自治团体 / tổ chức tự trị, tự quản

日本（にほん）には都道府県（とどうふけん）、市町村（しちょうそん）などの自治体（じちたい）がある。
In Japan, there are municipalities like prefectures, towns, cities and villages. / 日本有都、道、府、县、市、镇、村等自治体。/ Ở Nhật có các tổ chức tự quản ở các đơn vị hành chính thủ đô, phủ, tỉnh, thành phố, thị xã, làng v.v.

410 **知事**（ちじ） 名
governor / 首长，知事 / người đứng đầu tỉnh, tỉnh trưởng

新（あたら）しい知事（ちじ）が福祉（ふくし）を充実（じゅうじつ）させた。
The new governor worked to reinforce welfare programs. / 新任知事完善了社会福利制度。/ Tỉnh trưởng mới đã cho củng cố phúc lợi.

➕ 市長（しちょう） city mayor / 市长 / người đứng đầu thành phố, thị trưởng・町長（ちょうちょう） town mayor / 镇长 / người đứng đầu thị trấn

411 **応える**（こたえる） 動
respond / 响应，回应 / trả lời, đáp lại

今度（こんど）の知事（ちじ）は住民（じゅうみん）の期待（きたい）に応（こた）えるだろう。
The new governor will likely respond to the expectations of the residents. / 这次当选的知事应该能够满足市民们的期待了吧。 / Liệu tỉnh trưởng lần này có thể đáp lại kỳ vọng của người dân không nhỉ.

412 **住民**（じゅうみん） 名
residents / 居民，住民 / người dân, dân cư

新（あたら）しい施設（しせつ）ができて、住民（じゅうみん）の生活（せいかつ）が変（か）わった。
A new facility was built, and the lives of the residents changed. / 新设施建成后，居民们的生活也发生了改变。/ Có cơ sở mới, đời sống người dân đã thay đổi.

413 **身分証明書**（みぶんしょうめいしょ） 名
identification / 身份证 / giấy chứng minh, thẻ căn cước

図書館（としょかん）でカードを作（つく）る際（さい）は、身分証明書（みぶんしょうめいしょ）が必要（ひつよう）だ。
You need identification to create a membership card at the library. / 在图书馆办书卡时，需要身份证。/ Khi làm thẻ ở thư viện, cần có giấy chứng minh nhân thân.

414 **生年月日**（せいねんがっぴ） 名
birth date / 出生日期 / ngày tháng năm sinh

ここに生年月日（せいねんがっぴ）を書（か）いてください。
Please write your date of birth here. / 请在此处写上出生日期。/ Vui lòng viết ngày tháng năm sinh ở đây.

415 **署名〈する〉**（しょめい） 名
signature / 署名，签名 / sự ký tên, chữ ký

こちらに、ご署名（しょめい）をお願（ねが）いいたします。
Please sign here. / 请在此签名。/ Vui lòng ký tên ở đây.

➕ サイン〈する〉 signature / 签名，签字 / sự ký tên, chữ ký

416 修正〈する〉(しゅうせい)
名 correction, fix / 修改 / sự chỉnh sửa, sửa

住所が間違っているので、修正してください。
The address is wrong so, please correct it. / 地址写错了，请修改一下。/ Vui lòng sửa lại do địa chỉ bị sai.

➕ 修正テープ(しゅうせい) correction tape / 修正带 / keo xóa, bút xóa (dạng keo)

417 年金(ねんきん)
名 pension / 养老金 / lương hưu, tiền trợ cấp về hưu

国民は国に年金保険料を納めている。
The citizens pay pension premiums to the nation. / 国民向国家缴纳养老金。/ Người dân đóng tiền bảo hiểm lương hưu cho Nhà nước.

418 施設(しせつ)
名 facility / 设施 / cơ sở, địa điểm

市の新しい施設が、もうすぐできる。
The new city facility will be completed soon. / 市属的新设施马上就要建成了。/ Cơ sở mới của thành phố sắp hoàn thành rồi.

➕ 介護施設(かいごしせつ) nursing facility / 护理机构 / cơ sở điều dưỡng

419 ロッカー
名 locker / (带锁的) 储物柜 / tủ có khóa, tủ cất đồ

市のプールには無料で使えるロッカーがある。
The city pool has lockers that can be used for free. / 市属的游泳馆有能免费使用的储物柜。/ Hồ bơi của thành phố có tủ cất đồ có thể sử dụng miễn phí.

➕ コインロッカー coin locker (paid locker) / 投币储物柜 / tủ có khóa dùng tiền xu

420 建築〈する〉(けんちく)
名 construction / 建造 / kiến trúc

5年後に新しい区役所の建築が予定されている。
A new ward office is set to be built five years from now. / 5年后将建造新的区政府大楼。/ Kiến trúc mới của ủy ban quận được dự định vào 5 năm sau.

➕ 木造建築(もくぞうけんちく) wooden construction / 木造建筑 / kiến trúc bằng gỗ・建築家(けんちくか) architect / 建筑师 / kiến trúc sư

421 リニューアル〈する〉
名 renovation / 翻新，改装 / sự đổi mới, làm mới

市民ホールがリニューアルされた。
The city hall was rennovated. / 市民活动中心进行了翻新。/ Hội trường nhân dân thành phố đã được đổi mới.

422 近づける(ちか)
動 get close / 靠近 / cho (~) đến gần

ここは危ないので、子どもを近づけないでください。
It is dangerous here, so don't let the children go near. / 这里很危险，不要让孩子靠近。/ Ở đây nguy hiểm nên đừng cho trẻ đến gần.

➕ (～が) 近づく(ちか) (~ is) getting close / 接近，靠近 / (~) đến gần

423 福祉（ふくし）
名 **welfare / 福利，福祉 / phúc lợi**

この町（まち）は福祉（ふくし）が充実（じゅうじつ）している。
This town has good welfare programs. / 这座城镇的社会福利制度很完善。/ Thành phố này phúc lợi rất đầy đủ.

424 年度（ねんど）
名 **fiscal year / 年度 / năm tài khóa**

4月（がつ）から新（あたら）しい年度（ねんど）が始（はじ）まる。
The new fiscal year starts in April. / 4 月是新年度的开始。/ Từ tháng 4, năm tài khóa mới bắt đầu.

➕ 年度末（ねんどまつ） end of a fiscal year / 年度末 / cuối năm tài khóa

425 交替（こうたい）〈する〉
名 **altered / 轮流，交替 / sự thay phiên, đổi phiên**

市役所（しやくしょ）の福祉（ふくし）の担当者（たんとうしゃ）が交替（こうたい）した。
The welfare official at the city office has changed. / 市政府的福祉负责人换了。/ Người phụ trách phúc lợi của ủy ban thành phố đã thay đổi.

☞ Can also be written as "交代する" / 也写作"交代する" / Cũng viết là "交代する"

426 収集（しゅうしゅう）〈する〉
名 **collection / 收集，回收 / sự thu gom, thu thập**

ごみ収集（しゅうしゅう）のルールを町（まち）のホームページで調（しら）べる。
Check the town's webpage for the rules on garbage disposal. / 在市区的官网上查一下垃圾回收的规则。/ Tôi tìm hiểu quy định thu gom rác qua trang chủ của thành phố.

➕ ごみ収集車（しゅうしゅうしゃ） garbage collecting truck / 垃圾回收车 / xe rác

427 配布（はいふ）〈する〉
名 **handout / 配发 / sự phân phối, phân phát**

区役所（くやくしょ）はごみ出（だ）しのルールのパンフレットを配布（はいふ）している。
The ward office hands out pamphlets outlining the rules of garbage disposal. / 区政府在分发印有倒垃圾规则的宣传册。/ Ủy ban quận phân phát tập hướng dẫn quy định đổ rác.

➕ 配付（はいふ）する hand out / 配发，分发 / phân phối

☞ 配付 means to pass out things like exams / 写作"配付"时指分发教材等 là phát bài kiểm tra v.v.

428 処理（しょり）〈する〉
名 **manage / 处理 / sự xử lý**

自治体（じちたい）がこの地域（ちいき）のごみを処理（しょり）している。
The municipality handles this area's garbage. / 这个地区的垃圾由自治体负责处理。/ Tổ chức tự quản xử lý rác của khu vực này.

429 需要（じゅよう）
名 **demand / 需求 / nhu cầu**

自治体（じちたい）は老人（ろうじん）ホームの需要（じゅよう）に応（こた）えられない。
The municipality cannot respond to the demand for nursung homes. / 自治团体的养老院供不应求。/ Tổ chức tự quản không thể đáp ứng nhu cầu của viện dưỡng lão.

430 □ 名	提供〈する〉(ていきょう) **provide / 提供 / sự cung cấp**	役所(やくしょ)は生活(せいかつ)に必要(ひつよう)な情報(じょうほう)を提供(ていきょう)している。 The city office provides information necessary for living here. / 政府机关向人们提供了生活必须的信息。/ Ủy ban cung cấp thông tin cần thiết cho đời sống.
431 □ 名	用途(ようと) **usage / 用途 / sự sử dụng**	役所(やくしょ)では用途(ようと)のわからない支出(ししゅつ)は認(みと)められない。 The city office does not acknowledge expenses whose usage is unclear. / 政府机关不承认用途不明的支出。/ Ở ủy ban, không thể chấp nhận việc chi tiêu không rõ mục đích sử dụng.

これも覚(おぼ)えよう！ ⑫

接辞(せつじ)：とき② Affix: Time / 词缀：时间 / Phụ tố: Thời gian

• 新(しん)〜

新学期(しんがっき)	new school term / 新学期 / Học kỳ mới
新入学(しんにゅうがく)	entrance into a new school / 新入学 / Vào năm học mới
新入生(しんにゅうせい)	new students / 新生 / Học sinh, sinh viên mới (thường chỉ lớp đầu cấp)
新体制(しんたいせい)	new system / 新体制 / Thể chế, chế độ mới
新記録(しんきろく)	new record / 新记录 / Kỷ lục mới
新世界(しんせかい)	new world / 新世界 / Thế giới mới
新体操(しんたいそう)	rhythmic gymnastics / 艺术体操 / Thể dục nghệ thuật
新天地(しんてんち)	new world, new field of activity / 新天地 / Vùng đất mới, lĩnh vực mới
新生児(しんせいじ)	newborn / 新生儿 / Trẻ sơ sinh

Section 3
ふるさと

Hometown / 故乡 / Quê hương

432 □	故郷 (こきょう)	故郷の母から荷物が届いた。(こきょう・はは・にもつ・とど)
名	**hometown / 故乡，老家 / quê hương, quê nhà**	A package from my mother back home arrived. / 我收到了母亲从老家寄来的东西、/ Bưu kiện được gửi đến từ mẹ tôi ở quê nhà.
433 □	地元 (じもと)	①帰省して、地元の友達と会うのが楽しみだ。(きせい・じもと・ともだち・あ・たの) ②食料品は地元のスーパーで買う。(しょくりょうひん・じもと・か)
名	**hometown/local area / 本地，当地 / 家附近 / địa phương, bản địa, bản xứ**	① I am looking forward to going back home and meeting my friends from my hometown. ② I purchased food from the local supermarket. / ①回老家，跟当地的朋友们见面非常令人期待。②食材就在家附近的超市买。/ ① Tôi mong về quê gặp bạn bè bản xứ. ② Tôi mua thực phẩm ở siêu thị địa phương.

👉 ① a place one is affiliated with ② a place where one is living / ①与自己有关系的地方②自己住的地方 / ① Nơi có mối quan hệ ② Nơi bản thân đang sống

434 □	離れる (はな)	①ふるさとを離れて、もう10年になる。(はな・ねん) ②駅と商店街は、かなり離れている。(えき・しょうてんがい・はな)
動	**leave/far apart / 离开 / 距离远 / rời xa, cách xa**	① It's been 10 years since I left my hometown. ② The station and the shopping street is quite far apart. / ①离开家乡已经快10年了。②车站和商店街离得挺远的。/ ① Tôi rời quê hương cũng đã 10 năm. ② Nhà ga và phố mua bán cách nhau khá xa.

👉 ① moving from one place to another that is far away ② having space or an opening in between / ①从某地去另一个地方②有间距，有距离 / ① Đi xa từ nơi này đến nơi khác ② Có khoảng cách. Có cự ly

435 □	つかむ	①日本でチャンスをつかんで、親に家を買いたい。(にほん・おや・いえ・か) ②バスで隣にいた赤ちゃんが、私の腕をつかんだ。(となり・あか・わたし・うで)
動	**grasp/grab / 抓住，获得 / 抓住，揪住 / nắm bắt, nắm**	① I want to succeed in Japan and buy a house for my parents. ② The baby next to me on the bus grabbed my arm. / ①我想在日本抓住机会，然后给父母买房。②在公共汽车上旁边的宝宝抓住了我的手臂。/ ① Tôi muốn nắm bắt cơ hội ở Nhật và mua nhà cho bố mẹ. ② Đứa bé cạnh tôi trên xe buýt nắm lấy cánh tôi.

👉 ① make something one's possession completely ② hold in the hand firmly / ①完全成为自己的东西②用手握紧 / ① Làm cái gì đó thành của mình trọn vẹn. ② Nắm chặt bằng tay

436 □	帰省〈する〉(きせい)	夏休みと年末の年2回は帰省する。(なつやす・ねんまつ・ねん・かい・きせい)
名	**returning home / 回家乡 / sự về quê**	I return to my hometown twice a year, during summer vacation and at the end of the year. / 我每年回两次老家，分别在暑假和年末。/ Một năm tôi về quê 2 lần, kỳ nghỉ hè và cuối năm.

437 アクセス〈する〉

①この地域は東京からのアクセスが悪い。
②市のホームページにアクセスする。

名 access/access / 交通 / 接上，访问（网页）/ đường đi, truy cập, tiếp cận

① Access to Tokyo from this area is not convenient. ② Access the city's webpage. / ①这个地区到东京的交通不方便。②访问市政府的官方网站。/ ① Đường đi từ Tokyo đến khu vực này không tiện. ② Tôi truy cập vào trang chủ của thành phố.

① going to one's destination using some form of transportation ② connecting to the Internet / ①乘坐交通工具去目的地②联网 / ① Dùng phương tiện giao thông để đến đích. ② Kết nối mạng internet

438 改善〈する〉

子どもやお年寄りのために、町の交通が改善された。

名 improvement / 改善 / sự cải thiện, làm cho tốt lên

The city traffic has been improved for the children and elderly. / 为了儿童和老人，改善了城镇交通。/ Giao thông thành phố được cải thiện vì trẻ em và người già.

➕ 改良〈する〉 improvement / 改良 / sự cải thiện, làm cho tốt lên

439 行事

私の国には、いろいろな行事がある。

名 event / 仪式，活动 / sự kiện

There are many events in my country. / 我国有很多传统活动。/ Ở đất nước tôi có nhiều sự kiện khác nhau.

440 はるか〈な〉

この地方の祭りははるか昔から続いている。（副）

ナ形 副 distant/far away / 远远 / xa, xa xôi

This local festival has been continuously held since ancient times. / 这个地方的庙会活动从很久以前一直延续至今。/ Lễ hội địa phương này kế tục từ xa xưa.

441 誇り

自分のふるさとを誇りに思っている。

名 pride / 荣耀，骄傲 / sự tự hào

I am proud of my hometown. / 我为自己的故乡而感到自豪。/ Tôi tự hào về quê hương của mình.

➕ 誇る proud / 夸耀 / tự hào

442 載る

新聞に私の国の記事が載っていて、うれしかった。

動 run, be posted in/on something / 刊载 / đăng, đăng tải

I was happy to see an article about my country in the newspaper. / 报纸山刊载了有关我们国家的报道，我很高兴。/ Trên báo có đăng phóng sự về nước của tôi, tôi rất vui.

➕ （～を）載せる run / 刊登 / cho đăng (~)

443 宣伝〈する〉

ふるさとの良さを、もっと宣伝したい。

名 advertisement / 宣传 / sự quảng cáo, tuyên truyền

I want to advertise the good things about my hometown more. / 我想更多地宣传我的家乡有多好。/ Tôi muốn quảng cáo sự tốt đẹp của quê hương hơn nữa.

444 □ 名	作成〈する〉 さくせい draft, making / 制作 / sự soạn thảo, tạo, làm	国の文化を紹介するポスターを作成した。 A poster introducing the country's culture was drafted / 我制作了介绍我国文化的海报。/ Tôi làm áp phích giới thiệu văn hóa đất nước.
445 □ 動	見慣れる みなれる be familiar with, get used to seeing / 看惯 / nhìn quen, quen thuộc	国に帰ると、見慣れた景色が変わっていた。 When I returned to my home country, the familiar scenery had all changed. / 回国后，原本看惯了的景色都改变了。/ Khi về nước, những cảnh sắc quen thuộc đã thay đổi.

➕ 聞き慣れる get used to hearing / 听惯 / nghe quen

446 □ 名	近郊 きんこう suburb / 近郊 / ngoại ô	実家は東京の近郊にある。 My parents' home is in the suburbs of Tokyo. / 我的老家在东京近郊。/ Nhà bố mẹ ruột tôi ở ngoại ô Tokyo.
447 □ 動	描く えがく portray/draw / 描绘 / 画 / vẽ, miêu tả	①国で日本の留学生活を夢に描いていた。 ②妹がふるさとの風景を描いて、送ってくれた。 ① Back in my country, I used to dream of studying in Japan. ② My little sister drew a picture of my hometown's scenery and sent it to me. / ①我在国内时，一直在心里描绘着日本留学生活之梦②妹妹画了家乡的风景，寄给了我。/ ① Ở nước mình, tôi đã vẽ giấc mơ cuộc sống du học ở Nhật. ② Em gái tôi đã vẽ phong cảnh quê nhà gửi cho tôi.

👉 ① imagining in one's mind ② showing in picture or drawingalso written かく / ①在心里想②用绘画表达，也写作"かく" / ① Nghĩ trong đầu ② Thể hiện bằng tranh hay sơ đồ. Cũng đọc là " かく ".

448 □ 名	若者 わかもの young people / 年轻人 / giới trẻ, thanh niên	私の故郷では若者が減少している。 The number of young people is decreasing in my hometown. / 在我的家乡，年轻人越来越少了。/ Ở quê tôi số người trẻ đang giảm.
449 □ 名	Uターン〈する〉 ユー U-turn/U-turn / 回老家工作 / 调头 / quay về quê, quay đầu	①大学を卒業して、Uターン就職した。 ②渋滞だ。次の角でUターンしよう。 ① I want to return to my hometown to work after graduating from college. ② Let's make a U-turn at the next corner as the roads are crowded. / ①外地大学毕业后我回老家工作了。②堵车了。在下个路口掉头吧。/ ① Tốt nghiệp đại học, tôi quay về quê kiếm việc. ② Kẹt xe rồi. Hãy quay đầu ở góc tiếp theo thôi.

👉 ① going somewhere and then returning to one's hometown ② changing direction to the opposite direction as before is a vehicle / ①去其他地方然后再回故乡②开车时调转车头往回开 / ① Đi đến nơi khác rồi quay về quê. ② Xe hơi quẹo lại để đi về hướng cũ.

450 □ 名	行き来〈する〉(いゆき) go back and forth / 往返，来往 / sự đi lại	月に数回、故郷と東京を行き来している。 I travel between my hometown and Tokyo several times a month. / 每个月好几次往返于老家和东京。/ Một tháng vài lần tôi đi lại giữa quê nhà và Tokyo.
451 □ 動	担う(にな) to shoulder / 肩负，承担 / gánh vác	国の将来を担うために、日本に留学した。 I came to study in Japan for the future of my country. / 为了肩负起祖国的未来而去了日本留学。/ Để gánh vác tương lai đất nước, tôi đã du học Nhật Bản.

これも覚えよう！⑬

接辞：とき③ Affix: Time / 词缀：时间 / Phụ tố: Thời gian

• **再～**(さい)

再利用(さいりよう) reuse / 再利用 / Tái sử dụng

再開発(さいかいはつ) redevelop / 再开发 / Tái phát triển

再発見(さいはっけん) rediscover / 重新发现 / Tái phát hiện

再試験(さいしけん) reexamination / 补考 / Tái thử nghiệm

再検討(さいけんとう) reconsider / 重新讨论 / Cân nhắc lại, xem xét lại

再認識(さいにんしき) reacknowledge / 重新认识 / Nhận thức lại

再出発(さいしゅっぱつ) restart / 重新出发 / Xuất phát lại

再放送(さいほうそう) rerun / 重播 / Phát sóng lại

再生産(さいせいさん) reproduce / 再生产 / Tái sản xuất

交通

こうつう

Transportation / 交通 / Giao thông

452 □ 名	行き先 (い/ゆ さき)	ホームで電車の行き先を確認する。(でんしゃ い/ゆ さき かくにん)
	destination / 目的地 / nơi đi đến	Confirm the destination of the train at the platform. / 在站台上确认电车行驶的目的地。/ Tôi kiểm tra nơi tàu điện đi ở sân ga.

➕ 目的地 (もくてきち) destination / 目的地 / nơi đến

453 □ 名	方面 (ほうめん)	東京方面の電車が止まっているそうだ。(とうきょうほうめん でんしゃ と)
	direction / 方面，开往 / hướng	The train heading to Tokyo is apparently not moving. / 开往东京方向的电车好像停运了。/ Nghe nói tàu điện hướng Tokyo đang dừng.
454 □ 名	行き帰り (い/ゆ かえ)	学校への行き帰りはバスを利用している。(がっこう い/ゆ かえ りよう)
	going to and from / 往返 / sự đi và về	I use the bus to get to and from school. / 上学放学都坐公共汽车。/ Tôi sử dụng xe buýt để đi học và về nhà.

➕ 往復〈する〉(おうふく) round trip / 往返，来回 / khứ hồi, 2 chiều

455 □ 名	横断〈する〉(おうだん)	車が行き来する道を横断するときは注意しよう。(くるま い/ゆ き みち おうだん ちゅうい)
	cross / 穿，横穿 / sự băng qua	Be careful when crossing where cars are driving. / 横穿车来车往的道路时要注意安全。/ Khi băng qua đường có xe hơi qua lại, hãy cẩn thận.

➕ 横断歩道 (おうだんほどう) pedestrian crossing / 人行横道 / vạch băng qua đường

456 □ 名	通行〈する〉(つうこう)	この道は車は通行できない。(みち くるま つうこう)
	pass / 通行 / sự đi lại, lưu thông	Cars cannot take this road. / 这条路车辆不能通行。/ Con đường này xe hơi không thể lưu thông.

➕ 通行禁止 (つうこうきんし) no trespassing / 禁止通行 / sự cấm đi lại・通行止め (つうこうど) no entry / 禁止通行 / sự chặn đi lại

457 □ 名	歩行者 (ほこうしゃ)	歩行者がトラックにひかれた。(ほこうしゃ)
	pedestrian / 行人 / người đi bộ	The pedestrian was hit by a truck. / 行人被卡车轧了。/ Người đi bộ đã bị xe tải cán.

➕ 通行人 (つうこうにん) passer-by / 路人 / người đi đường

458 □ 副	絶えず (た)	この道路は絶えず車が通っている。(どうろ た くるま とお)
	constantly / 不断，无休止 / không dứt, không ngừng	Cars are always passing this road. / 这条马路不断有车通过。/ Con đường này xe hơi qua lại không dứt.

➕ 次々と (つぎつぎ) one after another / 接连不断 / liên tục, tiếp nối

459 **手段**（しゅだん）
名 **method / 手段，方式 / phương tiện**

ここへ行く（い）には、どの交通手段（こうつうしゅだん）が一番早い（いちばんはや）ですか。

What is the fastest transportation to get here? / 去这里采用什么交通方式最快呢？ / Để đi đến đây, phương tiện giao thông nào là nhanh nhất?

➕ 連絡手段（れんらくしゅだん） communication method / 交通方式 / phương tiện liên lạc

460 **公共**（こうきょう）
名 **public / 公共 / công cộng**

バスも電車（でんしゃ）も公共（こうきょう）の交通手段（こうつうしゅだん）だ。

Both buses and trains are public transportation. / 公共汽车和电车都是公共交通工具。/ Cả xe buýt lẫn tàu điện đều là phương tiện giao thông công cộng.

461 **運賃**（うんちん）
名 **transportation fare / 车费 / tiền cước, phí vận chuyển**

日本（にほん）は物（もの）だけでなく、運賃（うんちん）も高い（たか）。

In Japan, not only things but transportation fare is also expensive. / 日本不仅东西贵，车费也很贵。/ Nhật Bản không chỉ đồ vật mà phí vận chuyển cũng đắt đỏ.

462 **つかまる**
動 **hold on / 抓，抓住 / nắm, cầm**

電車（でんしゃ）がゆれるので、つり革（かわ）につかまった。

I grabbed the strap because the train was rocking. / 电车摇晃得厉害，所以我抓紧了吊环。/ Vì tàu điện lắc lư nên tôi nắm tay vịn.

463 **アナウンス〈する〉**
名 **announcement / 广播，报告 / loa thông báo, sự thông báo**

駅（えき）のアナウンスで事故（じこ）を知（し）った。

I learned of the accident through the announcement at the station. / 我通过车站广播得知发生了事故。/ Tôi biết tin vụ tai nạn nhờ thông báo của nhà ga.

➕ 車内（しゃない）アナウンス train announcement / 车内广播 / loa thông báo trong xe (tàu)

464 **見合わせる**（みあ）
動 **postpone, suspend operations / 推迟，延缓 / nhìn nhau, hoãn**

今（いま）、電車（でんしゃ）が運転（うんてん）を見合（みあ）わせている。

The train is not running now. / 现在电车暂时停运了。/ Bây giờ tàu điện đang hoãn hoạt động.

➕ 人身事故（じんしんじこ） accident resulting in personal injury or death / 人员伤亡事故 / tai nạn về người

465 **乱れる**（みだ）
動 **fall into disorder / 紊乱，混乱 / 不规范，乱七八糟 / xáo trộn, rối loạn, lung tung**

①電車（でんしゃ）の到着時間（とうちゃくじかん）がかなり乱（みだ）れている。
②最近（さいきん）、若者（わかもの）の日本語（にほんご）が乱（みだ）れてきた。

① The arrival times of the train fell into disorder. ② The Japanese spoken by young people recently are getting corrupt. / ①现在电车的到站时间发生了大幅的混乱。②最近，年轻人说的日语越来越不规范。/ ① Giờ tàu đến bị xáo trộn khá nhiều. ② Gần đây, tiếng Nhật của giới trẻ trở nên lung tung.

➕ （～を）乱（みだ）す disrupt / 弄乱 / làm (~) hỗn loạn, xáo trộn

👉 ① something that was in proper order falls into disorder ② rules and manners are not being maitained / ① 本来正常的东西变乱了 ②不遵守规矩或没有礼貌 / ① Những gì đang quy củ bị phá vỡ. ② Quy định, phép ứng xử không được gìn giữ.

385 ~ 501

466 □ 名	再開〈する〉(さいかい) restart, resume / 恢复，重新开始 / sự bắt đầu lại	しばらくして、運転(うんてん)が再開(さいかい)された。 Operation resumed after a while. / 过了一会儿，电车恢复运行了。/ Một lúc sau, (tàu điện) bắt đầu hoạt động trở lại.
467 □ 名	ＩＣカード(アイシー) IC card / 交通卡 / thẻ IC	電車(でんしゃ)でもバスでもＩＣ(アイシー)カードが便利(べんり)だ。 IC cards are convenient on both the bus and train. / 坐电车也好，坐公交车也好，用交通卡都很方便。/ Thẻ IC tiện lợi với cả tàu điện và xe buýt.
468 □ 名	免許(めんきょ) license / 许可 / sự cho phép, giấy phép	二十歳(はたち)で車(くるま)の運転(うんてん)免許(めんきょ)を取(と)った。 I received a driver's license at 20 years old. / 20岁时拿到了驾照。/ Tôi đã lấy giấy phép lái xe ở tuổi 20.
		➕ 免許証(めんきょしょう) license card / 许可证 / giấy phép, bằng cấp
469 □ 名	左右(さゆう) left and right / 左右 / trái phải	自転車(じてんしゃ)に乗(の)ったら、左右(さゆう)をしっかり見(み)て、交差点(こうさてん)を曲(ま)がる。 Look to your left and right carefully when turning at the intersection on a bicycle. / 骑自行车过路口时，要看清左右再转弯。/ Khi đi xe đạp phải nhìn kỹ trái phải rồi quẹo qua giao lộ.
		➕ 前後(ぜんご) front and back / 前后 / trước sau
470 □ 名	直線(ちょくせん) straight line / 直线 / đường thẳng	直線(ちょくせん)の道(みち)では車(くるま)がスピードを出(だ)しがちだ。 Cars tend to speed up on straight roads. / 在笔直的道路上车辆往往容易开得很快。/ Trên đường thẳng, người ta có khuynh hướng cho xe chạy tốc độ nhanh.
471 □ ナ形	なだらかな smooth, fluent / 平缓的，顺利的 / nhẹ, mềm	事故現場(じこげんば)はなだらかなカーブだった。 The scene of the accident was a gentle curb. / 事故发生在一个弧度平缓的弯道上。/ Hiện trường vụ tai nạn là góc cua nhẹ.
472 □ 名	間隔(かんかく) space / 间距 / khoảng cách	高速道路(こうそくどうろ)では前(まえ)の車(くるま)と間隔(かんかく)をあけて走(はし)る。 One needs to keep a distance from the car in front when driving on a highway. / 在高速公路上，和前方车辆保持距离行驶。/ Trên đường cao tốc thì chạy giữ khoảng cách với xe phía trước.
473 □ ナ形	スムーズな smooth / 流畅，顺畅 / trôi chảy, thuận lợi	今日(きょう)は渋滞(じゅうたい)もなく、車(くるま)はスムーズに進(すす)んでいる。 The car is moving smoothly with no traffic congestion. / 今天没有堵车，车辆行驶得很通畅。/ Hôm nay không bị kẹt xe, xe chạy bon bon.
		➕ 円滑(えんかつ)な smooth / 圆满，顺利 / trôi chảy, trơn tru

474 □ 動	指す (さ) **point / 指 / chỉ**	スピードメーターの針(はり)が 120 キロを指して(さ)いる。 The speedometer is pointing at 120 kph. / 计速器的指针指着 120 公里。/ Kim chỉ tốc độ chỉ 120km/h.
475 □ ナ形 副	のろのろ〈な / する〉 **slow/slowly / 迟缓，慢慢吞吞 / chầm chậm, chậm chạp, lờ đờ**	前(まえ)の車(くるま)がのろのろ走(はし)っている。(副) The car in front is driving slowly. / 前面的车开得慢吞吞的。/ Xe phía trước chạy chầm chậm.

➕ のろい slow / 迟钝 / chầm chậm, chậm chạp, lờ đờ

476 □ 副	ぐるぐる［と］ **around and around / 团团转 / loanh quanh, xoay**	道(みち)に迷(まよ)って、同(おな)じ道(みち)をぐるぐる回(まわ)った。 I got lost and keep going in circles on the same road / 迷路了，在同一条路上转来转去。/ Tôi lạc đường và loanh quanh lòng vòng cùng một con đường.
477 □ 名	パンク〈する〉 **flat tire / 爆胎 / sự nổ lốp, bể bánh xe**	高速道路(こうそくどうろ)でパンクしてしまった。 I got a flat tire on the highway. / 在高速公路上爆胎了。/ Xe bị nổ lốp trên đường cao tốc.
478 □ ナ形	慎重(しんちょう)な **cautiously / 慎重，小心 / thận trọng**	車(くるま)は慎重(しんちょう)に運転(うんてん)するべきだ。 One should drive a car carefully. / 开车要小心谨慎。/ Phải lái xe hơi thật thận trọng.
479 □ 慣	気(き)を抜(ぬ)く **relax one's attention / 疏忽大意 / lơ là, lơ đãng, bất cẩn**	道(みち)がすいていても、気(き)を抜(ぬ)いてはいけない。 One should be cautious even if the roads are clear. / 就算路上车少也不能大意。/ Dù đường có vắng cũng không được lơ là.

Section 5

産業（さんぎょう）

Industry / 产业 / Các ngành công nghiệp

480	生産（せいさん）〈する〉	私（わたし）の田舎（いなか）では米（こめ）の生産（せいさん）が盛（さか）んだ。
名	**production / 生产，产出 / sự sản xuất**	Rice production is popular in my hometown. / 我们农村盛产大米。/ Quê tôi phát triển sản xuất gạo.
481	供給（きょうきゅう）〈する〉	需要（じゅよう）と供給（きょうきゅう）のバランスは重要（じゅうよう）だ。
名	**provision / 供给 / sự cung cấp**	The balance of supply and demand is important. / 需求与供给的平衡很重要。/ Sự cân bằng giữa nhu cầu và cung cấp rất quan trọng.
482	栽培（さいばい）〈する〉	この地域（ちいき）では、いちごを栽培（さいばい）している。
名	**cultivation / 栽培 / sự trồng trọt**	Strawberries are grown around this area. / 这个地区栽培草莓。/ Vùng này trồng dâu.
483	農家（のうか）	野菜（やさい）は知（し）り合（あ）いの農家（のうか）から直接（ちょくせつ）買（か）っている。
名	**farmer / 农家 / nông dân**	I buy vegetables directly from a farmer that I know. / 蔬菜是我从认识的农户那里直接买来的。/ Tôi mua rau trực tiếp từ những nhà nông quen biết.
484	作物（さくもつ）	農家（のうか）の人達（ひとたち）は愛情（あいじょう）を込（こ）めて作物（さくもつ）を育（そだ）てている。
名	**produce / 作物 / hoa màu, cây trồng**	The farmers tend to their crops with care. / 农民们倾注心血，精心培育农作物。/ Những người nông dân trồng hoa màu với nhiều tình cảm.
485	漁業（ぎょぎょう）	父（ちち）は漁業（ぎょぎょう）で一家（いっか）を支（ささ）えている。
名	**fishery / 渔业 / ngư nghiệp, nghề chài lưới**	My father supports the family by working in the fishing industry. / 父亲靠打渔养活我们全家。/ Cha tôi cáng đáng cả nhà bằng nghề chài lưới.

➕ 漁村（ぎょそん） fishing village / 渔村 / làng chài・商業（しょうぎょう） business / 商业 / thương nghiệp・農業（のうぎょう） agriculture / 农业 / nông nghiệp・工業（こうぎょう） industry / 工业 / công nghiệp

486	栄（さか）える	この島（しま）は漁業（ぎょぎょう）で栄（さか）えている。
動	**prosper / 兴盛，繁荣 / phồn vinh, hưng thịnh**	This island prospers from the fishing industry. / 这个岛的渔业很兴盛。/ Hòn đảo này hưng thịnh nhờ nghề chài lưới.
487	普及（ふきゅう）〈する〉	コンピューターの普及（ふきゅう）で、IT 産業（さんぎょう）は成長（せいちょう）した。
名	**proliferation / 普及 / sự phổ cập, phổ biến**	The IT industry grew due to the proliferation of computers. / 随着电脑的普及，IT 产业得到了发展。/ Nhờ sự phổ biến của máy tính mà ngành công nghệ thông tin lớn mạnh.

488 急増〈する〉
きゅうぞう
名 **rapid increase / 急剧增加 / sự tăng nhanh, tăng đột ngột**

この辺りは最近観光客が急増している。
あた さいきんかんこうきゃく きゅうぞう

Recently, the number of tourists are increasing rapidly around here. / 最近，这一带的游客急剧增加。/ Gần đây, khu vực này khách du lịch tăng đột ngột.

➕ 激減（げきげん）〈する〉 drastic decrease / 激减 / giảm mạnh・激増（げきぞう）〈する〉 drastic increase / 激增 / tăng mạnh

489 情緒
じょうちょ
名 **atmosphere / 风情，情趣，情绪 / trữ tình, cảm xúc**

この町は情緒があるので、観光客が多く訪れる。
まち じょうちょ かんこうきゃく おお おとず

A lot of tourists visit this town because it has a lot of atmosphere. / 这座城镇别有风情，因此观光客蜂拥而至。/ Thành phố này trữ tình nên có nhiều khách du lịch tham quan.

➕ 異国情緒（いこくじょうちょ） foreign atmosphere / 异国风情 / cảm xúc như ở nước ngoài

490 向上〈する〉
こうじょう
名 **improvement / 提高 / sự tăng cường, nâng cao**

新しい技術で、この工場の生産性が向上した。
あたら ぎじゅつ こうじょう せいさんせい こうじょう

This factory's production improved due to new technology. / 新技术提高了这家工厂的生产力。/ Bằng kỹ thuật mới, việc sản xuất của nhà máy này được nâng cao.

491 構成〈する〉
こうせい
名 **structure / 构成，组织 / sự hình thành, tạo thành**

地元の商品を開発するため、チームが構成された。
じもと しょうひん かいはつ こうせい

A team was formed to develop local products. / 为了开发当地商品，成立了特别团队。/ Để khai thác sản phẩm của địa phương, đội đã được hình thành.

492 重視〈する〉
じゅうし
名 **emphasis, consideration / 重视 / sự xem trọng**

A国では観光やサービス産業を重視している。
こく かんこう さんぎょう じゅうし

Country A emphasises tourism and the service industry. / A国很重视观光和服务产业。/ Nước A xem trọng ngành công nghiệp du lịch và dịch vụ.

493 提案〈する〉
ていあん
名 **suggestion / 提案 / đề án**

地元の産業を生かした商品を提案する。
じもと さんぎょう い しょうひん ていあん

I suggested a product that took advantage of local industries. / 对能有效发挥本地产业优势的商品进行提案。/ Đưa ra đề án sản phẩm phát huy ngành công nghiệp của địa phương.

➕ 案（あん） plan / 方案 / đề án, đề nghị

494 検討〈する〉
けんとう
名 **consideration / 讨论，商讨 / sự cân nhắc, nghiên cứu, bàn thảo**

私の会社では新しい工場の建設を検討している。
わたし かいしゃ あたら こうじょう けんせつ けんとう

My company is thinking of building a new factory. / 我们公司在讨论新工厂的建设。/ Công ty tôi đang bàn thảo về việc xây dựng nhà máy mới.

495 □ ナ形	不可欠な (ふかけつ) **indispensable / 不可或缺的 / không thể thiếu**	この国には新しい産業が不可欠だ。(くに、あたら、さんぎょう、ふかけつ) New industries are indispensable in this country. / 这个国家不能缺少新兴产业。/ Ở nước này, ngành công nghiệp mới là không thể thiếu.
496 □ 動	妨げる (さまた) **prevent / 防碍，阻挠 / gây trở ngại, ảnh hưởng**	古いルールが新しい産業の発展を妨げている。(ふる、あたら、さんぎょう、はってん、さまた) The old rules are preventing new industries from developing. / 旧规定阻碍着新兴产业的发展。/ Quy định cũ gây trở ngại cho sự phát triển của ngành công nghiệp mới.
497 □ 動	生える (は) **grow / 长，长出 / mọc**	春になって、畑に雑草が生えてきた。(はる、はたけ、ざっそう、は) Spring has arrived, and weeds have started growing in the fields. / 春天到了，田里的杂草都长出来了。/ Đến mùa xuân, cỏ dại mọc đầy ruộng đồng.

also used for baby's teeth when they start growing in / 也用来表示婴儿长牙 / Cũng dùng cho răng của em bé.

498 □ イ形	著しい (いちじる) **drastic / 显著 / đáng kể**	1960年代の頃から機械工業が著しく進歩した。(ねんだい、ころ、きかいこうぎょう、いちじる、しんぽ) Mechanical engineering has advanced dramatically since the 1960s. / 从二十世纪六十年代左右开始，机械工业有了显著的进步。/ Từ khoảng những năm 1960, ngành công nghiệp cơ khí đã tiến bộ đáng kể.
499 □ 名	参考 (さんこう) **reference / 参考 / sự tham khảo**	このロボットは人間や動物の動きを参考にしている。(にんげん、どうぶつ、うご、さんこう) This robot uses the movement of humans and animals as reference. / 这个机器人的制作参考了人和动物的动作。/ Người máy này, chúng tôi đã tham khảo cử động của người và động vật.
500 □ 名	リスク **risk / 风险 / rủi ro**	農業には常に自然災害というリスクがある。(のうぎょう、つね、しぜんさいがい) Agriculture always entails the risk of natural diasters. / 农业总是面临着自然灾害的威胁。/ Trong ngành nông nghiệp thường có rủi ro về thiên tai.
501 □ 名	現地 (げんち) **site / 现场 / (nước, địa phương) sở tại, địa bàn**	A社は現地を調査して、新しい工場を建てた。(しゃ、げんち、ちょうさ、あたら、こうじょう、た) Company A conducted a field survey at the site and built a new factory there. / A公司做了实地调查之后建了一个新工厂。/ Công ty A đã khảo sát địa bàn và xây nhà máy mới.

N2

Chapter 5

学校で（がっこう）

At School / 学校篇 / Tại trường học

単語（たんご） No.

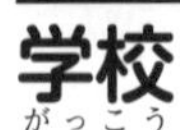

Section 1

学校（がっこう）

School / 学校 / Trường học

502 □ 動	教わる（おそ）	この学校（がっこう）で日本語（にほんご）だけでなく文化（ぶんか）や習慣（しゅうかん）も教わった（おそ）。
	learn / 受教，学习 / được dạy, học	I learned not only the Japanese language, but also Japanese culture and customs at this school. / 在这所学校，我除了日语之外，还学到了文化和风俗习惯。/ Ở trường này, không chỉ tiếng Nhật mà cả văn hóa và phong tục cũng được dạy.
503 □ 名	願書（がんしょ）	大学（だいがく）の願書（がんしょ）を締（し）め切（き）りまでに提出（ていしゅつ）する。
	application / 志愿书，申请书 / đơn, đơn xin	I will submit the university application before the deadline. / 在截止日期前提交大学入学申请书。/ Cho đến khi hết hạn, tôi sẽ nộp đơn vào đại học.

➕ 入学願書（にゅうがくがんしょ） application for (school, university) / 入学志愿书 / đơn nhập học

504 □ 名	推薦（すいせん）〈する〉	高校（こうこう）から大学（だいがく）に推薦（すいせん）してもらえることになった。
	recommendation / 推荐 / sự tiến cử, giới thiệu	The high school will recommend me to the university. / 我的高中把我推荐给了大学。/ Tôi đã nhận được sự tiến cử vào đại học từ trường cấp III.

➕ 推薦入試（すいせんにゅうし） entrance exam by commendation / 推荐生入学考试 / kỳ thi tiến cử・推薦状（すいせんじょう） recommendation letter / 推荐信 / thư tiến cử, thư giới thiệu・学校推薦（がっこうすいせん） recommendation from school / 学校推荐 / trường tiến cử, trường giới thiệu

505 □ 動	狙う（ねら）	彼（かれ）は有名（ゆうめい）な私立大学（しりつだいがく）を狙（ねら）っている。
	aim for / 瞄准，觊觎 / nhắm đến, hướng đến	He is aiming for a famous private university. / 他的目标是考上有名的私立大学。/ Anh ấy nhắm đến trường đại học tư nổi tiếng.
506 □ 名	意志（いし）	弟（おとうと）は強（つよ）い意志（いし）で留学（りゅうがく）を決（き）めた。
	will / 意志 / ý chí	My younger brother decided to study abroad with a strong will. / 弟弟下定决心去留学。/ Em trai tôi quyết định du học với ý chí mạnh mẽ.
507 □ 名	開始（かいし）〈する〉	この学校（がっこう）は9時（じ）に授業（じゅぎょう）を開始（かいし）する。
	start / 开始 / sự bắt đầu	Classes starts at 9:00 a.m. at this school. / 这所学校从 9 点开始上课。/ Trường này bắt đầu giờ học từ 9 giờ.
508 □ 名 副	通常（つうじょう）	学校（がっこう）は通常（つうじょう）、土日（どにち）と祝日（しゅくじつ）が休（やす）みだ。（副）
	usual/usually / 通常 / sự thông thường	The school is usually closed on weekends and holidays. / 学校通常双休日和节假日都放假。/ Trường học thông thường nghỉ vào thứ bảy, chủ nhật và ngày lễ.

509 担任〈する〉(たんにん)
名 **homeroom teacher / 负责人，班主任 / giáo viên chủ nhiệm**

私のクラスの担任は小林先生だ。
My homeroom teacher is Mr. Kobayashi. / 我们的班主任是小林老师。/ Giáo viên chủ nhiệm lớp tôi là thầy / cô Kobayashi.

510 受け持つ(うけもつ)
動 **in charge of / 掌管，负责 / đảm nhiệm, tiếp nhận**

田中先生は上級クラスを受け持っている。
Mr. Tanaka is in charge of the advanced class. / 田中老师负责高级班。/ Thầy / cô Tanaka đảm nhận lớp bậc cao.

➕ 受け持ち(うけもち) in charge of / 担任，负责 / sự đảm nhiệm

511 委員(いいん)
名 **representative, officer / 委员 / ủy viên, cán sự**

今年はクラス委員になった。
I became a class representative this year. / 今年当上了班委。/ Năm nay tôi trở thành cán sự lớp.

➕ 委員会(いいんかい) committee / 委员会 / ủy ban, hội đồng

512 なじむ
動 **get used to / 熟悉，习惯 / quen, quen thuộc**

学校生活に、やっとなじんできた。
I'm finally getting used to school life. / 终于习惯了校园生活。/ Cuối cùng tôi đã quen với đời sống học đường.

513 充実〈する〉(じゅうじつ)
名 **fulfilling / 充实 / sự đầy đủ, ý nghĩa, trọn vẹn**

日本に留学して以来、毎日が充実している。
Ever since I've arrived in Japan to study, my days are fulfilling. / 来日本留学之后，每天都很充实。/ Kể từ sau khi du học Nhật, mỗi ngày đều thật ý nghĩa.

➕ 充実感(じゅうじつかん) sense of fulfillment / 充实感 / cảm giác đầy đủ, ý nghĩa, trọn vẹn

514 高等〈な〉(こうとう)
名 ナ形 **superior/advanced / 高等，高度 / cấp cao, trình độ cao**

日本で高等な技術を学びたい。(ナ形)
I want to learn advanced technology in Japan. / 我想在日本学习高级技术。/ Tôi muốn học kỹ thuật cao ở Nhật

515 ステップ
名 **step/step / 台阶，过程 / 台阶 / bước tiến, bậc bước lên**

①進学は夢へのステップだ。
②バスのステップが低いと、高齢者が乗りやすい。
① Going on to higher education is a step towards my dream. ② It's easier for the elderly to board the bus when the steps are lower. / ①升学是向着梦想迈出的一步。②公交车的台阶较低的话，便于老年人上下车。/ ① Việc học lên là một bước tiến đến ước mơ. ② Bậc bước lên xe buýt thấp thì người cao tuổi dễ đi.

👉 ① the next step ② the platform used to get on and off the bus / ①下一个阶段②上下公交车时车门处的踏板 / ① Giai đoạn tiếp theo ② Bậc thang ở cửa lên xuống xe buýt

516 □	過程（かてい）	仕事の過程を上司に報告する。（しごと かてい じょうし ほうこく）
名	process / 过程 / quá trình	Report the progress of your work to your boss. / 向上级汇报工作的过程。/ Tôi sẽ báo cáo quá trình công việc lên cấp trên.

= プロセス

517 □	取り上げる（と あ）	①授業で日本の若者文化を取り上げた。（じゅぎょう にほん わかものぶんか と あ） ②子どもからゲームを取り上げた。（こ と あ）
動	take up/take away / 采用，接纳 / 没收，剥夺 / đưa vào, lấy đi, tịch thu	① The culture of Japan's youth was discussed in class. ② He took away the game console from the child. / ①课堂上讲了日本年轻人文化的相关内容。②（我）没收了孩子的游戏。/ ① Trong giờ học, văn hóa giới trẻ Nhật Bản đã được đưa vào. ② Tôi đã tịch thu game của con.

① adopt ② take away someone's things / ①使用②拿走对方的东西 / ① Đưa vào, tuyển dụng. ② Lấy đi đồ vật của người đối diện

518 □	欠ける（か）	①彼が欠けたら、大会に出られない。（かれ か たいかい で） ②固いものを食べたら、歯が欠けた。（かた た は か） ③無断で休むなんて、常識に欠ける。（むだん やす じょうしき か）
動	miss/chip/lack / 缺少 / 磕出缺口 / 缺乏 / thiếu, mất, khuyết, rụng	① We can't participate in the games without him. ② My tooth chipped when I bit on something hard. ③ Skipping class without explanation shows he lacks common sense. / ①缺了他就参加不了大赛了。②吃硬的东西，牙磕掉了一块。③竟然无故旷工，真是没有常识 / ① Nếu thiếu anh ấy thì không thể tham gia đại hội. ② Tôi ăn món cứng thì cái răng rụng mất tiêu. ③ Nghỉ không phép thì thật thiếu ý thức.

① a portion of something complete is broken ② a part is missing from the complete set ③ an element that should be there is missing / ①完整的东西有一部分坏了②应该齐全的东西有一部分没有了③缺乏应有的要素 / ① Vật hoàn hảo bị hư mất một phần. ② Vật lẽ ra phải đầy đủ thì bị mất một phần. ③ Thiếu yếu tố phải có.

519 □	優秀な（ゆうしゅう）	このクラスには優秀な学生が多い。（ゆうしゅう がくせい おお）
ナ形	highly capable / 优秀 / ưu tú, xuất sắc	There are many highly capable students in this class. / 这个班有很多优秀的学生。/ Ở lớp này có nhiều sinh viên ưu tú.

520 □	修了〈する〉（しゅうりょう）	3月で日本語学校を修了する。（がつ にほんごがっこう しゅうりょう）
名	completion / 结业，结束 / sự kết thúc, hoàn thành (việc học nói chung)	I will complete this Japanese language school in March. / 语言学校将在 3 月份结业。/ Tháng 3 tôi sẽ hoàn thành (chương trình học ở) trường tiếng Nhật.

＋ 修了証書（しゅうりょうしょうしょ） certificate (of completion) / 结业证书 / giấy chứng nhận kết thúc

521 □	ふさわしい	卒業式にふさわしい服装で出席する。（そつぎょうしき ふくそう しゅっせき）
イ形	suitable, fitting, appropriate / 合适，相称 / phù hợp	Attend the graduation ceremony wearing the appropriate attire. / 穿着合适的服装出席毕业典礼。/ Tôi dự lễ tốt nghiệp với trang phục phù hợp.

522 認識〈する〉(にんしき)
名 **realization / 认识 / nhận thức, ý thức**

学校(がっこう)では規則(きそく)を守(まも)るように生徒(せいと)に認識(にんしき)させる。
Make the students understand the need to follow school rules. / 让学生认识到在学校要遵守规定。/ Làm cho học sinh có ý thức giữ gìn quy định ở trường.

➕ 認識不足(にんしきぶそく) lack of realization / 认识不足 / thiếu nhận thức

523 語学学校(ごがくがっこう)
名 **language school / 语言学校 / trường học tiếng (ngoại ngữ)**

東京(とうきょう)の語学学校(ごがくがっこう)で勉強(べんきょう)している。
I am studying at a language school in Tokyo. / 在东京的语言学校学习。/ Tôi đang học tại trường học tiếng ở Tokyo.

これも覚(おぼ)えよう！⑭

➕ **接辞(せつじ)：感情等(かんじょうなど)①** Affix: Emotions, etc. / 词缀：情感等 / Phụ tố: Tình cảm v.v.

• **～感(かん)（自然(しぜん)に感(かん)じる思(おも)い、気持(きも)ち）**

責任感(せきにんかん)	sense of responsibility / 责任感 / Tinh thần trách nhiệm
一体感(いったいかん)	sense of unity / 集体感 / Cảm giác đồng nhất, tính thống nhất
親近感(しんきんかん)	sense of closeness / 亲近感 / Cảm giác gần gũi
満足感(まんぞくかん)	sense of satisfaction / 满足感 / Cảm giác thỏa mãn, hài lòng
違和感(いわかん)	sense of wrongness, uncomfortableness / 不协调的感觉，感觉奇怪 / Cảm giác khác biệt
嫌悪感(けんおかん)	hatred, disgust / 厌恶感 / Cảm giác ghê sợ, đáng ghét
安心感(あんしんかん)	sense of comfort / 安心感 / Cảm giác yên tâm
不安感(ふあんかん)	sense of unease / 不安感 / Cảm giác bất an
幸福感(こうふくかん)	sense of happiness / 幸福感 / Cảm giác hạnh phúc

Section 2

勉強（べんきょう）

Studying / 学习 / Học tập

524	学ぶ（まな）	日本で日本語と文化を学びたい。
動	learn / 学 / học	I want to learn Japanese and Japanese culture in Japan. / (我) 想在日本学习日语和（日本）文化。/ Ở Nhật, tôi muốn học tiếng Nhật và văn hóa.
525	学習〈する〉（がくしゅう）	一日の学習時間は8時間くらいだ。
名	learning / 学习 / việc học tập	I study about eight hours a day. / 我一天大概学习 8 小时。/ Thời gian học tập một ngày khoảng 8 tiếng.

➕ 学習法（がくしゅうほう） method of learning / 学习方法 / phương pháp học

526	学力（がくりょく）	大学に進学できる学力をつけたい。
名	academic ability / 学习能力 / học lực	I want to increase my academic ability enough to go to college. / 想具备能考上大学的学习能力。/ Tôi muốn có được học lực có thể vào đại học.
527	教養（きょうよう）	人には教養が必要だ。
名	education / 教养 / sự giáo dục, sự nuôi dưỡng	People need education. / 人要有教养。/ Con người cần sự giáo dục.
528	参考書（さんこうしょ）	どの参考書がいいか、先生に教えていただいた。
名	reference book / 参考书 / sách tham khảo	The teacher told me which reference books would be good for me. / 我向老师请教了哪本参考书比较好。/ Tôi được thầy / cô chỉ cho sách tham khảo nào tốt.

➕ 問題集（もんだいしゅう） exercise book / 练习题集 / sách bài tập

529	書き込む（かきこむ）	教科書に授業のメモを書き込む。
動	write down / 写上，填写 / viết vào	I wrote down notes from the lesson in the textbook. / 把课堂笔记写在教科书上。/ Tôi viết ghi chú trong giờ học vào sách giáo khoa.

➕ 書き込み（かきこみ） writing / 写上，记入 / sự viết vào

530	書き取る（かきとる）	会話問題を聞いて書き取る。
動	transcribe / 记录 / viết chính tả, (nghe rồi viết)	I listen to the conversation questions and transcribe them. / 听对话问题并记录下来。/ Tôi nghe câu hỏi hội thoại rồi viết.

➕ 書き取り（かきとり） dictation / 抄写，记录 / sự viết chính tả・聞き取る（ききとる） listen / 听写 / nghe hiểu

531 **記号**（きごう）
名 **symbol / 符号 / ký hiệu**

記号の「※」は「こめじるし」と読む。
This symbol is read "kome-jirushi" / 符号"※"读作"こめじるし"。/ Ký hiệu " ※ " đọc là "komejirushi".

532 **図**（ず）
名 **diagram / 图，图表 / hình minh họa**

遠藤先生は絵と図で、わかりやすく説明する。
Mr. Endo's explanations are easy to understand because he uses pictures and diagrams. / 远藤老师用画和图表简单易懂地进行说明。/ Thầy / cô Endo giải thích thật dễ hiểu bằng tranh và hình ảnh.

＋ 図形（ずけい） figure / 图形 / hình, hình minh họa

533 **下線**（かせん）
名 **underline / 下划线 / đường gạch dưới**

教科書のキーワードに下線を引く。
Underline the keywords in the textbook. / 在教科书上的关键词下面划线。/ Gạch dưới những từ khóa trong sách giáo khoa.

＝ アンダーライン

534 **法則**（ほうそく）
名 **law, rule / 法则，定律 / quy tắc, luật**

インターネットで引力の法則について調べる。
I did some research about the laws of gratitivity on the Internet. / 在网上查（万有）引力定律。/ Tôi tìm hiểu về quy tắc của lực hút qua mạng internet.

535 **志す**（こころざす）
動 **aspire / 立志于 / mong mỏi, khao khát, thiết tha**

学者を志して、努力を続ける。
I aspire to become a scholar and will continue to make efforts. / 我立志成为学者，并为之不断努力。/ Tôi mong trở thành học giả nên tiếp tục nỗ lực.

＋ 志（こころざし） aspiration / 志向，志愿 / ý chí, mong muốn

536 **徹夜〈する〉**（てつや）
名 **all night / 彻夜，通宵 / sự thức suốt đêm, thức trắng đêm**

昨日徹夜したので、今日はとても眠い。
I am very sleepy today because I stayed up all night yesterday. / 昨天通了个宵，所以今天非常困。/ Hôm qua tôi thức trắng đêm nên hôm nay rất buồn ngủ.

＋ 夜更かし〈する〉（よふかし） staying up late / 熬夜 / thức thâu đêm

537 **上達〈する〉**（じょうたつ）
名 **improvement / 提高 / sự tiến bộ, tiến triển**

半年で会話力が、かなり上達した。
My conversation skills improved substantially in the last six months. / 才半年时间，会话能力就有了很大的提升。/ Với nửa năm, năng lực hội thoại đã tiến bộ nhiều.

538 □	こつこつ［と］	①毎日(まいにち)こつこつと勉強(べんきょう)を続(つづ)けている。 ②靴(くつ)の音(おと)がこつこつと響(ひび)く。
副	**diligently / 刻苦，孜孜不倦 / 橐橐作响 / từng chút, lọc cọc**	① I study diligently every day. ② The sound of footsteps clacking resonated. / ①每天刻苦学习。②皮靴声橐橐作响。/ ① Hàng ngày tôi tiếp tục học từng chút từng chút. ② Tiếng giày vang lọc cọc.

☞ ① make effort steadily ② resonnate on a hard surface / ①勤奋努力②硬的东西碰撞的声音 / ① Nỗ lực đều đặn ② Âm thanh của vật cứng vang lên

539 □	地道(じみち)な	毎日(まいにち)、地道(じみち)に日本語(にほんご)を勉強(べんきょう)している。
ナ形	**steady, honest / 踏实 / đều đặn, vững chắc**	I study Japanese diligently every day. / 每天踏踏实实地学日语。/ Hàng ngày, tôi học tiếng Nhật đều đặn.
540 □	根気(こんき)	単語(たんご)は根気(こんき)よく覚(おぼ)えよう。
名	**patience / 毅力，耐心 / sự kiên nhẫn**	Learn vocabulary words patiently. / 背单词要有毅力。/ Hãy kiên nhẫn nhớ từ vựng.

➕ 根気強(こんきづよ)い very patient / 意志坚定，百折不挠 / nhẫn nại

541 □	効率的(こうりつてき)な	時間(じかん)を上手(じょうず)に使(つか)って、効率的(こうりつてき)に勉強(べんきょう)する。
ナ形	**effective / 高效的 / một cách hiệu quả**	Use your time wisely to study efficiently. / 擅用时间高效学习。/ Sử dụng thời gian thật khéo để học một cách hiệu quả.

➕ 合理的(ごうりてき)な rational / 合理的 / một cách hợp lý

542 □	旺盛(おうせい)な	好奇心(こうきしん)旺盛(おうせい)に新(あたら)しいことを学(まな)ぶ。
ナ形	**heartily / 旺盛 / mạnh mẽ, nồng nhiệt**	Have a great deal of curiosity and learn new things. / 怀着很强的好奇心学习新的东西。/ Học điều mới với lòng hiếu kỳ mạnh mẽ.

➕ 食欲旺盛(しょくよくおうせい)な eat heartily / 食欲旺盛 / ăn khỏe

543 □	基礎(きそ)	日本語(にほんご)の基礎(きそ)を、しっかり学(まな)びたい。
名	**basics / 基础 / căn bản, nền tảng**	I want to learn the basics of Japanese properly. / 想扎扎实实地打好日语基础。/ Tôi muốn học thật chắc căn bản tiếng Nhật.

➕ 基礎的(きそてき)な basic / 基础的 / một cách cơ bản

544 □	基本(きほん)	文法(ぶんぽう)の基本(きほん)を学(まな)んでから、会話(かいわ)を勉強(べんきょう)する。
名	**fundamentals / 基本 / cơ bản, căn bản**	Learn fundamental grammar first, then study conversation. / 学完语法的基本知识以后学习对话。/ Sau khi học căn bản văn phạm, sẽ học hội thoại.

➕ 基本的(きほんてき)な fundamental / 基本的 / một cách cơ bản

545 除く（のぞく）
動 aside from, excluding / 除去，去掉 / trừ ra, loại trừ

漢字を除けば、日本語の勉強は特に難しくない。
Studying the Japanese language is not so difficult except for the kanji. / 除了汉字以外，学日语不是特别难。/ Trừ Kanji ra, việc học tiếng Nhật không khó lắm.

546 現状（げんじょう）
名 current situation / 现状 / hiện trạng

先生に、現状では希望の大学は難しいと言われた。
My teacher told me that it will be difficult to get into my university of choice with my current grades. / 老师说按现状来看，（我）很难考上想上的大学。/ Tôi bị thầy / cô nói nếu với tình trạng hiện nay thì khó vào đại học đúng nguyện vọng.

547 おろそかな
ナ形 neglecting / 马虎，草率 / thờ ơ, sao lãng

学生は勉強をおろそかにしてはいけない。
Students should not neglect studies. / 作为学生，学习不能马虎敷衍。/ Sinh viên không được sao lãng việc học.

548 可能〈な〉（かのう）
名 ナ形 possibility/possible / 可能 / khả năng, có thể

努力すれば、不可能が可能になる。(名)
頑張れば、何だって可能だ。(ナ形)
Make the effort, then the impossible becomes possible. Anything is possible if you make an effort. / 只要努力，不可能会变成可能。只要加油，任何事都是可能的。/ Nếu nỗ lực, không thể sẽ trở thành có thể.Nếu cố gắng thì cái gì cũng có thể.

↔ 不可能〈な〉（ふかのう）　＋ 可能性（かのうせい） possibility / 可能性 / tính khả năng, khả thi

549 実現〈する〉（じつげん）
名 realization / 实现 / sự thực hiện

夢を実現するためには努力が必要だ。
You need to make efforts to make your dreams come true. / 要实现梦想就必须努力。/ Để thực hiện ước mơ, cần nỗ lực.

550 混同〈する〉（こんどう）
名 confusion / 混为一谈，混淆 / sự lẫn lộn, nhầm lẫn

似ている副詞は混同しやすい。
Similar adverbs are confusing. / 相似的副词容易混淆。/ Các phó từ giống nhau thì dễ nhầm lẫn.

＋ 公私混同〈する〉（こうしこんどう） mixing private and public / 公私不分 / lẫn lộn công tư

551 複数（ふくすう）
名 several / 复数，好几个 / số nhiều

日本語の名詞には単数形も複数形もない。
Japanese nouns do not have singular and plural forms. / 日语的名词没有单数形式和复数形式。/ Trong danh từ tiếng Nhật không có cả số ít lẫn số nhiều.

552 活用〈する〉（かつよう）
名 take advantage of / 活用，有效利用 / sự sử dụng hiệu quả, sự tận dụng

言葉を調べるときは、スマホを活用している。
Take advantage of your smartphone when looking up words. / 我会有效利用智能手机来查单词。/ Khi tra từ, tôi tận dụng điện thoại thông minh.

Section 3

試験（しけん）

Exam / 考试 / Thi cử

553 □ 名	挑戦〈する〉（ちょうせん） challenge / 挑战 / thử thách	今年、N2の試験に挑戦することにした。（ことし　しけん　ちょうせん） I decided to try taking the N2 exam this year. / 我决定今年去挑战N2的考试。/ Năm nay tôi quyết định thử thách với kỳ thi N2.

= チャレンジ〈する〉

554 □ 名	範囲（はんい） area / 范围 / phạm vi	次の試験の範囲は広い。（つぎ　しけん　はんい　ひろ） The next exam covers a wide range. / 下次考试的范围很广。/ Phạm vi bài thi sắp tới thì rộng.
555 □ 名	パターン pattern / 形式，模式 / kiểu, mẫu	文法の問題には、いろいろなパターンがある。（ぶんぽう　もんだい） There are various patterns to the grammar questions. / 语法题有很多形式。/ Câu hỏi văn phạm có nhiều kiểu.

＋ ワンパターン same pattern / 一种模式 / một kiểu, một mẫu

556 □ 連体	あらゆる various / 所有，一切 / tất cả	試験前にあらゆるパターンの問題をやってみた。（しけんまえ　もんだい） I tried solving different types of questions before the exam. / 考试前把所有形式的问题都试着做了。/ Trước kỳ thi, tôi đã làm thử tất cả các kiểu câu hỏi.

＋ ありとあらゆる of all sorts / 所有，一切 / một và tất cả

557 □ 名	課題（かだい） topic/issue / 题目 / 课题，任务 / đề tài, vấn đề	①小論文の課題は地球温暖化についてだった。（しょうろんぶん　かだい　ちきゅうおんだんか） ②日本には改善すべき課題が多くある。（にほん　かいぜん　かだい　おお） ① The topic of the short essay was about global warming. ② Japan has many issues that need to be improved. / ①小论文的主题是关于温室效应的。②日本有很多需要改善的课题。/ ① Đề tài tiểu luận là về trái đất ấm lên. ② Ở Nhật có nhiều vấn đề phải cải thiện.

☞ ① theme ② a problem that must be resolved / ①主题②必须要解决的问题 / ① Đề tài ② Vấn đề phải giải quyết.

558 □ 名	段落（だんらく） paragraph / 段落 / đoạn	最後の段落に重要なことが書かれている。（さいご　だんらく　じゅうよう　か） Something very important was written in the last paragraph. / 最后一段写着很重要的内容。/ Điều quan trọng được viết ở đoạn cuối cùng.
559 □ 名	箇所（かしょ） place / 部分，地方 / chỗ, điểm	問題に訂正箇所があった。（もんだい　ていせい　かしょ） There were corrections to the questions. / 问题中有修改订正了的部分。/ Trong câu hỏi có chỗ chỉnh sửa.

560 用紙（ようし）
名 **sheet / 用纸 / mẫu giấy**

問題と解答、２種類の用紙が配られた。
Two sheets, one for questions and one for answers, were passed out. / 发了试卷和答题卡。/ Tôi được phát 2 loại mẫu giấy, giấy đề thi và giấy trả lời.

➕ 問題用紙（もんだいようし） question sheet / 试卷，试题 / giấy đề thi・解答用紙（かいとうようし） answer sheet / 答题纸 / giấy trả lời・答案用紙（とうあんようし） answer sheet / 答案纸 / giấy đáp án

561 応用（おうよう）〈する〉
名 **application / 应用 / sự ứng dụng, áp dụng**

この問題は前に勉強した式を応用すれば、解ける。
This question can be solved by applying the equation we studied earlier. / 这个问题应用之前学的公式就能解答。/ Câu hỏi này nếu áp dụng công thức đã học lúc trước thì có thể giải được.

562 選択（せんたく）〈する〉
名 **selection / 选择 / sự lựa chọn, chọn lọc**

４つの中から一つを選択して、答えましょう。
Select one from the following four choices. / 请在四个当中选择一个作答。/ Hãy chọn 1 trong 4 câu để trả lời.

➕ 選択肢（せんたくし） choice / 选项 / các lựa chọn

563 当てはまる（あてはまる）
動 **fit / 合适 / đúng, thích hợp**

次の言葉の中から当てはまるものを選びましょう。
Select the appropriate answer from the following words. / 请在以下词语中选择合适的。/ Hãy chọn câu thích hợp từ những từ sau đây.

➕ (～を) 当てはめる（あてはめる） fit / 适用 / đúng với (~)

564 述べる（のべる）
動 **say / 陈述 / trình bày**

この段落で筆者が意見を述べている。
The author expresses her opinion in this paragraph. / 这个段落中，笔者陈述了自己的意见。/ Ý kiến của người viết được trình bày ở đoạn này.

565 言い換える（いいかえる）
動 **say differently / 换说法 / nói cách khác, đổi**

次の言葉を別の言葉に言い換えましょう。
Let's replace these words with other words. / 请将下面的词语换一种说法来表达。/ Hãy thay đổi cách nói của từ này bằng từ khác.

➕ 言い直す（いいなおす） say again / 换说法，改口 / nói sửa lại

566 考え込む（かんがえこむ）
動 **get caught up in one's thoughts / 苦思冥想 / suy nghĩ (một cách tập trung, chăm chú)**

問題が難しくて、考え込んでしまった。
The exam questions were difficult, and I was absorbed in thought. / 问题太难了，我陷入了冥思苦想之中。/ Câu hỏi khó nên tôi đã tập trung suy nghĩ.

567 □ 限る（かぎ）

動 **limit / 有限，限制 / 最好，顶好 / giới hạn, chỉ có**

①問題（もんだい）を解（と）く時間（じかん）は限（かぎ）られている。
②夏（なつ）はビールに限（かぎ）る。

① The time to answer the questions is limited. ② There is nothing better than beer in summer. / ①回答问题的时间有限。②夏天就是要喝啤酒。/ ① Thời gian giải đề thi có giới hạn. ② Mùa hè thì chỉ có bia là nhất.

☞ ① decide the range of something ② something that is the best / ①规定范围②最好 / ① Quyết định phạm vi ② Điều đó là tốt nhất

568 □ 紛らわしい（まぎ）

イ形 **confusing / 容易混淆，模糊不清 / mơ hồ**

N２になると、紛（まぎ）らわしい選択肢（せんたくし）も増（ふ）えてくる。

There are more confusing choices in N2 / 到了N2(考试)，会有更多容易混淆的选项。/ Lên N2 rồi thì những lựa chọn mơ hồ cũng tăng lên.

569 □ さっぱり（～ない）

副 **at all / 完全 / hoàn toàn (không ~)**

この問題（もんだい）は、いくら考（かんが）えてもさっぱりわからない。

No matter how much I think about this question, I can't figure it out at all. / 这个问题我想破脑袋也不会。/ Vấn đề này, có suy nghĩ bao nhiêu cũng hoàn toàn không hiểu.

570 □ 勘（かん）

名 **hunch / 感觉，直觉 / trực giác, linh cảm**

わからない問題（もんだい）は勘（かん）を働（はたら）かせて答（こた）える。

Use your hunch for questions you don't know the answer to. / 不会的问题都凭感觉回答。/ Những câu hỏi không hiểu thì tôi trả lời dựa vào trực giác.

➕ 直感（ちょっかん） gut feeling / 直觉 / trực cảm

571 □ 本番（ほんばん）

名 **real stage, real part / 正式 / buổi (ngày) chính thức, thực thụ**

試験（しけん）の本番（ほんばん）が近（ちか）づいてきて、緊張（きんちょう）している。

I am getting nervous as the day for the exam is approaching. / 离正式考试越来越近了，我很紧张。/ Ngày thi chính thức đến gần nên tôi căng thẳng.

➕ 当日（とうじつ） the day of / 当天 / ngày (diễn ra) chính thức

572 □ 迫る（せま）

動 **approach / 临近 / 逼近 / tiến gần, gần sát**

①試験（しけん）の日（ひ）が迫（せま）ってきた。
②彼（かれ）に危険（きけん）が迫（せま）っている。

① The day of the exam is getting closer. ② Danger is approaching him. / ①考试迫在眉睫。②他面临危险。/ ① Ngày thi đã đến gần. ② Nguy hiểm tiến sát anh ấy.

☞ ① time is getting closer ② distance is getting closer / ①时间越来越近②距离越来越近 / ① Thời gian đến gần ② Cự ly trở nên gần

573 □ 必死な（ひっし）

ナ形 **desperate / 拼命 / quyết tâm, hết sức**

合格（ごうかく）を目指（めざ）して、必死（ひっし）に頑張（がんば）った。

He worked desperately to pass the exam. / 以通过考试为目标拼命努力。/ Hướng đến việc thi đậu, tôi đã cố gắng hết sức.

➕ 一生懸命（いっしょうけんめい）〈な〉 with all one's might/earnest / 拼命 / hết sức mình, dốc hết sức

574 □ 副	いっせいに all at once / 一齐，同时 / đồng loạt	受験生(じゅけんせい)はいっせいに問題(もんだい)を読(よ)み始(はじ)めた。 The examinees started reading the questions all at once. / 考生们一齐开始看问题。/ Thí sinh dự thi đồng loạt bắt đầu đọc đề thi.
575 □ 名	終了(しゅうりょう)〈する〉 finished / 结束 / sự kết thúc,chấm dứt	「終(お)わりです」という声(こえ)で、試験(しけん)が終了(しゅうりょう)した。 The exam ended with a voice saying, "This is the end." / 随着一声"时间到"，考试结束了。/ Kỳ thi kết thúc bằng tiếng hô "Kết thúc".
576 □ 名	回収(かいしゅう)〈する〉 retrieve, collect / 回收 / sự thu hồi	試験終了後(しけんしゅうりょうご)、問題用紙(もんだいようし)と解答用紙(かいとうようし)が回収(かいしゅう)された。 The question and answer sheets were collected after the exam ended. / 考试结束后，试卷和答题卡都被收走了。/ Sau khi buổi thi kết thúc, giấy đề thi và giấy trả lời được thu hồi.
577 □ 名	採点(さいてん)〈する〉 grade / 评分 / việc chấm điểm	採点(さいてん)はコンピューターで行(おこな)われる。 The grading will be conducted by a computer. / 由电脑进行评分。/ Việc chấm điểm được tiến hành bằng máy tính.
578 □ ナ形	確実(かくじつ)な definitely / 准确，确实 / chắc chắn	彼(かれ)なら、合格(ごうかく)は確実(かくじつ)だと思(おも)う。 He will definitely pass the exam. / 我觉得他肯定能考过。/ Anh ấy thì tôi nghĩ đậu là cái chắc.

接辞(せつじ)：感情等(かんじょうなど)② Affix: Emotions, etc. / 词缀：情感等 / Phụ tố: Tình cảm v.v.

- **～観(かん)（見方(みかた)、考(かんが)え方(かた)）**

人生観(じんせいかん)	view on life / 人生观 / Nhân sinh quan
価値観(かちかん)	values / 价值观 / Giá trị quan
先入観(せんにゅうかん)	prejudice / 先入为主，成见 / Thành kiến, định kiến
世界観(せかいかん)	world view / 世界观 / Thế giới quan
結婚観(けっこんかん)	view on marriage / 婚姻观 / Quan niệm hôn nhân
職業観(しょくぎょうかん)	view on work / 职业观 / Quan niệm nghề nghiệp

大学・大学院

University, Graduate School / 大学・大学研究生院 / Đại học - Cao học

579 □ 名	受講〈する〉	田中教授の講義を受講することにした。
	attending the lecture / 上课，听课 / sự học, dự học	I decided to attend Prof. Tanaka's lecture. / 决定去听田中教授的课。/ Tôi quyết định dự học giờ của giáo sư Tanaka.
580 □ 動	書き留める	講義の内容を、しっかり書き留める。
	write down / 记下来 / ghi chép lại	I diligently took notes of the lecture. / 把课堂内容认真地记下来。/ Tôi ghi chép nội dung giờ học một cách đầy đủ.
581 □ 名	目標	経営学を学び、会社を経営するのが私の目標だ。
	goal, target / 目标 / mục tiêu	Studying business administration and starting my own company is my goal. / 学习经营学，将来经营自己的公司是我的目标。/Học kinh doanh và kinh doanh công ty là mục tiêu của tôi.
582 □ 名	心構え	大学では積極的に学ぼうとする心構えが必要だ。
	frame of mind / 思想准备 / sự chuẩn bị tinh thần	In college, one needs to be in a frame of mind to study enthusiastically. / 在大学必须要有好好学习的思想准备。/ Ở đại học cần có sự chuẩn bị tinh thần học hỏi một cách tích cực.

➕ 心掛け mental attitude / 留心，留意 / sự chuẩn bị tinh thần, sẵn sàng

583 □ 名	学問	大学は学問の場である。
	learning, study / 学问 / học vấn	The university is a place of learning. / 大学是做学问的地方。/ Đại học là môi trường học vấn.
584 □ 名	分野	この大学は科学の分野で知られている。
	field / 领域 / lĩnh vực	This university is known for its science field. / 这所大学因其科学领域而闻名于世。/ Trường đại học này nổi tiếng về lĩnh vực khoa học.

= ジャンル

585 □ 動	取り組む	来年は新しい研究に取り組みたい。
	engage / 全力对付，致力于 / nỗ lực, bắt tay (làm gì đó), đưa vào	I want to engage in a new research next year. / 明年我想致力于新的研究。/ Sang năm tôi muốn bắt tay vào nghiên cứu mới.

➕ 取り組み engagement / 对策，认真应对 / sự nỗ lực

586 □ **意欲** いよく

名 **enthusiasm / 热情，积极性 / ý chí, mong muốn, động lực**

この大学には意欲がある学生が多い。（だいがく・いよく・がくせい・おお）

There are many enthusiastic students in this university. / 这个大学里有很多积极向上的学生。/ Trường đại học này có nhiều sinh viên có ý chí.

587 □ **思いつく** おも

動 **come up with / 想出，突然想起 / nghĩ ra**

セミナーに参加して、論文のテーマを思いついた。（さんか・ろんぶん・おも）

I came up with the idea for my thesis after attending the seminar. / 参加了研讨会，想出了论文的题目。/ Tôi tham gia hội thảo chuyên đề và nghĩ ra đề tài luận văn.

＋ 思いつき（おも） fancy / 灵机一动，随便一想 / sự nghĩ ra

588 □ **発明〈する〉** はつめい

名 **invention / 发明 / phát minh**

社会に役立つ機械を発明したい。（しゃかい・やくだ・きかい・はつめい）

I want to invent a machine that is useful to society. / 想发明对社会有帮助的机器。/ Tôi muốn phát minh ra máy móc có ích cho xã hội.

＋ 発明家（はつめいか） inventor / 发明家 / nhà phát minh

589 □ **分析〈する〉** ぶんせき

名 **analysis / 分析 / sự phân tích**

データを分析して、結果をレポートにまとめる。（ぶんせき・けっか）

Analyze the data and write up a report about the findings. / 分析数据，把结果整理成报告。/ Tôi phân tích dữ liệu và tóm tắt kết quả vào bài báo cáo.

590 □ **継続〈する〉** けいぞく

名 **continuity / 继续，持续 / sự kế thừa, kế tục**

この研究は継続する価値がある。（けんきゅう・けいぞく・かち）

It is worth continuing this research. / 这个研究有继续进行下去的价值。/ Nghiên cứu này có giá trị kế thừa.

591 □ **ほんの**

連体 **just / 一点点 / chỉ (một chút)**

前回はほんの少し点が足らず、不合格だった。（ぜんかい・すこ・てん・た・ふごうかく）

He failed last time because he was short just a few points. / 上次的分数就差了那么一点点，（结果）没有及格。/ Lần trước chỉ vì thiếu một chút điểm mà tôi không đậu.

592 □ **受け入れる** う い

動 **accept / 接纳，接受 / tiếp nhận**

最近では、ほとんどの大学で留学生を受け入れている。（さいきん・だいがく・りゅうがくせい・う い）

Most universities accept overseas students these days. / 最近几乎所有的大学都招收留学生。/ Gần đây, hầu hết các trường đại học đều tiếp nhận du học sinh.

593 □ **キャンパス**

名 **campus / 校园 / khuôn viên**

この大学のキャンパスは、とても活気がある。（だいがく・かっき）

The campus of this university is very lively. / 这个大学的校园非常有活力。/ Khuôn viên trường đại học này rất sôi động.

594 休講〈する〉 きゅうこう
名 canceled class / 休讲，停课 / (giờ học) được nghỉ

先生の都合で今日は休講になった。
せんせい　つごう　きょう　きゅうこう
The class was canceled due to the professor's circumstances. / 因为老师有事，所以今天停课。/ Do thời gian biểu của giáo viên nên giờ học hôm nay được nghỉ.

595 講師 こうし
名 lecturer / 讲师 / giáo viên, người đứng lớp

大学には個性的な講師も多い。
だいがく　こせいてき　こうし　おお
There are many unique lecturers in this university. / 大学里有很多有个性的讲师。/ Ở đại học có nhiều giáo viên cá tính.

596 学会 がっかい
名 academic conference / 学会 / học hội

先週、日本語の学会に出席した。
せんしゅう　にほんご　がっかい　しゅっせき
Last week I attended an academic conference on the Japanese language. / 上星期出席了日语学会。/ Tuần trước, tôi đã tham dự học hội tiếng Nhật.

597 わずか［な／に］
ナ形 副 few/only little bit / 稍微，仅一点 / chỉ một chút, ít ỏi

このゼミに入れる学生は、ごくわずかだ。（ナ形）
はい　がくせい
There are only few students who can attend this seminar. / 能参加这个研究讨论小组的学生非常少。/ Số sinh viên có thể vào khóa học chuyên đề này rất ít ỏi.

598 論理的な ろんりてき
ナ形 logical / 逻辑性的 / một cách hợp lý, lý luận

日本語で論理的な文を書くのは大変だ。
にほんご　ろんりてき　ぶん　か　たいへん
It is difficult to write logically in Japanese. / 用日语写逻辑性的文章很困难。/ Viết câu văn lý luận bằng tiếng Nhật thật khó.

599 論じる ろん
動 argue, reason / 论述 / luận bàn, tranh luận

経済問題に関する意見を論じる。
けいざいもんだい　かん　いけん　ろん
We debated about economic issues. / 论述与经济问题相关的观点。/ Tranh luận ý kiến liên quan đến vấn đề kinh tế.

600 引用〈する〉 いんよう
名 quote / 引用 / sự trích dẫn

他人の論文を引用するときにはルールがある。
たにん　ろんぶん　いんよう
There are rules on how to quote someone else's paper. / 引用他人的论文时有一定的规则。/ Khi trích dẫn luận văn của người khác thì có quy định.

601 訳す やく
動 translate / 翻译 / dịch

論文を英語に訳して、雑誌で発表する。
ろんぶん　えいご　やく　ざっし　はっぴょう
The paper will be translated into English and presented in a magazine. / 把论文翻译成英语发表在杂志上。/ Dịch luận văn sang tiếng Anh và công bố trên tạp chí.

602 編集〈する〉 へんしゅう
名 edit / 编辑 / sự biên tập

この文は少し編集が必要だ。
ぶん　すこ　へんしゅう　ひつよう
This sentence needs to be slightly edited. / 这篇文章需要稍微编辑一下。/ Đoạn văn này cần biên tập một chút.

＋ 編集者 へんしゅうしゃ editor / 编辑，编者 / biên tập viên

603 □ 名	要旨 (ようし) summary / 要旨 / bản tóm lược, tóm tắt	レポートの要旨を800字程度にまとめた。(ようし, じていど) I summarized the report to about 800 words. / 用800字左右总结了报告的重点。/ Tôi đã tóm tắt bài bài tóm lược báo cáo trong khoảng 800 chữ.

➕ 要点 (ようてん) main point / 要点 / điểm quan trọng

604 □ ナ形	明確な (めいかく) clear / 明确 / rành mạch, rõ ràng	論文では言いたいことを明確にすることが重要だ。(ろんぶん, い, めいかく, じゅうよう) It is important to be clear about what you want to say in a research paper. / 在论文里，明确地表达论点很重要。/ Trong luận văn, làm rõ điều mình muốn nói rất quan trọng.
605 □ 動	挙げる (あ) raise, name / 举出 / đưa ra, nêu lên	具体的な例を挙げて、論文の主張をサポートする。(ぐたいてき, れい, あ, ろんぶん, しゅちょう) Support your argument in a research paper by naming concrete examples. / 举出具体的例子来支持论文的论点。/ Đưa ra ví dụ cụ thể để hỗ trợ cho chủ trương của luận văn.
606 □ 動	用いる (もち) use / 用 / sử dụng, áp dụng	データを用いて、問題を分析する。(もち, もんだい, ぶんせき) Use data to analyze the problem. / 用数据分析问题。/ Sử dụng dữ liệu để phân tích vấn đề.
607 □ 名	手書き (てが) handwritten / 手写 / bản viết tay, sự viết tay	手書きのレポートは受け付けません。(てが, う, つ) Handwritten papers will not be accepted. / 不接受手写的报告。/ Không tiếp nhận bài báo cáo viết tay.
608 □ 副	一気に (いっき) all at once / 一口气 / một hơi, một mạch	レポートを二日で一気に書いた。(ふつか, いっき, か) I wrote up the report in just two days. / 我用两天一口气写完了报告。/ Tôi đã viết bài báo cáo một mạch trong 2 ngày.
609 □ 名	完成〈する〉(かんせい) completion / 完成 / sự hoàn thành	何度も書き直して、やっとレポートが完成した。(なんど, か, なお, かんせい) I finally completed the report after rewriting it several times. / 修改了很多次，终于完成了报告。/ Tôi viết đi viết lại nhiều lần, cuối cùng cũng hoàn thành bài báo cáo.

Section 5

パソコン（スマホ）

Personal Computer (Smartphone) / 电脑（智能手机）/ Máy tính (Điện thoại thông minh)

610 □ 名	起動〈する〉(きどう) start / 启动 / sự khởi động	パソコンを起動する。 I booted up the computer. / 启动电脑。/ Khởi động máy tính.
		➕ 再起動〈する〉(さいきどう) restart / 重起 / sự tái khởi động
611 □ 名	本体(ほんたい) main unit / 机身，主体 / phần chính, đầu máy (vi tính v.v.)	このパソコンの本体は日本製だ。 This personal computer's main unit is made in Japan. / 这台电脑的主机是日本产的。/ Đầu máy tính này là hàng sản xuất tại Nhật.
612 □ 名	キーボード keyboard / 键盘 / bàn phím	彼はキーボードを見ずに入力できる。 He can type without looking at the keyboard. / 他能不看键盘打字。/ Anh ấy có thể đánh máy mà không nhìn bàn phím.
613 □ 名	ディスプレイ display / 显示器 / màn hình, sự hiển thị	大きなディスプレイだと、画面が見やすい。 It's easier to see the screen if the display is large. / 大的显示器看起来舒服。/ Nếu là màn hình lớn thì giao diện dễ xem.
614 □ 名	接続〈する〉(せつぞく) connection / 接上，连接 / sự kết nối	インターネットに接続して、検索する。 I accessed the Internet to conduct a search. / 联网检索信息。/ Kết nối mạng internet để tìm kiếm.
615 □ 名	検索〈する〉(けんさく) search / 查，搜索 / sự tìm kiếm	日本語研究の論文を検索する。 I searched for a research paper on the Japanese language. / 搜索日语研究的论文。/ Tìm kiếm luận văn nghiên cứu tiếng Nhật.
616 □ 名	転送〈する〉(てんそう) forward / 转发 / sự gửi chuyển tiếp	役に立ちそうな情報を友人に転送した。 I forwarded what appeared to be useful information to my friend. / 把看起来有用的信息转发给了朋友。/ Tôi đã gửi chuyển tiếp thông tin có vẻ có ích cho người bạn thân.
617 □ 名	文書(ぶんしょ) sentence / 文件 / văn bản	パソコンで文書を作る。 I wrote sentences using the personal computer. / 用电脑写文件。/ Soạn thảo văn bản bằng máy tính.
618 □ 名	設定〈する〉(せってい) setup / 设定 / sự định dạng	文字の設定を、もう少し大きくする。 Make the fonts slightly larger. / 把文字的字号再设置得大一些。/ Định dạng chữ lớn hơn một chút.

619 □ 名	余白（よはく） **margin / 空白 / lề giấy, sự chừa lề, canh lề**	上下（じょうげ）の余白（よはく）を2センチにする。 Set the top and bottom margins to be two centimeters. / 上下空出2厘米。/ Canh lề trên dưới 2 cm.
620 □ 名	フォント **font / 字体 / kiểu chữ, phông chữ**	細（ほそ）いフォントを選（えら）んで、メールを書（か）く。 Select small fonts to write an e-mail. / 选择细一点的字体写邮件。/Chọn kiểu chữ hẹp và viết e-mail.
621 □ 名	カーソル **cursor / 光标 / con trỏ**	カーソルが、うまく動（うご）かない。 The cursor isn't moving smoothly. / 光标无法顺畅地移动。/ Con trỏ hoạt động không tốt.
622 □ 名	改行（かいぎょう）〈する〉 **new sentence / 换行 / sự xuống hàng**	文章（ぶんしょう）が読（よ）みやすいように改行（かいぎょう）する。 Start a new line to make it easier to read the sentence. / 为了使文章读起来更容易理解而换行。/ Xuống hàng để dễ đọc câu văn.
623 □ 動	区切（くぎ）る **separate / 分，分割 / cách đoạn**	段落（だんらく）を区切（くぎ）るときには、改行（かいぎょう）して1字（じ）下（さ）げる。 Press start a new line and indent one character when starting new paragraphs. / 分段的时候要另起一行，再空一格。/ Khi cách đoạn thì xuống hàng, hạ khoảng cách xuống 1 ký tự.

➕ 区切（くぎ）り separation / 分段，段落 / sự cách đoạn

624 □ 動	貼（は）り付（つ）ける **paste / 贴，粘贴 / dán**	画像（がぞう）をコピーして、新規（しんき）ファイルに貼（は）り付（つ）ける。 Copy the image and paste it into a new file. / 复制图片粘贴到新文件里。/ Sao chép hình ảnh và dán vào tập tin mới.
625 □ 名	強調（きょうちょう）〈する〉 **emphasize / 强调 / sự nhấn mạnh**	文章（ぶんしょう）の中（なか）で強調（きょうちょう）したい文字（もじ）を太（ふと）くする。 Turn the letters you want to emphasize in the sentence into boldface. / 把文中要强调的文字加粗。/ Làm đậm chữ muốn nhấn mạnh trong đoạn văn.
626 □ 名	拡大（かくだい）〈する〉 **enlarge / 扩大 / sự mở rộng, làm lớn, phóng lớn**	写真（しゃしん）を少（すこ）し拡大（かくだい）して、保存（ほぞん）する。 Enlarge the photo a little and save. / 把照片放大一些再保存。/ Phóng lớn hình một chút và lưu lại.

↔ 縮小（しゅくしょう）〈する〉

627 □ 名	消去（しょうきょ）〈する〉 **delete / 删除，去掉 / sự xóa bỏ**	過去（かこ）のメールを消去（しょうきょ）した。 I deleted my past e-mails. / 把以前的邮件都删了。/ Tôi đã xóa các e-mail cũ.

628 □ 名	上書き保存〈する〉(うわがきほぞん)	作った文書を上書き保存した。
	overwrite save / 覆盖保存 / sự lưu đè (lên dữ liệu cũ)	I did an overwrite save of my writings. / 保存时选择了用新（写好的）文件替换了旧的。/Tôi đã lưu đè văn bản đã soạn.
629 □ 名	順序(じゅんじょ)	スマホのアイコンの順序を並び替える。
	order / 顺序 / thứ tự, trật tự, tuần tự	I changed the order of the icons on my smartphone. / 重新排列智能手机上（应用程序）的图标。/ Thay đổi trật tự các biểu tượng của điện thoại thông minh.
630 □ 名	印刷〈する〉(いんさつ)	完成した文書を印刷する。
	print / 打印，印刷 / việc in	I printed the completed document. / 把写好的文件打印出来。/ In văn bản đã hoàn thành.

➕ プリントアウト〈する〉 printout / 打印 / việc in ra

631 □ 名	プリンター	最近、プリンターの調子が悪い。
	printer / 打印机 / máy in	The printer hasn't been working properly these days. / 最近打印机不太好用。/ Gần đây, tình trạng máy in không tốt.
632 □ 名	インク	インクが少なくなってきたので、買っておこう。
	ink / 墨水 / mực	The printer is running out of ink, so I need to go buy some. / 墨水快没了，去买点来备着吧。/ Vì mực gần hết nên mua để sẵn thôi.

これも覚えよう！⑯

➕ **接辞：感情等③** Affix: Emotions, etc. / 词缀：情感等 / Phụ tố: Tình cảm v.v.

• ～心（持っている心）

好奇心(こうきしん)	curiosity / 好奇心 / Tính hiếu kỳ, tò mò
親切心(しんせつしん)	kindness / 热心肠 / Tình thân thiết
恐怖心(きょうふしん)	fear / 恐惧心 / Nỗi sợ hãi
対抗心(たいこうしん)	rivalry / 对抗心理 / Tinh thần đối kháng
反抗心(はんこうしん)	defiance / 反抗心理 / Tinh thần phản kháng
探究心(たんきゅうしん)	inquisitive mind / 探究心理 / Tinh thần học hỏi

N2

Chapter 6

会社で

かいしゃ

At the Office / 公司篇 / Tại công ty

Section 1

就職（しゅうしょく）

Finding Employment / 就职 / Tìm việc / Việc làm

633 □ 名

求人（きゅうじん）	求人のサイトをチェックする。
employment offers / 招聘 / tìm người	I checked a job search website. / 查看招聘网站上的信息。/ Kiểm tra trang web tuyển người.

➕ 求人広告（きゅうじんこうこく） classified ad / 招聘广告 / mục quảng cáo tìm người

634 □ 名

志望（しぼう）〈する〉	A社（しゃ）の営業（えいぎょう）を志望（しぼう）している。
desire / 志愿 / nguyện vọng	He wants to join the sales team of Company A. / 我希望能进入A公司的销售部门。/ Tôi có nguyện vọng vào ban kinh doanh của công ty A.

➕ 志望校（しぼうこう） school of choice / 志愿学校 / trường nguyện vọng・
第一志望（だいいちしぼう） first school of choice / 第一志愿 / nguyện vọng 1

635 □ 名

エントリー〈する〉	いくつかの企業（きぎょう）にエントリーした。
apply / 申请，报名 / sự vào, tiến vào, dự tuyển	I applied to several companies. / 我应聘了几家公司。/ Tôi đã dự tuyển vài doanh nghiệp.

➕ エントリーシート application sheet / 应聘申请表 / phiếu dự tuyển (lý lịch)

636 □ 動

携（たずさ）わる	福祉（ふくし）の仕事（しごと）に携（たずさ）わりたい。
take part, be involved / 参与，从事 / làm việc có liên quan	I want to take part in the welfare business. / 我想从事社会福利相关的工作。/ Tôi muốn làm việc có liên quan đến công việc phúc lợi.

637 □ 動

生（い）かす	専門（せんもん）が生（い）かせる仕事（しごと）をしたい。
take advantage of / 活用 / phát huy, tận dụng	I want to work where I can take advantage of my expertise. / 我想从事能发挥自己专业特长的工作。/ Tôi muốn làm công việc có thể phát huy chuyên môn.

638 □ 名

貴社（きしゃ）	ぜひ、貴社（きしゃ）で働（はたら）かせていただきたいです。
your esteemed company / 贵公司 / quý công ty	I truly want to work at your esteemed company. / 我很想为贵公司效力。/ Nhất định vui lòng cho tôi được làm việc ở quý công ty.

＝ 御社（おんしゃ）　⇔ 弊社（へいしゃ）

639 □ 名	御中 (おんちゅう) **and Company; Messrs; for the attention of ... / 公启 / kính gửi**	会社への手紙には会社名の後に「御中」と書く。 When writing to a company, address the company as "on-chu" after writing down the company name. / 给公司写信时在公司名后面写上"公启"。/ Thư gửi cho công ty thì viết " 御中 " sau tên công ty.
640 □ 名	動機 (どうき) **motive / 动机 / động cơ**	面接で志望の動機をうまく伝える。 Convey your motive clearly for applying to the company in the interview. / 面试时充分表达出自己的应聘动机。/ Trong buổi phỏng vấn, truyền đạt tốt động cơ nguyện vọng.

➕ 志望動機 (しぼうどうき) motive for application / 志愿动机 / động cơ nguyện vọng

641 □ 名	熱意 (ねつい) **enthusiasm / 热情 / thành ý, nhiệt tình**	面接では入社したいという熱意を見せた。 I showed my enthusiasm about working at the company in the interview. / 面试时展现出了自己想进入公司工作的热情。/ Trong buổi phỏng vấn, tôi đã cho thấy thành ý muốn vào công ty.
642 □ 名	学歴 (がくれき) **academic background / 学历 / lý lịch học tập**	履歴書に学歴や資格を書く。 Write down the schools you attended and any certification you have in your resume. / 在简历中写上学历和所取得的资格证等。/ Trong lý lịch viết lý lịch học tập và chứng chỉ.

➕ 高学歴 (こうがくれき) high academic achievement / 高学历 / học vấn cao

643 □ 名	不問 (ふもん) **unmentioned / 不问 / không hỏi**	求人広告に経験不問と書いてある。 The job advertisement says no experience is necessary. / 招聘广告上写着（从业）经验不限。/ Ở quảng cáo tuyển người có viết không đòi hỏi kinh nghiệm.

➕ 問わない (と) does not matter / 不问 / không hỏi・学歴不問 (がくれきふもん) academic background does not matter / 学历不限 / không hỏi lý lịch học tập・性別不問 (せいべつふもん) gender does not matter / 性别不限 / không hỏi giới tính・年齢不問 (ねんれいふもん) age does not matter / 年龄不限 / không hỏi tuổi

644 □ 名	制限〈する〉 (せいげん) **limit / 限制 / sự hạn chế, giới hạn**	求人広告に年齢の制限は書いていない。 There is no age limit written on the job advertisement. / 招聘广告上没有写年龄限制。/ Ở quảng cáo tuyển người, không viết giới hạn độ tuổi.

➕ 速度制限 (そくどせいげん) speed limit / 限速 / sự hạn chế tốc độ・
人数制限 (にんずうせいげん) limit on number of persons / 人数限制 / sự hạn chế số người

645 □ 名	特技 (とくぎ) one's strong point, special ablity / 特长 / sở trường, kỹ năng đặc biệt	私の趣味・特技は、テニスと料理です。 My hobby and specialty are tennis and cooking. / 我的爱好和特长是打网球和烹饪。/ Sở thích, sở trường của tôi là quần vợt và nấu ăn.
646 □ 名	協調〈する〉(きょうちょう) cooperation / 协调 / sự hòa đồng, hợp tác	面接では、同僚と協調できるかをチェックされる。 They check whether you can cooperate with colleagues at the interview. / 面试时会考察应聘者能否和同事协作。/ Ở buổi phỏng vấn, sẽ được kiểm tra có thể hợp tác với đồng nghiệp không.

➕ 協調性 (きょうちょうせい) cooperativeness / 协调性 / tính hòa đồng, hợp tác

647 □ ナ形	肝心な (かんじん) vital / 重要的 / chủ yếu, cốt lõi	日本の会社では協調性が肝心だ。 The ability to cooperate with others is vital in Japanese companies. / 在日企里，与人合作的能力是很重要的。/ Ở công ty Nhật, tính hợp tác là cốt lõi.
648 □ 名 副	精一杯 (せいいっぱい) to the best of my ability/to the best of my ability / 尽力，全力以赴 / hết sức mình, dốc hết sức	志望の会社に採用されたら、精一杯頑張りたい。(副) I want to do my best if I'm accepted in the company of my choice. / 如果被想进的公司录用的话，我一定会全力以赴。/ Nếu được tuyển vào công ty đúng nguyện vọng, tôi sẽ cố gắng hết sức mình.
649 □ 名	アピール〈する〉 appeal / 呼吁，宣传 / sự giới thiệu, làm nổi bật	面接で上手に自分をアピールできるか心配だ。 I am worried about whether I'll be able to sell myself in the interview. / 担心面试时能否充分地展示出自己的优点。/ Tôi lo lắng không biết liệu có thể giới thiệu mình tốt trong buổi phỏng vấn không.

➕ 自己 (じこ) アピール〈する〉 self-appeal / 自我宣传 / sự tự giới thiệu, tự làm nổi bật

650 □ 名	対応〈する〉(たいおう) respond / 应对 / sự ứng xử, trả lời	面接の質問に、しっかり対応できたと思う。 I think I was able to respond properly to the questions during the interview. / 面试时被问到的问题觉得自己都还回答得不错。/ Tôi nghĩ mình đã trả lời tốt các câu hỏi trong buổi phỏng vấn.
651 □ 名	合同〈する〉(ごうどう) joint / 联合 / sự kết hợp, chung, tập thể	いろいろな企業の合同説明会に参加した。 I participated in many joint company orientations. / 参加了各种企业的联合说明会。/ Tôi đã tham gia nhiều buổi thuyết minh tập thể của nhiều doanh nghiệp khác nhau.

➕ 合同発表 (ごうどうはっぴょう)〈する〉 joint announcement / 联合发布 / sự phát biểu tập thể

652 □ イ形	望ましい (のぞ) desirable / 合乎心意的 / được mong muốn, kỳ vọng	この会社では語学のできる人が望ましいそうだ。(かいしゃ ごがく ひと のぞ) This company desires people who can speak different languages. / 听说这家公司希望能招聘到会外语的人。/ Nghe nói công ty này muốn tuyển người có khả năng về ngôn ngữ.
653 □ イ形	好ましい (この) preferable / 讨喜 / được ưa chuộng, đáng mến	面接には黒か紺のスーツが好ましい。(めんせつ くろ こん この) Black or blue suits are preferable for interviews. / 参加面试宜穿黑色或深蓝色的西服套装。/ Trong buổi phỏng vấn, đồ vest đen hay xanh đậm thì được ưa chuộng.

➕ 好む (この) prefer / 喜欢 / yêu thích, ưa chuộng

654 □ 名 ナ形	公平〈な〉(こうへい) fair/fair / 公平 / sự công bằng, công bằng	この会社の採用は公平に決められる。(ナ形) (かいしゃ さいよう こうへい き) Admission in this company is decided in a fair manner. / 这家公司对于新员工的录用是比较公平的。/ Việc tuyển dụng của công ty này được quyết định công bằng.

↔ 不公平〈な〉(ふこうへい) ➕ 公正〈な〉(こうせい) fair/fair / 公正 / sự công chính, công chính

655 □ 副	せめて at least / 至少 / ít nhất, tối thiểu	せめて、一社だけでも内定が欲しい。(いっしゃ ないてい ほ) I want an official job offer from at least one company. / 希望至少能获得一家公司的内定录取。/ Tôi mong tối thiểu cũng được một công ty quyết định nội bộ.
656 □ 動	受け取る (う と) receive / 收，领 / nhận được	第一志望だった企業から、通知を受け取った。(だいいちしぼう きぎょう つうち う と) I received a notice from the company that I wanted to join the most. / 收到了最想进的那家公司发来的通知。/ Tôi đã nhận được thông báo từ doanh nghiệp nguyện vọng 1
657 □ 名	内定〈する〉(ないてい) official job offer / 内定录取 / quyết định nội bộ, tạm quyết định (thường dùng trong tuyển dụng)	三つの会社から内定をもらった。(みっ かいしゃ ないてい) I received an official job offer from three companies. / 三家公司都内定录取我了。/ Tôi đã nhận quyết định nội bộ từ 3 công ty.
658 □ 名	辞退〈する〉(じたい) decline / 辞谢，推辞 / sự từ chối	第一志望の会社以外は、すぐに辞退した。(だいいちしぼう かいしゃ いがい じたい) I immediately declined the job offers from companies that were not my first choice. / 除了最想进的那家公司，其他（公司）我都立刻推掉了。/ Ngoài công ty đúng nguyện vọng 1, tôi đã từ chối (các công ty khác) ngay.

659 □ 名	契約〈する〉(けいやく) **contract / 合同 / hợp đồng**	希望(きぼう)していた会社(かいしゃ)と契約(けいやく)できて、うれしい。 I am happy to be able to sign a contract with the company of my choice. / 能和想进的公司顺利签合同，非常开心。/ Được hợp đồng với công ty mình có nguyện vọng, tôi rất vui.

➕ 契約書(けいやくしょ) contract / 合同书 / bản hợp đồng・契約社員(けいやくしゃいん) contract employee / 合同工 / nhân viên hợp đồng

660 □ 名	入社〈する〉(にゅうしゃ) **joining the company / 入社 / sự vào công ty**	4月(がつ)の入社(にゅうしゃ)が、とても楽(たの)しみだ。 I am looking forward to joining the company in April. / 4 月就要进入公司工作了，很期待。/ Tôi rất mong đến ngày vào công ty vào tháng 4.

↔ 退社〈する〉(たいしゃ)

661 □ 動	心得る(こころえ) **be aware of / 明白 / thấu hiểu, nhận thức**	社会人(しゃかいじん)と学生(がくせい)との違(ちが)いを心得(こころえ)ておく。 I should be aware of the difference between being a student and a working adult. / 要明白参加工作的人和学生之间的区别。/ Nhận thức sự khác biệt giữa người đã đi làm và sinh viên.

➕ 心得(こころえ) awareness / 心得 / sự thấu hiểu, nhận thức

662 □ 名	社会人(しゃかいじん) **an adult, a full-fledged member of society / 走上社会的人，参加工作的人 / người đi làm, người đã ra ngoài xã hội**	先輩(せんぱい)から社会人(しゃかいじん)としての心得(こころえ)を教(おそ)わる。 My senior co-worker taught me the rules of being a full-fledged member of society. / 向前辈请教了走上社会之后应该注意的事情。/ Được người đàn anh dạy về nhận thức với tư cách người đi làm.
663 □ 名	自覚〈する〉(じかく) **self-awareness / 自觉 / tự giác**	就職後(しゅうしょくご)は社会人(しゃかいじん)としての自覚(じかく)を持(も)とう。 Have a sense of responsibility as an adult when you start working. / 就职之后就要有一个已经参加工作的人的自觉。/ Sau khi tìm việc, hãy tự giác với tư cách người đi làm.

➕ 自覚症状(じかくしょうじょう) noticable symptoms / 自觉症状 / triệu chứng tự nhận biết

664 □ 副	いよいよ **finally / 终于 / dần dần, rồi thì, cuối cùng**	いよいよ、春(はる)から社会人(しゃかいじん)だ。 Finally, I will be a full-fledged member of society in spring. / 终于，从春季开始要参加工作了。/ Rồi thì tôi cũng là người đi làm từ mùa xuân.

会社
かいしゃ

Company / 公司 / Công ty

665 **大企業** (だいきぎょう) 名
large companies / 大企业 / doanh nghiệp lớn, tập đoàn

日本の企業のうち、大企業は 0.3 パーセントだ。
Only 0.3% of all Japanese companies are large corporations. / 日本企业中，大企业占 0.3%。/ Trong số doanh nghiệp Nhật Bản, các doanh nghiệp lớn là 0.3%.

➕ 中小企業 (ちゅうしょうきぎょう) small and middle-sized companies / 中小企业 / doanh nghiệp vừa và nhỏ・一流企業 (いちりゅうきぎょう) blue-chip company / 一流企业 / doanh nghiệp hàng đầu

666 **大手** (おおて) 名
major / 大型 / lớn

A 社は大手ではないが、有名な会社だ。
Company A may not be major, but it is a very famous company. / A 公司不是大公司，但很有名。/ Công ty A tuy không lớn nhưng là công ty nổi tiếng.

667 **代表〈する〉** (だいひょう) 名
representative / 代表 / đại diện

私の会社は日本を代表するメーカーの一つだ。
My company is one of the major manufacturers in Japan. / 我们公司是日本有代表性的制造商之一。/ Công ty tôi là một hãng sản xuất đại diện Nhật Bản.

668 **民間** (みんかん) 名
private sector / 民间 / tư nhân

公務員ではなく、民間の企業で働きたい。
I don't want to be a public servant, I want to work at a private company. / 我不想当公务员，想在私企工作。/ Tôi muốn làm việc ở doanh nghiệp tư nhân chứ không phải nhân viên nhà nước.

669 **組織** (そしき) 名
organization / 组织，体系 / tổ chức

大企業は多くの組織で構成されている。
A major corporation is made up of many divisions. / 大企业是由很多组织构成的。/ Doanh nghiệp lớn được cấu thành từ nhiều tổ chức.

670 **従業員** (じゅうぎょういん) 名
employee / 员工，职工 / nhân viên

この会社の従業員は約 1,000 人だ。
This company has about 1,000 employees. / 这家公司约有 1000 名员工。/ Nhân viên của công ty này khoảng 1.000 người.

➕ 労働者 (ろうどうしゃ) laborer / 劳动者，工人 / người lao động

671 **新入社員** (しんにゅうしゃいん) 名
new employee / 公司新人 / nhân viên mới

4 月には新入社員の研修が行われる。
New employees will receive training in April. / 4 月对新员工进行培训。/ Việc đào tạo nhân viên mới được tổ chức vào tháng 4.

➕ 新入生 (しんにゅうせい) newcomer / 新生 / học sinh, sinh viên mới

672 □ 名	派遣社員 (はけんしゃいん) **temporary employee / 派遣职员 / nhân viên hợp đồng ngắn hạn**	A社は派遣社員ではなく、正社員を希望している。 Company A is looking for full-time employees, not temporary employees. / A公司想要招聘正式员工，而不是派遣员工。/ Công ty A muốn tuyển nhân viên chính thức chứ không phải nhân viên hợp đồng ngắn hạn.

➕ 派遣会社 (はけんがいしゃ) staffing agency / 派遣公司 / công ty tuyển dụng nhân viên hợp đồng

673 □ 名	オーナー **owner / 所有者，持有人 / người chủ**	彼は社長でもあり、オーナーでもある。 He is the president and owner of the company. / 他既是总经理，也是公司的所有者（老板）。/ Ông ấy vừa là giám đốc vừa là ông chủ.
674 □ 名	重役 (じゅうやく) **executive / 要职，重任，董事 / giám đốc, lãnh đạo**	新入社員なので、なかなか重役と会う機会がない。 I am a new employee and rarely have a chance to meet executives. / 因为是公司新人，所以很难有机会接触到公司的高层（董事）。/ Vì là nhân viên mới vào nên mãi không có cơ hội gặp cấp lãnh đạo.

➕ 役員 (やくいん) executive, director / 干事，干部 / lãnh đạo

675 □ 名	オフィス **office / 办公室 / văn phòng**	オフィスが郊外に移転した。 The office moved to the suburbs. / 办公室搬到郊区去了。/ Văn phòng đã chuyển ra ngoại ô.
676 □ 名	支給〈する〉 (しきゅう) **provision / 支付 / sự chu cấp, chi trả**	給料は月末に支給される。 Salaries are paid at the end of the month. / 工资月末支付。/ Tiền lương được chi trả vào cuối tháng.

➕ 支給額 (しきゅうがく) allowance / 支付金额 / tiền chu cấp, chi trả

677 □ 名	出世〈する〉 (しゅっせ) **climbing the corporate ladder / 出人头地，成功 / sự thăng tiến, thành đạt**	出世して、社長になりたい。 I want to go up the corporate ladder and become president. / 我想出人头地，自己当老板。/ Tôi muốn thăng tiến, trở thành giám đốc.
678 □ 名	昇進〈する〉 (しょうしん) **promotion / 晋升 / sự thăng tiến, thăng chức**	課長が部長に昇進した。 The section chief was promoted to chief director. / 科长晋升为部长了。/ Trưởng ban đã thăng chức lên trưởng phòng.
679 □ 名	転勤〈する〉 (てんきん) **relocation / 调职 / sự thay đổi chỗ làm (trong cùng một công ty)**	うちの会社は転勤が多い。 Our company demands employees to be relocated frequently. / 我们公司经常会有人员调动。/ Công ty tôi hay thay đổi chỗ làm.

680 赴任〈する〉(ふにん)
名 **take up the post / 赴任 / sự nhận chức**

家族を残して、大阪支社へ赴任する。(かぞく のこ おおさかししゃ ふにん)
I will leave my family behind to take up a post in the Osaka office. / 不带家人，只身去大阪分公司任职。/ Tôi để lại gia đình, đi nhận chức ở chi nhánh Osaka.

＋ 単身赴任〈する〉(たんしんふにん) take up the post without one's family / 工作调动时自己一个人去外地任职 / sự nhận chức đơn thân, công tác một mình trong thời gian dài

681 有給休暇(ゆうきゅうきゅうか)
名 **paid leave / 带薪假 / nghỉ phép có lương**

この会社は有給休暇が取りやすい。(かいしゃ ゆうきゅうきゅうか と)
It's easy to take paid leave in this company. / 这家公司很容易请到带薪休假。/ Công ty này dễ lấy phép có lương.

＝ 有休(ゆうきゅう)

682 人事(じんじ)
名 **personnel / 人事 / nhân sự**

ある日、人事の担当者に呼ばれた。(ひ じんじ たんとうしゃ よ)
One day the person in charge of personnel called me. / 有一天，我被人事负责人叫去了。/ Ngày nọ, tôi được người phụ trách nhân sự gọi lên.

683 人材(じんざい)
名 **talented persons / 人才 / nhân tài, nguồn nhân lực**

A社には今年も優秀な人材が集まった。(しゃ ことし ゆうしゅう じんざい あつ)
A lot of talented employees were gathered this year at Company A. / A公司今年也汇聚了很多优秀的人才。/ Năm nay, nguồn nhân lực ưu tú cũng lại tập trung vào công ty A.

684 人手(ひとで)
名 **manpower / 人手 / người làm việc, nhân công**

会社が忙しくなり、人手が足りない。(かいしゃ いそが ひとで た)
The company is becoming busy, and there isn't enough manpower. / 公司忙起来了，人手不够。/ Công ty trở nên bận rộn, không đủ người làm việc.

＋ 人手不足(ひとでぶそく) shortage of manpower / 人手不够 / sự thiếu người, thiếu nhân công

685 モニター
名 **monitor / 评论 / sự kiểm chứng, theo dõi**

お店や商品のモニターをして、ポイントをもらった。(みせ しょうひん)
I acted as a consumer monitor for shops and products to collect points. / 对商店或是商品进行评论获得了积分。/ Tôi kiểm chứng cửa tiệm và sản phẩm để nhận điểm tích lũy.

686 業績(ぎょうせき)
名 **business results / 业绩 / thành tích**

彼の会社は毎年業績が伸びている。(かれ かいしゃ まいとし ぎょうせき の)
His company is showing good business results every year. / 他们公司每年的业绩都在增长。/ Công ty của anh ấy thành tích mỗi năm đều tăng.

687 □	資本 しほん	①ビジネスマンは体が資本だ。 からだ しほん ②会社が資本金を増やした。 かいしゃ しほんきん ふ
名	capital / 本钱，重要的东西 / 資本 / vốn liếng, tiền vốn	① A healthy body is important to a businessman. ② The company increased its capital. / ①对商务人士来说身体是本钱。②公司增加了资本金。/ ① Người kinh doanh vốn liếng là sức khỏe. ② Công ty đã tăng thêm tiền vốn.

➕ ②資本金 しほんきん capital / 资本金 / tiền vốn

☞ ① something indispensable and important ② the basis for doing a major project / ①重要的，不可缺少的东西②做大事业的基础 / ① Thứ cần thiết, thứ không thể thiếu. ② Thứ trở thành căn bản khi làm kinh doanh.

688 □	方針 ほうしん	社長が今後の方針を述べた。 しゃちょう こんご ほうしん の
名	policy / 方针 / phương châm	The president talked about future policies. / 总经理陈述了今后的方针。/ Giám đốc đã trình bày phương châm từ nay về sau.
689 □	我々 われわれ	社会に貢献する企業になること、これが我々の方針だ。 しゃかい こうけん きぎょう われわれ ほうしん
代	our / 我们 / chúng tôi, chúng ta	Our policy is to become a company that contributes to society. / 成为对社会有贡献的企业，是我司的方针。/ Trở thành doanh nghiệp cống hiến cho xã hội - đây là phương châm của chúng ta.
690 □	製品 せいひん	あの企業は時代に合った製品を開発している。 きぎょう じだい あ せいひん かいはつ
名	product / 产品 / sản phẩm, thành phẩm, hàng hóa	That firm is developing products that meet the demands of modern society. / 那家企业在开发符合时代需求的产品。/ Doanh nghiệp đó phát triển sản phẩm phù hợp với thời đại.
691 □	売れ行き う ゆ	この商品は売れ行きがいいそうだ。 しょうひん う ゆ
名	sales demand / 销路 / tình hình bán hàng	This product is selling well. / 这个商品好像销路很好。/ Nghe nói tình hình bán sản phẩm này tốt.
692 □	売り上げ う あ	商品がヒットして、売り上げが伸びた。 しょうひん う あ の
名	sales / 销售额 / doanh thu bán ra	Sales increased because the product was a hit. / 商品大受欢迎，销售额增加了。/ Sản phẩm bán chạy nên doanh thu tăng lên.

➕ セールス sales / 销售，推销 / doanh số, sự bán hàng

693 □	コスト	この製品には予想以上にコストがかかりそうだ。 せいひん よそういじょう
名	cost / 成本 / chi phí	This product will be more costly than initially expected. / 这个商品的成本好像比预想的要高。/ Xem ra sản phẩm nay tốn chi phí hơn dự tính.

694 □	果たす (は)	大きな仕事が終わり、責任を果たした。(おお しごと お せきにん は)
動	**fulfill / 尽，实现 / hoàn thành, đạt được**	I fulfilled my responsibility by finishing this big job. / 完成了一项重要的工作，尽到了责任。/ Công việc lớn kết thúc, tôi đã hoàn thành nhiệm vụ.
695 □	得る (え)	上司の許可を得て、休暇を取った。(じょうし きょか え きゅうか と)
動	**receive / 获得 / có được**	I took some days off after receiving permission from my boss. / 获得上司的批准，请到了假。/ Được cấp trên cho phép, tôi đã lấy ngày nghỉ.
696 □	認める (みと)	①上司は部下の休暇を認めた。(じょうし ぶか きゅうか みと) ②自分の間違いを認めることが、成長につながる。(じぶん まちが みと せいちょう) ③この画家は世界に才能を認められた。(がか せかい さいのう みと)
動	**allow/acknowledge/ acknowledge / 认同 / 承认 / 认可，公认 / công nhận, chấp nhận**	① The boss permitted his subordinate's request for time off. ② Acknowledging your mistakes is part of growing as a person. ③ The talent of this painter was acknowledged by the world. / ①上司同意下属请假了。②承认自己犯的错误是有助于成长的。③这个画家的才能得到了全世界的认可。/ ① Cấp trên chấp nhận ngày nghỉ của cấp dưới. ② Chấp nhận sai lầm của bản thân sẽ dẫn đến trưởng thành. ③ Họa sỹ này được thế giới công nhận tài năng.

☞ ① deem a request to be appropriate ② accept an error ③ accept the value of something / ①申请通过②承认错误③价值被认可 / ① Đồng ý với những yêu cầu, đơn xin. ② Chấp nhận sai lầm v.v. ③ Đánh giá giá trị.

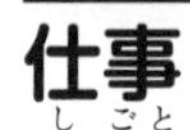

仕事(しごと)

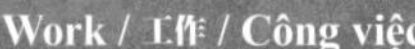

697 □ 名	ビジネス	日本(にほん)でビジネスチャンスをつかみたい。
	business / 商务，生意 / công việc, kinh doanh	I want to take advantage of business opportunities in Japan. / 想在日本抓住做生意的机会。/ Tôi muốn nắm bắt cơ hội kinh doanh ở Nhật.

➕ ビジネスマン business person / 商务人士 / doanh nhân

698 □ 動	就(つ)く	希望(きぼう)していた仕事(しごと)に就(つ)くことができた。
	take up a job / 就任，从事 / đạt được (công v iệc)	I was able to take up a job that I wanted. / 能从事自己想做的工作了。/ Tôi đã đạt được công việc mình mong muốn.
699 □ 名	生(い)きがい	仕事(しごと)に生(い)きがいを感(かん)じている。
	purpose of living / 价值，生活意义 / đáng sống, ý nghĩa sống	I feel very motivated about my work. / 从工作中感受到人生的意义。/ Tôi cảm thấy ý nghĩa trong công việc.
700 □ 名	やりがい	給料(きゅうりょう)よりやりがいが大切(たいせつ)だ。
	rewarding / 做事的意义 / đáng làm, giá trị	Doing something worthwile is more important than the pay. / 比起工资，工作的意义更重要。/ Giá trị việc làm quan trọng hơn tiền lương.
701 □ 動	抱(いだ)く	夢(ゆめ)を抱(いだ)いて、日本(にほん)で働(はたら)いている。
	hold / 怀揣 / ôm ấp	I am working in Japan, full of dreams. / 怀揣着梦想在日本工作。/ Tôi ôm ấp ước mơ và làm việc tại Nhật.
702 □ 名	打(う)ち合(あ)わせ〈する〉	今日(きょう)は3時(じ)から打(う)ち合(あ)わせがある。
	meeting / 商量，洽谈 / sự gặp gỡ bàn bạc, buổi trao đổi	There is a meeting from 3:00 p.m. today. / 今天3点有个商务洽谈会。/ Hôm nay có buổi trao đổi từ 3 giờ.

➕ 打(う)ち合(あ)わせる hold a meeting / 商量，洽谈 / gặp gỡ bàn bạc, trao đổi・会合(かいごう) meeting / 聚会 / hội họp

703 □ 名	アポイント	メールで打(う)ち合(あ)わせのアポイントを取(と)った。
	appointment / 约会，约见 / cuộc hẹn gặp	I sent an e-mail to make an appointment. / 用邮件预约了洽谈(时间)。/ Tôi đã hẹn gặp trao đổi qua e-mail.

🟰 アポ ➕ アポなし no appointment / 不预约就直接拜访 / không hẹn gặp

704 応対〈する〉 おうたい
名 handling, responding / 应对 / sự trả lời, ứng tiếp

今日は朝から電話の応対で忙しい。
I am busy handling phone calls from the morning today. / 今天从早上开始就一直忙于接电话。/ Hôm nay bận bịu từ sáng với việc trả lời điện thoại.

➕ 応接〈する〉 おうせつ reception / 接待 / ứng tiếp

705 伝言〈する〉 でんごん
名 message / 转告 / tin nhắn, lời nhắn

部長に伝言をお願いできますか。
Can you please pass along a message to the manager? / 可以麻烦您转告部长吗? / Vui lòng để lại tin nhắn cho trưởng phòng giùm tôi được không?

706 改めて あらた
副 again, once again, formally / 再，重新 / lúc khác

改めてこちらからご連絡します。
We will get back to you later. / 之后我会再联系您的。/ Tôi sẽ liên lạc lại vào lúc khác.

707 じかに
副 directly / 直接 / trực tiếp

この件は上司にじかに報告した方がいい。
This matter needs to be reported to the boss directly. / 这件事最好直接向上司汇报。/ Nên báo cáo trực tiếp vấn đề này với cấp trên thì tốt hơn.

708 プロジェクト
名 project / 项目 / dự án

大きなプロジェクトが、もうすぐ始まる。
A large project will start soon. / 有一项大型项目就要开始了。/ Dự án lớn sắp bắt đầu.

➕ プロジェクトチーム project team / 项目团队 / đội dự án

709 意図〈する〉 いと
名 intention / 意图，计划 / ý đồ

プロジェクトが意図した通りに進まない。
The project is not proceeding as intended. / 项目无法按计划进行。/ Dự án không tiến triển theo như ý đồ.

710 新たな あら
ナ形 new / 新 / mới

新たなプロジェクトが進んでいる。
A new project is ongoing. / 新项目正在进展之中。/ Dự án mới đang tiến triển.

711 組む く
動 join / 组，组织 / tổ chức, phối hợp

先輩とチームを組んで、新しい企画を立ち上げる。
I started a new project together with my senior co-worker. / 和前辈搭档，开始制订新企划案。/ Tôi kết hợp với người đàn anh và đưa ra kế hoạch mới.

633 ~ 777

712 □	取り引き〈する〉(と ひ)	うちの会社は一流企業と取り引きがある。
名	**deal / 交易 / giao dịch, quan hệ làm ăn**	We conduct business with blue-chip companies. / 我们公司和一流企业有生意往来。/ Công ty tôi có quan hệ làm ăn với doanh nghiệp hàng đầu.

➕ 取引先(とりひきさき) client, customer / 客户 / đối tác・クライアント client / 客户 / khách hàng

713 □	依頼〈する〉(い らい)	デザイナーにパンフレットのデザインを依頼する。
名	**request / 委托 / yêu cầu, nhờ, đề nghị**	I asked the designer to design the pamphlet. / 委托设计师设计宣传册。/ Yêu cầu nhà thiết kế thiết kế tập san giới thiệu.
714 □	任せる(まか)	次のプロジェクトを任された。
動	**put in charge / 委任 / giao phó**	I was put in charge of the next project. / 被委任负责下一个项目。/ Tôi được giao phó dự án sắp tới.
715 □	引き受ける(ひ う)	仕事の依頼を引き受けた。
動	**accept / 接下 / tiếp nhận, nhận lời, đảm nhận**	I accepted a job request. / 我接下了工作。/ Tôi nhận lời đề nghị công việc.
716 □	こなす	彼女はいつもスマートに仕事をこなす。
動	**manage, cope with / 运用自如，完成 / nắm vững, tiếp thu**	She always manages her work in a cool manner. / 她总能利落地完成工作。/ Cô ấy luôn tiếp thu công việc một cách thông minh.
717 □	成果(せい か)	上司に仕事の成果をほめられた。
名	**achievement / 成果 / thành quả**	My boss commended me for my work's achievement. / 工作成果得到了上司的表扬。/ Tôi được cấp trên khen ngợi thành quả trong công việc.
718 □	達成〈する〉(たっせい)	売り上げ目標を達成するために努力している。
名	**achievement / 达成 / sự đạt thành**	I am making efforts to meet the sales target. / 为达成销售目标而努力。/ Tôi nỗ lực để đạt mục tiêu doanh số bán ra.
719 □	作業〈する〉(さ ぎょう)	彼は、いつも効率よく作業を進める。
名	**work / 工作 / thao tác, tác nghiệp, công việc**	He is always efficient in the way he works. / 他总是能高效开展工作。/ Anh ấy luôn có thể tiến hành thao tác công việc hiệu quả.
720 □	保留〈する〉(ほ りゅう)	この件は、しばらく保留させてください。
名	**withhold, on hold / 保留 / sự bảo lưu, hoãn lại**	Please let me think about this case for a while. / 这件事请允许我暂且放一放。/ Về vấn đề này, vui lòng cho tôi bảo lưu một thời gian.

721 □ やり直す
なお
動 **redo / 重做 / làm lại**

ミスが見つかったので、もう一度やり直した。
み　いちど　なお

I found a mistake so I redid it. / 发现了错误，所以重新做了一次。/ Vì phát hiện ra lỗi sai nên tôi đã làm lại lần nữa.

722 □ 件
けん
名 **case / 事情 / vụ, trường hợp, vấn đề, công việc**

先日の件、お返事が遅れ、申し訳ございませんでした。
せんじつ　けん　へんじ　おく　もう　わけ

I'm sorry it took so long to respond to the earlier case. / 上次的事情，我回复晚了，非常抱歉。/ Trường hợp hôm trước, tôi hồi âm trễ, thành thật xin lỗi.

＋ 件名（けんめい） name of a case / 名称 / tên công việc

723 □ 急用
きゅうよう
名 **emergency / 急事 / công việc gấp**

急用ができ、午後の会議に出られなくなった。
きゅうよう　ごご　かいぎ　で

Something came up suddenly, so I won't be able to attend the afternoon meeting. / 突然有急事下午的会议出席不了了。/ Vì có việc gấp nên tôi không thể đến buổi họp buổi chiều.

724 □ 至急
しきゅう
名 副 **urgently / 火速，赶快 / cấp tốc, khẩn cấp**

至急、この資料をコピーしてください。(副)
しきゅう　しりょう

Please quickly copy this reference material. / 请火速复印一下这份资料。/ Hãy cấp tốc photo tài liệu này.

＋ 大至急（だいしきゅう） very urgently / 十万火急 / cực kỳ cấp tốc, khẩn cấp

725 □ 手順
てじゅん
名 **process / 步骤 / trình tự, thứ tự**

仕事の手順を早く覚えたい。
しごと　てじゅん　はや　おぼ

I want to quickly learn how to do my job. / 想快点记住工作的步骤。/ Tôi muốn nhanh chóng nhớ trình tự công việc.

726 □ 移動〈する〉
いどう
名 **moving / 移动 / sự di chuyển**

今移動中なので、後で連絡します。
いま　いどうちゅう　あと　れんらく

I'm on the move now so I will call back later. / 我现在正在路上，稍后与您联系。/ Bây giờ tôi đang di chuyển, sẽ liên lạc sau.

727 □ 大工
だいく
名 **carpenter / 木匠 / thợ mộc, thợ xây**

大工になって、自分の家を建てたい。
だいく　じぶん　いえ　た

I want to become a carpenter and build my own house. / 想当木匠造一栋自己的家。/ Tôi muốn thành thợ xây để xây nhà của mình.

728 □ ガードマン
名 **security guard / 警卫，保镖 / người bảo vệ**

身分証明書を忘れて、ガードマンに止められた。
みぶんしょうめいしょ　わす　と

I forgot my idenfication, and the security guard stopped me. / 忘了带身份证，被警卫拦下来了。/ Tôi quên thẻ chứng minh nhân thân nên bị bảo vệ chặn lại.

Section 4

上下関係

じょうげかんけい

Hierarchical Relationship / 上下级关系 / Quan hệ trên dưới

729 □ 名	地位 (ちい) position / 地位 / vị trí, địa vị	地位の高い人とは少し話しにくい。 It's a little difficult to speak to someone important. / 和地位高的人对话有点难。/ Hơi khó nói chuyện với người có địa vị cao.

➕ 身分 (みぶん) one's social standing / 身份 / thân phận, vị trí・肩書き (かたが) one's title / 头衔 / chức danh

730 □ 名	目上 (めうえ) someone who is your senior / 上级，长辈 / người trên	目上の人には敬語を使わないと失礼だ。 You need to speak in the honorific language to someone who is your senior. / 对上级和长辈不用敬语的话是不礼貌的。/ Không sử dụng kính ngữ với người trên thì thật thất lễ.

↔ 目下 (めした)

731 □ 名	敬意 (けいい) sense of respect / 敬意 / sự tôn kính, kính trọng	あの若者はお年寄りに敬意を持って話す。 That young person speaks to the elderly with respect. / 那个年轻人对老年人带着敬意说话。/ Bạn trẻ đó nói chuyện với người già một cách tôn kính.
732 □ 動	敬う (うやま) respect / 尊敬 / tôn kính, kính trọng	目上の人を心から敬う。 Sincerely respect someone who is your senior. / 由衷地尊经上级和长辈。/ Kính trọng người trên thật lòng.
733 □ ナ形	的確な (てきかく) accurate / 恰当，正确 / chính xác, xác đáng	先輩の的確なアドバイスは、ありがたい。 I am grateful for the shrewd advice from my senior co-worker. / 对前辈给出的中肯建议感激不尽。/ Lời khuyên xác đáng của đàn anh rất đáng quý.
734 □ 名	忠告〈する〉 (ちゅうこく) warning / 忠告，忠言 / lời cảnh cáo, nhắc nhở	祖父の忠告は今も役に立っている。 My grandfather's advice is still valuable to me today. / 祖父的忠告至今仍然让我受益匪浅。/ Lời nhắc nhở của ông tôi đến nay vẫn có ích.

➕ アドバイス〈する〉 advice / 建议 / lời khuyên

735 □ 名	サポート〈する〉 support / 支持 / sự hỗ trợ	新入社員は先輩達にサポートしてもらう。 New employees will be supported by senior co-workers. / 新员工由老员工们带领和协助。/ Nhân viên được các đàn anh đàn chị hỗ trợ.

736 □ 動 **いばる**

be bossy / 自以为是，摆架子 / kiêu căng, ngạo mạn

部下に対していばる上司には、なりたくない。
ぶか　たい　じょうし

I don't want to be a boss that bosses around his subordinates. / 不想当对部下摆架子的上司。/ Tôi không muốn trở thành cấp trên ngạo mạn với cấp dưới.

737 □ 動 **押し付ける**
お　つ

press / 强加于人，推压 / áp đặt, ép buộc

先輩に仕事を押し付けられた。
せんぱい　しごと　お　つ

A senior co-worker forced an assignment on me. / 被迫接受了前辈强加给我的工作。/ Tôi bị đàn anh áp đặt công việc.

738 □ 名 **ご無沙汰〈する〉**
ぶさた

not in contact for a long time / 久疏问候 / không liên lạc (trong thời gian dài)

先生、久しくご無沙汰しております。
せんせい　ひさ　ぶさた

Sir, I'm glad to see you after a long time. / 老师，好久不见 / 久未联系。/ Chào thầy / cô, đã lâu không liên lạc ạ.

739 □ 名 **恐縮〈する〉**
きょうしゅく

feel ashamed, feel humbled, feel obliged / 过意不去 / thật ngại, áy náy

ご無沙汰している先生から連絡があり、恐縮した。
ぶさた　せんせい　れんらく　きょうしゅく

I felt ashamed when my teacher who I haven't contacted for a long time called me up. / 久未联系的老师主动联系了我，觉得有些惶恐。/ Có liên lạc của thầy / cô đã lâu không gặp, tôi thấy thật áy náy.

740 □ 名 **信頼〈する〉**
しんらい

trust / 信赖，相信 / sự tin cậy, tin tưởng

あの先輩は信頼できる人だと思う。
せんぱい　しんらい　ひと　おも

I believe that senior co-worker can be trusted. / 我觉得那个前辈值得信赖。/ Tôi nghĩ đó là người đàn anh có thể tin cậy được.

741 □ 動 **従う**
したが

follow / 遵守，服从 / tuân theo, theo

社員は会社の規則に従わなければならない。
しゃいん　かいしゃ　きそく　したが

Employees must follow company rules. / 职员必须遵守公司规定。/ Nhân viên phải tuân thủ nội quy công ty.

742 □ 動 **うなずく**

nod / 点头，首肯 / gật đầu, gật gù

上司は私の話を、いつもうなずきながら聞いてくれる。
じょうし　わたし　はなし　き

My boss always nods in acknowledgement as he listens to me talking. / 上司总是一边点头一边听我说话。/ Cấp trên luôn vừa gật gù vừa nghe chuyện của tôi.

743 □ 名 **反論〈する〉**
はんろん

argue / 反驳 / phản biện, bác bỏ

会社のために上司の意見に反論した。
かいしゃ　じょうし　いけん　はんろん

I argued with my boss for the sake of the company. / 为了公司的利益反驳了上司的意见。/ Vì công ty, tôi phản biện ý kiến của cấp trên .

744 □ 動 **わびる**

apologize / 道歉 / xin lỗi

仕事のミスを上司にわびた。
しごと　じょうし

I apologized for my mistake at work to my boss. / 工作上失误了，向上司道了歉。/ Tôi xin lỗi cấp trên vì sai sót trong công việc.

➕ おわび apology / 致歉 / lời xin lỗi

745 **やる気（き）**
名 **eagerness / 干劲 / sự hứng thú, cảm hứng**
上司にやる気をアピールして、プロジェクトに参加した。
I showed my eagerness to my boss and was able to take part in the project. / 我向上司展现了自己的干劲，参加了这个项目。/ Tôi giới thiệu với cấp trên về sự hứng thú để tham gia vào dự án.

746 **お世辞（せじ）**
名 **flattery / 恭维，奉承 / sự tâng bốc, nịnh hót**
あの人はお世辞がうまい。
He is good at flattery. / 那个人很擅长恭维别人。/ Người đó nịnh hót giỏi.

747 **ごまをする**
慣 **flatter / 拍马屁 / xu nịnh**
上司にごまをするなんて嫌だ。
I don't want to curry favor with my boss. / 我讨厌对上司阿谀奉承。/ Tôi ghét kiểu xu nịnh cấp trên.

➕ ごますり flatterer / 拍马屁的人，阿谀奉承的人 / sự xu nịnh

748 **上等（じょうとう）な**
ナ形 **good quality / 上等 / cao cấp**
夏と冬に、クライアントに上等なワインを贈る。
I send expensive wine to my clients in the summer and winter. / 夏季和冬季，向客户赠送上等的红酒。/ Gửi rượu vang cao cấp đến khách hàng vào mùa hè và mùa đông.

➕ 高級な high class / 高级 / cao cấp

749 **苦痛（くつう）**
名 **pain / 苦痛，苦恼 / sự đau khổ**
残業が毎日続くのは苦痛だ。
Working overtime every day is stressful. / 每天加班真痛苦。/ Làm tăng ca cứ tiếp diễn hàng ngày thì thật đau khổ.

750 **夫人（ふじん）**
名 **wife of, Mrs. / 夫人 / phu nhân, người vợ**
今日、部長夫人に初めてお会いした。
I met the manager's wife today for the first time. / 今天第一次见到了部长夫人。/ Hôm nay tôi được diện kiến phu nhân trưởng phòng.

➕ 婦人 woman / 妇人 / phụ nữ, phu nhân, quý bà

751 **ベテラン**
名 **veteran / 专家，老手 / người giỏi, kỳ cựu**
ベテランの上司にクライアントの情報を教えてもらう。
My veteran boss will give me information about the client. / 我向经验丰富的上司请教了有关客户的事。/ Tôi được cấp trên kỳ cựu chỉ thông tin của khách hàng.

752 **平社員（ひらしゃいん）**
名 **employee with no title / 普通职员 / nhân viên quèn**
入社５年だが、まだ平社員だ。
I've been with the company for five years now but I still have no title. / 进公司 5 年了但还只是个普通职员。/ Tôi vào công ty đã 5 năm mà vẫn là nhân viên quèn.

これも覚えよう！ ⑰

接辞：職業等① Affix: Work, etc. / 词缀：职业等 / Phụ tố: Nghề nghiệp v.v.

• ～家（芸術的に優れた人）

作家	author / 作家 / Tác giả, nhà văn
画家	painter / 画家 / Họa sỹ
芸術家	artist / 艺术家 / nghệ sỹ
作曲家	composer / 作曲家 / Nhà soạn nhạc, người sáng tác
建築家	architect / 建筑师 / Kiến trúc sư
漫画家	cartoonist / 漫画家 / Tác giả manga, họa sỹ manga

• ～者（あることを専門的にする人）

医者	doctor / 医生 / Bác sỹ
記者	reporter / 记者 / Nhà báo, ký giả
科学者	scientist / 科学家 / Nhà khoa học
学者	scholar / 学者 / Học giả
役者	actor / 演员 / Diễn viên

• ～界（社会の分野）

学界	academic world / 学术界 / Giới học thuật
政界	world of politics / 政界 / Giới chính trị
財界	financial world / 金融界，财经界 / Giới tài chính
芸能界	entertainment world / 演艺界，娱乐圈 / Giới nghệ sỹ
医学界	medical world / 医学界 / Giới y khoa
業界	industry, industrial world / 业界 / Ngành nghề

退職・転職

たいしょく　てんしょく

Quitting Jobs, Changing Jobs / 辞职・转职 / Nghỉ việc - Chuyển chỗ làm

753 □ 名	退職〈する〉(たいしょく) resignation / 退职 / sự nghỉ việc	来月で今の会社を退職する。 I will quit this company next month. / 下个月就要离开现在的公司了。/ Tháng tới, tôi nghỉ việc công ty bây giờ.

＝ 辞める　＋ 退職届 letter of resignation / 辞呈 / đơn nghỉ việc・退職金 severance pay / 退职金 / tiền nghỉ việc・定年退職〈する〉 retirement / 退休 / về hưu

754 □ 名	転職〈する〉(てんしょく) changing jobs / 换工作，跳槽 / sự chuyển việc	もっとかせげる会社に転職したい。 I want to move to a company where I can earn more money. / 想跳槽去一家能赚到更多钱的公司。/ Tôi muốn chuyển việc sang công ty có thể kiếm nhiều tiền hơn.
755 □ 慣	首になる(くび) be fired, get sacked / 被解雇 / bị đuổi việc, bị sa thải	先週、会社を首になってしまった。 I was fired last week. / 我上周被公司解雇了。/ Tuần trước, tôi bị công ty sa thải mất rồi.
756 □ 名	リストラ〈する〉 layoff / 裁员 / người bị sa thải, sự sa thải (do cơ cấu lại)	会社の売り上げが下がり、リストラされた。 Company sales dropped, and I was laid off. / 公司的销售额下降，被裁员了。/ Doanh thu công ty giảm, tôi bị sa thải do cơ cấu lại.
757 □ 名	独立〈する〉(どくりつ) starting one's own business / 独立 / độc lập	いつか独立して、自分の会社を持ちたい。 One day, I want to start my own business and run my own company. / 希望有一天能从公司独立出来，创办自己的公司。/ Tôi muốn ngày nào đó sẽ độc lập, có công ty của riêng mình.
758 □ 副	着々［と］(ちゃくちゃく) steadily / 稳步地 / từng bước vững chắc	独立する準備を着々と進めている。 I am steadily preparing to start my own business. / 我正在稳步地为（从公司）独立出来做准备。/ Từng bước chuẩn bị độc lập.
759 □ 名 ナ形	フリー〈な〉 free/freely / 自由 / 免费 / tự do, miễn phí	①今はフリーで仕事をしている。(名) ②この雑誌はフリーです。ご自由にどうぞ。(ナ形) ① I am now freelancing. ② This magazine is free. Please go ahead and take it. / ①我现在是自由职业者。②此杂志免费，请自由取阅。/ ① Bây giờ tôi đang làm việc tự do. ② Tạp chí này miễn phí. Xin mời tự nhiên.

＋ ②フリーダイヤル toll-free number / 免费咨询电话 / số gọi miễn phí

① not belonging anywhere ② free / ①不属于任何地方，自由②免费 / ① Không thuộc vào nơi nào cả. Tự do. ② Miễn phí, không tốn tiền

760 □ 名	不平 (ふへい) complaint, gripes / 不满 / sự bất bình	彼は会社への不平を並べた末、辞めた。(名) He quit after complaining about the company. / 他罗列了对公司的诸多不满，最后辞职了。/ Sau những bất bình với công ty, anh ấy nghỉ việc.

➕ 不平不満 (ふへいふまん) discontent, grumbling / 不满 / sự bất bình bất mãn

761 □ 名 ナ形	満足〈な／する〉(まんぞく) satisfaction/satisfied / 满足 / sự hài lòng, thỏa mãn	今の仕事に満足していないので、転職したい。(名) I'm not satisfied with this job so I want to change jobs. / 对现在的工作不满意，想换工作。/ Vì không hài lòng với công việc bây giờ, nên tôi muốn chuyển việc.

➕ 自己満足 (じこまんぞく) self-satisfaction / 自我满足 / tự hài lòng

762 □ 名	辛抱〈する〉(しんぼう) perseverance / 忍耐 / sự nhẫn nhục, chịu đựng	あと3年は、この会社で辛抱するつもりだ。I plan to persevere at least three more years in this company. / 打算在这个公司再忍 3 年。/ Tôi định chịu đựng ở công ty này 3 năm nữa.

➕ 辛抱強い (しんぼうづよ) persevering / 有耐心，能忍 / giỏi chịu đựng

763 □ 副	ぐっと with a gulp / 使劲；哑口无言 / đè nén, chặt, nhiều	嫌なことがあっても、辞めずにぐっと我慢する。Even when something bad happens, I just bear it and don't quit. / 即使遇到了讨厌的事情也不辞职，使劲忍耐着。/ Dù có chuyện khó chịu đi nữa, tôi cố gắng đè nén, không nghỉ việc.
764 □ 動	負う (お) shoulder (the blame/ responsibility) / 承担，背 / gánh chịu	彼は仕事のミスの責任を負って、退職した。He took responsibility for the mistake at work and quit. / 他承担了工作失误的全部责任，辞职了。/ Anh ấy gánh chịu trách nhiệm phần lỗi trong công việc và nghỉ việc.
765 □ 動	溶け込む (とこ) blend in / 融入 / hòa nhập	会社の雰囲気に溶け込めず、転職した。He changed jobs as he couldn't fit in with the company's atmosphere. / 他还没融入公司的环境就跳槽了。/ Tôi không thể hòa nhập vào bầu không khí của công ty nên đã chuyển việc.
766 □ 慣	やむを得ず (え) out of necessity / 不得已 / bất đắc dĩ, không còn cách nào khác	やむを得ず、あと半年会社に残ることにした。I decided to stay with the company another six months out of necessity. / 不得已决定在这家公司再待半年。/ Bất đắc dĩ, tôi quyết định ở lại công ty thêm nửa năm.

767 立ち上げる(たあ)

①退職して、自分の会社を立ち上げた。
②パソコンを立ち上げる。

動 **start up/boot up / 成立/启动，开启 / thành lập, khởi động**

① I left the company and started my own. ② I booted up the computer. / ①离职后成立了自己的公司。②启动电脑。/ ① Tôi nghỉ việc và đã thành lập công ty của mình. ② Tôi mở máy tính.

① create a business or a company ② starting up a computer / ①做生意，开公司②启动电脑 / ① Bắt đầu công việc hay lập công ty. ② Khởi động máy tính.

768 試みる(こころ)

来年、独立を試みるつもりだ。

動 **attempt / 尝试 / thử**

I will attempt to start my own business next year. / 明年打算尝试（从公司）独立出来。/ Sang năm, tôi định thử làm riêng.

769 専念〈する〉(せんねん)

しばらく会社を休んで、育児に専念しようと思う。

名 **concentrate / 专注，专心 / sự chuyên tâm, tập trung**

I plan to take some time off work and concentrate on raising my child. / 想暂时辞去工作，专心带孩子。/ Tôi muốn nghỉ công ty một thời gian để tập trung nuôi dạy con.

770 悔やむ(く)

前の会社を辞めたことを悔やんでいる。

動 **regret / 懊恼，后悔 / hối hận, tiếc nuối**

I regret quitting the previous company. / 我很懊悔辞掉了之前的工作。/ Tôi hối hận vì đã nghỉ việc công ty trước đây.

= 後悔する(こうかい)

771 見送る(みおく)

①退職は、しばらく見送ることにした。
②友達を見送りに空港まで行った。

動 **forego/sent off / 搁置 / 目送，送 / theo dõi, xem xét lại, tiễn**

① I decided to forego quitting my job for a while. ② I went to the airport to see my friend off. / ①离职的事，我决定先放一放。②去机场送朋友。/ ① Tôi quyết định xem xét lại chuyện nghỉ việc. ② Tôi đi đến sân bay để tiễn bạn.

① quit doing something and wait for the next chance ② bid farewell to someone leaving / ①先不做，等下次机会②和要离开的人告别 / ① Ngưng làm việc đó, chờ đến cơ hội tiếp theo. ② Chào chia tay người ra đi.

772 逃す(のが)

この転職のチャンスを逃したくない。

動 **miss / 放过，错过 / bỏ lỡ**

I don't want to miss this chance to change jobs. / 不想错过这次跳槽的机会。/ Tôi không muốn bỏ lỡ cơ hội chuyển việc này.

773 重なる(かさ)

仕事でミスが重なり、自信を失った。

動 **pile up / 重叠，重复 / chồng chất**

Mistakes piled up at work and I lost my confidence. / 工作上重复出错，失去了信心。/ Tôi đánh mất tự tin khi lỗi chồng chất trong công việc.

774	引き止める（ひきとめる） 動 **restrain, detain / 劝阻，挽留 / ngăn chặn, can ngăn**	退職（たいしょく）したかったが、上司（じょうし）に引き止められた。 I wanted to quit, but my boss talked me out of it. / 本想辞职的，但被上司挽留了。/ Tôi muốn nghỉ việc nhưng bị cấp trên ngăn lại.
775	特殊〈な〉（とくしゅ） 名 ナ形 **unique/special / 特殊 / đặc thù**	この仕事（しごと）には特殊な能力（のうりょく）が必要（ひつよう）だ。（ナ形） You need special talent for this job. / 这个工作需要特定的能力。/ Công việc này cần có năng lực đặc thù.
776	身の回り（みのまわり） 名 **belongings / 身边的（事物）/ xung quanh mình**	明日（あした）退職（たいしょく）するので、身の回りの物（もの）を片付（かたづ）ける。 I will quit the company tomorrow so I'm collecting my belongings. / 明天要离职了，把身边的物品都收拾好。/ Ngày mai tôi sẽ nghỉ việc nên dọn dẹp những đồ đạc xung quanh mình.
777	状況（じょうきょう） 名 **circumstances / 状况 / tình trạng, tình hình**	会社（かいしゃ）の状況を見（み）て、退職届（たいしょくとどけ）を出（だ）すつもりだ。 I plan to submit my resignation depending on the company's circumstances. / 我打算看公司的状况再递交辞呈。/ Tôi định xem tình hình công ty rồi đưa đơn nghỉ việc.

➕ 情況（じょうきょう） situation / 情况 / tình trạng, tình hình

これも覚えよう！ ⑱

接辞：職業等② Affix: Work, etc. / 词缀：职业等 / Phụ tố: Nghề nghiệp v.v.

- ～師（学問などで特定の技能を持つ人）

医師	doctor / 医师 / Bác sỹ
教師	teacher / 教师 / Giáo viên
講師	lecturer / 讲师 / Giáo viên, người đứng lớp
技師	technician / 技术人员 / Kỹ sư
美容師	hairdresser / 理发师 / Thợ uốn tóc
看護師	nurse / 护士 / Y tá
調理師	cook / 厨师，烹饪师 / Đầu bếp

- ～士（一定の資格を持つ人）

弁護士	lawyer / 律师 / Luật sư
保育士	nursery school teacher, childcare worker / 保育员 / Bảo mẫu, giáo viên nhà trẻ
介護士	caregiver, nurse / 介护士（照顾病人的护工）/ Điều dưỡng viên
学士	bachelor / 学士 / Cử nhân
修士	master / 硕士 / Thạc sỹ
博士	doctor / 博士 / Tiến sỹ
宇宙飛行士	astronaut / 宇航员 / Phi hành gia

N2

Chapter 7

お気に入り

Favorites / 爱好篇 / Yêu thích

単語 No.

Section 1

競技（きょうぎ）

Competition / 竞技 / Thi đấu

	語	例文
778 □ 名	競技〈する〉（きょうぎ）	オリンピックの新しい（あたら）競技（きょうぎ）が決（き）まった。
	competition, event / 竞技, 比赛 / bộ môn thi đấu	They have decided on the new events for the Olympics. / 奥运会新增的比赛项目已经定下来了。/ Môn thi đấu mới trong Olympic đã được quyết.

➕ 競技場（きょうぎじょう） stadium / 竞技场 / sân thi đấu・競技会（きょうぎかい） competition / 竞技大会 / hiệp hội thi đấu

	語	例文
779 □ 動	競う（きそ）	8チームが優勝（ゆうしょう）を競（きそ）って戦（たたか）っている。
	compete / 竞争 / cạnh tranh, ganh đua	Eight teams are competing to win. / 8 支队伍为争夺冠军而战。/ 8 đội cạnh tranh chức vô địch.
780 □ 動	戦う（たたか）	次（つぎ）の試合（しあい）で人気（にんき）チーム同士（どうし）が戦（たたか）う。
	fight / 战斗 / chiến đấu, giao tranh	The two popular teams will compete in the next game. / 在下一场比赛中两支热门队伍将交战。/ Hai đội cùng được ưa thích giao tranh trận đấu tiếp theo.

➕ 対戦（たいせん）〈する〉 fight / 对战 / sự đối đầu, thi đấu

	語	例文
781 □ 名	勝負〈する〉（しょうぶ）	ライバルの選手（せんしゅ）と勝負（しょうぶ）して、負（ま）けた。
	contest, game / 决胜负 / sự thắng bại, sự thi đấu	I played against my rival player and lost. / 和对手一决胜负，结果输了。/ Tôi thi đấu với đối thủ cạnh tranh và đã thua.
782 □ 名	勝敗（しょうはい）	この試合（しあい）は、なかなか勝敗（しょうはい）が決（き）まらない。
	victory or defeat / 胜败 / sự thắng bại, kết quả thi đấu	It is taking a while for the winner of this match to be decided. / 这场比赛难分胜负。/ Trận đấu này mãi không phân thắng bại.

🟰 勝（か）ち負（ま）け ➕ 引（ひ）き分（わ）ける tie / 平局 / hòa, huề

	語	例文
783 □ 名	勝利〈する〉（しょうり）	ついに、我々（われわれ）のチームが大（おお）きな試合（しあい）で勝利（しょうり）した。
	win / 胜利 / thắng lợi	Our team finally won in a big game. / 我队终于在大型比赛上获胜了。/ Cuối cùng đội chúng tôi cũng giành thắng lợi ở trận đấu lớn.
784 □ 動	破る（やぶ）	ずっと優勝（ゆうしょう）を逃（のが）していた選手（せんしゅ）が、とうとうライバルを破（やぶ）った。
	defeat / 击败 / đánh bại, xé rách	The player who victory had for so long eluded finally defeated her rival. / 一直与冠军擦肩的选手终于击败了竞争对手。/ Vận động viên lâu nay bỏ lỡ chức vô địch cuối cùng đã đánh bại đối thủ cạnh tranh.

785 □ 動

やっつける

beat / 干掉，击败 / đánh đuổi

今日（きょう）こそ敵（てき）を<u>やっつけ</u>よう。

Let's beat our opponents today for sure. / 今天一定要干掉敌人。/ Ngày hôm nay hãy đánh đuổi kẻ thù.

786 □ 動

敗（やぶ）れる

defeated / 败北 / bị đánh bại, thua

逆転（ぎゃくてん）でライバルに<u>敗（やぶ）れて</u>しまった。

We marked a disappointing defeat to our rival despite the fact that our victory seemed certain. / 形势逆转，输给竞争对手了。/ Chúng tôi bị thua ngược đối thủ cạnh tranh.

＝ 負（ま）ける

787 □ 動

攻（せ）める

attack / 攻击，进攻 / tấn công

優勝候補（ゆうしょうこうほ）の選手（せんしゅ）が、積極的（せっきょくてき）に相手（あいて）を<u>攻（せ）めて</u>いる。

The player with the best bet to win is aggressively attacking the opponent. / 夺冠热门选手积极地向对手发起进攻。/ Vận động viên ứng viên cho chức vô địch tích cực tấn công đối thủ.

788 □ 名

逆転（ぎゃくてん）〈する〉

come-from-behind victory, comeback victory / 逆转 / sự xoay ngược, đổi ngược tình thế

試合（しあい）の最後（さいご）に<u>逆転（ぎゃくてん）した</u>。

We were able to make a comeback victory in the end. / 比赛最后局势发生了逆转。/ Chúng tôi đã xoay ngược tình thế vào cuối trận đấu.

789 □ 名

開会（かいかい）〈する〉

start / 开幕 / sự khai mạc

10時（じ）から<u>開会（かいかい）</u>式（しき）が行（おこな）われる。

The opening ceremony will start at 10:00 a.m. / 10点开始举行开幕式。/ Lễ khai mạc được tiến hành từ 10 giờ.

⇔ 閉会（へいかい）〈する〉　＋ 閉会式（へいかいしき） closing ceremony / 闭幕式 / lễ bế mạc

790 □ 名

中断（ちゅうだん）〈する〉

interruption, suspension / 中断，中止 / sự gián đoạn, dừng lại

大雨（おおあめ）で試合（しあい）が<u>中断（ちゅうだん）された</u>。

The game was temporarily suspended due to heavy rain. / 比赛因大雨中断了。/ Trận đấu bị gián đoạn vì cơn mưa lớn.

791 □ 名

延長（えんちょう）〈する〉

extension / 延长 / sự kéo dài, đấu thêm giờ

同点（どうてん）で試合（しあい）は<u>延長（えんちょう）</u>になった。

The game was extended because the teams had the same score. / 由于得分相同，比赛加时了。/ Do đồng điểm nên trận đấu đã đấu thêm giờ.

＋ 延長戦（えんちょうせん） extended game / 加时赛 / hiệp phụ

792 □ イ形

勇（いさ）ましい

mighty / 振奋人心，勇敢 / mạnh mẽ, vững chãi

選手達（せんしゅたち）の<u>勇（いさ）ましい</u>声（こえ）で、試合（しあい）が始（はじ）まった。

The game started with a mighty cry from the players. / 选手们振奋人心的呼声揭开了比赛的序幕。/ Trận đấu bắt đầu với tiếng hô mạnh mẽ của các vận động viên.

793 勢い（いきお）

①このチームは勢いがあるので、勝つだろう。
②この火事は火の勢いが強くて、消すことができない。

名 **force, energy/force / 气势 / 势头，形势 / uy lực, sức mạnh**

① This team is on the go so they will likely win. ② The force of the fire is so strong that we can't put it out. / ①这个队伍很有士气，应该能赢吧。②这场火的火势太大灭不掉。/ ① Đội này có sức mạnh nên hẳn sẽ thắng. ② Trận hỏa hoạn này do sức lửa mạnh nên không thể dập tắt được.

① active and energetic ② natural strength / ①有精神，有活力②自然的活动力 / ① Khỏe mạnh và tràn đầy sinh lực. ② Sức hoạt động của tự nhiên

794 さすが［に］

去年の優勝チームはさすがに強い。

副 **as one would expect / 到底，不愧 / quả là**

As one would expect, the team that won last year is strong. / 不愧是去年的冠军队伍还是强啊。/ Đội vô địch năm ngoái quả là mạnh.

795 観客（かんきゃく）

競技場に多くの観客が集まった。

名 **audience / 观众 / khán giả**

A large audience gathered at the stadium. / 比赛场馆里来了很多观众。/ Đông đảo khán giả đã tập hợp đến đấu trường.

796 敵（てき）

試合前に敵と味方に分かれて練習する。

名 **opponent / 敌人，对手 / đối phương, kẻ thù**

We split into ally and enemy teams to practice before the game. / 比赛前，分为敌我两方进行练习。/ Trước trận đấu, chia thành phe ta và phe đối phương để luyện tập.

↔ 味方（みかた）

797 グラウンド

グラウンドに観客の声が響いた。

名 **ground / 运动场 / sân bóng, sân**

The cheers of the audience resonnated throughout the playground. / 观众们的欢呼声响彻了整个运动场。/ Trên sân vang tiếng ủng hộ của khán giả.

798 順位（じゅんい）

去年より上の順位を目指したい。

名 **ranking / 名次 / thứ tự, thứ hạng**

I want to aim for a higher ranking than last year. / 争取取得比去年更高的名次。/ Tôi muốn nhắm đến thứ hạng cao hơn năm ngoái.

＋ ランキング ranking / 排行榜 / bảng xếp hạng

799 トレーナー
名 trainer/sweat shirt / 教练员 / 训练服 / huấn luyện viên, áo thể thao

①あの選手のトレーナーは厳しいらしい。
②このトレーナーは動きやすくて便利だ。

① That player's trainer seems to be strict. ② This sweatshirt is easy to wear and handy. / ①那个选手的教练员好像很严厉。②这件训练服穿着活动自如很方便。/ ① Huấn luyện viên của vận động viên đó hình như nghiêm khắc lắm. ② Áo thể thao này dễ cử động nên tiện lợi.

① someone managing the health condition of a sports player ② a shirt worn when playing sports, etc. / ① 管理运动选手身体状况的人 ②运动时穿的外衣 / ① Người quản lý sức khỏe v.v. của vận động viên trong thể thao. ② Áo mặc khi chơi thể thao.

800 指導〈する〉
名 instruction / 指导 / chỉ đạo, hướng dẫn

有名な選手に指導を受ける。

I am coached by a famous player. / 接受知名选手的指导。/ Tôi được vận động viên nổi tiếng chỉ đạo.

➕ 指導者 instructor / 指导员 / người chỉ đạo, người hướng dẫn

801 取り入れる
動 take in / 引进，采用 / đưa vào

今年から新しいトレーニング法を取り入れている。

I am taking in new training methods starting this year. / 今年引进了新的训练方法。/ Từ năm nay đưa vào phương pháp huấn luyện mới.

802 ハードな
ナ形 hard / 艰难 / cứng rắn, khắc nghiệt, vất vả

優勝するために毎日ハードな練習をこなす。

I practice hard every day to win. / 为了获胜，每天完成高强度的练习。/ Để vô địch phải hoàn thành bài luyện tập khắc nghiệt mỗi ngày.

➕ ハードトレーニング training hard / 高强度训练 / sự luyện tập khắc nghiệt

803 通用〈する〉
名 be valid, be accepted / 通用，通行 / thông dụng, được tiếp nhận

彼は世界に通用する選手になるはずだ。

I expect that he will become a player that is accepted by the world. / 他应该能成为一名被全世界认可的选手。/ Anh ấy chắc chắn sẽ trở thành vận động viên được cả thế giới tiếp nhận.

804 技
名 trick, technique / 技术、技艺 / chiêu thức, kỹ năng, kỹ xảo

彼女の技は誰もまねできない。

No one can imitate her technique. / 她的技术谁都模仿不了。/ Không ai có thể bắt chước chiêu thức của cô ấy.

➕ テクニック technique / 技巧 / kỹ thuật

805 今に
副 before long / 不久 / chẳng mấy chốc

彼は今にきっと一流の選手になる。

He will no doubt become a top notch player. / 他不久一定能成为一流选手。/ Anh ấy chẳng mấy chốc sẽ trở thành vận động viên hàng đầu.

Section 2

ファッション

Fashion / 时尚 / Thời trang

806 □ 名	格好 (かっこう) form, appearance / 打扮 / hình thức, bộ dạng, vẻ bề ngoài	そんな格好(かっこう)で外出(がいしゅつ)するのは、やめなさい。 Don't go outside looking like that. / 不要打扮成这样出门。/ Hãy ngưng ngay cái việc đi ra ngoài với bộ dạng đó đi.

➕ かっこいい cool / 帅，有型 / đẹp trai, phong độ・かっこ悪(わる)い not cool / 形象不好 / vẻ bề ngoài xấu xí, khó coi

807 □ 名	持ち物 (もちもの) belongings / 随身物品 / vật dụng	この女優(じょゆう)の持ち物(もちもの)は全(すべ)て有名(ゆうめい)ブランド品(ひん)だ。 The actress' belongings are all from a famous brand. / 这个女演员的随身物品都是名牌货。/ Tất cả những vật dụng nữ diễn viên này có đều là đồ hiệu nổi tiếng.
808 □ 慣	身につける (み) wear something/acquire skills / 穿着 / 掌握 / mặc, đeo, học hỏi, tiếp thu	①先生(せんせい)が身(み)につけているものはセンスがいい。 ②日本語(にほんご)を勉強(べんきょう)して、会話力(かいわりょく)を身(み)につけたい。 ① What the teacher is wearing is all fashionable. ② I want to study Japanese and acquire the ability to speak better. / ①老师的穿着很有品位。②我想学习日语，掌握会话能力。/ ① Những gì thầy / cô mặc trên người đều có gu thẩm mỹ. ② Tôi muốn học tiếng Nhật, trang bị năng lực hội thoại.

👉 ① wearing something ② becoming able to use the technique or knowledge / ①穿着打扮②通过学习掌握一门技术或者知识 / ① Mặc, đeo. ② Học để có thể sử dụng được kỹ thuật, tri thức.

809 □ 名	センス taste / 品位 / gu thẩm mỹ, cảm nhận	彼女(かのじょ)はセンスがよく、とても個性的(こせいてき)だ。 She has good taste in fashion and is very unique. / 她的品位很好，非常有个性。/ Cô ấy có gu thẩm mỹ tốt, rất cá tính.
810 □ イ形	ダサい uncool, unfashionable / 土，老土 / khó coi, xấu xí, lôi thôi	弟(おとうと)はセンスが悪(わる)く、服装(ふくそう)がダサい。 My younger brother doesn't have good taste in fashion and his clothes are terrible. / 弟弟没品位，穿着很土。/ Em trai tôi gu thẩm mỹ tồi, trang phục xấu xí.
811 □ 副	いまひとつ not quite / 差一点 / một chút, thiếu chút	この帽子(ぼうし)は私(わたし)にはいまひとつ似合(にあ)わない。 This hat doesn't really look good on me now. / 这顶帽子不怎么适合我。/ Cái nón này không hợp với tôi một chút.

〓 いまいち

812 スタイル

①彼女はモデルみたいにスタイルがいい。
②これが私のライフスタイルだ。

名 figure/style / 身材，体型 / 样式，方式 / thân hình, phong cách

① She has a good figure, just like a fashion model. ② This is my lifestyle. / ①她的身材跟模特一样好。 ②这是我的生活方式。/ ① Cô ấy thân hình đẹp như người mẫu. ② Đây là phong cách sống của tôi.

① figure ② style / ①外形，身材②样式 / ① Vẻ bề ngoài, thân hình. ② Hình thức

813 足元（足下）

彼は足元のおしゃれにも、こだわっている。

名 footing / 脚下，脚上 / bước chân (dưới chân)

He is particular about footware fashion. / 他连脚上穿的都很讲究。/ Anh ấy chú trọng đến cả việc sành điệu ở dưới chân. (Anh ấy sành điệu đến cả gót chân).

814 ウエスト

このスカートはウエストがきつい。

名 waist / 腰围 / vòng eo

This skirt is tight in the waist. / 这条裙子腰围太紧了。/ Cái váy này vòng eo bị chật.

815 見た目

妹は見た目は派手だが、性格は地味だ。

名 looks / 看起来 / vẻ bề ngoài

My little sister looks showy but her personality is actually quiet. / 妹妹看上去穿衣打扮很花哨，其实性格很朴实。/ Em gái tôi nhìn bề ngoài sặc sỡ nhưng tính cách thì giản dị.

＋ 外見 appearance / 外观，外貌 / bề ngoài, ngoại hình・
見かけ appearance, surface / 外表，外观 / vẻ bề ngoài

816 人目

彼女の服装は街の中でも人目を引く。

名 public eye / 旁人的目光 / sự quan tâm, chú ý của người xung quanh

Her clothes attract attention in public. / 她的穿着在路上很引人注目。/ Phục trang của cô ấy thu hút sự quan tâm của người trong phố.

817 色彩

この服は色彩は豊かだが、派手ではない。

名 coloring / 色彩 / sắc thái, màu sắc

This dress is colorful but not too flashy. / 这件衣服虽然颜色很丰富，但却不会太花哨。/ Cái áo này màu sắc đa dạng nhưng không sặc sỡ.

818 華やかな

妹は華やかな色が似合う。

ナ形 colorful / 华丽，耀眼 / tươi tắn,lộng lẫy

My little sister looks good in bright colors. / 妹妹适合鲜艳的颜色。/ Em gái tôi hợp với những màu tươi tắn.

819 鮮やかな

鮮やかなピンクのシャツが欲しい。

ナ形 bright / 鲜明 / rực rỡ, chói lọi

I want a shirt in bright pink. / 我想要一件颜色鲜亮的粉色衬衫。/ Tôi muốn có cái áo thun màu hồng rực rỡ.

820 □ 名	統一〈する〉(とういつ) **unified / 统一 / sự thống nhất**	上着とバッグの色を統一する。(うわぎ / いろ / とういつ) Match the color of the coat with the bag. / 统一外套和包的颜色。/ Thống nhất màu áo khoác và túi xách với nhau.

➕ 統一感(とういつかん) sense of unity / 统一性 / tính thống nhất, tổng thể

821 □ 名	フリーサイズ **one-size-fits-all / 均码 / kích cỡ tự do, một kích cỡ**	このＴシャツはフリーサイズだ。 This T-shirt is one-size-fits-all. / 这件 T 恤衫是均码的。/ Cái áo sơ-mi này kích cỡ tự do.
822 □ ナ形 副	ぶかぶか〈な / する〉 **loose/too large / 宽松，松垮 / thùng thình, to rộng**	この服はデザインは好みだが、ぶかぶかだ。(ナ形)(ふく / この) I like the design of this dress, but it's too big. / 这件衣服的设计我很喜欢，就是太大了。/ Cái áo này mẫu mã hợp sở thích của tôi nhưng rộng thùng thình.

➕ だぶだぶ〈な / する〉 loose/too large / 肥大 / thùng thình,lụng thụng

823 □ 名	生地(きじ) **material / 面料 / vải**	社長のスーツの生地は上等だ。(しゃちょう / きじ / じょうとう) The material of the president's suit is of high quality. / 社长西装的面料很高级。/ Vải đồ vest của giám đốc là cao cấp.

➕ 布(ぬの) fabric / 布 / vải

☞ can also be used when talking about food (eg. pizza crust) / 也可用于烹饪，如"披萨胚" / Cũng dùng trong nấu ăn như " ピザの生地 (vỏ bánh pizza)"

824 □ 名	綿(めん) **cotton / 棉 / sợi bông, vải cotton**	綿の服は着心地が、とてもいい。(めん / ふく / きごこち) Cotton clothes are comfortable to wear. / 棉制衣服穿起来很舒服。/ Áo quần vải cotton mặc có cảm giác dễ chịu.

🟰 コットン

825 □ 名	オーダーメイド **made-to-order / 定制 / hàng đặt**	オーダーメイドでスーツを作った。(つく) The suit was made-to-order. / 我定制了一套西装。/ Tôi đã đặt may đồ vest.
826 □ 名	サングラス **sunglasses / 墨镜 / kính mát, kính râm**	夏はサングラスが欠かせない。(なつ / か) Sunglasses are indispensable in the summer. / 夏天不能没有墨镜。/ Mùa hè không thể thiếu kính mát.
827 □ 動	(ボタンが) 取れる(と) **(button) come off / (钮扣) 掉下来 / (nút) bị sút ra**	このシャツはボタンが取れやすい。(と) The button comes off easily on this shirt. / 这件衬衫的钮扣很容易掉。/ Nút cái áo thun này dễ bị sút.

828 □ 名 **浴衣**（ゆかた） **yukata; informal cotton kimono / 浴衣 / yukata (kimono mùa hè của Nhật)**

新しい浴衣を着て、花火大会に行きたい。（あたら／ゆかた／き／はなびたいかい／い）

I want to wear my new yukata and go to the fireworks festival. / 我想穿着新浴衣去烟火大会。/ Tôi muốn mặc yukata mới đi lễ hội pháo hoa.

接辞：高程度①（せつじ：こうていど） Affix: High Degree / 词缀：高程度 / Phụ tố: Mức độ cao

- **大～（非常に）**（ひじょう）

【おお～】

大地震（おおじしん）	major earthquake / 大地震 / Động đất lớn
大急ぎ（おおいそ）	in a big rush / 十万火急 / Rất gấp, rất nhanh
大仕事（おおしごと）	big job / 重大任务，大事业 / Công việc lớn lao, trọng đại
大騒ぎ（おおさわ）	uproar / 大混乱，大吵大闹 / Náo động, ầm ĩ
大まじめ（おお）	dead serious, very serious / 一本正经 / Rất thành thật, rất chăm chỉ
大掃除（おおそうじ）	thorough cleaning / 大扫除 / Tổng vệ sinh, dọn dẹp
大喜び（おおよろこ）	jumping with joy / 大喜，欣喜若狂 / Rất vui mừng

【だい～】

大震災（だいしんさい）	earthquake disaster / 大震灾 / Thảm họa động đất
大事件（だいじけん）	major accident / 大事件 / Vụ án lớn
大問題（だいもんだい）	big problem / 重大问题 / Vấn đề lớn
大好評（だいこうひょう）	having an extremely good reputation / 大受好评 / Được đánh giá tốt, rất phổ biến
大人気（だいにんき）	extremely popular / 大受欢迎 / Rất được ưa chuộng, yêu thích
大評判（だいひょうばん）	great popularity / 轰动一时 / Được đánh giá cao, có tiếng tăm
大恋愛（だいれんあい）	passionate love / 轰轰烈烈的恋爱 / Tình yêu lớn

Section 3

エンターテインメント

Entertainment / 娱乐 / Giải trí

829 □ 名	イベント event / 活动 / sự kiện	週末のイベントが楽しみだ。 I'm looking forward to the weekend event. / 我很期待周末的活动。/ Tôi mong đến sự kiện cuối tuần ghê.
830 □ 名	アイドル idol / 偶像 / thần tượng	大好きなアイドルのコンサートには必ず行く。 I will definitely go to my favorite idol's concert. / 非常喜欢的偶像的演唱会，我一定会去。/ Chắc chắn tôi sẽ đi buổi hòa nhạc của thần tượng yêu thích.

➕ 芸能人(げいのうじん) celebrity / 艺人 / nghệ sỹ・タレント talent / 演员，艺人 / nghệ sỹ

831 □ 名	ステージ stage / 舞台 / sân khấu	アイドルがステージに現(あらわ)れた。 The idol appeared on stage. / 偶像出现在了舞台上。/ Thần tượng đã xuất hiện trên sân khấu.

➕ 舞台(ぶたい) stage / 舞台 / sân khấu, vũ đài

832 □ 名	興奮(こうふん)〈する〉 excitement / 兴奋 / sự phấn khích	会場(かいじょう)の空気(くうき)にファン達(たち)は興奮(こうふん)した。 The fans were excited with the atmosphere of the venue. / 现场的气氛让粉丝们兴奋起来了。/ Người hâm mộ phấn khích với không khí của hội trường.
833 □ 副	続々(ぞくぞく)［と］ one after another / 源源不断 / lần lượt, liên tục	会場(かいじょう)に続々(ぞくぞく)と人(ひと)が集(あつ)まった。 More and more people gathered at the venue. / 会场内源源不断聚集了很多人。/ Người người lần lượt tập hợp đến hội trường.
834 □ 名	演劇(えんげき) play / 话剧 / kịch	父(ちち)は演劇(えんげき)を見(み)に行(い)くのが趣味(しゅみ)だ。 My father's hobby is to go watch plays. / 去看话剧是父亲的爱好。/ Bố tôi có sở thích đi xem kịch.

➕ ［お］芝居(しばい) play / 戏剧，表演 / kịch, biểu diễn sân khấu

835 □ 名	劇場(げきじょう) theater / 剧场 / nhà hát, sân khấu	今度(こんど)の日曜(にちよう)に、劇場(げきじょう)に芝居(しばい)を見(み)に行(い)く。 I will go see a play at the theater next Sunday. / 这个星期天去剧场看表演。/ Chủ nhật này tôi sẽ đi xem kịch ở nhà hát.
836 □ 名	役者(やくしゃ) actor / 演员 / diễn viên	好(す)きな役者(やくしゃ)が出(で)る演劇(えんげき)を見(み)に行(い)った。 I went to see a play where my favorite actor is playing. / 我去看了喜欢的演员出演的话剧。/ Tôi đã đi xem kịch có diễn viên yêu thích xuất hiện.

837 主役（しゅやく）
名 **main role / 主演 / vai chính**

主役は今一番人気がある女優だ。
The main role is played by today's most popular actress. / 主演是现在最受欢迎的女演员。/ Vai chính là nữ diễn viên được hâm mộ nhất hiện nay.

838 セリフ
名 **line/words / 台词 / 话，言词 / lời thoại, ăn nói**

①役者はセリフを覚えるのも仕事だ。
②親に、よくそんなセリフが言えるわね。
① Learning their lines is part of an actor's job. ② How could you say that to your parents? / ①对演员来说背台词也是工作。②你居然对父母说得出这种话。/ ① Thuộc lời thoại cũng là công việc của diễn viên. ② Có thể ăn nói như vậy với bố mẹ nhỉ.

① words spoken by the characters of movies, etc. ② a special way of speaking to someone / ①戏剧中人物说的话②对人说的特别的说法 / ① Lời nhân vật xuất hiện trong phim v.v. ② Cách nói đặc biệt đối với người khác

839 演技（えんぎ）〈する〉
名 **acting/act / 演技 / 演戏 / sự diễn xuất, diễn kịch (giả tạo)**

①あの俳優はかっこいいが、演技は下手だ。
②彼女が泣いたのは、きっと演技だ。
① Tha actor is handsome but can't act at all. ② Her crying is probably an act. / ①那个演员虽然很帅但演技太差。②她哭肯定是装出来的。/ ① Diễn viên đó đẹp trai nhưng diễn xuất dở. ② Việc cô ấy khóc chắc chắn là diễn rồi.

＋ 芝居（しばい）〈する〉 play / 表演，戏剧 / sự diễn, diễn kịch・演じる（えんじる） act / 演，表演 / diễn xuất

① showing technique by words and movement ② doing something to deceive someone / ①通过语言或动作来进行表演的技巧 ②装模作样地做某事 / ① Cho xem kỹ năng bằng từ ngữ, động tác. ② Làm gì đó dối trá.

840 オーケストラ
名 **orchestra / 管弦乐 / hòa nhạc, dàn nhạc**

月に1回はオーケストラを聴きに行く。
I come to listen to the orchestra once a month. / 每月去听一次管弦乐。/ Mỗi tháng 1 lần, tôi đi nghe nhạc hòa tấu.

841 リズム
名 **rhythm / 节奏 / giai điệu**

リズムに合わせて、みんなで踊る。
We all dance to the rhythm. / 大家跟着节奏一起跳舞。/ Mọi người cùng hòa với giai điệu mà nhảy múa.

842 鑑賞（かんしょう）〈する〉
名 **observe, watch / 观摩，欣赏 / thưởng lãm, thưởng thức**

家で映画を鑑賞する。
I watch movies at home. / 在家看电影。/ Tôi thưởng thức phim ở nhà.

＋ 音楽鑑賞（おんがくかんしょう）〈する〉 listening to music / 音乐鉴赏 / sự thưởng thức âm nhạc・
芸術鑑賞（げいじゅつかんしょう）〈する〉 watching art / 艺术鉴赏 / sự thưởng lãm nghệ thuật

	語彙	例文
843	芸術家(げいじゅつか)	これは有名(ゆうめい)な芸術家(げいじゅつか)の物語(ものがたり)だ。
名	**artist / 艺术家 / nghệ sỹ, nghệ thuật gia**	This is a story about a famous artist. / 这是一位知名艺术家的故事。/ Đây là truyện kể của nghệ sỹ nổi tiếng.
844	監督(かんとく)〈する〉	この監督(かんとく)の映画(えいが)は全(すべ)て見(み)ている。
名	**director / 导演 / đạo diễn**	I've seen all of this director's movies. / 这个导演的电影我都看过。/ Tôi xem tất cả phim của đạo diễn này.
845	あらすじ	ネットであらすじを見(み)てから、映画(えいが)を見(み)に行(い)く。
名	**synopsis / 梗概 / tóm tắt, phác thảo**	I will read the synopsis on the Internet and then go see the movie. / 我在网上看了剧情梗概后再去看电影。/ Sau khi xem tóm tắt qua mạng, tôi đi xem phim.
846	ありふれた～	どこかで聞(き)いたようなありふれた話(はなし)は、つまらない。
連体	**commonplace / 平常 / cũ rích, xưa, tầm thường**	Commonplace stories that sound like something I have already heard before are boring. / 似乎是一件在哪里听说过的稀松平常的事情，没什么意思。/ Những chuyện xưa cũ như đã từng nghe ở đâu đó thì thật chán.
847	ばかばかしい	あの映画(えいが)はばかばかしいストーリーだが、面白(おもしろ)かった。
イ形	**silly / 荒谬，愚蠢 / ngu ngốc, nực cười**	That movie has a silly storyline, but it was entertaining. / 那部电影虽然讲了一个很荒谬的故事，但却很有意思。/ Phim đó nội dung thì ngu ngốc nhưng thú vị.

➕ ばからしい foolish / 傻，愚蠢 / ngu ngốc

	語彙	例文
848	退屈(たいくつ)〈な／する〉	昨日(きのう)の映画(えいが)は退屈(たいくつ)で、途中(とちゅう)で寝(ね)てしまった。(ナ形)
名 ナ形	**boring / 无聊 / buồn tẻ, chán ngắt**	Yesterday's movie was so boring, I fell asleep in the middle of it. / 昨天的电影很无聊，中途我睡着了。/ Bộ phim hôm qua chán ngắt, tôi đã ngủ gục giữa chừng.
849	人物(じんぶつ)	このドラマに登場(とうじょう)する人物(じんぶつ)は、みんなユニークだ。
名	**character / 人物 / nhân vật**	Every character appearing in this drama is unique. / 这部电视剧中出场的人物每个都很特别。/ Các nhân vật xuất hiện trong phim truyền hình này mọi người đều độc đáo.
850	場面(ばめん)	①主役(しゅやく)が死(し)ぬ場面(ばめん)で大声(おおごえ)で泣(な)いてしまった。 ②ビジネスの場面(ばめん)では敬語(けいご)を話(はな)すべきだ。
名	**scene/scene, situation / 场面，场景 / 场合 / cảnh, trường hợp, tình huống**	① I bawled at the scene where the main character died. ② You should use honorific language in business situations. / ①主角死的那一幕让我大哭了一场。②商务场合应该说敬语。/ ① Cảnh vai chính chết, tôi đã khóc thật to. ② Trong tình huống việc làm, phải nói kính ngữ.

👉 ① a scene from a film or play ② a scene where something took place / ①电影、话剧中的一个场景或一幕② 某事发生时的场景 / ① Một cảnh trong phim hay kịch. ② Tình trạng nơi xảy ra việc nào đó.

851 **展開〈する〉** (てんかい)

名 **development / 展开，发展 / sự triển khai, tiến triển, diễn tiến**

このゲームは予想できない展開で、面白かった。

This game is fun because its development is unpredictable. / 这个游戏的发展完全预料不到，很有意思。/ Game này không thể dự đoán được diễn tiến nên thú vị.

852 **テンポ**

名 **tempo/tempo / 速度 / 拍子 / nhịp độ, nhịp điệu**

①この話はテンポが速くて、あっという間に終わった。

②テンポの速い音楽の方が好きだ。

① The tempo of this story was fast and the story was over before I knew it. ② I like fast tempo music. / ①这件事进展得很快，一转眼就结束了。②我喜欢拍子很快的音乐。/ ① Câu chuyện này nhịp độ nhanh, chẳng mấy chốc đã kết thúc. ② Tôi thích nhạc có nhịp điệu nhanh hơn.

① the speed at which things progress ② the speed of a musical performance / ①事物进展的速度②音乐的演奏速度 / ① Tốc độ tiến triển của sự việc. ② Tốc độ diễn tấu của âm nhạc.

853 **評判** (ひょうばん)

名 **review / 评价，声望 / sự bình luận, đánh giá**

彼の映画は評判がいいが、私は好きではない。

His movie had good reviews, but I don’t like it. / 他的电影评价很好，但是我不喜欢。/ Phim của anh ấy được đánh giá cao nhưng tôi lại không thích.

854 **評価〈する〉** (ひょうか)

名 **evaluation / 评价 / sự đánh giá**

この監督の映画は海外で評価が高い。

Movies by this director gets good reviews overseas. / 这个导演的电影在海外评价很高。/ Phim của đạo diễn này được đánh giá cao ở hải ngoại.

＋ 好評 (こうひょう) good review / 好评 / sự đánh giá cao

855 **感想** (かんそう)

名 **impression, opinion / 感想 / cảm tưởng**

あの映画見たの？　感想聞かせて。

You saw that movie? Let me hear your opinion. / 那个电影看了吗？说说你的感想。/ Xem phim đó rồi hả? Cho tôi nghe cảm tưởng với.

＋ 感想文 (かんそうぶん) essay about the impression / 感想文 / văn cảm tưởng

856 **賞** (しょう)

名 **award / 奖 / giải thưởng**

人気映画の最新作が映画祭で賞をもらった。

The movie’s latest installment won a prize at the film festival. / 人气电影的最新作品在电影节上获奖了。/ Tác phẩm điện ảnh mới nhất được yêu thích đã nhận giải ở liên hoan phim.

＋ 受賞〈する〉 (じゅしょう) receiving the award / 获奖 / nhận thưởng, đoạt giải・大賞 (たいしょう) top award / 大奖 / giải thưởng lớn・グランプリ grand prix / 最高奖 / giải thưởng lớn

本
ほん

Book / 书 / Sách

857 **書物** (しょもつ) 名
book / 书籍 / sách, sách vở

子どもの頃(ころ)から書物(しょもつ)に親(した)しむことは大切(たいせつ)だ。
It is important to get familiar with books from an early age. / 从小让孩子多接触书籍很重要。/ Việc làm quen với sách từ nhỏ rất quan trọng.

➕ 書籍(しょせき) books / 书籍 / sách, sách vở

858 **絵本** (えほん) 名
picture book / 图画书 / truyện tranh minh họa

絵本(えほん)は子(こ)どもだけじゃなく、大人(おとな)にも人気(にんき)だ。
Children's books are popular not only among children, but also among adults. / 图画书不仅受小孩子喜爱，也受大人欢迎。/ Truyện tranh minh họa không chỉ trẻ em mà cả người lớn cũng yêu thích.

859 **作品** (さくひん) 名
work / 作品 / tác phẩm

この小説家(しょうせつか)の作品(さくひん)は世界中(せかいじゅう)で読(よ)まれている。
Works by this author are read around the world. / 这个小说家的作品被全世界的读者阅读。/ Tác phẩm của nhà văn này được đọc khắp thế giới.

➕ 名作(めいさく) masterpiece / 名作 / danh tác, tác phẩm nổi tiếng

860 **著者** (ちょしゃ) 名
author / 著者，作者 / tác giả

本屋(ほんや)で著者(ちょしゃ)のサイン会(かい)が開(ひら)かれている。
An author is holding an book signing at a book store. / 书店正在召开作者的签名会。/ Buổi ký tên của tác giả được tổ chức ở tiệm sách.

➕ 作者(さくしゃ) creator, artist / 作者 / tác giả・筆者(ひっしゃ) writer / 笔者 / tác giả, người viết

861 **書き手** (かきて) 名
writer / 作者，笔者 / người viết

この小説(しょうせつ)の書(か)き手(て)の気持(きも)ちが、わからない。
I don't understand the feelings of this novel's author. / 我不理解这本小说作者的心情。/ Tôi không hiểu cảm giác của người viết tiểu thuyết này.

↔ 読(よ)み手(て)

➕ 話(はな)し手(て) speaker / 说话人 / người kể, người nói・聞(き)き手(て) listener / 听话人 / người nghe

862 **ペンネーム** 名
pen name / 笔名 / bút danh

この著者(ちょしゃ)のペンネームはユニークだ。
This author's pen name is unique. / 这个作者的笔名很特别。/ Bút danh của tác giả này thật độc đáo.

➕ 本名(ほんみょう) real name / 本名 / tên thật・芸名(げいめい) stage name / 艺名 / nghệ danh

863 主人公（しゅじんこう）
名 **protagonist / 主人公 / nhân vật chính**

この物語（ものがたり）の主人公（しゅじんこう）は不思議（ふしぎ）な人物（じんぶつ）だ。
The protagonist of this story is a strange person. / 这个故事的主人公是个不可思议的角色。/ Nhân vật chính của truyện này là nhân vật kỳ ảo.

➕ ヒロイン heroine / 女主人公 / nhân vật nữ chính, nữ anh hùng・
ヒーロー hero / 男主人公，勇士 / nhân vật nam chính, anh hùng

864 ロマン
名 **romance / 浪漫 / sự lãng mạn**

彼（かれ）が書（か）くストーリーにはロマンがある。
His stories are romantic. / 他笔下的故事充满了浪漫色彩。/ Câu chuyện anh ấy viết có sự lãng mạn.

➕ ロマンティックな romantic / 浪漫 / lãng mạn・
ロマンティスト romantist / 浪漫主义者 / người lãng mạn

865 伝記（でんき）
名 **biography / 传记 / truyền ký, tiểu sử**

偉（えら）い人（ひと）の伝記（でんき）から生（い）き方（かた）を学（まな）ぶ。
I learn lessons on life from biographies of famous people. / 从伟人传记中学习人生态度。/ Học cách sống từ tiểu sử của những vĩ nhân.

866 人生（じんせい）
名 **life / 人生 / cuộc đời**

ある野球選手（やきゅうせんしゅ）の人生（じんせい）が本（ほん）になった。
The life of some baseball player became a book. / 一个棒球选手的人生被写成了一本书。/ Cuộc đời của vận động viên bóng chày nọ đã thành sách.

867 神話（しんわ）
名 **myth / 神话 / thần thoại**

この本（ほん）を読（よ）んでから、神話（しんわ）の世界（せかい）に夢中（むちゅう）だ。
Since reading this book, I've been crazy about the world of mythology. / 看了这本书后沉浸在了神话的世界中。/ Sau khi đọc quyển sách này, tôi đã đắm chìm trong thế giới thần thoại.

868 中世（ちゅうせい）
名 **Medieval Ages / 中世纪 / thời trung thế**

彼女（かのじょ）の本（ほん）を読（よ）んで、中世（ちゅうせい）に興味（きょうみ）を持（も）つようになった。
I became interested in the medieval ages after reading her book. / 读了她的书后，我对中世纪很感兴趣。/ Đọc sách của cô ấy, tôi trở nên quan tâm đến thời trung thế.

➕ 古代（こだい） ancient times / 古代 / thời cổ đại

869 文明（ぶんめい）
名 **civilization / 文明 / văn minh**

これは世界（せかい）の文明（ぶんめい）に関（かん）する本（ほん）だ。
This book is about world civilizations. / 这是一本关于世界文明的书。/ Đây là sách liên quan đến văn minh thế giới.

➕ 文明的（ぶんめいてき）な civil / 文明的 / một cách văn minh

870 □	忠実な ちゅうじつ	①この話は歴史に忠実に書かれている。 ②犬は主人に忠実だ。
ナ形	**faithful / 忠于 / 忠诚 / trung thực, trung thành**	① This story faithfully follows history. ② The dog is faithful to the owner. / ①这个故事写得很忠于历史背景。②狗对主人很忠诚。 / ① Câu chuyện này được viết trung thực với lịch sử. ② Chó rất trung thành với chủ nhân.

☞ ① same content as the original ② follow what one's superior is saying / ①与原型一致②对上级顺从 / ① Giống với nội dung ban đầu ② Ngoan ngoãn tuân theo người ở địa vị bên trên.

871 □	奇妙な きみょう	このまんがのストーリーは奇妙だ。
ナ形	**strange / 奇妙 / kỳ dị, lạ lùng**	The story of this comic is strange. / 这个漫画的故事很奇妙。 / Nội dung của truyện tranh này thật lạ lùng.
872 □	背景 はいけい	①この記事から事件の背景がわかる。 ②滝を背景に写真を撮った。
名	**background/background / 背景（抽象）/ 背景（具体）/ bối cảnh, nền**	① You can learn about the background of the incident from this article. ② I took a photo with the waterfall as a background. / ①从这篇报道中可以知道事件发生的背景。②以瀑布为背景照相。/ ① Có thể hiểu được bối cảnh vụ án từ bài phóng sự này. ② Tôi chụp hình lấy nền là thác nước.

☞ ① circumstances that cannot be observed ② the background of a photo / ①看不见的抽象情况②照片物体后面的景色 / ① Sự tình không thể thấy của sự việc. ② Quang cảnh phía sau hình chụp.

873 □	実際 じっさい	この小説の話は実際に起こったことだ。
名	**actuality / 实际 / thực tế**	The story in this novel is something that actually happened. / 这个小说的故事是真实发生过的。/ Câu chuyện của tiểu thuyết này là chuyện đã xảy ra trong thực tế.
874 □	文句 もんく	①文句の一つひとつに作家の個性が出ている。 ②文句ばかり言っていないで、行動しなさい。
名	**expression/complaint / 句子 / 抱怨 / câu văn, sự than phiền, cằn nhằn**	① The author's characteristic shows in all the expressions he uses. ② Quit grumbling and do something. / ①一字一句都体现着作家的个性。②不要老是抱怨，要行动起来。/ ① Cá tính của tác giả hiện lên trong từng câu văn. ② Đừng có than phiền không thôi, hãy hành động đi.

☞ ① words used in a sentence ② gripes and complaints / ①文章中的话②不满 / ① Từ ngữ trong văn chương ② Bất mãn, bất bình.

875 □	果たして は	①主人公は果たしてどうなるのだろうか。 ②果たして、天気予報通りに台風が来た。
副	**really/sure enough / 到底 / 果然 / rốt cuộc, quả nhiên**	① What is really going to happen to the protagonist? ② Sure enough, the typhoon came as predicted by the weather forecast. / ①主人公到底会怎么样呢？②果然如天气预报报道的那样台风来了。/ ① Rốt cuộc nhân vật chính sẽ ra sao nhỉ? ② Quả nhiên bão đến đúng như dự báo thời tiết.

① "really?" in question form ② as planned / ①疑问句中使用②预料之内 / ① Câu nghi vấn và thật ra ② Đúng như dự đoán

876 発想〈する〉
はっそう
名 **idea / 想法 / sự sáng tạo, ý tưởng**

こんな発想ができるなんて、彼は天才だ。
はっそう かれ てんさい
He is a genius for coming up with ideas like that. / 竟然能想出这种点子，他真是个天才。/ Có thể sáng tạo như thế này thì anh ấy đúng là thiên tài.

877 由来〈する〉
ゆらい
名 **origin / 由来 / nguồn gốc**

地名の由来について知りたいなら、この辞典がいい。
ちめい ゆらい し じてん
This dictionary is good if you want to know the origin of place names. / 想知道地名的由来的话，查这本词典好。/ Nếu muốn biết về nguồn gốc địa danh, quyển tự điển này tốt đấy.

878 空想〈する〉
くうそう
名 **imagination / 空想，架空 / sự không tưởng**

これは空想の世界の物語だ。
くうそう せかい ものがたり
This is an imaginary story. / 这是一个架空世界的故事。/ Đây là câu chuyện của thế giới không tưởng.

879 連想〈する〉
れんそう
名 **association / 联想 / sự liên tưởng**

この話は10年前の事件を連想させる。
はなし ねんまえ じけん れんそう
This story reminds me of an incident that occurred 10 years ago. / 这个故事让人联想到十年前发生的事件。/ Câu chuyện này làm tôi liên tưởng đến vụ án 10 năm trước.

880 解釈〈する〉
かいしゃく
名 **interpretation / 解释 / sự diễn giải, giải nghĩa**

本の解釈は一つではない。読む人が決めればいい。
ほん かいしゃく ひと よ ひと き
There is no single interpretation of a book. The reader should decide. / 对于书的解读不是只有一种。读者自己决定(如何理解)就好。/ Diễn giải về sách không chỉ có một. Người đọc quyết định là được.

881 発行〈する〉
はっこう
名 **publish / 发行 / sự phát hành**

新作が発行されて、100万部も売れている。
しんさく はっこう まんぶ う
A new work was published, and it sold 1 million copies. / 新作品发售，已经卖了100万部了。/ Tác phẩm mới được phát hành, bán được 1.000.000 bản.

882 生み出す
う だ
動 **create / 创作出，产出 / sáng tạo ra, tạo ra**

彼はデビュー以来、多くの名作を生み出している。
かれ いらい おお めいさく う だ
Since his debut, he has been creating many masterpieces. / 他出道以来创作了很多有名的作品。/ Kể từ khi ra mắt, anh ấy đã tạo ra nhiều tác phẩm nổi tiếng.

883 読書家
どくしょか
名 **avid reader / 爱读书的人 / mọt sách, người thích đọc sách**

読書家の父の影響で、私もよく本を読む。
どくしょか ちち えいきょう わたし ほん よ
I read a lot of books, due to the influence of my father who is an avid reader. / 受到爱看书的父亲的影响，我也经常看书。/ Chịu ảnh hưởng của người cha thích đọc sách, tôi cũng thường đọc sách.

＋ 勉強家(べんきょうか) industrial student / 爱学习的人 / người thích học・努力家(どりょくか) hard worker / 勤奋努力的人 / người nỗ lực

これも覚えよう！⑳

接辞：高程度②　Affix: High Degree / 词缀：高程度 / Phụ tố: Mức độ cao

• 超～（並みはずれて）

超満員	ちょうまんいん	extremely overcrowded / 拥挤不堪 / Chật cứng người
超能力	ちょうのうりょく	supernatural power / 超能力 / Siêu năng lực
超特急	ちょうとっきゅう	superexpress / 超级特快（列车）/ Cực nhanh
超音波	ちょうおんぱ	ultrasonic / 超声波 / Sóng siêu âm
超音速	ちょうおんそく	supersonic speed / 超音速 / Tốc độ siêu âm
超高層	ちょうこうそう	high-rise / 超高层 / Siêu cao tầng
超自然	ちょうしぜん	supernatural / 超自然 / Siêu nhiên

• 最～（その中で一番）

最高級	さいこうきゅう	best / 最高端（价格最高的）/ Cao cấp nhất
最上級	さいじょうきゅう	top-class / 最上乘（品质最好的）/ Cao cấp nhất, mức độ cao nhất
最高潮	さいこうちょう	peak / 最高潮 / Mực thủy triều cao nhất
最年長	さいねんちょう	eldest / 最年长 / Lớn tuổi nhất
最年少	さいねんしょう	youngest / 最年轻 / Nhỏ tuổi nhất
最優秀	さいゆうしゅう	best / 最优秀 / Xuất sắc nhất
最大級	さいだいきゅう	maximum / 最大级别（范围最大的）/ Cấp lớn nhất
最小限	さいしょうげん	minimum / 最小限度 / Giới hạn nhỏ nhất

趣味(しゅみ)・好(この)み

Hobby, Preference / 兴趣・爱好 / Sở thích - Ý thích

884 □ 習(なら)い事(ごと)

名 **lessons, learning something / 学习，技能 / việc học ngoại khóa**

子(こ)どもの頃(ころ)、ピアノなどの習(なら)い事(ごと)をしていた。

I used to take lessons for piano and other things when I was a child. / 小时候我学过钢琴什么的。/ Thuở nhỏ, tôi đã học ngoại khóa piano v.v.

➕ けいこ practice / 学习，练功，排练 / luyện tập, học ngoại khóa

885 □ こだわる

動 **be particular/be bothered / 讲究 / 追究 / chú trọng, câu nệ**

①母(はは)は外出(がいしゅつ)するとき、靴(くつ)にこだわる。
②そんなことに、いつまでこだわっているの？

① My mother is particular about shoes when she goes out. ② How long do you intent to be bothered about something like that? / ①妈妈外出时对穿什么鞋很讲究。②这种事情你要追究到什么时候？ / ① Khi mẹ tôi ra ngoài, bà luôn chú trọng giày dép. ② Cứ câu nệ chuyện như thế đến khi nào?

👉 ① claiming preferences for minor details ② being needlessly particular about things / ①容易被忽视的地方也有主张②在意鸡毛蒜皮的事情 / ① Dù có bị coi thường cũng vẫn chủ trương ý thích. ② Lưu tâm chuyện nhỏ nhặt không cần lưu tâm.

886 □ こだわり

名 **preference, obsessiveness / 讲究 / đặc trưng, phong cách riêng**

彼(かれ)はコーヒーの入(い)れ方(かた)にこだわりがある。

He has strong preferences about the way he brews coffee. / 他泡咖啡的方式很有讲究。/ Anh ấy có phong cách riêng trong việc pha cà phê.

887 □ 凝(こ)る

動 **be wrapped up in, be passionate about / 热衷于，讲究 / tập trung, đắm chìm, say mê**

最近(さいきん)、父(ちち)は釣(つ)りに凝(こ)っている。

My father has been passionate about fishing these days. / 最近爸爸迷上了钓鱼。/ Gần đây, bố tôi say mê đi câu.

➕ 凝(こ)り性(しょう) perfectionist / 热衷于某一事情的性格。 / sự chuyên tâm

888 □ 熱中(ねっちゅう)〈する〉

名 **absorption / 热衷 / sự say mê**

弟(おとうと)はオンラインゲームに熱中(ねっちゅう)している。

My younger brother is addicted to online games. / 弟弟沉迷于网络游戏。/ Em trai tôi say mê game online.

889 □ コレクション〈する〉

名 **collection / 收藏 / sự sưu tầm, bộ sưu tập**

海外(かいがい)の絵(え)をコレクションしている。

I have a collection of drawings from overseas. / 我收藏外国画。/ Tôi sưu tầm tranh hải ngoại.

➕ コレクター collector / 收藏家 / nhà sưu tầm

890 **多彩な**
たさい
ナ形 **varying / 丰富多彩 / đa dạng**

先生は多彩な趣味を持っている。
せんせい たさい しゅみ も
The teacher has many hobbies. / 老师有丰富多彩的爱好。/ Thầy / cô có nhiều sở thích đa dạng.

891 **素人**
しろうと
名 **novice / 门外汉，新手 / người nghiệp dư**

写真を始めたが、まだまだ素人だ。
しゃしん はじ しろうと
I started doing photography, but I'm still a novice. / 我虽然开始玩摄影了，但还是个新手。/ Tôi bắt đầu chụp ảnh nhưng vẫn còn là người mới nghiệp dư thôi.

↔ 玄人（くろうと）

892 **初心者**
しょしんしゃ
名 **beginner / 初学者 / người mới bắt đầu**

この教室は茶道の初心者でも、ていねいに教える。
きょうしつ さどう しょしんしゃ おし
This class teaches tea ceremony to beginners thoroughly. / 这个茶道班对初学者也会耐心地教导。/ Lớp học này dạy kỹ cho cả những người mới bắt đầu học trà đạo.

＋ 初歩（しょほ） first step / 入门 / sơ bộ, bước đầu

893 **本格的な**
ほんかくてき
ナ形 **serious / 正式的 / một cách thực thụ**

本格的に絵を習うことにした。
ほんかくてき え なら
I decided to learn drawing seriously. / 我决定正式开始学习画画。/ Tôi quyết định học vẽ một cách thực thụ.

894 **名人**
めいじん
名 **master / 名人，能手 / chuyên gia, danh nhân, người giỏi lĩnh vực nào đó**

父は自分のことを「釣りの名人」と呼んでいる。
ちち じぶん つ めいじん よ
My father calls himself "a master fisherman." / 爸爸把自己称作"钓鱼能手"。/ Bố tôi tự gọi mình là "chuyên gia câu cá".

＋ 達人（たつじん） expert / 高手，能人 / chuyên gia, người thành thạo

895 **共通〈する〉**
きょうつう
名 **common / 共同 / cùng chung**

彼との共通の趣味はクラシック音楽だ。
かれ きょうつう しゅみ おんがく
Our common hobby is classical music. / 我和他共同的爱好是古典音乐。/ Sở thích chung (của tôi) với anh ấy là nhạc cổ điển.

896 **ブーム**
名 **fad / 热潮，流行 / trào lưu, cơn sốt**

ジョギングがブームになって、何年も経つ。
なんねん た
It's been several years since jogging became a fad. / 跑步成为一股热潮，已经几年了。/ Chạy bộ trở thành trào lưu cũng đã mấy năm.

＋ マイブーム personal fad / 最爱 / trào lưu của riêng mình

897 **アウトドア**
名 **outdoor / 户外 / hoạt động ngoài trời**

週末はいつも、アウトドアを楽しんでいる。
しゅうまつ たの
I enjoy playing outdoors every weekend. / 我周末通常享受户外活动。/ Cuối tuần tôi luôn vui thú các hoạt động ngoài trời.

＝ アウトドアアクティビティ ↔ インドア

＋ アウトドアライフ outdoor life / 户外生活 / cuộc sống ngoài trời, cuộc sống giữa thiên nhiên

898 編み物 (あもの)
名 **knitting / 编织物 / đồ đan móc**

母から編み物を教わっている。(はは あもの おそ)
I am learning how to knit from my mother. / 妈妈教我编织东西。/ Tôi được mẹ dạy đan móc.

➕ 編む (あ) knit / 编织 / đan, móc

899 手品 (てじな)
名 **magic / 戏法，魔术 / trò ảo thuật**

宴会で趣味の手品を見てもらった。(えんかい しゅみ てじな み)
I had people watch my magic performance at the party. / 我在宴会上表演了自己业余爱好的魔术。/ Ở buổi tiệc, tôi được mọi người xem sở thích ảo thuật.

➕ マジック magic / 魔术 / trò ảo thuật・マジシャン magician / 魔术师 / nhà ảo thuật

900 占い (うらな)
名 **fortune-telling / 占卜 / sự bói toán**

占いが好きで、本を買って勉強している。(うらな す ほん か べんきょう)
I like fortunetelling, so I bought a book to study it. / 我喜欢占卜，所以买了书在学习。/ Tôi thích xem bói nên mua sách về học.

➕ 占う (うらな) tell one's fortune / 占卜，卜卦 / bói toán・星座占い (せいざうらな) astrology / 占星 / sự bói theo sao chiếu mệnh・血液型占い (けつえきがたうらな) fortune-telling using blood type / 血型占卜 / sự bói theo nhóm máu・手相占い (てそううらな) palm reading / 手相占卜 / sự bói chỉ tay

901 手話 (しゅわ)
名 **sign language / 手语 / ngôn ngữ ký hiệu**

先月から手話の教室に通い始めた。(せんげつ しゅわ きょうしつ かよ はじ)
I started going to sign language classes last month. / 我从上个月开始上手语培训班。/ Từ tháng trước tôi bắt đầu đi học lớp ngôn ngữ ký hiệu.

902 伝統 (でんとう)
名 **tradition / 传统 / truyền thống**

留学をきっかけに、日本の伝統に興味を持った。(りゅうがく にほん でんとう きょうみ も)
Since studying abroad, I have become more interested in Japanese traditions. / 以留学为契机，对日本传统开始感兴趣了。/ Nhờ du học là động cơ mà tôi quan tâm đến truyền thống Nhật Bản.

➕ 伝統的な (でんとうてき) traditional / 传统的 / một cách truyền thống

903 作法 (さほう)
名 **manners / 礼法，礼仪 / nghi thức xã giao, lễ nghi**

日本で生け花や茶道の作法を学びたい。(にほん い ばな さどう さほう まな)
I want to learn ikebana and tea ceremony manners in Japan. / 我想在日本学习插画以及茶道的礼法。/ Tôi muốn học các lễ nghi cắm hoa, trà đạo ở Nhật.

904 撮影〈する〉(さつえい)
名 **photography / 摄影 / sự chụp ảnh, quay phim**

先週、風景や建物を、たくさん撮影した。(せんしゅう ふうけい たてもの さつえい)
I photographed a lot of scenery and buildings last week. / 上周拍了很多风景和建筑。/ Tuần trước, tôi đã chụp nhiều phong cảnh và công trình xây dựng.

➕ 記念撮影〈する〉(きねんさつえい) commemorative photos / 纪念照 / sự chụp ảnh kỷ niệm

905 □	レンズ	このレンズはカメラより高かった。
名	**lens / 镜头 / ống kính**	This lens was more expensive than the camera. / 这个镜头比照相机还要贵。/ Ống kính này đắt tiền hơn máy chụp.
906 □	宝くじ	毎週月曜日に宝くじを買う。
名	**lottery / 彩票 / vé số**	I buy the lottery every Monday. / 我每周一都买彩票。/ Thứ hai hàng tuần tôi mua vé số.
907 □	当たる	①宝くじで10万円当たった。②野球のボールが当たって、腕にけがをした。
動	**win/hit / 中(奖)/ 打到，撞到 / trúng, đụng**	① I won 100,000 yen in the lottery. ② The baseball hit me and injured my arm. / ①彩票中了10万日元。②被棒球打到，手臂受伤了。/ ① Tôi trúng vé số 100.000 yên. ② Tôi bị trúng banh bóng chày nên bị thương ở cánh tay.

⟷ 外れる

＋ (～を) 当てる win, hit / 撞，打，碰 / trúng (~)・当たり win / 打中，命中 / sự trúng

① happen as expected ② bump into something / ①如愿②撞到东西 / ① Đúng với mong đợi ② Đụng trúng vật

908 □	コツ	ギターがうまくなるコツを知りたい。
名	**tip / 诀窍 / bí quyết**	I want to know tips on improving my guitar performance. / 我想知道弹好吉他的诀窍。/ Tôi muốn biết bí quyết để trở nên giỏi guitar.
909 □	瞬間	決定的瞬間の動画をサイトにアップする。
名	**moment / 瞬间 / khoảnh khắc**	I uploaded a video of the decisive moment on the website. / 我把记录了决定性瞬间的视频传到网站上。/ Tải lên trang web hình ảnh động của khoảnh khắc mang tính quyết định.
910 □	組み合わせる	四角い箱を組み合わせて棚を作る。
動	**combine / 组合 / kết hợp, lắp ghép**	I made a shelf by combining square boxes. / 把方形的箱子组装起来，做一个架子。/ Tôi lắp ghép các hộp vuông để đóng kệ.

＋ 組み合わせ combination / 组合 / sự kết hợp, lắp ghép

911 □	身近〈な〉	好きな物は、いつも身近に置いておきたい。(名) 世間は身近な問題に興味を持つ。(ナ形)
名 ナ形	**close/familiar / 身边 / sự thân cận, gần gũi**	I want to keep my favorite things around me always.The world is interested in problems that are close to you. / 喜欢的东西总是想放在身边。/ Tôi luôn muốn đặt các đồ vật yêu thích gần mình.Con người quan tâm đến các vấn đề gần gũi với mình.

N2

Chapter 8

自然・レジャー

しぜん

Nature, Entertainment / 自然・休闲篇 / Thiên nhiên - Thư giãn

気候と天気(きこうとてんき)

Climate and Weather / 气候与天气 / Khí hậu và Thời tiết

912 □ 名 **気候**(きこう)

climate / 气候 / khí hậu, thời tiết

この辺(あた)りは一年中温暖(いちねんじゅうおんだん)な気候(きこう)だ。

The weather is temperate all year around here. / 这一带全年都气候温暖。/ Khu vực này khí hậu ấm áp quanh năm.

➕ 天候(てんこう) weather / 天气，气候 / thời tiết

913 □ 名 **シーズン**

season / 季节 / mùa

一番(いちばん)いいシーズンを選(えら)んで、旅行(りょこう)に行(い)く。

I chose the best season to go on a trip. / 选择最好的季节去旅游。/ Tôi chọn mùa tốt nhất để đi du lịch.

➕ シーズンオフ off season / 淡季 / hết mùa, qua mùa

914 □ 名 **四季**(しき)

four seasons / 四季 / bốn mùa

日本(にほん)には、春(はる)、夏(なつ)、秋(あき)、冬(ふゆ)の四季(しき)がある。

Japan has four seasons; spring, summer, autumn and winter / 日本有春、夏、秋、冬四个季节。/ Nhật Bản có 4 mùa, xuân, hạ, thu, đông.

➕ 春夏秋冬(しゅんかしゅうとう) spring, summer, autumn, winter / 春夏秋冬 / xuân hạ thu đông

915 □ 動 **ふくらむ**

budding/swell / 鼓起 / 膨胀 / nở phồng, to lớn

①桜(さくら)のつぼみがふくらみ始(はじ)めた。
②入学(にゅうがく)が決(き)まり、期待(きたい)に胸(むね)がふくらむ。

① The cherry blossoms are budding. ② I've been accepted by the school, and my chest swells in expectation. / ①樱花的花蕾开始鼓起来了。②学校确定后，满心期待。/ ① Nụ hoa sakura bắt đầu nở phồng lên. ② Được quyết định nhập học, kỳ vọng trong tôi trở nên to lớn.

➕ (～を) ふくらます swell, blow up / 扩张，扩展 / làm cho (~) phồng lên

👉 ① flower buds becoming plump ② becoming large, expanding / ①花朵鼓起来要开放②变大 / ① Nụ hoa căng nở. ② Trở nên to lớn

916 □ 名 **梅雨**(つゆ)

rainy season / 梅雨 / mùa mưa

春(はる)が終(お)わり、もうすぐ梅雨(つゆ)が始(はじ)まる。

Soon, spring will end, and the rainy season will begin. / 春天结束了，马上要梅雨季节了。/ Mùa xuân kết thúc, chuẩn bị vào mùa mưa.

➕ 梅雨入(つゆい)り entering the rainy season / 入梅 / sự vào mùa mưa・梅雨明(つゆあ)け end of rainy season / 出梅 / sự hết mùa mùa mưa・梅雨前線(ばいうぜんせん) seasonal rain front / 梅雨前线 / đường front (khoảng cách giữa 2 khối khí) mùa mưa

👉 梅雨前線 is read "baiu-zensen" / ＊"梅雨前線"读作"ばいうぜんせん" / "梅雨前線" đọc là "baiu zensen".

917 □ 名	初夏（しょか） early summer / 初夏 / đầu hè	真夏（まなつ）ではなく、初夏（しょか）が好（す）きだ。 I like early summer, not mid-summer. / 我喜欢初夏而不是盛夏。/ Tôi thích đầu hè, không phải giữa hè.
918 □ 名	温帯（おんたい） temperate zone / 温带 / vùng ôn đới	温帯（おんたい）では4つの季節（きせつ）がある。 The temperate zone has four seasons. / 温带有四个季节。/ Ở vùng ôn đới có 4 mùa.

➕ 熱帯（ねったい） tropical zone / 热带 / nhiệt đới・亜熱帯（あねったい） subtropical zone / 亚热带 / cận nhiệt đới

919 □ 動	属（ぞく）する belong to / 属于 / thuộc	日本（にほん）は温帯（おんたい）に属（ぞく）するが、亜熱帯化（あねったいか）してきた。 Japan belongs to the temperate zone, but it's turning subtropic. / 日本虽属于温带，但渐渐亚热带化了。/ Nhật Bản thuộc vùng ôn đới nhưng đã bị cận nhiệt đới hóa.
920 □ 名	確率（かくりつ） probability / 概率 / xác suất	明日（あした）の降水確率（こうすいかくりつ）は100パーセントだ。 Tomorrow's precipitation percentage is 100%. / 明天的降水概率是100%。/ Xác suất trời mưa ngày mai là 100%.
921 □ 名	夕立（ゆうだち） evening shower / 骤雨，（雷）阵雨 / mưa giông	夕立（ゆうだち）が降（ふ）る前（まえ）に家（いえ）に帰（かえ）ろう。 Let's go home before the evening shower comes. / 在下阵雨之前回家吧。/ Truước khi mưa giông ập xuống, hãy về nhà thôi.
922 □ ナ形	にわかな before we know it / 突然 / đột ngột	空（そら）がにわかに暗（くら）くなってきた。 The skies turned dark before we know it. / 天空突然暗了下来。/ Bầu trời đột ngột trở tối.

➕ にわか雨（あめ） rain shower / 阵雨 / mưa rào

923 □ 動	覆（おお）う cover / 覆盖，遮盖 / bao phủ	空（そら）が黒（くろ）い雲（くも）に覆（おお）われている。 Dark clouds are covering the skies. / 天空乌云密布。/ Bầu trời bị bao phủ với những đám mây đen.
924 □ ナ形	びしょびしょな soaked / 湿透 / ướt sũng, sũng nước	突然雨（とつぜんあめ）に降（ふ）られて、びしょびしょになった。 I was soaked by the sudden rain. / 突然下起了雨，我被淋得湿透了。/ Cơn mưa thình lình ào xuống, tôi bị ướt sũng.

➕ びしょぬれ soaked, sopping wet / 淋成落汤鸡 / ướt sũng

925 □ ナ形 副	あいにく〈な〉 I'm afraid, unfortunately / 不凑巧 / đáng tiếc, không may	今日（きょう）はあいにくなお天気（てんき）ですね。（ナ形） I'm afraid we have bad weather today. / 今天不凑巧天气不好。/ Hôm nay không may thời tiết xấu nhỉ.

926 □ 名	吹雪 ふぶき blizzard / 暴风雪 / bão tuyết	明日は吹雪になりそうだ。 (あした ふぶき) It seems there will be a blizzard tomorrow. / 明天好像有暴风雪。/ Ngày mai có lẽ có bão tuyết.
927 □ 動	凍える こご freeze / 冻僵 / đóng băng, đông cứng	北国の冬は凍えそうな寒さだ。 (きたぐに ふゆ こご さむ) Winters in the northern countries are freezing cold. / 北国的冬天冷得要把人冻僵了。/ Cái lạnh mùa đông vùng phía bắc như muốn đóng băng.
928 □ 動	冷え込む ひ こ get colder / 骤冷 / lạnh cóng	今朝は、とても冷え込んでいた。 (け さ ひ こ) This morning was very cold. / 今天早晨天气骤冷。/ Sáng nay trời lạnh cóng.

➕ 冷え込み (ひ こ) chill / 严寒 / sự lạnh

929 □ 名 ナ形	陽気〈な〉 ようき weather/cheerful / 天气好，阳光，活力 / tiết trời, vô tư, thoải mái	今日は陽気がいい。(名) (きょう ようき) 彼は本当に陽気な人だ。(ナ形) (かれ ほんとう ようき ひと) We have good weather today. He is truly a very happy person. / 今天阳光很好。/ Hôm nay tiết trời tốt. Anh ấy là người thoải mái.

👉 the noun refers to weather,while the na adjective refers to bright, active personality / 名词时指“气候、天气”，形容词时指“开朗、活泼的性格” / Danh từ chỉ “khí hậu, thời tiết”, tính từ loại Na chỉ “tính cách tươi vui, thoải mái”

930 □ 名	日和 ひより weather condition / 晴天，好天气 / tiết trời (thời tiết) đẹp, lý tưởng	今日は洗濯日和になりそうだ。 (きょう せんたく びより) Today is a good day to do laundry. / 今天应该会是洗衣服的好天气。/ Xem ra thời tiết hôm nay lý tưởng để giặt đồ.

➕ 散歩日和 (さんぽびより) good day to walk / 散步的好天气 / thời tiết lý tưởng để đi dạo・
行楽日和 (こうらくびより) good day to go play / 出游的好天气 / thời tiết lý tưởng để đi chơi, đi picnic

931 □ 名	日差し ひざ sunlight / 阳光 / ánh nắng	今日は日差しが強いので、傘をさして出かける。 (きょう ひざ つよ かさ で) The sunlight is strong today, so I use a parasol when I go out. / 今天太阳很大，所以要打伞出门。/ Hôm nay nắng gắt nên tôi che dù ra ngoài.
932 □ 副	いっそう yet / 更，越发 / hơn hẳn	雨はいっそう強くなった。 (あめ つよ) The rain is getting stronger. / 雨下得更大了。/ Mưa lớn hơn hẳn.

933 □ 副	一段と (いちだん) further / 越发 / hơn hẳn một bậc	暑(あつ)さが一段(いちだん)と厳(きび)しくなってきた。 The heat is getting worse. / 天气越发炎热起来了。/ Cái nóng trở nên khắc nghiệt hơn hẳn một bậc.
934 □ ナ形	急速な (きゅうそく) suddenly / 骤然 / nhanh chóng, cấp tốc	今日(きょう)は明(あ)け方(がた)、急速(きゅうそく)に冷(ひ)え込(こ)んだ。 It suddenly became chilly this morning. / 今天一早骤然降温。/ Sáng sớm hôm nay trời lạnh nhanh chóng.
935 □ 副	ぐんぐん［と］ steadily / 猛然地，稳步地 / dần dần (một cách vững vàng)	朝(あさ)からぐんぐん気温(きおん)が上(あ)がっている。 The temperature has been rising steadily since morning. / 早上开始气温不断升高。/ Từ sáng, nhiệt độ dần dần tăng.
936 □ 副	いくぶん somewhat / 稍微，几分 / hơi, một chút	雨(あめ)はいくぶん弱(よわ)くなった。 The rain is getting somewhat weaker. / 雨势小了一点。/ Mưa đã nhỏ hơn một chút.

＝ いくらか

937 □ 副	めっきり remarkably / 显著 / rõ ràng, trông thấy	年末(ねんまつ)が近(ちか)くなり、めっきり寒(さむ)くなった。 The year's end is approaching and it's turning remarkably cold. / 临近年末，天气明显变冷了。/ Gần cuối năm, trời lạnh trông thấy.
938 □ 副	あまりに［も］ too much, so much / 过于 / quá	今年(ことし)の夏(なつ)はあまりにも暑(あつ)い。 This year's summer is so hot. / 今年夏天太热了。/ Mùa hè năm nay thật là nóng quá.
939 □ 名	差 (さ) difference / 差，差别 / khoảng cách, sự khác biệt	今週(こんしゅう)は昼間(ひるま)と夜(よる)の気温(きおん)に差(さ)がある。 This week, there is not much difference in temperature between day and night. / 本周昼夜温差较大。/ Tuần này nhiệt độ ban ngày và ban đêm có sự khác biệt.
940 □ 名 副	本来 (ほんらい) in and of itself/originally / 本来，原来 / vốn dĩ, về cơ bản, từ trước đến nay	この地域(ちいき)は本来(ほんらい)、雪(ゆき)は降(ふ)らない。(副) It doesn't normally snow in this area. / 这个地区原来不下雪的。/ Vùng này từ trước đến nay không có tuyết rơi.

Section 2

台風・地震
たいふう　じしん

Typhoon, Earthquake / 台风・地震 / Bão - Động đất

941 □ 名	接近〈する〉 せっきん **approach / 接近，靠近 / sự tiếp cận, đến gần**	台風が日本に接近している。 たいふう　にほん　せっきん A typhoon is approaching Japan. / 台风正在接近日本。/ Bão đang đến gần Nhật Bản.
942 □ 動	備える そな **prepare / 防备 / chuẩn bị, phòng bị, đối phó với**	台風に備えて、社員は早めに退社した。 たいふう　そな　しゃいん　はや　たいしゃ The employees left work early in preparation for the typhoon. / 为防备台风，职员们都提前下班了。/ Để đối phó với cơn bão, nhân viên công ty đã về sớm.
943 □ 名	砂 すな **sand / 沙子 / cát**	砂を袋に詰めて、家の前に積む。 すな　ふくろ　つ　いえ　まえ　つ Stuff sand into bags and pile them in front of the house. / 把沙子装进袋子，堆在家门前。/ Nén cát vào bao và chất trước nhà.
944 □ 動	あふれる **overflow / 溢出，满溢 / tràn, ngập**	大雨で川の水があふれている。 おおあめ　かわ　みず The river is overflowing due to the heavy rain. / 因大雨河水泛滥。/ Nước sông tràn đầy vì cơn mưa lớn.

➕ 洪水（こうずい） flood / 洪水 / nước lụt, ngập lụt, lũ lụt

945 □ 名	降水量 こうすいりょう **rainfall / 降雨量 / lượng nước mưa**	今月、この地域では例年にない降水量を記録した。 こんげつ　ちいき　れいねん　こうすいりょう　きろく This area marked record-breaking rainfall this month. / 本月这个地区出现了史无前例的降雨量。/ Tháng này, khu vực này đã ghi kỷ lục về lượng nước mưa chưa từng có hàng năm.

➕ 雨量（うりょう） amount of rainfall / 雨量 / lượng mưa・降雪量（こうせつりょう） amount of snow / 降雪量 / lượng tuyết rơi

946 □ 名	観測〈する〉 かんそく **observe / 观测 / sự quan trắc, đo đạc**	最近、日本の各地で地震を観測している。 さいきん　にほん　かくち　じしん　かんそく Earthquakes are observed all over Japan recently. / 最近日本各地都在观测地震。/ Gần đây, người ta đo đạc động đất ở các địa phương trong Nhật Bản.
947 □ 名	大気 たいき **atmosphere / 大气 / không khí, khí trời**	今週は大気が不安定だ。 こんしゅう　たいき　ふあんてい This week, the atmosphere is unstable. / 本周气压不稳定。/ Tuần này không khí không ổn định.

➕ 気圧（きあつ） atmospheric pressure / 气压 / khí áp

948 荒れる
あ

動 **get rough/get rough / 乱 / 粗糙 / (biển) động, (da) khô, nứt nẻ**

①天気予報によると、明日は海が荒れるそうだ。
てんきよほう　あした　うみ　あ
②最近、肌が荒れて仕方ない。
さいきん　はだ　あ　しかた

① According to the weather forecast, the seas will be rough tomorrow. ② My skin is getting so rough these days. / ①据天气预报报道，明天海浪很大。②最近皮肤粗糙真没办法。/ ① Theo dự báo thời tiết, ngày mai biển động. ② Gần đây da tôi bị khô không chịu nổi.

① weather worsens ② skin loses its smoothness / ①天气情况糟糕②皮肤等不光滑 / ① Thời tiết trở nên khắc nghiệt. ② Da dẻ trở nên không còn mềm mại, trơn láng.

949 傾く
かたむ

動 **tilt/decline / 倾斜 / 衰落 / nghiêng, có chiều hướng đi xuống**

①台風で大きな木が傾いた。
たいふう　おお　き　かたむ
②不景気で会社が傾いている。
ふけいき　かいしゃ　かたむ

① The large tree tilted because of the typhoon. ② The company is going down because of bad business. / ①大树被台风吹歪了。②由于不景气，公司萎靡不正。/ ① Cái cây lớn đã bị nghiêng vì bão. ② Công ty trở nên sa sút vì tình hình kinh tế ảm đạm.

① something tilts ② losing force or energy / ①东西偏斜②形势不好 / ① Vật trở nên nghiêng ② Mất đi sức mạnh.

950 またぐ

動 **step over / 跨越 / băng qua, vượt qua**

倒れた木をまたいで、先に進む。
たお　き　さき　すす

Step over the fallen tree and continue to move forward. / 跨过倒下的树继续往前走。/ Tôi băng qua cái cây bị ngã để tiến về phía trước.

951 応答〈する〉
おうとう

名 **response / 回应 / tiếng đáp trả ,sự hồi âm**

家が崩れた現場で名前を呼んだが、応答がない。
いえ　くず　げんば　なまえ　よ　おうとう

I called his name at the site of the fallen house, but there was no answer. / 在房子坍塌的现场呼喊他的名字，却没有回应。/ Ở hiện trường nhà bị sụp đổ, tôi gọi tên mà không có tiếng đáp trả.

952 静まる
しず

動 **quiet down / 平息 / tĩnh lặng, lắng xuống, dịu đi**

夜になって、雨も風も静まった。
よる　あめ　かぜ　しず

The rain and wind calmed down by nighttime. / 入夜，风雨都平静了下来。/ Trời tối thì mưa, gió cũng dịu đi.

953 もたらす

動 **cause / 带来，招致 / gây nên, mang đến**

台風が、この地域に大きな被害をもたらした。
たいふう　ちいき　おお　ひがい

The typhoon caused great damage in this region. / 台风给这个地区造成了很大损失。/ Cơn bão đã gây nên thiệt hại lớn cho khu vực này.

954 及ぼす
およ

動 **impact, influence / 波及，影响到 / gây hại, gây ảnh hưởng**

台風が農業に大きな被害を及ぼした。
たいふう　のうぎょう　おお　ひがい　およ

The typhoon caused major damage to agriculture. / 台风给农业造成了巨大的损失。/ Cơn bão đã gây ảnh hưởng to lớn đến nông nghiệp.

955 □ 動	及ぶ（およ） extend to / 波及，达到 / đến mức, đạt mức	地震の被害は数十億円に及んだ。（じしん ひがい すうじゅうおくえん およ） The damage caused by the earthquake amounted to several billion yen. / 地震造成的损失达到数十亿日元。/ Thiệt hại do động đất đạt mức hàng tỉ yên.
956 □ 動	去る（さ） leave / 离开 / rời đi, bỏ đi	大型の台風が、ようやく去った。（おおがた たいふう さ） The large typhoon finally left. / 大型台风终于过去了。/ Cuối cùng, cơn bão lớn cũng rời đi.
957 □ 副	ひとまず for the time being / 暂且 / tạm thời, trước mắt	台風が去り、ひとまず安心だ。（たいふう さ あんしん） The typhoon is gone, so we can relax for the time being. / 台风已过，暂且可以放心了。/ Cơn bão đi rồi, tạm thời yên tâm.
958 □ 名	直後（ちょくご） immediately after / 紧跟着 / ngay sau khi	スマホが鳴った直後、地震が起きた。（な ちょくご じしん お） The earthquake occurred right after the smartphone's alarm went off. / 手机刚一响，紧接着就发生了地震。/ Ngay sau khi điện thoại thông minh reo thì động đất xảy ra.

↔ 直前（ちょくぜん）

959 □ 名	行動〈する〉（こうどう） action / 行动 / hành động, hoạt động	地震です。皆さん、落ち着いて行動してください。（じしん みな お つ こうどう） It's an earthquake. Everyone act calmly. / 地震了。请大家冷静地采取行动。/ Động đất! Mọi người hãy bình tĩnh hành động!

＋ 自由行動（じゆうこうどう） free activities / 自由行动 / sự tự do hoạt động・団体行動（だんたいこうどう） group activities / 团体行动 / hoạt động tập thể

960 □ 名 副	万一（まんいち） in case/in case / 万一，不测 / chẳng may	万一、大地震が起きたときに備えておく。（副）（まんいち おおじしん お そな） Be prepared in case of a major earthquake. / 为防备万一发生大地震的情况做好准备。/ Chuẩn bị sẵn để chẳng may, động đất xảy ra.

👉 used for negative things / 用于不好的情况 / Dùng vào việc không tốt.

961 □ 名	傾向（けいこう） tendency / 倾向 / khuynh hướng	台風などの天災が最近増える傾向にある。（たいふう てんさい さいきん ふ けいこう） The occurance of natural disasters like typhoons is on the rise. / 台风等天灾最近有增多的倾向。/ Gần đây, thiên tai như bão v.v. có khuynh hướng tăng lên.
962 □ 動	達する（たっ） reach / 达到 / đạt	台風の被害は5億円に達した。（たいふう ひがい おくえん たっ） The damage caused by the typhoon reached 500 million yen. / 台风造成的损失达到了 5 亿日元。/ Thiệt hại của cơn bão đến 500 triệu yên.

963 □ 名 災害(さいがい) disaster / 灾害 / tai họa

常に(つね)災害(さいがい)に備え(そな)ておくことが大切(たいせつ)だ。

It is important to always be ready for a disaster. / 防患于未然很重要。/ Luôn chuẩn bị sẵn phòng tai họa là việc quan trọng.

➕ 天災(てんさい) natural disaster / 天灾 / thiên tai・人災(じんさい) man-made disaster / 人祸 / tai họa do con người gây ra

これも覚え(おぼ)よう！ ㉑

➕ 接辞(せつじ)：印象(いんしょう)・感想等(かんそうなど)① Affix: Impression, Opinion, etc. / 词缀：印象・感想等 / Phụ tố: Ấn tượng - Cảm tưởng v.v.

• ～やすい

(簡単(かんたん)に～できる)

書き(き)やすい easy to write / 容易写 / Dễ viết

見(み)やすい easy to see / 容易看 / Dễ nhìn

話し(はな)やすい easy to speak / 容易说话 / Dễ nói chuyện

食べ(た)やすい easy to eat / 容易食用 / Dễ ăn

飲み(の)やすい easy to drink / 容易饮用 / Dễ uống

わかりやすい easy to understand / 簡单易懂 / Dễ hiểu

相談(そうだん)しやすい easy to consult / 容易沟通 / Dễ trao đổi, nói chuyện

(そうなる傾向(けいこう)が強(つよ)い)

汚れ(よご)やすい soiled easily / 容易脏 / Dễ vấy bẩn

切れ(き)やすい cut easily / 容易断 / Dễ đứt

変わり(か)やすい changes easily / 善变 / Dễ thay đổi

間違え(まちが)やすい easy to mistake / 容易搞错 / Dễ sai, dễ nhầm lẫn

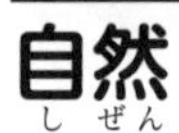

自然

しぜん

Nature / 自然 / Thiên nhiên

964 □ 名	大地 (だいち) land / 大地，土地 / trái đất, vùng đất	アフリカの大地(だいち)を、いつか訪(おとず)れたい。 I want to visit the land of Africa one day. / 我希望有一天能踏足非洲大陆。/ Tôi muốn tham quan vùng đất châu Phi một ngày nào đó.
965 □ ナ形	広大な (こうだい) vast / 广阔的 / bao la, rộng lớn	広大な(こうだい)森林(しんりん)には多(おお)くの動物(どうぶつ)がいる。 There are many animals in the vast forest. / 广阔的森林里住着很多动物。/ Khu rừng bao la có nhiều động vật.
966 □ 名	砂漠 (さばく) desert / 沙漠 / sa mạc	ここから先(さき)は、砂漠(さばく)がどこまでも続(つづ)いている。 From here, the desert stretches on forever. / 从这里再往前就是绵延不绝的沙漠了。/ Từ đây trở đi là sa mạc kéo dài đến vô tận.

➕ 砂丘(さきゅう) dune / 沙丘 / đồi cát

967 □ 名	谷 (たに) valley / 山谷 / thung lũng	谷(たに)の間(あいだ)を川(かわ)が流(なが)れている。 The river runs along the valley. / 山谷间流淌着一条河。/ Giữa thung lũng có dòng sông chảy.
968 □ 名	滝 (たき) waterfall / 瀑布 / thác nước	ナイアガラの滝(たき)はカナダとアメリカの境(さかい)にある。 Niagara Falls is located at the border of Canada and the United States. / 尼亚加拉瀑布位于加拿大和美国的边境处。/ Thác Niagara nằm ở ranh giới Canada và Mỹ.
969 □ 名	岸 (きし) shore / 岸 / bờ, ven	川(かわ)の向(む)こうの岸(きし)まで泳(およ)げるだろうか。 Will I be able to swim to the opposite shore? / 不知能否游到河对岸。/ Liệu có thể bơi đến bờ bên kia của dòng sông.
970 □ 名	海辺 (うみべ) seashore / 海边 / ven biển, bờ biển	海辺(うみべ)の町(まち)に住(す)むのが昔(むかし)からの夢(ゆめ)だ。 It was always my dream to live in a town by the sea. / 能住在海滨城市是我一直以来的梦想。/ Sống ở thành phố ven biển là ước mơ từ xưa của tôi.

➕ 浜辺(はまべ) beach / 海滨，湖滨 / bờ biển

971 □ ナ形	透明な (とうめい) transparent, clear / 透明的 / trong suốt	海(うみ)が透明で(とうめい)、魚(さかな)が泳(およ)いでいるのが見(み)える。 The sea is so clear I can see the fish swimming. / 海是透明的，我能看见鱼游来游去。/ Biển trong suốt, có thể thấy cá đang bơi lội.

972 **底** そこ
名 **bottom / 底 / đáy**

この海は透明で、底まで見えそうだ。(うみ とうめい そこ み)

The sea is so clear I think I can see all the way to the sea floor. / 这片海是透明的，清澈见底。/ Biển này trong suốt có thể nhìn thấy tận đáy biển.

➕ 海底(かいてい) sea floor / 海底 / đáy biển

973 **生き物** いきもの
名 **creature / 活物，生灵 / sinh vật, động vật**

生き物は大切に飼わなければならない。(い もの たいせつ か)

Animals should be kept with great care. / 生灵需要很用心地养育。/ Phải nuôi các con vật một cách cẩn thận.

974 **生物** せいぶつ
名 **organism, creature / 生物 / sinh vật**

研究者が森林で生物に関する調査を行う。(けんきゅうしゃ しんりん せいぶつ かん ちょうさ おこな)

The researcher conducts research of life forms in the forests. / 研究者在森林中进行关于生物的调查 / Nhà nghiên cứu tiến hành khảo sát liên quan đến sinh vật ở rừng rậm.

975 **植物** しょくぶつ
名 **plant / 植物 / thực vật**

庭で、いろいろな植物を育てている。(にわ しょくぶつ そだ)

I grow different plants in the garden. / 在院子里栽培着各种各样的植物。/ Trong vườn, tôi trồng nhiều loại thực vật.

976 **芽** め
名 **bud / 芽 / mầm**

春が訪れて、花の芽が出た。(はる おとず はな め で)

The flower buds are appearing with the approach of spring. / 春天到了，花儿冒出了嫩芽。/ Mùa xuân đến, mầm hoa xuất hiện.

977 **人間** にんげん
名 **human / 人，人类 / con người**

人間は自然とうまく付き合いながら生きてきた。(にんげん しぜん つ あ い)

Humans have lived in harmony with nature. / 人类是与自然和谐相处，生存至今的。/ Con người vừa sống vừa giao tiếp khéo léo với thiên nhiên.

➕ 人類(じんるい) humanity / 人类 / nhân loại

978 **天然** てんねん
名 **natural / 天然 / thiên nhiên**

天然の資源を大事に使う。(てんねん しげん だいじ つか)

Use natural resources carefully. / 珍惜使用自然资源。/ Sử dụng trân trọng nguồn tài nguyên thiên nhiên.

➕ 天然ガス(てんねん) natural gas / 天然气 / khí thiên nhiên・天然自然(てんねんしぜん) nature / 纯天然 / thiên nhiên tự nhiên

979 **日光** にっこう
名 **sunlight / 阳光 / ánh nắng mặt trời, nắng**

公園に行って、日光をたくさん浴びる。(こうえん い にっこう あ)

Go to the park and bathe in plenty of sunlight. / 去公园，尽情地沐浴阳光。/ Đi công viên và tắm thật nhiều ánh nắng mặt trời.

➕ 日光浴(にっこうよく)〈する〉 sun bathing / 日光浴 / sự tắm nắng

980 昇る（のぼる）
動 rise / 升起 / lên, (mặt trời) mọc

朝日が昇る光景は美しい。（あさひ のぼ こうけい うつく）
The scene where the sun is rising is beautiful. / 朝阳升起时的景色很美。/ Cảnh mặt trời lên thật đẹp.

⇔ 沈む（しず）

981 日陰（ひかげ）
名 shadow / 背阴处 / bóng râm

日陰と日なたでは気温が3度くらい違う。（ひかげ ひ きおん ど ちが）
There is about a three-degree difference between being in the sun and being in the shade. / 背阴处和向阳处的气温差有3度左右。/ Nhiệt độ bóng râm và ánh nắng khác nhau khoảng 3 độ.

⇔ 日なた（ひ）

982 夕焼け（ゆうや）
名 sunset / 晚霞 / hoàng hôn đỏ rực

夕焼けがきれいだ。明日は晴れるだろう。（ゆうや あした は）
The sunset is beautiful. Tomorrow will likely be sunny. / 晚霞如此之美，明日定是晴天。/ Hoàng hôn đỏ thật đẹp. Hẳn là ngày mai trời sẽ nắng ráo.

983 飛び回る（とびまわる）
動 fly around / 飞来飞去 / 跑来跑去，奔波 / bay quanh, bay khắp nơi

①この島では、いろいろな種類の鳥が飛び回っている。（しま しゅるい とり と まわ）
②彼は一年中、仕事で世界を飛び回っている。（かれ いちねんじゅう しごと せかい と まわ）
① Various birds are flying around this island. ② He is traveling around the world for business all year round. / ①这个岛上有各种各样的鸟飞来飞去。②他整年都为工作在全世界奔波。/ ① Hòn đảo này có nhiều loài chim bay lượn. ② Suốt năm, vì công việc anh ấy bay khắp thế giới.

☞ ① fly around in the sky ② run around busily / ①在空中到处飞②忙碌地到处走动 / ① Bay quanh trên không trung. ② Đi chỗ này chỗ kia một cách bận rộn

984 鳴く（なく）
動 cry / 叫，鸣 / (động vật) kêu, hót, hú, gáy

森の中で鳥が鳴いている。（もり なか とり な）
The bird is chirping in the woods. / 森林中鸟儿在鸣叫。/ Chim đang hót trong rừng.

985 し［い］んと〈する〉
副 quietly / 寂静 / im lặng, lặng phắc như tờ

森の中は何も聞こえず、しんとしている。（もり なか なに き）
Nothing can be heard in the woods; it's dead calm. / 森林里什么声音都听不到，一片寂静。/ Trong rừng, không nghe thấy gì cả, lặng phắc như tờ.

＋ ひっそり［と］〈する〉 in obscurity / 寂静，鸦雀无声 / yên tĩnh, tĩnh lặng

Section 4

休日（きゅうじつ）

Holiday / 休假 / Ngày nghỉ

986 □ 名	休息（きゅうそく）〈する〉 rest / 休息 / nghỉ giải lao, nghỉ ngơi	休（やす）みの日（ひ）は休息（きゅうそく）のために使（つか）う。 Use the day off to rest. / 休假日就休息。/ Ngày nghỉ, tôi dùng để nghỉ ngơi.
987 □ 副	ゆっくり〈する〉 slowly / 悠闲 / thong thả, chậm rãi	休日（きゅうじつ）は時間（じかん）を忘（わす）れて、ゆっくりする。 I relax and forget about time on my day off. / 休假日忘记时间悠闲地度过。/ Ngày nghỉ, tôi thong thả quên thời gian.
988 □ 副	ごろごろ〈する〉 idly / 闲着没事 / lăn qua lăn lại, nằm không, mô tả tiếng động ầm ầm	休（やす）みの日（ひ）は家（いえ）でごろごろするのが一番（いちばん）だ。 The best thing to do on a day off is to do nothing and relax at home. / 休息日在家里闲着什么都不做最舒服了。/ Ngày nghỉ, sướng nhất là nằm lăn ở nhà.
989 □ 副	だらだら［と］〈する〉 drag out / 散漫 / lê thê, uể oải, lừ đừ	だらだらと一日（いちにち）過（す）ごしてしまい、夜（よる）、後悔（こうかい）した。 I did nothing all day and regretted it at night. / 自由散漫地过了一天，到了晚上很后悔。/ Uể oải cả ngày, đến tối tôi lại hối hận.
990 □ 副	のびのび〈する〉 feel relaxed / 悠然自得 / thong dong, nhàn nhã	昨日（きのう）試験（しけん）が終（お）わった。久（ひさ）しぶりにのびのびできる。 The exams finished yesterday. I can relax once and for all. / 昨天考试结束了，难得可以悠闲一阵了。/ Hôm qua, kỳ thi đã kết thúc. Lâu lắm tôi mới được thong thả.
991 □ 動	くつろぐ relax / 放松，惬意 / nghỉ ngơi, thư giãn	家（いえ）でくつろぎながら、映画（えいが）を見（み）る。 I'm relaxing at home while watching movies. / 在家里放松地看电影。/ Tôi vừa thư giãn ở nhà vừa xem phim.
992 □ 動	こもる be confined in, filled with / 闭门不出 / 满是烟雾 / rúc, đọng	①休（やす）みの日（ひ）は、家（いえ）にこもってゲームをしている。 ②台所（だいどころ）に魚（さかな）を焼（や）いた臭（にお）いがこもっている。 ① I play games all day at home on my days off. ② The smell of burnt fish filled the kitchen. / ①休息日宅在家里打游戏。②厨房里满是烤焦鱼的烟味。/ ① Ngày nghỉ, tôi rúc ở nhà chơi game. ② Mùi cá nướng đọng trong bếp.

➕ ①引（ひ）きこもる shut oneself up in / 幽闭，闭门不处 / khép kín trong nhà, không giao tiếp

① staying inside and not leaving at all ② the smell remains inside and fills the space / ①在室内不出去②味道等没出去，占满了整个空间 / ① Vào trong và không ra ngoài. ② Mùi không thoát ra ngoài, đầy ở không gian đó.

912 ~ 1047

993 □	ぐうぐう	①疲れていたのか、ぐうぐう寝てしまった。 ②おなかがぐうぐう鳴っている。
副	**snoring (sound) / 呼呼大睡 / 咕咕叫 / (ngủ) khò, (bụng) sôi rột rột**	① I must have been tired, for I fell deeply asleep. ② My stomach is growling. / ①可能是太累了，呼呼大睡。②肚子咕咕叫。/ ① Không biết có phải vì mệt không mà tôi ngủ khò mất tiêu. ② Bụng sôi rột rột.

① sleeping soundly ② sound emitted when hungry / ①睡得很香的样子②肚子饿得直叫 / ① Tình trạng ngủ say ② Bụng đói nên kêu

994 □	どっと	①平日の疲れが週末にどっと出た。 ②映画を見て、観客がどっと笑った。
副	**rush out/suddenly / 突然出现 / 突然一齐 / thình lình ập đến, cùng ồ lên**	① The fatigue of the weekdays seemed to hit me suddenly over the weekend. ② The audience bursted out laughing while watching the movie. / ①工作日积累的疲劳，一到周末就爆发出来了。②看电影时观众们突然齐声笑了起来。/ ① Mệt mỏi của ngày thường ập đến vào cuối tuần. ② Xem phim, khán giả cùng cười ồ.

① a large amount comes out all at once ② many people speaking in a loud voice all at once / ①大量的东西一齐出现②很多人一起发出很大的声音 / ① Vật có nhiều xuất hiện cùng lúc ② Nhiều người cùng nhau phát ra tiếng lớn.

995 □	切り替える	日曜は気持ちをオフに切り替える。
動	**switch / 改换，切换 / chuyển đổi, thay đổi**	I switch to relax mode on Sundays. / 星期日把心情转换到放松模式。/ Chủ nhật chuyển tâm trạng sang trạng thái nghỉ ngơi.
996 □	あれこれ	休みの日も、あれこれやることが多い。(副)
名 副	**this and that/this and that / 这个那个 / việc này việc kia, cái này cái nọ**	There are many things to do during my days off from work, too. / 休息日也有这个那个很多要做的事情。/ Ngày nghỉ cũng có nhiều việc này việc kia phải làm.

＝ あれやこれや

997 □	芝生	公園で芝生の上に寝て、本を読む。
名	**lawn / 草地 / bãi cỏ**	I lay back on the lawn in the park to read a book. / 躺在公园的草地上看书。/ Tôi nằm trên bãi cỏ ở công viên đọc sách.
998 □	転がる	公園のベンチに座っていたら、ボールが転がってきた。
動	**roll / 滚转 / lăn**	The ball rolled toward me when I was sitting on a bench in the park. / 在公园的长椅上刚坐下，一个球滚了过来。/ Tôi đang ngồi trên băng ghế công viên thì quả bóng lăn đến.

＋ (～を) 転がす roll / 滚动 / lăn (~), làm cho (~) lăn, đổ

999 うなる

動 **growl/groan / 吼 / 发呜呜声 / gừ, kêu rên**

①散歩中の犬がこちらを見て、「ウーッ」とうなった。
②試験問題があまりに難しくて、思わずうなった。

① A dog on a walk saw me and growled at me. ② The test question was so difficult that I groaned. / ①一只正在散步的狗朝我这边看过来，发出了威胁的低吼声。②考试题目太难了，我不禁发出了无奈的声音。/ ① Chú chó đang đi dạo nhìn về phía tôi và "gầm gừ". ② Đề thi khó đến nỗi tôi bất giác kêu rên.

① an animal emitting a low voice to scare the opponent off ② emitting a low voice as if one is in pain and cannot speak / ①野兽发出的威胁的声音。②很痛苦却无法言说时发出的低声。/ ① Thú vật cảnh giác, kêu bằng giọng thấp ② Khổ sở đến nỗi kêu bằng giọng thấp mà không ra từ ngữ.

1000 ボート

名 **boat / 小船 / thuyền**

湖で彼女とボートに乗る。

I rode in a boat with her on the lake. / 我和她在湖上乘船。/ Tôi đi thuyền với bạn gái trên hồ.

1001 こぐ

動 **row / 划（船）/ chèo**

私はボートをこぐのが得意だ。

I am good at rowing a boat. / 我划船划得很好。/ Tôi giỏi chèo thuyền.

1002 展覧会

名 **exhibition / 展览会 / cuộc triển lãm**

散歩のついでに、展覧会を見に行った。

I went to see the exhibition while I was taking a walk. / 我出去散步，顺便去看了展览会。/ Tiện đường đi dạo, tôi đi xem triển lãm.

➕ 展示会 show / 展示会 / cuộc triển lãm, trưng bày

1003 ばったり

副 **run into/fall flat / 偶然 / 叭地一下 / tình cờ (chạm mặt), (ngã) sầm**

①美術館でばったり友達に会った。
②マラソンでゴールして、ばったり倒れた。

① I ran into a friend at the museum. ② He fell flat after he passed the finish line of the marathon. / ①我在美术馆偶然遇到了朋友。②马拉松冲刺后，叭地一下倒下了。/ ① Tôi tình cờ chạm mặt người bạn ở bảo tàng mỹ thuật. ② Chạy việt dã đến đích, tôi ngã sầm.

① by coincidence ② falling suddenly / ①意外相遇②突然掉下或倒下 / ① Tình cờ, ngẫu nhiên ② Thình lình ngã ra

1004 はらはら〈する〉

副 **nervously / 担心 / hồi hộp, phấn khích**

野球の試合ではらはらしながら、弟を応援した。

I nervously cheered for my little brother at the baseball game. / 观看棒球比赛时提着心为弟弟加油。/ Tôi phấn khích ủng hộ em trai trong trận đấu bóng chày.

➕ ひやひや〈する〉 uneasily / 提心吊胆 / hồi hộp, căng thẳng

1005 □	［お］墓(はか)	月(つき)に1回(かい)、我(わ)が家(や)のお墓(はか)に行(い)く。
名	**grave / 坟墓 / mộ**	I visit the family grave once a month. / 我一个月去扫一次墓。/ Mỗi tháng 1 lần, tôi đi thăm mộ gia đình.

➕ 墓地(ぼち) gravesite / 墓地 / nghĩa trang・［お］墓参(はかまい)り〈する〉 visiting the grave / 扫墓，上坟 / sự viếng mộ

1006 □	突(つ)っ込(こ)む	休日出勤(きゅうじつしゅっきん)で、鞄(かばん)に書類(しょるい)を突(つ)っ込(こ)んで出(で)かけた。
動	**stuff / 塞入 / xông vào, đâm vào, nhét vào**	I stuffed my documents in the bag and left for work on a holiday. / 休息日要上班，我把文件塞进包里就出门了。/ Do đi làm ngày nghỉ, tôi nhét hồ sơ vào cặp rồi đi
1007 □	見渡(みわた)す	山(やま)に登(のぼ)って、遠(とお)くを見渡(みわた)す。
動	**glance / 眺望，远望 / nhìn quanh, nhìn bao quát**	Climb the mountain and take in the distant view. / 爬上山眺望远处。/ Tôi leo lên núi và nhìn bao quát ra xa.
1008 □	眺(なが)める	①山(やま)を眺(なが)めると、リラックスできる。 ②毎晩(まいばん)寝(ね)る前(まえ)に家族(かぞく)の写真(しゃしん)を眺(なが)める。
動	**glance/gaze / 眺望 / 注视，凝望 / ngắm, nhìn**	① I can relax when I glance at the mountain. ② I gaze at the family photos before going to sleep every night. / ①眺望远山能感到放松②每天晚上睡前凝视家人的照片。/ ① Ngắm núi non thì có thể thư giãn. ② Mỗi tối, trước khi ngủ, tôi ngắm hình gia đình.

👉 ① looking at something in the distance carefully ② looking at something carefully / ①眺望远方②一动不动地注视 / ① Nhìn kỹ những vật ở xa. ② Nhìn chăm chăm cái gì đó

1009 □	眺(なが)め	ここからの眺(なが)めは最高(さいこう)だ。
名	**view / 风景 / tầm nhìn, tầm mắt**	The view from here is wonderful. / 从这里看过去的风景最棒。/ Tầm nhìn từ đây thật tuyệt vời.
1010 □	かすかな	天気(てんき)は悪(わる)いが、かすかに富士山(ふじさん)が見(み)える。
ナ形	**faint / 微弱，隐约 / thấp thoáng**	The weather is bad, but we can faintly see Mt. Fuji in the distance. / 虽然天气不好，但是隐约可以看见富士山。/ Thời tiết xấu nhưng vẫn có thể thấy núi Phú Sỹ thấp thoáng.
1011 □	おぶう	寝(ね)てしまった子(こ)どもをおぶって帰(かえ)った。
動	**carry on one's back / 背 / cõng, địu**	I carried home the sleeping child on my back. / 我背着熟睡的孩子回来了。/ Tôi cõng con đã ngủ ra về.

🟰 背負(せお)う ➕ おんぶ〈する〉 carrying on one's back / 背 / sự cõng, địu

1012	最適な（さいてき） ナ形 **best / 最适合 / thích hợp nhất**	日曜日は外出に最適な天気だった。（にちようび、がいしゅつ、さいてき、てんき） Sunday had the best weather for an outing. / 星期天的天气最适合外出了。/ Ngày chủ nhật thời tiết thích hợp nhất để đi ra ngoài.
1013	余裕（よゆう） 名 **room/capacity / 富余，余裕 / 从容 / thời gian rảnh, dư sức, phần dư, thong thả**	①今年は休む余裕はなさそうだ。（ことし、やす、よゆう） ②彼には余裕が見られる。成績はもっと伸びそうだ。（かれ、よゆう、み、せいせき、の） ① I don't think there is room for taking time off on the holidays this year. ② He seems to have more capacity. His grades will likely improve more. / ①今年好像没什么时间休息。②他很从容，成绩还有很大的提升空间。/ ① Năm nay xem ra không có thời gian rảnh nghỉ ngơi. ② Có thể thấy anh ấy dư sức. Xem ra thành tích còn có thể tăng hơn nữa.

① having room, space ② not having reached the limit yet, still having room for more / ①富余，有宽裕②态度从容，不慌不忙 / ① Có sự dư dả, thong dong ② Chưa đạt đến giới hạn, vẫn còn có sức dư.

これも覚えよう！㉒
（おぼ）

接辞：印象・感想等②（せつじ、いんしょう、かんそうなど） Affix: Impression, Opinion, etc. / 词缀：印象・感想等 / Phụ tố: Ấn tượng - Cảm tưởng v.v.

- **～づらい（それをするのが難しい）**（むずか）

聞きづらい（き）	hard to hear / 听不清 / Khó nghe, khó hỏi
見づらい（み）	hard to see / 看不清 / Khó nhìn, khó thấy
歩きづらい（ある）	hard to walk / 不好走 / Khó đi bộ
使いづらい（つか）	hard to use / 不好用 / Khó sử dụng
入りづらい（はい）	hard to enter / 不好进 / Khó vào

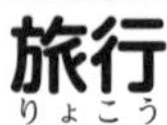

旅行
りょこう

Travel / 旅行 / Du lịch

1014 □	旅 たび	初めて一人で旅をした。
名	travel / 旅行 / chuyến đi, hành trình	I traveled alone for the first time. / 第一次一个人去旅行了。/ Lần đầu tiên tôi thực hiện chuyến đi một mình.

➕ 一人旅 traveling alone / 一个人的旅行 / du lịch một mình・個人旅行 private travel / 自由行 / du lịch cá nhân

1015 □	レジャー	今年は夏のレジャーを楽しむ予定だ。
名	leisure activities / 闲暇 / sự thư giãn, trò giải trí	I plan to enjoy summer activities this year. / 我打算好好享受夏天的闲暇时光。/ Năm nay tôi dự định vui thú thư giãn mùa hè.

➕ 娯楽 fun activity / 娱乐 / trò giải trí, tiêu khiển

1016 □	訪れる おとずれる	①ここは週末になると、多くの観光客が訪れる。②もうすぐ桜の季節が訪れる。
動	visit/arrive / 拜访 / 来临 / thăm viếng, đến thăm	① A lot of tourists visit here on the weekends. ② The cherry blossom season will arrive soon. / ①这里一到周末，就会有很多游客到访。②樱花的季节很快就要来了。/ ① Nơi đây vào cuối tuần có nhiều du khách đến thăm. ② Mùa hoa anh đào sắp đến.

👉 ① going somewhere for a purpose ② a condition or time period arrives / ①为了某种目的去某处②某种状态或时期到来 / ① Đi đến nơi nào đó với mục đích. ② Tình trạng, thời kỳ nào đó đến

1017 □	体験〈する〉 たいけん	異文化に接する体験は、きっと将来の役に立つ。
名	experience / 体验 / sự trải nghiệm	Experience with different cultures will definitely be useful in the future. / 接触体验不同的文化以后肯定会有用的。/ Trải nghiệm tiếp xúc với văn hóa khác biệt chắc chắn có ích cho tương lai.
1018 □	冒険〈する〉 ぼうけん	たまには少し冒険してみたい。
名	adventure / 冒险 / sự phiêu lưu, mạo hiểm	Sometimes I want to go on a little adventure. / 偶尔想稍微冒险一下。/ Thỉnh thoảng tôi muốn phiêu lưu một chút.
1019 □	見聞き〈する〉 みきき	旅行で知らないことを見聞きしたい。
名	see and hear / 见闻 / nghe nhìn, học hỏi	I want to go on a trip to see and hear things I've never seen or heard before. / 我想在旅行中看到、听到一些不知道的事情。/ Tôi muốn nghe nhìn những gì chưa biết bằng du lịch.

1020 □ **巡る**（めぐ）

動 **go around/surrounding / 巡游 / 围绕 / dạo quanh, đi quanh, xoay quanh**

①世界遺産を巡るのが夢だった。（せかいいさん・めぐ・ゆめ）
②税金を巡る問題が起きている。（ぜいきん・めぐ・もんだい・お）

① My dream was to travel to different world heritage sites. ② There is a problem involving taxes. / ①巡访世界遗产曾是我的梦想。②围绕税款发生了问题。/ ① Vòng quanh các di sản thế giới là ước mơ của tôi. ② Nổ ra vấn đề xoay quanh tiền thuế.

➕ ①名所巡り（めいしょめぐ） visiting famous sites / 周游名胜 / dạo quanh thắng cảnh

☞ ① move around here and there ② related to something / ①到处巡访②与某事相关 / ① Đi quanh nơi này nơi kia. ② Liên quan đến việc đó.

1021 □ **プラン**

名 **plan / 计划，方案 / kế hoạch**

夏休みのプランを立てる。（なつやす・た）

I made plans for the summer vacation. / 制定暑假的计划。/ Tôi lên kế hoạch cho kỳ nghỉ hè.

➕ 計画（けいかく） plan / 计划 / kế hoạch

1022 □ **思い立つ**（おもいたつ）

動 **come up with / 决心做 / nghĩ đến, nảy ra**

連休中、急に旅行を思い立った。（れんきゅうちゅう・きゅう・りょこう・おもいた）

I suddenly came up with the idea to go on a trip during the long holiday. / 连休中突然决定去旅游。/ Trong kỳ nghỉ dài ngày, thình lình tôi nảy ra ý đi du lịch.

1023 □ **豪華な**（ごうか）

ナ形 **luxurious / 豪华 / lộng lẫy, hào nhoáng**

世界を巡る豪華な船旅をしてみたい。（せかい・めぐ・ごうか・ふなたび）

I want to go on a luxurious trip around the world by ship. / 我想体验环游世界的豪华邮轮之旅。/ Tôi muốn thử đi du lịch bằng tàu thuyền lộng lẫy vòng quanh thế giới.

1024 □ **手配〈する〉**（てはい）

名 **arrangement/search / 安排 / 通缉 / chuẩn bị, sắp xếp, truy lùng**

①旅行会社でホテルと飛行機を手配した。（りょこうがいしゃ・ひこうき・てはい）
②手配されていた犯人が、やっと捕まった。（てはい・はんにん・つか）

① The travel agency arranged the hotel and flight. ② The fugitive was finally arrested. / ①旅行社安排了酒店和航班。②终于抓到了通缉犯。/ ① Tôi đã chuẩn bị khách sạn và máy bay ở công ty du lịch. ② Cuối cùng, thủ phạm bị truy lùng cũng đã bị bắt.

➕ ②指名手配〈する〉（しめいてはい） searching for suspect / 通缉令 / truy lùng tội phạm

☞ ① preparing for work or travel ② identifying a criminal for arrest / ①为工作或旅行等做准备②为了逮捕犯人做的指令 / ① Chuẩn bị cho công việc hay du lịch v.v. ② Chỉ đích danh để bắt được thủ phạm

1025 □ **前もって**（まえ）

副 **beforehand / 提前 / trước**

現地の友達に前もって連絡しておこう。（げんち・ともだち・まえ・れんらく）

I will contact my friend at the site in advance. / 提前联系好当地的朋友吧。/ Liên lạc sẵn trước với bạn bè ở nơi đến.

1026 便（びん）
名 flight / 航班 / chuyến

出発（しゅっぱつ）は午後（ごご）の便（びん）になった。
I will depart on an afternoon flight. / 去程航班变成了下午的航班。/ Xuất phát chuyến buổi chiều.

＋ フライト flight / 飞行，航班 / chuyến bay

1027 空席（くうせき）
名 vacancy / 空座位 / ghế trống

飛行機（ひこうき）に空席（くうせき）があって、よかった。
I'm glad there was a vacancy on the airplane. / 飞机还有空位，太好了。/ Máy bay có ghế trống, thật may.

1028 超過（ちょうか）〈する〉
名 excess / 超重 / vượt quá

荷物（にもつ）が多（おお）すぎて、空港（くうこう）で超過料金（ちょうかりょうきん）を払（はら）った。
I had too much luggage and had to pay an excess luggage fee at the airport. / 行李太多，我在机场支付了超重的费用。/ Hành lý quá nhiều nên tôi đã trả tiền quá ký ở sân bay.

＋ オーバー〈する〉 over / 超过 / vượt quá

1029 飛（と）ぶ
動 fly / 飞 / bay

飛行機（ひこうき）は時間通（じかんどお）りに飛（と）んだ。
The airplane took off on time. / 飞机按时起飞了。/ Máy bay đã bay đúng giờ.

＋ 離陸（りりく）〈する〉 take off / 起飞 / cất cánh・着陸（ちゃくりく）〈する〉 landing / 着陆 / hạ cánh

1030 思（おも）いがけず
副 unexpectedly / 意想不到 / tình cờ, không ngờ

思（おも）いがけず、知（し）り合（あ）いと同（おな）じ便（びん）だった。
I unexpectedly found myself on the same flight as an old aquaintence. / 没想到和熟人坐的是同一个航班。/ Không ngờ cùng chuyến bay với người quen.

＋ 思（おも）いがけない unexpected / 没料想到 / không ngờ

1031 引（ひ）き返（かえ）す
動 return / 返回，折回 / quay lại, quay ngược lại

行（い/ゆ）きの便（びん）はエンジントラブルで、空港（くうこう）に引（ひ）き返（かえ）した。
The outbound flight returned to the airport due to engine trouble. / 去程的飞机由于引擎故障，折返机场了。/ Chuyến bay vòng đi đã quay lại sân bay do trục trặc động cơ

1032 間（ま）もなく
副 soon / 不久，即将 / chốc lát, sắp sửa, chẳng bao lâu

バスは間（ま）もなく目的地（もくてきち）に着（つ）く。
The bus will soon reach its destination. / 巴士即将到达目的地。/ Xe buýt sắp đến nơi.

1033 宿泊（しゅくはく）〈する〉
名 stay / 住宿 / sự lưu trú, ngủ trọ

町（まち）の中心（ちゅうしん）にあるホテルに宿泊（しゅくはく）した。
I stayed at a hotel in the middle of the city. / 我住了市中心的酒店。/ Tôi đã lưu trú ở khách sạn nằm ở trung tâm thành phố.

1034 大幅な（おおはば）
ナ形 **major / 大幅度 / lớn, rộng, nhiều**

連休中は旅行代が大幅に上がる。（れんきゅうちゅう りょこうだい おおはば あ）
Travel expenses rise drastically during long holidays. / 连休期间旅行费用大幅上涨。/ Trong kỳ nghỉ dài ngày, tiền du lịch tăng lên nhiều.

1035 旅先（たびさき）
名 **travel destination / 旅行目的地 / nơi đi du lịch, điểm đến**

旅先から友達に、はがきを送った。（たびさき ともだち おく）
I sent a card to my friend from where I was visiting. / 旅途中给朋友寄了明信片。/ Từ nơi đi du lịch, tôi đã gửi bưu thiếp cho bạn.

1036 各地（かくち）
名 **each place / 各地 / các nơi, các địa phương**

連休に友達と日本の各地を回るつもりだ。（れんきゅう ともだち にほん かくち まわ）
I plan to travel around Japan during the long holiday with my friend. / 我打算连休时和朋友到日本各地旅游。/ Tôi định đi vòng quanh các nơi ở Nhật với bạn trong kỳ nghỉ dài ngày.

1037 名所（めいしょ）
名 **sites / 名胜，景点 / danh lam thắng cảnh**

観光の名所をガイドブックで調べる。（かんこう めいしょ しら）
I researched popular tourist spots using a guidebook. / 我在旅游指南上查找观光名胜。/ Tôi tìm hiểu các danh lam thắng cảnh du lịch bằng sách hướng dẫn du lịch.

➕ 観光名所（かんこうめいしょ） tourist sites / 观光名胜 / thắng cảnh du lịch, điểm tham quan nổi tiếng

1038 市場（いちば）
名 **market / 市场 / thị trường, chợ**

外国の市場には見たこともない野菜がある。（がいこく いちば み やさい）
Vegetables I have never seen before are sold at markets in foreign countries. / 国外的（菜）市场里有我没见过的蔬菜。/ Ở chợ nước ngoài, có loại rau tôi chưa từng thấy bao giờ.

1039 免税店（めんぜいてん）
名 **duty free shop / 免税店 / cửa hàng miễn thuế**

空港の免税店で化粧品を買った。（くうこう めんぜいてん けしょうひん か）
I bought cosmetics at the airport duty free shop. / 我在机场的免税店买了化妆品。/ Tôi đã mua mỹ phẩm ở cửa hàng miễn thuế trong sân bay.

➕ 免税品（めんぜいひん） duty free items / 免税商品 / hàng miễn thuế

1040 風景（ふうけい）
名 **scenery / 风景 / phong cảnh**

目の前の風景を、しっかりと記憶しておこう。（め まえ ふうけい きおく）
I will firmly commit to memory the scenery in front of me. / 好好记住眼前的风景吧。/ Hãy ghi phong cảnh trước mắt vào ký ức thật kỹ.

➕ 夜景（やけい） night scenery / 夜景 / cảnh đêm

1041 海水浴（かいすいよく）
名 **sea swimming / 海水浴 / sự tắm biển**

ホテルの近くに海があるので、海水浴もできる。（ちか うみ かいすいよく）
The beach is near the hotel, so I can go swimming. / 酒店附近就有海，所以可以去海边玩水。/ Vì gần khách sạn có biển nên có thể tắm biển.

1042 □ 動	もぐる **dive / 潜水，潜入 / lặn**	こんな美(うつく)しい海(うみ)にもぐれるなんて、感動(かんどう)する。 It is amazing to be able to dive in such a beautiful ocean. / 能够潜到这么美的海里，我很感动。/ Có thể lặn dưới biển đẹp thế này thật là cảm động.

➕ ダイビング diving / 潜水 / sự lặn

1043 □ 名	跡(あと) **track, trace / 痕迹 / dấu vết**	砂(すな)の上(うえ)に、足(あし)の跡(あと)がはっきり残(のこ)った。 Footprints were left clearly on the sand. / 沙子上留下了清晰的脚印。/ Trên cát còn rõ dấu chân.

➕ 足跡(あしあと) footprint / 脚印 / dấu chân・城跡(しろあと) castle ruin / 城址 / di tích thành cổ

1044 □ 名	位置(いち) **location, position / 位置 / vị trí, địa điểm**	スマホで現在(げんざい)の位置(いち)を調(しら)べる。 I can check my current location using the smartphone. / 我用智能手机查我现在所在的位置。/ Tìm hiểu vị trí hiện tại bằng điện thoại thông minh.
1045 □ 名	めいめい **each individual / 各个，分别 / từng người, mỗi người**	朝(あさ)はめいめい好(す)きなものを皿(さら)にとって食(た)べる。 Everyone will individually put what they want to eat on their plates for breakfast. / 早上把喜欢的东西分别盛到盘子吃。/ Buổi sáng từng người lấy món ưa thích vào dĩa và ăn.
1046 □ 副	しばしば **often / 经常，屡次 / thường, nhiều lần**	ハワイの観光地(かんこうち)で、しばしば日本人(にほんじん)を見(み)かけた。 I often see Japanese at tourist attractions in Hawaii. / 在夏威夷的景点，常常能看到日本人。/ Tôi nhiều lần nhìn thấy người Nhật ở các thắng cảnh ở Hawaii.
1047 □ 名	出来事(できごと) **occurence / 发生的事，变故 / sự kiện**	旅行(りょこう)での出来事(できごと)は、全部(ぜんぶ)いい思(おも)い出(で)だ。 Everything that occurred during the trip became fun memories. / 旅途中发生的事都是美好的回忆。/ Những sự kiện trong chuyến đi du lịch tất cả đều là kỷ niệm đẹp.

これも覚(おぼ)えよう！㉓

接辞(せつじ)：印象(いんしょう)・感想等(かんそうなど)③ Affix: Impression, Opinion, etc. / 词缀：印象・感想等 / Phụ tố: Ấn tượng - Cảm tưởng v.v.

• **～にくい**

(簡単(かんたん)に～できない)

読(よ)みにくい	hard to read / 难读 / Khó đọc
使(つか)いにくい	hard to use / 难用 / Khó sử dụng
扱(あつか)いにくい	hard to handle / 难处理 / Khó xử lý
言(い)いにくい	hard to say / 难说 / Khó nói
わかりにくい	hard to understand / 难懂 / Khó hiểu
はきにくい	hard to sweep / 难穿 / Khó mang (giày, dép)
付(つ)き合(あ)いにくい	hard to get on with / 难打交道 / Khó giao tiếp

(なかなかそうならない)

壊(こわ)れにくい	hard to break / 难坏 / Khó hư
破(やぶ)れにくい	hard to tear / 难破 / Khó rách
割(わ)れにくい	hard to crack / 难碎 / Khó bể
焦(こ)げにくい	hard to burn / 难焦掉 / Khó bị cháy

N2

Chapter 9

健康のために

けんこう

For Your Health / 健康篇 / Vì sức khỏe

Section 1

体と健康（からだ　けんこう）

Body and Health / 身体与健康 / Cơ thể và sức khỏe

1048 □ 名	測定〈する〉(そくてい) **measurement / 测定，测量 / sự đo lường, đo đạc**	学校で身長と体重を測定した。(がっこう しんちょう たいじゅう そくてい) I measured my height and weight at school. / 在学校测量了身高和体重。/ Tôi đã đo cân nặng và chiều cao ở trường.

➕ 身体測定(しんたいそくてい) body measurement / 体检 / sự đo chiều cao cân nặng

1049 □ ナ形	定期的な(ていきてき) **periodic / 定期的 / một cách định kỳ**	定期的に健康診断を受けている。(ていきてき けんこうしんだん う) I get regular health check-ups. / 我定期接受健康检查。/ Khám sức khỏe theo định kỳ.
1050 □ 名	血圧(けつあつ) **blood pressure / 血压 / huyết áp**	最近、血圧が高い。(さいきん けつあつ たか) My blood pressure is high these days. / 最近血压很高。/ Gần đây, huyết áp cao.

➕ 高血圧(こうけつあつ) high blood pressure / 高血压 / cao huyết áp・
低血圧(ていけつあつ) low blood pressure / 低血压 / huyết áp thấp

1051 □ 名	体力(たいりょく) **physical strength / 体力 / thể lực**	体力も気力も問題ない。(たいりょく きりょく もんだい) There is nothing wrong with my stamina or mental toughness. / 体力和精力都没问题。/ Cả thể lực lẫn khí lực đều không có vấn đề.

➕ 気力(きりょく) mental strength / 精力 / sinh lực

1052 □ 名	心身(しんしん) **body and soul / 身心 / tinh thần và thể chất**	健康のためには心身のバランスが大切だ。(けんこう しんしん たいせつ) The balance between the body and soul is important for your health. / 为了健康，保持身心平衡很重要。/ Để có sức khỏe tốt, sự cân bằng tinh thần và thể chất là quan trọng.
1053 □ ナ形	健やかな(すこ) **healthy / 健康的 / mạnh khỏe**	子ども達はみんな、健やかに成長した。(こ たち すこ せいちょう) The children all grew up healthy. / 孩子们都健康地长大了。/ Con cái tất cả đều trưởng thành mạnh khỏe.
1054 □ 動	かたよる **unbalanced / 不均衡，失衡 / chênh lệch, mất cân bằng**	最近、栄養がかたよっている。(さいきん えいよう) My diet has not been well-balanced recently. / 最近营养不均衡。/ Gần đây, tôi bị mất cân bằng dinh dưỡng.

1055 小柄な（こがら）
ナ形 small built / 小个，身材矮小 / nhỏ con, nhỏ người

彼女は、どちらかと言うと小柄な方だ。
If anything, her built is on the small side. / 她算是块头小的。 / Cô ấy nếu mà nói thì thuộc dạng nhỏ con.

↔ 大柄な（おおがら）

1056 寿命（じゅみょう）
名 duration of life / 寿命 / tuổi thọ

日本人女性は世界一寿命が長い。
Japanese women have the longest life expectancy in the world. / 日本女性的寿命是世界上最长的。 / Phụ nữ Nhật có tuổi thọ cao nhất thế giới.

＋ 平均寿命（へいきんじゅみょう） average life expectancy / 平均寿命 / tuổi thọ trung bình・死亡（しぼう）〈する〉 death / 死亡 / tử vong

1057 一般に（いっぱん）
副 generally / 一般，通常 / thông thường

一般に、男性より女性の方が寿命が長い。
Generally, women have a longer life-span than men. / 一般来说相比男性，女性的寿命更长。 / Thông thường nữ giới có tuổi thọ cao hơn nam giới.

1058 手首（てくび）
名 wrist / 手腕 / cổ tay

毎日、手首で血圧を測っている。
I measure my blood pressure using my wrist every day. / 我每天通过手腕测量血压。 / Hàng ngày tôi đo huyết áp ở cổ tay.

＋ 足首（あしくび） ankle / 脚腕 / cổ chân

1059 かかと
名 heel / 脚后跟 / gót chân

歩きすぎて、かかとが痛む。
My ankle hurts from walking too much. / 走太多路了，脚后跟很疼。 / Tôi đi bộ nhiều quá nên gót chân bị đau.

1060 つま先（さき）
名 toe / 脚尖，指尖 / đầu ngón chân

靴を脱いで、つま先を伸ばす。
Take off your shoes and stretch your toes. / 脱下鞋子，伸伸脚趾头。 / Tháo giày và duỗi đầu ngón chân.

1061 血管（けっかん）
名 blood vessel / 血管 / huyết quản

年とともに血管が弱くなる。
My blood vessels get weaker as I grow older. / 随着年龄的增长，血管功能会变弱。 / Cùng với thời gian (tuổi tác), huyết quản trở nên yếu đi.

1062 さらさら〈な / する〉
ナ形 副 smooth/smoothly / 干燥清爽感 / mềm mại, trơn tru, thông suốt

たまねぎを食べると、血液がさらさらになるらしい。（ナ形）
Blood flows more smoothly when you eat onions. / 听说吃洋葱的话，能使血液循环变得通畅。 / Nghe nói ăn hành tây thì máu lưu thông tốt.

1048 ~ 1161

1063	筋肉 きんにく 名 **muscle / 肌肉 / cơ bắp**	毎日、筋肉をトレーニングしている。 I train my muscles every day. / 我每天都练肌肉。/ Hàng ngày, tôi rèn luyện cơ bắp.

➕ 筋肉痛 (きんにくつう) muscle pain / 肌肉酸痛 / đau cơ

1064	障がい しょう 名 **disability / 毛病，障碍 / khuyết tật**	耳に軽い障がいを持っている。 I have a slight hearing disability. / 我有一点轻微的听力障碍。/ Tôi có khuyết tật nhẹ ở tai.

➕ 障がい者 (しょうがいしゃ) physically challenged / 残疾人 / người khuyết tật

1065	乗り越える の　こ 動 **overcome / 克服，战胜 / vượt qua**	人より努力して、障がいを乗り越えた。 I overcame my disability by working harder than other people. / 比别人更加努力，从而克服了障碍。/ Tôi đã nỗ lực hơn người để vượt qua khuyết tật.
1066	傷跡 きずあと 名 **scar / 伤疤 / vết thẹo**	かいたところに傷跡が残った。 A scar was left behind where I scratched. / 挠过的地方留下了疤。/ Ở chỗ gãi còn lại vết thẹo.

➕ 傷口 (きずぐち) wound / 伤口 / miệng vết thương

1067	いびき 名 **snoring / 鼾声 / tiếng ngáy**	自分のいびきの音で目が覚めた。 I woke up to the sound of my own snoring. / 我被自己的鼾声吵醒了。/ Tôi choàng tỉnh vì tiếng ngáy của mình.

➕ 寝言 (ねごと) sleep talking / 梦话，胡话 / nói mớ

1068	体が持つ からだ　も 慣 **one's body will last / 身体承受得了 / đủ sức**	この忙しさでは体が持たない。 I'm so busy that I am ruining my health. / 忙成这样，身体会受不了的。/ Bận rộn như vầy thì không đủ sức chịu đựng.

Section 2

病気になる前に

びょうき まえ

Before Getting Sick / 生病前 / Trước khi đổ bệnh

1069 □ 名	休養〈する〉(きゅうよう) **rest / 休养 / sự nghỉ dưỡng, nghỉ ngơi**	医者(いしゃ)に、少(すこ)し休養(きゅうよう)をとった方(ほう)がいいと言(い)われた。 The doctor told me I need to rest a little. / 医生跟我说休养一段时间比较好。/ Tôi được bác sỹ nói nên nghỉ ngơi một chút.
1070 □ 名	疲労〈する〉(ひろう) **fatigue / 疲劳 / sự mệt mỏi, lao lực**	疲労(ひろう)がたまる前(まえ)に休(やす)むようにしている。 I try to rest before I get too tired. / 我尽量在疲劳累积起来前休息。/ Trước khi mệt mỏi dồn lại, tôi cố gắng nghỉ ngơi.
1071 □ 名 ナ形	不調〈な〉(ふちょう) **fail/failing / 不舒服 / (tình trạng) không khỏe**	体(からだ)の不調(ふちょう)を感(かん)じたら、すぐに病院(びょういん)に行(い)く。(名) I go to the hospital immediately if I feel something is wrong with my body. / 我感到身体不舒服的话，马上就去医院。/ Nếu cảm thấy cơ thể không khỏe thì đi bệnh viện ngay.

⟷ 好調〈な〉(こうちょう)

1072 □ 名	体調(たいちょう) **body condition / 身体状况 / tình trạng cơ thể, sức khỏe**	体調(たいちょう)を崩(くず)したので、会社(かいしゃ)を休(やす)んだ。 I took a day off work because I felt ill. / 我身体不舒服，所以向公司请假了。/ Vì cơ thể không khỏe nên tôi đã nghỉ làm.

＋ 体(からだ)を壊(こわ)す become ill / 弄坏身体 / gây hại cho sức khỏe, bị bệnh

1073 □ 副	やや **a little / 稍微，有点儿 / hơi, chút chút**	少(すこ)し寝(ね)たら、体(からだ)がやや楽(らく)になった。 I felt a little better after I slept a little. / 睡了一会，身体舒服一点了。/ Ngủ một chút thì tôi thấy cơ thể hơi khỏe hơn.
1074 □ 名	寝心地(ねごこち) **the feeling in bed / 睡时的感觉 / nằm thoải mái, dễ chịu**	寝心地(ねごこち)のいい枕(まくら)を買(か)ったら、よく寝(ね)られるようになった。 I was able to sleep better after I bought a comfortable pillow. / 自从买了舒适的枕头以后，睡得好了。/ Mua được cái gối nằm thoải mái, tôi đã có thể ngủ ngon.
1075 □ 連体	大(たい)した **quite / 了不得的 / 了不起，惊人的 / to tát, trọng đại, đáng kể**	①大(たい)したことはないと思(おも)っても、病院(びょういん)に行(い)く。 ②中学生(ちゅうがくせい)でオリンピック選手(せんしゅ)とは、大(たい)したものだ。 ① I go to the hospital even if I don't think it's quite that serious. ② Being an Olympian at junior high school is quite a feat. / ①虽然我觉得没什么大事，还是去医院。②才中学生就是奥运选手，太了不起了。/ ① Dù cho là không đáng gì nhưng vẫn đi bệnh viện. ② Học sinh cấp II mà là vận động viên Olympic thì thật đáng kể.

👉 ①used in negative form to mean "not so much" ②be amazed by the degree of excellence / ①不值一提(后接否定) ②程度很惊人 / ① Thể phủ định, không đến mức đó. ② Thán phục vì mức độ tuyệt vời.

1076 念のため（ねん）
慣
just in case / 以防万一 / để bảo đảm, để chắc chắn

症状は軽いが、念のため病院で診てもらう。
The symptoms are light, but I will go to the hospital just in case. / 症状很轻，但以防万一还是去医院看看。/ Triệu chứng bệnh tuy nhẹ nhưng để chắc chắn tôi khám ở bệnh viện.

1077 通院〈する〉（つういん）
名
visiting the hospital / 跑医院 / đi bệnh viện

月に1回、検査のために通院している。
I go to the hospital once a month for an examination. / 每个月去医院检查一次。/ Mỗi tháng 1 lần, tôi đi bệnh viện để xét nghiệm.

1078 レントゲン
名
X-ray / X 光 / X-quang

念のため、レントゲンを撮ってもらった。
I had an X-ray taken just in case. / 以防万一，去照了 X 光。/ Để cho chắc, tôi đã chụp X-quang.

1079 さらに
副
further/more / 再进一步 / 更加 / hơn nữa

①一度検査をして、さらに詳しく検査する。
②雨はさらに強くなってきた。
① I will be examined once, and on top of that, I will go through a more detailed examination after that. ② The rain is getting stronger. / ①检查过一次后，要再做进一步详细的检查。②雨下得更大了。/ ① Xét nghiệm 1 lần rồi còn xét nghiệm kỹ hơn nữa. ② Mưa trở nên lớn hơn.

① on top of, or ② furthermore, more / ①再②越发，更加 / ① Ngoài ra, còn nữa ② Càng tăng, hơn nữa

1080 おとろえる
動
deteriorate / 衰弱，衰退 / sa sút, yếu đi, suy nhược

筋肉がおとろえないように運動している。
I exercise to keep my muscles in shape. / 为了防止肌肉萎缩，我坚持锻炼。/ Tôi vận động để cơ bắp không bị yếu đi.

1081 きたえる
動
train / 锻炼 / rèn luyện, mài giũa

かぜをひかないように体をきたえる。
I work out to avoid catching colds. / 为了预防感冒，我锻炼身体。/ Tôi rèn luyện cơ thể để không bị cảm.

1082 適度な（てきど）
ナ形
moderate / 适量，适度 / vừa phải, chừng mực

健康のために適度な運動が必要だ。
Moderate exercise is necessary for good health. / 为了健康，适量的运动是必要的。/ Vì sức khỏe, cần vận động vừa phải.

1083 予防〈する〉（よぼう）
名
prevention / 预防 / sự phòng chống, ngừa

クリームで日焼けを予防する。
I prevent sunburn using sunscreen lotion. / 涂防晒霜防止晒黑。/ Tôi phòng ngừa rám nắng bằng kem chống nắng.

＋ 予防注射〈する〉（よぼうちゅうしゃ） imunization shot / 预防接种 / chích ngừa

1084 □ 補給〈する〉
名 **replenish / 补充，补给 / sự bổ sung, thêm vào**

熱中症を防ぐために水分を補給した。
I replenished myself with water to avoid a heat stroke. / 为了防止中暑，补充了水分。/ Để phòng chứng sốc nhiệt, tôi đã bổ sung nước.

➕ 補う supplement / 弥补，补充 / bù đắp, bổ sung

1085 □ 不足〈する〉
名 **lacking / 不足，不够 / sự thiếu**

ビタミンが不足しているようだ。
I seemed to lack vitamins. / 好像是缺乏维生素。/ Xem ra thiếu vitamin.

➕ 睡眠不足 lacking sleep / 睡眠不足 / sự thiếu ngủ・水分不足 lacking water / 水分不足 / sự thiếu nước・勉強不足 lacking studies / 学习不足 / sự học hành thiếu sót, thiếu hiểu biết・運動不足 lacking exercise / 运动不足 / sự thiếu vận động

1086 □ サプリメント
名 **supplement / 营养品，保健品 / viên bổ sung, bổ trợ, thuốc bổ**

毎日、サプリメントをとっている。
I take supplements every day. / 我每天吃营养品。/ Hàng ngày tôi uống thuốc bổ.

1087 □ 取り戻す
動 **take back / 恢复 / lấy lại**

規則正しい生活をして、健康を取り戻した。
I regained my health by better regulating things in my life. / 我通过规律的生活恢复了健康。/ Nhờ sinh hoạt đúng giờ giấc mà tôi đã lấy lại sức khỏe.

1088 □ ワクチン
名 **vaccine / 疫苗 / vắc-xin**

病院で新しいワクチンを注射してもらった。
I received a new vaccine shot at the hospital. / 我去医院打了新疫苗。/ Tôi được tiêm vắc-xin mới ở bệnh viện.

1089 □ 加入〈する〉
名 **join / 加入，参加 / tham gia, gia nhập, vào**

保険に加入して、病気の治療に備えている。
I prepared for my medical treatment by getting health insurance. / 我买了保险，以备治病之需。/ Tôi vào bảo hiểm để trang bị cho việc chữa bệnh.

1090 □ 医師
名 **doctor / 医生，大夫 / bác sỹ**

よい医師がいる病院を探している。
I'm looking for a hospital that has good doctors. / 我在找一家有好医生的医院。/ Tôi đang tìm bệnh viện có bác sỹ giỏi.

1091 □ くれぐれも
副 **earnestly / 反复地，周到仔细 / lúc nào cũng, luôn luôn**

くれぐれもお体をお大事になさってください。
Please do take care of yourself. / 请多加保重。/ Vui lòng lúc nào cũng giữ gìn sức khỏe.

1048 ~ 1161

これも覚えよう！㉔

接辞：状況① Affix: Situation / 词缀：状况 / Phụ tố: Tình trạng

• 反〜（反対の）

反比例	inverse proportion / 反比例 / Tỉ lệ nghịch
反体制	anti-establishment / 反体制 / Phản chế độ
反作用	reaction / 反作用 / Phản tác dụng
反政府	anti-government / 反政府 / Phản chính phủ
反社会	anti-social / 反社会 / Phản xã hội

• 逆〜（方向が反対の）

逆輸入	reverse import / 再进口 / Tái nhập khẩu
逆効果	adverse effect / 反效果 / Tác dụng ngược
逆回転	reverse turn / 反转 / Xoay ngược
逆コース	reverse course / 反航向 / Lộ trình ngược

症状
しょうじょう

Symptoms / 症状 / Triệu chứng bệnh

1092 □ ナ形	具体的な (ぐたいてき) specific / 具体的 / một cách cụ thể, chi tiết	今の症状を具体的に教えてください。(いま しょうじょう ぐたいてき おし) Please let me know your symptoms specifically. / 请具体地说一下现在的症状。/ Vui lòng cho tôi biết cụ thể triệu chứng bệnh hiện nay.

⇔ 抽象的な (ちゅうしょうてき)

1093 □ 名	程度 (ていど) degree / 程度 / mức độ	痛みの程度を人に説明するのは難しい。(いた ていど ひと せつめい むずか) It's difficult to explain the degree of pain. / 很难向别人说明疼痛的程度。/ Khó mà giải thích cho người khác biết mức độ cơn đau.
1094 □ 副	ぼうっと〈する〉 absent-mindedly/faintly / 精神恍惚，发呆 / 朦胧，隐约 / thẫn thờ, lờ mờ	①最近、祖父はぼうっとしていることが多い。(さいきん そふ おお) ②向こうにぼうっと山が見える。(む やま み) ① Recently, my grandfather has often been absent-minded. ② The mountain can be seen faintly in the distance. / ①最近祖父常常发呆。②对面的山隐约可见。/ ① Gần đây, ông tôi nhiều lúc thẫn thờ. ② Có thể thấy lờ mờ ngọn núi đằng kia.

＋ ぼんやり〈する〉 vaguely / 模糊不清 / mờ ảo, lờ mờ

☞ ① lacking concentration, blacking out ② an uncertain condition / ①精神不集中，恍惚②不清晰 / ① Không có sức tập trung, tình trạng thừ người ② Trong tình trạng không rõ ràng

1095 □ ナ形 副	ふらふら〈な / する〉 dizzy/staggeringly / 摇晃，蹒跚 / hoa mắt, choáng váng	今朝から頭がふらふらしている。(副) (けさ あたま) My head has been feeling dizzy since the morning. / 从今天早上开始头就晕晕的。/ Từ sáng, đầu óc tôi choáng váng.
1096 □ 名	意識 (いしき) consciousness / 意识 / ý thức, sự nhận biết	頭を打って、意識を失った。(あたま う いしき うしな) I hit my head and lost consciousness. / 撞到头，失去了意识。/ Bị té giập đầu, bất tỉnh (mất ý thức).

＋ 無意識〈な〉(むいしき) unconscious/unconsciously / 无意识 / sự không có ý thức, vô thức

1097 □ 動	しゃがむ crouch / 蹲下 / khuỵu xuống, cúi xuống	めまいがして、その場にしゃがんだ。(ば) I felt dizzy and crouched down on the spot. / 头晕目眩，就地蹲下了。/ Tôi chóng mặt và khuỵu xuống tại đó.

1098 視野（しや）

名 field of view / 视野 / 眼界 / tầm nhìn, tầm mắt

①最近周り（さいきんまわ）が見（み）えにくく、視野（しや）が狭（せま）くなった。
②視野（しや）を広（ひろ）げるために留学（りゅうがく）を決（き）めた。

① Recently, my field of view is getting narrower and I can't see around me too well. ② I decided to study abroad to broaden my perspective. / ①最近看不清周围，视野变窄了。②为了开阔眼界，我决定去留学。/ ① Gần đây, khó nhìn thấy xung quanh, tầm nhìn trở nên hẹp đi. ② Để mở rộng tầm mắt, tôi quyết định du học.

+ ①視界（しかい） visibility / 视野 / tầm nhìn, tầm mắt

① an area that can be seen from a given point ② a way of thinking / ①能看到的范围②对事物的看法 / ① Phạm vi có thể nhìn từ đó ② Cách nhìn, cách nghĩ về sự vật

1099 呼吸（こきゅう）〈する〉

名 breath / 呼吸 / hô hấp, hít thở

寝（ね）ている間（あいだ）に呼吸（こきゅう）が止（と）まることがあるらしい。

Apparently, it is possible to stop breathing while sleeping. / 听说睡着的时候会出现呼吸暂停的情况。/ Trong lúc ngủ, hình như có khi ngừng thở.

+ 深呼吸（しんこきゅう）〈する〉 deep breath / 深呼吸 / hít thở sâu

1100 詰（つ）まる

動 stuff/pack / 堵塞，不通 / 装满 / nghẹt, đầy ắp

①鼻（はな）が詰（つ）まって、苦（くる）しい。
②スーツケースにお土産（みやげ）が詰（つ）まっている。

① My nose is stuffed, and I have difficulty breathing. ② The suitcase is packed with souveniers. / ①鼻塞很难受。②行李箱里装满了土特产。/ ① Mũi bị nghẹt nên khổ sở. ② Trong va li đầy ắp quà.

+ （～を）詰（つ）める pack / 塞满，填满 / đóng, nén, lèn chặt

① stop in the middle and don't go any further ② full to the point that more no more can fit in / ①有东西卡住变得不畅通②东西装得满满的，没有空隙 / ① Dừng lại giữa chừng không tiến hơn được ② Nhiều đến mức không thể vào được nữa.

1101 耐（た）える

動 bear / 忍受 / chịu đựng

腹痛（ふくつう）がひどく、耐（た）えられない。

My stomach hurts so much that I can't bear it. / 腹痛难忍。/ Tôi đau bụng kinh khủng, không thể chịu nổi.

+ こらえる persevere / 忍受 / chịu đựng, nhẫn nhịn

1102 便秘（べんぴ）〈する〉

名 constipation / 便秘 / bón

便秘（べんぴ）が続（つづ）いているので、薬（くすり）を飲（の）んだ。

My constipation has been persistent, so I took some medicine. / 因为一直便秘，所以我吃药了。/ Vì bị bón kéo dài nên tôi đã uống thuốc.

+ 下痢（げり）〈する〉 diarrhea / 拉肚子 / tiêu chảy

1103 ～気味（ぎみ）
接辞
feeling, a touch of / 有点…的倾向 / cảm giác, hơi có vẻ

かぜ気味（ぎみ）で、気分（きぶん）がすっきりしない。
I don't feel good as I seem to have a cold. / 有点要感冒的样子，很不舒服。/ Do có vẻ bị cảm nên cảm giác không vui vẻ.

＋ 疲（つか）れ気味（ぎみ） rather tired / 有点儿累 / cảm giác mệt mỏi ・ 太（ふと）り気味（ぎみ） rather fat / 有点儿胖 / cảm giác mập lên ・ やせ気味（ぎみ） rather thin / 有点儿瘦 / cảm giác ốm đi

1104 寒気（さむけ）
名
shivers / 发冷，寒冷 / sự ớn lạnh, cơn ớn lạnh

かぜなのか、寒気（さむけ）がする。
Maybe I've got a cold, because I'm getting the shivers. / 可能是感冒了，身体发冷。/ Không biết có phải bị cảm không mà thấy ớn lạnh.

＋ 悪寒（おかん） chill / 恶寒，发冷 / sự ớn lạnh, cơn ớn lạnh

1105 ねじる
動
sprain / 拧，扭 / trặc, xoay, vặn

転（ころ）んで、足（あし）をねじった。
I fell and sprained my foot. / 我摔倒扭到脚了。/ Tôi bị té trặc chân.

＋ （～が）ねじれる twist / 扭曲，拧弯 / (~) xoăn, cong

1106 しっしん
名
rash / 湿疹 / phát ban, nổi mẩn

腕（うで）のしっしんが、かゆくて寝（ね）られない。
My arm's rashes are so itchy that I can't sleep. / 手上的湿疹痒得我睡不着。/ Cánh tay nổi mẩn ngứa không thể nào ngủ được.

1107 はれる
動
swell / 肿胀 / sưng

ねじったところが赤（あか）くはれてきた。
The part I twisted turned red and swelled up. / 扭到的地方红肿起来了。/ Chỗ bị trặc sưng đỏ lên.

1108 しきりに
副
frequently / 频繁地，不断地 / không ngừng, liên tục

彼（かれ）は腕（うで）のしっしんをしきりにかいている。
He keeps scratching his rashes on his arm. / 他不断地挠手腕上的湿疹。/ Anh ấy không ngừng gãi chỗ nổi mẩn ở cánh tay.

1109 異常（いじょう）〈な〉
名 ナ形
abnormality/abnormal / 异常，异常的 / sự bất thường, bất thường

検査（けんさ）で心臓（しんぞう）に異常（いじょう）が見（み）つかった。（名）
An abnormality in the heart was found during the exam. / 检查后发现心脏有异常。/ Phát hiện bất thường ở tim nhờ xét nghiệm.

＋ 異常気象（いじょうきしょう） abnormal weather / 异常天气 / hiện tượng thời tiết bất thường

1110 伴（ともな）う
動
accompanied by / 伴随着 / phát sinh, kèm theo, có

この病気（びょうき）は痛（いた）みを伴（ともな）うようだ。
It seems this illness is accompanied by pain. / 这个病会伴随着疼痛感。/ Hình như bệnh này kèm theo đau đớn.

1111	単なる (たん)	彼の症状は単なるかぜではないようだ。(かれ しょうじょう たん)
連体	**just a / 只是，仅仅 / đơn thuần**	These symptoms do not appear to be just a cold. / 他的症状好像不只是感冒。/ Triệu chứng bệnh của anh ấy xem ra không đơn thuần là bị cảm.
		= ただの　+ 単に (たん) just / 仅，只 / đơn giản, đơn thuần
1112	伝染〈する〉(でんせん)	この病気は伝染する可能性はないそうだ。(びょうき でんせん かのうせい)
名	**contagion / 传染 / sự truyền nhiễm**	There seems to be no possibility of this illness infecting others. / 听说这个病好像没有传染性。/ Nghe nói bệnh này không có khả năng truyền nhiễm.
		+ 伝染病 (でんせんびょう) contagious disease / 传染病 / bệnh truyền nhiễm・感染〈する〉(かんせん) infection / 感染 / sự lây nhiễm
1113	反応〈する〉(はんのう)	くしゃみや鼻水は、花粉のアレルギー反応の症状だ。(はなみず かふん はんのう しょうじょう)
名	**response / 反应 / phản ứng**	Sneezing and a runny nose are symptoms of pollen allergy. / 打喷嚏和流鼻涕是花粉过敏的症状。/ Hắt hơi, sổ mũi là triệu chứng bệnh phản ứng dị ứng với phấn hoa.

Section 4

病気と治療
びょうき ちりょう

Illness and Treatment / 生病与治疗 / Bệnh và điều trị

1114 □ **病む** (や)

動 **ill / 得病，忧伤 / đau**

現代は心を病んでいる人が少なくない。(げんだい こころ や ひと すく)

There are quite a number of people today that are suffering mentally. / 现代社会有心理疾病的人不少。/ Hiện nay không ít người bị đau tim.

This is a relatively old expression / 比较老套的说法 / Cách nói hơi xưa

1115 □ **負傷〈する〉** (ふしょう)

名 **injury / 受伤 / vết thương**

事故で負傷し、救急車で運ばれた。(じこ ふしょう きゅうきゅうしゃ はこ)

I was injured and carried in an ambulance. / 在事故中受伤，被救护车送走了。/ Bị thương do tai nạn và được chuyển đi bằng xe cấp cứu.

➕ 負傷者 (ふしょうしゃ) injured person / 伤员 / người bị thương

1116 □ **重体** (じゅうたい)

名 **serious condition / 病危 / tình trạng nguy kịch**

車にひかれた人が重体になっている。(くるま ひと じゅうたい)

The person who was run over by a car is in serious condition. / 被车轧到的人病危了。/ Người bị xe hơi tông đang trong tình trạng nguy kịch.

➕ 重傷 (じゅうしょう) seriously injured / 重伤 / bị thương nặng・軽傷 (けいしょう) slightly injured / 轻伤 / bị thương nhẹ

1117 □ **熱中症** (ねっちゅうしょう)

名 **heat stroke / 中暑 / chứng sốc nhiệt, say nắng**

この季節は熱中症に気をつけなければいけない。(きせつ ねっちゅうしょう き)

This season, you have to be careful of heat stroke. / 这个季节要小心中暑。/ Mùa này phải chú ý chứng sốc nhiệt.

1118 □ **細菌** (さいきん)

名 **bacteria / 细菌 / vi khuẩn, vi trùng**

傷口から細菌が入ったようだ。(きずぐち さいきん はい)

Bacteria seemed to have entered from the wound. / 好像从伤口进入细菌了。/ Xem ra vi khuẩn đã vào từ miệng vết thương.

➕ ウイルス virus / 病毒 / vi-rút

1119 □ **つまずく**

動 **trip/setback / 绊，绊倒 / 受挫 / vấp, sẩy chân, trượt chân**

①つまずいて転んでしまい、足を骨折した。(ころ あし こっせつ)
②それは人生で初めてつまずいた出来事だった。(じんせい はじ できごと)

① I tripped and fell, and broke my leg. ② That was my first setback in life. / ①绊了一跤，腿摔骨折了。②那是我人生第一次受挫。/ ① Tôi bị vấp té và gãy chân. ② Đó là sự kiện sẩy chân lần đầu tiên trong đời.

① one's feet bumps into something while walking ② fall in the middle of something / ①行走时脚尖被东西绊到②中途失败 / ① Đi và chân va phải cái gì đó ② Thất bại giữa chừng

1120	医療 (いりょう) 名 healthcare, medical service / 医疗 / y tế	日本の医療は、かなり進んでいる。 Japanese medical service has progressed significantly. / 日本的医疗非常先进。/ Y tế Nhật Bản khá phát triển.

➕ 医療機関 (いりょうきかん) medical institution / 医疗机构 / cơ quan y tế・医療技術 (いりょうぎじゅつ) medical technology / 医疗技术 / kỹ thuật y tế

1121	高度〈な〉 (こうど) 名 ナ形 high degree/advanced / 高度，先进 / trình độ cao, cao độ	この病院なら、高度な医療が受けられる。（ナ形） This hospital offers advanced medical care. / 在这家医院的话，可以接受先进的治疗。/ Nếu là bệnh viện này thì có thể tiếp nhận nền y tế trình độ cao.
1122	実績 (じっせき) 名 result, experience / 实际成果 / thành tích thực tế	手術の実績で病院を選ぶ。 I will choose my hospital based on their track record for surgery. / 我通过看医院过去的手术情况来选择医院。/ Chọn bệnh viện bằng thành tích thực tế.
1123	負担〈する〉 (ふたん) 名 burden / 负担 / phí tổn, gánh vác	この病気は治療費の負担が大きい。 The medical bill for this illness is a big burden. / 这种病治疗费用的负担很大。/ Bệnh viện này phí tổn điều trị lớn.
1124	適用〈する〉 (てきよう) 名 application / 适用 / sự áp dụng	この病気の治療には保険が適用される。 Insurance can be used to pay for the treatment of this illness. / 这种病的治疗可以使用保险。/ Việc điều trị bệnh này được áp dụng bảo hiểm.
1125	手当て (てあて) 名 treatment / 治疗，处理 / sự chăm sóc, trợ cấp	けがをしたので、すぐに手当てをした。 I was injured and was treated immediately. / 受伤后立刻处理了伤口。/ Vì bị thương nên tôi đã chăm sóc ngay.
1126	尽くす (つくす) 動 do everything / 尽力 / dốc hết sức, dốc cạn	医者は母の治療に全力を尽くしてくれた。 The doctor did everything he could to treat my mother. / 医生尽全力为我妈妈医治了。/ Bác sỹ đã dốc toàn lực chữa trị cho mẹ tôi.
1127	薬品 (やくひん) 名 medicine / 药品 / dược phẩm, thuốc men	薬品の扱いには十分に注意する。 You have to be extra careful when handling medicine. / 药品管理要十分注意。/ Hãy chú ý cẩn thận trong việc sử dụng thuốc men.

➕ 薬品会社 (やくひんがいしゃ) pharmaceutical company / 制药公司 / công ty dược phẩm

1128 □ 作用〈する〉（さよう）
名 **effect / 作用 / tác dụng**

説明書を読んで、薬の作用を知る。
I read the explanation leaflet and learned about the effects of the medicine. / 看说明书了解药的效果。/ Đọc giấy hướng dẫn, tôi biết được tác dụng của thuốc.

1129 □ 目安（めやす）
名 **an aim, standard / 大致目标，头绪 / độ chừng, tiêu chuẩn**

大人は1回3粒を目安に飲んでください。
Adults need to take about three tablets each time. / 大人 1 次大概吃 3 粒。/ Người lớn thì vui lòng uống theo tiêu chuẩn 1 lần 3 viên.

1130 □ 副作用（ふくさよう）
名 **side effect / 副作用 / tác dụng phụ**

薬の副作用で気分が悪くなることがある。
I sometimes feel ill as an side effect of taking this medicine. / 药物的副作用有时会让身体不舒服。/ Do tác dụng phụ của thuốc, có khi cảm thấy khó chịu.

1131 □ 余計［に］（よけい）
副 **unnecessarily/in excess / 更加 /（比普通人）更多 / hơn (ngoài mong muốn), nhiều hơn, không cần thiết, dư thừa**

①薬を飲んだら、余計に気分が悪くなった。
②人より余計にリハビリをした。
① I felt worse after taking the medicine. ② I did my rehabilitation exercises more often than others. / ①吃了药后，身体更不舒服了。②比一般人做了更多复健。/ ① Uống thuốc rồi thì cảm giác khó chịu hơn. ② Tôi đã tập vật lý trị liệu nhiều hơn người khác.

① more than before ② more than normal / ①比之前更加②比通常多 / ① Hơn lúc trước ② Nhiều hơn bình thường

1132 □ 余計な（よけい）
ナ形 **excessive / 不必要的 / không cần thiết**

家族に余計な心配をかけたくない。
I don't want my family to worry more. / 不想让家人有不必要的担心。/ Tôi không muốn gia đình lo lắng không cần thiết.

1133 □ もむ
動 **massage / 按摩，揉 / đấm bóp, chà xát**

肩が凝ったので、友達にもんでもらった。
I had stiff shoulders, so my friend massaged me. / 我肩膀酸痛，所以让朋友帮我按摩了。/ Do bị đau nhức vai nên tôi nhờ bạn đấm bóp.

＋ マッサージ〈する〉 massage / 按摩 / mát-xa

1134 □ 告げる（つ）
動 **tell / 告知 / sự thông báo, thông cáo**

医師に病名を告げられ、ショックだった。
I was shocked to hear the name of my illness from the doctor. / 被医生告知病名后，我很受打击。/ Được bác sỹ thông báo tên bệnh, tôi bị sốc.

＋ 告知〈する〉（こくち） notification / 告知，告示 / sự thông báo, thông cáo

1048 ~ 1161

Section 4

1135 覚悟〈する〉(かくご)
名 **preparation / 觉悟 / sự sẵn sàng, chuẩn bị tinh thần**

医者と話し、最悪の場合を覚悟した。(いしゃ はな さいあく ばあい かくご)

I talked with the doctor and prepared for the worst. / 和医生谈话时，我做好了接受最坏结果的准备。/ Tôi nói chuyện với bác sỹ và chuẩn bị tinh thần cho trường hợp xấu nhất.

1136 看病〈する〉(かんびょう)
名 **nursing / 照看，护理 / sự chăm bệnh**

かぜをひいて、彼女に看病してもらった。(かのじょ かんびょう)

I caught a cold, and she took care of me. / 感冒时请她照顾我了。/ Tôi bị cảm nên nhờ bạn gái chăm bệnh.

1137 配慮〈する〉(はいりょ)
名 **consideration / 关怀，照料 / sự lưu tâm, lo lắng**

あの医師は患者への配慮が不足している。(いし かんじゃ はいりょ ふそく)

That doctor is not considerate enough of his patients. / 那个医生对病人的关怀不够。/ Bác sỹ đó thiếu lưu tâm đến bệnh nhân

1138 遺伝〈する〉(いでん)
名 **hereditary / 遗传 / sự di truyền**

この病気は遺伝するらしい。(びょうき いでん)

This illness is apparently hereditary. / 这种病好像会遗传。/ Nghe nói bệnh này di truyền.

＋ 遺伝子 (いでんし) gene / 遗传因子 / gen di truyền

1139 克服〈する〉(こくふく)
名 **overcome / 克服 / sự khắc phục, chinh phục**

病気を克服して、仕事に戻った。(びょうき こくふく しごと もど)

I overcame the illness and returned to work. / 战胜了疾病，重新回到了职场。/ Tôi khắc phục bệnh và quay lại công việc.

1140 リハビリ
名 **rehabilitation / 复健，康复治疗 / vật lý trị liệu, phục hồi chức năng**

しばらくは、病院でリハビリを続ける。(びょういん つづ)

I will continue my rehabilitation exercises in the hospital for a while. / 暂时要在医院持续做康复治疗。/ Tôi tiếp tục tập vật lý trị liệu ở bệnh viện một thời gian.

＝ リハビリテーション

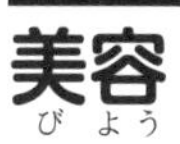

美容

Beauty / 美容 / Làm đẹp

1141 □ 名	肌（はだ） **skin / 皮肤 / da**	冬は肌が乾燥しやすい。（ふゆ・はだ・かんそう） My skin easily dries out in the winter. / 冬天皮肤很容易干燥。/ Mùa đông da dẻ dễ bị khô.

➕ 素肌（すはだ） bare skin / 素颜 / da tự nhiên

1142 □ 名	手入れ（ていれ）〈する〉 **care / 保养，维修 / sự chăm sóc**	毎日、素肌の手入れに時間をかける。（まいにち・すはだ・ていれ・じかん） I take my time every day to care for my bare skin. / 每天花时间保养皮肤。/ Hàng ngày tôi bỏ thời gian để chăm sóc làn da tự nhiên.
1143 □ 名	ケア〈する〉 **care / 保养 / sự chăm sóc**	お風呂の後の素肌のケアは欠かせない。（ふろ・あと・すはだ・か） It is necessary to take care of your bare skin after taking a bath. / 泡澡后，皮肤的保养必不可少。/ Sau khi tắm, không thể thiếu việc chăm sóc làn da tự nhiên.

➕ スキンケア skin care / 皮肤保养 / sự chăm sóc da・
ヘアケア hair care / 护发 / sự chăm sóc tóc

1144 □ 名	維持（いじ）〈する〉 **maintenance / 保持，维持 / sự duy trì**	きれいな肌を維持したい。（はだ・いじ） I want to maintain clear skin. / 我想保持好的皮肤状态。/ Tôi muốn duy trì làn da đẹp.

🟰 キープ〈する〉 ➕ 保つ（たもつ） to maintain / 保持 / duy trì

1145 □ 名	機能（きのう）〈する〉 **function / 功能 / tính năng, chức năng**	ようやく肌の機能が回復した。（はだ・きのう・かいふく） The function of my skin finally returned. / 皮肤机能终于恢复了。/ Cuối cùng chức năng của làn da đã hồi phục.
1146 □ 副	かえって **rather / 反倒，相反地 / ngược lại**	マッサージをしたら、かえって顔にしわが増えた。（かお・ふ） The wrinkles on the face worsened with the massage. / 按摩后脸上的皱纹反而变多了。/ Mát-xa rồi thì ngược lại, nếp nhăn trên mặt tăng lên.

1147 □	刺激(しげき)	①この化粧品(けしょうひん)は刺激(しげき)が強(つよ)くて、肌(はだ)が赤(あか)くなる。 ②旅行(りょこう)は、いろいろな刺激(しげき)を受(う)けるので楽(たの)しい。
名	stimulation / 刺激 / sự kích thích, thúc đẩy, động lực	① This cosmetic is too strong and causes my skin to redden. ② Having a lot of stimulation while travelling can be fun. / ①这种化妆品刺激性很强，(使用后）皮肤会泛红。②旅行可以得到各种外界刺激，所以很愉快。/ ① Loại mỹ phẩm này kích thích mạnh nên da trở nên đỏ. ② Vì nhận được nhiều động lực khi du lịch nên rất vui.

➕ 刺激的(しげきてき)な stimulative / 刺激性的 / một cách kích thích

☞ ① caused by the reaction of sensory organs ② caused by externally exciting things / ①感官反应的原因 ②来自外部的使人兴奋的原因 / ① Nguyên nhân phản ứng của giác quan ② Nguyên nhân làm cho phấn khởi từ bên ngoài

1148 □	かさかさ〈な／する〉	かかとが乾燥(かんそう)して、かさかさだ。(ナ形)
ナ形 副	dry, flaky/dry / 干巴巴，干燥 / khô ráp, nhám	My ankle is dry. / 脚后跟很干燥，不光滑。/ Gót chân bị khô nên nhám.
1149 □	低下(ていか)〈する〉	素肌(すはだ)の機能(きのう)が低下(ていか)している。
名	weaken / 下降 / sự suy giảm, kém đi	The function of my bare skin is weakening. / 皮肤机能下降。/ Chức năng làn da bị suy giảm.
1150 □	くっきり〈する〉	日焼(ひや)けの跡(あと)がくっきりついてしまった。
副	clearly / 清楚地，明显地 / rõ ràng	The sunburn left a clear tan line. / 晒黑的痕迹清楚地留了下来。/ Vết rám nắng bị thấy rõ ràng.
1151 □	つや	皮膚(ひふ)のつやが、だんだんなくなってきた。
名	glossiness / 光泽 / độ bóng	My skin's glossiness is gradually fading. / 皮肤渐渐失去了光泽。/ Độ bóng của da dần dần mất đi.
1152 □	脂肪(しぼう)	運動(うんどう)を止(や)めたら、脂肪(しぼう)がついてしまった。
名	fat / 脂肪 / mỡ, chất béo	I put on fat after I quit exercising. / 停止运动后，脂肪增多了。/ Nếu ngưng vận động là mỡ xuất hiện.

➕ 体脂肪(たいしぼう) body fat / 身体脂肪 / mỡ trong cơ thể

1153 □	肥満(ひまん)〈する〉	肥満(ひまん)は健康(けんこう)によくない。
名	obesity / 肥胖 / béo phì	Obesity is bad for your health. / 肥胖对身体不好。/ Béo phì không tốt cho sức khỏe.
1154 □	減量(げんりょう)〈する〉	ダイエットで減量(げんりょう)に成功(せいこう)した。
名	weight loss / 减少体重 / sự giảm cân, giảm trọng lượng	I succeeded in losing weight by going on a diet. / 通过控制饮食减重成功。/ Tôi đã giảm cân thành công nhờ ăn kiêng.

1155 □ ナ形	急激な（きゅうげき） drastic / 急剧的 / cấp tốc, khẩn cấp	急激なダイエットは、かえって後で太る。 A drastic diet rather makes you gain weight later. / 减肥减得太猛，过后很容易反弹。/ Ăn kiêng cấp tốc thì ngược lại về sau sẽ mập lên.
1156 □ 副	一向に（いっこう）（〜ない） the least bit, at all / 一点也，全然 / hoàn toàn (không ~)	半年もダイエットしているのに、一向にやせない。 I've been on a diet for six months, but I still can't lose weight at all. / 我减肥减了半年，却一点儿也没瘦。/ Đã ăn kiêng nửa năm rồi mà hoàn toàn không ốm đi.
1157 □ イ形	疑わしい（うたが） doubtful / 可疑的，值得怀疑的 / đáng nghi, khả nghi	このダイエット食品の効果は疑わしい。 The effects of this diet food are questionable. / 这个减肥食品的效果令人怀疑。/ Hiệu quả của thực phẩm ăn kiêng này thật đáng nghi ngờ.
1158 □ 名	姿勢（しせい） posture/attitude / 姿势 / 态度 / tư thế, thái độ	①姿勢をよくすれば、太らない。 ②人間は、いくつになっても学ぶ姿勢が大切だ。 ① You won't get fat if you maintain good posture. ② It is important for people to have a willingness to learn no matter how old you get / ①姿势正确的话就不会胖。②人无论到了多少岁，学习的态度都很重要。/ ① Nếu tư thế đúng sẽ không bị mập. ② Con người quan trọng là thái độ học tập dù có bao nhiêu tuổi đi nữa.

① body posture ② readiness when doing something / ①身体的姿势②做事的态度 / ① Tư thế, kiểu dáng cơ thể ② Tinh thần khi làm gì đó

1159 □ 動	（医者（いしゃ）に）かかる visit (a doctor) / 看医生 / đi (bác sỹ), đi bác sỹ điều trị	去年から、美容外科の医者にかかっている。 I have been visiting a cosmetic surgeon since last year. / 去年开始看美容外科的医生。/ Từ năm ngoái, tôi đi bác sỹ thẩm mỹ ngoại khoa.
1160 □ 名	依存（いぞん）〈する〉 dependent / 依存，依赖 / sự phụ thuộc, lệ thuộc, nghiện ~	きれいになるために手術に依存する女性が多い。 There are many women who become dependent on surgery to become beautiful. / 有很多女性为了变得漂亮而依赖手术。/ Nhiều phụ nữ nghiện phẫu thuật để trở nên đẹp hơn.

＋ アルコール依存症（いぞんしょう） alchoholic / 嗜酒症 / chứng nghiện rượu

1161 □ 動	映す（うつ） show / 照（镜子）/ soi, chiếu	鏡に顔を映しながら、笑顔を作る。 Form a smile while showing your face on a mirror. / 一边照镜子，一边微笑。/ Tôi vừa soi mặt trong gương vừa tạo mặt cười.

＋ （〜が）映る（うつ） show / 映，照 / (~) soi, chiếu・放映（ほうえい）〈する〉 broadcasting, televising / 放映 / sự chiếu phim, phát sóng

これも覚えよう！㉕

接辞：状況② Affix: Situation / 词缀：状况 / Phụ tố: Tình trạng

• 各～（それぞれの）

各国（かっこく） each country / 各国 / Các nước

各地（かくち） each location / 各地 / Các địa phương

各位（かくい） you all / 各位 / Các vị (cách nói trịnh trọng)

各自（かくじ） each one / 各自 / Tự bản thân từng người, các cá nhân

各種（かくしゅ） every kind / 各种 / Các loại

各家庭（かくかてい） each family / 各家庭 / Các gia đình

各界（かっかい） various circles / 各界 / Các giới

• 諸～（さまざまな）

諸外国（しょがいこく） foreign countries / 诸外国 / Nhiều nước ngoài khác nhau

諸国（しょこく） countries / 诸国 / Nhiều nước khác nhau

諸事情（しょじじょう） various reasons / 诸种情况 / Nhiều sự tình khác nhau

諸説（しょせつ） various theories / 诸种说法 / Nhiều thuyết khác nhau

諸先輩（しょせんぱい） various seniors / 诸前辈 / Nhiều đàn anh, đàn chị khác nhau

諸問題（しょもんだい） various problems / 诸种问题 / Nhiều vấn đề khác nhau

諸島（しょとう） several islands / 诸岛 / Nhiều đảo khác nhau

諸君（しょくん） you all / 诸位 / Các quý vị

諸悪（しょあく） various evils / 诸恶 / Những việc tồi tệ, những việc xấu

N2

Chapter 10

ニュース

News / 新闻篇 / Tin tức

			単語 No. (たんご)
1	トラブル・事件（じけん）	Trouble, Incidents / 纠纷・事件 / Rắc rối - Sự cố	1162~1194
2	事故（じこ）	Accidents / 事故 / Tai nạn	1195~1222
3	政治（せいじ）	Politics / 政治 / Chính trị	1223~1254
4	社会（しゃかい）	Society / 社会 / Xã hội	1255~1290
5	世界・環境（せかい・かんきょう）	World, Environment / 世界・环境 / Thế giới - Môi trường	1291~1326

Section 1

トラブル・事件（じけん）

Trouble, Incidents / 纠纷・事件 / Rắc rối - Sự cố

1162	騒音（そうおん）	騒音を巡って、アパートでトラブルが起きている。
	名 **noise / 噪音 / tiếng động, tiếng ồn**	There is an issue at the apartment regarding excessive noise. / 公寓里围绕着噪音问题发生了纠纷。/ Xoay quanh tiếng ồn, ở căn hộ đã xảy ra xích mích.
1163	続出（ぞくしゅつ）〈する〉	最近、近所でのトラブルが続出している。
	名 **appear one after another / 相继发生，不断发生 / sự liên tục xuất hiện, xảy ra**	There has been trouble occuring in the neighborhood one day after another recently. / 最近邻里之间的纠纷接连发生。/ Gần đây, xích mích láng giềng liên tục xảy ra.
1164	思（おも）わず	近くで大声が聞こえたので、思わず窓から外を見た。
	副 **couldn't help / 不假思索地，无意识地 / bất giác, bất chợt**	I heard a loud voice and couldn't help looking out the window. / 听到附近有大的声响，我想也没想就看向了窗外。/ Do nghe tiếng động lớn gần đây, tôi bất giác nhìn ra ngoài từ cửa sổ.
1165	一方（いっぽう）	①近所の人間関係は悪化する一方だ。 ②一方の話だけを聞いても、問題は解決しない。
	名 **keep on/one side / 一直，越来越 / 单方面 / một chiều, mặt khác, đơn phương**	① Neighborhood relations keep on getting worse. ② The problem will not be solved by listening to only one side of the story. / ①邻里之间的关系越来越差。②只听单方面说的话解决不了问题。/ ① Mối quan hệ với hàng xóm cứ trở nên xấu. ② Có nghe chuyện của một phía cũng không thể giải quyết vấn đề.

☞ ① lean toward a single direction ② one of two things / ①一直倾向于一方面②两者之中的一个 / ① Chỉ thiên về một hướng nào đó ② 1 trong 2 cái

1166	対立（たいりつ）〈する〉	ごみ捨てが原因で近所同士が対立している。
	名 **confrontation / 对立，其冲突 / sự đối lập**	The neighbors are confront each other about garbage disposal. / 邻居们因为倒垃圾的问题起冲突了。/ Vì lý do vứt rác mà cùng là hàng xóm với nhau trở nên đối lập.
1167	拒否（きょひ）〈する〉	彼らは話し合いを拒否した。
	名 **deny / 拒绝 / sự phủ nhận, bác bỏ, từ chối**	They refused to discuss the matter. / 他们拒绝对话。/ Họ từ chối nói chuyện với nhau.

1168 **訴える**
うった

①騒音トラブルで相手を訴えた。
②彼女は昨日から頭痛を訴えている。

動 **sue/claim / 起诉 / 诉说 / khiếu nại, kiện, kêu, méc**

① I sued the other person over excessive noise. ② She has been claiming about a headache since yesterday. / ①因噪音问题起诉了对方。②她昨天开始一直说头痛。/ ① Do xích mích tiếng ồn mà tôi đã khởi kiện bên kia. ② Cô ấy kêu đau đầu từ hôm qua.

① apply to an official organization like the judicial court ② tell others of your feelings or situation / ①向法院提出裁决申请②向他人诉说心情或状态 / ① Yêu cầu khiếu kiện lên cơ quan công. ② Truyền đạt cảm giác, tình trạng của mình cho người khác

1169 **裁判〈する〉**
さいばん

できれば裁判など、したくない。

名 **trial, lawsuit / 审判 / sự xét xử, kết án**

I don't want to go to court, if possible. / 可以的话我不想告上法庭。/ Nếu được tôi không muốn xét xử này nọ

＋ 裁判所 court / 法院 / tòa án・裁判官 judge / 法官 / quan tòa, trọng tài

1170 **関わる**
かか

①あの人には関わらない方がいい。
②命に関わるような、けがではない。

動 **involve/affect / 关联，瓜葛 / 涉及 / liên quan, ảnh hưởng**

① It's best not to be inolved with that person. ② It's not a life-threatening injury. / ①你最好别和那个人扯上关系。②这伤不危及性命。/ ① Với người đó thì không nên liên quan. ② Không phải là vết thương ảnh hưởng đến tính mạng.

① being related to something ② possibility of having a bad influence / ①有关系②有可能有不好的影响 / ① Có quan hệ ② Có khả năng đem lại ảnh hưởng xấu

1171 **はねる**

車が通ったとき、泥がはねてスカートが汚れた。

動 **splash / 溅 / văng, bắn, nhảy**

The skirt got dirty from being splashed with mud when a car drove by. / 车开过时泥溅了起来把裙子弄脏了。/ Khi xe chạy ngang qua, bùn bắn lên làm cái váy bị dơ.

＋ ジャンプ〈する〉 jump / 跳跃 / cú nhảy, sự nhảy

1172 **犯罪**
はんざい

最近、この辺りで犯罪が増えている。

名 **crime / 犯罪 / tội phạm**

Crime has been increasing around here recently. / 最近这一带犯罪增加了。/ Gần đây, khu vực này tội phạm tăng lên.

＋ 強盗 robbery / 强盗 / sự trộm cắp, tên trộm・殺人 murder / 杀人 / sự giết người

1173 **暴れる**
あば

駅前で男が暴れている。

動 **be violent / 胡闹 / tức giận, gây ầm ĩ, quậy phá**

A man is being violent in front of the station. / 车站前面有个男的在闹事。/ Trước nhà ga, người đàn ông đang gây ầm ĩ.

1174 □ 乱暴〈な／する〉（らんぼう）
名 ナ形
violence/violently / 粗暴 / sự bạo loạn, thô lỗ, thô bạo

彼は怒って、ドアを乱暴に閉めた。(ナ形)
He slammed the door shut in anger. / 他生气了，粗暴地关上了门。/ Anh ấy tức giận và đóng cửa một cách thô bạo.

1175 □ 暴力（ぼうりょく）
名
violence / 暴力 / sự bạo lực

どんな理由があっても、暴力はいけない。
Violence is not good, whatever the reason. / 无论有什么理由，都不能使用暴力。/ Dù có lý do gì đi nữa, bạo lực là không được.

1176 □ おどかす
動
threaten / 威胁，恐吓 / 吓唬 / dọa, đe dọa, hù dọa

①このままでは合格しないと、親におどかされた。
②暗い場所で友達をおどかした。
① My parents threatened me by saying that I won't pass like this. ② I surprised my friend in a dark place. / ①父母吓唬我说这样下去合格不了。②躲在暗处吓朋友一跳。/ ① Tôi bị bố mẹ đe nếu cứ như vầy mà không đậu thì không được. ② Tôi hù người bạn ở chỗ tối.

① make the other feel afraid ② surprise / ①让对方害怕②吓人一跳 / ① Bị đối phương làm cho sợ hãi ② Làm cho giật mình

1177 □ 侵入〈する〉（しんにゅう）
名
enter / 侵入 / sự xâm nhập, đột nhập

犯人は、この窓から侵入したようだ。
The criminal entered from the window. / 犯人好像是从窗户闯入室内的。/ Hình như thủ phạm đột nhập từ cửa sổ.

1178 □ のぞく
動
look into / 窥视 / nhìn trộm, loại trừ

怪しい男が家の中をのぞいている。
A suspicious man was looking into the house. / 有一个可疑的男人在往房子里窥视。/ Người đàn ông khả nghi nhìn trộm trong nhà.

1179 □ 見知らぬ（みしらぬ）
連体
unknown / 陌生 / không quen biết, lạ

見知らぬ人に突然声をかけられた。
Someone I don't know suddenely started talking to me. / 被陌生人突然叫住了。/ Tôi bị người lạ mặt cất tiếng gọi thình lình.

＋ 見知らぬ町（みしらぬまち） unknown town / 陌生的城镇 / thành phố lạ

1180 □ 近寄る（ちかよる）
動
approach / 挨近，靠近 / đến gần, tiến gần

後ろから知らない男が近寄ってきた。
A man I don't know approached me from behind. / 一个陌生男子从后方靠近了过来。/ Từ phía sau, người đàn ông không quen biết đến gần.

1181 □ 縮まる（ちぢまる）
動
contract, shrink / 缩短 / ngắn lại, thu nhỏ

あまりに怖い思いをして、命が縮まった。
I almost had a heart attack from fear. / 经历了很可怕的事情，折寿了。/ Sợ đến mức tuổi thọ ngắn lại.

＝ 縮む（ちぢむ） ＋ (〜を) 縮める（ちぢめる） squeeze / 缩短，缩小 / thu gọn, làm nhỏ lại

No.	語	例文
1182 □	無理やり むり 副 forcibly / 硬是，强逼 / miễn cưỡng, bị ép buộc	暗い道で無理やりバッグを取られた。 くら みち むり と My bag was forcibly stolen on a dark road. / 在黑暗的街道上被强行抢走了包。/ Tôi bị ép lấy mất cái túi ở con đường tối.
1183 □	捜査〈する〉 そうさ 名 investigation / 搜索，调查 / sự điều tra	警察が事件を捜査している。 けいさつ じけん そうさ The police are investigating the incident. / 警察正在对案件进行调查。/ Cảnh sát đang điều tra vụ án.
1184 □	確定〈する〉 かくてい 名 confirmation, decision / 确定 / sự xác định	いろいろな証拠から、その男が犯人だと確定した。 しょうこ おとこ はんにん かくてい Given the evidence, the man was confirmed to be the criminal. / 从很多证据上能确定这个男人就是犯人。/ Từ nhiều chứng cứ, đã xác định được người đàn ông đó là thủ phạm.
1185 □	明らかな あき ナ形 obvious / 明显，明明白白 / rõ ràng, minh bạch	あの男が犯人であることは明らかだ。 おとこ はんにん あき It is obvious that man is the criminal. / 很明显那个男人就是凶手。/ Việc người đàn ông đó là thủ phạm đã rõ ràng.
1186 □	一致〈する〉 いっち 名 match / 一致，符合 / sự thống nhất, giống nhau, nhất trí	犯人の特徴と証言者の話が一致した。 はんにん とくちょう しょうげんしゃ はなし いっち The criminal's characteristics matched what the witness described. / 犯人的特征和证人说的一致。/ Đặc trưng của thủ phạm và lời nói của nhân chứng thống nhất với nhau.
1187 □	自ら みずか 副 oneself / 自己，亲自 / tự mình	犯人が自ら警察に現れた。 はんにん みずか けいさつ あらわ The criminal turned himself into the police. / 凶手自己出现在警察局。/Thủ phạm đã tự mình xuất hiện ở chỗ cảnh sát.
1188 □	居場所 いばしょ 名 address, whereabouts / 住处，所在地点 / nơi ở	犯人の居場所が、わかった。 はんにん いばしょ I know where the criminal is. / 知道了犯人所在地点。/ Đã biết được nơi ở của thủ phạm.
1189 □	持ち主 も ぬし 名 owner / 持有者，所有人 / chủ nhân	警察が自転車の持ち主を調べている。 けいさつ じてんしゃ も ぬし しら The police are investigating the owner of the bicycle. / 警察在调查自行车的主人。/ Cảnh sát đang điều tra chủ nhân của chiếc xe đạp.

1190 □ あくまで［も］

①事件が解決するまで、あくまで捜査を続ける。②この金額はあくまでも目安で、変更の可能性がある。

副 **to the end/just / 彻底 / 终归 / kiên trì đến cùng, gì thì gì**

① No doubt they will continue the investigation until the case is solved. ② The price is just an estimate, and there is a possibility that it will change. / ①直到案件解决为止，彻查下去。②这个金额再怎么说都只是大概，有变化的可能性。/ ① Cho đến khi giải quyết được vụ án, tiếp tục điều tra đến cùng. ② Số tiền này gì thì gì cũng chỉ là ước chừng, có thể thay đổi.

① until the end, without limit ② set a particular limit / ①没有限制，做到底②限定在一定的范围内 / ① Không có giới hạn, cho đến cuối cùng. ② Giới hạn trong một phạm vi nhất định.

1191 □ 実に

これは実に不思議な事件だ。

副 **quite / 实在，确实 / quả thực**

This is quite a strange case. / 这确实是个不可思议的案件。/ Đây quả thực là vụ án bí ẩn.

1192 □ 困難〈な〉

彼は多くの困難を乗り越えて、頑張っている。(名)
警察は困難な事件を一つひとつ解決する。(ナ形)

名 ナ形 **difficulty/difficult / 困难 / sự khó khăn, vất vả**

He is working hard, overcoming various difficulties. The police solved a very difficult case. / 他克服了很多困难，一直很努力。/ Anh ấy cố gắng vượt qua nhiều khó khăn. Cảnh sát giải quyết vụ án khó khăn từng chút một.

1193 □ 改める

彼は今は生活を改め、まじめに暮らしている。

動 **change for the better / 重改，修正 / sửa đổi, cải thiện, đổi mới**

He has changed his lifestyle for the better and lives seriously. / 他现在改变了生活方式，认真地生活着。/ Bây giờ anh ấy thay đổi sinh hoạt, sống nghiêm túc.

1194 □ ようやく

20年前に起こった事件がようやく解決した。

副 **finally / 终于 / cuối cùng rồi cũng**

A case that occurred 20 years ago was finally solved. / 20年前发生的案件终于解决了。/ Vụ án xảy ra 20 năm trước cuối cùng cũng được giải quyết.

事故

じこ

Accidents / 事故 / Tai nạn

1195 □ 名	発生〈する〉 はっせい **occurrence / 发生 / sự phát sinh**	高速道路で大きな事故が発生した。 A big accident occurred on the expressway. / 高速公路上发生了重大事故。/ Phát sinh tai nạn lớn trên đường cao tốc.
1196 □ 動	相次ぐ あいつ **follow in succession / 相继发生，接连不断 / liên tục, liên tiếp**	未だに飲酒運転が相次いでいる。 There is still drunken driving occuring one after another. / 至今酒驾事件仍在不断发生。/ Đến nay lái xe trong tình trạng uống rượu vẫn liên tục diễn ra.
1197 □ 動	飛び出す と だ **leap out / 跳出来，飞出来 / chạy ra, nhảy ra, phóng ra**	いきなり、自転車が道に飛び出してきた。 A bicycle suddenly leaped out onto the road. / 一辆自行车突然窜了出来。/ Thình lình, chiếc xe đạp phóng ra đường.
1198 □ 名 副	一瞬 いっしゅん **in a flash/for a moment / 一瞬间 / khoảnh khắc, trong khoảnh khắc**	それは一瞬の出来事だった。（名） 一瞬、その人が昔の彼女に見えた。（副） It happened in a flash.For a moment, she looked like my old girlfriend. / 那是一瞬间发生的事情。一瞬间，他看到了曾经的女朋友。/ Đó là sự kiện (diễn ra) trong khoảnh khắc.Trong khoảnh khắc, tôi thấy người đó như bạn gái cũ.
1199 □ 連語	あり得ない え **unthinkable / 不能想像 / không thể nào, không thể chấp nhận, không thể có**	こんなに狭い道路でスピードを出すなんて、あり得ない。 It's unthinkable to speed along like that on such a narrow road. / 在这么窄的路上开这么快，真是难以想象。/ Chạy tốc độ nhanh ở con đường hẹp thế này thì thật không thể nào chấp nhận.

↔ あり得る う/え

1200 □ イ形	荒っぽい あら **rough / 粗暴 / thô lỗ, cẩu thả**	彼は運転が荒っぽいので、よく事故を起こす。 He drives rough and is often involved in accidents. / 他的驾驶技术很粗糙，经常造成事故。/ Anh ta lái xe cẩu thả nên thường gây tai nạn.
1201 □ 名	少年 しょうねん **boy / 少年 / thiếu niên**	16 歳の少年が運転して、事故を起こした。 A 16 year old boy was driving and caused an accident. / 16 岁的少年开车发生了交通事故。/ Thiếu niên 16 tuổi đã lái xe và gây tai nạn.

＋ 少女 しょうじょ girl / 少女 / thiếu nữ・青年 せいねん young man / 青年 / thanh niên・中年 ちゅうねん middle-aged man / 中年 / trung niên

1202 取り締まり（とりしまり）
名 **crackdown / 管制，取締 / sự quản chế, quản lý**

この道路は警察の取り締まりが厳しくなっている。
The police's crackdown on this road is getting stricter. / 警察对这条路的管制严格了起来。/ Cảnh sát quản chế con đường này nghiêm ngặt hơn.

＋ 取り締まる crack down, police / 管束，管理 / quản chế, quản lý

1203 防止〈する〉（ぼうし）
名 **prevention / 防止 / sự đề phòng**

交通事故を防止するために、警察が取り締まっている。
The police are cracking down to prevent traffic accidents. / 为防止交通事故，警察严加管理。/ Cảnh sát quản chế để phòng tai nạn giao thông

＋ 危険防止 prevention of hazards / 防止危险 / đề phòng nguy hiểm

1204 事情（じじょう）
名 **circumstance/situation / 实情 / 情况 / sự tình, tình hình**

①警察が運転手に事故の事情を聞いている。
②山田教授は世界の経済事情に詳しい。
① The police are asking the driver about the circumstances of the accident. ② Prof. Yamada knows a lot about the situation of the world's economy. / ①警察在问司机事故时的情况。②山田教授对世界经济情况很熟悉。/ ① Cảnh sát đang hỏi tài xế về tình hình tai nạn. ② Giáo sư Yamada am hiểu về tình hình kinh tế thế giới.

☞ ① reason an incident happened ② various information related to something / ①发生的原因②和其有关的各种信息 / ① Nguyên nhân xảy ra chuyện đó ② Nhiều thông tin liên quan đến việc đó

1205 有無（うむ）
名 **with or without / 有无，是否有 / việc có hay không**

警察が事故の目撃者の有無を調べている。
The police are checking to see whether there were witnesses to the accident. / 警察在调查是否有目击证人。/ Cảnh sát đang điều tra xem có người chứng kiến vụ tai nạn hay không.

1206 目撃〈する〉（もくげき）
名 **witness / 目击 / sự mục kích, chứng kiến**

事故を目撃した人を警察が探している。
The police are looking for someone who witnessed the accident. / 警察在找目击了事故的人。/ Cảnh sát đang tìm người chứng kiến vụ tai nạn.

＋ 目撃者 witness / 目击者 / nhân chứng・証言〈する〉 testimony / 证词 / lời khai làm chứng

1207 判断〈する〉（はんだん）
名 **judgement / 判断 / sự đánh giá, phán đoán**

警察はトラックの運転手の不注意だと判断した。
The police judged it to be due to the carelessness of the truck driver. / 警察判定是卡车司机不小心。/ Cảnh sát phán đoán tài xế xe tải đã không cẩn thận.

1208 □ 動	見逃す(みのがす) let slip/overlook, miss / 放过 / 看漏，错过 / bỏ sót, bỏ lỡ	①一瞬(いっしゅん)の出来事(できごと)だったので、犯人(はんにん)を見逃(みのが)した。②彼(かれ)は大(おお)きなビジネスチャンスを見逃(みのが)した。① It happened so suddenly that I missed the criminal. ② He missed a major business opportunity. / ①因为是瞬间发生的事情，放跑了犯人。②他错过了一个很大的生意机会。/ ① Do sự việc xảy ra trong khoảnh khắc nên đã bỏ sót tội phạm. ② Anh ấy đã bỏ lỡ cơ hội kinh doanh lớn.

① to leave it as it is without noticing ② leave it as it is without taking advantage of it / ①没注意到，就这么错过了②没有用到，就这么错过了 / ① Do không nhận ra nên để nguyên ② Không sử dụng mà để nguyên

1209 □ 名	行方(ゆくえ) whereabouts / 行踪 / hành tung, hướng đi	警察(けいさつ)がGPSで逃(に)げた車(くるま)の行方(ゆくえ)を追(お)っている。The police are looking for the whereabouts of the fleeing car using GPS. / 警察用GPS追踪逃逸车辆的行踪。/ Cảnh sát đang đuổi theo hướng đi của chiếc xe bỏ chạy bằng GPS.
1210 □ 副	未だに(いまだに) still / 仍然，还 / đến nay vẫn, bây giờ	死亡事故(しぼうじこ)を起(お)こした犯人(はんにん)は未(いま)だに捕(つか)まっていない。The criminal who caused the deadly accident has still not been caught. / 造成了死亡事故的犯人至今仍未抓到。/ Đến nay vẫn chưa bắt được tội phạm gây ra vụ án tử vong.
1211 □ 名 ナ形	不明(ふめい)〈な〉 unknown/unknown / 不明 / sự không rõ, không minh bạch	事故(じこ)の原因(げんいん)は未(いま)だに不明(ふめい)だ。(ナ形) The cause of the accident is still unknown. / 事故原因至今不明。/ Nguyên nhân của vụ tai nạn đến nay vẫn chưa rõ.

➕ 行方不明(ゆくえふめい) whereabouts unknown / 行踪不明 / sự mất tích

1212 □ 名	過失(かしつ) negligence / 过失 / sự cẩu thả, lơ đễnh, sai lầm	彼(かれ)は過失(かしつ)による事故(じこ)で、逮捕(たいほ)された。He was arrested for negligence in the accident. / 他因过失造成事故，被逮捕了。/ Anh ấy đã bị bắt do cẩu thả gây tai nạn.
1213 □ 動	誤る(あやまる) make a mistake, fail / 失误，搞错 / sai lầm, mắc lỗi	母(はは)は運転(うんてん)を誤(あやま)って、事故(じこ)を起(お)こした。My mother caused an accident by failing to drive properly. / 母亲开车时失误引发了事故。/ Mẹ tôi mắc lỗi lái xe nên gây ra tai nạn.
1214 □ 動	もめる argue / 发生纠纷 / tranh chấp, cãi cọ	事故現場(じこげんば)で運転手同士(うんてんしゅどうし)がもめている。The drivers are arguing at the scene of the accident. / 司机们在事故现场争吵。/ Ở hiện trường tai nạn, tài xế các bên cùng tranh chấp.

➕ もめ事(ごと) argument / 纠纷 / sự tranh chấp

1215 予期(よき)〈する〉 名

その事故(じこ)は全(まった)く予期(よき)できなかった。

prediction / 预期，预料 / sự dự đoán

That accident could not be predicted. / 这个事故完全没有预料到。/ Tai nạn đó hoàn toàn không thể dự đoán được.

➕ 予期(よき)せぬ unexpected / 无法预料 / không dự đoán được

1216 流(なが)す 動

①被害者(ひがいしゃ)の親(おや)は涙(なみだ)を流(なが)して犯人(はんにん)の逮捕(たいほ)を訴(うった)えた。
②好(す)きな音楽(おんがく)を流(なが)しながら、料理(りょうり)を作(つく)る。

flow/flow / 流下，流淌 / 播放 / chảy, làm cho trôi đi, mở nhạc

① The parent of the victim demanded the arrest of the criminal in tears. ② I cook while playing my favorite music. / ①受害者的父母流着眼泪，控诉要把犯人绳之以法。②放着喜欢的音乐做料理。/ ① Bố mẹ nạn nhân chảy nước mắt đòi bắt tội phạm. ② Tôi vừa mở nhạc yêu thích, vừa nấu ăn.

➕ (～が) 流(なが)れる flow / 流淌 / (~) chảy, trôi, (nhạc) vang lên

☞ ① water moves along ② make someone listen to things like music / ①水流动的样子②播放音乐 / ① Làm cho nước chuyển động. ② Cho nghe nhạc v.v.

1217 爆発(ばくはつ)〈する〉 名

大(おお)きな化学工場(かがくこうじょう)が爆発(ばくはつ)した。

explode / 爆炸 / vụ nổ

A large chemical factory exploded. / 大型化工厂发生了爆炸。/ Nhà máy hóa học lớn đã phát nổ.

☞ also used for emotions, such as "exploding in anger" / 也有"怒りが爆発する"这种用于表示感情的情况 / Cũng dùng cho tình cảm như "cơn giận bùng phát" v.v.

1218 抜(ぬ)く 動

①工事(こうじ)の手(て)を抜(ぬ)いたことで大事故(だいじこ)が起(お)こった。
②お風呂(ふろ)のお湯(ゆ)を抜(ぬ)く。

leave off/take out / 抽手 / 放掉，除掉 / làm ẩu, cẩu thả, gỡ, tháo, nhổ, kéo

① A major accident occurred due to careless construction. ② Pull the plug of the bathtub. / ①施工时稍有松懈，引发了大事故。②放掉浴室的热水。/ ① Do xây dựng cẩu thả mà tai nạn lớn đã xảy ra. ② Tháo nước ở bồn tắm.

➕ ②(～が) 抜(ぬ)ける go through / 脱落 / (~) sót, thiếu, rụng, rút lui

☞ ① not doing something that needs to be done ② losing something that was there; can also mean pulling out something long like hair / ①不做必须要做的事情②去掉有的东西，也有拔掉头发等长的东西的意思 / ① Không làm việc phải làm ② Làm cho cái đã có mất đi. Cũng có nghĩa kéo những vật dài như tóc.

1219 火災(かさい) 名

工場(こうじょう)で爆発(ばくはつ)があり、火災(かさい)が発生(はっせい)した。

fire / 火灾 / hỏa hoạn, sự cháy

There was an explosion at the factory and a fire started. / 工厂发生了爆炸，引发了火灾。/ Có vụ nổ ở nhà máy và phát sinh hỏa hoạn.

➕ ビル火災(かさい) fire in a building / 大楼火灾 / tòa nhà bị cháy・森林火災(しんりんかさい) forest fire / 森林火灾 / cháy rừng

1220	消防車（しょうぼうしゃ） 名 **fire engine / 消防车 / xe chữa cháy**	消防車（しょうぼうしゃ）が何台（なんだい）も工場（こうじょう）に向（む）かっている。 Several fire engines went towards the factory. / 好几辆消防车驶向工厂。/ Đến mấy xe chữa cháy đang hướng đến nhà máy.
1221	少（すく）なくとも 副 **at least / 至少 / tối thiểu là, ít nhất cũng**	爆発（ばくはつ）で少（すく）なくとも5人（にん）が大（おお）けがをした。 At least five people were seriously injured by the explosion. / 爆炸造成了至少 5 人重伤。/ Ít nhất 5 người bị thương nặng trong vụ nổ.
1222	救助（きゅうじょ）〈する〉 名 **rescue / 救助 / sự cứu giúp, cứu hộ**	事故（じこ）の被害者（ひがいしゃ）は、すぐに救助（きゅうじょ）された。 The victim of the accident was immediately rescued. / 事故受害者很快就获救了。/ Nạn nhân của vụ tai nạn đã được cứu hộ ngay lập tức.

接辞（せつじ）：名詞化（めいしか）① Affix: Nominalization / 词缀：名词化 / Phụ tố: Danh từ hóa

• **～性（せい）（人（ひと）や物（もの）が持（も）つ性質（せいしつ））**

可能性（かのうせい）	possibility / 可能性 / Tính khả năng, khả thi
人間性（にんげんせい）	humanity / 人性 / Nhân tính, bản tính con người
国民性（こくみんせい）	national character / 国民性 / Tính dân tộc
将来性（しょうらいせい）	future prospect / 将来的可能性 / Tính tương lai
必要性（ひつようせい）	necessity / 必要性 / Tính cần thiết
重要性（じゅうようせい）	importance / 重要性 / Tầm quan trọng
多様性（たようせい）	diversity / 多样性 / Tính đa dạng
危険性（きけんせい）	danger / 危险性 / Tính rủi ro, nguy hiểm
安全性（あんぜんせい）	safety / 安全性 / Tính an toàn
植物性（しょくぶつせい）	vegetable / 植物性 / Tính thực vật
動物性（どうぶつせい）	animal / 动物性 / Tính động vật

1162 ~ 1326

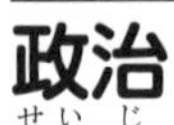

政治
せいじ

Politics / 政治 / Chính trị

1223 □ 名	政策 せいさく policy / 政策 / chính sách	選挙の前に、それぞれの政党の政策を調べる。 I researched the policies of each political party before the election. / 选举前调查各政党的政策。/ Trước bầu cử, tôi tìm hiểu chính sách của từng đảng phái chính.
1224 □ 動	治める おさ govern / 治理 / trị, thống trị, cai trị	政府は国を正しく治めなければいけない。 The government must govern the country fairly. / 政府必须正确治理国家。/ Chính phủ phải cai trị đất nước đúng đắn.

➕ (～が) 治まる is governed / 安定，平息 / (~) yên ổn, ngừng

1225 □ 名	政党 せいとう political party / 政党 / đảng chính trị	この候補者は政党に属していない。 This candidate doesn't belong to any political party. / 这个选举候选人不属于任何政党。/ Ứng viên này không thuộc đảng phái chính trị.

➕ 与党 ruling party / 执政党 / đảng cầm quyền・野党 opposition party / 在野党 / đảng đối lập

1226 □ 動	掲げる かか mention/hold up / 主张，高举 / 悬挂，张贴 / đưa ra, giương cao	①この政党は福祉の充実を政策に掲げている。 ②バスガイドが旗を掲げて客を待っている。 ① This party talks about improved welfare being its party policy. ② The bus guide waits for the passengers while holding up a flag. / ①这个政党主张完善福利政策。②巴士导游举着旗帜等游客。/ ① Đảng phái chính trị này đưa ra chính sách nâng cao phúc lợi. ② Hướng dẫn viên xe buýt giương cao cờ chờ khách.

👉 ① presenting a belief or opinion ② raising something high enough for people to be able to see / ①表达主义或主张②为了让人看见举起来 / ① Thể hiện chủ nghĩa và chủ trương ② Đưa lên cao để người khác nhìn thấy.

1227 □ 名	外交 がいこう diplomacy / 外交 / ngoại giao	政府は外交の問題を一つずつ解決している。 The government resolves diplomatic issues one by one. / 政府在一一解决外交问题。/ Chính phủ giải quyết từng vấn đề ngoại giao.

➕ 外交官 diplomat / 外交官 / nhà ngoại giao

1228 コメント〈する〉
しゅしょう こくほうもん
名 **comment / 评价，评语 / bình luận**
首相がA国訪問についてコメントした。
The prime minister commented on his visit to country A. / 首相就访问 A 国发表了评论。/ Thủ tướng bình luận về việc viếng thăm nước A.

1229 発言〈する〉 はつげん
名 **comment / 发言 / sự phát ngôn, phát biểu**
政治家の発言が世間で問題になっている。
せいじか はつげん せけん もんだい
The politician's comments have been deemed problematic by the public. / 政治家的发言造成了舆论问题。/ Phát biểu của chính trị gia trở thành vấn đề trong xã hội.

➕ 失言〈する〉 しつげん improper remark / 失言 / sự lỡ lời

1230 国会 こっかい
名 **Diet / 国会，议会 / quốc hội**
国会の生放送を見る。
こっかい なまほうそう み
Watch the Diet session live. / 观看国会的直播。/ Xem truyền hình trực tiếp quốc hội.

1231 議論〈する〉 ぎろん
名 **debate / 议论，讨论 / sự tranh luận**
国会で予算に関する議論が続いている。
こっかい よさん かん ぎろん つづ
Debate on the budget is continuing in the Diet. / 国会在继续讨论预算的相关问题。/ Các cuộc tranh luận liên quan đến ngân sách tiếp tục diễn ra ở quốc hội.

1232 延びる の
動 **extend / 延期，延长 / kéo dài, giãn ra**
国会の日程が延びた。
こっかい にってい の
The Diet's schedule was extended. / 国会的日程延期了。/ Lịch làm việc của quốc hội kéo dài thêm.

➕ （～を）延ばす の extended / 延长，延 / kéo dài (~), trì hoãn

1233 大臣 だいじん
名 **minister / 大臣 / bộ trưởng**
お金の問題で大臣が交替した。
かね もんだい だいじん こうたい
The minister was replaced due to a financial scandal. / 因财务问题，大臣换人了。/ Bộ trưởng đã thay đổi do vấn đề tiền bạc.

➕ 総理大臣 そうりだいじん prime minister / 总理大臣 / thủ tướng・外務大臣 がいむだいじん foreign minister / 外务大臣 / bộ trưởng bộ Ngoại giao

1234 議員 ぎいん
名 **parliamentarian / 议员 / nghị sỹ**
彼は国会議員になるのが夢らしい。
かれ こっかいぎいん ゆめ
His dream seems to be to become a parliamentarian. / 成为国会议员好像是他的梦想。/ Hình như ước mơ của anh ấy là trở thành nghị sỹ quốc hội.

➕ 市会議員 しかいぎいん city assembly member / 市议会议员 / nghị sỹ thành phố・
区会議員 くかいぎいん ward assembly member / 区议会议员 / nghị sỹ quận

1235 選挙〈する〉 せんきょ

名 election / 选举 / việc bầu cử

来月、全国的な選挙が行われる。
らいげつ ぜんこくてき せんきょ おこな

Next month national elections will be held. / 下个月将举行全国性的选举。/ Tháng tới, bầu cử toàn quốc sẽ được tiến hành.

➕ 選挙権 せんきょけん right to vote / 选举权 / quyền bầu cử・候補者 こうほしゃ candidate / 候补 / ứng cử viên

1236 演説〈する〉 えんぜつ

名 speech / 演说 / sự diễn thuyết, bài diễn thuyết

選挙の候補者が駅前で演説する。
せんきょ こうほしゃ えきまえ えんぜつ

The candidates of the election hold a speech in front of the station. / 选举的候选人在车站前演讲。/ Ứng viên tuyển cử sẽ diễn thuyết trước nhà ga.

1237 支持〈する〉 しじ

名 support / 支持 / sự ủng hộ

どの政党を支持するかは国民の自由だ。
せいとう しじ こくみん じゆう

The citizens have the right to support any party they wish to. / 支持哪个政党是国民的自由。/ Ủng hộ đảng phái nào là tự do của người dân.

➕ 支持率 しじりつ support rate / 支持率 / tỉ lệ ủng hộ・支持者 しじしゃ supporter / 支持者 / người ủng hộ

1238 各々 おのおの

名 each one / 各自，诸位 / mỗi, từng

会場で各々、候補者の名前を書いて箱に入れる。
かいじょう おのおの こうほしゃ なまえ か はこ い

Each person should write the name of the candidate and put it in the box at the polls. / 在会场的每个人写上候选人的名字，然后放入箱中。/ Ở hội trường, từng người viết tên ứng viên và bỏ vào thùng.

➕ 各自 かくじ each one / 各自 / mỗi người, từng người

1239 ばく大な だい

ナ形 enormous / 莫大，庞大（数量）/ to lớn, khổng lồ

選挙にはばく大な費用がかかる。
せんきょ だい ひよう

The elections costs a lot of money. / 选举要花费巨额的费用。/ Bầu cử tốn chi phí khổng lồ.

1240 不正〈な〉 ふせい

名 ナ形 wrongdoing/wrong / 不正当 / sự bất chính, bất chính

選挙活動で不正は許されない。（名）
せんきょかつどう ふせい ゆる

国会議員が不正な行為で逮捕された。（ナ形）
こっかいぎいん ふせい こうい たいほ

Wrongdoing is impermissible in election activity.The parliamentarian was arrested for wrongdoing. / 选举活动中不允许有不公正的行为。/ Trong hoạt động bầu cử, bất chính không được tha thứ. Nghị sỹ quốc hội đã bị bắt vì hành vi bất chính.

1241 思想 しそう

名 thought / 思想 / tư tưởng

日本には思想の自由がある。
にほん しそう じゆう

There is freedom of thought in Japan. / 日本思想自由。/ Ở Nhật có sự tự do tư tưởng.

1242 改正〈する〉 かいせい

名 revision / 改正，修正 / sự thay đổi, chỉnh sửa

犯罪に関する法律が改正された。
はんざい かん ほうりつ かいせい

The laws on crime were revised. / 修订了与犯罪有关的法律。/ Luật liên quan đến tội phạm đã được sửa đổi.

1243	実施〈する〉 じっし 名 enforcement / 实施，实行 / sự thực thi, tiến hành	明日から新しい法律が実施される。 Tomorrow, a new law will come into effect. / 明天开始实行新法。/ Từ ngày mai, luật mới được thực thi.
1244	要素 ようそ 名 element / 要素 / nhân tố, yếu tố	政治家にとって、スピーチ力も不可欠な要素だ。 The ability to deliver a good speech is an indispensable element to being a politician. / 对政治家来说，演讲能力是不可或缺的要素。/ Với chính trị gia, năng lực hùng biện là yếu tố không thể thiếu.
1245	成立〈する〉 せいりつ 名 formation / 成立 / sự thành lập	今年度の予算が成立した。 This year's budget passed. / 本年度的预算成立了。/ Dự toán ngân sách năm tài khóa lần này đã được thành lập.
1246	事実 じじつ 名 fact / 事实 / sự thật	政府は国民に事実を伝えなければならない。 The government must tell the truth to the people. / 政府必须要告知国民事实。/ Chính phủ phải truyền đạt sự thật cho người dân.
1247	隠す かく 動 hide / 隐藏 / che giấu	あの政治家は何かを隠しているようだ。 That politician seems to be hiding something. / 那个政治家好像有所隐藏。/ Chính trị gia đó như đang che giấu điều gì.

➕ (～が) 隠れる(かく) hide / 藏 / (~) trốn, ẩn nấp

1248	抱える かか 動 have/carry / 有 / 抱 / đối mặt, ôm	①この国は大きな問題を抱えている。 ②おばあさんが大きな荷物を抱えている。 ① This country has a major problem. ② That old lady is carrying a large piece of luggage. / ①这个国家有很大的问题。②奶奶抱着很大的行李。/ ① Đất nước này đang đối mặt với vấn đề lớn. ② Bà lão đang ôm gói hành lý lớn.

👉 ① accept something that must be solved ② hold something as if hugging it / ①承受着不得不解决的问题 ②抱着东西 / ① Tiếp nhận việc phải giải quyết ② Cầm như ôm đồ vật.

1249	支配〈する〉 しはい 名 dominate, rule / 支配 / sự chi phối, cai trị	A大統領は、あの国を30年も支配していた。 President A has been ruling the country for 30 years. / A总统统治了那个国家整整30年。/ Tổng thống A đã cai trị nước đó những 30 năm.
1250	非難〈する〉 ひなん 名 criticize / 责难，指责 / sự trách móc, đổ lỗi	若者の多くが大統領の経済政策を非難している。 Many young people are criticizing the president's economic policy. / 很多年轻人都指责总统的经济政策。/ Nhiều người trẻ trách móc chính sách kinh tế của tổng thống.

1162 ~ 1326

1251 □ 名	要求（ようきゅう）〈する〉 demand / 要求 / sự yêu cầu, đòi hỏi	国民（こくみん）は大統領（だいとうりょう）に辞任（じにん）を要求（ようきゅう）した。 The people demanded the resignation of the president. / 国民要求总统辞职。/ Người dân yêu cầu tổng thống từ chức.
1252 □ 名	デモ〈する〉 demonstration / 示威游行 / cuộc biểu tình, sự biểu tình	先週（せんしゅう）の日曜日（にちようび）にデモが行（おこな）われた。 Last Sunday, a demonstration was held. / 上周日发生了示威游行。/ Chủ nhật tuần trước, cuộc biểu tình đã được tổ chức.
1253 □ 副	およそ about / 大约 / khoảng chừng	およそ10万人（まんにん）がデモに参加（さんか）した。 About 100,000 people participated in the demonstration. / 大约10万人参加了游行。/ Khoảng chừng 100.000 người đã tham gia biểu tình.

＝ おおよそ

1254 □ 名	関連（かんれん）〈する〉 related / 关联 / sự liên quan	私（わたし）は政治（せいじ）関連（かんれん）のニュースをよく見（み）る。 I often watch political news. / 我常看和政治有关的新闻。/ Tôi thường xem tin tức liên quan đến chính trị.

これも覚（おぼ）えよう！ ㉗

接辞（せつじ）：名詞化（めいしか）② Affix: Nominalization / 词缀：名词化 / Phụ tố: Danh từ hóa

• ～み（それを感（かん）じる状態（じょうたい））

新鮮（しんせん）み	freshness / 新鲜感 / Sự tươi mới
強（つよ）み	strength / 强项 / Độ mạnh, sức mạnh
弱（よわ）み	weakness / 弱项 / Độ yếu, điểm yếu, sự yếu đuối
温（あたた）かみ	warmth / 温情，温度 / Sự ấm áp
ありがたみ	gratitude / 恩惠，感谢之意 / Sự cảm kích, cảm tạ
深（ふか）み	depth / 深意，深度 / Sự sâu sắc

社会(しゃかい)

Society / 社会 / Xã hội

1255 □ 名	反映(はんえい)〈する〉 reflection / 反映 / sự phản ánh	国民(こくみん)の意見(いけん)を反映(はんえい)した社会(しゃかい)であってほしい。 I wish for a society that is refelctive of the will of its citizens. / 希望是一个国民的意见能得到反馈的社会。/ Tôi mong đây là xã hội phản ánh ý kiến người dân.
1256 □ 名	貢献(こうけん)〈する〉 contribute / 贡献 / sự cống hiến	ボランティアとして社会(しゃかい)に貢献(こうけん)したい。 I want to contribute to society by volunteering. / 想作为志愿者为社会做贡献。/ Tôi muốn cống hiến cho xã hội với tư cách tình nguyện viên.
1257 □ 名	寄付(きふ)〈する〉 donation / 捐款 / sự quyên góp	恵(めぐ)まれない子(こ)ども達(たち)のために、毎年(まいとし)寄付(きふ)している。 I make donations every year for children in need. / 为了那些不幸的孩子每年都捐款。/ Hàng năm,tôi quyên góp cho những đứa trẻ không may mắn.

➕ 募金(ぼきん)〈する〉 donation / 募捐 / tiền quyên góp

1258 □ 名 ナ形	平等(びょうどう)〈な〉 equality, fair / 平等 / sự bình đẳng, bình đẳng	世界(せかい)の人(ひと)が平等(びょうどう)な社会(しゃかい)を望(のぞ)んでいる。(ナ形) People around the world are hoping for a fair society. / 世界上人人都期望社会平等。/ Con người trên thế giới đều mong muốn xã hội bình đẳng.

➕ 男女平等(だんじょびょうどう) gender equality / 男女平等 / nam nữ bình đẳng・不平等(ふびょうどう)〈な〉 inequality, unequal / 不平等 / sự bất bình đẳng, bất bình đẳng

1259 □ 名	復興(ふっこう)〈する〉 reconstruction / 复兴 / sự phục hưng	社会(しゃかい)が災害(さいがい)からの復興(ふっこう)をサポートする。 Society supports the reconstruction after a disaster. / 社会援助受灾地复兴重建。/ Xã hội hỗ trợ cho phục hưng từ thảm họa.
1260 □ 名	義務(ぎむ) duty / 义务 / nghĩa vụ	税金(ぜいきん)を払(はら)うのは国民(こくみん)の義務(ぎむ)の一(ひと)つだ。 Paying taxes is one of the duties of a citizen. / 纳税是国民的义务之一。/ Đóng thuế là một nghĩa vụ của người dân.
1261 □ 名	制度(せいど) system / 制度 / chế độ	年金(ねんきん)制度(せいど)の見直(みなお)しが求(もと)められている。 There is demand for revision of the pension system. / 人们要求重新审视养老金制度。/ Người ta đang yêu cầu xem xét lại chế độ lương hưu.

1162 ~ 1326

1262 □ 景気（けいき）
名 economy / 经济状况 / tình hình kinh tế

景気が徐々に回復している。
けいき　じょじょ　かいふく

The economy is gradually recovering. / 经济状况逐渐回暖。 / Tình hình kinh tế đang dần hồi phục.

➕ 不況（ふきょう） recession / 不景气 / sự xuống dốc, ảm đạm, khủng hoảng・
不景気（ふけいき）〈な〉 bad economy, hard times/stagnant / 不景气 / sự ế ẩm, khó khăn

1263 □ インフレ
名 inflation / 通货膨胀 / sự lạm phát

私の国ではインフレが続いている。
わたし　くに　つづ

Inflation continues in my country. / 我国持续通货膨胀。 / Lạm phát đang tiếp diễn ở đất nước tôi.

＝ インフレーション　↔ デフレ

1264 □ 加速（かそく）〈する〉
名 speed up / 加速 / sự gia tốc, làm tăng

新しい政策が景気回復を加速させることを願う。
あたら　せいさく　けいきかいふく　かそく　ねが

I pray that the new government policy will speed economic recovery. / 希望新政策能推进经济复苏。 / Tôi mong chính sách mới sẽ làm tăng nhanh việc hồi phục kinh tế.

1265 □ 上回る（うわまわ）
動 surpass, outdo / 超过 / vượt hơn

国民の収入が昨年を上回った。
こくみん　しゅうにゅう　さくねん　うわまわ

Citizens' income for this year surpassed that of last year. / 国民收入超过了去年。 / Thu nhập của người dân vượt hơn năm ngoái.

↔ 下回る（したまわ）

1266 □ 予測（よそく）〈する〉
名 forecast / 预测 / sự dự đoán

経済の専門家が将来の日本経済を予測する。
けいざい　せんもんか　しょうらい　にほんけいざい　よそく

Experts of economics forecast the future of Japan's economy. / 经济学家预测未来日本的经济形势。 / Chuyên gia kinh tế dự đoán kinh tế Nhật Bản trong tương lai.

1267 □ 見解（けんかい）
名 view / 见解 / quan điểm

首相が日本経済の現状について見解を述べた。
しゅしょう　にほんけいざい　げんじょう　けんかい　の

The prime minister commented on his view of the current situation of the Japanese economy. / 首相表达了对日本经济现状的看法。 / Thủ tướng trình bày quan điểm về hiện trạng kinh tế Nhật Bản.

1268 □ 増す（ま）
動 increase / 增加，增长 / làm tăng

需要が増せば、物の値段は下がる。
じゅよう　ま　もの　ねだん　さ

The price will drop if we can increase demand. / 需求增长的话，物价就会下降。 / Giá sẽ hạ nếu làm tăng nhu cầu.

1269 □ 水準（すいじゅん）
名 standard / 水平，水准 / tiêu chuẩn

国民の生活水準は徐々に下がっている。
こくみん　せいかつすいじゅん　じょじょ　さ

The living standard of citizens is gradually dropping. / 国民的生活水平在逐渐下降。 / Tiêu chuẩn sinh hoạt của người dân dần hạ xuống.

1270 □ ナ形	深刻な しんこく serious / 严峻的 / trầm trọng, nghiêm trọng	少子化は深刻な問題だ。 しょうしか しんこく もんだい The declining birthrate is a serious problem. / 少子化是个很严峻的问题。/ Giảm sinh là vấn đề nghiêm trọng.
1271 □ 動	呼びかける よ call on / 呼吁，招呼 / kêu gọi	政府は国民に節電を呼びかけた。 せいふ こくみん せつでん よ The government asked its citizens to save electricity. / 政府呼吁国民节约用电。/ Chính phủ kêu gọi người dân tiết kiệm điện.
1272 □ 名	世間 せけん society, public, people / 世间，世上 / xã hội, thế gian	ある事件が世間の注目を集めている。 じけん せけん ちゅうもく あつ A particular incident is coming to the attention of society. / 某事件引起了舆论关注。/ Vụ án nọ tập trung sự chú ý của xã hội.
1273 □ 動	驚かす おどろ surprise / 震惊 / gây ngạc nhiên	青色 LED の発明は世間を驚かした。 あおいろ はつめい せけん おどろ The invention of blue LED was a surprise to society. / 蓝色 LED 的发明震惊了世界。/ Phát minh LED màu xanh khiến cả thế giới ngạc nhiên.
1274 □ 名	ニーズ needs / 需求 / nhu cầu	企業は若者のニーズに応えて、商品を作る。 きぎょう わかもの こた しょうひん つく Companies respond to the needs of the young people when creating products. / 企业制作商品满足年轻人的需求。/ Doanh nghiệp tạo ra sản phẩm đáp ứng nhu cầu của người trẻ.
1275 □ 名	了承〈する〉 りょうしょう understanding / 同意，谅解 / sự chấp nhận, công nhận	国は住民の了承を得ないまま、開発を進めた。 くに じゅうみん りょうしょう え かいはつ すす The government went ahead with the development without the consent of the residents. / 国家没有征得居民的同意就进行开发了。/ Nhà nước đã tiến hành khai thác mà không có được sự chấp nhận của người dân.

➕ 了解〈する〉 りょうかい acknowledgement / 了解，同意 / sự lý giải, hiểu rõ

1276 □ 名	個人情報 こじんじょうほう private information / 个人信息 / thông tin cá nhân	個人情報は確実に守られるべきだ。 こじんじょうほう かくじつ まも Private information should be protected at all costs. / 个人信息应该得到切实保护。/ Thông tin cá nhân phải được bảo vệ chắc chắn.

➕ マイナンバー Individual Number so-called “my number” / 个人号码 / mã số cá nhân

1277 □ 名	プライバシー privacy / 隐私 / sự riêng tư	これはプライバシーに関わることだ。 かか This is related to personal privacy. / 这事关系到隐私。/ Đây là việc liên quan đến sự riêng tư.

1278 定着〈する〉（ていちゃく） 名

SNS は若者の間で、すっかり定着した。

settle, become common / 稳定，固定 / sự định hình

The use of SNS has become common among young people. / SNS 在年轻人中已经完全普及了。/ SNS đã định hình chắc chắn trong giới trẻ.

1279 両立〈する〉（りょうりつ） 名

日本では、仕事と育児の両立は、なかなか難しい。

coexistence / 两立 / sự thực hiện cả hai vẹn toàn

It is difficult to raise children while working in Japan. / 在日本想要工作育儿两不误，太难了。/ Ở Nhật khó mà thực hiện cả hai việc làm việc và nuôi con vẹn toàn.

1280 システム 名

日本の宅配便のシステムは世界から注目されている。

system / 系统 / hệ thống

The Japanese delivery system is attracting attention from around the world. / 日本的快递系统收到全世界的关注。/ Hệ thống chuyển phát của Nhật được thế giới quan tâm.

1281 煙（けむり） 名

たばこの煙は周りの人に迷惑だ。

smoke / 烟 / khói

The smell of smoke is annoying to the people around you. / 香烟的烟味对周围的人来说是困扰。/ Khói thuốc lá làm phiền người chung quanh.

1282 公（おおやけ） 名

大統領が公の場で世界平和について発言する。

public / 公共 / công, công cộng

The president will give a speech on world peace in public. / 总统在公共场合做了有关世界和平的演说。/ Ở nơi công cộng, tổng thống phát biểu về hòa bình thế giới.

➕ 公的な（こうてき） public / 公共的 / mang tính công

1283 マスコミ 名

マスコミが首相の会見に集まり、取材している。

mass media / 传媒 / truyền thông đại chúng

The media gathered to report on the prime minister's media conference. / 媒体们聚集在首相见面会上，进行采访报道。/ Giới truyền thông đại chúng tập trung đến buổi họp báo của thủ tướng để lấy tin.

＝ マスコミュニケーション ➕ 口コミ（くち） word of mouth / 口碑 / truyền miệng, lời đồn

1284 メディア 名

メディアを通して世界の状況を知る。

media / 媒体 / phương tiện truyền thông

I learn about the world situation through the media. / 通过媒体来了解世界的情况。/ Thông qua phương tiện truyền thông để biết tình hình thế giới.

1285 取材〈する〉（しゅざい） 名

テレビ局が消費者の傾向を取材する。

information collecting / 采访 / sự phỏng vấn, điều tra

The TV station is gathering information about consumer trend. / 电视台对消费者的消费倾向进行了采访。/ Đài truyền hình phỏng vấn khuynh hướng người tiêu dùng.

1286 □ 名	報道〈する〉 ほうどう **reporting, coverage / 报道 / sự đưa tin, truyền thông**	マスコミがこの事件(じけん)を、いっせいに報道(ほうどう)した。 The media all reported on this incident. / 媒体们都对这个事件进行了报道。/ Truyền thông đại chúng nhất loạt đưa tin về vụ án này.
		➕ 報道番組(ほうどうばんぐみ) news program / 报道节目 / chương trình thời sự
1287 □ 名	中継〈する〉 ちゅうけい **broadcast / 转播 / sự phát sóng (truyền hình, truyền thanh)**	オリンピックが現地(げんち)から世界(せかい)に中継(ちゅうけい)された。 The Olympics wre broadcast around the world from the venue. / 奥运会从现场转播至全世界。/ Olympic được phát sóng từ thành phố đăng cai ra thế giới.

➕ 生中継(なまちゅうけい)〈する〉 live broadcast / 直播 / sự phát sóng (truyền hình, truyền thanh) trực tiếp・衛星中継(えいせいちゅうけい)〈する〉 satellite broadcast / 卫星转播 / sự phát sóng vệ tinh

1288 □ 名	訂正〈する〉 ていせい **correction / 改正，修正 / đính chính, sửa chữa**	ニュース番組(ばんぐみ)でアナウンサーが間違(まちが)いを訂正(ていせい)した。 The announcer corrected the mistake on the news program. / 新闻节目中主持人修正了错误。/ Phát thanh viên đính chính sai lầm trong chương trình tin tức.
1289 □ 副	ただちに **immediately / 立刻 / ngay lập tức**	そのニュースはただちに世界中(せかいじゅう)に広(ひろ)まった。 That news quickly spread around the world. / 这个新闻立刻传遍了全世界。/ Tin đó ngay lập tức đã lan rộng khắp thế giới.
1290 □ 名	コマーシャル **commercial / 广告 / quảng cáo**	人気(にんき)のある番組(ばんぐみ)にはコマーシャルが多(おお)い。 A lot of commercials run during popular programs. / 受欢迎的节目有很多广告。/ Chương trình được yêu thích thì có nhiều quảng cáo.

Section 5

世界・環境
せかい　かんきょう

World, Environment / 世界・环境 / Thế giới - Môi trường

1291 □ 名	国旗 こっき national flag / 国旗 / quốc kỳ	弟は世界の国旗に、とても詳しい。 My younger brother knows the national flags of countries around the world very well. / 弟弟对世界各国的国旗非常了解。/ Em trai tôi rất rành về quốc kỳ trên thế giới.
1292 □ ナ形	様々な さまざま various / 多种多样 / nhiều, khác nhau	世界には様々な文化がある。 There are various cultures around the world. / 世界上有各种各样的文化。/ Thế giới có nhiều nền văn hóa khác nhau.
1293 □ 名	国籍 こくせき nationality / 国籍 / quốc tịch	様々な国籍の人が日本に留学している。 People of various nationalities come to study in Japan. / 各种国籍的人在日本留学。/ Nhiều người của nhiều quốc tịch khác nhau đến Nhật du học.
1294 □ 名	先進国 せんしんこく developed nation / 发达国家 / nước phát triển	先進国のトップが集まって、会議を開く。 Leaders of developed nations gather to hold a meeting. / 发达国家的领导人汇聚一堂，举行会议。/ Lãnh đạo của các nước phát triển tập trung mở hội nghị.

＋ 発展途上国（はってんとじょうこく） developing nation / 发展中国家 / nước đang phát triển・
後進国（こうしんこく） underdeveloped nation / 发展中国家 / nước chậm phát triển

1295 □ 名	呼称 こしょう name / 叫法，称呼 / sự xưng hô, cách gọi	グルジアの呼称はジョージアに変わった。 The pronounciation of the country name Georgia changed from “Gurujia” to “Jorjia” in Japan. / 在日本格鲁吉亚的叫法从“グルジア”改成了“ジョージア”。/ Cách gọi Gruzia đã thay đổi thành Georgia.
1296 □ 名	宗教 しゅうきょう religion / 宗教 / tôn giáo	宗教を巡る問題が世界中で起きている。 Problems related to religion are occuring around the world. / 世界各地都发生着围绕宗教的问题。/ Các vấn đề xoay quanh tôn giáo xảy ra khắp thế giới.
1297 □ 名	異文化 いぶんか different culture / 异文化 / văn hóa khác biệt	異文化の中で習慣や文化を学ぶ。 Learn the customs and culture from a different civilization. / 在不同的文化中学习风俗和文化。/ Học phong tục và văn hóa trong nền văn hóa khác biệt.

＋ 異文化交流（いぶんかこうりゅう）〈する〉 cross-cultural exchange / 异文化交流 / giao lưu văn hóa khác biệt

1298	否定〈する〉(ひてい) 名 **deny / 否定 / sự phủ định**	異文化は否定せず、積極的に学ぶべきだ。(いぶんか / ひてい / せっきょくてき / まな) Do not deny different cultures; instead, try to actively learn from them. / 不应该否定不同的文化，而要积极学习。/ Không phủ định văn hóa khác biệt mà phải tích cực học tập. ↔ 肯定〈する〉(こうてい)
1299	移民〈する〉(いみん) 名 **immigrant / 移民 / sự di dân, dân di cư**	欧米諸国が移民を受け入れている。(おうべいしょこく / いみん / う / い) The United States and European nations are accepting immigrants. / 欧美各国都接受移民。/ Các nước Âu Mỹ tiếp nhận di dân.
1300	見方(みかた) 名 **view / 看法，见解 / cách nhìn, quan điểm**	留学してから、ものの見方が変わった。(りゅうがく / みかた / か) I began to see things differently after studying abroad. / 留学了以后对事物的看法发生了改变。/ Sau khi du học, cách nhìn sự vật của tôi đã thay đổi.
1301	権利(けんり) 名 **right / 权利 / quyền lợi**	どんな人にも生きる権利がある。(ひと / い / けんり) Every human has a right to live. / 不论是什么的人，都有生存的权利。/ Bất kỳ người nào cũng đều có quyền sống.
1302	支援〈する〉(しえん) 名 **aid / 支援 / sự chi viện, viện trợ, giúp đỡ**	世界には支援が必要な国が多くある。(せかい / しえん / ひつよう / くに / おお) There are many countries around the world that need help. / 世界上需要援助的国家有很多。/ Thế giới có nhiều nước cần viện trợ.
1303	飢える(う) 動 **starve / 饥饿 / đói**	世界の飢えた子ども達を救いたい。(せかい / う / こ / たち / すく) I want to save the starving children around the world. / 我想救助世界上那些饥饿困扰的孩子们。/ Tôi muốn cứu những đứa trẻ bị đói trên thế giới.
1304	占める(し) 動 **occupy, fill / 占据 / chiếm**	A国では、貧しい人達が全体の半分を占めている。(こく / まず / ひとたち / ぜんたい / はんぶん / し) Half of the population of country A is poor. / 在A国贫民占全体人口的一半。/ Ở nước A, người nghèo chiếm một nửa toàn thể (dân số).
1305	かつて 副 **earlier / 曾经 / trước đây, đã từng**	かつてここには高度な文明が存在した。(こうど / ぶんめい / そんざい) At one time, an advanced civilization existed here. / 曾经这里存在过高度文明。/ Trước đây nơi này đã tồn tại nền văn minh cao độ.

1306 主張〈する〉(しゅちょう)
名 claim / 主张 / chủ trương, ý kiến

各国が、それぞれの立場を主張する。(かっこく、たちば、しゅちょう)
Each country expresses its own stance. / 各国都坚持各自的立场。/ Các nước chủ trương lập trường của riêng mình.

➕ 自己主張〈する〉(じこしゅちょう) one's own claim / 自我主张 / ý kiến bản thân, cái tôi

1307 交渉〈する〉(こうしょう)
名 negotiation / 交涉 / sự đàm phán, cuộc đàm phán

アメリカと中国が経済問題に関して交渉する。(ちゅうごく、けいざいもんだい、かん、こうしょう)
The United States and China are negotiating about economic issues. / 中美就经济问题进行交涉。/ Mỹ và Trung Quốc đàm phán liên quan đến vấn đề kinh tế.

1308 比較〈する〉(ひかく)
名 comparison / 比较 / sự so sánh

アジア各国の経済を比較して、意見を述べなさい。(かっこく、けいざい、ひかく、いけん、の)
Compare the economy of the Asian nations and give your opinion. / 请比较亚洲各国的经济情况，阐述一下看法。/ Hãy so sánh kinh tế các nước châu Á và nêu ý kiến.

➕ 比較的(ひかくてき) comparatively / 比较 / mang tính so sánh

1309 危機(きき)
名 crisis, emergency / 危机 / nguy cơ, khủng hoảng

首相は世界経済に危機が迫っていると述べた。(しゅしょう、せかいけいざい、きき、せま、の)
The prime minister said the world economy is turning critical. / 首相称世界经济危机四伏。/ Thủ tướng trình bày khủng hoảng đang đến gần kinh tế thế giới.

➕ 経済危機(けいざいきき) economic crisis / 经济危机 / khủng hoảng kinh tế

1310 テロ
名 terrorism / 恐怖袭击 / khủng bố

世界中でテロが起きている。(せかいじゅう、お)
Terrorism is occuring around the world. / 世界各地都有发生恐怖袭击。/ Khủng bố xảy ra khắp thế giới.

1311 悲劇(ひげき)
名 tragedy/tragedy / 悲惨 / 悲剧 / thảm kịch, bi kịch

①戦争は悲劇だ。(せんそう、ひげき)
②ギリシャ悲劇を見に行った。(ひげき、み、い)
① War is a tragedy. ② I went to see a Greek tragedy. / ①战争很悲惨。②去看了希腊悲剧。/ ① Chiến tranh là thảm kịch. ② Tôi đã đi xem bi kịch Hy Lạp.

👉 ① an incident of misery ② a play with a sad ending / ①凄惨的事②结局很悲的剧 / ① Sự kiện bi thảm ② Kịch có kết thúc buồn

1312 現に(げん)
副 indeed / 现在 / thực tế là, hiện thực

戦争はなくならない。現に、今も続いている。(せんそう、げん、いま、つづ)
War never disappears. Indeed, it's ongoing even now. / 战争无法结束，至今仍然持续着。/ Chiến tranh không mất đi. Thực tế là bây giờ nó vẫn còn tiếp diễn.

1313 □ 名	少子化 (しょうしか) **declining birthrate / 少子化 / sự giảm sinh**	世界で少子化と高齢化が進んでいる。(せかい しょうしか こうれいか すす) Declining birthrates and aging populations are progressing around the world. / 全世界的少子化和老龄化越来越严重。/ Tình trạng giảm sinh và già hóa trên thế giới đang tiến triển.

➕ 少子高齢化 (しょうしこうれいか) declining birthrate and aging population / 少子老龄化 / sự giảm sinh & già hóa

1314 □ 副	主に (おも) **mainly / 主要 / chủ yếu**	世界の人口は主にアフリカで増えている。(せかい じんこう おも ふ) The world's population is increasing, mainly in Africa. / 世界人口的增长主要集中在非洲。/ Dân số thế giới chủ yếu tăng ở châu Phi.
1315 □ 名	環境 (かんきょう) **environment / 环境 / môi trường**	地球の環境に強い関心を持っている。(ちきゅう かんきょう つよ かんしん も) I have a strong interest in the earth's environment. / 我对地球环境十分关注。/ Tôi quan tâm mạnh mẽ đến môi trường trái đất.

➕ 環境問題 (かんきょうもんだい) environmental issues / 环境问题 / vấn đề môi trường・家庭環境 (かていかんきょう) family environment / 家庭环境 / môi trường gia đình・教育環境 (きょういくかんきょう) educational environment / 教育环境 / môi trường giáo dục・自然環境 (しぜんかんきょう) natural environment / 自然环境 / môi trường tự nhiên

1316 □ 名	温暖化 (おんだんか) **global warming / 气候变暖, 温室效应 / hiện tượng (trái đất) ấm lên**	温暖化を防ぐ方法を、みんなで考えよう。(おんだんか ふせ ほうほう かんが) Let's all think of a way to prevent global warming. / 大家一起想一想防止气候变暖加剧的方法吧。/ Mọi người hãy cùng nhau suy nghĩ phương pháp phòng chống hiện tượng trái đất ấm lên.

🟰 地球温暖化 (ちきゅうおんだんか)

1317 □ 名	開発〈する〉(かいはつ) **development / 开发 / khai thác, phát triển**	ここは30年前に海を埋めて開発された。(ねんまえ うみ う かいはつ) This place was developed by reclaiming land from the sea 30 years ago. / 这里30年前是填海开发出来的。/ 30 năm trước nơi đây được lấp biển để khai thác.
1318 □ 名	調査〈する〉(ちょうさ) **research / 调查 / điều tra, khảo sát**	温暖化の影響を調査する。(おんだんか えいきょう ちょうさ) Research the impact of global warming. / 调查温室效应的影响。/ Khảo sát ảnh hưởng của hiện tượng trái đất ấm lên.
1319 □ 名	エネルギー **energy / 能源 / năng lượng**	エネルギーは世界共通の問題だ。(せかいきょうつう もんだい) Energy is a global issue. / 能源是全球性问题。/ Năng lượng là vấn đề chung trên thế giới.

➕ エネルギー資源 (しげん) energy resources / 能源资源 / nguồn năng lượng

1162 ~ 1326

1320 □ 名 ナ形	無限〈な〉(むげん) **infinity/infinite / 无限 / sự vô hạn, vô hạn**	天然資源は無限ではない。(ナ形) Natural resources are not infinitely available. / 天然资源不是无限的。/ Nguồn tài nguyên thiên nhiên không phải vô hạn.

➕ 無限大〈な〉(むげんだい) infinity/infinite / 无限大 / sự vô tận, vô tận

1321 □ 名	節電〈する〉(せつでん) **saving electricity / 节电 / sự tiết kiệm điện**	資源を大切にするために節電する。 Save electricity to protect resources. / 为珍惜资源节约用电。/ Để quý trọng nguồn tài nguyên, tiết kiệm điệm.

➕ 節水〈する〉(せっすい) saving water / 节水 / sự tiết kiệm nước

1322 □ 名	エコ **ecology / 环保 / (thân thiện với) sinh thái, môi trường, tự nhiên**	うちのエコカーは電気をためておける。 Our eco-car can store electricity. / 我们家的环保车能储电。/ Xe hơi thân thiện với môi trường của chúng tôi có thể trữ điện.

〓 エコロジー ➕ エコバッグ eco-bags / 环保袋 / túi (giỏ) thân thiên với môi trường

1323 □ 名	省エネ(しょう) **energy conservation / 节能 / sự giảm thiểu năng lượng**	省エネが地球の温暖化を防ぐ。 Energy conservation will prevent the earth from warming. / 节约能源可以防止全球变暖问题加剧。/ Giảm thiểu năng lượng phòng chống hiện tượng trái đất ấm lên.
1324 □ 名	汚染〈する〉(おせん) **pollution / 污染 / sự ô nhiễm**	A国では工場が増え、自然環境を汚染している。 Factories are increasing in country A and polluting the natural environment. / A国的工厂增加，自然环境遭到污染。/ Ở nước A, nhà máy tăng khiến ô nhiễm môi trường tự nhiên.

➕ 環境汚染(かんきょうおせん) environmental pollution / 环境污染 / sự ô nhiễm môi trường

1325 □ 名	面積(めんせき) **area / 面积 / diện tích**	世界で森林の面積が減少している。 Forest areas are decreasing around the world. / 世界上森林面积正在减少。/ Diện tích rừng trên thế giới đang giảm.
1326 □ 動	守る(まもる) **protect/abide / 保护 / 遵守 / bảo vệ, gìn giữ, tuân thủ**	①みんなで大切な自然を守っていく。 ②法律は全ての国民が守らなければならない。 ① Protect precious nature together with everyone. ② Laws must be abided by every citizen. / ①我们一起保护重要的大自然。②所有国民必须遵守法律。/ ① Mọi người cùng nhau bảo vệ thiên nhiên quý giá. ② Tất cả người dân đều phải tuân thủ pháp luật.

① trying to avoid negative influence ② following rules / ①不受不好的影响②遵守规定 / ① Để không chịu ảnh hưởng của những gì xấu ② Tuân theo quy tắc v.v.

これも覚えよう！ ㉘

接辞：名詞化③　Affix: Nominalization / 词缀：名词化 / Phụ tố: Danh từ hóa

• ～さ（そうであること）

めでたさ	happiness / 可喜可贺之处 / Sự vui mừng
良さ	merit / 好的地方，好处 / Sự tốt đẹp
美しさ	beauty / 美 / Vẻ đẹp
静かさ	quietness / 安静 / Sự yên tĩnh
やさしさ	kindness / 好，温柔 / Sự tử tế, vẻ hiền dịu
おいしさ	deliciousness / 美味 / Độ ngon, vị ngon

• ～風（そういう感じがすること）

和風	Japanese style / 和风，日本风 / Kiểu (phong cách) Nhật
西洋風	Western style / 西洋风，欧美风 / Kiểu (phong cách) Tây
ＯＬ風	like a working woman / OL 风，职业女性风 / Kiểu (phong cách) nữ nhân viên văn phòng
サラリーマン風	like a working man / 上班族风 / Kiểu (phong cách) nhân viên văn phòng
学生風	like a student / 学生风 / Kiểu (phong cách) sinh viên

N2

Chapter 11

様子・イメージ

ようす

Appearance, Image / 模样・印象篇 / Trạng thái - Hình ảnh

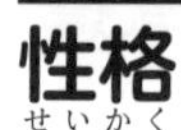

性格
せいかく

Personality / 性格 / Tính cách

1327 **人柄** (ひとがら) 名 **personality / 人品 / nhân cách, tính cách, tính tình**

彼は人柄がよく、友達がとても多い。(かれ ひとがら ともだち おお)
He is good-natured and has many friends. / 他人品很好，朋友很多。/ Anh ấy tính tình tốt đẹp, nên có rất nhiều bạn.

+ 家柄 (いえがら) ancestry / 门第，家世 / dòng tộc, gia đình・土地柄 (とちがら) local color / 当地风俗 / phong tục địa phương

1328 **性質** (せいしつ) 名 **disposition/property, characteristic / 品质 / 性质 / bản tính, tính chất**

①彼は穏やかな性質の持ち主だ。(かれ おだ せいしつ も ぬし)
②この家は燃えにくい性質の材料で建てられている。(いえ も せいしつ ざいりょう た)
① He has a gentle personality. ② This house is built of material that doesn't burn easily. / ①他是一个品性温和的人。②这个房子采用了不易燃的材质所建。/ ① Anh ấy là người có bản tính ôn hòa. ② Căn nhà này được xây bằng vật liệu có tính chất khó cháy.

① a tendency that a person has had since he/she was born ② the tendency or function that a thing has / ①人出生以来就有的性格②东西所有的倾向、作用 / ① Khuynh hướng con người có được từ khi sinh ra. ② Khuynh hướng, sự vận động mà sự vật có

1329 **向く** (む) 動 **be fit/face / 适合 / 朝 / phù hợp, quay về hướng**

①私は性格的に教師に向いていると思う。(わたし せいかくてき きょうし む おも)
②名前を呼ばれたので、声がする方を向いた。(なまえ よ こえ ほう む)
① I think I'm fit to be a teacher. ② Someone called my name and I turned to face the direction from where I heard my name. / ①我的性格比较适合做老师。②有人叫我名字，所以转向了声音的方向。/ ① Tôi nghĩ tính mình phù hợp với nghề giáo viên. ② Vì được gọi tên nên tôi quay về hướng có tiếng gọi.

+ ①向き (む) direction / 朝向 / chiều hướng, thích hợp cho

① fitting ② orienting the body in a certain direction / ①适合②把身体转过去 / ① Hợp ② Cố định cơ thể với điều đó

1330 **温厚な** (おんこう) ナ形 **mild-mannered / 温厚，敦厚 / hòa nhã, ôn hòa**

兄は昔から温厚な人柄で、誰からも好かれている。(あに むかし おんこう ひとがら だれ す)
My big brother has always been mild-mannered and was loved by all. / 哥哥从前到现在一直是个性格温厚的人，人见人爱。/ Anh trai tôi là người có tính hòa nhã từ xưa nên bất kỳ ai cũng quý mến.

+ 温和な (おんわ) gentle / 温和，温暖 / ôn hòa

1331 **社交的な** (しゃこうてき) ナ形 **outgoing / 善于社交 / có tính xã giao**

妹は人見知りな私と違って、とても社交的だ。(いもうと ひとみし わたし ちが しゃこうてき)
Unlike me, who is shy, my younger sister is very outgoing. / 妹妹和怕生的我不同，非常善于社交。/ Em gái tôi rất xã giao, khác với tôi rất nhút nhát.

➕ 内向的な（ないこうてき） shy / 内向 / có tính nội tâm

1332 ☐ ナ形	活発な（かっぱつ） active / 活泼 / hoạt bát	あの姉妹の姉はおとなしく、妹は活発だ。 Concerning the two sisters, the elder sister is quiet and the younger sister is active. / 那对姐妹的姐姐很安静，妹妹很活泼。/ Người chị trong hai chị em đó thì trầm tĩnh, còn cô em thì hoạt bát.
1333 ☐ 名 ナ形	頑固〈な〉（がんこ） stubbornness/stubborn / 顽固 / sự bướng bỉnh, ngoan cố	私の頑固な性格は父の遺伝だ。（ナ形） I get my stubbornness from my father. / 我顽固的性格是遗传我爸。/ Tính bướng bỉnh của tôi là di truyền từ bố.
1334 ☐ ナ形	素朴な（そぼく） simple / 朴素 / chất phác, quê mùa, thô kệch	彼は昔から派手なことが嫌いで、素朴な性格だ。 He was always a simple person who disliked brash things. / 他从以前开始就不喜欢花哨的，性格很朴实。/ Anh ấy tính cách chất phác, từ xưa đã ghét những gì lòe loẹt.
1335 ☐ 名 ナ形	無邪気〈な〉（むじゃき） naïve/innocent / 天真无邪 / sự ngây thơ, trong sáng	彼女は子どものように無邪気な性格だ。（ナ形） She is naive like a child. / 她的性格像孩子一样天真无邪。/ Cô ấy tính cách ngây thơ như trẻ con.
1336 ☐ ナ形	謙虚な（けんきょ） humble / 谦虚 / khiêm nhường, khiêm tốn	私の上司は誰に対しても謙虚だ。 My boss is humble towards anyone. / 我的上司对谁都很谦虚。/ Cấp trên của tôi khiêm nhường với bất kỳ ai.
1337 ☐ 名 ナ形	無口〈な〉（むくち） reticence/quiet / 沉默寡言 / tính ít nói, kín tiếng	私はおしゃべりなので、無口な人が好きだ。（ナ形） I am talkative, so I like quiet people. / 我是个话唠，所以喜欢不爱说话的人。/ Tôi hay trò chuyện nên thích người ít nói.
1338 ☐ 名	人見知り〈する〉（ひとみし） shy / 怕生 / tính nhút nhát, bẽn lẽn	人見知りする性格なので、友達が少ない。 I'm shy, so have I don't have many friends. / 因为性格怕生，所以朋友很少。/ Vì tính cách nhút nhát nên tôi ít bạn.
1339 ☐ 名 ナ形	おく病〈な〉（びょう） coward/cowardly / 胆小，懦弱 / tính nhát gan	おく病な性格を変えて、いろいろなことに挑戦したい。（ナ形） I want to change my cowardly personality and try many new things. / 想改掉懦弱的性格，挑战各种各样的事。/ Tôi muốn thay đổi tính cách nhát gan để thử thách làm nhiều việc.

➕ おく病者（びょうもの） coward / 胆小鬼 / người nhát gan

1340 大胆な（だいたん）
ナ形
daring / 大胆 / bạo dạn, táo bạo

おく病（びょう）な性格（せいかく）なので、大胆（だいたん）な人（ひと）がうらやましい。

I am cowardly, so I envy daring people. / 因为我的性格很懦弱，所以我羡慕那种胆子大的人。/ Vì tính cách nhút nhát nên tôi rất ghen tỵ với người bạo dạn.

➕ 小心（しょうしん）な timid / 慎重，小心 / nhút nhát, hẹp bụng, nhỏ mọn

1341 なれなれしい
イ形
over-familiar / 自来熟的，过分亲昵的 / suồng sã

彼（かれ）は初（はじ）めて会（あ）ったのに、なれなれしい人（ひと）だ。

Even though this was my first time meeting him, he is acting a little too familiar with me. / 才第一次和他见面，他是个特别自来熟的人。/ Lần đầu tiên gặp mà anh ấy thật suồng sã.

➕ よそよそしい distant / 冷漠，疏远 / hờ hững, lạnh nhạt・フレンドリーな friendly / 友善，友好 / thân thiện

1342 厚（あつ）かましい
イ形
brazen / 厚颜无耻 / đanh đá, đáo để

彼女（かのじょ）が、あんなに厚（あつ）かましい人（ひと）とは知（し）らなかった。

I didn't know she was such a brazen person. / 没想到她居然是这么厚颜无耻的人。/ Tôi không biết cô ấy là người đanh đá đến thế.

➕ 図々（ずうずう）しい bold / 厚脸皮 / vô duyên, trơ trẽn

1343 欲張（よくば）り〈な〉
名 ナ形
greed/greedy / 贪婪 / tính tham lam, tham lam

妹（いもうと）は欲張（よくば）りで、何（なん）でも欲（ほ）しがる。（ナ形）

She is greedy and wants everything. / 妹妹很贪婪，什么都想要。/ Em gái tôi tham lam, cái gì cũng muốn.

➕ 欲張（よくば）る boss around / 贪，贪图 / tham lam

1344 ねばり強（づよ）い
イ形
persistently, tenaciously / 坚韧的，有毅力的 / kiên nhẫn, kiên trì

あきらめず、ねばり強（づよ）く頑張（がんば）ろう。

Don't give up, work with persistence. / 别放弃，顽强地努力到最后吧。/ Không bỏ cuộc, hãy cố gắng kiên trì.

1345 大（おお）ざっぱな
ナ形
rough, not particular / 粗枝大叶 / đại khái, sơ sài

彼（かれ）は大（おお）ざっぱな性格（せいかく）だが、お金（かね）についてはけちだ。

He isn't too particular about things but is stingy about money. / 他的性格粗枝大叶的，但对钱很抠门。/ Anh ấy tính tình đại khái nhưng lại keo kiệt chuyện tiền nong.

1346 だらしない
イ形
sloppy, weak / 邋遢 / 不像话 / lôi thôi, bừa bãi, lỏng lẻo, yếu đuối

①あの人（ひと）の服装（ふくそう）は、いつもだらしない。
②部下（ぶか）に注意（ちゅうい）できないなんて、部長（ぶちょう）はだらしない。

① That person always dresses sloppily. ② A manager who can't redress his subordinates is weak. / ①那个人的穿着打扮一直很邋遢。②不敢提醒部下这种部长真是不像话。/ ① Trang phục của người đó lúc nào cũng lôi thôi. ② Không thể lưu ý được cấp dưới thì trưởng phòng thật yếu đuối.

☞ ①not being proper ②weak, cowardly, can also be described as "だらしがない" / ①不整洁②懦弱,没有勇气,也说"だらしがない" / ① Không đàng hoàng ② Yếu đuối, không có dũng khí. Cũng nói là " だらしがない"

1347 □ ナ形	ルーズな loose / 散漫，松懈 / lỏng lẻo, lề mề	彼(かれ)は時間(じかん)にルーズで、いつも人(ひと)を待(ま)たせる。 He is never punctual and always makes people wait. / 他的时间观念很差，总是让人等他。/ Anh ấy giờ giấc lề mề, lúc nào cũng bắt người khác đợi.
1348 □ 名 ナ形	短気(たんき)〈な〉 short-tempered/short-tempered / 性急 / tính nóng nảy, nóng nảy	すぐに怒(おこ)る短気(たんき)な人(ひと)とは付(つ)き合(あ)えない。(ナ形) I can't deal with short-tempered people who get angry easily. / 我和那种性子急动不动就发火的人处不来。/ Tôi không thể giao tiếp với người tính khí nóng nảy, hay giận.

= 気(き)が短(みじか)い

1349 □ 名 ナ形	ひきょう〈な〉 cowardice/unmanly / 卑鄙，卑怯 / sự bần tiện, hèn hạ	彼(かれ)のやり方(かた)はひきょうだ。(ナ形) His way of doing things is cowardly. / 他的做法很卑鄙。/ Cách làm của anh ta thật hèn hạ.

＋ ひきょう者(もの) coward, traitor / 卑鄙的人 / người bần tiện

1350 □ 名	プライド pride / 自尊 / lòng kiêu hãnh, tự hào	妹(いもうと)は、かなりプライドが高(たか)い。 My younger sister is really too proud. / 妹妹的自尊心很强。/ Em gái tôi lòng kiêu hãnh rất cao.
1351 □ ナ形	典型的(てんけいてき)な typical / 典型的 / mang tính điển hình	彼(かれ)はまじめで時間(じかん)に厳(きび)しい。典型的(てんけいてき)な日本人(にほんじん)だ。 He is serious and strict about time. He's a typical Japanese. / 他很认真很守时，是个典型的日本人。/ Anh ấy nghiêm túc và nghiêm khắc trong thời gian. Là người Nhật điển hình.
1352 □ 名	要領(ようりょう) be to the point / 要领，要点 / sự nắm bắt công việc, thao tác	今年(ことし)の新入社員(しんにゅうしゃいん)は要領(ようりょう)がいい。 The new employees this year know how to swim in the tide. / 公司的新人都很精明能干。/ Nhân viên mới năm nay nắm bắt công việc tốt.
1353 □ 名	乗(の)り upbeat / 劲头 / sự hòa nhập, hòa đồng	彼女(かのじょ)は乗(の)りがいいので、すぐ友達(ともだち)ができる。 She is upbeat and makes friends easily. / 她很会来事，很快就能交到朋友。/ Cô ấy hòa nhập tốt nên có thể kết bạn ngay.
1354 □ 名	物事(ものごと) things / 事物 / sự vật sự việc	彼(かれ)は物事(ものごと)をじっくりと観察(かんさつ)して、判断(はんだん)する。 He makes a decision after observing things very carefully. / 他对事物仔细观察后再进行判断。/ Anh ấy chăm chú quan sát sự vật rồi quyết định.

1355 反面 (はんめん)
名 other side / 另一面 / mặt trái, mặt khác, phản diện

彼女(かのじょ)は温厚(おんこう)な反面(はんめん)、冷(つめ)たいところもある。
She is good-natured, but can at times be cold-hearted. / 她温厚性格的背后，也有冷淡的一面。/ Cô ấy một mặt nồng ấm nhưng mặt khác, cũng có điểm lạnh lùng.

これも覚(おぼ)えよう！ ㉙

接辞(せつじ)：否定(ひてい)① Affix: Negation / 词缀：否定 / Phụ tố: Phủ định

- 無～（～がない）

【む～】

無意味 (むいみ)	meaningless / 无意义 / Không có nghĩa
無関心 (むかんしん)	uninterested / 不闻不问，不感兴趣 / Không quan tâm
無許可 (むきょか)	unauthorized / 没有许可 / Không phép
無責任 (むせきにん)	irresponsible / ①无责任②没有责任感 / Không có trách nhiệm, vô trách nhiệm
無関係 (むかんけい)	unrelated / 没有关系 / Không liên quan
無意識 (むいしき)	unconscious / 无意识 / Không có ý thức, vô thức
無計画 (むけいかく)	unplanned / 没有计划性 / Không kế hoạch
無差別 (むさべつ)	indiscriminate / 无差别 / Không phân biệt
無制限 (むせいげん)	limitless / 无限制 / Không giới hạn
無免許 (むめんきょ)	unlicensed / 无证 / Không có bằng, không có giấy phép
無表情 (むひょうじょう)	expressionless / 无表情 / Không bày tỏ cảm xúc

【ぶ～】

無遠慮 (ぶえんりょ)	brazen / 无所顾虑 / Không e ngại
無作法 (ぶさほう)	ill-mannered / 没有规矩 / Vô phép, bất lịch sự
無愛想 (ぶあいそう)	unfriendly / 不和善，冷淡 / Không hòa đồng

いい気分(きぶん)

Feeling Good / 好心情 / Cảm giác thoải mái

No.	語	例文
1356 □	快適(かいてき)な ナ形 comfortable / 舒适 / sảng khoái, dễ chịu, thoải mái	このホテルは、とても快適(かいてき)だ。 This hotel is very comfortable. / 这个酒店很舒适。/ Khách sạn này rất thoải mái.
1357 □	快(こころよ)い イ形 pleasant / 愉快，高兴 / dễ chịu, du dương	この音楽(おんがく)は快(こころよ)い気分(きぶん)にさせてくれる。 This music makes me feel good. / 这个音乐能让人心情愉悦。/ Âm nhạc này khiến tôi có cảm giác dễ chịu.
1358 □	心地(ここち)よい イ形 comfortable / 畅快，惬意 / dễ chịu, thích thú, êm ái	窓(まど)から心地(ここち)よい風(かぜ)が入(はい)ってきた。 Comfortable wind blew through the window. / 窗边吹进一阵舒爽的风。/ Từ cửa sổ, làn gió dễ chịu thổi vào.
1359 □	すがすがしい イ形 refreshing / 神清气爽 / khỏe khoắn, sảng khoái	試験(しけん)が終(お)わって、すがすがしい気分(きぶん)だ。 I feel refreshed with the exams over. / 考试结束了，我感觉神清气爽。/ Kết thúc kỳ thi, tâm trạng thật sảng khoái.
1360 □	リフレッシュ〈する〉 名 refreshed / 放松，振作精神 / sự làm mới, làm cho tỉnh người	週末(しゅうまつ)はテニスをして、リフレッシュする。 I refresh by playing tennis over the weekend. / 我周末打网球，换个心情放松放松。/ Cuối tuần tôi chơi quần vợt cho tỉnh người.
1361 □	穏(おだ)やかな ナ形 calm / 平静，平稳 / ôn hòa, thanh thản, yên ả	いつも穏(おだ)やかな気持(きも)ちでいたい。 I always want to be calm. / 我希望能一直心平气和。/ Tôi muốn lúc nào cũng trong tâm trạng thanh thản.
1362 □	心強(こころづよ)い イ形 encouraging / 有把握的，胆壮的 / ủng hộ, động viên tinh thần	彼(かれ)がいてくれると、とても心強(こころづよ)い。 I feel very encouraged when he is here. / 有他在，我觉得心里很有底。/ Khi có anh ấy, tôi cảm thấy được động viên tinh thần mạnh mẽ.
1363 □	恋(こい)しい イ形 long for, miss / 想念 / nhung nhớ	さっきまで会(あ)っていたのに、彼女(かのじょ)が恋(こい)しい。 I was with her just a moment ago, but I already miss her. / 刚刚还在一起，但我又想念她了。/ Mới gặp lúc nãy mà đã nhung nhớ cô ấy rồi.
1364 □	前向(まえむ)き 名 positive / 向前，积极向上 / tích cực, hướng về phía trước	彼(かれ)はいつでも前向(まえむ)きに努力(どりょく)する。 He is always positive and makes an effort. / 他一直积极向上地努力着。/ Anh ấy luôn nỗ lực hướng về phía trước.

⇔ 後(うし)ろ向(む)き ＋ ポジティブな positive / 积极 / tích cực

1365 □ イ形	めでたい happy / 可喜可贺 / đáng mừng, vui mừng	最近、家族にめでたいことが続いている。 Happy things are happening one after another to my family these days. / 最近家里不断有喜事。/ Gần đây, liên tục có nhiều việc đáng mừng trong gia đình

➕ おめでとう congratulations / 恭喜 / chúc mừng

1366 □ ナ形	ラッキーな lucky / 幸运的 / may mắn	今日は何だかラッキーな日だ。 For some reason, today is a lucky day. / 今天真是个幸运的日子。/ Hôm nay là ngày may mắn sao đó.

⟷ アンラッキーな

➕ 幸運〈な〉 luck/lucky / 幸运的 / vận may, may mắn・ついてる lucky / 走运 / may mắn

1367 □ 名 ナ形	幸福〈な〉 happiness/happy / 幸福 / niềm hạnh phúc, hạnh phúc	彼女と出会ってから､穏やかで幸福な毎日だ。(ナ形) Since meeting her, my days have been full of happinnes and joy. / 和她相遇后每天都是稳稳的幸福。/ Sau khi gặp gỡ cô ấy, mỗi ngày của tôi đều êm ả và hạnh phúc.

⟷ 不幸〈な〉

1368 □ 動	張り切る enthusiastic / 紧绷，拉紧，干劲十足 / hăng hái, sẵn sàng	彼は入社後、張り切って仕事に取り組んでいる。 He has been enthusiastically engaged in work since joining the company. / 他进入公司以后，干劲十足地投入到工作中。/ Sau khi vào công ty, anh ấy hăng hái nỗ lực làm việc.
1369 □ 副	わくわく〈する〉 exciting / 期待 / hồi hộp, phấn khởi	もうすぐ夏休みだ。わくわくする。 It's almost summer vacation and I feel so excited. / 马上就要放暑假了，我满怀期待。/ Sắp đến mùa hè rồi. Thật phấn khởi.
1370 □ 副	そわそわ[と]〈する〉 nervous / 坐立不安 / sốt ruột	デートの日の朝はそわそわと落ち着かない。 I feel nervous on the morning of the date. / 约会那天早上，我坐立不安难以平静。/ Sáng hôm hẹn hò, tôi sốt ruột đứng ngồi không yên.
1371 □ 副	うっとり[と]〈する〉 spellbound / 陶醉 / như bị thôi miên, say đắm, lãng đãng	好きな歌手のコンサートで、うっとりした気分になる。 I'm spellbound at the concert of my favorite singer. / 听喜欢的歌手的演唱会，我听得陶醉忘我。/ Tôi như bị thôi miên trong buổi hòa nhạc của ca sỹ mình yêu thích.

1372	すっと〈する〉 副 feel refreshed / 痛快 / nhẹ nhàng, nhẹ nhõm	言いたいことを全部言って、胸がすっとした。 I feel refreshed, having said everything I wanted to say. / 把想说的都说了，我感觉很痛快。/ Tôi nói hết những gì muốn nói và thấy trong lòng nhẹ nhõm.
1373	気分転換〈する〉 名 change of pace / 转换心情 / sự thay đổi tâm trạng	カラオケで気分転換して、すっきりした。 I feel refreshed after having a change of pace with karaoke. / 唱唱卡拉 OK 转换一下心情，现在痛快了。/ Tôi thay đổi tâm trạng bằng cách hát karaoke và thấy sảng khoái.

接辞：否定② Affix: Negation / 词缀：否定 / Phụ tố: Phủ định

• **不～（～が足りない）**

不可能	impossible / 不可能 / Không thể, thiếu khả năng
不自然	unnatural / 不自然 / Không tự nhiên, thiếu tự nhiên
不景気	bad economy / 不景气 / Kinh tế khó khăn, buôn bán ế ẩm
不公平	unfair / 不公平 / Không công bằng, thiếu công bằng
不必要	unnecessary / 不必要 / Không cần thiết
不完全	incomplete / 不完全 / Không hoàn thiện, thiếu hoàn thiện
不自由	disabled / 不自由 / Không được tự do, cách nói tránh với những người khuyết tật
不人気	unpopular / 不受欢迎 / Không được ưa chuộng
不まじめ	insincere / 不认真 / Không chăm chỉ, không nghiêm túc
不合格	failure, disqualification / 不及格 / Không đậu
不安定	unstable / 不稳定 / Không ổn định
不透明	unclear / 不透明 / Không trong sáng, không minh bạch

Section 3

ブルーな気分(きぶん)

Feeling Down / 坏心情 / Cảm giác buồn bã

1374 ゆううつ〈な〉 名 ナ形
depression/feel depressed / 忧郁，闷闷不乐 / u uất, ảm đạm
一日中雨(いちにちじゅうあめ)だと、ゆううつになる。(ナ形)
I feel depressed when it rains all day. / 下一整天雨的话，心情也会变得郁闷。/ Mưa cả ngày thật ảm đạm.

1375 みじめな ナ形
miserable / 可怜，惨不忍睹 / đáng thương, khốn khổ
今(いま)のみじめな生活(せいかつ)を早(はや)く終(お)わらせたい。
I want to end this miserable life as soon as possible. / 我想早点儿结束现在悲惨的生活。/ Tôi muốn mau kết thúc cuộc sống khốn khổ hiện nay.

1376 つらい イ形
painful, depressing / 痛苦，难过 / buồn, khổ sở, đau khổ, khắc nghiệt, vất vả
親友(しんゆう)が病気(びょうき)になってしまい、とてもつらい。
My best friend became ill and I am very depressed. / 好朋友得了病，我心里很难过。/ Bạn thân tôi bị bệnh, thật buồn.

1377 心細(こころぼそ)い イ形
lonely / 心中不安的，心中没底的 / cô đơn, trơ trọi
日本(にほん)へ来(き)たばかりの頃(ころ)は、とても心細(こころぼそ)かった。
I felt very lonely when I just arrived in Japan. / 刚来日本的时候，我无依无靠觉得心中不安。/ Khi mới đến Nhật, tôi rất cô đơn.

1378 弱気(よわき)〈な〉 名 ナ形
weakness/hesitance, timidness / 软弱，怯弱 / sự yếu đuối, nhát gan
いつもは強気(つよき)な彼(かれ)が、今日(きょう)はなぜか弱気(よわき)だ。(ナ形)
That aggressive man is acting timid today for some reason. / 一向很强势的他为何今天如此怯弱。/ Lúc nào cũng mạnh mẽ vậy mà không hiểu sao hôm nay lại yếu đuối.

↔ 強気(つよき)〈な〉

1379 落(お)ち込(こ)む 動
depressed / 消沉 / buồn bã, suy sụp
彼女(かのじょ)にふられて、落(お)ち込(こ)んでいる。
She dumped me so I'm depressed. / 被女友甩了，很消沉。/ Tôi bị bạn gái chia tay, nên buồn bã.

1380 失望(しつぼう)〈する〉 名
disappointment / 失望 / sự thất vọng
友達(ともだち)のひきょうなやり方(かた)に心(こころ)から失望(しつぼう)した。
I am truly disappointed with my friend's cowardly methods. / 对朋友卑鄙的做法，我从心底里感到失望。/ Tôi thật sự thất vọng với cách làm hèn hạ của bạn mình.

＋ 失望感(しつぼうかん) sense of disappointment / 失望感 / cảm giác thất vọng

1381 絶望〈する〉(ぜつぼう)

名 no hope / 绝望 / sự tuyệt vọng

何(なに)をやってもうまくいかない。人生(じんせい)に絶望(ぜつぼう)してしまいそうだ。

Nothing goes the way I want it to, no matter what I do. I feel like giving on life. / 我什么都做不好，快对人生绝望了。/ Làm gì cũng không suôn sẻ. Gần như tuyệt vọng với cuộc đời.

+ 絶望的(ぜつぼうてき)な hopeless / 绝望的 / một cách tuyệt vọng・絶望感(ぜつぼうかん) sense of hopelessness / 绝望感 / cảm giác tuyệt vọng

1382 傷(きず)つく

動 be hurt / 受伤 / tổn thương

弟(おとうと)は、すぐに傷(きず)つくタイプだ。

My younger brother is easily hurt. / 弟弟是那种很容易受伤的类型。/ Em trai tôi thuộc típ người dễ tổn thương.

+ (～を) 傷(きず)つける hurt (someone) / 伤害 / gây tổn thương (~)

1383 わずらわしい

イ形 a pain / 麻烦 / phiền phức, phiền toái

ときどき、人間関係(にんげんかんけい)がわずらわしくなる。

Sometimes I find human relations to be a pain. / 有时人际关系会变得很麻烦。/ Thỉnh thoảng, quan hệ con người trở nên phiền phức.

1384 うんざり〈する〉

副 sick of / 厌倦，厌烦 / chán ngán, ngán ngẩm

彼(かれ)の言(い)い訳(わけ)には、もううんざりだ。

I am sick of his excuses. / 我已经对他的借口厌烦了。/ Ngụy biện của anh ấy thật ngán ngẩm.

+ うざい pestering / 厌烦，烦 / phiền hà, phức tạp, ngán ngẩm

uzai is an informal term used by young people / "うざい" 是年轻人的说法 / うざい là cách nói chỉ của người trẻ

1385 戸惑(とまど)う

動 perplexed / 不知如何是好 / phân vân, băn khoăn

初(はじ)めての仕事(しごと)で戸惑(とまど)ってしまった。

I was perplexed during my first time on the job. / 因为是我的第一份工作，所以我不知如何是好 / Là công việc đầu tiên nên tôi cứ băn khoăn.

+ 戸惑(とまど)い perplexed / 困惑 / sự phân vân

1386 ためらう

動 reluctant / 犹豫 / do dự, lưỡng lự

街(まち)で部長(ぶちょう)に会(あ)ったが、声(こえ)をかけるのをためらった。

I saw the manager on the street but was reluctant to call out to him. / 我在街上遇到部长，但犹豫要不要打招呼。/ Tôi gặp trưởng phòng ở phố mà cứ do dự chuyện gọi hay không.

1387 申(もう)し訳(わけ)ない

イ形 feel bad, feel apologetic / 实在抱歉 / cảm thấy có lỗi, khó tha thứ

去年(きょねん)は帰国(きこく)せず、両親(りょうしん)には申(もう)し訳(わけ)ないことをした。

I feel bad toward my parents for not returning home last year. / 我去年没能回国，觉得很对不起父母。/ Năm ngoái tôi không về nước nên cảm thấy có lỗi với bố mẹ.

1388 □	すまない	長い間苦労をかけて、すまなかったね。(ながい あいだ くろう)
イ形	**sorry / 对不起，抱歉 / xin lỗi**	I'm sorry for making you go through all this trouble for so long. / 真是过意不去，让你吃了这么长时间的苦。/ Bắt anh phải lao động cực nhọc thời gian dài, xin lỗi nhé.
1389 □	仕方［が］ない (しかた)	私がうそをついたのだから、彼が怒っても仕方ない。(わたし かれ おこ しかた)
イ形	**cannot be helped / 没有办法 / đành chịu, không còn cách nào khác**	I lied, so it can't be helped that he is angry. / 是我撒了谎，他要生气也没有办法。/ Vì tôi nói dối nên anh ấy giận cũng đành chịu.

= しょうがない

1390 □	しまった	しまった！　宿題、忘れた！(しゅくだい わす)
感	**oh dear / 糟糕 / tiêu rồi, chết rồi, thôi rồi**	Oh dear! I forgot my homework! / 糟糕！我忘了作业了！/ Thôi rồi! Quên bài tập rồi!
1391 □	恐れる (おそ)	私は、いつも失敗を恐れている。(わたし しっぱい おそ)
動	**fear / 害怕，恐惧 / sợ, e sợ, khiếp sợ**	I am always afraid of failure. / 我一直都很害怕失败。/ Tôi luôn sợ thất bại.
1392 □	情けない (なさ)	テストで0点を取るなんて、情けない。(てん と なさ)
イ形	**pitiful / 无法同情的，可悲可叹的 / đáng buồn, đáng trách, tội nghiệp**	How pitiful to get a zero on the exam. / 考试竟然考了 0 分，真是太难为情了。/ Bài kiểm tra mà 0 điểm thì thật đáng trách.
1393 □	恥 (はじ)	駅の階段で転んで、恥をかいた。(えき かいだん ころ はじ)
名	**embarrassment / 耻辱，羞愧 / sự xấu hổ, mắc cỡ**	I was embarrassed for falling down the station stairs. / 在车站楼梯上摔倒了，真是丢脸。/ Tôi bị ngã ở cầu thang nhà ga, thật xấu hổ.
1394 □	別に（～ない）(べつ)	今、別に悩みはない。(いま べつ なや)
副	**not particularly / （没有）特别 / ngoài ra, (không có gì) đặc biệt**	I don't particularly have anything worrying me now. / 现在没有什么特别的烦恼。/ Bây giờ tôi không có trăn trở gì đặc biệt.

often used in negative sentences / 多用于否定 / Phần nhiều trong câu phủ định.

1395 □	構わない (かま)	あんな人に何を言われても、構わない。(ひと なに い かま)
連語	**do not care / 无所谓 / không sao, không bận tâm**	I don't about anything someone like that says. / 那样的人对我说什么我都无所谓。/ Bị người như thế nói gì cũng chẳng sao.

Section 4

プラスのイメージ

Positive Image / 积极印象 / Hình ảnh tích cực

1396 □ 副	はきはき〈する〉 clearly / 干脆，爽快 / quả quyết, sinh động, rõ ràng	生徒は先生の質問にはきはき答えた。 The student answered the teacher's question clearly. / 学生干脆利落地回答了老师的问题。/ Học trò trả lời câu hỏi của thầy / cô thật rõ ràng.
1397 □ ナ形	清潔な clean / 清洁 / sạch sẽ	このデパートはトイレを清潔に保っている。 The toilet of this department store is always clean. / 这个商场的洗手间一直保持得很干净。/ Trung tâm thương mại này giữ nhà vệ sinh sạch sẽ. ↔ 不潔な
1398 □ ナ形	客観的な objective / 客观的 / mang tính khách quan	社長の意見は、いつも客観的だ。 The president's opinion is always objective. / 社长的意见一直很客观。/ Ý kiến của giám đốc luôn mang tính khách quan. ↔ 主観的な
1399 □ ナ形	冷静な calm / 冷静的 / điềm tĩnh, bình tĩnh	彼女は何があっても、冷静に対応する。 She always responds calmly whatever happens. / 她无论发生什么都冷静地应对。/ Dù có chuyện gì, cô ấy cũng bình tĩnh ứng phó.
1400 □ ナ形	もっともな understandable / 理所当然的 / đương nhiên, đúng đắn, có lý	彼女が怒るのはもっともだと思う。 It is understandable that she gets angry. / 我认为她生气也是理所当然的。/ Tôi nghĩ cô ấy tức giận là đúng rồi.
1401 □ 名	謙そん〈する〉 humble / 谦逊 / sự khiêm tốn, khiêm nhường	日本には謙そんの文化がある。 Japan has a culture of being humble. / 日本有自谦的文化。/ Nhật Bản có văn hóa khiêm nhường
1402 □ イ形	若々しい young / 年轻 / trẻ trung, đầy sức sống	私の祖母は外見も気持ちも若々しい。 My grandmother looks and feels young. / 我祖母不论外表还是心态都很年轻。/ Bà tôi trẻ trung cả về bề ngoài lẫn tinh thần.
1403 □ ナ形	ユニークな unique / 独特的 / duy nhất, độc đáo	ユニークな建築物を見るのが好きだ。 I like to see unique architecture. / 我喜欢看独特的建筑物。/ Tôi thích ngắm những công trình kiến trúc độc đáo.
1404 □ 名	唯一 only / 唯一 / sự duy nhất	彼は唯一信頼できる人だ。 He is the only person I trust. / 他是唯一可以信赖的人。/ Anh ấy là người duy nhất có thể tin cậy được.

1405 □ 名	洗練〈する〉 せんれん	彼の小説は文章が洗練されている。 かれ しょうせつ ぶんしょう せんれん
	finess / 千锤百炼，考究 / vẻ lịch sự, tinh tế	His sentences in his novel have finess. / 他的小说遣词造句十分讲究。/ Câu văn trong tiểu thuyết của anh ấy được làm cho tinh tế.
1406 □ 名	品 ひん	彼女の言葉づかいは、とても品がある。 かのじょ ことば ひん
	elegance / 品位 / phẩm chất, phẩm giá	Her words are very elegant. / 她的措辞很有品味。/ Cách sử dụng ngôn từ của cô ấy rất quý phái

➕ 品格 ひんかく dignity / 品格，品质 / phẩm cách・上品な じょうひん in good taste / 高雅，上等 / tốt, lịch thiệp, tao nhã・下品な げひん in bad taste / 下流，下等 / kém chất lượng, tầm thường, thấp kém

1407 □ 副	広々［と］〈する〉 ひろびろ	広々としたキッチンは、とても使いやすい。 ひろびろ つか
	spacious / 宽敞，广阔 / rộng lớn, rộng rãi	A spacious kitchen is easy to use. / 宽敞的厨房用起来很方便。/ Căn bếp rộng rãi rất dễ sử dụng.
1408 □ ナ形 副	ふわふわ〈な／する〉	このパンはふわふわしていて、おいしそうだ。(副)
	soft, spongy/softly / 蓬松柔软 / mềm mại, êm ái	This bread is soft and looks tasty. / 这个面包很松软，看起来很好吃。/ Cái bánh mì này xốp mềm, trông thật ngon.
1409 □ 副 連体	断然 だんぜん	私は断然こっちの絵が好きだ。(副) わたし だんぜん え す
	definitely/definitely / 断然，绝对 / rõ ràng, hoàn toàn	I definitely prefer this drawing. / 我绝对是喜欢这幅画的。/ Tôi hoàn toàn thích bức tranh này.
1410 □ ナ形	結構な けっこう	①結構な物を、ありがとうございました。 けっこう もの ②十分いただいたので、もう結構です。 じゅうぶん けっこう
	nice/fine / 完美的，漂亮的 / 足够 / tốt, đủ, được	① Thank you for this nice gift. ② I've had enough, I'm fine now. / ①这么好的东西，真是谢谢。②我已经拿了很多了，真的够了。/ ① Cám ơn món đồ rất tốt. ② Tôi đã nhận đủ rồi, được rồi ạ.

👉 ① very good ② need no more / ①很好②再多就不要了 / ① Vô cùng tốt ② Không cần hơn nữa

1411 □ ナ形	見事な みごと	彼の作品は、いつも見事だ。 かれ さくひん みごと
	stunning / 卓越，精彩 / đẹp, tuyệt vời	His works are always stunning. / 他的作品总是很出彩。/ Tác phẩm của anh ấy luôn tuyệt vời.
1412 □ ナ形	貴重な きちょう	留学は、とても貴重な経験だ。 りゅうがく きちょう けいけん
	precious / 贵重，宝贵 / quý giá, quý trọng	Studying abroad is a precious experience. / 留学是很宝贵的经验。/ Du học là kinh nghiệm rất quý giá.

➕ 貴重品 きちょうひん valuables / 贵重物品 / đồ quý giá

1413 □ 名 ナ形	質素〈な〉 しっそ	無駄のない、質素な生活を送っている。(ナ形) むだ しっそ せいかつ おく
	frugality/frugal / 朴素，简朴 / sự giản dị , giản dị	I live a frugal life with no waste. / 过着不铺张浪费的简朴生活。/ Sống cuộc sống giản dị không hoang phí.

⇔ 贅沢〈な〉

1414 ナ形	同様な (どうよう) same as / 同样，一样 / tương tự	今までと同様に、これからもよろしくお願いします。 I'm looking forward to working with you the same way as before. / 往后也一如既往，请多多关照。/ Trong tương lai, tôi cũng xin được giúp đỡ như từ trước đến nay.

これも覚えよう！ ㉛

接辞：否定③ Affix: Negation / 词缀：否定 / Phụ tố: Phủ định

• **非～（～ではない）**

非日常 (ひにちじょう) extraordinary / 非日常 / Bất thường, không như thường nhật

非公開 (ひこうかい) undisclosed / 非公开 / Không công khai

非公式 (ひこうしき) unofficial / 非正式 / Không chính thức

非常識 (ひじょうしき) lack of common sense / 没有常识，荒唐 / Thiếu kiến thức phổ thông

非科学 (ひかがく) unscientific / 非科学 / Không khoa học

• **未～（まだ～ない）**

未使用 (みしよう) unused / 未使用 / Chưa sử dụng

未確認 (みかくにん) unidentified / 未确认 / Chưa kiểm tra, chưa xác nhận

未解決 (みかいけつ) unsolved / 未解决 / Chưa giải quyết

未開発 (みかいはつ) undeveloped / 未开发 / Chưa phát triển

未完成 (みかんせい) incomplete / 未完成 / Chưa hoàn thành

未経験 (みけいけん) unexperienced / 无经验 / Chưa trải qua

未成年 (みせいねん) underaged / 未成年 / Vị thành niên, chưa trưởng thành

Section 5
マイナスのイメージ

Negative Image / 消极印象 / Hình ảnh tiêu cực

1415 □	憎らしい（にくらしい）	兄は、いつも憎らしいことを言う。（あに・にく・い）
イ形	exasperating, hateful / 可憎 / đáng ghét, ghê tởm	My elder brother always says something annoying. / 哥哥总是说些让人讨厌的话。/ Anh tôi luôn nói những chuyện đáng ghét.
1416 □	強引な（ごういん）	兄の友人に強引に食事に誘われた。（あに・ゆうじん・ごういん・しょくじ・さそ）
ナ形	forceful / 强硬 / ép buộc	My elder brother's friend forced me to join for dinner. / 被哥哥的朋友硬拉去吃饭了。/ Tôi bị bạn của anh trai ép đi dùng bữa.
1417 □	うっとうしい	①梅雨に入って、うっとうしい天気が続く。（つゆ・はい・てんき・つづ） ②彼はおしゃべりで、うっとうしい。（かれ）
イ形	dreary/annoying / 沉闷 / 啰嗦，烦 / u ám, buồn rầu, ủ dột, nhặng xị, ồn ào	① Dreary weather continues as we enter the rainy season. ② He is talkative and annoying. / ①进入梅雨季节，每天都是阴郁的天气。②他很爱说话，非常烦人。/ ① Vào mùa mưa, thời tiết cứ u ám kéo dài. ② Anh ấy nói nhiều, thật nhặng xị.

👉 ① the weather is bad ② annoying and obstructive / ①天气不好②啰嗦碍事 / ① Thời tiết không đẹp ② Phiền toái, ồn ào

1418 □	やっかい〈な〉	やっかいな仕事を引き受けてしまった。(ナ形)（しごと・ひ・う）
名 ナ形	troublesome/troublesome / 麻烦，恼人 / sự phiền phức ; rắc rối	I accepted a troublesome task. / 我接了个棘手的工作。/ Tôi lỡ nhận công việc phiền phức.
1419 □	とんでもない	①彼は非常識で、とんでもないやつだ。（かれ・ひじょうしき） ②A「合格できたのは先生のおかげです。」（ごうかく・せんせい） B「とんでもない。Aさんの努力の結果ですよ。」（どりょく・けっか）
イ形	unbelievable/not at all / 骇人听闻 / 哪儿的话 / quá đángkhông thể nào, không dám đâu	① He has no common sense and is an unbelievable person. ② A: I was able to pass the test because of you, teacher. B: Not at all. It is a result of your effort. / ①他是个毫无常识，不像话的家伙。②A："我能合格，多亏了老师。" B："哪里的话，都是你自己努力的结果。" / ① Anh ấy là người thiếu nhận thức, thật quá đáng. ② A: Em thi đậu là nhờ thầy / cô. B: Không đâu. Đó là kết quả nỗ lực của A đấy

👉 ① so bad that it's unthinkable ② denying someone else's words as a form of humility / ①过分得无法想像②否定对方的说法，表示谦虚 / ① Tệ đến mức bình thường không thể nào nghĩ được ② Phủ định, khiêm nhường trước lời nói của người kia

1420 □	安易な（あんい）	安易に人を信じて、だまされてしまった。（あんい・ひと・しん）
ナ形	easy / 轻易 / dễ dàng, đơn giản	I trusted people too easily and ended up being fooled. / 亲信了别人，被骗了。/ Tôi dễ dàng tin người nên đã bị lừa.

1421 □ ナ形	無難な（ぶなん） safe, passable / 说得过去，无可非议 / an toàn, vừa phải, chấp nhận được	彼（かれ）の答（こた）えは、いつも無難（ぶなん）だ。 His answers are always passable. / 他的回答总是让人无可非议。/ Câu trả lời của anh ta luôn chấp nhận được.
1422 □ ナ形	平凡な（へいぼん） ordinary / 平凡的 / bình thường, bình lặng	平凡（へいぼん）な毎日（まいにち）で退屈（たいくつ）だ。 It's boring as the days are ordinary. / 过着平凡的日子，每天都很无聊。/ Mỗi ngày bình lặng thật buồn tẻ. ↔ 非凡（ひぼん）な
1423 □ イ形	みっともない miserable / 不像样，不体面 / thiếu lịch sự, không đứng đắn, hổ thẹn	そんなみっともない服装（ふくそう）で出（で）かけるの？ Do you plan on going out in such miserable clothes? / 你真要穿成这副模样出去吗？ / Đi ra ngoài với bộ quần áo không đứng đắn như vậy sao?
1424 □ イ形	見苦しい（みぐる） ugly / 难看，丢脸 / xấu, khó coi	彼（かれ）は負（ま）けたくせに怒（おこ）っている。見苦（みぐる）しい。 He lost the fight but is angry. It looks ugly. / 他输了还发火。真丢脸。/ Anh ấy đã thua mà còn tức giận. Thật khó coi.
1425 □ イ形	みにくい ugly / 难看，丑陋 / xấu xí, khó coi	兄弟（きょうだい）だから、お金（かね）のことでみにくい争（あらそ）いをしたくない。 We're brothers, so I don't want to be involved in an ugly argument about money. / 因为是兄弟，所以不想为了钱而斗得难看。/ Vì là anh em nên tôi không muốn vì chuyện tiền bạc mà tranh chấp khó coi.
1426 □ ナ形	ぼろぼろな falling apart / 破破烂烂 / rách nát, tả tơi	このコートはぼろぼろだ。もう捨（す）てよう。 The coat is falling apart. I should throw it away. / 这件大衣破破烂烂的，丢掉吧。/ Cái áo choàng này đã rách nát rồi. Vứt thôi.
1427 □ ナ形	あわれな pitiful / 悲哀的 / đáng thương	あわれな子（こ）どもの話（はなし）を聞（き）き、涙（なみだ）が出（で）た。 Hearing the story about a poor child made me cry. / 我听着一个可怜孩子的故事，眼泪掉了下来。/ Nghe câu chuyện về đứa bé đáng thương, tôi chảy nước mắt.
1428 □ イ形	乏しい（とぼ） lacking / 缺乏 / thiếu thốn, hạn hẹp, keo kiệt, bần cùng	彼（かれ）は想像力（そうぞうりょく）が乏（とぼ）しく、話（はな）していてもつまらない。 He lacks imagination and is not fun talking to. / 他缺乏想象力，说话很是无趣。/ Anh ấy nghèo trí tưởng tượng, có nói chuyện cũng chán. ↔ 豊（ゆた）かな

1429 □ 名 ナ形	中途半端〈な〉(ちゅうとはんぱ) **halfway/half-hearted / 半途而废 / nửa chừng, nửa vời**	弟は、することがいつも中途半端だ。(ナ形) Everything my younger brother does is half-hearted. / 弟弟做什么都总是半途而废。/ Em trai tôi luôn làm gì cũng nửa chừng.
1430 □ 副	まごまご〈する〉 **flustered / 慌张，不知所措 / lúng túng, hoang mang, loay hoay**	ＡＴＭの操作がわからず、まごまごした。 I didn't know how to operate the ATM and was flustered. / 我不会操作 ATM 机，一时不知所措。/ Tôi loay hoay, không biết cách thao tác máy ATM.
1431 □ 名	矛盾〈する〉(むじゅん) **contradiction / 矛盾，相左 / mâu thuẫn, trái ngược**	彼の話は矛盾している。 His story doesn't make sense. / 他的话很矛盾。/ Câu chuyện của anh ấy thật mâu thuẫn.
1432 □ 副	にやにや〈する〉 **grinning / 嗤笑 / cười giả tạo, màu mè**	人を見て、にやにやするのはやめなさい。 Stop grinning when you look at someone. / 不要见到人就笑眯眯的。/ Hãy ngưng ngay cái trò nhìn người ta rồi cười giả tạo đi.
1433 □ 名 ナ形	でこぼこ〈な／する〉 **bump/bumpy / 凹凸不平 / lồi lõm, gập gềnh**	学校の前の道はでこぼこだ。(ナ形) The road in front of the school is bumpy. / 学校前面的道路凹凸不平。/ Con đường trước trường gập ghềnh.

also written "凸凹" / 也写作"凸凹" / Cũng có cách viết "凸凹"

1434 □ 名	それなり **passable / 相应的，恰如其分 / trong chừng mực nào đó**	このドラマは評判が悪いが、それなりに面白い。 The drama isn't popular, but I find it reasonably interesting. / 这部电视剧虽然评价不好，但还是蛮有意思的。/ Bộ phim truyền hình này tuy bị đánh giá thấp nhưng trong chừng mực nào đó thì thú vị.

N2

Chapter 12

間違えやすい表現

まちが　ひょうげん

Frequently Mistaken Expressions / 容易误用的表达 / Cách nói dễ nhầm lẫn

Section 1

慣用句①気・心・胸

かんようく　き　こころ　むね

Idioms (1) Energy, Heart, Mind / 惯用语①気·心·胸 / Thành ngữ (1) Tính khí - Tâm hồn -Tâm trạng

1435 □

気が早い (きがはやい)	旅行は来週なのに、もう準備するなんて気が早い。(りょこう・らいしゅう・じゅんび・きがはやい)
hasty / 性急 / nôn nóng	The trip is next week so you're being too hasty for starting preparations. / 下周才去旅行，现在就做准备也太着急了吧。/ Tuần sau mới đi du lịch mà bây giờ đã chuẩn bị rồi thì đúng là nôn nóng.

➕ せっかち〈な〉 impatient, restless / 性急 / nôn nóng, lanh chanh

1436 □

気が重い (きがおもい)	仕事でミスした翌朝は、とても気が重い。(しごと・よくあさ・きがおもい)
dispirited, depressed / 心情沉重 / cảm thấy chán nản, nặng nề	The morning after making a mistake at work makes me feel very depressed. / 工作上犯了错，第二天早上心情很沉重。/ Buổi sáng sau khi mắc sai lầm trong công việc thì lòng thật nặng nề.

1437 □

気が合う (きがあう)	鈴木さんとは、とても気が合う。(すずき・きがあう)
get along well / 合得来 / hợp tính	I get along very well with Mr. Suzuki. / 我和铃木很合得来。/ Tôi rất hợp tính với anh / chị Suzuki.

➕ 馬が合う (うまがあう) get along well / 气味相投，投缘 / hợp nhau

1438 □

気が利く (きがきく)	木村さんは、よく気が利く人だ。(きむら・きがきく・ひと)
thoughtfuls / 善于察言观色 / chu đáo, quan tâm, ân cần	Mr. Kimura is a very thoughtful person. / 木村很善于察言观色。/ Anh / chị Kimura là người rất ân cần.

1439 □

気がつく (きがつく)	①駅に着いてから、忘れ物に気がついた。(えき・つ・わすれもの・き) ②彼女は、よく気がつく人だ。(かのじょ・き・ひと)
notice/attentive / 意识到 / 仔细周到 / nhận thấy, nhớ ra, để ý , chu đáo	① I noticed that I forgot something when I arrived at the station. ② She is a very attentive person. / ①到了车站，意识到忘了东西。②她是个无微不至的人。/ ① Sau khi đến nhà ga, tôi mới nhận ra để quên đồ. ② Cô ấy là người rất chu đáo

👉 ① learning something that one did not know until then ② be attentive to details / ①知道了不知道的事②注意细节 / ① Biết việc cho đến giờ đã không biết ② Để ý những việc nhỏ, chi tiết

1440 □

気が強い (きがつよい)	妹は気が強いが、そんなところも可愛いと思う。(いもうと・きがつよい・かわいい・おも)
aggressive / 好强，倔强 / cá tính, mạnh mẽ	My little sister is very aggressive, but I find that cute too. / 妹妹虽然好强，但这点我也觉得很可爱。/ Em gái tôi mạnh mẽ nhưng tôi nghĩ điểm đó cũng đáng yêu.

↔ 気が弱い (きがよわい)

1441 □	気(き)が小(ちい)さい	彼(かれ)は気(き)が小(ちい)さいのに、大(おお)きなことを言(い)う。
	timid / 小心眼，气量小 / nhỏ nhen, hẹp bụng	He is timid but can talk big. / 他心眼那么小却说大话。/ Anh ấy tính tình nhỏ nhen mà toàn nói chuyện to tát.
1442 □	気(き)を遣(つか)う	そんなに気(き)を遣(つか)わないでください。
	worry about / 担心，费心 / giữ ý, lo lắng	Don't worry about it, please. / 请不要那么费心。/ Xin đừng giữ ý như thế.
1443 □	気(き)が進(すす)まない	飲(の)み会(かい)に誘(さそ)われたが、あまり気(き)が進(すす)まない。
	don't feel up to it / 不起劲 / không hứng thú	I was invited to a drinking party but I don't feel up to it. / 虽被叫去喝酒，但没什么兴致。/ Tôi được mời đi ăn uống nhưng không hứng thú lắm.
1444 □	気(き)にかかる	昨日(きのう)のテストの結果(けっか)が気(き)にかかる。
	worry about / 挂念 / lo lắng	I am worried about the results of yesterday's test. / 对昨天考试的结果一直放不下心。/ Tôi lo lắng về kết quả bài kiểm tra hôm qua.

➕ (〜を)気(き)にかける have in one's mind / 放在心上 / lo lắng, quan tâm

1445 □	気(き)にくわない	あの人(ひと)の態度(たいど)は気(き)にくわない。
	dislike, unable to stomach / 反感 / bất mãn, không ưa	I don't like his attitude. / 那个人的态度真让人反感。/ Thái độ của người đó thật không ưa.
1446 □	心(こころ)が通(かよ)う	二人(ふたり)は言葉(ことば)はわからなくても、心(こころ)が通(かよ)っている。
	undertand each other / 心灵相通 / thấu hiểu nhau	The two don't understand the language but are communicating by heart. / 两个人就算语言不通，也能心意相通。/ Hai người tuy ngôn ngữ không hiểu nhưng tâm hồn thì thấu hiểu nhau.
1447 □	心(こころ)が狭(せま)い	人(ひと)のミスが許(ゆる)せないなんて、心(こころ)が狭(せま)い人(ひと)だ。
	petty-minded / 心胸狭隘 / hẹp lòng, hẹp hòi	He is so petty-minded that he can't forgive people's mistakes. / 不能原谅别人的过失，真是心胸狭隘的人。/ Không thể tha thứ cho lỗi lầm của người khác thật là người hẹp hòi.

↔ 心(こころ)が広(ひろ)い

1448 □	心(こころ)が動(うご)く	試験(しけん)の前日(ぜんじつ)に飲(の)み会(かい)に誘(さそ)われ、心(こころ)が動(うご)いた。
	moved, tempted / 动心，动摇 / dao động, xáo động	I was tempted when they invited me for drinks on the day before the exam. / 考试前一天有人叫我去喝酒，我有点动心。/ Tôi bị dao động khi được mời đi ăn uống trước ngày thi.

1449 □	心を配る (こころ くば)	彼女は常に周囲に<u>心を配って</u>いる。(かのじょ つね しゅうい こころ くば)
	be considerate / 关心，注意 / quan tâm, chu đáo	She is always considerate of the people around her. / 她总是关心着身边的事。/ Cô ấy thường quan tâm đến chung quanh.
		➕ 心配り (こころくば) consideration / 关怀，照料 / sự quan tâm, chu đáo
1450 □	心を引かれる (こころ ひ)	日本に来て、茶道に<u>心を引かれた</u>。(にほん き さどう こころ ひ)
	attracted / 吸引人 / bị thu hút	I was attracted to tea ceremony upon arriving to Japan. / 来日本后，我迷上了茶道。/ Đến Nhật, tôi bị thu hút bởi trà đạo.
1451 □	心を許す (こころ ゆる)	佐藤さんは田中さんにだけ<u>心を許して</u>いる。(さとう たなか こころ ゆる)
	trust / 没有戒心 / tin tưởng, thật lòng	Mr. Sato trusts only Mr. Tanaka. / 佐藤只对田中没有戒心。/ Anh / chị Sato thật lòng tin tưởng mỗi anh / chị Tanaka.
1452 □	胸が痛む (むね いた)	ニュースで事件を知って、<u>胸が痛んだ</u>。(じけん し むね いた)
	pained / 心痛 / đau lòng, xót xa	I was pained when I heard the about incident over the news. / 看新闻知道了这个事件，我感到很心痛。/ Qua tin tức tôi biết về vụ án và thấy thật đau lòng.
1453 □	胸が一杯になる (むね いっぱい)	両親のやさしい言葉に<u>胸が一杯になった</u>。(りょうしん ことば むね いっぱい)
	have a lump in one's throat / 感动 / xúc động, cảm xúc dâng trào	I had a lump in my throat after hearing my parents' kind words. / 父母温情的话语让我很感动。/ Tôi trở nên xúc động trước những lời nói yêu thương của bố mẹ.
1454 □	胸をはずませる (むね)	留学生活を前に<u>胸をはずませて</u>いる。(りゅうがくせいかつ まえ むね)
	heart leaps / 满心欢喜，激动 / hồi hộp, háo hức, lòng rộn ràng	My heart is leaping with joy at being able to studying abroad. / 留学生活即将开始，我内心很激动。/ Lòng tôi rộn ràng trước cuộc sống du học.

Section 2

慣用句②頭・顔

かんようく　あたま　かお

Idioms (2) Head, Face / 惯用语②头部・脸部 / Thành ngữ (2) Đầu - Mặt

1455	頭が痛い（あたま いた） **troubled / 头疼 / lo lắng, bận tâm, đau đầu**	日本は生活費が高いので、頭が痛い。 （にほん せいかつひ たか あたま いた） I'm troubled over Japan's expensive living expenses. / 日本的生活费很高昂，令我头疼。/ Tôi đau đầu vì chi phí sinh hoạt đắt đỏ ở Nhật.
1456	頭が固い（あたま かた） **stubborn / 顽固 / cứng đầu, bảo thủ**	父は頭が固くて、話し合いができない。 （ちち あたま かた はな あ） My father is stubborn, so I can't talk with him. / 爸爸很固执，没有办法交流。/ Cha tôi đầu óc bảo thủ, không thể nào nói chuyện.
1457	頭にくる（あたま） **be mad / 生气，恼怒 / bực mình, phát cáu, xóc óc**	あの人の態度には本当に頭にくる。 （ひと たいど ほんとう あたま） His attitude really makes me mad. / 那个人的态度真让人生气。/ Thật sự phát cáu với thái độ của người đó.
1458	頭が下がる（あたま さ） **respect, humbled / 佩服 / khâm phục, kính trọng, cúi đầu**	彼女の努力には頭が下がる。 （かのじょ どりょく あたま さ） I respect all the effort she's making. / 对她的努力佩服得五体投地。/ Tôi cúi đầu trước những nỗ lực của cô ấy.
1459	顔が広い（かお ひろ） **know a lot of people / 人脉广 / xã giao, quen biết rộng**	社長は顔が広くて、有名人の知り合いも多い。 （しゃちょう かお ひろ ゆうめいじん し あ おお） The president knows a lot of people, including celebrities. / 社长的人脉很广，认识很多有名的人。/ Giám đốc quen biết rộng, người quen nổi tiếng cũng nhiều.
1460	顔を出す（かお だ） **drop by / 露脸 / xuất hiện, ló mặt, có mặt**	忙しいが、飲み会に少しだけ顔を出した。 （いそが の かい すこ かお だ） I was busy, but dropped by the drinking party briefly. / 虽然很忙，我还是在酒会上露了下脸。/ Bận bịu nên tôi chỉ có mặt một chút ở buổi ăn uống.
1461	目がない（め） **love, addicted to / 盲目 / mê, ghiền, không có mắt**	私は甘い物に目がない。 （わたし あま もの め） I love sweets. / 我对甜食毫无抵抗能力。/ Tôi ghiền đồ ngọt.
1462	目が離せない（め はな） **can't take one's eyes off of, can't stop watching / 移不开眼 / không thể rời mắt**	好きなドラマから目が離せない。 （す め はな） I can't stop watching my favorite drama. / 无法从喜欢的电视剧移开眼。/ Tôi không thể rời mắt khỏi bộ phim truyền hình ưa thích.

Section 2

1463 □	目が回る (め まわ)	毎日残業で目が回る忙しさだ。 (まいにちざんぎょう め まわ いそが)
	feel giddy, head is spinning / 头晕眼花，非常忙 / hoa mắt, tối mắt tối mũi	I have been working overtime every night, and I'm so busy my head is spinning. / 每天加班，忙得团团转。/ Ngày nào cũng làm ngoài giờ, bận hoa cả mắt.
1464 □	目に浮かぶ (め う)	寂しくなると、国の両親の顔が目に浮かぶ。 (さび くに りょうしん かお め う)
	imagine, think of / 浮现在眼前 / hiện lên trước mắt, nhớ đến	When I'm lonely, I think of my parents' faces back home. / 孤单时，眼前会浮现出父母的脸庞。/ Khi buồn bã, gương mặt bố mẹ ở trong nước hiện lên trước mắt.
1465 □	目にする (め)	駅のホームで乗客同士のけんかを目にした。 (えき じょうきゃくどうし め)
	witness / 看到 / chứng kiến, bắt gặp	I witnessed passengers fighting with each other on the station platform. / 我在车站站台上看到了乘客吵架。/ Ở sân ga, tôi bắt gặp những người cùng là hành khách cãi nhau.

☞ this means seeing something by chance / 偶然看到的意思 / Có nghĩa tình cờ thấy

1466 □	目に付く (め つ)	目に付くところにポスターを貼ろう。 (め つ は)
	notice / 显眼 / đúng tầm nhìn, đúng tầm mắt	Let's put up the poster where it can be seen. / 把海报贴在显眼的地方吧。/ Hãy dán áp phích đúng tầm mắt.
1467 □	目を疑う (め うたが)	バッグの値段があまりに高くて、目を疑った。 (ねだん たか め うたが)
	unable to believe / 不相信自己的眼睛 / không tin vào mắt mình	The bag was so expensive that I couldn't believe what I saw. / 这个包的价格高得离谱，我不敢相信我的眼睛。/ Giá của cái túi đắt đến nỗi tôi không tin vào mắt mình.
1468 □	目を向ける (め む)	日本ばかりではなく、世界の出来事にも目を向けよう。 (にほん せかい できごと め む)
	be aware, be concious of / 关注 / hướng tầm mắt	Let's be conscious about not only what is going on in Japan, but about what is happening around the world as well. / 不仅是日本，我们也关注一下世界上其他地方发生的事情吧。/ Không chỉ Nhật mà hãy hướng tầm mắt đến cả những sự kiện trên thế giới.
1469 □	目を通す (め とお)	会議の資料に、ざっと目を通す。 (かいぎ しりょう め とお)
	glance / 过目，浏览 / nhìn qua, xem qua, lướt mắt	I took a glance at the meeting reference notes. / 大致过目会议的资料。/ Xem lướt qua tài liệu cuộc họp.
1470 □	耳が痛い (みみ いた)	母から最近の成績について言われ、耳が痛い。 (はは さいきん せいせき みみ いた)
	be painfully true / 听来刺耳 / xấu hổ, ngại, rát tai	My mother's remarks about my recent grades were painfully true. / 妈妈老说最近成绩的事情，我都听烦了。/ Bị mẹ nói về thành tích gần đây, tôi đến rát cả tai.

1471	耳が遠い (みみ とお) **hard of hearing / 耳背 / lãng tai**	祖父は最近少し耳が遠くなった。(そふ さいきんすこ みみ とお) My grandfather is becoming hard of hearing. / 祖父最近开始有点耳背了。/ Gần đây ông tôi trở nên lãng tai.
1472	耳にする (みみ) **hear / 听到 / nghe, đến tai**	彼について悪いうわさを耳にした。(かれ わる みみ) I heard bad rumours about him. / 听到了关于他的不好的传言。/ Tiếng đồn không hay về anh ấy đã đến tai tôi.

this means hearing something by chance / 偶然听到的意思 / Có nghĩa tình cờ nghe

1473	耳を傾ける (みみ かたむ) **listen / 倾听 / lắng tai nghe**	みんなが先生の話に耳を傾けた。(せんせい はなし みみ かたむ) Everyone listened to the teacher's story. / 大家都认真听老师说。/ Mọi người lắng tai nghe câu chuyện của thầy / cô.
1474	耳を疑う (みみ うたが) **doubt / 怀疑自己听到的 / không tin vào tai mình**	これまでにない大事件のニュースを聞いて、耳を疑った。(だいじけん き みみ うたが) I couldn't believe what I heard when I heard about the unprecedented news. / 在新闻上听了闻所未闻的大事件，真不敢相信自己的耳朵。/ Nghe tin tức về vụ án lớn chưa từng có lâu nay, tôi không tin vào tai mình.
1475	口がうまい (くち) **glib / 嘴甜，花言巧语 / khéo ăn nói, dẻo mồm dẻo miệng**	彼は口がうまいから、気をつけた方がいい。(かれ くち き ほう) He is glib, so be careful. / 他这个人花言巧语的，最好小心为妙。/ Anh ấy dẻo mồm dẻo miệng, nên cẩn thận thì hơn.
1476	口が堅い (くち かた) **able to keep a secret / 守口如瓶 / kín miệng**	親友は口が堅いので、何でも相談できる。(しんゆう くち かた なん そうだん) My friend is able to keep a secret, so I can confide anything in her. / 好朋友嘴很严，我什么都可以和他商量。/ Bạn thân tôi rất kín miệng nên có thể trao đổi bất kỳ chuyện gì.
1477	口が軽い (くち かる) **unable to keep a secret / 嘴快，说话轻率 / ba hoa, lắm mồm**	口が軽い人に秘密を話してはいけない。(くち かる ひと ひみつ はな) Don't share your secret with someone who can't keep a secret. / 不要把秘密告诉嘴不严的人。/ Không được nói chuyện bí mật với những người lắm mồm.
1478	口が重い (くち おも) **be incommunicative / 少言寡语 / lầm lì, ít nói**	彼は口が重いから、話が盛り上がらない。(かれ くち おも はなし も あ) He is a man of few words, so the conversation remains dull. / 他是个少言寡语的人，说话时活跃不了气氛。/ Anh ấy ít nói nên câu chuyện không được sôi nổi lắm.

1479 □ 口(くち)が滑(すべ)る

つい口(くち)が滑(すべ)って、友達(ともだち)の秘密(ひみつ)を話(はな)してしまった。

make a slip of the tongue / 失言，说走嘴 / thốt ra, lỡ lời

He told his friend's secret with the slip of his tongue. / 一不小心把朋友的秘密说出去了。/ Tôi lỡ buột miệng nói ra bí mật của người bạn.

➕ 口(くち)を滑(すべ)らす let something slip / 说漏嘴 / buột miệng, lỡ lời

1480 □ 口(くち)が悪(わる)い

あの人(ひと)は口(くち)が悪(わる)いし、不親切(ふしんせつ)だ。

have a dirty mouth / 说话刻薄 / độc mồm độc miệng

He has a dirty mouth and is a mean person. / 那个人说话刻薄，不友善。/ Người đó độc mồm độc miệng và không tử tế.

1481 □ 口(くち)にする

①自分(じぶん)の意見(いけん)は、よく考(かんが)えてから口(くち)にしなさい。

②どんな料理(りょうり)も口(くち)にしてみなければ、おいしいかどうかわからない。

mention/eat / 说出 / 尝 / đưa ý kiến, ăn

① Give your opinion after thinking it through carefully.
② You can't tell if a dish is good or bad until you've had it. / ①把自己意见好好考虑以后再说出来。②不论什么料理不尝一下的话不知道好吃不好吃。/ ① Hãy suy nghĩ kỹ rồi hẵng nói ra ý kiến của mình. ② Dù là món ăn gì đi nữa mà nếu không ăn thử thì không thể biết ngon hay không.

☞ ① giving one's own opinion ② eat / ①说自己的意见②吃 / ① Nói ý kiến của mình ② Ăn

1482 □ 口(くち)に合(あ)う

日本料理(にほんりょうり)は外国(がいこく)からの客(きゃく)の口(くち)に合(あ)ったようだ。

suit someone's taste / 合口味 / hợp khẩu vị

Japanese food seems to suit the customers from overseas. / 日本料理似乎很合外国客人的口味。/ Hình như món ăn Nhật hợp khẩu vị khách nước ngoài.

↔ 口(くち)に合(あ)わない

1483 □ 口(くち)を出(だ)す

あなたは、この件(けん)に口(くち)を出(だ)さないでください。

have a say, stick one's nose into / 说出口 / chen vào, dính vào, cắt ngang

Please do not stick your nose into this case. / 你不要把这件事情说出去。/ Bạn đừng dính vào vụ này.

Section 3

慣用句(かんようく)③体(からだ)

Idioms (3) Body / 惯用语③身体部位 / Thành ngữ (3) Cơ thể

1484	手(て)がふさがる busy / 腾不出手来，没空闲 / bận rộn	今(いま)手(て)がふさがっているので、後(あと)でお手伝(てつだ)いします。 I'm busy now so I'll help you later. / 我现在腾不出手来，等一会儿来帮你。/ Bây giờ tôi đang bận, để tí nữa tôi sẽ giúp.
1485	手(て)が空(あ)く free / 有空 / rảnh tay	手(て)が空(あ)いたので、何(なに)かお手伝(てつだ)いしましょうか。 I'm free now so can I help you? / 我有空了，我帮你做点什么吧。/ Tôi đang rảnh tay, tôi giúp bạn làm cái gì đó nhé.
1486	手(て)がかかる take a lot of dealing with / 费事 / khó, tốn công	これは、ずいぶん手(て)がかかる仕事(しごと)だ。 This requires a lot of work. / 这是个相当麻烦的工作。/ Đây là công việc khá tốn công.
1487	手(て)が離(はな)せない be in the middle of something / 抽不开身 / đang dở tay, không thể rời	すみません。今(いま)、手(て)が離(はな)せないんですが…。 Sorry, I'm in the middle of something. / 对不起。现在我抽不开身……/ Xin lỗi. Bây giờ tôi đang dở tay nên…
1488	手(て)に入(い)れる acquire / 入手，得到 / đạt được, có được	ずっと欲(ほ)しかったバッグを手(て)に入(い)れた。 I acquired the bag that I really wanted. / 入手了一个一直想要的包。/ Tôi đã có được cái túi mong mỏi lâu nay.
1489	手(て)にする take hold of, get hold of / 弄到手，拿在手里 / 获得 / cầm lên, giành được, đạt được	①デパートの売(う)り場(ば)で、きれいなピアスを手(て)にした。 ②サッカーの大会(たいかい)で優勝(ゆうしょう)を手(て)にした。 ① I got a hold of a beautiful pierced earring at the department store corner. ② We clinched our victory in the soccer tournament. / ①我在商场专柜买到了漂亮的耳环。②在足球比赛上获胜了。/ ① Ở quầy bán trong trung tâm thương mại, tôi cầm đôi bông tay đẹp lên. ② Chúng tôi đã giành được chức vô địch ở giải bóng đá.
1490	手(て)につかない can't concentrate / 心不在焉 / không hứng thú, không tập trung	彼女(かのじょ)のことを思(おも)うと、勉強(べんきょう)が手(て)につかない。 I can't study when I think of her. / 一想到她，我就没心思学习了。/ Cứ nghĩ đến cô ấy là tôi không tập trung học được.

Note to 1488: ➕ (～が) 手(て)に入(はい)る able to acquire / 得到 / có được

Note to 1489: 👍 ① hold in one's hand ② make things like an award one's own / ①弄到手②获胜，获奖 / ① Cầm trên tay ② Lấy được giải thưởng v.v. làm của mình

1491	手(て)をつける	おとといからゲームに夢中(むちゅう)で、宿題(しゅくだい)に手(て)をつけていない。
	start working on / 着手 / đụng tay đến	I have been playing the game like crazy since two days ago and haven't started doing my homework yet. / 前天开始一直沉迷于游戏，作业还没开始做。/ Từ hôm kia tôi say sưa chơi game mà không đụng tay đến bài tập.
1492	手(て)を貸(か)す	悪(わる)いけど、ちょっと手(て)を貸(か)してくれない？
	give a hand / 帮忙 / cho mượn đỡ một tay, giúp đỡ	Sorry, but can you give me a hand? / 不好意思，能帮我个忙吗？ / Xin lỗi nhưng có thể cho tôi mượn đỡ một tay một chút không?
1493	手(て)を休(やす)める	仕事(しごと)の手(て)を休(やす)めて、コーヒーを飲(の)んだ。
	take a break / 休息，暂停 / nghỉ tay	I took a break from work and had some coffee. / 把工作放下，去喝了杯咖啡。/ Nghỉ tay làm việc, uống cà phê.
1494	手(て)を抜(ぬ)く	手(て)を抜(ぬ)かないで、最後(さいご)まで努力(どりょく)しなさい。
	be lazy, slack / 松懈，偷工减料 / chiếu lệ, qua loa, nơi tay	Don't get lazy, work hard until the end. / 不要松懈，坚持努力到最后。/ Đừng có qua loa, hãy nỗ lực đến cùng.
1495	腕(うで)がいい	彼(かれ)は料理(りょうり)の腕(うで)がいい。
	skillful / 手艺好 / có tay nghề, giỏi	He is good at cooking. / 他做菜手艺很好。/ Anh ấy có tay nghề nấu ăn giỏi.
1496	腕(うで)を磨(みが)く	料理(りょうり)の腕(うで)を磨(みが)こうと、教室(きょうしつ)に通(かよ)っている。
	improve skills / 磨练手艺 / luyện tay nghề, nâng cao kỹ năng	I am attending classes to improve my cooking skills. / 我想提高做菜的手艺，所以在上烹饪课。/ Tôi đến lớp học để rèn luyện tay nghề nấu ăn.
1497	腕(うで)が上(あ)がる	いつの間(ま)にか料理(りょうり)の腕(うで)が上(あ)がった。
	skills have improved / 手艺增进 / tay nghề, trình độ tăng cao	My cooking skills improved before I knew it. / 不知不觉做饭的手艺好起来了。/ Chẳng mấy chốc, tay nghề đã tăng lên.

➕ 腕(うで)を上(あ)げる improve one's skills / 提高手艺 / nâng cao trình độ

1498	肩(かた)を落(お)とす	弟(おとうと)はテストで不合格(ふごうかく)になり、肩(かた)を落(お)とした。
	be discouraged / 沮丧 / buông xuôi hai vai, thất vọng	My younger brother failed the test and got discouraged. / 弟弟考试不及格，非常沮丧。/ Em trai tôi không đậu bài kiểm tra, buông xuôi cả hai vai.

1499	腹が立つ (はら た) **get angry / 生气，恼怒 / tức giận, bụng tức anh ách**	兄の言葉に、いちいち腹が立つ。(あに ことば はら た) My elder brother's words are really annoying. / 我对哥哥说的每一句话都感到很生气。/ Tôi tức anh ách vì mỗi lời nói của anh trai.
1500	腹を抱える (はら かか) **laugh hard / 捧腹 / ôm bụng mà cười**	テレビ番組を見て、腹を抱えて笑った。(ばんぐみ み はら かか わら) I watched a TV program and laughed hard. / 看电视节目看得捧腹大笑。/ Tôi đã ôm bụng cười khi xem chương trình tivi.
1501	足が出る (あし で) **go over budget / 超出预算 / đi quá giới hạn, quá độ**	買い物をしすぎて、足が出てしまった。(か もの あし で) I bought too much and went over budget. / 买了太多东西，超出预算了。/ Tôi đã đi quá giới hạn khi mua sắm quá nhiều.
1502	足を伸ばす (あし の) **go futher to / 去（更远的地方）/ đi thêm một chút**	散歩のついでに、美術館まで足を伸ばした。(さんぽ びじゅつかん あし の) While taking a walk, I decided to go to the musuem since I was out. / 散步时顺便连美术馆也去了。/ Sẵn tiện đi dạo, tôi đi thêm chút đến bảo tàng mỹ thuật.
1503	足を運ぶ (あし はこ) **travel to / 特地去 / đến, quá bộ**	暑い中、足を運んでいただき、申し訳ありません。(あつ なか あし はこ もう わけ) Thank you for traveling all the way in the heat. / 这么热的天，还让您特地跑一趟，真是不好意思。/ Thật có lỗi khi để anh / chị quá bộ đến đây trong trời nóng bức.
1504	足を引っ張る (あし ひ ぱ) **be in the way / 拖后腿 / gây cản trở, ngáng chân**	自分のミスでチームの足を引っ張った。(じぶん あし ひ ぱ) I was in the way of the team with my mistake. / 因为自己的过失，拖了整个队的后腿。/ Tôi đã ngáng chân cả đội do lỗi của mình.

副詞（ふくし）

Adverb / 副词 / Phó từ

1505	何かと（なに）	最近、何かと忙しい。（さいきん、なに、いそが）
副	one way or another / 各方面 / cách này hay cách khác, gì thì gì, kiểu gì cũng	I am busy one way or another. / 最近各种事情很忙。/ Gần đây kiểu gì cũng bận.
1506	何だかんだ（なん）	母は何だかんだとうるさい。（はは、なん）
副	one thing or another / 种种 / chuyện gì cũng, chuyện này chuyện kia	My mother is always nagging about one thing or another. / 妈妈总是唠叨这个唠叨那个，很烦。/ Mẹ tôi chuyện gì cũng ồn ào.
1507	なぜか	今日はなぜか食欲がない。（きょう、しょくよく）
副	for some reason / 不由得，不知怎的 / tại sao đó	For some reason, I don’t have an appetite. / 今天不知怎的食欲不好。/ Hôm nay chẳng hiểu sao không muốn ăn

👉 なぜ is the reason, here being used as a word to ask for the cause / “なぜ” 是理由，询问原因 / なぜ là lý do. Từ hỏi nguyên nhân

1508	何だか（なん）	何だか今日は気が重い。（なん、きょう、き、おも）
副	somehow / 总觉得 / có chút gì đó	Somehow I feel depressed today. / 今天总感觉心情沉重。/ Hôm nay có chút gì đó nặng nề trong lòng.
1509	何しろ（なに）	最近、疲れ気味だ。何しろ仕事が忙しい。（さいきん、つか、ぎみ、なに、しごと、いそが）
副	at any rate / 不管怎样，总之，反正 / dù gì đi nữa	I’m a bit tired these days. At any rate, I’m busy at work. / 最近有点儿累。总之工作很忙。/ Gần đây, cảm giác mệt mỏi. Dù gì đi nữa, là do công việc bận rộn.
1510	何とも（～ない）（なん）	彼のことなんて、もう何とも思っていない。（かれ、なん、おも）
副	nothing at all / 真的，什么也 / (không~) chút nào	I don’t feel anything about him at all. / 我对他的事情已经一点儿也不在意了。/ Chuyện của anh ấy, tôi chẳng nghĩ đến nữa.
1511	どうか	この件、どうかよろしくお願いいたします。（けん、ねが）
副	please / 务必 / vui lòng	Please take care of this case. / 这件事务必拜托了。/ Vụ việc này, xin vui lòng giúp đỡ.
1512	どうにか	ぎりぎりの点だったが、どうにか試験に合格できた。（てん、しけん、ごうかく）
副	somehow, in some way / 总算，想办法 / bằng cách nào đó, cuối cùng rồi cũng	The points were barely enough, but somehow I passed the test. / 分数刚过及格线，总算及格了。/ Điểm sát nút nhưng cuối cùng cũng đã đậu kỳ thi.

1513 どうしても

副 **by all means, inevitably / 无论如何也要 / 怎么也 / bằng mọi giá,nhất định, làm cách nào cũng (không thể)**

①どうしても志望大学に合格したい。
②どうしても論文が書けない。

① I want to get into the university of my choice by all means. ② I simply can't write my thesis. / ①我无论如何都想考上自己想去的那所大学。②怎么也写不出论文。/ ① Tôi muốn bằng mọi giá đậu đại học nguyện vọng. ② Làm cách nào cũng không thể viết được luận văn.

① strong intention ② no matter what / ①意志很坚定，表示"一定要" ②怎么做也 / ① Ý chí mạnh mẽ. Nhất định muốn ~ ② Làm thế nào cũng

1514 どうせ

副 **anyway / 反正 / đằng nào cũng, tiện thể**

うちのチームなんか、どうせ勝てない。

Our team can't win anyway. / 我们对反正也赢不了。/ Đội mình đằng nào cũng không thể thắng.

1515 どうやら

副 **evidently / 好歹，多半 / xem ra, có vẻ**

どうやら明日は暑くなりそうだ。

Evidently, tomorrow will be a hot day. / 明天天气多半会热起来。/ Xem ra ngày mai trời có vẻ nóng.

1516 とにかく

副 **in any case / 姑且，总之 / tóm lại, nói chung, dù thế nào**

店は満席かもしれないが、とにかく行ってみよう。

The shop may be full, but, in any case, let's go. / 虽然店里可能没位子了，姑且去看看吧。/ Có thể tiệm hết chỗ nhưng dù thế nào thì cũng đi thử đã.

= ともかく　+ とりあえず tentatively / 姑且 / tạm thời, trước mắt

1517 とても（～ない）

副 **by any possibility / 怎么也（不）/ hoàn toàn (không thể ~)**

今の日本語力では、とても日本で就職できない。

There is no way I can find a job in Japan with my current Japanese ability. / 以我现在的日语水平，不可能在日本找到工作。/ Với năng lực tiếng Nhật bây giờ thì hoàn toàn không thể kiếm việc làm ở Nhật.

1518 より

副 **do more / 更 / hơn nữa**

今後はよりいっそう努力するつもりだ。

I will make more efforts in the future. / 今后打算加倍努力。/ Từ nay về sau, tôi định sẽ nỗ lực hơn nữa.

+ なおいっそう further / 更加 / hơn thế nữa, vượt xa

よりいっそう (all the more) can also be used if one wants to express something with emphasis / 想要强调时也说"よりいっそう" / Cũng nói " よりいっそう " khi muốn nhấn mạnh.

1519 いかに

副 **how / 如何 / như thế nào, biết bao nhiêu**

日本の技術がいかに進んでいるか、よくわかった。

I know well just how developed Japanese technology is. / 终于明白了日本的技术是如何发展的。/ Tôi đã hiểu rõ kỹ thuật của Nhật phát triển biết bao nhiêu.

1520 □ 副	いかにも	あの子はいかにも賢そうだ。
	indeed / 的确，实在 / quả thật, đúng là	That child looks wise indeed. / 那个孩子真的很聪明。/ Đứa bé đó quả thật thông minh.

Section 5

接続表現
せつぞくひょうげん

Conjunctive Expressions / 接续表达 / Cách nói nối

1521 **それで** 接続
and then / 因此 / do đó, vì vậy

日本は物価が高い。それで、バイトをしている。
Prices in Japan are high. So I'm working part-time. / 日本的物价很高，因此我在做兼职。/ Vật giá ở Nhật đắt đỏ. Do đó, tôi làm thêm.

＝ だから

＋ そのため for that reason / 因此，所以 / vì vậy・その結果 as a result / 因此，所以 / kết quả là

1522 **そこで** 接続
so, accordingly / 于是，因此 / do vậy

友達と食事する予定だ。そこで、ネットで評判のいい店を調べた。
I was supposed to eat with my friend. So I looked up a popular restaurant on the Internet. / 和朋友约了吃饭，于是在网上查了评价好的店。/ Tôi dự định dùng bữa với bạn. Do vậy, tôi tìm cửa tiệm được đánh giá tốt bằng internet.

1523 **すると** 接続
then / 于是，随后 / thế là

部下を叱った。すると、彼女は泣き出した。
I scolded my subordinate. Then, she started crying. / 责骂了下属后，下属（她）哭了起来。/ Tôi đã mắng cấp dưới. Thế là, cô ấy òa khóc.

1524 **なぜなら** 接続
because / 因为 / lý do là

彼女は人気がある。なぜなら、気が利くからだ。
She is popular. That's because she is considerate of others. / 她很受欢迎，是因为她很细心周到。/ Cô ấy rất được yêu mến. Lý do là cô ấy rất ân cần.

＝ なぜかというと

1525 **というのも** 接続
the reason being / 是因为 / là bởi vì

最近、少しやせた。というのも、忙しいからだ。
I lost a little weight recently, which is because I'm busy. / 最近瘦了是因为很忙。/ Gần đây, tôi ốm đi một chút. Là bởi vì bận rộn quá.

＝ というのは

1526 **つまり** 接続
in other words / 总之，也就是说 / nghĩa là

明日はテストだが、勉強しない。つまり、あきらめたということだ。
The test is tomorrow, but I'm not studying. In other words, I have given up. / 明天虽然有考试，但我不想复习了。也就是说，我已经放弃治疗了。/ Ngày mai kiểm tra nhưng không học. Nghĩa là đã bỏ cuộc.

＋ 要するに all in all / 总而言之 / nghĩa là・すなわち that is to say / 也就是说 / có nghĩa là

1527 □ いわゆる

弟はゲームが大好きで、いわゆるオタクだ。

連体 **so-called / 所谓的 / nói cách khác**

My younger brother loves games, and is a so-called 'otaku'. / 弟弟很喜欢打游戏，也就是所谓的宅男。/ Em trai tôi rất thích chơi game, nói cách khác là otaku.

1528 □ その上

この本はわかりやすい。その上、値段も安い。

接続 **furthermore / 而且 / hơn nữa**

This book is easy to understand. Furthermore, the price fairly agreeable. / 这本书很简单易懂，而且很便宜。/ Quyển sách này dễ hiểu. Hơn nữa, giá lại rẻ.

＝ それに

1529 □ そればかりか

先輩にごちそうしてもらった。そればかりか、家まで送ってもらった。

接続 **not only that but / 不仅如此 / không chỉ vậy**

My senior friend treated me to dinner. Not only that, he drove me home. / 前辈请我吃了饭，不仅如此还送我回了家。/ Tôi được đàn anh chiêu đãi. Không chỉ vậy, còn được chở về tận nhà.

＝ そればかりでなく

1530 □ しかも

日本の冬は寒い。しかも、雪が降る。

接続 **moreover / 而且 / chưa kể, hơn nữa**

Winter in Japan is cold. Moreover, it snows. / 日本的冬天很冷，而且还下雪。/ Mùa đông Nhật Bản lạnh. Chưa kể còn có tuyết rơi.

1531 □ また

彼は留学生だ。また、画家でもある。

接続 **and / 还，而且 / ngoài ra**

He is an overseas student. And he is an artist. / 他是留学生，还是个画家。/ Anh ấy là du học sinh. Ngoài ra, còn là họa sỹ.

1532 □ しかし

けんかをして謝った。しかし、彼女は許してくれなかった。

接続 **but / 但是 / nhưng**

We fought and I apologized. But she wouldn't forgive me. / 吵架后我道歉了，但她没有原谅我。/ Chúng tôi cãi nhau và tôi đã xin lỗi. Nhưng cô ấy không tha lỗi cho tôi.

＋ だが but / 但是 / nhưng・けれども but / 但是 / tuy nhiên

1533 □ ところが

昨日は飲み会だった。ところが、急に中止になった。

接続 **whereas / 然而，但是 / tuy vậy, nhưng mà**

Yesterday, there was supposed to be a drinking party. But it was suddenly canceled. / 明天本来有聚餐，可是突然取消了。/ Hôm qua là buổi ăn uống. Nhưng không ngờ bị hủy.

expressing the speaker's feeling of surprise / 表示说话人很意外的心情 / Thể hiện sự bất ngờ của người nói.

1534 □	それでも	彼は謝ってきた。それでも、許せなかった。
接続	even then / 即便如此 / dù vậy	He apologized. Still, I couldn't forgive him. / 他来道歉了，但即便如此我也无法原谅他。/ Anh ấy đến xin lỗi. Dù vậy, tôi không thể tha thứ.
1535 □	(それ)にもかかわらず	この店のサービスは最悪だ。それにもかかわらず、客は多い。
接続	despite / 尽管如此 / vậy mà, bất chấp (điều đó)	The service of this store is horrible. Despite this, it has many customers. / 这家店的服务太差了，但尽管如此客人还是很多。/ Dịch vụ của tiệm này quá tệ. Vậy mà, khách lại đông.
1536 □	そうはいっても	勉強は嫌いだ。そうはいっても、しないわけにはいかない。
接続	having said that / 即便这么说 / dù nói vậy	I hate studying. Having said that, I can't avoid it. / 我讨厌学习，但即便这么说也不是不学。/ Tôi ghét học. Dù nói vậy cũng phải học.

➕ といっても although one might say / 就算如此也 / có nói vậy cũng

1537 □	それにしては	彼はアメリカに5年も留学していた。それにしては、英語が下手だ。
接続	considering / 即便如此却 / vậy mà	He has studied in the United States for five years. Considering that, his English is not good. / 他在美国留学了5年，但即便如此英语却很糟糕。/ Anh ấy du học Mỹ những 5 năm. Vậy mà tiếng Anh thật dở.
1538 □	一方	A大学は東京にある。一方、B大学は地方にある。
接続	meanwhile / 另一方面 / mặt khác, ngược lại	University A is in Tokyo. On the other hand, University B is in the countryside. / A大学在东京，而B大学在地方城市。/ Đại học A nằm ở Tokyo. Ngược lại, đại học B nằm ở địa phương.

➕ それに対して on the other hand / 与此相对 / ngược lại

1539 □	ただ	毎年、海外旅行に行く。ただ、去年は行けなかった。
接続	just / 但是，只是 / có điều, tuy nhiên	I travel abroad every year. But I couldn't go last year. / 我每年都出国旅行，只有去年没去成。/ Hàng năm tôi đều đi du lịch nước ngoài. Có điều, năm ngoái không đi được.
1540 □	ただし	テストは3時まで。ただし、延長する場合もある。
接続	provided, however / 只是，不过 / tuy nhiên, nhưng	The test is until 3:00 p.m. However, the time may be extended. / 考试3点结束，不过也有可能会延长时间。/ Bài kiểm tra đến 3 giờ. Tuy nhiên, có trường hợp kéo dài.

➕ もっとも but then, however / 最 / nhưng

1435 – 1546

1541 □ なお

明日(あした)は運動会(うんどうかい)です。なお、昼(ひる)ご飯(はん)はめいめい持(も)ってきてください。

接続 **in addition, additionally / 还，另外 / ngoài ra, hơn nữa, trái lại**

Tomorrow is sports day. Additionally, make sure to bring your own lunches. / 明天是运动会。另外，请各自带午餐来。/ Ngày mai là hội thao. Ngoài ra, mọi người hãy tự mình đem theo cơm trưa.

1542 □ または

お問(と)い合(あ)わせは、メールまたはお電話(でんわ)でどうぞ。

接続 **or / 或者 / hoặc là**

Please send inquiries by e-mail or phone. / 请通过邮件或者电话咨询。/ Vui lòng hỏi qua e-mail hoặc điện thoại.

= あるいは

1543 □ それとも

会議(かいぎ)は月曜日(げつようび)がいいですか。それとも、火曜日(かようび)がいいですか。

接続 **or / 或者，还是 / hay là**

Is it alright to schedule the next meeting on Monday? Or would you prefer Tuesday? / 会议是放在周一还是周二？ / Cuộc họp vào ngày thứ hai được không? Hay là thứ ba?

1544 □ ところで

授業(じゅぎょう)を終(お)わります。ところで、マリアさんの欠席(けっせき)理由(りゆう)を誰(だれ)か知(し)っていますか。

接続 **by the way / 另外（转换话题时用）/ mà này, nhân tiện**

Class is over for today. By the way, does anyone know the reason for Maria's absence? / 现在下课。对了，有谁知道玛丽亚为什么没来吗？ / Giờ học kết thúc. Mà này, có ai biết lý do bạn Maria vắng mặt không?

1545 □ さて

さて、次(つぎ)の問題(もんだい)に進(すす)みましょう。

接続 **now / 那么 / nào, và bây giờ**

Now, let's go on to the next question. / 那么我们就来看下个问题吧。/ Nào, chúng ta tiến đến câu hỏi tiếp theo.

1546 □ それでは

それでは、これで今日(きょう)の授業(じゅぎょう)を終(お)わります。

接続 **well / 那么 / bây giờ thì, vậy thì**

Well, this is the end of today's class. / 那么今天的课就上到这里。/ Vậy thì, giờ học hôm nay kết thúc tại đây.

= では + それなら in that case / 这么说的话，那么 / nếu vậy・それじゃ if so / 那么 / vậy thì・じゃ then / 那么 / vậy

まとめて覚えよう！

いろいろな意味を持つ動詞 Verbs With Many Different Meanings / 有很多意思的动词 / Động từ mang nhiều ý nghĩa khác nhau

• **あがる・さがる**

家に**上がる**（＝入る）・**上げる**（＝入れる）

腕が上がる・**腕を上げる**（＝上手になる）

成績が**上がる**（＝よくなる・高くなる）⇔成績が**下がる**（＝悪くなる・低くなる）

風呂から**上がる**（＝出る）

発表で**あがる**（＝緊張する）

線の内側に**下がる**（＝後ろに移動する）

• **あげる・さげる**

大声を**上げる**（＝出す）

例を**あげる**（＝示す）

頭を下げる（＝頭を低くする・あいさつする）

皿を**下げる**（＝片付ける）

• **かかる・かける**

電話が**かかる**（＝つながる）・電話を**かける**（＝する）

手間が**かかる**（＝必要だ）・手間を**かける**（＝使う・費やす）

インフルエンザに**かかる**（＝病気になる）

迷惑がかかる（＝影響がある）・**迷惑をかける**（＝影響を与える）

エンジンがかかる（＝エンジンが動く）・
エンジンをかける（＝エンジンを動かす）

ふとんを**かける**（＝上にかぶせる）

アイロンを**かける**（＝使用する）

声をかける（＝呼ぶ・誘う）

• 立つ・立てる

席を**立つ**（＝離れる）

うわさが立つ（＝うわさが広がる）

煙が**立つ**（＝上に上がる）

計画を**立てる**（＝作る）

音を**立てる**（＝出す）

• つく・つける

味が**つく**（＝加わる）・味を**つける**（＝加える）

パワーが**つく**（＝生まれる）・パワーを**つける**（＝生む・添える）

見当がつく（＝見当がはっきりする）・**見当をつける**（＝見当をはっきりさせる）

勝負がつく（＝勝負が決まる）・**勝負をつける**（＝勝負を決める）

差がつく（＝差がはっきりする）・**差をつける**（＝差をはっきりさせる）

• 出る・出す

授業に**出る**（＝出席する）

結果が**出る**（＝わかる）

新商品が**出る**（＝発売される）・新商品を**出す**（＝発売する）

元気が**出る**（＝生まれる・起きる）・元気を**出す**（＝生む・起こす）

大声が**出る**（＝外に現れる）・大声を**出す**（＝外に現す）

テレビに**出る**（＝人の前に現れる）

宿題を**出す**（＝与える）

本が出る（＝出版される）・**本を出す**（＝出版する）

実力を**出す**（＝発揮する）

• **とれる・とる**

痛みが**取れる**（＝なくなる）

お金を**取る**（＝盗む）

汚れが**取れる**（＝なくなる）・汚れを**取る**（＝除く）

資格を**取る**（＝取得する）

バランスを取る（＝うまく調整する）

睡眠を取る（＝眠る）

責任を**取る**（＝引き受ける）

連絡を取る（＝連絡する）

メモを取る（＝メモする）

休暇を**取る**（＝自分のものにする）

新聞を**取る**（＝注文して配達してもらう）

社員を**採る**（＝採用する）

50音順単語索引 おんじゅんたんごさくいん

Vocabulary Index in Syllabic Order / 50音图顺序索引 / Danh mục từ vựng theo thứ tự 50 chữ cái tiếng Nhật

う

す

ち

と

<著者> アークアカデミー
1986年創立。ARCグループ校として、ARC東京日本語学校、アークアカデミー新宿校、大阪校、京都校、ベトナムハノイ校がある。日本語教師養成科の卒業生も1万人を超え、日本語を通して社会貢献できる人材育成を目指している。

監修　遠藤 由美子（えんどう ゆみこ）
早稲田大学大学院日本語教育研究科修士課程修了
アークアカデミー新宿校校長

執筆　山田 光子（やまだ みつこ）
立教大学文学部教育学科卒業、ARC東京日本語学校講師

協力　関 利器（せき りき）
ARC東京日本語学校専任講師

はじめての日本語能力試験
N2 単語 2500 ［英語・中国語・ベトナム語版］

2016年10月26日　初版　第1刷発行
2024年 4月 5日　初版　第10刷発行

著　者	アークアカデミー
翻訳・翻訳校正	Yvonne Chang/Red Wind（英語） ALA中国語教室 彭博 / 胡奥琦（中国語） NGUYEN DO AN NHIEN（ベトナム語）
イラスト	花色木綿
装丁	岡崎裕樹
編集・DTP	有限会社ギルド / 有限会社ブルーインク
発行人	天谷修身
発行所	株式会社アスク 〒162-8558 東京都新宿区下宮比町2-6 TEL 03-3267-6864　FAX 03-3267-6867 https://www.ask-books.com/
印刷・製本	日経印刷株式会社

　Printed in Japan　ISBN978-4-87217-984-2